THE QUEEN'S QUARRY

The Petralist · Book 5

THE QUEEN'S QUARRY

The Petralist · Book 5

FRANK MORIN

Whipsaw Press

The Queen's Quarry

Book 5 of the Petralist
This is a work of fiction. All the characters and events portrayed in this book are fictional, and any resemblance to real people or incidents is purely coincidental.

Ebook ISBN: 978-1-946910-06-6
Paperback ISBN: 978-1-946910-07-3
Hardcover ISBN: 978-1-946910-08-0

A Whipsaw Press Original

Edited by Joshua Essoe
(http://www.joshuaessoe.com/)

Cover art by Brad Fraunfelter
(http://www.bfillustration.com/)

Illustrations by Jared Blando
(http://www.theredepic.com/)

Book design by Kathryn Morin
First Whipsaw printing May, 2019

Acknowledgements

The Queen's Quarry is here! I'm so thrilled to get this epic adventure into your hands. I know you're going to love it. I do.

As usual, I owe many more people for their assistance, encouragement, and inspiration than I can name individually. There are a few that stand out, though, and I need to mention them because they know where I sleep.

My family, of course. They're my biggest fans and my most brutal critics. They hold me to the highest possible standard, and you should all thank them for insisting I push the limits with every book. Jenny is the heart and soul of my world. Going on a quarter century married together, and she keeps our relationship fresh and fun, and fills my world with humor and inspiration. Kate and Kyle, my brain trust and sounding boards. Emily, my nutritional support agent (she brings me cookies), and her undying enthusiasm. And Jacob, whose relentless energy and good humor inspire me.

Thanks again to my Fast Rollers, the beta readers who devour every word, even though they read early drafts that aren't nearly so incredible. Your support keeps me focused and energized.

As usual, Joshua Essoe produced an edit as epic as the novel. This time, my draft worked better than usual and he actually said, "You should be proud." Yeehah!

Brad Fraunfelter produced yet another gorgeous cover, and Jared Blando took my rough sketches and turned them into two new, fantastic maps. This team is unstoppable.

And THANK YOU to all of you fans who share my enthusiasm for this work, and who encourage me to keep going, hound me for release dates for the next novel, and tell your friends about these stories. Without you, none of this would be possible.

The Northern Reaches
Varvakis
Orlov
Platov
River Angara
Krashnov
Lake Pgasino
River Slenet
Valeska Rivers
Althing
Jagdish
Granadure
Edduritz
Dagmanson
R. Anok
Finnlaugur
Ravinder
River Sanjit
Prahalad
Obrion
R. Macantacht
R. Baol
R. Beegrin
The Eastern Sea
The Broken Water
Donleavy
Maninder
The Western Sea
Sea of Olcan
Sehravad
Ozlem
Hayreddin
Murex
Tabnit
Mahzun
Tabnit
The Known World

GRANADURE
N
W E
S
GRANITE MINE
ALASDAIR
QUARTZ-ZINC GOLD MINE
THE WICK
PUMICE MINE
BASALT MINE
MARBLE MINE
MERKLAND
SLATE MINE
OBRION
CRANN
TRODAIRE
SAOL RIVER
DONLEAVY
MACANTACHT RIVER
FREASTAL
GRANITE MINE
BASALT MINE
GRANITE MINE
CASUR
MULRENNAN
CARRAIG
DEIFUR
LIMESTONE MINE
RAINEACH
LAIGE
SANDSTONE MINES
CHOSTALAN
SPEIRMOR
RADHARC
THE DESERT
THE LANDS OF
OBRION
BLANDO

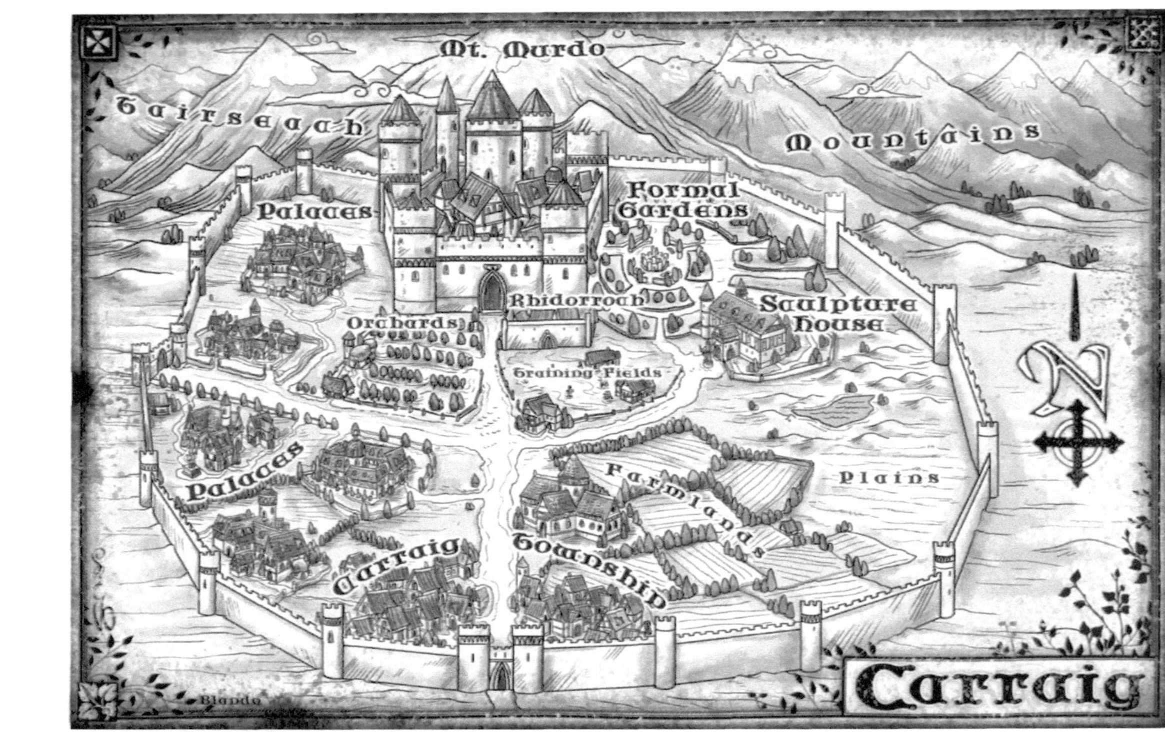

Mt. Murdo
Gairseach
Mountains
Palaces
Formal Gardens
Rhidorroch
Sculpture House
Orchards
Training Fields
Palaces
Farmlands
Plains
Carraig Township
Blando
Carraig

Mt Osterwald
Merkland
Abwehr Mts
Inner Gate
Outer Gates
The Cliffs
Army Camp
Watchtower
Badurach Pass
Blando

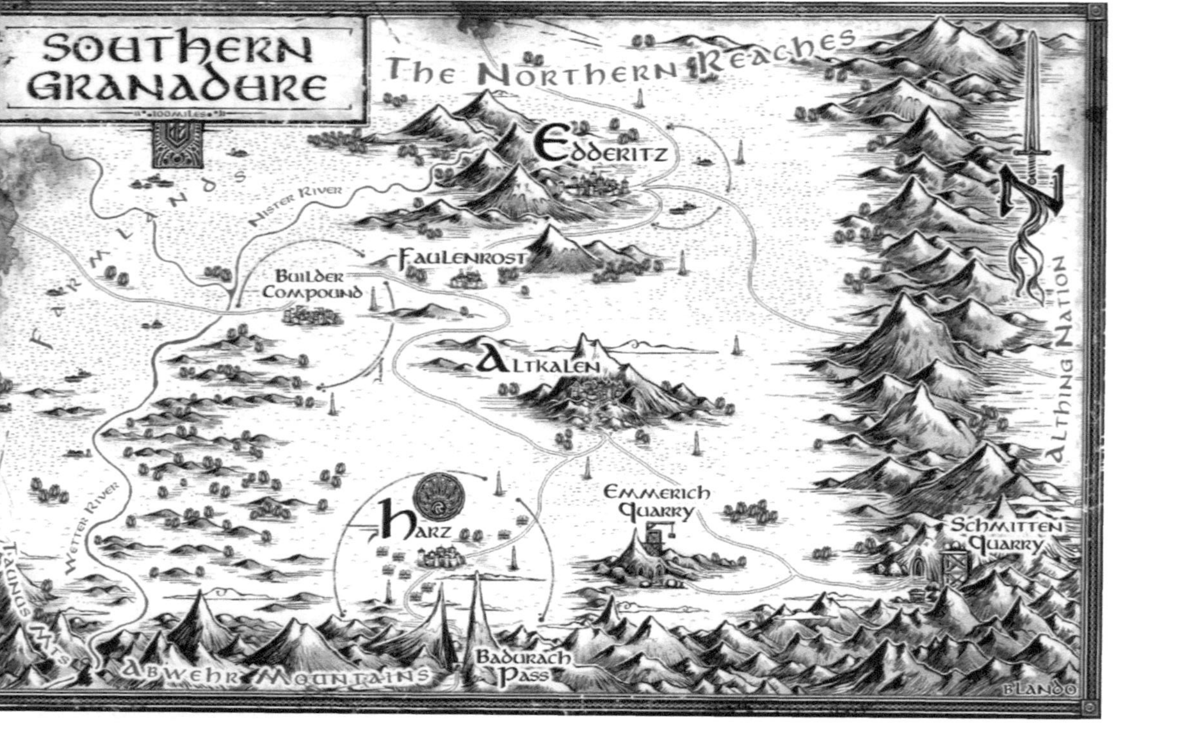

Southern Granadure
100 Miles
The Northern Reaches
Edderitz
Nister River
Farmlands
Faulenrost
Builder Compound
Altkalen
Althing Nation
Harz
Emmerich Quarry
Schmitten Quarry
Wetter River
Taunus Mts
Abwehr Mountains
Badurach Pass
BLANDO

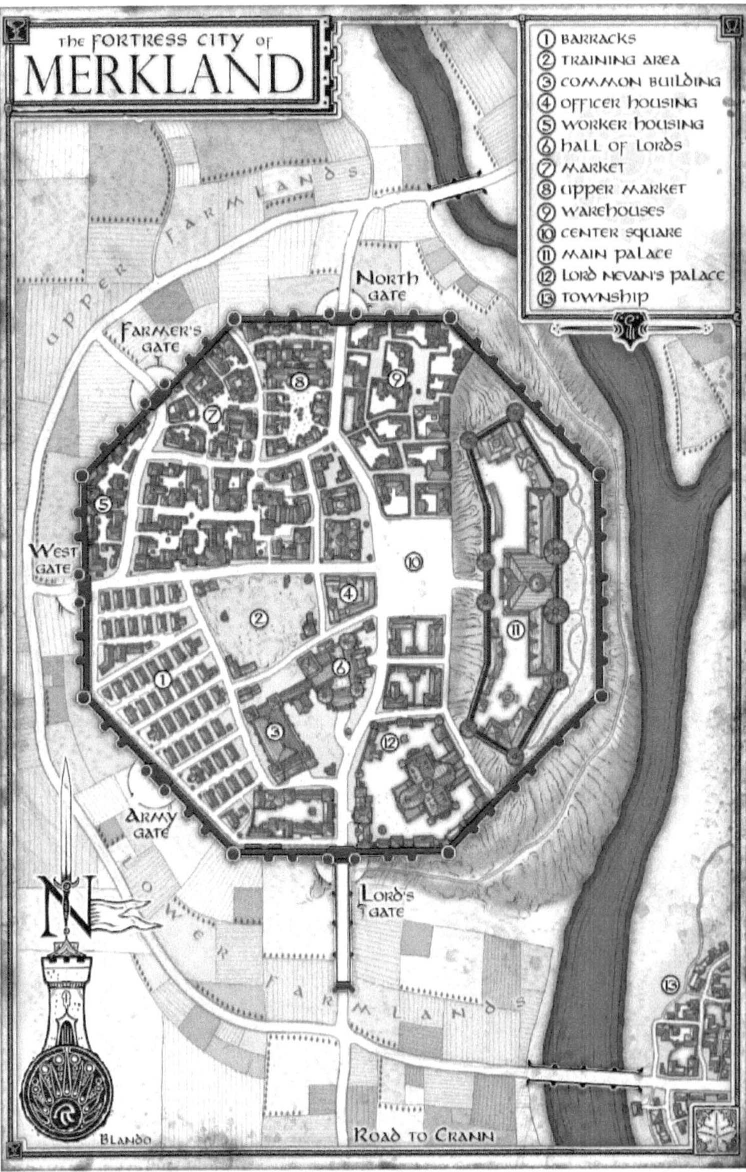

THE FORTRESS CITY OF
MERKLAND

1 BARRACKS
2 TRAINING AREA
3 COMMON BUILDING
4 OFFICER HOUSING
5 WORKER HOUSING
6 HALL OF LORDS
7 MARKET
8 UPPER MARKET
9 WAREHOUSES
10 CENTER SQUARE
11 MAIN PALACE
12 LORD NEVAN'S PALACE
13 TOWNSHIP

UPPER FARMLANDS
NORTH GATE
FARMER'S GATE
WEST GATE
ARMY GATE
LOWER FARMLANDS
LORD'S GATE
N
BLANDO
ROAD TO CRANN

The City of
Donleavy
S
Blando

THE CHALLENGES OF DEALING WITH COMPLICATED FRIENDS

Connor backpedaled across the hard, frozen ground, barely avoiding the whistling tip of a sword that slashed the cold air half an inch from his chin. Aifric pursued in the quick, graceful dance of obsidian. Connor smiled, tapped limestone, and focused it on his teeth. They started to glow.

"Are you trying to get me to knock out those pretty teeth?" Aifric asked, speaking in the merciless tones of her Student Eighteen persona.

It never ceased to amaze Connor how everything about her changed when she slipped on a different personality. A grim expression replaced Aifric the Healer's ready smile. He'd lost count of how many times her practice sword had bruised him right through his battle leathers in the past two days of intense practice.

"Admit it. They distracted you a little." Connor released limestone.

"You need more than shiny teeth to win," she said, lunging again. He barely parried before she could skewer him.

"I'll find a way," he promised.

"Try hitting me for once." She chuckled, stepped back a pace, and motioned him to pause.

Connor gladly lowered his sword and dagger and checked to make sure he hadn't moved too far to the edge of the practice area. Student Eighteen had knocked him into a tent once and hit him four times before he could roll free.

The light dusting of snow wasn't thick enough to cover the charred scars marking the place where Ingrid had died, along with the monstrous elfonnel. It happened on that very spot on the high mountain plateau, just north of Badurach Pass.

When Connor thought of all of the death and suffering that had resulted from the Obrioner invasion, he felt a deep sense of frustration.

They'd failed to kill High Lord Dougal in Alasdair, and he'd raised the terrifying, ancient Queen Dreokt from her centuries-long slumber. Connor still hadn't effectively begun spreading the truth about patronage to his countrymen either.

The wind gusted, shaking the tents huddling on the icy mountain pass on three sides of the practice field as it raced south toward Obrion. Dark, ominous storm clouds were piling along the northern horizon. They'd been building all day, and the air felt heavy with the weight of the impending storm.

The unusually warm weather they'd been enjoying had fled south, and temperatures had plummeted all day. The mid-afternoon sunlight felt weak and timid. Winter was finally arriving and seemed eager to make up for lost time.

Good thing they were camped on a barren, battle-scarred plateau, high atop the rugged Maclachlan Mountains. No, in Granadure they were called the Abwehr Mountains. Not that it mattered. A fierce winter storm would freeze him just as gleefully, no matter the name.

Kilian stepped onto the practice area and approached. The lanky, ancient Dawnus looked like a man still in his prime, with only a few streaks of gray in his black hair that faded to blue on the ends. As usual, he ignored the cold and dressed only in charcoal-colored trousers and a black leather jacket over a white linen shirt. Pinpoints of fire danced in his blue eyes. He wore his sword and dagger sheathed, a pair of leather gloves tucked into his wide, leather belt.

"I think that bout went better," Connor said as Kilian neared.

Kilian chuckled. "Next time try fighting more than glowing."

Student Eighteen nodded agreement. "I figured you'd get tired of blocking my sword with your ribs so often." She wore dark gray furs over her soldier's uniform. Her thick, brown hair hung past her shoulders, but was pulled back from her face by a fur-lined, leather cap. Her deep brown eyes watched him with her assassin's alert gaze.

"Very funny. I was trying to explore strategic misdirection," Connor said, frustrated that his glowing teeth hadn't affected her more.

When Mattias set his teeth glowing, they seemed to distract every girl he met. Even Verena had seemed affected far too much.

As usual, his thoughts turned to Verena and her lingering coma, but he pushed his worries for her aside. Aifric raised her sword, and she liked helping him re-focus by cracking him with it.

Kilian retreated a step and said, "Again. Focus this time."

As if focusing would help him defeat a Mhortair assassin. Still, when Student Eighteen shifted closer, Connor tapped obsidian and lunged. He struck with both sword and dagger, moving with perfect balance, his entire body tuned to fight.

Obsidian pulsed through his limbs, so different from the itchy-crawly feel of granite or the coursing energy of basalt. Obsidian flowed like words whispered on a distant wind, and somehow it improved his agility and reflexes. Obsidian helped him learn faster and move with unmatched grace. It also helped him read his opponent and anticipate her moves.

Unfortunately, Student Eighteen anticipated better than he did.

She leaned and twisted, somehow managing to slip just past his practice blades. The two of them spun apart, wooden blades lashing out and cracking as they connected half a dozen times in three seconds.

In that moment, Connor felt one with the fight as they shifted and flowed around each other in the deadly, obsidian-fueled dance. He drew deep from the igneous stone, one of his primary affinities, which he had absorbed in its powdered form through his skin before the fight. Its power infused him, heightening his senses to the point where he captured every minute detail of the moment.

As he dragged in great gulps of the thin mountain air, it didn't seem to fill his lungs enough. It carried the scents of leather and frozen sweat floating on the humid smell of impending snow. The creaking of their battle leathers sounded sharp and clear, as did the crunch of their boots and the swish of practice swords slicing the air. The crashing of their weapons echoed with staccato intensity.

The other reason Connor loved tapping obsidian was that it always triggered the sound of Verena's soft laughter in his mind. That heart-warming sound helped ease his constant terror that she might never awaken from her coma, or that even if she did, her mind might have suffered some permanent, incurable wound.

That was one of the reasons he'd insisted on training so hard with obsidian since returning to the Grandurian side of Drumwhindle Pass. When he trained, it was as if Verena stood close beside him, her blue eyes watching every move. He could almost feel the soft touch of her hand on his shoulder, whispered encouragement buried within the laughter.

Every muscle moved in perfect harmony. The sword and dagger were like extensions of his hands and he knew exactly where they would strike. With obsidian-fueled confidence, Connor stood against Student Eighteen with the skill of a warrior with months of intense training experience instead of barely two days.

For a moment he even held his own.

Her predatory expression hardened and Connor marveled again at how her features seemed to alter in her different persona. Her oval-shaped face that seemed so open and honest as Aifric seemed more angular and menacing as Student Eighteen. Her eyes were harder, her voice harsh and merciless.

She increased the tempo little by little until their blades blurred as they lashed out, parried, slashed, and stabbed. He had seen Blades dueling before, always amazed by their fluid grace, their deadly speed, and their incredible control.

Living the moment felt a thousand times better.

The two of them shifted across the circular practice ground, situated on the southern end of the Grandurian army camp that huddled below the broken peaks of Badurach Pass. Nearby tents flapped in the gusting wind that cut through his battle leathers and chilled his sweaty forehead.

Few spectators watched their duel. Most people not assigned a specific duty were smart enough to stay inside the relative warmth of their tents, or huddle around the huge bonfires that strove to drive back the chill.

Kilian paced nearby, watching their every move. Connor had yet to see him sweat in their practice sessions.

Of course, the fact that they ended so fast might have something to do with that. He hadn't lasted more than three seconds against Kilian. Student Eighteen had lasted five, and she was an acknowledged master among the Allcarvers in camp.

Obsidian enhanced many attributes, but it did not offer the super-human speed of basalt. In his centuries-long life, Kilian had mastered basalt like no other. When he fought, he seemed to blur, limbs moving with breathtaking speed. Most other Wingrunners only knew how to run with basalt, but Connor was learning that there might be many aspects to speed still to be learned. He looked forward to studying the concepts with Kilian.

With an abrupt reversal, Student Eighteen slipped under Connor's high slashing sword and cracked her weapon against his ribs. The blow struck hard enough to add a new bruise to his growing collection. Connor danced back, rubbing his side.

"Better." She sheathed her weapons without even bothering to look. They just slid into place like sweetbreads plunging down Hamish's gullet. No hesitation, and no chance of missing.

"Not good enough," Connor grumbled.

He was grateful for a rest, although he bet he could have kept fighting for hours under that Obsidian-induced battle high. He loved that he could spend so much time practicing with the amazing stone. He'd only established affinity with obsidian during the fight with the elfonnel at the Carraig, only to have Dougal use his obsidian affinity to try seizing Connor's mind. The threat of that mind control had prevented Connor from daring obsidian much since then. Only now that he felt confident Dougal was too far to make another attempt could he practice openly with it.

Kilian said, "You're making solid progress. In the next bout, I want you to try something different."

"What?"

"Win."

Connor rolled his eyes. Student Eighteen grinned and said, "I think you've advanced to the point I should demonstrate what a really thorough beat-down feels like."

"Don't you remember Catriona's hugging days at the Carraig? I know what it feels like to get beat up," he reminded her quickly. Those were not happy memories.

Her smile shifted to Aifric's warm, friendly one. "Don't worry, Connor. I promise to heal you when Student Eighteen finishes the lesson."

As the two of them settled into fighting stances again, Connor decided he definitely needed to change tactics.

He really needed to figure out a way to cheat.

2

BREAKING RECORDS

Connor wished Hamish was around. He could really use some of that skunk extract. Unfortunately, Hamish had left days before to take the refugees of Alasdair north to the Emmerich quarry to settle into their new homes, arranged by Kilian and Wolfram.

Connor hoped his family was handling the change all right. With Hamish to help shepherd the transition, maybe there wouldn't be too many problems.

Student Eighteen moved toward him, weapons held casually, not hiding the fact that she expected to beat him easily. If he stuck to his training, she definitely would.

Using obsidian, he'd progressed with astonishing speed. Somehow he not only learned the fighting techniques and principles more quickly, but retained the knowledge better. Even his muscle memory felt like he'd been practicing for months instead of days.

He felt confident of his chances in a one-on-one duel against any non-obsidian warrior. That didn't help him with Student Eighteen, though. Before he could figure out a plan, she closed in a rush, wooden blade snapping out toward his sword hand.

No way he'd let her disarm him in the first strike. Connor deflected the blow and drove an elbow toward her face. She'd expected him to strike with his dagger, so the elbow strike almost landed.

She was just too fast, though, and ducked under it. That left him open. Somehow she sheathed her dagger, slapped him a stinging blow across the face with her left hand, and drew the knife again before he could bring his own dagger to bear.

Connor retreated, rubbing his cheek. The cold made the sting worse. "Ow."

She chuckled. "Good improvisation. If you'd connected, it might have worked."

"I'll get you," he promised.

She beckoned him on, her expression amused.

So he circled instead of attacking. Tapping obsidian was like standing before a window in his mind that was only opened partway. To tap more, he pulled the window open wider, allowing more sound to pour in, igniting greater power throughout his entire body. He concentrated that power into his mind, accelerating his thoughts, considering and discarding a dozen crazy ideas for beating her. He really needed to learn Kilian's fighting tricks, but even if he knew them, Student Eighteen would never give him time to purge obsidian and absorb basalt.

He needed porphyry.

The idea ignited in his mind like a Solas lantern and for a second Aifric and the entire practice ground faded from his sight. All of his senses were overwhelmed by the raging need for more porphyry.

The glorious, inhuman power of the rampager could defeat Aifric. He'd beat her down, rip off her arms so she couldn't hit him again, drink her blood to—

Connor shook himself violently and nearly fell over as he fought down the horrific images that had flooded his mind. He began to pant, and sweat dripped into his eyes and made them burn. His muscles quivered, as if he'd been fighting at full intensity for hours.

Student Eighteen lowered her weapons, her expression concerned. "Are you all right, Connor?"

He held up a hand, glad she didn't attack in his moment of distraction. He felt as weak and nauseous as a kitten spun in a sack for half an hour. "Give me a second."

Kilian drew closer, his expression grave. "It's the porphyry, isn't it?"

Hearing the word triggered a renewed craving and Connor took a staggering step toward Kilian, growling with the need. He realized with a shock that he was gripping his sword, as if to strike.

"Do you have any? Even a little?" he couldn't help asking.

Kilian shook his head. "I don't. It was all destroyed, and taking even a tiny bit would probably seal your addiction for life. I am still hopeful the craving will subside."

Connor crouched and drove his wooden dagger several inches into the hard, rocky soil. "It doesn't feel like it's passing. It's been getting worse every day since Alasdair."

"I'll call Aifric," Student Eighteen offered.

"No, thanks." Connor forced himself to his feet and took a deep, shuddering breath. He hated what porphyry was doing to him, feared that growing craving more than he wanted to admit. He'd fight it down, somehow. He refused to give Uncle Martys the final victory by succumbing to the craving and becoming a blubbering fool.

"Fight me instead. Obsidian seems to help some."

"I'm not sure you're up for it."

"Do it," he snapped more harshly than he planned. "Don't hold back."

She shrugged. "Maybe you're right, Connor. Pain tends to bring clarity. I'm thinking you need a lot of both."

"Nothing permanent," Kilian warned.

"Aifric's ready, so he'll eventually recover from all but a mortal wound," she said, her tone calm and clinical.

"I feel overwhelmed by your concern," Connor told them dryly.

The threat of impending pain did help clear his mind, as did the obsidian when he tapped it again. He still needed a new approach to beat Student Eighteen, though.

They had both promised not to use metamorphic stones in the duel. It had seemed a reasonable promise, particularly given the location. The entire border region was still dangerously unstable. Earthquakes rattled the area constantly, although they'd diminished in intensity in the days since the catastrophe at Alasdair.

He hoped that marked a permanent easing of the unsettled elements, but doubted it. Tempting the powerful metamorphic stones was still extremely dangerous. That very morning he'd tried slate and extended feelers of thought down into the earth beneath their camp and felt the distant energy building again.

Connor glanced up at the broken peak of Mount Macduib. No, it was Mount Osterwald on this side. The jagged, broken peaks that had lorded over the pass were a stark reminder of the danger of tapping tertiaries too deeply.

So that left secondaries.

Connor began circling again, and Student Eighteen seemed willing to let him make the first strike. Her obvious confidence made him more eager than ever to flip the duel against her.

Sedimentary stones weren't usually considered great battle stones. Sandstone could heal damage he took. He had the sculpted sandstone pendant with its unrivaled healing power, but he'd used it so much in recent weeks the fist-shaped pendant was looking more like a shapeless, rough oval. It wouldn't last much longer.

That left limestone. As his affinity with that light-triggering stone had deepened in the past couple of days, he'd learned that the stone was potentially far more powerful than he'd ever understood. Maybe it was because he was now ascended through the first threshold, but it offered the one possible advantage.

In the past couple of days, he'd learned that light was not exactly what he'd always thought. Limestone actually acted more like a gateway to light. It wasn't quite like the tertiary-affinity gateways to the elements. Maybe a baby brother gateway.

When light flowed past, he sensed it moving like invisible waves, but when he drew it to him, it rolled up his skin like particles of bright sand. Kilian had confirmed that light did indeed act as both a wave and a stream of particles, but no one was really sure why. Rolling those particles up into his teeth was the secret to making them glow.

What if he made Student Eighteen's teeth glow? That might just distract her enough for him to get in a solid hit.

"Are you going to fight, or defeat me with boredom?" She demanded.

"You asked for it."

Connor launched himself at her, striking with every bit of skill she had taught him. The two of them plunged into the most intense Allcarver duel Connor had ever experienced. They spun and twisted, slashed and stabbed, flowing around each other like twin-bladed whirlwinds.

It was amazing. Connor grinned as he fought.

Until she caught him under the chin with the hilt of her sword. The world spun as Connor tumbled off his feet. Somehow she hit him six more times before he could crash to the ground, his body aching, his head spinning.

"That's more like it," Student Eighteen said.

Then her features shivered a bit and her Aifric smile returned. She extended a helping hand, and when he accepted it, healing power flowed into him. She made a tsking sound and muttered, "Take it easy, Eighteen."

Connor wondered what would happen if the two of them got into a real fight in that head of theirs. Would her other personalities pile on and escalate it into a mental riot, or would they help calm the two captive roommates? He reminded himself to ask her later to explain more about how she could tap different affinities from her alternate personalities.

Aifric released him and her features shifted back to the Mhortair assassin. She reached for her weapons.

To tap limestone, he only needed skin contact, and he had a piece hanging from a leather cord around his neck. Limestone was the last major affinity stone that he had connected with. It had always seemed reluctant to answer his call, as if still moping over that fact. Thankfully he'd spent so much time with it recently that he connected quickly for once.

He didn't want the stone itself to glow, but concentrated through it to the light streaming past. The sunlight now felt heavier, the waves discernible to his limestone sense. Some of the closest waves flickered across his skin, allowing him to feel the individual particles. Their touch eased the chill, as if they contained heat as well as light.

Student Eighteen saluted. "Time for the real lesson."

Time to light up the match.

Connor tugged at the streaming sunlight pouring between them and twisted it. He was hoping to wrap her with it, momentarily blind her, and create a distraction for the half second he would need to wipe that bored expression off her face.

Instead, the light twisted into an eye-bending pattern. She looked momentarily distorted, as if he was looking at her through rippling water.

He nearly released it to try again, but Student Eighteen frowned. He was accomplishing something. So he intensified his efforts. Maybe he could distract her with that strange distortion effect.

She'd drilled into him the need for constant movement in their practice sessions, so he slipped to his right.

She didn't turn to follow.

Her expression turned concerned and she lowered her weapons, taking a step toward where he'd been. "Connor, are you all right?"

That was an unexpected bonus. Connor slipped farther to the right, barely allowing himself to breathe. He raised his sword, ready to deflect if she pulled some kind of new trick, but the Assassin still didn't turn to follow him.

"What are you doing?" she asked, frowning at empty space where he'd been.

She took another step in that direction, her guard down, the perfect opportunity to strike. It might be a trick, so he decided to find out.

Connor lunged from the side and slashed his sword across her ribs.

Only when he moved did she react, looking startled.

Too late. He hadn't actually thought that would work, so he hit her harder than he'd intended, sending her staggering.

Student Eighteen regained her balance instantly, but did not counterattack. Instead she looked from him to the spot he'd been standing before. "How did you do that?"

"I'm just that good," he teased.

"No, I mean, you sort of faded away. For a second it looked like you were literally melting on the spot. I've never seen anything like it."

Kilian drew closer and said, "I'd be surprised if you had."

Student Eighteen asked him, "Did you see it too, or am I cracked?"

He gave her an amused smile. "I can't claim that mind of yours is normal, but you weren't imagining things."

"What are you talking about? I was just playing with limestone, trying to distract you with a little glow."

"I didn't see anything glowing. I swear I saw you fade away, then reappear over there."

"Really? Wow. You mean, like I disappeared or something?"

That was perhaps the most amazing failed attempt to use a power stone ever.

"Something like that," Kilian said, a bemused smile on his face. "You have an exceptional knack for stumbling upon abilities that others often have to work at for months."

"I thought his talent was breaking things," Student Eighteen said with a smile that grew more radiant as she shifted back to Aifric.

Connor shrugged. "Today I'm breaking records, I guess. So what did I do?"

Kilian gestured him to remove the chain with the piece of limestone, then took it and held it up. "One of the subtle and tricky aspects to limestone now available to you since your ascension. You've already discovered you can now manipulate light better. What you just did was bend the light around Aifric. It changed what she saw."

"Really?" Connor and Aifric asked together.

"Really. It's a technique I haven't used in ages. I was never that good at it, not like my father, but you seem to have a knack for it. My father called it Mirage, and it has tremendous potential."

Aifric frowned in concentration, shaking her head and poking herself in the temple. "Cut it out. It's my turn."

"What's going on?" Connor asked, worried the mirage had affected her more than she'd explained.

"Student Eighteen wants to drive. She's not happy that you've rediscovered mirage. It's one of the powers the Mhortair are sworn to stamp out."

Connor felt relieved she hadn't surrendered control to the deadly Assassin. "Can you remind her that she's already decided some of those directives are pretty dumb?"

He watched her closely as she paced away, muttering to herself, hands balled into fists. Part of him really wanted to eavesdrop on that singular argument, but he didn't want to push Student Eighteen any farther. He thought back to the day when she'd been ordered by Mister Five to assassinate him. She had held steel to every kill location on his body but had refused to end his life. She had made her choice, and he would trust her to remain true to her oath.

Aifric returned, looking relieved. "She's all right now. Thanks for reminding us of our oath. Sometimes loyalties get a bit twisted around you, Connor."

"Friends have to do that to each other sometimes." He glanced at Kilian and added, "And sometimes we have to share truth with people who might not necessarily want to hear it."

"You're absolutely right. We need that patronage revolution of yours now more than ever."

"Don't get distracted," Aifric chided Connor as he took the limestone back and studied the little greenish stone closely.

"So explain mirage, please. I had planned to blind Student Eighteen, but when I directed the light toward her, it sort of twisted instead."

"That's mirage in a nut shell. Most Solas focus so hard and so long on merely triggering light from limestone they struggle to recognize it can do more, even when they ascend and gain access to its more subtle and startling powers."

"That explains it, then. I'm so new to limestone, I'm working with pure creative brilliance here."

Aifric rolled her eyes. "It's a good thing I like you, Connor, or I'd let Student Eighteen teach you some more humility."

Kilian said, "Call it what you will. It's an important discovery. You twisted the light out of its normal pattern and anchored the new pattern to Aifric. That caused the distortion that made her see you melting away instead of seeing you move."

"I definitely need to practice this more," Connor said with a grin.

The concept had tons of potential. No doubt when he explained it to Hamish, he'd recommend they try waltzing right into the kitchen tents and sneaking fresh sweetbreads without the cooks turning their long-handled wooden spoons against them.

Kilian said, "We'll work on it. It's a good idea for me to practice some more too, if only to be prepared against limestone trickery from my mother."

"Is she good at mirages?" Aifric asked nervously.

That was a scary thought. From what he'd heard about Queen Dreokt, she was already far too dangerous without perhaps tricking them into seeing things that weren't there, or jumping out of thin air when they weren't ready.

"Not really. She all but ignores the primary and secondary affinity stones. She was the ultimate elemental battle Petralist. Not even my father could match her for raw elemental power."

"Well that's encouraging," Connor said dryly.

Aifric asked, "Can Connor access any new abilities with obsidian too?"

That was a good question. He'd love a new advantage against Student Eighteen.

But Kilian shook his head. "No. Obsidian is the only primary affinity stone that offers a threshold specific to itself. Connor can tap a deeper measure of obsidian than he could have prior to ascension, and that offers significant advantages, as you've already witnessed."

"So I've been learning faster than normal?"

Aifric nodded. "Even most Blades require weeks to pick up what you have in the past couple of days."

Connor grimaced. "I don't have that much time."

"So why is obsidian different?" Aifric asked.

"It seems to be an exception in a lot of ways," Connor agreed.

"That's because it was the first-ever power stone."

"What?" Aifric exclaimed.

Connor shook his head in disgust. "You can't just drop shocking truths on us like that without a little more buildup."

Just like when Kilian had casually revealed that he was the original prince of Obrion, son of the dreaded Queen Dreokt, and that Evander was his nephew. Those were wasted opportunities. For a guy with so much style, he seemed to have a blind spot when it came to ancient, mind-stretching secrets.

Kilian smiled. "Sorry. I forget sometimes how much is new to so many of you."

"It's new because you've kept it all secret for three hundred years," Connor reminded him.

"What did you mean?" Aifric asked.

"Just what I said. My parents were the first-ever Petralists, and obsidian was the first-ever successful affinity stone."

Connor asked, "How is that possible?"

"I know only a little. When they came to this continent, they were already powerful Petralists. I was born here and learned only bits and pieces of their history. They almost never spoke about it. I believe they were essentially magical researchers, working with a vast power too great to control. They figured out how to tap some of it by using stones as a form of intermediary buffer."

Connor rubbed his temples where a headache was starting behind his eyes. He almost wished Kilian hadn't started explaining. He was having enough trouble just learning about the different affinities and how to master them.

Aifric said, "Where did your parents come from?"

"I have no idea. They would never say, but it doesn't really matter. Just know that obsidian acts slightly different than most other power stones for reasons that we don't fully understand."

"Do you think your mother would explain it to you?" Connor asked.

Kilian barked a humorless laugh. "Not on my life. Even before her mind broke and she spent three centuries entombed under Alasdair as an elemental monster, she was tight-lipped about those truths."

"We have to find a way to kill her," Aifric said in a cold, hard voice, her hand dropping to one of her daggers. She'd shifted back to Student Eighteen without Connor noticing.

"I completely agree with your people on that point," Kilian said.

Connor asked, "But how? She stopped you in Alasdair even though she was weakened. Then she flew away as easily as a Builder."

"That was perhaps our best opportunity to remove her," Kilian admitted, his expression troubled. "That's why we're training so hard now. You must master your full range of affinities if you are to stand with me against her."

Connor tried to look enthusiastic, but the lump of dread in his throat made it hard to breathe.

"I think you'll need more than that," Student Eighteen said.

Kilian nodded. "We'll need everything we can come up with. She is by far the most powerful Petralist alive. We'll need our full might, plus the help of the Mhortair and a good deal of luck to have any hope of stopping her."

"And that's assuming she's not surrounded by the entire Obrioner army when we find her," Connor said.

Kilian's expression turned fierce, with flames igniting in his eyes. "She doesn't own them yet."

"It won't take her long," Student Eighteen warned.

Connor said, "So we don't have much time to figure out how to start spreading word about patronage and start our revolution."

Kilian nodded, then gave Connor a warning look. "Don't mention your revolution plans when we meet with Shona and Rory to sign the peace treaty later."

"That's really happening?" Connor asked. He'd thought talks of an official peace treaty for pausing hostilities was pretty foolish. No one was going to fight with winter finally howling down over them.

Kilian nodded. "It's happening. It's an important symbolic gesture."

Student Eighteen snorted. "So they feel clever when they break it and invade in the spring?"

Connor chuckled. "In that case, I'm all for it. They'll feel doubly foolish when we break the treaty first."

3

THE MOST IMPORTANT LIES NEED TO BE WRITTEN DOWN

Several hours later, Connor and Kilian flanked General Wolfram, who looked impressive dressed in full parade uniform, his legendary mustaches carefully groomed.

The three of them walked through the southern end of the Badurach Pass in a pocket of remarkable calm. Wind shrieked as it howled past on either side, channeled by the high walls of vertical stone close on either side, but it did not so much as ruffle Kilian's blue-tipped, black hair.

Kilian still wore only his light leather jacket, even though the fierce winter storm had indeed crashed over the high mountain pass with a savage vengeance that literally snatched the breath away. Connor walked beside Kilian, awed by the man's mastery of the elements. They both tapped just enough marble to ward against the intense, bone-numbing cold that crept south along with the brutal storm. Kilian regularly placed a hand on Wolfram's shoulder, sharing precious warmth with him too.

Connor glanced back the way they'd come, but couldn't see more than a few feet back through the narrow pass, cumbered by piles of rubble from the cracked and broken summits that made walking treacherous. Snow billowed around their little pocket of calm like an ever-changing sheet, whipped to a frenzy by the brutal wind.

Connor tapped soapstone. He'd already downed a mixture of powdered stone and water, and now he imagined the gateway to elemental water like a door in his mind, filled with crashing waves. The doorway to elemental fire, reached through the bit of marble wedged under his tongue, stood back-to-back with the watery doorway. The doorway to marble, wreathed in crimson flame, already stood partly ajar, allowing him to access elemental fire and create heat directly through that conduit. There was certainly none to draw upon from their surroundings.

When Connor pried open the doorway to soapstone, he instantly connected with water. Soapstone responded to his call better than any other metamorphic stone. He could walk with water and fire together without much trouble.

Air was always a challenge, though. It was fickle and unruly on the best of days. Connor always imagined the gateway to air like a trapdoor overhead. Thrusting his affinity senses up through that doorway connected with elemental air. Pulling the door down toward him allowed him to tap quartzite internally, enhancing his senses.

He pushed the door up, and his senses burst upward into the storm, connected with water, fire, and air. Only the queen could manage more than two tertiary affinities together. Even the mighty Kilian was limited to a Dawnus power of fire and water.

Connor sucked in a sharp breath. "Wow. I've never felt anything like this."

The mighty storm churning south over the mountains loomed in his elemental senses, dark and foreboding. Winds tore across the landscape in a frenzy. Usually he could sense a bit about the winds he touched, their history and purpose, but not in that moment. The wind felt wild, panicked, like a spooked stallion. Well, a stallion that could run hundreds of miles an hour and scream like a thousand pedras caught in a bloodlust frenzy.

Kilian spoke loudly over the screaming wind. "I suspect the turbulence my mother released helped intensify it." He gave Connor a serious, warning look. "Don't meddle with it."

"I won't." He was tempted to, though.

Kilian leaned a bit closer. "I'm serious, Connor. Tampering with the weather is tricky business on a good day, and this storm is already in a rage. Don't give it an excuse to turn into the storm of the century."

"I won't," he promised again, but had to wonder what that would look like. Maybe if the peace talks didn't go well, he could try it on the Obrioner side.

The sheer energy of the storm dwarfed all the power he'd ever harnessed as a Petralist. His affinities might grant him access to the elements, but these elements were completely untamed. Through soapstone, he felt the snow, helpless under the wind's onslaught, hurled against men and stone with such intensity the hard little flakes felt like hornets fired from Hamish's speedsling.

The storm still could not ignore Kilian, though. The ancient Dawnus had drawn snow into a protective wedge behind them, fusing the snow into sheets that parted the wind and storm around them, just wide enough to leave them in their protective, calm bubble. It was similar to how he parted the waters of the rivers when they rode the marvelous underwater Slide against the current.

Connor felt tempted to reach farther and grapple with the weather to see if he could ease the intensity of the storm or deflect it to the west.

He'd never felt such a storm. But Kilian was still watching him, so he resisted the urge.

As soon as they stepped beyond the end of the pass, called Drumwhindle on the Obrioner side, the wind smacked Connor in the side of the face with a brutal cross breeze, as if chiding him for huddling in the protective confines of the broken pass. In three seconds, the wind whipped Wolfram's well-groomed mustaches into a tangled mess. He frowned at Kilian.

Connor looked to Kilian too, expecting to see him extend the shielding around them, but Kilian only glanced at him and asked, "What are you waiting for?"

Connor glanced south to where the Obrioner welcoming party waited for them twenty paces away, at the end of the narrow stone causeway that connected the wide plateau with the pass. The causeway was barely ten yards wide, spanning a deep gorge that the wind seemed to love playing in.

General Rory, flanked by Tomas and Cameron and several officers, withstood the battering from the weather through sheet determination. He kept his craggy face impassive. Well, what Connor could see of it was impassive. Rory and his men were bundled in heavy furs, their hoods concealing most of their features.

As General Wolfram strode purposefully toward the Obrioners, Connor seized the whipping snow and pushed it out into another wedge-shaped, defensive barrier upwind of their position. He loved the feeling of the wind and snow parting around it, cut like a thrown pudding. In a few seconds, he adjusted the angle and height of his shield to overlap with the one Kilian maintained behind them, enlarging the calm space enough to encompass the Obrioners as they drew near.

Rory pushed his hood back and shook Wolfram's hand firmly.

"Well met, General, and congratulations on your promotion," Wolfram said.

Rory said, "I'm glad we meet with a handshake instead of with crossed swords. Come. Let's get out of this insane weather."

Connor had to wonder why they hadn't employed Spitters to shield them from the weather like Kilian had just taught him. Surely someone else understood the trick. Did they fear tampering with any of the elements that much, or were their Spitters occupied with other duties?

With so much snow to play with, a full team of Spitters, coordinating their efforts closely, could launch a devastating attack. Kilian, Wolfram, and Connor represented a tempting target. Would they dare strike during a meeting about peace?

If the talks failed for any reason, they'd have a great excuse.

Rory nodded to Kilian, who gave him a roguish salute. Then he looked at Connor and gestured toward the storm. "This isn't your doing, is it?"

"I take full responsibility for shielding you now, but I haven't even started playing with the rest of the weather yet," Connor replied as he shook Rory's hand enthusiastically. "I'm happy to try if you like."

Rory grimaced. "Please don't. This causeway makes me nervous on the best of days."

That was a good point. That narrow bridge of stone might not represent much of a challenge to Hamish and Verena with their flying machines, but Connor didn't doubt many people felt absolutely weak in the knees crossing it, even without the wind clawing at them.

Connor said, "I'll leave it alone unless I'm forced to change my mind."

He felt that was a pretty nice way to warn Rory not to allow any underhanded tricks during the meeting. Unleashing the storm of the century on Rory's army would be the perfect way to counter any such foolishness.

Tomas and Cameron greeted Connor with their normal enthusiasm, and for a moment he worried he might stumble right off the causeway as they pounded his back so hard he stumbled.

Tomas said, "No offense, Connor, but I don't want this storm broken."

"Might just upset it," Cameron agreed.

Connor was thrilled to see them and hoped they'd join the treaty talks. Their easy banter and unabashed lack of respect for most authority always helped settle his nerves.

They crossed the causeway with the wind battering Connor's shields. If it broke free, it could easily drag them over the edge and into a five-thousand-foot free fall. Connor decided he'd have to try it on a less formal day. He was getting better with quartzite. With that much open air, he'd surely snag a helpful current before hitting the bottom.

Probably.

The Obrioner camp looked as empty as the Grandurian side. Despite extra tie-downs, tents shook and flapped in the intense storm, and no one moved around outside. Connor doubted more than a token force remained up on the plateau anyway. Most of the army was probably fleeing for the safety of Merkland's famous white granite walls.

The Grandurian army was just as depleted. The majority of the forces had left the day before, retreating north toward Altkalen. He didn't envy them that trip. Not only were they marching through a blizzard, but their Petralists couldn't dare ease the journey much. The land was dangerously unstable almost all the way north to Altkalen.

The battle for Harz had broken it, leaving the land heaving with earthquakes and fiery fissures. The unprecedented earthquake triggered by Queen Dreokt had intensified the problems to the point of complete destabilization.

Entire mountains had shaken themselves apart, burying Alasdair under a mile of rubble. The shaking had spread all the way to the border and cracked the twin peaks of Drwumwhindle Pass. Mini earthquakes were common, and Sappers couldn't risk walking with earth in any mean-ingful way. Flameweavers had almost as much trouble tapping fire, which seemed eager to boil out of control.

Soapstone didn't seem to pose quite as much risk, and Longseers had no issue using quartzite internally to enhance their senses. Few ever tried focusing it to wield external air, and even if the area wasn't so unstable, air was always a fickle thing.

That meant the fighting was over for now, despite what people might want. The Obrioners wanted the treaty to save face after their failed inva-sion and to give them time to figure out what the return of Queen Dreokt meant.

The Grandurians wanted the treaty to make the Obrioners think they believed the ruse, and to give them time to figure out how to respond to the threat the queen posed. And to give Connor time to launch his revolu-tion of Guardians.

If he succeeded, the treaty might prove very useful after all. He didn't want Granadure invading a distracted Obrion, and with the treaty in place, he felt a little more confident they'd show restraint.

Instead of taking them to the command tent, Rory led them to High Lord Dougal's enormous palace tent. Connor was surprised that Rory would confiscate Dougal's palace, but at least it now had an honorable occupant.

They passed through a pair of solid oak doors into an enormous, plush entry hall. The thick canvas walls did an admirable job blocking out the howling storm. Thick rugs covered the ground, with tapestries hanging from interior walls made of white birch planking. Braziers of coals stood in the corners, keeping the room pleasantly warm. It might be a tent, but it felt as solid inside as any stone palace.

Shona stood waiting for them, flanked by several other officers and three handmaids, all dressed in House Dougal's colors. Shona was a high lady, Dougal's daughter, and she looked resplendent in a blue satin gown with a low enough neckline to accentuate her full figure without over-doing it. Her blond hair, nearly back to shoulder length after the times Connor had burned it off, was pulled back from her face with a simple silver circlet that definitely hinted at wanting to be a crown.

Connor nearly laughed. Shona was beautiful, manipulative, clever, and deadly. She had shared with him her dream of one day rising to rule, using him as her path to ascension.

Her hazel eyes settled on him and she gave him a dazzling smile. Often in the past, despite what he knew of her, that smile had still made it hard to think straight. Today it didn't work. His worry for Verena consumed all his available emotion and insulated him from Shona's heart games.

He would have preferred it if Shona had returned to Merkland instead of taking part in the treaty talks. She was devious and brilliant and made him nervous. They'd spent far too much time together, much of it with her trying to seduce and manipulate him into marrying her so she could control his powers and launch her own plans for national conquest.

They'd managed to create some good memories too, and those still tugged at his mind, creating that hated sense of hesitation around her. He didn't want Shona, but he'd never managed to entirely break from her. Even during the recent war, she'd found ways to twist and complicate his life. He felt surprised to realize that despite everything, he still didn't hate her. He couldn't ever trust her, though. Complicated was the word that best described how he felt toward Lord Dougal's devious daughter.

Connor was tempted to tap limestone and experiment with that mirage effect he'd just learned. Could he make Shona believe her hair was on fire again? He grinned at the mental image of the poised and beautiful Shona suddenly yelping and swatting at her own head.

She gave him an annoyed looked. She couldn't know what he was grinning at, but it was clear her carefully planned greeting hadn't produced the desired effect.

But Shona didn't let that interrupt her for long. She approached and extended her hands to Wolfram. "General. It's a pleasure to see you again."

General Wolfram made a courtly bow over her hand. "Lady Shona, I'm thrilled that you will be in attendance for this historic meeting."

A tall soldier standing to Shona's right sniffed in disdain. "Not so historic. Granadure is once again buying time, but you will rejoin Obrion sooner or later."

Connor recognized the arrogant, angry voice of Lord Flichity, representative of High Lord Lenox. He'd dared chide Dougal about their loss at Altkalen and challenge Dougal's orders to retreat back to the border. Now that Dougal's trap at Alasdair to destroy Kilian and entrap Connor again had failed, no doubt Flichity was raging about the peace accord.

Kilian spoke before Wolfram could. He took a half step closer and said softly, "We haven't signed anything yet, Flichity. I doubt anyone would mind if you and I stepped outside for a moment if you feel the need for a final duel."

Flichity recoiled from Kilian, his face draining of color and his manner changing to near panic. "No need for hostilities today. I completely support General Rory and High Lady Shona's decisions."

"Wise choice," Kilian said simply.

Wolfram's mustaches twitched, perhaps concealing a smile. Connor wasn't actually an official delegate, so he didn't feel bad at all when he caught Flichity's eye, gave him a wide smile, and winked. Flichity's expression hardened, but he didn't dare speak his outrage.

Rory offered Shona his arm and they led the party down a wood-paneled hall, then into a large office. The huge desk on the far side of the room was probably Dougal's personal work space, and Connor was tempted to take a look in the drawers. He'd love to discover a detailed outline of Dougal's convoluted plans. He doubted Dougal had exhausted all of his contingencies. It would be nice to not feel two steps behind the legendarily clever nobleman next time they faced him.

The group settled into padded wooden chairs around a long, black table. A single document already sat at the head of the table, beside a gold-tipped feather quill and an ink well in the shape of a pedra's open, double-jawed mouth.

Connor suspected most such occasions would drag on as the gathered lords and ladies felt obligated to make long-winded, meaningless speeches about good will and trust, which not even they would actually believe. Thankfully, neither Wolfram nor Rory felt the need.

Shona looked like she wanted to, but just sighed and waved them on. While the two generals discussed specific terms, including renewing limited trade across the border, her expression turned thoughtful, worry lines creasing her normally smooth face.

The process took far less time than Connor had feared, and within an hour they finalized the simple document and each signed it. Connor had to wonder how the peace accord would affect relationships with the five nations of the Arishat League. Led by the nation of Althing, they had all begun mobilizing to respond to the threat of invasion by Obrion. Would they believe that peace had been restored?

Not when they heard about the dread Queen Dreokt's return.

As soon as the last signature was dry on the paper and congratulatory handshakes shared around the room, Connor asked, "Shona, have you found your father yet?"

"Why, so you can kill him?" Shona asked, one fine eyebrow raised, her tone carefully neutral.

"Dying is something he'll get around to soon enough." He didn't bother responding to the silent offer he read in her eyes. She'd flat-out told him she'd help assassinate her father if he'd marry her so they could rise to power together. Her unwavering conviction of the rightness of her claim to rule would be admirable if it wasn't so psycho.

Rory said, "Enough talk of dying, lad. The latest report claimed that Queen Dreokt showed up in Donleavy and seized the throne yesterday."

Tomas, who stood with Cameron on either side of the door spoke up. "I heard King Turriff and his family surrendered power without a fight."

Cameron grunted, his ugly face turned uglier with a scowl. "That ain't right. Even if she's his upteenth grandmother, one has to defend their rights."

Lord Flichity glowered. "Watch your tongues, fools. We don't share rumors about our king with the enemy."

Rory gestured toward the outer wall of the office that shook slightly under the howling wind. "No one is attacking anyone through this mess."

Kilian said, "Invading Obrion is not our concern. You have bigger problems."

"You know about her, don't you?" Shona asked, studying Kilian closely.

Connor nearly blurted out, *She's his mother, after all.* But realized they didn't know, and Kilian might not want them to.

"I know her," Kilian said with a grimace. "She is the reason you don't need to fear us."

"Because she could drive you out?" Lord Flichity guessed eagerly.

"No you fool, because she is completely insane. She's totally unbalanced, but also immensely powerful. You have no concept of the destruction she's about to unleash upon you all."

Shona looked shaken. "My father is still with her. That's about the only thing that's clear."

Connor asked, "How could she just walk into Donleavy and take the throne? Aren't there defenses in place to protect King Turriff?"

"There should be. He wouldn't just step down, not without some kind of argument," Shona conceded.

"She is the rightful queen," Lord Flichity declared, and actually tipped his nose up a bit, as if that might make his idiocy sound more impressive.

Rory said, "But she's been in elemental hibernation for centuries. King Turriff is no fool. He might have ceded to her out of fear, but he would have tried to arrange to remain as her regent to assist with the transition, or something. We've heard nothing of the sort."

"It's worse than that. From what I heard, he not only surrendered the throne, but she's taken the entire royal family as her personal servants," Shona said with a grimace.

Lord Flichity spat, "Simply shameful. The man has no dignity."

"Probably worse than that," Kilian said. "What exactly did the report say? Any detail could prove helpful."

Lord Flichity snapped, "To you! But we're not allies. Why is it that I alone seem to remember this?"

"Because you're the only one who doesn't see there are better options available," Connor suggested.

Rory waved Flichity to silence and gestured at the treaty they just signed. "We have a peace accord in place. All things considered, I recommend you convince yourself we can trust it, and that perhaps working together we can avert a greater disaster."

Lord Flichity muttered under his breath. Connor tapped quartzite in time to catch the word, "Fool."

He decided Lord Flichity needed close watching. He seemed far too similar to Dougal, if not half so clever.

Shona said, "The most reliable report I received from my father wasn't very long, nor did he go into great detail. He stated the queen reclaimed her throne, that he served as her closest advisor, and the King

Turriff and his entire family now also served her. The queen called them the only worthy servants to her rule."

Tomas grunted. "You'd think with as much sleep as she's gotten, she'd be a little less abrasive."

"Maybe she's like those Striders. Make them sit still too long and they go wild," Cameron suggested.

Kilian said, "She has used the term 'worthy servant' in the past, but only for those whose loyalty remained absolute."

"The king's honor is impeachable," Lord Flichity declared.

"But she could never trust his loyalty, not completely," Shona said with a frown.

Kilian said solemnly, "I suspect your King Turriff and his family are not the same people you knew."

"What do you mean?" Rory asked with a frown.

"She has the power to influence the minds of those around her, and her technique is the mental equivalent to a sledgehammer. A resisting mind is like a piece of hard stone." He glanced at Connor. "What happens when you strike a rock with a sledgehammer?"

"It breaks."

The warm room suddenly felt cold.

4

THE POWER OF FOOD DIPLOMACY

Hamish sat at the high table at the front of a huge barn converted into an assembly and feasting hall at Emmerich township. He shared the long table with the leaders of both Emmerich and Alasdair. The large building still smelled like hay, potatoes, and beets, which had only been cleared out the day before.

The enormous barn was packed with people, both the locals of Emmerich who had survived the unexpected attack by the fire-bound elfonnel, as well as all the displaced villagers from Alasdair. The two groups were roughly equivalent in size and sat in distinct groups on opposite sides of the central aisle running down the room.

They regarded each other with a mixture of curiosity and distrust. The low murmur of hundreds of voices in two different languages mixed far more freely than their owners.

Hamish decided before the next feast he would shift tables around to remove that center aisle. That might make it easier to begin integrating the groups. He had only arrived at Emmerich with the refugees from Alasdair the day before. People in both countries were raised to mistrust and even hate each other, and here he was trying to get these two groups to live and work together in peace.

No problem.

The challenges they faced plagued Hamish's every waking moment and nearly robbed him of his appetite. When Connor suggested he take the lead in the effort and prove it was possible, Hamish had agreed with his normal good cheer.

Inside, he'd wanted to shout at Connor that he was cracked.

In his defense, Connor had a lot on his mind. Verena was still lying unconscious and no one knew if she'd ever awaken and recover. Connor also had all that affinity training to focus on with Kilian, and as much as he tried not to share his worry, Hamish had seen how much the transformation into that horrible rage monster had affected Connor.

And then there was the whole revolution thing Connor kept talking about. Yes, it was necessary. No, there was no one else who could do it. And of course now with the dread risen from her granite tomb, Obrion would surely be thrown into chaos. That might present the perfect opportunity for the Guardians to throw off the shackles of lies that the Petralist high houses used to keep them in a state of ignorance and slavery.

Hamish understood all that, probably better than Connor or Kilian gave him credit for. But while they were focusing on the high-level plans and deep, arcane secrets no one else could touch, Hamish worried about all the things they hadn't considered yet.

As he scanned the long barn full of nervous villagers, he tried to enjoy the fact that they'd made it so far alive and all together. That alone was a miracle, but perhaps the greatest challenges lay ahead.

How would war and revolution affect hundreds of other villages like Alasdair? They couldn't resettle all of Obrion in Emmerich Valley.

Hamish did hope he could show that the people of the two nations could get along. They could take the first small steps in demonstrating to the world that change was possible.

All Hamish had to do was help break through centuries of prejudice. If only those five tons of bacon hadn't been lost and buried with Alasdair. That stash alone could have engendered tremendous goodwill. That was the kind of international diplomacy that everyone could understand.

Lord Wenzel, the lord of Emmerich, who sat at the center of the high table to Hamish's left, stood. The low rumble of hundreds of whispered conversations immediately faded to silence.

The last day had been extremely busy as the folks from Alasdair, under the enthusiastic direction of Hendry and Lilias, pitched in to help their hosts. Together they worked clearing the rubble from the elfonnel attack, rebuilding broken homes, and trying to resettle an entire town. Nothing helped build bridges better than actually building bridges. And houses.

Thankfully a Sapper had already been dispatched from General Wolfram to help, along with a squad of Rumbler workmen. With their enhanced strength the work was progressing very quickly. The Sapper had already raised numerous earthen buildings. They were actually a lot more comfortable and warm than Hamish had feared. Without that assistance, he doubted the folks from Alasdair would have met such a warm welcome. The resources of Emmerich would have been stretched beyond their capacity.

Lord Wenzel spoke, his baritone voice echoing well through the cavernous barn. Unlike the weak Lord Gavin of Alasdair, the tall Lord Wenzel radiated a sense of confident authority. His graying hair and manicured beard added to the impression of a man in charge.

"My friends and my people, with the Tallan's blessing, we can enjoy this feast and each other's company in safety. It is with great enthusiasm that I look to the future. Despite the trials we have all faced in recent days, it is clear that together we can not only survive, but thrive."

The little speech was met with a ripple of applause from the Grandurians, but looks of confusion from the folks of Alasdair. None of them spoke Grandurian yet, although Hamish was already working with Lord Wenzel's family to teach them.

Lord Wenzel smoothly transitioned to Obrioner and repeated the same opening remarks. Despite an obvious ripple of revulsion from the Alasdairians at the mention of the Tallan's blessing, Hendry and Lilias led the applause from where they sat to Hamish's right at the high table.

Another man and his wife sat on the opposite side of Lord Wenzel and Lady Theda. Merten was the Grandurian equivalent to the Ashlar. In Granadure the title was Quader, pronunced kva-de. He was a solid, dependable man, so much like Hendry that Hamish dared feel confident they might just figure out how to coexist.

Theda and Lilias had already begun organizing their women into a joint organization. Their efficient leadership could rival the best military officers Hamish had met.

The Obrioners clearly appreciated hearing their native tongue directly from Lord Wenzel, and Hamish was grateful that he made the effort to include them. He could have asked Hamish to interpret. His Obrioner was good but not great. Many people felt self-conscious about speaking a non-fluent tongue, especially in front of a large group of native speakers who couldn't help but recognize the thick accent.

All of Lord Wenzel's family spoke at least a little Obrioner. Hamish was grateful that they seemed eager to help lead language lessons for both the newcomers and their own townsfolk.

Lord Wenzel launched into only a brief monologue, showing great restraint for a lord. He seemed to understand that remarks made before a feast needed to be short. Otherwise the food would create a distraction that even the most ardent supporters would have a hard time ignoring.

When he finished, Lord Wenzel raised his hands again and said loudly, "Let the feasting begin!"

Everyone dug in with enthusiasm. Although the range of foodstuffs available for the feast had been slim, the quantities were plentiful. Lilias and the women of Alasdair had done a remarkable job creating familiar Obrioner food out of the local Grandurian fare.

Hamish noted that the food being passed around the heavy feasting tables was as segregated as the people and their languages. He leaned a bit closer to Hendry and Lilias and asked, "What do you think about sharing the food across the aisle?"

Hendry said, "I thought that's what they were doing already."

Lilias poked him in the ribs. "He means sampling each others' dishes.

We do need to figure out how to appreciate each other's cooking sooner rather than later."

Hamish turned to Lord Wenzel and repeated the suggestion in Grandurian. Both Lord Wenzel and Lady Theda also agreed, as did Merten and his wife, Karola.

So Hamish left the high table, grabbed a long platter piled high with Obrioner sausages and minced beef pies. Of course, the sausages were Grandurian, but the Alasdairian ladies had cooked and seasoned them the way they did at home. And Hamish hadn't seen anything to rival the famous Obrioner meat pies anywhere in Granadure.

He carried the platter across to the Grandurian side, placed it on a table in the middle of their packed rows with a flourish, and said in Grandurian, "Enjoy."

The locals greeted the meat pies with distrust, but helped themselves to the sausages. Most of them ended up exchanging disgusted glances with their neighbors.

"You'll get used to it," he assured them.

Over the next ten minutes, he moved back and forth across the hall, overseeing the distribution of the food platters across opposite sides of the room so everyone got a chance to sample at least a little bit of something new.

Every ten seconds, he wished for his amazing flying Builder battle suit. Walking was just such a chore, one he'd tried to avoid whenever possible while wearing the suit. The memory of it getting shredded by Martys in his horrifying rampager form still made Hamish shiver. Connor had helped heal the worst of his scarring, but he'd always wear a few, particularly those across his shoulder. Jean thought they made him look brave.

He shouldn't have been surprised by hesitation to try new foods, although he was surprised by how many pushed away the strange dishes after only small samples. He loved Grandurian food, loved exploring new tastes. He'd even discovered several dishes at the Builder compound that were now some of his all-time favorites.

When Hamish returned to the high table, where they'd also shared their food around, Hendry looked up from a spoonful of button-sized spatzle, unable to conceal his grimace. "I'm not sure this was such a good idea."

Lilias snatched the spoon from him and popped the soft noddles into her mouth. "I don't know what you're talking about. These are delicious."

"I've always thought so," Hamish said.

"I guess it'll take some getting used to," Hendry said with a little sigh.

It seemed the majority of the people in the room shared that sentiment. They'd grow accustomed to each other's food eventually. The ladies would play the critical role in helping everyone adjust.

In the meantime, Hamish forced himself to feast with near-normal enthusiasm. If he let the enormous weight of responsibility and worry wear him down, he wouldn't be able to help anyone.

While they ate, Lady Theda asked Hendry in her elegant Obrioner accent, "How did the cutting go today?"

"Better than I expected."

Merten nodded agreement and spoke in Grandurian. Hamish translated. "Your cutters are very skilled. My men were impressed. They hadn't been sure you Obrioners would be able to keep up."

Hendry smiled. "The techniques are a little different, but obsidian is not as hard as granite. My concern is that my men will grow soft quarrying this glassy stone."

Lord Wenzel laughed. "I suspect our quotas will rise, so I am glad we have your help."

Hamish scanned the tables for the cutters. Out of all of the people, they seemed most friendly with each other. Despite the threat of the impending storm, they had put in a full day at the quarry, the first since the disaster. Hamish had already heard that it had been exceptionally productive, even though all the man-made infrastructure at the quarry had been destroyed by the elfonnel attack.

Hendry added, "The only surprise today was how strange the obsidian felt."

Lilias said, "You just told us it's easier to quarry."

"It's not that. The quarrying process we can handle."

"Then what do you mean?" Lady Theda asked.

Hendry hesitated before speaking. "It's a little strange, but the stone itself feels odd. Granite always has a strong, enduring feel to it. Alasdair White especially. It's so familiar, we barely notice."

Hamish leaned closer, intrigued by the comment. As a Builder he knew exactly what Hendry was talking about, but he had grown up all his life in Alasdair as the only person who ever admitted that different stones tasted different. "But obsidian feels different?"

Hendry nodded. "Obsidian feels kind of flighty, honestly."

Lord Wenzel and his wife laughed, but the Quader looked thoughtful. Through Hamish he said, "We too know our stone well. To me, working with obsidian energizes me. I often work all day without hardly feeling tired."

Lord Wenzel said with a smile. "I'm sure you Obrioners will get used to working our stone."

He did not seem interested in pursuing the question. He was not a Petralist, so maybe he didn't try to dwell too deeply on questions of power stone. His wife was an Allcarver, and she looked more intrigued. Perhaps she could help Hamish dig into the question further. He definitely planned to.

How the cutters unlocked the tiny fraction of diorite power they used in their chisels and hammers was a mystery. They weren't Petralists, but nor were they Builders. So what were they?

His deeper thoughts were interrupted by the arrival of dessert. Hamish eagerly grabbed dishes from both nations. Again Lord Wenzel insisted that the food be passed around between both groups. Hamish expected those delicious desserts would better convince people that the food across the border was worth considering.

He watched people carefully as they cautiously tried unfamiliar sweets. Most were definitely better received, but he was still amazed by how many pushed the desserts aside after only tiny trial bites.

Hamish would have to mingle around the room again at the end of the meal to help deal with those leftovers. In a time of war, rations had to be managed carefully. He couldn't take the risk that any of those desserts might get discarded.

"How can you people eat this?" Stuart demanded, pushing his plate roughly away. He sat at one of the closer tables with his younger siblings and with the rest of Hendry and Lilias's family.

Hamish wanted to fly over there and slap him a couple of times. He didn't need Stuart's big mouth making things any harder. Hamish had actually started hoping Stuart might think before speaking sometimes. The responsibility for caring for his younger siblings after their idiot parents had died in the first battles of Alasdair weighed heavily on him. He was seen as a rising leader among the ranks of the cutters, but now he was acting like the blockheaded Stuart Hamish had grown up with.

Hamish had changed too, though. Even though he didn't have a replacement flying suit yet, he felt confident he could put the heavily-muscled Stuart in his place if he had to. As tempting as that was, it probably wouldn't help things either. So instead, Hamish spotted one of his favorite desserts. The platter of powder-coated, jelly-filled krapfen sat on the high table. Only one piece remained. Hamish snatched it up and brought it to Stuart.

"Here. Try this."

Stuart recoiled, as if Hamish had asked him to try licking a live snake. "Grandurian food is disgusting."

Although most of the Grandurians did not understand, his tone and manner clearly communicated what he was saying. Hamish fought down the image of dumping Stuart head-first into the town well.

He leaned a little closer and said softly but intently, "Stuart, these people have accepted us into their homes. I heard that one of their cutters even allowed you to use his chisel today. So do you think insulting them is the best response?"

Stuart glared again but took the pastry. "Fine. I'll eat it this once."

"And look like you enjoy it."

"You owe me."

"We'll talk after you eat it."

Stuart took a deep breath and, with an expression like one about to plunge his hand into an open flame, shoved the entire pastry into his mouth. He chewed quickly, clearly planning to swallow the entire thing to avoid having to endure the taste longer than absolutely necessary.

After the first couple of frenzied bites, Stuart stopped. His eyes widened and his mouth dropped open in amazement. Since it was full of half-eaten pastry, the sight was rather gross, but Hamish still laughed.

"So, what was that about all Grandurian food being disgusting?"

Stuart didn't speak, but closed his eyes as he slowly savored the krapfen. Only after he swallowed did he say, "I never imagined something so wonderful. How is it possible?"

Hamish chuckled again and clapped Stuart on his beefy shoulder. Many of those who had been glowering at Stuart's antics earlier were now openly grinning. Nothing like a little food diplomacy.

Hamish said loudly in Grandurian, "Even the most obstinate block-head is vanquished by your cooking."

The comment elicited a round of laughter, and even some clapping. Hamish asked, "Who baked this dish?"

He glanced around, expecting to congratulate whichever mother had brought her best baking game to this first feast. She had done perhaps more to help break the ice between the two groups than anyone else.

He noticed several people looking behind him, and he was surprised when he turned to see Stefanie, Lord Wenzel's seventeen year-old daughter standing. She was a plump, blonde, happy girl, who Hamish already immensely liked. She had volunteered to help translate and lead language classes. And she could cook.

With everyone staring at her, she flushed, little spots of color rising in her cheeks, serving to make her look even prettier. She accepted Hamish's compliment with a nod and a smile.

"Wow."

The soft word, barely above a whisper, would have been inaudible if Hamish had been standing even a foot farther from Stuart. He glanced down to find Stuart staring at Stefanie with a look of unabashed adoration on his face.

Hamish nearly laughed, but embarrassing Stuart would undo everything he had just accomplished. So he clapped Stuart on the shoulder again, shaking him out of his rapt reverie.

Stefanie had noticed Stuart's attention, but did not look displeased by his interest. Torben, her burly older brother did, though.

Hamish returned to his seat, content with the breakthrough he had helped broker. Hopefully the goodwill would continue to grow enough to withstand the imminent and likely challenge Torben would make. Grandurian older brothers took their responsibility to honor duel any potential suitors very seriously. Torben was a cutter, and Stuart's equal in size so the match would be interesting.

Hamish chuckled to himself as he polished off the last of the food at the high table.

"You seem awfully proud of yourself," Lilias said. She looked more nervous than happy about Stuart's obvious infatuation with Lord Wenzel's daughter.

Hamish grinned. "I'm just thinking about how Stuart will react when he learns Stefanie is a Rumbler."

5

LOOK DEEP. SEE CLEAR.

J ean settled onto a short wooden stool beside one of the marvelous healthbeds in the long, brightly lit recovery room of the hospital in Faulenrost. The tidy beds marched down both sides of the room, positioned under tall windows with the drapes thrown wide to enjoy the fading afternoon sunlight. A huge storm was sweeping toward them from the north so darkness would arrive early.

For the moment, the room was quiet, and most of the patients lying in their healthbeds recovering from injuries or illnesses seemed at peace. Several had family members visiting. Four white-jacketed Healers moved among their patients.

Jean alone sat beside the last bed and the terribly sick little girl sleeping fitfully on it. Barely ten years old, the girl looked exhausted, her features drawn from her life-threatening ordeal.

Her name was Else and she had scratched her arm on a rusty nail three days prior. The cut was so minor, her family hadn't bothered to bring her to the Healers until it grew red and inflamed. Infection was one of the ailments that Healing power could not easily cure. That had surprised Jean and given her an opportunity to really help.

Most of the time, her herbs and tonics weren't necessary. The Healers with their marvelous sandstone power could heal cuts, broken bones, and even many internal injuries with the touch of a hand. Patients usually recovered within hours after treatment, relaxing on a healthbed, soaking in the gentle flow of healing power. Jean felt it as she leaned over Else's bed, like a waft of warm air against her skin, easing her concerns and invigorating her.

Jean used a piece of soft cloth to gently bathe the girl's sweaty forehead with cool water. The way her bedclothes stuck to her suggested the fever sweat had spread all over. That was a good sign. If the fever had broken, maybe they were finally winning the fight against the insidious infection.

For a couple of days, she had feared they would lose the girl. She'd visited three times a day, despite her many other duties, adjusting the dosage and composition of her herbal remedies to find the best solution for the unusually difficult infection.

Else blinked open her eyes and managed a weak smile. "Hello, Lady Jean." Her voice sounded stronger too.

She loved the fact that she could understand Else's words. She'd been studying Grandurian with Carolin, the elegant mistress of the Faulenrost Girls Academy, who also worked with Jean on her management team.

"Just call me Jean," she replied in broken Grandurian.

Understanding what other people said came easier than forming the strange sounds herself. Far too often people gave her odd stares, warning her that she'd again messed up the words. One time she'd tried to tell Bruno, the huge master blacksmith, that she wanted to meet to discuss designs for a new flying craft.

He'd laughed loudly and explained that it sounded like she'd said she wanted help burning a latrine for dinner.

She had gotten better.

That didn't mean the girl would drop the 'lady' honorific. Lord Eberhard had proclaimed Jean the hero of Schwinkendorf, and the people of the town had enthusiastically adopted her as their favorite new daughter. Her initial embarrassment at all the attention was fading under the realization that it wouldn't change, and that at least her new position helped her get things done.

And she had a lot to do. Somehow she'd been appointed to oversee the effort of coordinating with Builders to provide temporary workshops in Faulenrost. She also headed the committee responsible for rebuilding Schwinkendorf, and Lord Eberhard had enthusiastically supported her idea for a new school of higher learning. He'd immediately appointed her as its first head mistress.

Her days were packed so full of meetings and planning with her ever-growing management teams that she found it increasingly difficult to slip away and visit the hospital. She'd found a way, though. Else's life depended on it.

Else said, "Yes, Lady Jean. I will."

Jean chuckled and brushed the girl's hair from her forehead and checking her temperature. She really did feel much cooler. "How are you feeling today?"

"Tired, but better, I think." She finished with more of a question than a statement, looking up at Jean with nervous hope.

"Let's check your injury." She took Else's bandaged hand, but approaching footsteps drew her attention.

An aged Healer was heading in their direction. Healer Karlmann was

Lord Eberhard's chief physician. He possessed a profound understanding of the human body and how to heal it, but his own body was failing. His wispy, gray hair framed an ancient, lined face with the hint of a scraggly beard. His blue eyes were weak, his skeletal hands shaky, and he walked with a pronounced stoop. But he possessed a happy smile, a rich, friendly voice, and thankfully he spoke Obrioner.

"Lady Jean, I heard you'd come again. How is our young patient?"

Jean rose and curtsied. "She is much improved. How are you feeling today?"

"Old," he said with a wheezing chuckle.

She helped him to the chair on the other side of Else's bed. He grumbled about the attention, but did not refuse. Jean had felt intimidated by the old Healer when they'd first met. He hadn't bothered hiding his impatience at her herbal healing, but had allowed her to visit the hospital without restriction. No doubt at first he'd just humored her because she was a favorite of Lord Eberhard, but he too had been drawn to Else's case.

In the past couple of days they'd spent as much time together as Jean could spare, discussing various treatment options and the limitations and advantages of their different approaches. She'd grown to respect his depth of wisdom and experience, and she'd sensed that he'd been surprised, then intrigued by some of her questions and by the potential help her herbal remedies offered.

"I brought you something," she told him, extracting a ceramic jar of warm tea from her many-pocketed apron and removing the stopper for him. "It's a mixture of herbs that should help ease your aches and revitalize some of your energy."

Karlmann chuckled. "Not even you or I can stop aging, young Jean."

"But we can help ease the journey."

"Indeed. Thank you, my dear." He sipped the tea and gave her an appreciative nod. She'd added extra honey. She knew he had a bit of a sweet tooth.

He represented another interesting case for the limits of Healing powers. With his amazing abilities, he'd extended his productive lifespan significantly. He hadn't told her his exact age, but she suspected he was well over a hundred.

If he possessed a tertiary affinity, no doubt he could have extended his life even further. She longed to interview Kilian and Evander about their longevity. If she could isolate the reasons their unusually powerful affinities granted them such remarkably long lives, could she find a way to adapt it for use by others? The ramifications were staggering.

Karlmann sipped his tea again, then placed one trembling hand on Else's forehead. His eyes might not work very well, but his inner sense saw more than anyone Jean had ever known. Sometimes she felt jealous. If only she could see and feel what he could. Even if she lacked the ability to apply healing power directly to her patients, that added information could guide her remedies so much more effectively.

Karlmann grunted with satisfaction. "The fever is broken. The infection is in full retreat." He gave Else an encouraging smile. "I suspect you'll be well enough to return to your family in a couple more days."

"Thank you." The girl closed her eyes, a smile on her lips. The tea Jean had given her would help her sleep.

Jean breathed a sigh of relief as she gently stroked Else's forehead. She hated the thought of losing any patients. Infection was an enemy she loathed and would fight with every ounce of skill.

"You saved this girl," Karlmann told her with an approving smile.

"I had a lot of help."

"I ensured she had the energy her body needed to continue fighting, but your remarkable herbs turned the tide."

Jean flushed under the praise, even though it was true. "It still seems remarkable that you can't sweep away infection as easily as you mend shattered bones and stop internal bleeding."

Karlmann had explained that infection and some diseases were like tiny armies of monsters that invaded patients. Healers could bolster the patient's natural defenses, but that did not guarantee the patient would win the fight.

The aged Healer said, "Infection is one of the few enemies I do not always conquer. I wish we could find a way to magnify our healing sight like the Pathfinders can their vision. If we could study the disease more closely, perhaps we could better determine how to fight it."

"That's a great idea," Jean exclaimed, pulling out her ever-present notebook and pencil.

Karlmann chuckled. "I miss that boundless enthusiasm of youth. I spoke only hypothetically, my dear."

"But it's a good idea."

"An impossible one."

Jean flashed a determined smile. "Impossible ideas are sort of my specialty."

He raised his jar of tea in salute. "Indeed, You have a knack for creative thinking, and access to some exceptional friends."

Jean prodded, "What other ideas can you suggest?"

He sipped his tea again before speaking. "If you can indeed help the Builders figure out a way to magnify healing sight, or a way to visualize the tiny particles of disease, it could prove the most monumental mechanical of all time. Make sure you do not only look at infection, though. I recommend you look at molds too."

Jean grimaced. She hated mold. It smelled like disease and represented the corruption and decay of living things.

Karlmann noted her look. "Usually, mold is exactly what it appears, but a few years ago as part of my studies, I cultivated infection in a laboratory. Ultimately, the effort proved fruitless, but at one point some mold began growing on one of the infection dishes. Where that mold grew, the infection died."

"Really?" Jean had never considered one type of decay might overpower another.

"Indeed. I do not know the reasons, but if you develop a way to study tiny things, please take a look for me."

"I will," Jean promised, jotting a few more notes. She wasn't sure what good studying mold might do, but she would humor the old man anyway.

"What other problems have you been chewing on?" he asked as she finished her notes.

Jean flipped to the page where she kept that exact list. She scanned it quickly. Most were items that required far more research before she understood the question well enough to pick Karlmann's remarkable brain. But one caught her attention.

"Do you have any idea what triggers double-tap sickness in Agor Petralists? Why can they not use two primary-affinity stones, but they can use multiple secondary or tertiary affinities at the same time?"

"Never the easy questions for you. I am not an affinity researcher, but I have a colleague in Edderitz who is. I will send a letter asking her opinion. I personally believe the limitation is tied to the inner-focused nature of primary affinity stones."

That was what she suspected. She planned to ask more, but the far door opened and Gisela rushed inside. The pale-haired Althin approached, notebook and papers clutched in one hand. She'd assumed the role of Jean's primary secretary and scribe, and she tried her best to manage Jean's increasingly busy schedule.

Gisela was very organized and very skilled, and Jean had no doubt she was copying everything down to report to her mother in Althing. That was a small price to pay. Gisela had also requested resources from her mother, who had promised to dispatch several leading research scientists. With their help developing the curriculum for the new school, Jean felt confident her dreams of building an institution for higher learning to accelerate Builder efforts could really materialize.

Jean rose and told Karlmann, "See you tomorrow."

THE DANGERS OF TOO MUCH ALONE TIME

Three days stuck in a tent during a blizzard was not Connor's definition of fun.

The storm continued to intensify until Connor worried the howling wind might rip the entire Grandurian camp right off the mountain. The whipping snow might have buried them all if not for the Water Moccasins working in shifts to deflect it away.

Despite their every attempt to use the snow-laden air to turn the winds, the calm never lasted. The storm grew too fierce. Walls of snow built up around the camp, reaching twenty feet at one point. But then the shifting winds changed again and whipped those piles of snow back into the air for the Water Moccasins to chase again.

Connor tempted those wild currents once by tapping external quartzite, but the winds raged with unrivaled insanity. Individual air currents seemed to scream as they tore past, filled with so much energy they would probably race down the length of the continent before slowing.

Only one answered his call when he tugged at it. He hoped to wrap it around the camp to help deflect the other currents away. Instead the current plunged down upon his little tent and blasted right through the fabric walls, shredding it in a heartbeat and scattering his meager possessions.

While the snow and wind assaulted them with brutal ferocity, the cold crept in like a stalking nuall, threatening to suck the life out of the unwary or foolish. That cold deepened to nose-hair-freezing levels, then to all-exposed-skin-killing levels. Even Kilian finally donned a woolen sweater under his leather jacket.

Thankfully the storm had given ample warning of its approach, and the Grandurians knew how to prepare for nasty weather. Less than a thousand troops remained in camp as Wolfram's escort. The Rumbler companies worked hard to upgrade every tent into weather-proof shelters.

The tents were arranged in tight formation, and special winter tents were pitched right around each of them. Those winter tents were made of thicker canvas, reinforced with wood and steel beams against the fierce elements. They took the brunt of the storm and helped insulate the inside tents in tiny pockets of relative calm.

Most of the troops were packed four men to a tent, with a small iron brazier for heat. After his disaster with the wind, no one felt comfortable bunking with Connor, so that left him alone in a spare tent. The quartermaster warned him sternly not to destroy another one. The extra space proved useful for pacing impatiently.

Actually, he enjoyed the first day of enforced rest. He needed a chance to recover from recent insanely busy days thwarting Dougal's invasion. By the second day, however, he felt eager for something productive to do. Spending much time outside was folly, and he felt reluctant to tamper with the weather again.

The cold kept worsening. It crept into his double tent, despite keeping the brazier fully stoked. Connor had to tempt marble and add extra heat to keep from freezing. Luckily fire responded without issue.

Meals were simple things, with everyone rotating in shifts through the long, low dining hall, which was one of the few Sapper-raised earthen buildings. If not for the instability of the elements, the Sappers could have easily raised substantial buildings to shield everyone.

Many of the soldiers liked to play card games, but they seemed uneasy when Connor offered to join. He doubted they still resented the fact that he was Obrioner. They might feel concerned about playing the Blood of the Tallan, but he couldn't tell if they felt more nervous about beating him or losing to him.

Connor spent several hours practicing with limestone, playing with the odd qualities of light. He fine-tuned his affinity with the stone until it blazed with light at the first flicker of his will.

Mirage was a lot more fun, but it proved difficult to trick himself. He knew what was happening, so he had to work a lot harder to believe the strange sights that appeared in front of him. He needed someone to practice on.

Lingering alone in his tent left him bored. So of course his mind turned to Verena. Fears haunted him. What if she never awoke? Had he already lost her forever but didn't know it yet? What if she did wake up, but her mind or body was broken beyond repair?

That seemed like the worst possible outcome. Verena loved life, loved to fly and to build mechanicals. She was strong and confident and clever. What would she do if she awoke and could no longer walk? Or if she'd somehow lost her Builder gift? Would she despair, or would she find new purpose for her life?

Would it include him?

Not knowing drove him to distraction. The need to go to her was so strong, he nearly attempted tampering with the weather again.

He resisted the urge, barely, but hated every second of delay. The peace accord was signed, so they didn't need him there any more.

As much as he loved thinking of Verena, those constant fears would drive him crazy. He had to think of something else. That's when more dangerous cravings would creep in, like tendrils of cold fastening to his heart.

Porphyry.

Always the hunger remained, lurking in the darker corners of his heart and mind, eager to tug at his conscious thoughts and fill his soul with restless hunger.

The basic craving for porphyry was still relatively easy to banish, but the hunger returned again and again, growing more clever every time. Porphyry granted him the power to kill Martys, just as it had helped him survive the elfonnel. It was his greatest affinity, so why push it away? As a rampager, he would be immune to the cold, could howl louder than the storm. So why not find some, transform, and cower the storm like he could any living thing?

He had no porphyry. Kilian said he had no more either.

But what if Kilian was lying?

Connor eventually broke free of that dangerous train of thought. He hated how porphyry ate at him, hated the fact that he couldn't simply cast the hunger away. Hated the part of him that longed to relent and tempt porphyry again.

So he bundled himself into warm furs, tapped marble for additional warmth, and dared the short run through the shrieking wind and the brutal cold to the dining hall. It wasn't meal time, but the hall was the one possible gathering place, so many soldiers loitered there, attempting to escape their own boredom.

Connor found a quiet corner to watch some men playing at cards. One skinny fellow, filled with the nervous energy of a Wingrunner, was playing a complex dice game with a pair of Blades. Connor decided he'd make the perfect test case to play with mirage again.

He carefully reached out to the waves of light emanating from the nearest glowing brazier, diverted them past the Wingrunner's face, and twisted them into a knot. He hadn't figured out how to control the images people saw, so he waited to see how the soldiers would interpret the changes. Maybe that would help him learn to fine-tune the skill.

Luckily the bright light glinting off shining steel armor and weapons contrasted well with the dark leather straps and sheaths. The more the contrast, the better the twisting effect.

He only had to wait about two seconds. The two Blades jumped to their feet, swords and daggers leaping to hand, their gazes locked onto a spot several inches to the left of the Wingrunner.

"Tallan's grace, what is it?" One of the men exclaimed. The other just lunged, stabbing the empty air and shouting in surprise when the movement apparently changed what he saw.

The Wingrunner rolled right off his chair and leaped into a fracked sprint, his expression horrified, the color draining from his face. Shouting like a lunatic, he ran right into the outer earthen wall, bounced off, and crashed onto his back.

Connor cringed and released the light. The men blinked in confusion and looked around suspiciously. The other men and women who had been quietly playing cards all rose to their feet, hands on weapons, calling questions.

"I don't know what happened," the Wingrunner insisted. "All of a sudden, the dice turned into spiders trying to crawl up my arm."

One of the Blades shook his head. "That wasn't what I saw. The chair next to you stood up and sprouted arms. Looked like some kind of bizarre conjuring. Looked like it was going for the back of your head, but when I tried to dispatch it, it just disappeared."

The other Blade said, "I saw something similar, but not exactly the same."

Connor drew closer, fascinated by what he was learning. It seemed that the minds of those affected by mirage supplied the images to give meaning to the twisted light patterns. Did they always see fears or things that worried them, or could he create patterns that would better suggest what they should see?

If he could, then mirage could truly help him turn invisible or offer unprecedented advantages when facing a powerful foe. He could confuse or distract, or trick someone into fighting an imaginary enemy. Could he use it to duplicate himself, make it look like there were half a dozen Connors in the room?

The men looked embarrassed that they alone had seen something strange. A few of their friends at the next table joked that they couldn't handle a couple days of isolation and were already cracking.

As they returned to their game, Connor slipped away to his tent, eager to practice more. With the storm shaking the tent, flapping the heavy canvas and isolating him in his little piece of calm, no one would bother him. Maybe not until after the storm ended.

So Connor spent the next hour trying to trick himself into seeing his bed turn into a pedra. The first time, he only triggered memories of the great stone pedra that Kilian and Ilse had conjured together, and the desperate fight against the pedras in bloodlust frenzy. For a second, he saw the disgusting, double jaws of the pedra that had snatched him out of Rory's little army snapping toward his head again.

The next attempt, he actually saw an image take shape sitting on his bed. It looked like a baby elfonnel, no bigger than a toddler, charging across the bed and attacking his pillow, its many snakelike tongues snapping up feathers as it savaged the helpless bedding. As weird as that was, he felt even more unsettled by the unexpected urge to pick up the little beast and pet it.

The next several attempts produced an exploding cake shaped like a pedra, a fireplace with a large ham on a spit and, most unexpected, the image of Hamish trying to force-feed an outhouse to a torc. Connor laughed himself to exhaustion after the last one.

As he lay on his bed, he considered the different images and how he'd managed to produce them. He'd thought he would need to try forcing the light into specific patterns, creating the image he wanted the person to see, but that wasn't how it worked at all. His mind had reacted more to the broader strokes of the twisted light, taken the general shapes and filled them with images that best fit them, even if those images didn't match the specific details he was trying to add.

So how could he produce specific images? Practice.

As soon as he twisted the light again, a new image formed, but it wasn't a pedra. He found himself looking at Verena, lying prone on the bed, her pretty face composed and calm. Her huge blue eyes opened and joy burned like marble in his heart when she smiled.

Then Mattias leaned over her and kissed her.

The sight shocked him so much that Connor forgot he was fooling himself with the mirage. He shouted with rage, lunged and snatched Mattias off the ground. A rampager-like fury roared through him and he hurled Mattias away from Verena with all his strength.

The mirage evaporated just as his bed, which he had just thrown, collided with the wall of the tent and uprooted the entire thing, smashing it into the outer tent and nearly unseating that one too. The back wall of the tent overturned the brazier, sending hot coals spilling into the room, setting some of the canvas alight.

Connor managed to grab a piece of marble and prevent the fire from spreading. He didn't recover from that shocking mirage until he'd righted the tent, arranged his clothing stand to hide the holes burned in the canvas, and dropped onto his battered bed.

Why did he see that? He was getting worse, not better. Although he knew the sight of Verena kissing Mattias again was a lie, something dredged up from the dark recesses of his worried mind, it still infuriated him.

He hadn't been tapping granite or slate when he lifted and threw the bed. It was a light camp model, but he still should have struggled to throw it so hard. He tapped his sandstone pendant, sending a flicker of healing power down through his body along with his healer senses. He could examine himself more completely than any non-Healer ever could.

He really was stronger. His muscles hadn't changed, but they felt denser, more packed with power. He wasn't sure if it was a result of his ascension, or of his deeper connection with earth. He hadn't tapped granite or slate in days, but perhaps some residual benefit of the many times he had used the stones in the past weeks still lingered?

The enforced inactivity would have been a great time to pick Kilian's brain about deeper magic like his enhanced strength or managing mirages, but Kilian spent the majority of his time with Wolfram and the army commanders. They counseled about logistics for wintering the army in Altkalen, contingency plans for monitoring the border, and response plans should Obrion break the truce.

Kilian did take the time to pull Connor aside the next day. "I heard there was a bit of a ruckus in the meal tent yesterday. Some unexpected sights startling some of the soldiers."

Connor sighed. Sometimes it was no fun spending so much time with someone who knew so much. "I was just practicing with mirages. I didn't mean to cause such a stir."

"What do you think mirages are?" Kilian asked with a smile. "You bend the light which tricks the eye, so the mind of that person has to fill in the gap. Usually they fill it with fears."

"I know that now." He wished he'd understood before tricking himself into seeing Mattias kiss Verena.

"Don't attempt mirages alone, and don't tamper with the storm. And don't walk with slate here. Marble has acted almost normal during the storm, but don't use it once things return to normal. In fact, don't tempt the elements anywhere south of Altkalen."

"I haven't. I won't," Connor promised, annoyed at Queen Dreokt and High Lord Dougal for making such a mess of things. They'd wrecked everyone's access to the elements. That seemed particularly mean-spirited and selfish.

Kilian fixed him with a serious gaze. "Good. Don't start. I think the border is secure, at least for a while. I'll be traveling north to Altkalen in the coming days to help Anton and his Sappers try to calm the elements. The city is probably safe, but the sooner we begin reversing the damage Dougal did, the better."

"How do you reverse unstable elements?" When a cow got unruly, a good slap to the rump could often set it back on the path, but he suspected slapping the elements might only make them kick harder.

"With great care. Once we're ready to try, I'll let you know. You can give us a hand."

"I'm usually better at breaking things than fixing them," Connor pointed out, thinking about the arguments with Verena and wishing for the thousandth time that he'd apologized sooner, taken more time to understand her point of view.

"Don't limit yourself. Different moments call for different talents."

"Verena is in Altkalen. I plan to visit her, so I'll be there." It might be insane to try fiddling with the elements, but he couldn't think of better company to try than Kilian and Anton.

First he needed to visit Verena. He had hated the idea of letting Mattias take her back to the citadel of Altkalen for better care, but that was preferable to letting Mattias take her farther north to his estates near Edderitz. He'd pushed for that, but been overruled. No doubt he would try again if rumors started that Altkalen was in danger.

If they could settle things down, Mattias would lose that argument. Connor could not allow him to isolate Verena.

"She's receiving the best possible care," Kilian assured him. "Saskia already has a healthbed, and Mattias promised the best Healers."

"I know. It's just. . ." Connor trailed off, hesitating to voice aloud his constant worries. They had too much to say to each other, too much to do together for her to slip away.

He decided he simply couldn't wait any longer. "Tomorrow I'm leaving for Altkalen."

"If you wait a couple more days, I can run it with you. I doubt we'll get a windrider, but we can make the journey pretty fast."

"I know the way. You don't need me here anymore, and I need to check on her."

"Very well. Say hello for me when she wakes."

"I will." He appreciated Kilian's confidence that her waking was a foregone conclusion.

He slept fitfully that night while his tent snapped and boomed in the constant wind. By the next morning, the storm finally slackened to little more than a blustery gale. Gusts still howled occasionally, but lacked the intensity of the past few days. Snow lay in windblown drifts ranging from six inches to over eight feet.

The chill felt warm by comparison to the past couple days. The clouds actually fractured, allowing dazzling sunlight to sparkle across the snow fields.

Connor found a pair of Wingrunner shaded goggles.

Then he started to run.

7

SNOW DAY!

Connor all but flew across the snow-laden landscape. Deep drifts concealed the road, turned many trees into little more than pointed snow mounds, and sparkled in the bright morning sunlight like they'd swallowed a company of Solas.

Connor flashed across the surface, his fracked legs moving so fast he barely scuffed the top layer of snow. The fracking felt unusually painful in the crisp, cool air. The pain faded almost immediately, though, and Connor risked a glance down at his blurring legs and his changed physique.

A lot of people fear change, but Striders and Wingrunners had more reason than most. Human legs could only move forward and back so fast, but basalt broke that boundary by breaking legs. The thigh fractured, forming a new joint as the upper leg swung out at a forty-five-degree angle. The new joint allowed the upper leg to rotate in full circles without the lower leg needing to follow. The intensely painful process took only a couple of heartbeats, but unlocked incredible new speeds.

The first time Connor successfully fracked, the sight of his freakish new legs had distracted him and he'd tripped. Since then he usually didn't look, didn't think about how his legs moved, but just embraced the thrill of running so fast he sometimes wondered if he might outrun the day and catch up with the previous night again.

Now Connor laughed as he threw himself into a race against his own shadow. The miles fell away, but he scarcely noticed. His shadow kept up the entire way. He wondered if he could pull ahead using limestone. He ran so fast that even with a Wingrunner face mask to shield his nose and mouth, the wind nearly made it impossible to breathe.

He'd left his custom armor packed, with orders to ship it to Altkalen. He wore solid boots, but unless he slowed, he wouldn't really need them.

The cold wind cut through his insulated Wingrunner baggy pants. He also wore a soft, sheep-leather jacket, lined with fur and padded with wool, a thick, woolen cap, and wool-lined leather gloves.

He could tap a little marble to keep himself warm like Kilian preferred. Kilian was the master of fire and water, but Connor still hesitated to tap marble too often. Life was crazy enough without embracing the wild, reckless burn of fire all the time.

As Connor sprinted tirelessly over the snowy landscape toward the lower valleys, he tapped a little limestone. The connection came immediately, and the streaming sunlight became clearer to his limestone vision. He enjoyed the shimmering waves of light cascading across the landscape, although he deflected some of it away from himself to reduce the glare.

Then he simply ran.

Basalt speed was freedom unlike anything else in the world. Connor flashed down the mountain, legs blurring, breathing evenly, exulting in unrivaled speed. Running with Donald or even Dietmar was always fun, but he hadn't gotten much alone time in recent weeks of battles and bloodshed.

As he ran, he let his thoughts settle to silence that reflected the stillness of the high mountains. The rushing wind alone filled his ears, drowning out the fast patter of his boots skipping across the snow. He was glad he had decided to run north alone. The bright, chill morning seemed to replenish his reserves, and he found himself smiling through chilled lips.

In minutes he reached the first steep switchback that descended a wide bluff for over a thousand feet. A beautiful, forested valley spread below for three more miles before dropping down to even lower slopes.

That slope offered way too much fun to ignore. At the first switchback turn, Connor simply leaped off the edge, threw his arms out wide as he soared out over empty space, and embraced quartzite.

The air felt exhausted. As Connor cast his thoughts out wide, he found only weak currents limping south, dragged after the fast-moving storm. The storm, fueled by the turbulent, unruly elements had spent all that energy and left the land, the snow, and the air temporarily slumbering.

As Connor flew out over the land, untethered to any element, to any restraint, he enjoyed freedom that not even Verena and Hamish could feel in their marvelous Builder flying machines. For a moment Connor soared, alone and untouchable.

Flying like that, he could imagine Verena zipping up beside him in her Swift, giving him that special smile she reserved only for him, and pivoting so he could step aboard and fly with her. The image felt so real, he actually looked around for her.

The empty sky mocked him, reminding him that she might never fly again.

Connor shouted a wordless cry of defiance, refusing to accept that possibility. Verena would return. She had to. He shouted again, the sound lost in the wide open air, and his fears seemed to mock him. That fear and the anger it triggered stirred the beast in his heart and for a second the yearning for porphyry swept through him, setting his limbs shaking with the memory of the unrivaled might he enjoyed as a rampager.

"No!" Connor shouted aloud and drove thoughts of porphyry from his mind.

Instead he focused on his tertiary affinities and touched all four elements. Briefly, and not deep enough to unlock any of their marvelous powers, but just enough to feel them. And in that moment of untethered flight, the elements touched his mind with more clarity than ever before.

Each element was different. Each one walked with different strides, different focus. He'd never noticed those differences so clearly. It felt like floating through the air with four close friends flying beside him. He cherished each friendship, but each affinity was unique.

Air was wild and flighty, bold but undisciplined. It loved exploring the world and leaping over every mountain without hesitation, without worry about consequences. It refused to be cowed, but would rush in to help if the inclination struck it. For the first time, Connor felt as if air was like a girl, with long, wind-blown tresses, a quick smile and a ready laugh, but with a mischievous gleam in her sky blue eyes.

Earth flew beside air like a slightly disapproving uncle. Earth was solid, dependable, methodical, and careful. Slow to anger, but unrivaled in fury. Earth was a builder of mountains, a protector of nations. Earth was a giant of a man, and in Connor's mind he envisioned earth like Evander. For the first time he sensed that earth secretly envied air her freedom and loved her caresses, even though they would eventually wear away the majestic peaks he worked so hard to raise.

On Connor's other side flew water and fire, like eager lovers who couldn't stay apart, but couldn't quite manage to bear each other's company. Water was a beautiful, poised woman, mature and strong, dependable and incapable of yielding against direct pressure, but also flexible and nimble, able to flow into any shape she chose. Fire seemed a hot-headed youth who lived every moment with every ounce of life he could summon, but lacked staying power. He destroyed in a heartbeat of blistering heat, but also possessed a tender heart, capable of warm caring when calmed.

Connor was so amazed by the insights, so intrigued by the new clarity that he felt from the elements that he nearly forgot he wasn't actually flying. He was falling, with style.

And in a second, he'd splatter with spectacular effect across the snowy landscape.

So he extended a hand to soapstone and she responded, as she always did, without hesitation and without placing any conditions on their bond. The entire landscape glowed in Connor's water senses as he plunged through the gateway and became one with water. He seized the snow piled high in the meadow he was about to crash into and piled it into a fifty-foot pillar of soft powder.

He plummeted into it, blasting snow in every direction. His speed bled away and he settled to a full stop six inches from the frozen, rocky ground. Lying face first in the snow, he laughed with relief and with the wonder of simply exploring his affinities.

When he rose to his feet, he brushed the piles of snow away with a flicker of thought. "That's even more fun than flying."

His frozen cheeks ached with the movement, so he sucked on a piece of marble, savoring the spicy explosion of flavor. He kept the tap rate minute, just enough to warm his insides, then again tapped basalt.

Connor rocketed north, pouring on the speed. He fracked again, then max-tapped, outrunning the fastest arrow.

In minutes, he descended to the lowlands and neared the long Harz Valley where one of the most brutal battles of the invasion had taken place. Streamers of black smoke rose into the still air. That marked the beginning of the broken lands. As much as he wanted to see the devastation with his own eyes, he didn't want to deal with any delays.

So he banked wide to the east around Harz, running up a long saddle between a pair of stubby peaks and soaring off the summit. Several fast miles later he discovered faint distortions in the snow, the first indication that tens of thousands of feet had marched past recently.

As he continued north, the tracks became clearer. The army was forced to move at the snail's pace of walking soldiers. He was running at least fifty times that fast, and he caught up with them a couple minutes later.

They had stopped for the midday meal and their huge numbers filled a small valley to bursting. Connor spotted a pair of hovering windriders watching the back trail and waved, confident the Longseers stationed there would recognize him.

As he rounded a final bend and closed on the stationary army, a company of Wingrunners leaped out of concealment on both flanks and joined him. Connor slowed to match their top speed and waved to Dietmar, the cocky Wingrunner from Ilse's company.

"What's the good word?" he called.

Dietmar jabbed a thumb toward the stationary army as they ran past on the left flank. "Not so good, boy. This lot can barely walk five miles a morning. Thanks for stopping by. Gives us a chance to stretch our legs a bit."

"I'm surprised you haven't run ahead to Altkalen to inform them the army's coming."

Dietmar snorted. "Been there four times since we started the march."

"How are things there?"

He knew what Connor was asking. He shook his head sadly. "She hasn't woken up yet."

"Maybe today."

Connor suddenly didn't feel like chatting. He waved good-bye and accelerated again, leaving the astonished Dietmar vainly trying to speed up in his wake.

Maybe he shouldn't have revealed his full speed, but he wasn't worried about those men blabbing. No basalt runner that Connor had ever met would openly admit anyone else was faster.

When Connor rounded the front of the army, he spotted Ilse, Marshal Gunter, and several of the other senior officers, but did not stop. His good humor had faded under a renewed need to get to Verena as fast as possible.

He waved again and sped up. The road north was covered in deep snow. No doubt the Water Moccasins would clear the path for the army, but Connor decided that even though he wouldn't stop, he could still help.

So he tapped soapstone and formed an invisible plow radiating out at an angle to either side. Snow billowed and rolled aside like a drawn curtain just in time for him to race through.

Ten minutes later, he shot up the long slope south of Altkalen to the enormous valley that held the sprawling trading metropolis.

Altkalen.

8

BIG SURPRISES IN LITTLE PACKAGES

Every other city Connor had ever seen, lumped together in one place, would probably not fill a tenth of Altkalen. Sure, the Carraig possessed majestic palaces, but the huge Grandurian metropolis was so vast, it filled a sprawling plain for miles in every direction.

Unfortunately, Verena would be in the citadel, the huge castle that lorded over the richest part of the city where the rulers and nobles lived. That area lay across a wide river, on the northern edge of Altkalen. Connor was approaching from the south, so he'd have to traverse the entire expanse, crowded with over half a million people.

He slowed as he neared the city and passed through the sprawling cattle pens and tent communities of the herdsmen. The area smelled so much better covered by two feet of snow. Most of the animals huddled together in herds, close to the enclosures where they were fed.

One of those pastures had been converted into a holding area for the hundreds of Obrioner prisoners captured during the recent battle. The initial, rough earthen walls had been expanded into a fully enclosed earthen compound, with smooth, curving walls merging into a domed roof that rose over forty feet into the air.

Good thing, or those prisoners would have frozen in that blizzard. He reminded himself to check on Ivor. Officers were housed separately, and Connor needed to speak with his friend. He hoped Ivor was handling his captivity well, and he suspected Ivor could help plan his Guardian revolution.

That too would have to wait until he checked on Verena.

It seemed that the entire population of Altkalen had decided to come out into the streets to celebrate the end of the storm. Connor fumed as he slowed to a pitiful jog when he reached the press of the lower town.

People seemed eager to block traffic in big, chatty crowds, enjoying the clear calm after the long storm.

There in the poorer, southern sections of the city, the buildings lacked the self-importance to rise more than three stories over the narrow streets that they huddled close beside. Most were sheathed in simple, unpainted wood or volcanic rock. The people dressed in sturdy workers' clothing, simple in design, and usually somber in color.

The streets smelled clean, a rare treat that many people commented on. Connor tried to conceal his impatience as he wove through the press. It took nearly an hour to just reach the wider avenues and the enormous trading houses of the merchant district. The thick throngs of people there had to compete with entire caravans of wagons, mules, and camels.

The clear, cool air carried thousands of smells. The scent of cook fires hung close over the city, the bluish smoke reluctant to rise into the strangely still sky. Perfumes, roasting meat, spices, and the odor of many people pressed close together clashed in sometimes jarring ways. Mingled with it all was the fouler scents of animal droppings, the fish market that Connor accidentally walked too close to, and one open sewer pit that maintenance workers were trying to unplug. Connor felt grateful that he had not been tapping quartzite to his nose.

If anything, the crowds grew thicker the farther north he moved into the city. Servants in sensible shoes hurried about their errands while well-dressed merchants and their wives haggled in loud, good-natured voices while they blocked the lanes. No one seemed to be in a hurry except for Connor.

He tried shifting closer to the buildings, hoping to skirt the crowds, but street vendors were already claiming most of that area. They all seemed to think the best way to help him enjoy the day was to try to delay him with their best deals.

Finally, exasperated, Connor climbed a ladder rising up the wall of a tall basket weaver's guild. When he reached the roof and looked out, the sea of people seemed never-ending. Usually he liked being around people, and he had never understood people who feared crowds. In that moment he did. He was tempted to embrace soapstone to flood the streets, or summon some fiery legs to walk above the crowd.

He was no longer south of Altkalen, so Kilian's warnings to avoid tertiary-affinity stones no longer applied so much. With a feeling of immense relief, Connor wedged a tiny piece of marble under his tongue and a little piece of quartzite into his cheek.

The air hung limp and tired over the city, worse than it had felt in the wilds to the south. He wondered if all those people breathing tired it out more. Luckily, Connor was not too far from the gorge that held the river, with its beautifully colored banks and shoals. He found a rare, enthusiastic gust of wind rushing down that gorge, as if enjoying the fact that it could race there without anyone noticing. He gave it a tug, and was thrilled when it responded to his call, whipped around him, and lifted him high into the air.

The rush of wind rattled the rooftops and drew many gazes. He heard many startled exclamations as he rose on the current. Connor waved, happy to leave them all behind.

Unfortunately ever-fickle air quickly grew bored serving him. In his mind, Connor sensed her toss her wild hair and wink before she abandoned him and fled.

She'd accomplished what she needed to, though. Connor switched to marble and formed a wide set of fiery wings, eliciting a wave of applause from the spectators below. Connor waved again, then banked north. Fancy palaces, manor houses, and the huge expanse of the central citadel seemed to beckon him on from across the river.

The still air did little to help his flight, but neither did it impede it. Connor angled slightly downward to pick up speed as he flew over the river gorge. He wasn't using all that much marble. Again it generated the image of an impetuous youth, urging him to draw deeper, to unleash him across the city.

"Maybe next time," Connor said with a grin. Talking to the elements like people might be a sign that his mind was cracking, but he couldn't feel anxious about that possibility while riding with fire across the clear sky.

As he flew, he realized the city was clear of snow. It hadn't clogged the streets, nor did it cling to the rooftops. The pastures farther south had some, but the snowline ended abruptly at the city limits. He wondered if the hundreds of hot springs bubbling under the plain heated it enough to melt everything.

Lots of people thronged the richer northern sections of town, but the crowds seemed far less dense than on the southern bank. Connor glided most of the way to the outer citadel wall before touching down.

The guards recognized him and gave him no trouble. So he rushed inside, planning to race through the confusing maze of corridors and hallways that he remembered from his last visit. The halls were busy, filled with servants, soldiers in the blue and gray of the city watch, officials carrying scrolls and parchments, and finely-dressed lords and ladies. Thankfully no one seemed interested in speaking with him. Everyone moved about with purpose, as if eager to catch up on all the work that hadn't been done during the blizzard.

Eventually Connor reached Saskia's personal tower and jogged up the flight of stairs to the lowest level. Saskia was Mattias's sister, and the Lady Marshall of the city. At the entrance to the tower, Connor reached a simple, stone-walled anteroom. Four guards with Saskia's golden lion epaulettes on the shoulders of their uniforms blocked the way.

Their leader, a solid-looking sergeant who looked annoyed by the duty, grew suspicious when he realized Connor was Obrioner. Connor wasn't feeling very patient, so he wrapped the man in streamers of fire, water, and earth.

They quickly summoned him a guide. They probably also sent for reinforcements, but luckily the eager young servant girl who arrived, dressed in Saskia's colors of teal and white, recognized him. She said something in quick Grandurian that reassured the soldiers, then she curtsied to Connor.

She looked barely twelve years old. Her light brown hair, which reminded him of Verena's, was tied back in a ponytail. Her high-pitched voice fit her perfectly. "Lord Connor, I've been sent to fetch you."

Connor chuckled. "I'm not a lord. Just call me Connor."

The suggestion seemed to shock her, but she recovered quickly and beckoned him after her. "If you'll follow me, please."

She led him deeper into the citadel and up at least seven flights of steps. They reached an area he recognized as Saskia's personal quarters.

The last time he'd visited Altkalen, he'd spent time in her study and her library. The memory of the morning before the battle of Altkalen came to mind, when he found Verena and Saskia in her private study before dawn. That was the morning Verena had gifted to him his marvelous new suit of armor.

The girl brought Connor to a slightly less ornate hallway that he did not remember. She stopped at an impressive wooden door, carved with bright red roses and some other gilded flower he didn't recognize.

Connor pushed open the door and stepped through, entering a long, plush waiting room. The floor was tiled in black marble, with several rugs of pure white positioned in strategic locations. Connor avoided walking on the rugs with his dirty boots. Several couches and overstuffed chairs clustered in small groups around the room. A pair of tall windows in the right-hand wall overlooked a snowy courtyard, and a door next to the windows opened onto a narrow balcony. The second doorway across the room was closed, with a white-robed Healer sitting in a comfortable chair, reading a scroll.

She looked up as Connor approached, and her soft blue eyes radiated the gentle confidence of most Healers he had known.

"I'm looking for Verena," Connor said.

The woman, who was older, but not old, gave him one of those comforting smiles that Healers often used when trying to make people feel comfortable receiving bad news. "She's resting right now."

The smile only stoked his impatience. "Has she stirred?"

"I'm not authorized to discuss the specifics of her care with anyone outside of the Lady Marshall's family without authorization. Are you a relation?"

He wanted to say, "Not yet, but as soon as she wakes up I'd like to talk with her about that."

He wasn't sure that was the right way to start the conversation though, so he only said, "I'm a close friend."

A voice spoke behind them. "Oh let him in Abigail. This is Connor."

Lady Marshall Saskia stood in the doorway behind him. She was dressed in her noble finery, as if she had just finished a meeting with the ruling council. Her long hair was tied up in a fancy pattern atop her head that probably took four assistants half an hour to weave. She looked regal.

Saskia was a little taller than Verena and her same age. She'd been Verena's best friend at the Grandurian academy. She was pretty and looked more confident than the last time he'd seen her. She seemed to have really grown into her role as Lady Marshal.

She gave him a warm smile and added, "Just make sure to wipe off those dirty boots first."

Connor crossed to her and bow over her hands. "Saskia, it's so good to see you."

"I'm glad you're back. She hasn't moved, but she's resting well." Saskia did not bother trying to make one of her lilting limericks, nor did she try to hide her worry.

After he removed his boots, they entered the next chamber together. There he spotted Verena and his heart sang with joy. She lay peacefully on an enormous fourposter bed. The covers were drawn up under her shoulders, with her arms lying on top. Her midnight black hair framed her face, and for a moment Connor just stared. She looked so beautiful and so peaceful, her face turned just a little so he could see the profile of her little button nose and her lips parted slightly while she breathed.

His worries faded away, and a jubilant laugh bubbled in his throat. He wasn't sure Saskia would approve so he tried to swallow it and ended up coughing instead.

Saskia hit him on the back hard enough to make him stumble. Her slender build concealed a Sapper's strength. "Are you all right?"

"I'm fine. Thanks."

Only when he again looked to Verena did the difference in her appearance finally register.

"What happened to her hair?" he exclaimed. He'd always loved Verena's sandy locks, similar in shade to his own. "Did someone dye it?"

Saskia said, "Her hair changed color on its own. No one knows why."

She didn't look like she was joking. He couldn't imagine anyone playing a practical joke on Verena in a coma. When he glanced at the Healer, she shrugged and nodded. "It is a mystery."

Connor moved to the bedside and took one of Verena's hands. As always, her skin was warm to the touch, and he took that as a good sign. He studied her hair and fingered one lock. It felt the same, still soft and slightly curly, but definitely black. He marveled at how something as simple as the color of her hair could make her seem more exotic and alluring than ever. He decided he liked it.

"Verena, can you hear me?" he asked softly, not caring that his voice shook in front of Saskia and Abigail.

He dearly wished Verena's eyes would pop open and she'd exclaim that she'd only been waiting for his arrival to wake up.

It didn't happen.

Verena did not move. Connor glanced over at Saskia who had joined him beside the bed. Her eyes glittered, but he wasn't sure if it was because of unshed tears, or if she was just tapping limestone. He'd seen her make her skin glow, although he hadn't ever seen her limit it to her eyes.

She spoke softly. "This mattress rests on a framework built out of two healthbeds."

Abigail the Healer said, "Physically she has recovered extremely well. All of her other wounds are healed. The healthbed maintains her muscle tone. When she awakens she'll be able to resume normal activities almost immediately."

"Is her mind . . . ?" Connor couldn't finish the question, wasn't sure how to ask it.

Abigail gave him an apologetic smile. "Injuries of the mind are the most difficult. She's been given everything she needs."

"And although Abigail arrived only recently in Altkalen, she's become Verena's primary care giver," Saskia added.

Abigail made a tiny bow to acknowledge the compliment. "I am determined to be present when she finally awakens."

Connor appreciated the woman's dedication to Verena. "Thank you for taking such good care of her."

"It is my duty and my pleasure, although for now we can do little more than wait for her to work things out in there and find her way back to the surface."

Connor squeezed Verena's hand gently, somehow hoping the contact helped.

Saskia placed a comforting hand on his shoulder. "Mattias comes in here every day to speak to her and to sing to her." She hesitated before adding, "You're welcome to visit as long as you like."

Connor appreciated the fact that she was not trying to block his access. He wasn't sure how she felt about him dating Verena, or the fact that Mattias was trying so hard to win Verena back. Saskia had seemed friendly when he was first introduced to her as Verena's boyfriend, but maybe her attitude was changing. She was Mattias's sister after all.

"Thank you."

Saskia and Abigail retreated and closed the door gently behind them. Connor pulled a stool close to the side of the bed. It was probably the same one that Mattias used. He sat for a long moment simply holding

Verena's hand, staring at her face, and enjoying her presence. That tiny contact eased his worries and calmed his heart. She looked so perfect, so healthy, he couldn't doubt she would eventually awaken.

At one point he leaned closer, brushed her cheek with his fingers, and breathed the gentle, clean scent of her. He was tempted to kiss her lips, but didn't feel right about it. He needed to wait until she woke up, until they talked through things and she settled the question of him or Mattias.

He desperately hoped they could find a way to reconcile. He could not imagine what his life might become if she chose Mattias. The thought filled him with panic, but what more could he do about it?

So he sat with her and just talked. He told her about everything that had happened since her injury. He described the terrifying night saving everyone from Alasdair as the mountains collapsed behind them. He described Hamish's efforts to help everyone settle in Emmerich, and how grateful he felt knowing Hamish was there to help them.

He discussed the peace accord and his hopes that the fighting would end and that they could find a way to deal with the queen, and that maybe she wouldn't be so bad after all. He described the crazy winter storm and his run north, related Jean's efforts to help oversee the rebuilding effort and the new school, and his hopes for how much she would accomplish.

After that, he just talked, speaking whatever came to mind. He shared his concerns about the responsibilities being placed on him by Kilian, the possibility of having to help fight the dreaded queen. He described the wonder of discovering new abilities since his ascension.

He admitted, "I doubt he's told me everything. Kilian keeps secrets better than Aifric. He's hinted there are other hazards I have to understand. I wish you were there to help me figure it out."

When she still didn't react, he shared with her his worries that he wouldn't be able to live up to all the high expectations people had about Blood of the Tallan, and his desire to just be left alone for a while, even though he knew that would probably not happen.

Eventually his words ran out, but just sitting beside her helped him feel at peace in a way that he had not for a while.

Finally, he tapped the profound power of his sandstone pendant and poured a flood of warm healing into her. He sensed no lingering injuries, but could not see into her mind, so he filled it with healing. She was receiving excellent care, but he felt better knowing he was giving her everything he possibly could.

Then he kissed her forehead and whispered, "I love you, Verena. Come back to me."

Abigail was waiting patiently in the sitting room. Connor promised that he'd return every day.

He wasn't sure where to go next, and needed a moment to gather his thoughts. So after he retrieved his boots, he stepped through the outer door to that narrow balcony overlooking a courtyard piled with drifts of snow. The air was cool and he breathed deep.

Then the door to the balcony banged open and a boy rushed out. He zipped along the balcony with Wingrunner speed.

It was Nicklaus, the little boy whose capture the year before by Dougal's men had sparked all of the battles of Alasdair and Connor's first meeting with Shona and with Verena. In a flash, Nicklaus reached the end of the balcony beside him and leaped over the railing without slowing.

He waved and laughed as he started the long fall.

Connor didn't even have time to try to catch him. They were several stories above the little courtyard, and even with all the deep snow, Nicklaus was probably going to at least break his legs.

As Nicklaus fell toward the snowy garden below, he laughed again, the loud clear pealing of childish joy.

Connor had not realized he was insane.

Nicklaus raised his hands above his head, clasped together, and a jet of air erupted from between them. The air whooshed down over him, whipping his hair in every direction, flapping his clothing on his little body, and arrested his fall. Nicklaus hung there, three stories above the ground, in a perfect hover. It took Connor a couple of astonished seconds to realize what he was seeing.

Nicklaus had just activated quartzite. Not as a Petralist, but as a Builder. He had also run with Wingrunner speed.

Verena had said the Nicklaus showed the potential for a unique gift, but she had never explained what that was. Now Connor understood why Dougal had risked so much to kidnap the little boy.

He was a Petralist and a Builder.

A harried-looking woman rushed out onto the balcony, moving fast enough that she also had to have affinity with basalt. She leaned over the rails, caught sight of Nicklaus who was now slowly drifting toward the ground, and shouted in an exasperated tone.

"Master Nicklaus! You promised."

She glanced at Connor and he said, "Chasing kids off balconies wasn't in the job description, was it?"

"He's such a good boy, but sometimes . . . " She made a wringing gesture with her hands.

Connor laughed, thinking of his younger brother, Wallace. "I think I could find some chains."

She sighed. "I tried that once, but he got his hands on some marble and burned right through them."

Connor wanted to ask more, but she continued, "He's not much of a flier yet, but thankfully he hovers pretty well. He's so eager to train with Verena that he insisted on coming to Altkalen for the winter."

Connor said, "We're all hoping Verena wakes up soon."

"Excuse me, my lord, I have to find a way down there before he escapes again. He loves hiding in the citadel."

Connor pulled a vial of soapstone mixture out of his belt pouch, downed it in a single gulp, and said, "I'll try to slow him down for you."

Then he jumped over the rail.

9

OPTIMISM IS SOMETIMES THE BEST DEFENSE

Shona stepped from her open-topped carriage in the center of Merkland Township, barely giving General Rory a chance to scramble out ahead of her and offer his hand.

"Thank you, General," she said with a nod as she looked around.

The township was packed to bursting with people. Soldiers in uniforms of every realm crowded around cook fires and steel drums full of hot coals for warmth. Wagoneers cursed loudly as they drove their teams through the press, pulling wagons piled high with crates of food-stuffs and winter supplies. The air was laden with thousands of voices and the clatter and din of a city-sized population squeezed into the confines of the small township.

The sounds echoed back from the high walls of snow, piled to the east from the Spitters after the recent blizzard. The cobbled streets were clear, and thankfully the temperature had risen to almost above freezing.

Shona wore a thick, snowy white, ermine fur coat with no hood. She never covered her head when visiting her troops. They needed to see their leaders to fully enjoy the moment.

Even Rory wore a wool greatcoat over his battle leathers, although otherwise he seemed impervious to the cold. As Lord Nevan followed Shona out of the carriage, Rory said in an approving tone, "Settlement of the troops is progressing better than I'd feared."

Officers and merchants were gathered nearby to give reports and no doubt petition for more aid. Shona would let Nevan and Rory handle the specifics. She needed to be present to see the troops and to be seen of them. Rory and Nevan would ensure the twenty thousand troops that had descended upon Merkland for the winter were well cared for.

Nevan sniffed, his long nose already red from the chill air. He wore a black nuall fur coat, draped with the gold chains of his office. "Certainly you could have received the reports in your father's office, Lady Shona." He was a brilliant administrator, but preferred working from the warmth of the main palace, across the river.

Shona glanced in that direction, between a couple of stately homes of some of the wealthier merchants who oversaw operations in the township. On the far western back of the Macantact River, a high bluff rose in steep cliffs for over fifty feet, with the famous white walls of Merkland City rearing another twenty feet higher still. The turrets and towers of her palace home seemed to pierce the sky beyond.

"Nonsense, Nevan," she told him with a smile. "My duty is clear. With the army returned from the border, we must see to their needs."

Rory grunted, "Would be simpler if the Sentries could raise barracks like normal."

He didn't usually complain, but many of his soldiers had suffered from exposure during the recent blizzard, and that made Rory grumpy. With the land so unstable, Sentries could only work at a tentative pace, if at all. Most of the Petralists were housed in the city, but not even Merkland could absorb the many thousands of regulars too.

"We'll get it sorted, Rory," Shona promised as she swept past toward the group waiting to greet them. She spent a few minutes listening to their needs, assuring them support was coming, and offering words of encouragement.

The reports were better than she'd feared. Several large warehouses had already been converted into barracks, and more would be available in the coming days. Luckily warehouse space was readily available since the vast quantities of supplies that had been stockpiled in them through the summer had been shipped to the front during the invasion.

Morale seemed to be pretty good, and as Shona toured the town with the local officials, troops greeted her with smart salutes and great respect.

They cheered Rory.

She felt an unexpected flash of irritation at that. Rory walked among his troops, shaking hands, gripping shoulders, greeting an astonishing number of men and women by name and asking with obvious concern about their well being. Soldiers responded with enthusiasm, and when he promised more aid soon, they believed him. And not just troops from her realm, either. Many who wore the uniform of other realms seemed just as loyal to Rory as his own Fast Rollers.

Shona considered that as they followed the single main road through the center of town, along the gently curving course of the river. Her father had appointed Rory general primarily to counter the threat posed by Kilian and Connor, but had he understood how brilliant that decision really was? Rory was a well-respected tactician and legendary warrior, but he was proving an inspired leader, a man the troops could rally behind.

With Rory doing such a fantastic job encouraging the troops, the merchants pulled Shona and Nevan aside to complain about interruption of the river trade. Much freight passed through the realm by ship and barge up the wide Macantact. Moving all that freight in and out of the city was the primary responsibility of the township, with its many docks and extensive warehouse facilities here in the accessible lowlands across the river. When Shona pointed out that trade would continue briskly through the winter this year and Nevan promised to restore their warehouses as soon as new barracks could be built, they seemed pleased.

After Rory finished discussed specifics of troop barracks assignments and training schedules, he pulled Nevan and Shona to one side. "Lady Shona, have you considered spreading troops out through the nearby towns to help lessen the pressure on Merkland?"

"Impossible, General. Not with the current situation in Donleavy."

Rory frowned. "How does that affect us here? I've seen the latest reports. Queen Dreokt is turning everything upside down in Donleavy, but we're talking about winter quarters for my troops."

"You heard that she's actually executed many officials, and even some lords and ladies?" Nevan asked.

Shona grimaced. The news out of Donleavy was growing increasingly dire. The queen insisted on interviewing everyone at court, and the number of people who did not survive those interviews was growing at an alarming rate. The woman seemed intent on a full cleanse of the political quagmire of the capital. Such barbaric heavy-handedness was rocking the nation.

Shona said, "Obrion is facing an unstable political situation in the short term. We don't yet know what we'll be called upon to do once the dust settles. Will we invade Granadure again, or will the peace treaty hold while we deal with internal matters?"

"You're worried if your father falls to Dreokt that one of his rivals might attack?" Rory asked, sounding surprised.

"My father appears to have secured a solid position serving the queen." Despite the lack of specifics, her father sounded optimistic. No doubt he saw opportunity to not only renew the war effort but also expand his own influence.

Lord Nevan said, "Open fighting between high families is rare, but not unheard of."

"So we might face attack?"

"Or see an opportunity to assist a struggling neighbor," Shona added, putting a more positive spin on the possibility of conquering neighboring realms. Rory would need that kind of justification to support any such plan. He didn't see other Obrioners as enemies and would be reluctant to lead his troops in such an attack.

The possibility existed, though. Others were already seeing it. A few of her father's more vocal opponents, including the annoying Lord

Flichity, were already preparing to leave for their home realms with at least some of their troops.

It was a delicate situation, compounded by the uncertainty in Donleavy. Leaving the bulk of their forces in Merkland under Rory's command might weaken them in a critical moment. But they could not withdraw all of their troops either. That might suggest to the queen that they no longer supported a war agenda, which she might wish to pursue.

Shona continued. "Given the situation, we cannot spread our own troops out to neighboring townships with so many troops from other realms wintering in Merkland."

"And we can't send the others to the townships for fear they may seize unguarded territory," Rory finished for her. "Very well, but that means Merkland will face the brunt of the expense for wintering them."

"For now, you have my full support to do whatever we must to keep our entire army safe, secure, and ready for battle," Shona said.

Lord Nevan smiled. "And of course we've already sent letters to the lords of every other realm, requisitioning more supplies and funds to help defray the cost."

Rory grunted again and allowed the hint of a smile. "I should have known."

Shona led the way back to her carriage, satisfied with the trip. "Everything appears to be in order here."

"The troops appreciate your attention and the fact that you care so much for their comfort," Rory said.

"Of course I care. These are my troops. A good leader never squanders valuable assets."

As they carriage headed for the north side of the township and the bridge spanning the Macantact to return to the city, Shona sat back in her plush, cushioned seat. "You've both done excellent work. Keep everything running smoothly until I return."

"Return?" Rory asked.

"I've been summoned to Donleavy."

Rory grimaced. Nevan already knew, but the news still worried him. "Donleavy is not a place I would recommend you visit now," Rory said.

"Nonsense. It's the perfect time to visit."

Rory looked at her like she'd cracked. "You clearly are not worried about surviving your interview with the queen, but it's a dangerous time. People act in unexpected ways when they face danger."

"It's a time of opportunity," Shona assured him. "My father appears to be well positioned. He can bring me up to date on the situation, and together we can ensure that our realm remains strong through Queen Dreokt's return."

She sorely wished her father had sent more details, but the lack of specifics meant he expected his communication might be read by unfriendly eyes. That was not uncommon, but at the moment the question was whose eyes? Someone loyal to the new queen, to King Turriff, or someone else?

Shona thought back to the discussion during the peace treaty signing. "That Kilian knew about the queen. Do you trust what he said?"

Rory rubbed his chin. "Kilian is a legend on the battlefield, but I never took him for a liar. I believe he was speaking in earnest. He seemed genuinely concerned about what she would do. I wish I had gotten a chance to speak with Connor. He might have been able to tell us more."

"I had hoped to do the same," she admitted with a frown.

Getting a quiet moment alone with Connor had been one of Shona's primary objectives during the peace accord meeting. It frustrated her that she had failed. Connor had been so distant, it was obviously the wrong moment to approach him again.

She blamed that vixen wench Builder.

As always, thinking of Verena set Shona's blood boiling. The vile Grandurian had somehow wormed her way into Connor's heart right under Shona's nose. Shona berated herself again for having bungled her time with Connor so badly.

She had been so focused on planning their rise to power and how much good they would accomplish together, she had not given the present the attention it deserved. She should have enjoyed the quiet moments they had together and built their relationship more carefully. Instead of trying to force his support, she should have ensured that his needs were met.

Knowing that he was so close across the border was like a constant thorn in her side. She felt a powerful urge to march into Granadure and demand to speak with him before leaving for Donleavy. Unfortunately, that would only drive him away. Connor needed careful enticing and constant encouragement.

Exactly what the rest of the nation needed.

If only she had Connor by her side, she would travel to the capital with even more confidence. Her plans were in disarray, but the unsettled political field would surely offer new opportunities.

The queen was an unknown, but Shona felt confident in quickly discovering the queen's strengths and weaknesses. The only person she knew who might be as good at judging people and sensing how to position themselves to best advantage was Ivor. Somehow he had been captured in the fighting at Altkalen and she was not sure of his current fate.

No doubt her father had already discovered the loyalties and secrets of most of the major players at court. His brilliant mind, enhanced by obsidian, worked at an unmatched level. She could draw much information from him, but wondered if his agenda of conquest might be clouding his vision.

Where her father seemed intent on using a hammer to shatter opposition, Shona preferred to use a gentle caress. Once she understood how to deal with the queen, she could figure out a plan with her father. Let him lead the conquering army into Granadure and finally subdue them. Let him spend the rest of his life bringing the rest of the continent to heel.

Shona wanted to help make Obrion mighty again. She yearned for the day when the entire continent could be united again under one ruler. The expense for building armies and monitoring nervous neighbors was staggering. Serving a central ruler would remove all that. Only then could the continent again rival the greatness that it enjoyed before the Tallan wars.

Queen Dreokt had done it once. Hopefully she could do it again, with Shona and her father assisting, and rising to greatness at her side. All Shona needed to do was survive the near-term turbulence.

And win Connor back.

Nevan spoke, pulling her back to the present. "We will keep you posted on the situation here. I received word that Lord Torcall is en route from Curadh. He will no doubt feel slighted that my return blocked his ascension to the post of interim administrator."

Lord Torcall was one of the most powerful local lords serving Dougal. The Curadh quarry produced excellent quartzite, making the city second only to Merkland in size and wealth in all of Dougal's realm. If Nevan hadn't returned from the nearly-empty Carraig during winter repairs, Torcall would have been the likely choice for administrator.

Rory grunted. "Torcall is too proud by half."

"But useful all the same," Shona said.

"If he's coming, that means Logan will rush in on his heels too."

Lord Nevan said, "Indeed. Lord Logan hates the thought of missing anything. He'll support my appointment since it diminishes any new power to Torcall."

The political maneuvering of the lesser lords of her realm usually interested Shona, but at the moment she found herself growing impatient with them. Lord Logan lacked any Petralist power, but he ruled the wealthy town of Inverurie, along with the vast wealth its gold mine produced. The long-standing rivalry between Torcall and Logan was a source of much of the intrigue at Dougal's court.

She said, "Keep them in line, Nevan. This isn't the time for any escalation of their squabbles."

"I'd love an excuse to clap them both in irons in a cold cell for a few days," Rory said with a grim smile. "Nothing like a little forced humility to help reset priorities."

Nevan gave him an appreciative smile. "As much as I too would enjoy such a sight, I believe I can keep them in check. Their presence here will likely draw many of the lesser lords and ladies from their towns. The political games will help the dreary winter days pass more easily."

"Send me updates directly. My father will be busy securing our position at court. I don't want him distracted. Is there anything else of note I should know about before I leave?"

Rory said, "One of my spies in the Grandurian camp reported the Builder Verena was seriously injured in Alasdair. She has not yet recovered, and there's a good chance she'll never awaken again."

He kept his voice carefully neutral. Shona knew all too well his conflicted loyalties regarding Connor, Verena, and especially Anika. She appreciated that he stayed true to the course and fulfilled his duties with exactness, as always, but he would need to resolve that conflict soon. A commander could not afford distractions, and he was now playing far too critical a role to hesitate.

She snapped, "And every day she lingers is one more day before Connor's mind can start clearing."

Lord Nevan said, "Connor seemed to possess exceptional cleverness. I'm sure he'll make the right choice eventually."

That vile Builder had lacked the good grace to die in Altkalen like she was supposed to. Now she had the audacity to linger in a coma, distracting Connor and preventing him from moving forward with his life.

"Keep me posted on any developments in her case. Craigroy suggested there was another resource who might be able to help us bring closure there. Once you receive word, I'll be able to implement plans to help Connor come back around to our side."

Like her father always said, people's emotions ran deep around important moments like birth, marriage, and death. Those were times of transition, and Shona planned to guide Connor to a more intelligent course as soon as Verena died.

As the carriage clattered across the long bridge arcing over the river, Shona looked out over the dark blue expanse, feeling better. "If you need anything else from me, Craigroy will be overseeing all correspondence."

"When does the speedcaravan leave?"

"It's waiting for me now. I expect to embark within the hour."

It would take her to Donleavy where she would craft a new plan for her future. And Connor's.

WHEN SMILING IS HARDER THAN PUNCHING

As Connor fell toward the courtyard where Nicklaus was just touching down, he tapped soapstone and formed the piles of snow into a tall, spiraling, grooved ramp. He landed on the top and whooshed down into the slide. He laughed as he gained speed, twisting around and around as he slid to the ground and shot out the bottom, skidded across the icy pavement, and plowed to a stop in a thick drift of snow.

Connor shook all the snow off with a thought as he stood and extended his arms for applause.

Nicklaus eagerly obliged and said something in Grandurian. When Connor frowned, not understanding, the boy smoothly switched to Obrioner. "Can I try?"

"Sure."

Nicklaus had grown a lot in the months since Connor had last seen him. He was probably already seven. His blond hair was long, hanging past his ears, and his blue eyes sparkled with glee as Connor lifted him into the air using a slender arm of snow.

When Connor deposited him in the top of the slide, Nicklaus whooped. A second later, air erupted behind him as he activated a piece of quartzite and accelerated rapidly.

Nicklaus made four turns before bursting over the edge of the slide and shooting across the courtyard. He shuttered the blasting quartzite, and Connor piled snow in front of him with a tug of thought. The cushioning snow caught him just before he crashed into the stone wall of the outer edge of the court.

Nicklaus bounded out of the snow laughing and shouted, "Again!"

"Not like that," Connor laughed.

Nicklaus's lips were chattering from cold, but he didn't seem to care.

Connor brushed away the snow and tapped a bit of marble to warm himself. Then he gripped Nicklaus's hands and poured warmth into him too.

The boy grimaced. "Mom won't let me play with marble yet."

That sounded like a very smart decision.

Connor pointed at the slide and tapped soapstone again. In seconds he converted the curving ramp into a tube.

Nicklaus grabbed his hand and exclaimed with childish enthusiasm, "You come too! I'll race you."

Racing down one tube would be interesting. "Okay. But first, did I see you using quartzite like a Builder, but also running like a Strider?"

Nicklaus placed his hands on his hips and gave Connor a disgusted look. "We're in Granadure. We call basalt Petralists Wingrunners. Didn't you know that?"

"Sorry. I meant Wingrunner."

"Then yes. I love running fast, don't you?"

"It's one of my favorite things in the world."

Tomas and Cameron would give Connor a legendary beating for admitting that, even though he loved granite too.

The newly reconfigured slide worked perfectly, although Connor could not keep up with the quartzite-speeding Nicklaus. So he tapped quartzite and tried to draw the air down to help him out.

The resulting mini tornado of snow and wind scoured the tiny garden courtyard clear of snow before Connor could get the wind to cut it out. He swore he could hear a mischievous chuckle on the wind.

Nicklaus laughed hysterically. "Longseer. Too much air inside the head gets in the way trying to use it outside! Gotta be a Builder like me!"

"I'm better at it than most," Connor insisted.

That only made Nicklaus laugh again. "I'm glad I didn't make affinity with quartzite. I had to test first with marble like Uncle Kilian. I'm Dawnus, just like him."

Connor gaped. Only the most powerful Petralists discovered their powers as children, and even then it was rare to establish a tertiary affinity, let alone a Dawnus gift before their teen-age years. Nicklaus might grow to rival Kilian for raw power.

"When I was at the Carraig, I got to be an undercover general," Connor told Nicklaus, who looked dutifully impressed. "I was pretending to be Dawnus, and I used marble and soapstone. I even told them my name was Kilian."

"That was a great choice. Uncle Kilian is the best."

"When did you discover you also have Builder powers?"

"Just a little bit before I was kidnapped that time. Mother kept me in the palace for months after that." He scowled at that memory. "Now I finally get a chance to come to Altkalen and Verena won't wake up."

Connor's smile faded and Nicklaus added, "Don't worry. Mattias says she'll wake up soon."

"I'm sure of it." He appreciated the boy's confidence, but since when did Mattias spend time with Nicklaus? And how often did they discuss Verena?

A thick wooden door led back inside, but it was locked. They had to pound on it for a minute before Nicklaus's nanny finally arrived. She had sought a less dangerous route down to the courtyard from Verena's room. She chided Nicklaus for running away, but he only winked at Connor. No doubt it was going to be a busy afternoon for that woman.

Connor considered Nicklaus's special gift as he headed back up into Saskia's tower. He wanted to ask her what she knew about it. The possibility of Petralists also being Builders had never dawned on him, and the ramifications were incredible. If Dougal had managed to keep Nicklaus, what might he have accomplished through the little boy?

It was a terrifying thought.

The tower was larger than it appeared from the outside, with wide, curving hallways of paneled wood and enormous tapestries. Connor hoped to find Saskia again, but as he exited a long, stone stair on the fourth floor, he ran into Mattias. He was dressed in a well-tailored suit, one of his swords swinging at his hip.

That hallway was much finer, with a smooth, black-tiled floor and stone walls hung with gilt-framed paintings of landscapes and portraits of important people Connor didn't know. The gently arced ceiling was tiled in an intricate mosaic depicting the entire continent.

Mattias smiled when he saw Connor, but unfortunately did not set his teeth glowing. Connor was eager for that moment so he could do it too. He couldn't wait to see the look on Mattias's face. And if that didn't impress Mattias enough, Connor would be happy to demonstrate what a mirage could do.

He needed to test if Longseers could pierce mirage with their enhanced vision. Mattias was very skilled, but wasn't ascended, so maybe it would still work on him.

"I heard you arrived in town today," Mattias said, extending his hand.

Connor took it, wishing he had taken the time to purge basalt and absorb granite. One of his favorite dreams was still the moment when he'd get to throw Mattias out a window.

"I ran up from the border today. The army should be here in a day or two."

"I also heard you attended the signing of the peace accord. I wish I had been there."

"Why?" Connor asked suspiciously, trying to read Mattias's expression.

"There's widespread doubt that they came to the table with real intent. I would have liked to look into their eyes and try to read their sincerity."

Mattias didn't bother asking Connor his opinion, so he shared it anyway. "They were serious for now, but that treaty won't stop them when they change their mind. With the crazy weather we're having, I'd be surprised if anyone had tried anything before spring anyway."

"We'll be ready for them if they do," Mattias said confidently.

Connor didn't share anything about the plans he and Kilian were making to foster a revolution among the Guardians in Obrion. Mattias didn't need to know, and the two of them weren't exactly close friends.

"With things so quiet around here, I imagine you'll have to return to Edderitz to resume your other duties," Connor said. He couldn't wait for Mattias to travel hundreds of leagues from Verena. He wasn't sure he kept his eagerness out of his voice.

"There's no hurry," Mattias assured him a bit smugly. "With my father's health so poor, Crown Prince Theodor has agreed to allow me to stay down here for a while to help my sister with her duties."

"That's nice," Connor managed.

Mattias's smile faded and he gestured toward a nearby wooden door. "I have something to discuss with you."

He led Connor inside. It was a simple meeting room, with little more than a long table and several chairs. Mattias drew back the drapes to allow some light into the room, then gestured to a seat. Connor took it and Mattias took one across from him.

"We both know why we're both here," Mattias said in a conversational but not quite friendly voice.

"Verena."

"She's receiving the best possible care. It's just a matter of time before she wakes." He spoke with the same forced assurance Connor used, the result of telling himself that fact over and over until he could not imagine any other outcome.

Connor wondered if Mattias was better at self-delusion than he. He desperately wished Verena would awaken, but as a commoner in Obrion, he had grown up with too many disappointments to not recognize that bad things happened.

All he said was, "Could be any time."

Mattias leaned a little closer. "That's my concern. When she awakens, she's going to need peace and rest."

"Then you should probably leave right now," Connor said evenly.

Mattias did not smile. "What she does not need is a lot of confusion, heartache, and fighting."

"Exactly. I'll tell her you send your best."

Mattias's calm expression cracked, and for a moment he looked annoyed, but quickly regained control. "I like you Connor. I appreciate all you've done to help our country."

Connor felt obligated to say, "Thank you. I appreciate the effort you took in helping train me in quartzite."

"I honestly think we could be really good friends."

"We probably could have been if you hadn't started kissing Verena and trying to steal her away from me," Connor pointed out, his voice turning harder, despite his best efforts to conceal his anger.

"What did you expect me to do? If you were in my position and had a chance to maybe win her back, wouldn't you try?"

Connor wanted to shout, *She's with me! Back off.* He hated to admit Mattias might have a point. "I know you care about her. I can't imagine anyone who knows Verena not caring, but you had your chance and you let her go. Verena moved on, and I'm not going to allow you to confuse her."

Connor was ready to fight Mattias right there, even though he only had basalt. No doubt Mattias had obsidian ready and Connor had seen him fight. He was one of the most skilled Allcarvers Connor had ever seen. He had leaped into battle against the entire pack of rampagers and actually survived for several seconds until Connor swept them away in a flood and killed most of them.

None of that mattered in that moment, though.

Mattias raised his hands in a placating gesture. "I didn't bring you in here to fight. I brought you in here to offer a truce."

Connor still preferred the idea of throwing Mattias out that big window, but the suggestion surprised him enough that he asked, "Truce?"

"We both love Verena. She knows it. We know it. We don't need to fight about it because it's not our decision. It's hers."

"She made the decision and chose me."

"She did, but then you did some rather stupid things, Connor, and I believe there is now a question in her mind about the right course."

"I think you've been listening to yourself in the mirror with your teeth glowing a little too often. There's no question."

A torrent of fear and guilt burst from where he usually kept it bottled up in his heart and he fought to keep his breathing even. He had acted the fool, had allowed Shona to manipulate him again, had lost focus. He and Verena had both made some bad choices, but his errors were so much worse. He longed for nothing more than a chance to tell her how sorry he felt.

Would he get that chance? Would she forgive him? Or would he see her awaken only to watch her return to Mattias? The thought filled him with dread and fury, and for a second the beast stirred in his heart.

No. He refused to let porphyry undermine his will. He could never risk tempting porphyry again. He had nearly killed his own family the last time. He'd never forgive himself if he ever hurt Verena.

"Then you should not be afraid to agree to the truce," Mattias said, watching him closely. Connor wondered how much of his fears and worries Mattias could read.

"What exactly are you suggesting?"

"I propose that we don't argue, don't fight, and don't pressure her when she awakens. She needs time to recover. We'll both be there to support her and to help her." He leaned a little closer and added more intently, "We will leave her free to make her choice and we'll both agree to accept that choice. Only a man lacking honor would make her life difficult with a lot of useless drama."

"So you agree to not scream or whine or complain or throw a tantrum when she confirms that she's with me?" Connor asked.

Mattias took a long, slow breath, his fingers clenching, as if he was rethinking the offer. After several seconds he said, "Yes. When you agreed to the same thing."

Mattias waited, his gaze locked onto Connor's. Connor really wished he had taken the opportunity to throw Mattias out that window earlier. Now it was too late.

If he refused to agree, Mattias would take that to mean that he was immature and that he did not care about Verena. No doubt he would explain it that way to Saskia and the two of them would do their best to bar Connor from Verena's side.

That would guarantee when she woke up only Mattias would be there to comfort and help her. As much as Mattias claimed to want to accept her decision, Connor had no doubt that he would do everything in his power to sway her choice.

Unfortunately, Connor did not have the resources to counter all the good that Mattias was doing for her. She needed the Healers, the healthbeds, and the constant care that only the citadel with its thousands of servants and workers and Petralists could provide. He loved Verena too much to put her at risk.

So he nodded and said in a strong, clear voice. "I agree."

SOMETIMES CRYING IS THE BEST MEDICINE

Connor and Mattias parted without further comment, and Connor marched toward the citadel exit. He needed some open air. He should go visit Ivor. From what he'd heard, the prisoners were being treated well, especially the officers. He couldn't imagine Ivor not maneuvering himself into the best possible position.

Hopefully his friend would be eager for something to do. He needed Ivor to help the Guardians fight for freedom. He might even be able to get Ivor released into his custody for that effort.

He reached the ground level and was crossing a wide atrium where seven different hallways converged when a familiar voice called, "Connor, there you are!"

"Aifric?"

She jogged up to him, dressed in an ankle-length, fur-lined coat over her normal Healer whites. Her thick, brown hair bounced as she moved, and her deep, brown eyes twinkled with humor.

"How did you get to Altkalen?" Connor asked.

"I caught a ride in the daily windrider. I heard you came to visit Verena."

"I did. Have you seen her yet?" Verena might be getting excellent care, but Connor trusted Aifric more than any other Healer.

She nodded. "The Healers here are very good."

Connor hesitated, but couldn't help asking, "Do you think she'll wake up soon?"

Aifric squeezed his hand and gave him an encouraging smile. "I'd say chances are very good, but with mind injuries, there's no telling how long we'll have to wait."

"We'll wait however long it takes," Connor promised, trying not to show his disappointment.

Aifric gestured toward one of the hallways to their left. "Have you had lunch yet?"

"No." As soon as she asked the question, his stomach rumbled, as if it had been waiting for a chance to remind him that running all the way from the border might be fun, but it took enormous amounts of energy. Ivor would have to wait. "I'm starving."

"Figured as much." She led him through a wide tower, then down to a subterranean level. There, Aifric pushed through a pair of wide but otherwise unremarkable wooden double doors.

A wave of delicious scents seized Connor by the nose. He breathed deep the aromas of roasting pork, fresh-baked bread, and a mix of spices that almost rivaled the intense flavor of marble.

"What is this place?" he asked as they stepped into a tile-lined entry hall, with another door on the far side. Racks of diners' coats hung to their left. Most looked like officers' uniforms.

"This is one of the senior officers' dining halls," Aifric said, leading him toward the opposite door where a portly, middle-aged soldier stood at a tiny podium desk. As soon as she identified Connor, the man rushed to open the door for them.

"One of the perks of being famous is good food sometimes," she told him as shed led him between tables and booths scattered around the long, low room. Plenty of space separated each of them to allow for private conversations. The floor was clad in hardwood, the walls draped in expensive tapestries, and soft lighting kept the room in perpetual near-twilight.

They selected a small booth near the back of the room, and a waiter soon brought them a huge meal of venison sauerbraten, smothered in a delicious sauce Hamish would love. It was spicy, but sweet, and seemed to magnify the natural flavors of the meat. Connor ate an extra plate for his friend.

Only after he finished his third helping did he wave off the relieved-looking waiter. "That was delicious."

"I usually prefer eating in officers dining halls whenever possible," Aifric said. Although she had only eaten a fraction as much as Connor, she looked satisfied. "The food is better, as is the eavesdropping."

"Is that why we're here?" Connor asked, wondering if she planned to switch to a different persona. He didn't think she had any secret missions, but maybe he was about to find out.

"Not today." Her features shifted slightly, the soft oval face of Aifric the Healer turning harder, more predatory, and her voice changed to a colder, deadlier tone.

Student Eighteen fixed her penetrating gaze on him. "The queen is back, Connor. We've never faced a danger so dire."

"That's what I'm afraid of."

She twirled her knife through her fingers. "I can't protect you from her. I don't know if anyone can, but I can make sure you're as well prepared as possible for when we do face her."

"I appreciate that," he said, although he was starting to wonder what Varvakis was like up in the frozen north in winter. He was tempted to go find out.

"You've discovered mirage, Connor."

"And you decided you don't need to kill me," he reminded her.

She smiled, but it was a cold, humorless smile. "You're our best chance for defeating her. Stop worrying about that."

He breathed a little easier, but having an Assassin as his personal Healer tended to make it hard to not worry sometimes.

"Mirage is an ability that has not been used since the Tallan Wars."

"Kilian could do it."

"But he admitted he hasn't. Yet you discovered it, even though you don't understand how it works."

"I've been practicing. It doesn't make a lot of sense yet."

"That's because mirage plays tricks that the mind fills in."

"Kilian said something like that too." Connor leaned back in his chair to ease his over-full stomach. "The real trick is figuring out what people are going to see, how their minds will fill in those gaps."

"The only way to do that is with chert."

"That's great," Connor said sarcastically. "I don't have chert."

"I do." She drew from the pocket of her Healer coat a small piece of gray stone.

With great excitement, Connor took it and fingered its sharp edges. "It looks like flint."

"It's related. The two are often mistaken for each other. If you strike chert with steel, it'll spark just like flint. Our deposit is the only known power-grade variant."

"So how does it work?" Connor asked, rubbing a finger over the hard, gray stone.

"Chert is sedimentary, so affinity is established like sandstone or limestone."

Great. He'd just gotten limestone to stop moping about how it was the last affinity stone he'd established affinity with. He wasn't sure it would be thrilled that it wasn't the new kid any more, or if it would start moping again, thinking he'd abandoned it for a fancy new stone.

Only one way to find out.

Connor glanced around the dining hall. There were other diners, but it was far from full. The main rush probably wouldn't begin for an hour or so. "Do you think this is the best place to try this?"

Student Eighteen nodded. "While people are eating, they're usually relaxed, not on their guard, and often their thoughts wander. It's a perfect time to read their emotions, and even tweak them if needed."

"I don't plan to tweak anyone." Making a connection with the stone would be plenty. He focused on it, willing the connection to materialize.

Nothing happened.

Limestone had taken more effort than other stones. He wasn't sure if that was because of how many affinities he'd already established. He was Blood of the Tallan, and that supposedly meant he could use every power stone, but was there a limit? Would he have to sever affinity with another stone in order to link to chert?

Was that even possible? Which would he choose? He couldn't imagine losing any of his powers, even though he'd only acquired most of them recently. He'd grown up suppressing his curse, but in the last year he'd come to depend up on it. Without his affinity powers, he'd have died many times.

So he needed to make chert work.

"Don't get angry at it," Student Eighteen said softly, leaning closer, an amused expression on her face. "It can take a little time."

"How did you know . . .?"

She chuckled. "As if I'd teach you to use chert and not tap it myself."

"So you can sense my feelings?"

"If I need to. You're not exactly subtle."

"I can be," he muttered.

She only smiled wider.

Connor closed his eyes and focused, again rubbing the stone. He tried to relax, tried to open himself to the connection, but he wasn't sure what it would feel like. He didn't expect a rush of warm strength like sandstone, or a burst of light like limestone.

What, then?

A slow minute passed as he concentrated, ready for any manifestation. He was trying so hard to pick up some kind of sense from the stone that at first he completely dismissed the soft whispers that began sounding in his ears. Then he realized, they weren't sounding in his ears, but in his mind.

Connor sat up straighter, focusing on those distant whispers, little more than suggestions of soft conversation, beyond the limits of his hearing. That's when he noticed flickers of temperature against his skin.

The feeling was odd, as if someone was sliding invisible pieces of crystal against his skin. Some were hot, at least one icy cold, but most fell into a narrower range between warm and cool.

He frowned. "I think I've got something. It's like whispers in my mind, but also hot and cold touches on my skin."

Student Eighteen gave him an approving nod. "That's chert."

"Chert is kind of weird."

"So are people."

"Good point."

"Those whispers aren't words. You won't understand them until you ascend again."

"Weird," Connor repeated.

"But useful, nonetheless. Those whispers hint at the mental state of the person you are sensing. The flickers of heat and cold on your skin are another clue. The two work together to help you understand your target."

"I'm not targeting anyone."

She indicated the room around them. "You're not focusing chert, so its effects spread out all around. You're feeling the emotional states of everyone in the room. As you focus on a particular individual, those whispers and feeling on your skin will sharpen."

"I thought it would be more useful," Connor said, frowning down at the little gray stone. "It's pretty vague."

"Try focusing. Firing an arrow into the sky isn't very useful either, but an aimed shot is deadly."

Connor glanced around and selected a larger table with six officers chatting around it. Most of them looked content after their meal and conversed in friendly tones. The whispers in his mind seemed calm and uninteresting, while the flickers of temperature were stuck right in the lukewarm zone.

One fellow proved more interesting. He seemed to be carrying most of the conversation. He was laughing and talking loudly, gesturing with his hands, cracking jokes, and looking like he was enjoying himself.

Chert told a different story. The skin of Connor's forearm closest to the man turned cool. The whispers in his mind sounded soft, but fearful.

"What's wrong with the loud fellow?" Connor asked.

"I figured you might notice him. It's a common tale. A lot of people try to hide fear or nervousness by overcompensating. People like that are easily influenced by magnifying those fears. They either become so rowdy that they create distractions, or they break down, surprising people they've been fooling, and creating even better distractions.

Connor wasn't interested in wrecking the guy's day. "Can't we help them feel better?"

"Temporarily, sometimes. We can't fix people's minds for them. We can only push them a little. That doesn't change their outlook on life. Intensifying or weakening their current emotions is most productive, but with practice you can learn to carefully introduce new emotions and guide your target to an entirely different focus."

The ramifications were enormous, and a little disturbing. "I'm glad not a lot of people can use this stone."

She nodded. "It'll never be a mainstream stone, even if Obrion or Granadure learn where it's quarried. The deposit is small, the stone lacks much power, and it drains quickly."

"Good."

Now that she mentioned it, the little stone he held had already shrunk noticeably in his hand.

Connor spent another moment flicking his chert senses around the room, conferring with Student Eighteen about what chert revealed about each person. Most of the officers were pretty straight-forward, their emotional state exactly matching their external state.

Then he noticed a woman sitting in the corner, eating silently alone. The whispers from her came rapid, urgent, and the feel against his skin turned icy cold.

"What about her? She looks calm, but I get a feeling of near-panic and also terrible loss."

Aifric considered the woman for a moment. "I suspect she lost someone dear to her in the recent fighting. I would not be surprised if she did something abrupt and possibly fatal to herself pretty soon."

"Suicide?" Connor asked, his voice rising a little higher than he intended. He glanced at the woman again, thinking about the crazy battle of Altkalen. A lot of people had died, although fewer than if the fighting had gone against them.

"Can we do something for her?" he asked.

"Like I said, most of the time we can only affect minor, temporary changes."

"Let me try," Connor urged. He felt an intense need to help the woman, but didn't dare walk up to her and say, *Hey, I sense you're planning to kill yourself. Bad idea.*

"It's not the first test I would recommend. It probably won't make a lot of difference, but go ahead. Aifric approves too."

Knowing she was watching gave him a little more confidence.

"What do I do?"

"Reading people is easy. You're just taking the emotions they're emitting. Trying to influence someone requires a deeper connection."

Connor closed his eyes and allowed the whispered emotions from the woman to fill his mind. He drew that icy chill emanating from her into his own heart.

For a moment he just felt cold and a bit unsettled by the urgent whispering that tugged at his thoughts, as if on the cusp of becoming clear. Then the connection suddenly solidified, like a conduit snapping into place between them. Her emotions boiled down that link and Connor felt her crushing loss, overwhelming grief, lack of hope, and inability to see a brighter future.

He rocked back in his seat, gripping the edge of the table with suddenly tense hands as he sucked in a long, shuddering breath. He wanted to drop the connection, escape that terrible link, but he couldn't.

He understood her.

If Verena died, he would probably feel the same way. For a moment as the emotions washed through him he blinked back tears, facing that most horrible of possible futures as if it had already happened.

Student Eighteen touched his hand and said softly, "This is the hardest part. Some lack the natural empathy to make such a deep link, and few manage it without extensive practice, but I can see you feel her. I should have realized your ascension would change things." Her own voice was tinged with sorrow. She must have also linked to the woman.

Connor nodded, fighting to rise above the torrent of grief and loss. He reminded himself over and over that Verena was not dead, that she wouldn't die. It helped clear his mind. "What do we do now?"

"Depends on what you want to do. If my mission was to assassinate her, I wouldn't need to bother. I could just amplify her current emotions, echoing them back to her. She'd finish herself off for me."

Connor grimaced. "I'm glad that's not our mission."

"Me too. I sense she's got inner strength, but it's been eclipsed by her loss. In time, she'll regain her balance and learn to heal."

"We need to give her the time, but how?"

"I can't tell you exactly. Empathy is a personal thing. Just like you have to feel the emotion, you have to feel the solution."

"Give me a hint at least," he implored.

She hesitated and glanced at the woman again. "Like I said, I sense strength in her. Consider how you can help her tap that strength again."

That wasn't as useful as Connor hoped. He was starting to wish he'd never insisted on trying to help. No, he was glad for the chance, he just wished it wasn't so difficult. So painful.

Relationships and emotions were always difficult, though. Even he and Verena struggled, despite how deeply they cared for each other. He was willing to fight to salvage their special bond, and he realized he was willing to fight to help this nameless woman regain the will to face the next day with hope.

Her loved one had already died, but maybe she had other things to live for, to focus on? Connor closed his eyes again and embraced the emotions radiating from the woman. Aifric had said he could send emotions back. As the connection deepened, he felt the link, sensed the conduit could indeed feed in reverse.

He held the image in his mind of waves of emotion radiating back to the woman from him, like those invisible beams of light he saw when tapping limestone. Then he focused on all the reasons that still inspired him to hope.

He thought of happy memories with Verena, memories he would always cherish, even if she slipped away forever. They would be tinged with sorrow, but still powerful. He thought of the first time he'd kissed her, of the first time she punched him, of the intimate moment when he healed her leg, that night he learned about Nicklaus and realized she had been telling the truth. He smiled to himself as he thought of the first time they flew together, of the sight of her in her custom battle leathers, of her cheeks flushed with the thrill of discovery in her workroom.

For several minutes, he forgot where he sat, forgot about Aifric, even forgot about the woman he was trying to help. He allowed himself to walk those wonderful memories, and he felt peace settle gently over his heart.

Verena might die. She might even leave him for Mattias when she awoke. Either of those events would devastate him, but they wouldn't change the past. They would not make it impossible to find a happy future.

Student Eighteen gently gripped his hand, drawing him from his reverie. Tears glittered in her eyes, and embracing chert as he was, he read her approval.

She said softly, "I'm impressed, Connor. I think you can stop now."

He blinked a couple of times and glanced at the woman in the corner. She had pushed her plate aside and was huddled in her chair, sobbing uncontrollably. Two other women officers had rushed to her side and were comforting her. Several others were moving in that direction.

Connor felt embarrassed as he sensed sorrow pouring off the woman in waves. The temperature of the emotions had risen from hopeless icy cold to the chill of a long winter night.

Connor released chert and withdrew his empathic senses. "Sorry. I thought I could help."

Student Eighteen's voice shifted to the warmer tones of Aifric. she chuckled and shook her head. "For one with such a knack at this, you're pretty dense, Connor. You did help. A lot. I blame the ascension."

"But look at her. She's a wreck." Connor barely caught himself before gesturing at the grieving woman.

Aifric nodded. "Exactly. She has released her anguish. Crying is good. It helps one deal with sorrow. This is the first step to actually dealing with her trauma, not getting destroyed by it."

"I hope you're right."

Switching back to Student Eighteen, she rose and winked. "I don't think you've ever seen me wrong."

Connor laughed and followed her toward the exit. Then he admitted, "That was a lot more intense than I had expected. I'm exhausted."

"Too bad because we're going up onto the wall so I can teach you to use serpentinite."

1 2

WHEN YOU REALIZE YOU WEREN'T NEARLY SCARED ENOUGH

Shona relaxed in a padded armchair in the front enclosed compartment of the speedcaravan, facing an enormous window that spanned the entire front wall. She gazed out at the panoramic view as the marvelous craft ascended the long final slope before reaching Donleavy.

The speedcaravan was one of the few marvels still remaining from the days of wonder before the Tallan wars. The long, sleek craft slid along raised rails, gliding so smoothly that it seemed to be floating more than sliding. Each metal cabin, oblong in shape, about forty feet long, and connected by wobbly bridges, served a different purpose.

She was the only passenger. The speedcaravan was reserved for high nobility and urgent communications. Usually the closer it drew to Donleavy, the more people tried to find an excuse to win one of the privileged seats on board.

Not this trip.

Instead of needlessly stopping at each of the cities along the way for non-existent passengers, the speedcaravan only slowed. Workers who manned the acceleration gears at the stations launched her toward the next stop. She wasn't sure how it worked, but somehow the long, tubular wagon of the speedcaravan shot down the track without needing any additional propulsion, sliding with enough energy to reach the next stop.

Since she hated Verena above all other living souls, she made a point of not inquiring further. She appreciated the smooth, fast journey down half the length of Obrion, but she felt that focusing on the marvelous accomplishment of the ancient Builders somehow gave Verena yet another victory.

Instead she focused her thoughts on the capital and her growing worries that she might have underestimated the danger. It seemed the turmoil was even worse than they'd been told. No wonder people who lacked her connections felt hesitant to visit. Part of her was eager to find out what was going on and meet the queen. The part of her that looked forward to a long and healthy life was growing increasingly nervous.

The last car on the speedcaravan was a sleeping compartment, and she had tried to rest earlier in the trip, but sleep had refused to come. The middle car was the dining car with an extensive staff prepared to make palace-worthy meals at any time, day or night.

In the front car, the huge windows gave her unrestricted views of the countryside and she loved watching the scenery slide past. She hated that Connor could fly with Verena and enjoy sights that she'd never see.

The speedcaravan topped the final rise, slowed from the long climb up from the lowlands. The breathtaking city of Donleavy came into view, and Shona allowed herself a moment to simply enjoy the vista. The speedcaravan route circled part way around Donleavy, following the crest of a long hill overlooking the lower reaches of the city, offering panoramic views.

Donleavy was built high in the northern reaches of the Tairseach Mountain range that thrust up out of the farmlands of central Obrion. The Carraig was less than a hundred miles away if one could fly directly south like a Builder, but the jagged peaks between the school and the capital made the journey many times longer. The city clung to seven levels of wide bluffs that climbed the north face of the mountain. A deep canyon fell away to the east in steep cliffs, and the majestic Mealt Falls plunged from the inaccessible peak of Mount Raasay that lorded over the city. The long, silvery falls fell over four hundred feet and thundered into the center of the High Palace, the great wonder of Donleavy.

The sight took her breath away, as it had both times she'd visited Donleavy in the past. The Carraig, with its tightly packed palaces and soaring towers sought to impress by sheer magnitude of architecture. Donleavy embraced the breathtaking scenery and indomitable landscape and melded it into its architecture in a way no other city could match.

The High Palace was made of several parts. The central palace encircled the falls that plunged right through its heart into the wide Loch Mealt. The enormous palace extended out over that loch for more than a hundred yards and rose in five stories of solid granite, more than two hundred yards across. Long wings extended farther, becoming the western and eastern palaces. The western palace extended a full quarter mile and reared seven stories, with frost-rimmed towers and spires rising in graceful splendor even higher.

Her father's tower was located there, close to the central palace. Shona loved the view of the falls plunging down the cliff nearby. The rushing water and the spray that billowed high along the mountain kept her rooms cool and comfortable in the summer. Firetongues heated that mist in the winter to keep the palace warm even in the worst weather.

The eastern palace extended to the outer edge of the cliff and rose in tiered levels, with the famous windowed wall at the top level overlooking the panoramic vista. The royal family lived there, which meant it was now Queen Dreokt's residence.

The throne room seemed to hover four stories directly above the central palace, standing atop nine graceful, granite towers. Elegant walkways circled the towers at each level, but Shona stared only at the throne room. Its famous domed roof of translucent blue quartzite from the Glenmuick quarry made it look like a giant jewel floating in front of the waterfall.

Only the nine towers of the lore masters of each affinity rose above the throne room, reaching up to encircle the silvery falls like grasping fingers. The gray granite towers were inlaid with vertical stripes of their particular affinities, and the soapstone tower was capped by a rooftop walkway so the senior master Spitter could stand within arm's reach of the mighty falls.

Shona forced herself to tear her gaze away from the magnificent palace to glance across the rest of the city. The Mealt flowed out of the loch and cascaded down seven additional waterfalls, with smaller pools at the base of each one. The final pool, simply named the Eas, was long, but narrow, and exceptionally deep. Shona had heard that the river seeped out the porous rock at the bottom and traversed three thousand feet down through the mountain before emerging again on the lower plain to join the mighty Macantact River.

Shona had never visited Donleavy in winter, and the city looked beautiful under blankets of freshly fallen snow. She enjoyed the view as the speedcaravan slid on raised bridges from one tier to the next on its course toward the High Palace, which occupied the entire highest level. The rest of the city was built upon the wide steps of the seven waterfalls, and the populace of the city was just as strictly segregated along economic and social lines. The palaces and properties of the highest nobility occupied the second highest level, while the rest of the nobles lived, worked, and shopped in the third. Lower classes lived and worked in the levels below, but Shona doubted she'd ever venture there.

She wasn't sure if the waterfalls ever froze. The constant pounding of the falls kept the lochs from freezing solid, but much of the city was rimed with sparkling ice from the spray.

The end terminal for the speedcaravan was built into the basement of the central palace, and the speedcaravan slowed as it approached. Her father had once explained to her that resistance blocks were built into the tracks to help dissipate the caravan's energy. Somehow they worked to bring it to a stop in the perfect position every time, despite the fact that the weight changed depending on the number of passengers and the cargo.

Once the speedcaravan settled with a gentle shudder into its cradle in the terminal, Shona rose and headed for the exit. A woman in her father's colors, who acted as Shona's chief handmaiden during the voyage, was already holding a fur-lined, knee-length coat for her. Shona had brought few personal effects. Her rooms in her father's tower were already stocked with gowns and appropriate court apparel.

She swept out of the speedcaravan and spotted her father's delegation waiting nearby. But she stopped abruptly as a nearby woman shifted to block her path.

"Watch yourself," Shona snapped.

The woman was heavily bundled against the cold. She gave a barely adequate curtsy and pushed back the hat that had fallen down over her eyes. "Beg your pardon, Lady Shona."

It was Connor's Aunt Ailsa, the sculptress from the Carraig. For a second Shona was not sure what to say. The sight of Ailsa triggered a flurry of memories. Some were dark, filled with the anxious worry from playing the great game of the school, but most centered on Connor.

Ailsa stepped closer, her expression serious. She nodded toward the compartment Shona just exited. "Step inside, Shona. I need a moment of your time, and your life depends on listening to what I have to say."

The intensity of her green-eyed stare ignited again all of Shona's nervous worries about her summons. The delegation was approaching. She needed to go.

"What are you doing here?" she hissed.

"No time for chatting." Ailsa gestured with a leather-covered portfolio. "My excuse for being here is to study the speedcaravan. I hope to find a way to replicate its functionality through sculpted stones."

"Is that possible?"

"I doubt it," Ailsa admitted with a flicker of a smile. "But it gives me an excuse, and these days that's barely enough. Now get inside and listen to me, or you will cease to exist before this day is through."

Ailsa was not one to make idle threats, so Shona waved the delegation to wait, then stepped back inside. Ailsa was one who always seemed to know more than she should and could find answers. That was exactly what Shona needed.

"What danger are you referring to?" She asked when they stood inside alone.

"You've heard of the coup, but you're walking into a trap that few have survived in recent days," Ailsa said gravely. "The queen seeks worthy servants. Everyone who arrives with a summons like you must present themselves to her for an interview. Most of them do not survive. The lucky ones are executed."

Shona's fears redoubled. "I can't leave."

"No. It's too late for that. No doubt Dreokt would take that as a sign of guilt and dispatch an execution squad to track you down. I believe you are one of the few people clever enough to understand and utilize the information I'm about to share with you."

"I'm listening." More than that, Shona felt terrified, desperate to hear what Ailsa had to say. She tried to keep her expression neutral, though. No sense giving Ailsa too much advantage.

Ailsa edged closer and whispered, even though they stood alone in the speedcaravan. "The queen is an ancient Petralist. She has powers not seen since the Tallan wars. No one is prepared when they meet her."

Her absolute assurance set Shona's heart racing even faster. "But you can help me?"

Ailsa considered her for a moment, and the hesitation drove Shona's anxiety to a fever pitch. What if she refused to share the information after all? What if this was some kind of tease, some kind of retribution for how Shona had treated Connor at the Carraig? She prepared arguments, ways to convince Ailsa that she had done what she had thought was best.

But Ailsa spoke. "The queen possesses powers unavailable to anyone else I know about. She can read the minds of those with whom she speaks."

Shona paled. Invading the minds of others was the worst form of personal violation. No secrets could be kept, no privacy.

Ailsa added, "And that's not the worst of it. She also has a terrifying ability to influence those minds that she touches."

That seemed a bit far-fetched.

Ailsa read her expression. "You'll see it for yourself, and if you fail your interview, you will more than see, unless she executes you outright."

Shona paced away, her thoughts a dizzying blur. "So how can you help?"

"If you're as clever as I believe you are, if you focus carefully, and if you're more than a little lucky, you might survive."

"If I fail, she'll know you tried to help me, won't she?"

Ailsa flashed a tight grin. In that moment, she reminded Shona of Connor and his daring. "All life is a risk, and I'm willing to take this risk for you."

"Why?" Shona wished she had taken the time to learn more about Ailsa.

"Because I think we will be able to help each other. I can help you survive today. We will need each other to continue surviving here."

Shona extended her hand. "I accept your proposal. What do I do?"

Ailsa took her hand, her calloused grip strong. "There is no defense against the queen's ability to touch your mind. You need to understand this truth. Most of those who have suffered since she took over have tried to conceal their thoughts and present a false face to the queen. Such duplicity enrages her, and she has at times done terrible things to people whose service she needs. Her mood swings dramatically from one moment to the next, and there's no telling what she'll do, but there are ways to position yourself to not draw her wrath."

"How?"

"You may not be able to block her access to your mind, but the trick that few people seem to realize is to present a mind that is uninteresting, or one that would take too much effort for her to decipher."

Ailsa tapped Shona on the side of the head. "Any time you are in her presence, you must present a consistent, simple, yet compelling mindset. Your father is her foremost counselor at the moment, so she may already be predisposed to like you. I recommend you focus on your father. Think about him and nothing else. Fill your mind with thoughts of pride for what he has accomplished, and with the single, overruling desire to make him proud and do his will."

As Shona considered that Ailsa added, "If you do this, she will see in you a daughter determined only to serve her father. From the insights I've gathered in recent days attending her, such an image would be most likely to make a positive impression. As a result, you become a person whose mind she does not need to delve deeper into."

Shona nodded, understanding. "I see how that could work. It's simple but brilliant. If she touches my thoughts, she finds nothing surprising or even very interesting, but something she approves. I can do that."

Ailsa gave her an encouraging nod. "I thought you might. If your concentration lapses, if you let your thoughts wander, or if you react too strongly to any of her surprising antics, you may draw her attention again. If she decides further investigation is warranted, there may be no hope for you."

Shona wanted to ask more, but Ailsa gestured toward the waiting delegation. "We've lingered long enough. We don't want the queen to glean from any other mind that there was anything unusual about your arrival. She's incredibly smart and absolutely ruthless."

Shona stepped out of the carriage and Ailsa followed, her hat once again pulled low over her face. She slipped away along the track and seemed to blend into the background, completely uninteresting.

The delegation waiting for Shona consisted of four soldiers in dress uniforms and a man she did not recognize, but who dressed as one of her father's personal attendants. He looked to be in his twenties, tall, with strong features. His black hair was carefully groomed, and he bowed over her hand with perfect etiquette.

"Welcome to Donleavy, Lady Shona. I am Ian. It is my pleasure to escort you to your father in his tower."

"Thank you, Ian, but where is Goshka?" Her father usually sent his elderly valet to meet her, and she had been looking forward to seeing his familiar face.

"Goshka is no longer with us. He made the mistake of expressing a contrary opinion in the presence of the queen."

"Oh, no," Shona breathed. The man was one of his father's oldest servants. Hearing of his death in such a matter-of-fact way reinforced Ailsa's warnings.

"It may comfort you to know that the queen herself executed him on the spot," Ian offered, his expression still carefully neutral. "I am told it is a great honor for a servant to die by her hand."

"That's not exactly comforting," Shona said coldly.

"I apologize," Ian said. His careful facade cracked for a second and he glanced around, moving his eyes more than his head. He spoke in a low voice intended for her ears alone, "Take great care what you say and who you speak with here, Lady Shona. Donleavy is a dangerous place right now and you're a newcomer. If you survive today, things will start making sense."

"Thank you," she said softly.

He gave her an encouraging smile. "We're all wishing you great success." Then his expression turned carefully neutral again and he said more loudly, "If I may escort you to your father."

Shona had planned to ask Goshka additional questions, but doubted Ian would again risk breaking out of his role. From what she was seeing, he had taken a great risk to even share that much with her.

So she studied the people they passed as they climbed the grand central stair up to the main level of the central palace. The enormous entry atrium rose five stories to gilded ceilings, with seven staircases leading off to the main halls. The falls plunged down along the rear of the vast room behind a wall of tall, pivoting windows that stood closed, shielding the hall from the billowing spray.

The palace was busy as always, but it seemed unusually quiet. People moved about quickly, with their heads down, their expressions a mask of false happiness, but it was far too easy to read their fear.

She caught people casting glances in her direction, but they did not speak. When she spotted a girl she knew from the Carraig, she raised a hand in greeting, but the girl turned and hurried away, her expression terrified. For a second, Shona felt hurt, but then realized she hadn't survived her interview yet. The girl probably did not want the queen gleaning any suggestion that they were friends until Shona proved her worthiness.

That thought chilled her with an even deeper fear. The queen had only just returned, but already she'd cowered the proud populace to a degree Shona never would have believed. Residents of Donleavy must feel like the world had turned upside down. Donleavy was the seat of power in Obrion and the home of the great game of houses. Politics and intrigue were the norm, where lies and half-truths and double crosses were daily occurrences. People in Donleavy appreciated astute political maneuvering and all the baggage that came with it. The queen threatened to destroy their entire way of life.

Ian led Shona to the western palace and up to her father's tower. When Shona entered their luxurious apartment, she found him dressed in full, formal finery. He'd been waiting for her and swept her into a welcoming hug that he held several seconds longer than normal.

"Shona, I'm so glad you came quickly. Any delay would have been unwise. Quick, change into one of your gowns."

He looked healthy, but tired and drawn. Her father was always a master at concealing his true emotions, but Shona could read him better than anyone. She read tension in his eyes and nervousness in his grip on her arms.

"I was hoping to speak with you for a few minutes about what's going on here."

He took a deep, shuddering breath, something she had only seen him do once or twice in her entire life. "There is no time. The queen is aware of your arrival, and she has already sent for us to attend her."

He gestured toward her room. "I took the liberty of picking out a suitable gown. Attendants are already waiting to help you."

She resisted his push in that direction. "Father, I've heard rumors about her. Please explain the situation. Surely she can wait a minute or two."

Dougal attempted to give her a reassuring smile, but couldn't quite manage it. That more than confirmed her worst fears. "The queen is the ultimate Petralist, wielding power that we have been seeking to restore for over three hundred years. We celebrated power that was but a shameful shadow of the truth. She is power, and we must embrace this opportunity and serve her."

"It doesn't sound like we have a choice," Shona said, shocked by his attitude more than by his words. He spoke as if trying to convince both of them. She'd never seen him like this. He was always the person in control, the man who knew more than anyone else.

Not anymore.

"We will serve her, and that service grants us access to that power." He looked deep into her eyes and added forcefully, "There are some risks, but if we help our queen secure her throne, she will deal with our enemies and establish an unbreakable rule across the entire continent. However, you cannot show any doubts. You cannot show any hesitation, any criticism of anything she ever says, or even think anything that she might disapprove of. If you do, not even I could save you."

She started asking another question, her mind whirling with questions and the growing fear that she would die within the next hour, but he grabbed her hands, his expression one of fearful excitement.

"My dear Shona, you are my pride and joy. If anyone can survive an interview with the queen and benefit from it, it's you. I trust you. I've trained you well. You are the most capable young woman I know." He gave her an encouraging grin. "If you survive today, we'll have time to discuss everything. It will be wonderful. Hurry."

Shona allowed him to push her to her bedroom, with his words ringing in her ears. He had spoken the exact same words Ian and Ailsa had.

If you survive today.

13

THE DEEPER SOUND OF SOUNDS

Connor followed Aifric onto the battlements atop the citadel's outer wall. The late afternoon sunlight bathed the city of Altkalen in soft orange light, setting the western-facing windows glittering like diamonds.

They stood alone on a shadowed section of the wall, overlooking one of the large gates facing one of the bridges over the river. A wide courtyard just inside the wall was bustling with activity. The wall was patrolled by the citadel guard, but it also appeared to be a popular place for couples to stroll together as evening settled over the city.

Connor loved the unparalleled feeling of discovery he experienced when establishing affinity with a new power stone. He couldn't imagine what it must be like for other Petralists who might only get to enjoy it once. A few others managed a secondary affinity with a sedimentary stone, and fewer still with a metamorphic, tertiary-affinity. Only a handful in every generation unlocked Agor or Dawnus dual powers.

The recent training with chert had left him a bit shaken from the intense emotional journey, but surely serpentinite would be far simpler. Before Aifric could begin the training, a couple came strolling past. The pretty blonde woman who clung to the arm of a tall, muscular officer, glanced at her, then looked again. With an exclamation of joy, she rushed over.

She spoke excitedly in Grandurian and seemed to know Aifric.

Aifric coughed, the movement masking the little shudder as she smoothly shifted personalities. Her features softened, her eyes seeming to grow wider and more vulnerable, and her voice rose to a higher, sweeter pitch.

She hugged the woman enthusiastically and spoke in Obrioner. "It's so good to see you Alena, but what are you doing so far south?"

Alena looked startled by the shift in language, but transitioned smoothly with a laugh. "What about you? I can't believe your boorish father would let you come to Altkalen so soon after the fighting."

Aifric-Cacilia shrugged, a mischievous look in her eyes. "You assume he approved."

"Oh, you can be such a dare," Alena gushed in mock shock, although she looked thrilled to hear of Cacilia's disobedience.

"Don't tell anyone I'm here."

"Your secret is safe with me," Alena assured her. She glanced at Connor and her eyes widened with new delight. "Tallan be praised, you're the Blood of the Tallan!" She added excitedly, "Oh, such a scandal."

Connor tried to protest, but Cacilia shushed him and took his arm. She tried to look demure and asked, "Am I wicked for trying to comfort this deserving hero while he waits for his love to awaken?"

"Not at all," Alena assured her with mock sincerity and obvious delight.

Connor couldn't bear the thought of generating rumors that he might be unfaithful to Verena. He had enough to straighten out with her already, but when he tried to protest, Cacilia shushed him again.

She declared, "Then I shall have to work harder."

Alena glanced at her officer, who looked eager to resume their private walk, then said, "You must come visit me, Cacilia. I'm only here another week."

"Of course," Cacilia assured her.

After the couple left, Aifric shivered, her features shifting back to Student Eighteen and she frowned after Alena. "Such a fool. She's the perfect friend for shallow Cacilia."

"What was that all about?" Connor demanded.

Student Eighteen sighed. "Cacilia is one of my Grandurians. She's my version of the daughter of an arrogant lordling in southwest Granadure who oversees an important quartzite quarry. Her entire purpose is to generate rumors to infuriate him."

"Why?"

"The man discovered and nearly captured Mister Five's wife, who is one of our best infiltrators."

"Wow. How did he manage that?"

"I was sent to discover that very fact. In the guise of my Longseer officer from northern Granadure I visited his quarry on the pretense of inspecting their processes. I learned that the man has a perfect memory. He remembers everything he's ever seen or heard or thought."

"How is that possible?"

She shrugged. "It's a very rare condition. It was also unknown to Mister Five's wife. The man caught her in a lie. Once he grew suspicious, her mission was compromised."

"So did you, ah, punish him?" Connor asked awkwardly. He didn't want to say the word assassinate.

"Killing him wouldn't have been productive, but I have punished him." She nodded toward the distant form of Lady Alena. "I created Cacilia based on his daughter. I look a little like her, but I periodically go about in her guise, spreading rumors that will eventually get back to him."

"What does that accomplish?"

"Like I said, he's arrogant. With his perfect memory, he considers everyone else little better than buffoons. So when he hears rumors about his daughter, he knows they're false since he keeps her at home at all times. So he browbeats the messengers and makes enemies. He damages his own reputation and reduces his influence in circles of power."

"That's terrible." It was better than killing him, but it was far from nice.

"He does the damage to himself. I just give him a chance to demonstrate his poor qualities. Perhaps the rumors will encourage his daughter to take a chance and try living her own life on her own terms someday."

Connor thought about that, but she said, "Enough distraction. On to serpentinite."

She extracted from a pocket a small rock and handed it to him. It felt rough and uneven, but in the deepening shadows he couldn't see it clearly. So he used a small piece of limestone to create a soft glow.

"I see where it gets the name." Serpentinite had a mottled exterior of shades of green and blue, and even a little red. It looked quite a bit like the skin of a serpent.

"Different variants have different coloration, but all power-grade serpentinite I've ever seen looks pretty similar to this. It's found only rarely on the surface, although our lore masters suggest there may be much more underground."

Connor turned it over in his hand, savoring that sense of wonder. "Affinity with this metamorphic stone is a doorway to manipulate sound?"

She grinned. "Sound is amazing. Sounds become visible to us and we can control them."

"How do you envision the gateway?" He'd learned from Ivor the trick to thinking of each gateway as a physical doorway in his mind. He wondered what personality serpentinite would eventually manifest.

"I don't see the gateway, I hear it. Affinity with serpentinite triggers a sound in the mind. That's the focal point to connect with it."

"What will I hear?" With twilight settling over the city, sounds seemed muted already. Distant conversations, occasional shouts, the braying of a donkey, slamming doors, and the myriad other sounds of such a huge city made a constant background jumble.

"We all hear something different, something that holds a special meaning for the person."

"What do you hear?"

She hesitated. "We don't usually discuss our sounds. They're personal."

"Oh. Sorry. Forget about it."

"It's all right. I'm willing to share it with you." She gave him a wicked grin. "We are rumored to be having a scandalous dalliance after all."

Connor rolled his eyes. "Do you really want Verena getting angry with you when she wakes up?"

Her grin evaporated. "Good point. When I tap serpentinite, I hear the sound of laughter."

"Really?" Connor had expected something more Mhortairish, maybe the sound of a crossbow bolt slicing an apple into eighteen identical pieces, or the sound of a soft footfall in the darkness.

"I hear a child's joy-filled laughter, the first laughter I ever heard. I found it fascinating."

"You remember the first time you heard someone laugh?"

She nodded. "I was eleven, in Ravinder, practicing infiltration techniques in a tiny, nameless town near the northernmost of the nine famous lakes."

"What? You never heard laughter before?"

She shook her head. "Jagdish is a very stern community. There's no laughter in the kill academy, and that same intensity is reflected through the rest of the enclave."

"Wow. I can't imagine a place where people don't laugh."

"It seemed normal growing up, but looking back I see the strangeness of it," she admitted. "So for me, the sound of serpentinite is the sound of laughter. It is the sound that opened my mind to new possibilities."

That was pretty deep. Connor hoped his serpentinite sound didn't turn out to be something shallow and foolish, like the sound of Hamish's championship belch, or the sound of smacking lips after a particularly good sweetbread. Maybe it would be the sound of Verena's laughter like he always heard when he tapped obsidian. He would love that.

So he focused on the stone and tried to clear his mind. He stood like that for several minutes, eyes closed, just breathing and letting the sounds of the city wash over him, waiting for one to snatch his attention.

When nothing happened, he was tempted to tap quartzite to his ears. He could hear so much better that way, but would serpentinite resist establishing affinity while he was also walking with another metamorphic stone?

The wind picked up. It rushed past, growing quickly into a powerful gale. Only when he opened his eyes did he realize there was no wind.

Student Eighteen stood patiently watching him, her hair motionless around her head. Her clothing did not flap in the strong wind, and neither did his. And yet, he clearly heard wind.

"You hear something," Student Eighteen said.

"I don't understand, though. All I hear is wind."

It continued rushing through his mind, tugging at a memory that he couldn't quite bring into focus. He liked something about that wind, but at the moment it didn't make much sense.

"Wind? Are you sure?"

He shrugged. "Better than hearing Hamish chewing, I guess."

Connor focused on that sound and willed his senses to connect with it, extend out through it the way they did through the other elemental gateways.

All of a sudden, the city lit up with a cascade of lights. He gaped as he watched streams of light bouncing all around the city. Most were soft, flickering around like fireflies, but some were bright and shot into the sky with tremendous energy.

"What is all that?" he asked, double-checking that he hadn't accidentally activated limestone.

He gaped anew when his words flowed out his mouth as a stream of blue light. He heard the sounds, but he saw them too. And as he focused on them, he felt them, like water from the Wick flowing past his fingers.

The sounds radiated away from him, but then suddenly stopped and returned to flit around Student Eighteen's upraised left hand like moths around a flame.

"Seeing sounds is only the first benefit of serpentinite."

Her words gushed forth with the same bluish light as his, and again she caught them, this time circling them around her right hand.

Connor reached out to touch the glowing words, and he heard his own voice again, speaking those words. Laughing, he mentally tugged at the words, drawing them to himself.

"Speaking softly like we are, the sounds are rather weak, and they'll fade away in a moment unless we grant them more energy to sustain them."

Without warning, Aifric shouted, a loud wordless cry. The sound erupted from her mouth, glowing a vibrant yellow. She caught it and pulled it back to her. It circled her head, moving at twice the speed of the more sedate blues.

"No one else heard that shout, did they?"

She shook her head. "I prevented it from leaving."

"How is that possible? Sound moves so fast, but you caught it before it moved ten feet."

"That's one of the mysteries of serpentinite. It accelerates our processing of sound somehow so we can see it and manipulate it in the tiny fraction of a second before it would reach others."

Connor noted that none of the sounds of their voices escaped into the night. They all bounced back from an invisible barrier. Most of their words faded to violet, then to nothing as their energy drained away.

"I never knew sound could be so much fun," he said and caught the words the way Aifric had. They vibrated against his invisible senses like fish on a line. Their energy tingled down his serpentinite awareness, and somehow he understood how to push more energy back to them to sustain or amplify them. Or pull that energy and suck the life out of them.

He frowned. "Longseers can amplify voices too."

"But they only amplify sound as it is generated. We own sound."

She took that last statement, caught it in her hands, and pulled it apart. Connor watched in fascination as she split the words, re-ordered some of them, mashed the remainder together to form new ones, then extended the final product for him to touch.

"Amplify sound only can they manage, but not own them like us."

"Wait, you changed some words."

"It takes a little practice, but once we understand a person's voice, we can easily mimic it." She extracted from a pocket a crystal, cut into a perfect geometric pattern, like a sphere with flat sides. About the size of her pinky fingernail, it reflected the lights with brilliant clarity.

She held it up for him to see. "We can even capture sounds and preserve them for long periods of time with these."

"What is it?" Connor asked, touching the hard, cool crystal.

"This is a special strain of diamond, cut into a decahedron, and imbued with serpentinite power. I can capture sounds within and maintain them indefinitely by applying a little energy weekly."

Connor whistled softly, enjoying how the sharp sound bounced around him with bright green intensity. "A diamond like that is worth a fortune."

"We have a large deposit of diamonds. Their value is in their unique sound-preserving capabilities."

"What sounds do you save?" Connor could think of lots of sounds he'd love to listen to again later, but Aifric might not appreciate all of them. Most of all, he wished for the sound of Verena's voice. He carried it in his heart, but he'd love to carry it in his pocket too.

"This diamond holds the last words of Mister Five."

"Really?"

"I am saving them to share with my father when he hunts me down. If I'm lucky, I'll have time to use them before he takes my life."

"I'm still hoping Sir didn't deliver the message." Connor's problems seemed a little less dire when he compared them to hers. She had defied Mister Five. By her people's barbaric rules, her own father would be tasked to lead the kill team to execute her to restore the family honor.

"I have't heard from him, so I must assume he returned to Jagdish." She gave him a reassuring smile. "I have no plans to die easily, and this is one weapon in the arsenal I'll use to preserve my life and help you."

"You've helped me already. Teaching me chert and serpentinite is something no one else could do."

Her smile turned rueful. "And yet, to my people it will be one more crime I must pay for."

Connor was moved by how much she had sacrificed for him, how determined she was to follow the path she knew to be right. "I'll help you restore your good name. We could go to your home together and explain things."

Aifric laughed, but shook her head. "You do realize they'd try to kill you as soon as they learned you're Blood of the Tallan."

"A lot of people try to kill me. You changed your mind. Maybe they will too."

"Don't bet your life on it."

Connor took her hand and said with deadly intensity, "You've sworn to help me. I don't let people kill my friends."

"Thank you, Connor. I appreciate that, but I must take care of my people. With the queen risen, perhaps they will see reason. For now, back to practicing."

Connor spent the next hour learning from her how to manipulate and master sound. He learned to divert sounds away from specific people, but not others, how to absorb sounds and prevent their escape, and how to magnify sounds until they boomed like thunderclaps.

Student Eighteen showed him how to examine sounds and memorize their unique structure. The light represented their frequency, but they also contained pitch and inflection. He learned to chop sounds apart, rebuild them, and fill in resulting gaps in ways that sounded natural. It was a little scary to think how he could actually change what a person said so that others heard something completely different than what they intended. He could do it so fast that he could disrupt ongoing discussion at the speed of speech.

"I see why you Mhortair love this stone. You can sneak up on a target in absolute silence."

"We can deny them the ability to call out for help. We can squash their dying scream."

She was more than a little scary talking about killing so coldly, but Connor knew she had a good heart. He decided he didn't want to know any more specifics about any of her kill missions.

She said, "But think more on other ways to use it. We can create wonderful confusion and distractions that can sometimes allow us to slip unseen through areas where we might otherwise be forced to kill."

She completed the lesson by showing him how to generate sounds beyond the range of human hearing. With eyes closed, he learned to send out waves of high-pitched sound and catch the echoes to create a map of his surroundings in his mind.

"So we can see in the dark," Connor laughed.

As they tested the limits, Connor discovered that he could hear sounds in a wider range than she could. She decided it must be due to his ascension, and they agreed to test the theory later.

"Maybe we could test it on Kilian," Connor suggested. "See if we can draw his attention with sounds no one else can hear. He's ascended even higher than I have."

"But he doesn't have affinity with quartzite or serpentinite," Aifric pointed out. "So I'd be surprised if he could hear more than most.

"Other ascended Longseers might, though."

She nodded. "Keep that in mind when using the technique."

Connor asked, "So what do you call users of chert and serpentinite?"

"We call Mind Killers those who master chert, and Silent Killers those who alone can hear the true sound of silence."

"Did the same person come up with both of those?"

"I don't know. Why?"

"They're good names, but pretty similar."

She shrugged. "Our targets don't care what we call ourselves as they die, Connor."

"Good point."

He did want to test out the sound of silence idea. What would absolute silence sound like? Probably like a sweetbread with no flavor.

They finished the training by eavesdropping on people passing through the gate below, then creating new sentences in those same mimicked voices. Connor took to the technique so fast he could soon keep up with Aifric.

She gave him a disgusted look. "It took me weeks to learn this."

"Guess I'm back to breaking records."

She rolled her eyes. "I could throw you over the battlement so you could practice breaking legs."

Connor caught sight of a group of Crushers approaching across the bridge and got an idea. "One more test, and I promise to be terrible at voices for at least a week." He nodded toward the Crushers. "Mattias might have agreed to get along, but I can't imagine him not trying to make it difficult for me to spend time with Verena. I'm going to give him something else to worry about."

She raised one eyebrow. "Aifric suggests the plan may not be wise, but Rith heartily approves."

"And you?"

She shrugged. "I haven't killed anyone in days. I could take care of Mattias for you."

"Let's try it my way first, okay?" He didn't actually want Mattias dead. Not yet. Once Mattias accepted the fact that Verena belonged with Connor, hopefully he'd move back to Edderitz. Problem solved.

It took Connor only a moment to perfect a copy of Mattias's voice. He knew all too well the sound of his rival so he crafted some words and cast them off the wall, sending them in a wide arc before draining away most of their energy and floating them past the Longseer of the group of Crushers. They'd sound like a distant whisper, perhaps bounced back from the river chasm.

"I don't know why everyone is so in awe of the Crushers."

The Longseer stiffened and gestured to his companions to quiet as he turned his head and listened harder.

Connor continued, making Mattias's voice sound scornful. *"Sure, they're good soldiers, but with all that special training and all those mechanicals Verena keeps inventing for them, who wouldn't be? I could defeat any three of them any day of the week."*

The Longseer shared the words with his comrades, and the angry group stormed in through the gate, already shouting for Mattias to show himself.

Connor laughed long and loud, but prevented the sounds from reaching anyone but Student Eighteen. He doubted any serious harm would come of the prank. Mattias worked closely with Lukas after all, but he'd have some fast talking to do, and the distraction might keep him from interfering with Connor's visits to Verena for a couple days.

"That might not have been wise," Aifric pointed out through a smile. "Word will get back to him, and he'll figure out it was you."

"He might, but the brightest thing about Mattias is his smile."

"Have a care, nonetheless. We succeed because no one knows what we can do, so they don't know to question what they hear. If the truth spreads, we risk diminishing our own effectiveness."

She had a point, but then again, would it be such a bad thing to reduce the effectiveness of the rest of her clan? He needed to think about that. He needed Aifric, but at some point, it might be worth it to spread the word about the Mhortair so they couldn't victimize the rest of the world so easily.

14

____

THERE'S ALWAYS A BRIGHT SIDE. MAYBE.

Shona paused with her father in the glass-walled antechamber situated directly below the throne room. All nine towers that supported the throne room high above the central palace contained long spiraling stairs that all led here.

The floor was tiled in patterns of rippling blue and silver, as if mimicking the never-ending waterfall that streamed past the enormous window in the southern wall. Flowering plants in ceramic vases stood between each stairwell, but the room lacked any other ornamentation. A white-marbled grand staircase rose to wide, gilded double doors that led into the throne room itself.

"Are you ready?" Dougal asked, sounding unusually breathless. She wasn't sure if he was winded, excited, or afraid.

She felt all three emotions and her voice shook. "I hope so."

He took her hands, his expression grave. "You must be sure, my dear. This is your moment, Shona. Focus now. Think only positive thoughts. Fill your mind with the desire to serve, to do your duty, and to meet the legendary queen and learn at her feet."

Shona nodded, not trusting herself to speak. Her mouth had gone dry in a fit of nerves worse than anything she'd felt going into battle. At least in battle, she knew she had a chance to win, a chance to survive through her own cunning and strength.

Today her survival hung solely on the whim of a mad . . . No, she refused to even think that. Instead she steeled her mind, focused her thoughts like Ailsa explained, settled her expression into a mask of simple enthusiasm. Her armor today was her long, charcoal gown and a carefully prepared facade that matched both internally and externally.

She took a deep breath and nodded. "I'm ready."

Dougal swept up the staircase and the guards stationed at the top swung them open for him. Half a step behind, Shona entered the throne room. Despite her nervousness, she still felt the same, undiminished sense of wonder as she stepped into the marvelous room again.

The floor, made of rare, transparent quartzite crystals from the Glenmuick quarry, created the illusion that everyone walked on the billowing waterfall spray. That floor had always made Shona nervous, but as she stepped onto it, she wished it was her worst worry.

The outer, domed wall of blue-tinged, translucent quartzite bathed the scene in soft light from three sides. Only the rear of the throne room, directly across from Shona, broke the pattern with its bank of windows and their fantastic view of the waterfall plunging past. The air smelled of clean mountain water like it did through most of the city, but in the throne room, it was tinged with perfumes that tried to mask worry and fear.

The rushing of the falls created a constant background noise that usually helped mask the many whispered conversations between nobility. Today the many high nobility, officers, and courtiers who stood in tiny clusters around the room, all oriented toward the throne, remained absolutely silent. Shona's already tense nerves ratcheted another notch tighter. Everyone focused on the queen with desperate intensity, although more than a few turned at her entrance, looking eager for any distraction.

All of that served only as the backdrop for the queen, and she drew Shona's attention like a max-tapped Solas in a pitch-black cave. Queen Dreokt sat on the Obrioner throne, looking completely at ease in the famous stone chair. Crafted from the best pieces of all nine affinity stones, it was a masterwork of art and power.

Shona wasn't sure what she expected, but the slender woman with gray-streaked, golden hair and piercing blue eyes emanated power in near-palpable waves. She wore a gorgeous gown of deep blue, trimmed in intricate gold thread along the bodice. The heavy golden crown of Obrion stood on a stand beside the throne, but she wore a delicate golden tiara that included every affinity stone, mounted in ornate brackets.

King Turriff and his entire family, dressed in finely-cut servants uniforms, stood to either side of the throne's raised dais, focused entirely on their queen, looking eager to serve.

As Shona approached, she noted a rack of weapons standing to the left of the throne, within arm's reach of the queen. It was an incongruous sight in that room where weapons were barred except on the royal guard. The gilded rack held a sword, a long-handled hammer, several wicked-looking knives, a whip, and a simple leather glove with a long cowl that would extend back up to the elbow.

It did not encourage happy thoughts.

The deep baritone voice of the royal caller boomed across the room, echoing repeatedly from the domed exterior. "Presenting High Lord Dougal and High Lady Shona."

Shona strode between the ranks of onlookers, head high, acting like she belonged there. If she believed it, maybe they would.

Her father stopped several yards short of the dais and bowed low. Shona curtsied while he said, "Your Royal Majesty, I am deeply honored for this opportunity to present my daughter, Shona."

"Present yourself, child," the queen said in a soft but commanding voice.

Shona stepped a little closer and curtsied again. "Your Majesty, it is my great honor to meet you."

Queen Dreokt's glowing blue eyes seemed to drink in her entire vision, and Shona felt a touch against her mind, a flicker like a caress, but inside her head. She kept her thoughts focused on her father, her desire to do her duty, and her eagerness to serve her queen.

The touch became harder, like a hand pressing down on her brain. She forced herself not to flinch, not to move, and kept her thoughts unchanged.

Queen Dreokt spoke in a happy, almost girlish tone. "Oh, it's so refreshing to meet a young person who understands their place in the world so clearly."

Shona blinked as those mesmerizing eyes released her. The queen grinned at her like an old friend. She almost sighed with relief, but caught herself just in time. Her muscles quivered with tension, and she felt exhausted, but she maintained her position without moving.

Queen Dreokt made a beckoning gesture. "Come here, child."

Shona approached, stepping right onto the raised dais when the queen beckoned her even closer. She felt acutely aware of everyone's stares. Up close, the force of the queen's gaze felt like a palpable weight on her shoulders.

When Shona dropped her gaze the queen made a tsking sound. "No child, look at me."

Shona looked into her eyes and they blazed with inner light, again consuming her vision. For a moment her mind froze, her muscles became rigid, and she forgot to breathe.

Then the queen blinked, releasing her, and Shona sagged visibly before catching herself.

Queen Dreokt abruptly rose to her feet. Shona stumbled back in surprise, tripped on the edge of he dais, and fell hard to her backside. She grunted from the impact and glanced around, already feeling humiliated and expecting a wave of laughter from the watching nobility.

None of them had seen her fall.

Everyone had dropped to their knees, heads bowed, some shaking with fear. Shona got the distinct impression that bad things usually resulted from the queen rising. Her fear escalated to near panic as she realized she was the cause of the queen's wrath this time. What would the woman do to her?

She looked toward her father, who had dropped to one knee. He glanced at her, fear in his eyes, but she read the terrifying truth there too. He was powerless to help her survive whatever punishment the queen was planning.

Queen Dreokt stepped closer and Shona scrambled to her knees like the others. Her dress caught on her legs, nearly toppling her over again, but she tapped a bit of granite to strengthen her core and managed to remain upright, head bowed, hands trembling against the cool crystalline floor. She stared down at the billowing spray, like ever-shifting clouds beneath her, and wondered if that might be the last thing she saw.

"You are a lovely girl," the queen said in a surprisingly approving tone.

Shone risked looking up. The queen stood at the edge of the dais, studying her as one would consider a prize pet. "Strong and well-learned. I sense ambition, but wrapped thoroughly in a desire to serve your masters."

"Thank you, Your Majesty," Shona said, proud and more than a little surprised that her voice did not shake.

Queen Dreokt stepped down from the dais to stand beside her. Shona dropped her gaze again, wondering if the punishment would come now, and which weapon the queen would use to strike her down. Ian had said it was considered a great honor to be executed personally by the queen, but she had hoped to survive a little longer.

She hadn't really accepted the possibility that she might die today. She had overcome many challenges in her life. Sure, reports suggested that many had perished, but those men and women weren't Shona. Now that she faced the moment where she might actually die, helpless to defend herself, she felt truly powerless for the first time in her life.

The feeling was so foreign, she very nearly broke down in tears. Only a lifetime of discipline kept her in place, silent, poised, outwardly calm, but her fears very nearly distracted her from the purpose Ailsa had drilled into her.

Shona realized her thoughts were slipping and wrenched them back to focus on her father and her desires to serve him and the queen in whatever capacity they required. The terror that set her heart racing and her hands sweating against the cool floor lent her desire to serve more humility than usual, and in that moment she would honestly and gratefully have accepted whatever duty might be imposed upon her.

Queen Dreokt did not strike. She said nothing, but walked a slow circuit around Shona, who managed to remain perfectly still, fighting to keep her breathing under control. Out of the corner of her eye, she watched the queen's progress, her gown swooshing softly along the floor, her footsteps inaudible beneath the constant rumble of the waterfall. No other sound broke the absolute, tense stillness of the throne room. The queen's perfume drifted down to her, a surprisingly pleasant, floral scent. Shona only hoped the queen could not smell her rank fear.

The slow circuit seemed to take forever as the queen paced around Shona, her thoughts and intent a mystery. Shona wanted to scream from the tension, from not knowing which second the queen would strike, or what mistake she had made to seal her fate. All she could do was kneel in breathless anticipation, trying to keep her mind centered on her duty. She couldn't tell if the queen was still reading her thoughts, but didn't dare assume she wasn't.

It felt like hours later when the queen abruptly returned to her throne, sat with a flourish, and said, "Rise, my child."

Shona stood on wobbly legs, trying to straighten her twisted dress without drawing attention to the movement. Behind her, the gathered witnesses rose too. Shona caught hints of surprised whispers. They had honestly expected her to die while kneeling before the queen. Now that Queen Dreokt again sat on the throne, the weapons rack was once more within easy reach.

Queen Dreokt did not reach for a weapon, but gave Shona a motherly smile. "You're an exceptional young lady."

"Thank you, Your Majesty," Shona managed, her dry throat rasping, the sound barely more than a whisper. She dared consider that maybe she had survived after all.

"And yet you have established no secondary affinity."

Shona's nervous tension flooded back. Was this the moment when she failed the interview? She forced herself to look up into the queen's eyes again. If she was to die, she would face her fate like the high lady she'd trained all her life to become.

Queen Dreokt laughed, a happy sound, like that of a young child. She actually clapped her hands together and nodded in approval. "Yes. Yes, I like you child. In fact, you must attend me daily."

Shona nearly screamed, but she couldn't even let herself think all the thoughts she wanted to. It took all of her training, all of her willpower, but she managed a grateful smile and curtsied.

"Thank you, my queen. Serving you is my greatest desire."

"And service to me brings with it the greatest rewards," The queen said, her tone shifting to one of grave self-importance in the blink of an eye. She extended a hand, holding something.

Shona accepted it and was surprised to find a tiny piece of limestone. Before she could formulate a question, the queen touched Shona on the cheek.

A shock rippled through her from that touch and Shona staggered, her muscles quivering uncontrollably. She dropped to one knee, shaking, trying to understand what had happened. How had the queen done that? What had she done?

Why did the room look brighter?

She blinked a couple of times, then focused on the piece of limestone still clutched in her hand. Light burst between her fingers as if she held a piece of the sun.

Shona gasped and opened her hand. Sure enough, the limestone was blazing, filling the room with green-tinged light. The quartzite dome absorbed it and glowed in response, brightening the room even further. Shona became aware of the connection to the limestone, like a gentle warmth along her palm. The affinity was part of her, familiar as if it had always been there, but was now suddenly awakened.

Shona laughed and looked up into the queen's smiling face. "How is it possible? I mean, I've never managed even a flicker from limestone before." She realized with horror that she'd addressed the queen like an equal and quickly apologized.

Queen Dreokt made a dismissive gesture. "My child, your enthusiasm warms my heart. Your primary affinity was so strong it clouded your mind to other possibilities. The potential always existed within you. I just poked it to life like stirring a sleeping ember."

She laughed then, as if she'd said something hysterically funny. Shona didn't understand, but curtsied again. "Thank you so much!"

Perhaps the queen could help her discover a tertiary affinity?

Queen Dreokt's laughter cut off as abruptly as it began and her expression changed instantly back to serious. Shona very nearly shuffled farther away. Had the queen heard that thought, disapproved of it?

Queen Dreokt spoke loudly, casting her gaze across the room. "Thus are my worthy servants rewarded."

She waved Shona back, but added in a friendly tone, "Be sure to attend me daily in the afternoons, my dear. I think we'll become excellent friends."

"I will, Your Majesty," Shona said as she retreated to her father.

With a thought, she shuttered the limestone's power. She wanted to test it, explore the new affinity she'd just miraculously gained, but didn't dare cause an interruption that might trigger the queen's anger.

Her father gave her a restrained hug and whispered fiercely, "Well done, Shona."

"Thank you, Father."

She had so much to think about, so much to understand, but Queen Dreokt spoke again, her tone regal and disapproving. "And now you will all witness the punishments that must come to those unworthy servants who disappoint me."

She waved to the outer door. It opened, and a pair of Boulders dragged a terrified looking man into the room.

15

SOME NIGHTMARES KEEP GETTING WORSE

Shona sidled to her right a pace to see around a portly lord dressed in a rich doublet of crimson and steel of house Feichin to get a better look at the poor man getting dragged toward the queen.

He didn't look like a criminal. Probably around her own age, his handsome face had that open, innocent look of sheltered nobility who knew little of strife or warfare. He looked terrified, but also a bit confused.

She felt sorry for him. Even if his infraction turned out to be minor, dragging him to the throne in front of all the assembled nobility created a sense of existing guilt. She'd fallen into the trap of snap judgments before. She thought back to that frustrating day when she'd made perhaps her stupidest mistake with Connor.

She'd supported Carbrey's decision to hang Connor for treason. He'd just burned her hair, burned the weakening powder they so desperately needed. In her rage, she'd turned on him and set the stage for Verena to slip into his heart.

Queen Dreokt stared down at the frightened man forced to kneel before her dais, her expression disapproving. Silence settled over the assembly as everyone craned a bit closer to learn the man's terrible infraction.

The man prostrated himself and cried, "I'm so sorry, Your Majesty. Whatever I did, I promise not to do it again. Please forgive me."

"Whatever you did?" She snapped angrily. "You fool. You don't even realize your fault."

He shook his head violently. "I am a fool, but I'm a loyal subject. Please teach me how to be better."

She glared down at him. "You dared ascend the mountain yesterday. Do you deny this?"

He rose to a kneeling position, looking confused. "I did. I was hunting an Icy Snowdrop for my beloved. Look."

He withdrew from inside his tunic a little wooden box, as long as his hand. Shaking with haste and fear, he carefully pried open the lid, extracted an exquisite flower and held it up. "I've kept it close to my heart ever since I found it."

The delicate snowy petals drooped down from an icy-blue heart. Shona had seen the rare flower only twice. It was prized as an exceptional symbol of love and coveted by enamored young men as ideal gifts during courtship.

"It is lovely," Queen Dreokt breathed, leaning a bit closer.

The young man dared extend it for her to take. "They bloom only on the peaks above Donleavy, and only after snowstorms. Please, take it as an apology."

The queen accepted it and sat back on her throne, examining the flower. A little smile played across her face as she stroked one snowy petal, and the man visibly relaxed. Shona dared breathe a little easier. Flowers were known to soften every woman's heart, but could the fragile little gift really assuage the queen's fury?

"I appreciate this gift, and I will treasure it," Queen Dreokt said in that same happy, almost-little-girl voice.

Then her expression changed in the blink of an eye back to wrath and she glared down at the man. "But you still dared climb the mountain above me, dared look down upon me as if you were somehow better."

The man paled in terror, but Shona exchanged a confused look with her father. That was what offended her?

Queen Dreokt's expression turned sorrowful and she spoke in a motherly voice. "My dear boy, lessons must be taught, or order cannot be maintained."

The man began to weep, begging for forgiveness, swearing he hadn't realized what he did was so wrong. Who could have imagined such an offense?

The queen's expression did not change. She gave no outward indication of tapping any affinity stone, but the poor, doomed man suddenly pitched over, clutching at his head, screaming.

Shona took half a step back, as did most of those assembled. The man rolled and writhed on the floor as wisps of steam began hissing out his ears, nose, open, screaming mouth, and even around his eyes.

Then his scream faded and he slumped against the clear floor, unmoving. The hissing steam continued to rise from every opening in his body. Shona frowned as she studied him. His skin was turning brown, almost as if. . . .

The smell of boiled meat wafted across the room, and Shona gagged and held her breath when she realized what it was. She'd experienced death in many forms on the battlefield so she maintained discipline better than some of the courtiers who knew nothing but sheltered palace life.

When they realized they were smelling the man cooking in his own blood, several of them vomited. Of course then they scrambled to try mopping up the mess with their fine clothing, weeping with fear as they muttered apologies in the queen's direction.

She ignored them, but crinkled her nose at the smell. With a dismissive wave of her hand, the quartzite under the dead man's feet flowed aside, allowing his body to tumble down into the boiling mists of the Mealt and disappear into the loch far below.

Then the floor under one fat woman, who was blubbering hysterically as she tried vainly to wipe her vomit from the floor, also disappeared. Her scream echoed out of the obscuring mists for several seconds, even after she must have crashed into the loch and died.

A powerful wind gusted up into the room through those holes in the floor, flapping robes and well-groomed hair. It smelled of chill mountain air, heavy with water from the mists. In seconds that wind scoured the room clean of the stench of the dead man as well as the smell of vomit. Then the wind faded back to calm silence and the floor flowed back into place.

Shona marveled at the queen's amazing and seemingly casual mastery over the elements. She wielded higher forms of power, available only to those who had ascended, with terrifying ease.

No Spitter Shona knew could boil a man's blood. The human body shielded its liquid too well. The thought of her own blood beginning to boil terrified her more than most other ways of dying. Such a death would deny her the ability to fight to defend herself. She would have to suffer like that poor fool, helpless and without hope.

The queen's unrivaled power drove home the fact that they were now enslaved to a being much more powerful than any of them. Shona could not imagine how anyone could ever hope to be free again.

One of the other courtiers, a pretty young woman who had been standing close to the fat lady who just plummeted to her death, suddenly took an angry step forward. Her face was blotchy from tears and terror, her long, black hair disheveled.

"You're insane! You—" Her angry shriek cut off abruptly and she fell to her knees, eyes wide with horror.

"Silence!" Queen Dreokt leaped to her feet, her expression rabid with fury. She snatched up a short, curved knife from the rack at her side and took a step toward the woman who just dared insult her.

"You unworthy cur!" she shrieked, raising the knife as if to throw it.

Nobles and courtiers alike scrambled away from the woman. Every face reflected the same terror that Shona felt. But Queen Dreokt did not throw the dagger. Instead she crumpled it into a twisted mass of steel in one hand. The idle gesture spoke volumes about her strength. Shona herself could twist a sword into a knot, but not one-handed.

The queen tossed the mangled knife back onto the rack and King Turriff himself rushed over to snatch it up and replace it with his own belt dagger. His expression remained perfectly neutral, as if he was serving desserts at banquet instead of watching murder in his own throne room.

The queen's expression changed to one of parental concern and she spoke in a tender voice. "But you can become worthy. I will grant you forgiveness and show you the way."

The woman screamed again, a high-pitched wail of suffering, as if her innards were getting ripped apart. The scream cut off as quickly as if the queen had slashed her throat. The woman convulsed off the ground, climbing to a kneeling position, her expression of horror melting away into a look of ecstatic joy.

She looked like she was remembering her happiest memory. Shona frowned as the woman's hands fell to her side and she knelt for a moment in perfect stillness. Then she rose smoothly to her feet and declared in a joyous voice, "All hail the queen of glory!"

The woman raised worshipful hands and rushed to the queen, dropping to her knees before her. When Queen Dreokt extended one hand in blessing, the woman kissed it with desperate thanksgiving. Shona felt sick. The woman was clearly not acting. She was eagerly, almost desperately, worshiping the queen.

"Rise, my worthy servant," Queen Dreokt said, and the woman glided to her feet and joined the royal family standing to the queen's left.

Gone was her terror and anger. She looked perfectly calm, perfectly content, her eyes empty of intelligence. She looked like a different person. No, she looked like a person devoid of personality.

Horror chilled Shona's heart. What had the queen just done? She was starting to understand what Ailsa had said about the lucky people getting executed.

A soft voice spoke in a whisper close beside Shona. "The queen shows great favor for one so unworthy."

She spun to find an elegant young woman standing beside her. The girl had to be about her same age, but she didn't recognize her.

"Pardon me?" Shona asked, pitching her voice low enough that the constant rumble of the nearby waterfall would drown out her words before they reached anyone else. The distraction helped her regain her calm. She couldn't afford to dwell on the horror of what she'd just witnessed.

The girl made a brief curtsy. "I apologize for startling you, Lady Shona, but I am sent to inform you that the queen's afternoon audiences start at the second bell and usually end by the fourth."

"Thank you," Shona said cautiously, frowning at the girl. There was something familiar about her after all.

"You have been chosen to attend her every afternoon, so it is important you arrive promptly ten minutes early."

Recognition struck like a hammer-blow, and Shona's legs suddenly felt weak. "Catriona?"

The princess made another little curtsy. "I am honored that you know my name."

"Catriona, don't you remember me?" Shona whispered, peering closer, trying to match the pudgy, dumpy, unremarkable princess she remembered with the tall, graceful, beautiful young woman speaking with her.

Wait, this woman was taller. She glanced down to make sure the princess wasn't wearing extra-high heels. No, Catriona had simply grown several inches and now rivaled Shona's height. Her figure looked exquisite, and her features delicate and regal. Her hair hung to her waist in thick, loose curls. No wonder Shona hadn't recognized her. Her own mother might not.

"My memory isn't what is used to be," Catriona admitted demurely, ducking her chin a bit in embarrassment. "Thankfully, everything I need to remember to serve our lady queen is still in place." Her smile revealed perfect teeth. "Those found worthy to serve are granted wonderful blessings by the queen's patronage. She possesses the healing powers of a goddess. She can even correct deformities of birth."

Shona had never considered Catriona deformed. Uninspiring for sure, but not deformed. Her sense of horror deepened and she barely kept from running screaming from the room. The queen had rebuilt Catriona into someone new.

Into a worthy servant.

Shona glanced at the rest of the royal family. They had not undergone such dramatic physical transformation, but she didn't doubt that the queen had scrambled their brains too, leaving them empty puppets, good for nothing but serving her.

No wonder King Turriff hadn't tried any crafty double-cross. He was dead. What remained was not a man, but a vacant shell.

The queen's voice startled her out of her reverie, and she actually jumped. Queen Dreokt again sat on her throne, a look of regal displeasure on her face.

"Does no one here understand basic courtesy? Must I teach even such fundamentals? Apparently so." She sighed in a long-suffering way and declared, "Be it known to all that no one is allowed to stand higher than their queen. Not in this palace. Not on the cliffs. Not anywhere! On penalty of death."

She rose and continued, "If I deign to descend into the city, all must descend lower than I." She glanced around the room and her mood darkened. "I read your confusion, as if you consider such basic signs of respect some great thing. Have no fear, my children, I will mold you into worthy servants."

Shona only barely kept from gaping, and was grateful her father's shoulder blocked her from the queen's direct gaze. She wasn't sure if the queen could read her mind from across the room, but she had definitely lost focus for a moment.

The proclamation was awe-inspiringly insane.

The queen's voice changed to a pleasant, conversational tone. "Do any of you have a problem with this, or wish to contest my will?"

The only people stupid enough to pick up that challenge must have already died.

"Dougal, you will see that all understand this decree. I will be seriously displeased if I must make another example out of anyone." She idly crushed the beautiful flower and dropped it beside the throne.

High Lord Dougal bowed and stepped closer to the throne. "I will see it done, my queen." He hesitated and added, "May I ask a point of clarification?"

Shona nearly gasped. How could he dare tempt her wrath?

"What is it, Dougal," Queen Dreokt asked, her tone bored and impatient. "You know I prefer you deal with the minutia."

"I am happy to," he assured her quickly. "With this new edict, I must point out that at times our servants are assigned tasks that might require them to ascend to all levels of the palace at any time. Delaying their duties might adversely impact your own schedule."

Queen Dreokt turned thoughtful. "I see your point. The palace functions must not be hindered. Very well, any servants assigned official duties that take them higher in the castle must bow in the direction of the throne room and apologize three times."

"Thank you for your gracious consideration," Dougal stated and began to withdraw, but Queen Dreokt raised her hand to forestall him.

She glanced around the room. "It is imperative that our nobility always possess greater privileges than our servants."

"Indeed," Dougal said.

Many of the assembled appeared to relax, clearly expecting her to rescind the ridiculous decree. Shona did not allow herself to hope for so much. She had already learned not to make any assumptions around the queen.

Queen Dreokt nodded to herself, as if coming to a decision. "Therefore it is my will that any nobility who wear an eoin feather, plucked fresh daily from a live a bird, are worthy to stand anywhere in the castle, should their duties require it."

Shona caught many looks of confusion and annoyance, but they all faded quickly. Such a bizarre command might be strange, but they could make it work. No doubt eoin farmers were about to earn unexpected fortunes.

Queen Dreokt added, "It is imperative that the feathers be harvested by your own hand. Furthermore you must arise from your beds in the morning before I do, or your laziness proclaims to all your slothful and unworthy state. None such are worthy to wear the feather."

She then waved a hand and declared, "Dismissed."

As Shona hurried away with her father, she wondered how long she could handle standing daily for hours in the presence of that madwoman.

The day her concentration broke, would the queen execute her or break her mind and make her a worthy puppet?

16

CHOCOLATE PUDDING SIMMERING OVER AN OPEN FLAME

Hamish banked the Storm wide around the town of Faulenrost to pass over the snow-covered field of Schwinkendorf valley where the Builder compound used to be. The deep snows from the recent blizzard had already been cleared from the work sites and rebuilding was again under way. From that height it was easy to see the layout of the new town taking shape. He recognized Jean's ordered mind in the regular streets already marked out on the frozen turf.

The skeletal frameworks of two large buildings were already nearly complete. The first was positioned near the center of town and he hoped it was the new dining hall. It was huge enough that Jean probably incorporated his recommendations for expanded kitchens.

He did not linger, but banked back toward Faulenrost and opened wide the rear thrusters. The fast little craft could cover a lot of distance. Its unrivaled speed helped ease the lingering ache at the loss of his flying suit.

Hamish hoped Jean was ready to help him build a new and better one. She'd expressed interest in helping him test and fine-tune his last suit. He had big plans for the new one. He couldn't wait to discuss them with her.

The Storm was packed with power stones and supplies. The tiny supply bed at the back was stuffed to bursting, and the other eight seats were piled high. He'd crammed his personal gear into the storage boxes underneath. Hamish loved flying the Storm, but nothing could really replace his suit. He felt naked without it. Even if Jean hadn't gotten around to preparing a workroom for him, he'd brought along enough supplies to build several from scratch, if needed.

Despite the bitter cold of the high altitudes, Hamish was only dressed in linen trousers and a cotton shirt under his many-pocketed leather jacket. He'd applied Verena's trick of using a shieldstone to create a protective canopy over the Storm. He'd even added a little piece of marble in a metal pot. The tiny flame created enough heat to warm the space and make the trip through the wintry landscape downright pleasant.

He planned to drag Jean away from her work long enough to slip away in the Storm with a nice meal. Maybe they could watch the sunset from five thousand feet. It would be nice to get a little quiet time together.

Hamish passed once over Faulenrost. The picturesque Grandurian town looked even prettier in the wintry landscape. He activated his long-vision goggles and scanned the crowds of waving people. He recognized many, both locals and refugees from the Builder compound who had settled there until New Schwinkendorf was built.

Most windriders landed on the outskirts of town in a field of packed earth set aside for them, but Hamish spotted Jean emerging from the manor house near the town square. He very nearly leaped out of the Storm to fly down to her, but bumped his head on the shieldstone canopy and remembered he was not wearing his flying suit. So he slowed and dropped the Storm straight down into the town square.

He deactivated the shieldstone and leaped out to meet Jean without bothering to don his heavy coat. The air was chilly but not brutally cold, and Jean rushed up and jumped into his arms. His heart sang with the joy reserved for her alone and he spun her around once, loving the feel of her in his arms.

She wore a long, downy jacket, but no hat. Her long, blond hair was braided, her cheeks flushed from the cold, and her bright blue eyes sparkled with joy.

He drew her close and kissed her passionately, exulting in the fact that she kissed him back just as enthusiastically. She smelled like herbs and winter skies, and somehow of flowers.

When she finally let him breathe again she gushed, "Welcome home!"

"It's good to be back."

He grabbed his jacket, then followed her into the inn where he spent a few minutes greeting old friends and chatting with people about the rebuilding efforts and the schedule for more supplies. He confirmed that the peace treaty had been signed, which elicited a round of cheering and calls for drinks.

Jean spent a moment speaking with Liesa, the plump, jolly old woman who ran the inn with her husband. Hamish joined them and Liesa gave him a hug.

"Welcome back, Builder. Food is ready."

"You're my favorite person," he told her warmly.

"I doubt that," she laughed, pushing him and Jean toward a small back room where they could talk while he ate. It wasn't yet time for dinner, but Liesa herself brought in a large platter for him. She knew him so well.

"How is the work going?" Hamish asked between bites of the inn's famous roasted pork. "I saw the construction out in the valley."

"The blizzard slowed us down, but we're making progress. We have some workrooms already functioning here in town. The Althing scientists arrived yesterday to help with the school, and they're amazing."

Her eyes sparkled with enthusiasm as she told him about all the progress they had already made in so many areas of study. She'd accomplished so much in the days since he'd last seen her that his mind whirled.

"We should go fly together," he said when she took a breath.

She nodded eagerly. "As soon as I show you your new suit."

Hamish dropped his fork. "What? As in it's finished already?"

She laughed and kissed him, looking so excited she could barely contain herself. He trusted Jean completely, but could she and Dierk really have rebuilt his suit to the same level of craft as the original?

She rose and took his hand. "Come on. I'll take you to the workroom. On the way, you can tell me how everyone is doing at Emmerich. How is Gran?"

He stuffed the rest of the food into a sack he kept in a pocket for exactly those occasions. While they walked through town, Hamish told her about the efforts to settle the folks from Alasdair in Emmerich, the challenges of communication and rebuilding, the mistrust slowly changing to cautious acceptance, and the surprising budding courtship between Stuart and Stefanie.

Jean laughed when she heard about it. "I can't imagine Stuart courting a Grandurian!"

"She's pretty, and she cooks great. I think Stuart almost had a heart-stomp when he realized she was a Petralist. She lifted him right off the ground when he asked her to dance at the festival Lord Wenzel proclaimed to celebrate the end of the blizzard."

Jean laughed. "Is her family okay with it?"

Hamish grimaced. "I don't think they believed it at first, but the two of them seem seriously interested in each other. Hopefully I'll get back before her brother decides to beat Stuart to a pulp. They take the brother honor responsibility very seriously."

"As they should." She gave him a mischievous grin. "You know, Gran still has a special tonic for you. Since I don't have any brothers, she's going to stand in and make you take the challenge."

Hamish shuddered. Mhairi made the most disgusting tonics on a good day. She knew he'd built up his resistance to them through sheer stubbornness. He could only imagine what she might come up with for a special occasion.

"Your grandmother is doing great. Not many communities in Granadure have non-Petralist healers so she fascinates them. She took a page right out of one of your notebooks and started a healing school. She has half a dozen of the local girls already enrolled. She's extremely busy, and she looks very happy."

Jean looked relieved. "I'm so glad. I was worried she would miss me too much."

"Everyone misses you, but she's found a way to keep busy."

They chatted as they walked through town hand in hand, and everything felt right in the world. By the time they reached the large barn at the outskirts of town, converted into a Builder workshop, he felt like he had never left. He never wanted to leave her side again, and hated that he would have to.

The inside of the workroom was filled with piles of stone, partially constructed mechanicals, crates full of supplies, work tables covered with tools, and a brand-new smashpack machine. It smelled like broken stone, grease, and fresh-baked cookies.

It felt like home. Hamish took a deep breath and broke into a wide grin. Stepping into a Builder workroom was a special joy.

"Looks like Dierk took his team to the other workroom," Jean said as she led him through the clutter. "He'll be happy to see you."

"Dierk's the best," Hamish agreed.

She placed a hand on his arm, her expression turning more serious. "Having you here for a while will hopefully cheer him up. He is still so torn up about Ingrid's death and so angry at the Obrioners. It's not healthy."

"I'll do what I can to help," he promised. Thinking about Ingrid still filled him with aching sorrow. He still felt like he should have figured out a way to save her.

Jean gave him a hug and said softly, "We all miss her, but it was no one's fault that she's gone but the elfonnel." Then she forced a smile and drew him deeper into the workroom. "Come on. There's so much to see."

Hamish decided the best way to honor Ingrid would be to keep developing amazing mechanicals. So he forced a grin to math Jean's. "I wouldn't have believed that you could capture the heart of Schwinkendorf in a barn in Faulenrost, but you did. I can imagine we're back in the Builder compound right now."

The comment obviously pleased her, and Jean led him around a pair of tall standing cabinets. On the other side, in an open workspace that seemed a little less cluttered than the rest of the workshop, stood Hamish's new suit.

He laughed. He'd been a fool to doubt that there was anything Jean couldn't do.

"It looks amazing!" But no doubt she hadn't thought of enhancing it like he planned to.

With a flicker of thought, Hamish triggered the quartzite blocks in his jacket and jumped. With loud, whooshing jets, each of the quartzite stones ignited for just a second in a tight sequence he'd worked out in Emmerich. The brief but intense thrusts catapulted Hamish into a half-twisting somersault, right over the suit to land on the opposite side. He landed on his feet, facing back at Jean, and extended his hands in victory.

Looking dutifully impressed, Jean clapped. "That's new."

"I've got plans to enhance my next suit," he told her as he slowly walked around the fantastic suit.

Jean's smile turned a bit mischievous. "I'm sure we can fit that in somewhere between the other enhancements I already added."

That piqued his interest, so he studied the suit more closely. It looked similar, but he instantly spotted several improvements. An outer layer of leather and steel now covered the armored jacket of overlapping, hardened granite leaves. She had lined the inside of the jacket with more leather, then with an enhanced water bladder, followed by another padded jerkin. It would be a little bulkier than his last suit, but he could already tell that she'd at least doubled the stop-bash properties.

Jean showed him the water bladder. "We added some ribbing within the bladder to increase strength and encourage better force dispersion. That gave us another fifty percent improvement."

"Wow." Hamish whistled softly in appreciation.

The water bladder was a key component. He already could have taken a punch from a max-tapped Rumbler and survived, but might have cracked some granite leaves and gotten bruised. The hard outer layer transferred the impact into the water, which dispersed it around his body to dissipate the force. With a fifty percent better force dispersion, he could stay in the fight unhurt a lot longer.

"And since we already knew the performance targets as we built it this time, we were able to test each component more thoroughly and calibrate everything for additional improvements."

She'd suggested that with rigorous testing she could improve his last suit dramatically, even more than they'd manage in the hectic days before the battle of Altkalen.

The new boots were slightly bigger too. In addition to the large quartzite thruster he expected to find in each one, she had added three smaller blocks. She explained how he could use those blocks to fine-tune his directional control or amplify the force of the main block. The new configuration resulted in thirty percent more power.

"You might be able to keep up with the Storm now."

Hamish whistled again. His suit had performed remarkably well, especially given the fact that he had done no specialized testing. He had just attached the biggest block he could fit without it getting in the way of walking.

This was as much Jean's suit as his now. He squashed an unexpected flash of annoyance that she'd done so much and made so many decisions without him. No doubt he would have agreed to every suggestion had he been there with her. Instead he focused on how proud he felt of her. His Jean was becoming a top-rate mechanical designer. He itched to put on the suit and test it out.

They spent a few more minutes discussing other enhancements. The suit carried better armaments and more of them, including defensive stones like marble puking dooms, gushing soapstone, and blind coal worked into the arms and helmet.

She pointed out several shieldstones. "We built on the research you started on shaping shieldstones to affect the shape of the resulting shield. Brilliant work, by the way. We proved your theories and fine-tuned them. We can produce stronger defensive shields using less than half the power output. So you can generate more shields, they can last longer, but consume less stone."

"I was planning on testing the use of shaped shields while flying. If I could use them to cut air resistance when I reach full speed, I might be able to accelerate even more, but with less power consumption."

She kissed his cheek. "Great idea. We hadn't gotten that far yet, but it's the next logical step."

"Have I told you yet today that I love you?"

"Saying it again never hurts," she said, giving him that special smile that melted his insides.

So he told her. Twice. That earned him another kiss, but did not distract her from the suit for long.

When she detailed the offensive weaponry, he almost wished they had not signed the peace treaty so he could test it against real Petralists. The suit now sported two side-holstered speedslings with longer revolving canisters that held more hornets. Several little diorite-tipped missiles were recessed in each arm. They were propelled by marble or quartzite. Spikes could snap into position to extend beyond his knuckles to allow him to punch with devastating force.

Hamish laughed. "It's going to take me three days to test all this out and make sure I understand how all of the enhancements work."

She grinned. "I'm glad you like it. There's more we haven't even covered yet, but maybe now you'll stick around for a little while."

He took her hands and turned serious. "Now that we have peace, I'm hoping I'll get to spend most of the winter here."

She sighed. "I hope you can visit a lot. There's so much I can't do without your here, but with the queen returned, Connor is going to need you too."

"I'm sure he will, but I'm hoping we'll still find some time to relax."

She took his face in her hands and kissed him seriously. "You're a good man. Once Verena is awake, Connor won't need us quite so much, but for now he does."

"He's in Altkalen right now. I'll need to head up there in a few days. What else are you working on?"

They exited the workroom and returned to Lord Eberhard's manor where Jean had set up an office. Bruno, Artur, and Carolin were all there, discussing in rapid Grandurian one of their latest mechanical tests. Hamish greeted them all warmly and listened in amazement as they described all of the work they were doing to help rebuild the Builder workshops, New Schwinkendorf, and the school. Jean really had assembled a magnificent team.

Bruno, the huge master blacksmith, clapped Hamish on the shoulder and said with great pride, "I'm also spearheading an effort with your brilliant girl to develop an outer protective armor for when you need to do battle against the strongest Petralists."

"That would be amazing."

"We're still brainstorming the best designs, but haven't settled on a plan yet," Jean said in Grandurian. Her accent was a little rough, but Hamish adored it. He wasn't surprised she'd started learning Grandurian. "I'm glad you're here to help. We need that creative flair of yours."

"Let's see what you've got. How many cookies do you have handy?" Hamish always worked best when riding a sugar high.

Bruno extracted from a cabinet several square pieces of parchment and spread them on the table. They contained rough sketches and notes exploring possible armored frameworks.

As Hamish scanned them, Bruno jabbed one meaty finger at the parchments. "Your suit has tremendous agility and flexibility. For most encounters, that should be enough to keep you safe. However, if you get drawn into a long bash fight or have to face a tertiary, you'll still be in great danger."

"I've been thinking about that too," Hamish admitted.

He had designed his suit to allow him to fight Petralists, but there were still things he couldn't do. The ease with which Martys had ripped his suit apart in rampager form had highlighted that fact. Hamish had been thinking about additional enhancements he could make, but Jean and Bruno were proposing a whole new level.

As he stared down at the rough sketches, new ideas started bubbling across his mind like chocolate pudding simmering over an open flame. He quickly discarded several of their initial ideas, including one that looked sort of like the Storm, but with wheels and heavier armor. Something like that could prove very effective on roads, but not in rougher terrain. He also pushed aside one design that looked like a huge humanoid suit, similar to his, but ten times larger.

"Wait, I like that one," Jean protested, and Bruno nodded agreement.

Hamish shook his head. "Won't work. My suit functions as well as it does because I do all the work to stand and move. A suit that big, shaped like a man, would be too unsteady. We'd spend so much power trying to keep it upright and moving like a person, it would become too complicated. Too much opportunity for failure."

Jean sighed and exchanged a crestfallen look with Bruno. "That's why we need you, Hamish. I can take your ideas and fine-tune them, but you're the Builder. You're the creative genius."

Hamish marveled at her. He'd never imagined that he might be better than her at anything other than eating, or belching, or distance puking. To hear her admit she needed him inspired and daunted him more than a little.

"I really need a cookie."

Bruno and Artur laughed and both extracted small coins from their belt pouches, then pushed them across to Carolin, who was smiling with victory. She extracted a small package wrapped in brown paper from her purse and passed it to Hamish. "I told them."

Hamish eagerly unwrapped the package. It held a dozen crescent-shaped cookies, coated with fine, white sugar. The Grandurian vanillekipferl was one of his favorites.

He saluted Carolin with a cookie. "You're a rare lady."

The first cookie tasted like a dream come true. The soft, sugar-coated outer layer wrapped a crunchy heart. Hamish closed his eyes as he savored the cookie. Somehow he ate four more before opening his eyes.

The others watched him with open amusement, although Artur, the master carpenter, was starting to look concerned by how fast the pile of cookies was disappearing. Hamish sighed and offered the package to them all. One had to make certain sacrifices when working with a team.

As the others munched on cookies too, Hamish reached that state of cookie ecstasy, where he often found his best creative brilliance. And once again, the cookie did not fail to deliver. A simple, but brilliant idea struck like the smell of bacon in the morning.

Hamish grabbed a piece of parchment and one of Jean's pencils and started drawing rapidly. The others drew closer, watching but not asking questions for several minutes until he completed the initial sketch. It was rough, but the more he thought about it, the more excited he felt.

"A ball?" Bruno asked, looking confused.

"A sphere," Hamish corrected. "Think about it. It doesn't need wheels. The whole thing's a giant wheel."

"Even you'd get dizzy spinning in a sphere long enough," Carolin pointed out.

"But maybe we could set up some kind of harness to keep you upright," Jean said thoughtfully, her pencil poised over her notebook, quivering slightly as she thought. Hamish hadn't even noticed her pull it out. "A spherical shape could be very strong, could offer tremendous defensive potential."

Bruno took the pencil and added a bunch of lines criss-crossing through the center of the sphere. "If we reinforced internally, it would be very hard to break, even for Petralists."

"And between the support beams, we could pack it with offensive mechanicals," Hamish added eagerly. He loved how quickly they were embracing the idea.

Jean said, "Especially if we design the outer shell with some kind of plates that could slide out of the way."

That triggered a wave of suggestions from the rest of the team. Hamish grinned as they dove into the creative process he loved so much. They needed more cookies, or even better, a cake. But in the meantime, the team threw out dozens of great ideas, from the best ways to craft the shell, to the best mechanicals to include, to ways to power it and make it move. If they packed in half those ideas into that sphere, it would have to stand over ten feet tall.

Excellent.

Eventually Bruno's sugar-induced enthusiasm faded and he sat back, his chair creaking under his weight. "This is a very ambitious project. We've never built anything like it. Nothing even close. We may not be able to make it work."

"We'll make it work," Hamish promised. It was too brilliant not to make work. They might need to eat a few dozen cookies to keep the pure, sugar-induced inspiration rolling, but that was a price he was happy to pay.

Gisela entered the room and waved. She handed a rolled scroll to Jean. "Ailsa has writing from Donleavy. She is bringing important news and information about speedcaravan."

Jean took the scroll and Hamish asked, "What is Ailsa doing in Donleavy? That place sounds crazy-dangerous." He didn't know Ailsa well, but she'd always seemed more intelligent than that.

Gisela shrugged. "It is also the placing of most important information gathering."

Jean unrolled the scroll and scanned it quickly. Hamish did not bother trying to read it too. Jean could read ten times faster, and she would share the important information with him.

She whistled softly. "We'll need to copy this and send it on to Kilian and to Connor at once. The queen is more dangerous than I imagined."

"I have already doing that," Gisela said. "I am agreeing with you. The queen has making much turmoil in Obrion."

Hamish started to ask for more details, but Jean interrupted. "By the Tallan's glory, this is wonderful!"

She had only lived in Granadure for weeks, but she had already picked up on some of their sayings. No other Obrioner Hamish knew would use the Tallan's name in a good way. Even Connor seemed to hesitate. Jean had already made the mental transition. Once she knew truth, she embraced it.

"What is it?" He and Bruno asked at the same time.

Jean gestured down at the parchment. "Ailsa sent information about the speedcaravan. How it runs, how it accelerates, and how it slows."

"We know it uses quickened basalt, but I've never had a chance to study it," Hamish said.

Jean handed him the parchment. "She included some diagrams. Look at that gearing. That's exactly the kind of mechanical brilliance we need to make your big armor work."

Bruno leaned over Hamish's shoulder as he studied the scroll, and he recognized the importance of those gears quicker than Hamish. He laughed and clapped Hamish on the back so hard that he almost knocked him out of his seat.

"This Ailsa is a brilliant woman. Please make me a copy of this section too."

"I will having it prepared within the hour," Gisela said. She took the scroll and left. Jean looked like she wanted to chase after her to read it again, but Hamish held her hand.

"We'll learn more from it when we all have our own copies."

Jean's smile faded. "From what I read there, you're going to need that armored shell sooner rather than later."

17

DON'T QUESTION REALLY GOOD IDEAS

Connor was surprised to learn that Saskia had assigned him a comfortable apartment in one of the citadel towers. It was not exactly close to where Verena slept, but it wasn't too far away either. Clearly she hadn't consulted Mattias about the decision. No doubt he would've assigned Connor a sagging bunk in a shepherd stable down at the far southern edge of Altkalen.

The next day, after spending an hour at Verena's side, he sent for Ivor. He was eager to speak with him.

Ivor looked surprisingly good when he stepped through the door into Connor's sitting room. Instead of his battle-stained uniform, he wore a fashionable outfit, as if we was a minor Grandurian noble. His leather boots held a mirror shine and he wore an expensive fur-trimmed leather coat.

Connor grinned as he quickly crossed the room to grip Ivor's extended hand. He felt immensely relieved to see Ivor looking so well. Even though he knew Ivor's unmatched ability to read a situation and position himself advantageously, he had worried Ivor might have been treated badly. He was probably the most powerful Petralist captured in the battle of Atlkalen, and he'd done a lot of damage before Connor defeated him.

"Ivor, I'm so glad to see you."

"You seem to be doing pretty well," Ivor said approvingly as he moved deeper into the room.

"Me? Look at you. I thought you were a prisoner, but you look like you're on vacation."

Ivor gave him a confident smile. "It's not my fault that some of the senior officers like to play cards."

Connor groaned. "You'd think they'd learn."

"Took them way too long. I even won a meteor hammer."

"They let you keep a weapon?" Connor asked, surprised that even Ivor could manage that.

"No. The guards are storing it for me, along with some other gear deemed too dangerous for a prisoner to keep in their cell. But I've arranged daily instruction. It's an amazing weapon."

"I've always wanted one of those," Connor admitted. Made of braided steel cables and capped with spiked steel balls, meteor hammers were the trademark weapon of the Grandurian fast movers.

"The training is key. Nearly brained myself the first time I tried it."

They dropped into overstuffed chairs near the fire and spent several minutes catching up with each other. Ivor's experience as a prisoner at Altkalen certainly did not reflect those of most of the others, but it sounded like they were all being treated fairly. Connor wondered if Grandurian prisoners were treated so well in Obrion.

Ivor had a way with people. He could read them and position himself for best advantage. He'd been Connor's primary opponent in the Tir-raon, but they'd somehow still become very good friends.

Ivor had used his skills to leverage access to the senior officers and Altkalen nobility. He'd not only won a new wardrobe and a new weapon, but gained a surprising degree of freedom.

He fixed Connor with a serious look. "I'm really starting to like the people here, but this is not home. I heard you helped get a peace accord signed. Will they let us leave soon?"

"I'm sure they will, although I haven't heard when. Might be a while still."

"Don't get me wrong. Once the dust settles, I'd love to come back to spend a summer, but I've got a life I need to return to back home."

Connor grinned at the thought of what Ivor could accomplish with full freedom. The people of Altkalen were clever traders, but he doubted they were quite ready for that. "I wouldn't be surprised if you ended up with your own tower here in the citadel."

"That would be fun, but what of Verena? Has she awakened yet?" Ivor asked with real concern in his voice.

Of course Ivor would know about Verena, and Connor appreciated that he cared. "Not yet. The healers say it's just a matter of time."

"She'll be all right. That girl of yours is a strong one."

"Thanks," he said sincerely.

Ivor leaned back in his chair and regarded Connor thoughtfully. "I'm glad you're back in town, but you didn't send for me to have a simple social visit, did you?"

Connor shook his head. "You don't miss much. The accord may have been signed, but I wouldn't claim peace is about to break out. What have you heard about Queen Dreokt?"

"Not much. My contacts have been pretty tight-lipped, although they all seem pretty nervous."

"The more I learn about her, the more nervous I get too." Connor related the events around Alasdair, defeating Martys, then the terrifying earthquake that the newly-risen queen triggered. He explained what he'd heard about Kilian's confrontation with her and his failure to destroy her.

Ivor let out a low whistle. "If Kilian couldn't kill her, what are the rest of us supposed to do?"

"That's the question, isn't it?"

Ivor considered that for a moment. "So she's wreaking havoc in Obrion while Granadure grows ever more worried, and you're thinking this is the perfect opportunity to start a revolution."

"Again, you don't miss much."

Ivor laughed. "A lot less than you. Your first bright revolutionary idea was to try recruiting the heirs of the ruling class. Not the smartest move I've ever seen. Have you kissed Shona yet?"

Connor grimaced. Shona had maneuvered him into agreeing to one final passionate kiss before he could speak with his troops and try spreading the truth of patronage. That attempt had failed a miserable death. Worse, they'd been interrupted before he could get that kiss over with.

Of course Verena had seen Shona preparing to kiss him. When she angrily confronted him, they'd argued. He still cringed to think of the things they'd said to each other. Worse, that fight had given Mattias the opening to worm his way back into her life.

Verena had to wake up. Connor not only had to prevent Mattias from simply stealing her away, but had to somehow reconcile with Verena. He loved her, and he knew she loved him, but things had gotten so messed up.

He sighed and rubbed a hand through his hair. "I saw Shona at the treaty signing, but we didn't really talk."

"Good. Shona knows how to play you too well. Your best defense is to stay far away from her."

Connor nodded. "Shona is not the concern right now. I need your help. You were a Guardian a lot longer than I was, and you know the system better than I do. How do I spread the word about patronage?"

Ivor hesitated. "I appreciate what you're trying to do. The problem is, I'm not sure starting a revolution is the best way for me to plan my home-coming and enjoy a relaxing honeymoon."

Connor had hoped Ivor might see beyond that personal inconve-nience, but Ivor always positioned himself for best advantage. He was careful and methodical, and when he struck, he usually won. Those skills had helped him rise through the ranks of Guardians, had secured him a very advantageous marriage into a high house, and very nearly won him the Tir-raon.

But a revolution would threaten some of those hard-fought gains. So Connor said, "I mentioned that most prisoners will have to stay a while. If you help me, I think I could get you released early. You might be able to get back to your new house that much sooner."

Ivor considered that. "Tempting. You might be surprised, but I'm actually really looking forward to marrying Alyth. I haven't known her for long, but I miss her." He added softly, "Hoping for too much can be a dangerous thing, but I think we actually might be able to build a good life together."

Ivor rarely shared so much with anyone. Connor felt honored that Ivor trusted him so much.

"I bet you will, if the queen doesn't destroy all the high houses out of hand. From what I hear, there's no telling what she might do. Come help me, Ivor. Help me free our people, and I'll get you back to Alyth. Who knows, by helping me plan the revolution, you might be able to ensure your new house comes out ahead."

"You have a point, and as much as I'm enjoying my time here in Altkalen, freedom would be better. You'd have to promise to get me some power stones again, though."

"You haven't gotten any since the battle?" That surprised Connor. With how good Ivor was at gaining advantage, he had assumed his friend had gotten his hand on a supply.

Ivor shook his head. "The Grandurians here might be foolish in cards, but not that foolish."

"Do you blame them? You're one of the most dangerous Petralists alive."

"And you're going to need to give me some stones if I agree to help." Ivor's expression turned intense. "I've never gone so long without tapping any affinity. It's driving me crazy. Do you have any idea what that feels like?"

Connor nodded. "More than you know."

Just thinking about the need for porphyry triggered a wild craving in the pit of his stomach that made his hands clench. He had to take several deep breaths, and was grateful he was not tapping granite. He might have crushed the arms of the chair before regaining control.

The need for porphyry was a constant hunger, a distracting menace that could easily drive him insane. His worry for Verena and his recent practice with limestone, chert, and serpentinite had kept him distracted enough to handle it, but whenever he thought about it, the wild hunger returned with renewed fury.

The intensity of it scared him, and he worried that one day he might not be able to contain it. The craving made the furious rampager beast stir in his heart, filling his mind with thoughts of destruction and violence. If he ever lost control, how many people would he hurt before snapping out of it?

What if he didn't recover? What if it drove him to madness?

Ivor noted his reaction. "I'm no Healer, but even I can tell something's not right. What's going on, Connor?"

"Like I told you, I had to use porphyry and transform into a rampager to defeat Martys and save my family." Just saying the word porphyry aloud made him want to howl with the need for more powder. "Using it is extremely dangerous and enormously addictive. I need it now. It's like a living thing. If this keeps up, I'm not sure how long I'll be able to control myself."

Ivor grimaced. "Addictions are nasty things. I've known a couple of people who got addicted to herbs from one of the healers at an outpost where I served. The healer was an unscrupulous fellow who used those addictions to gain power over strategically-placed people. Even when he was discovered and executed, it took them months to wean themselves off the chemicals. I was told they would have died if they didn't have small doses to keep them sane. Do you have any more porphyry?"

Connor shook his head. "If I had it, I'd be using it." He could not imagine having access to it and not succumbing to its call.

"Maybe Kilian can get you some."

Connor shook his head. "Their only supply was destroyed. The only one who knows where to get it is High Lord Dougal, but he's with Queen Dreokt."

Ivor grimaced. "What a Tallan-twisted irony. You were the only one who could save us at the Carraig, and it sounds like you had no other choice but to use porphyry again to defeat Martys. I hate to think it could destroy you eventually."

Connor nodded. He'd railed in silent rage against that bitter irony. It felt good to talk about it with Ivor.

Ivor said, "I'll think about it. Maybe there's a way I can help. In the meantime, do you know any herbalists who might be able to help? You can't just ignore an addiction."

"Will you help me plan a revolution?" Connor asked. He needed to focus on something else. Ivor might be well-meaning, but the conversation was driving him mad.

"If you can have me freed, give me access to all of my affinity stones, and get me back to Alyth soon, we might have a deal."

Connor was not sure he was ready to fuel all of Ivor's affinities. He trusted Ivor, but if his big friend decided to make a break for the border, even Connor would have a hard time stopping him.

A knock at the door interrupted his reply and a courier wearing General Wolfram's colors entered the room. He handed Connor a message tube, saluted, and withdrew.

Ivor leaned closer, interested, as Connor extracted a scroll. "What does it say?"

Connor scanned the scroll and whistled softly. "It's from my Aunt Ailsa. She's in Donleavy, and she's serving the queen."

The news worried him immensely. The last he'd known, she was safely back in her mansion outside of Raineach, slowly filling new orders for sculpted stones. Why would the queen have sent for her?

He quickly scanned the drawings and descriptions of the speedcaravan mechanical. No doubt Jean and Hamish would be drooling over that, but it didn't really make sense to him. He focused on the description of the queen's erratic behavior and unrivaled powers. He shivered at the description of how she had broken the minds of the king and his family and other high nobles and ladies.

"She sounds terrible," Ivor said gravely as he read over Connor's shoulder.

Then he gasped and pointed farther down the scroll where Ailsa included a list of some of the other nobility who had been summoned to Donleavy for interviews. "Alyth is on the list!"

Ivor's face drained of color, and his hands shook. He really did care about the girl.

He paced away, then spun back to Connor. "We have to do something. The queen seems completely unbalanced. There's no telling what she might do to Alyth."

"I told you. We need to start the revolution to free the people, and—"

Ivor cut him off. "There's no time for that. Alyth will reach the capital in a matter of days. We need to intercept her and get her out of there."

When Connor hesitated, Ivor added, "You know you can get me to Donleavy."

Connor shook his head. "Donleavy is not where I need to go. You said yourself, don't start at the top."

Ivor took a deep breath and forced himself to calm. He resumed his seat, but the fists remained clenched. "I need your help Connor, and you need mine. We can help each other. You take me to Donleavy, help me rescue Alyth, and bring her back here to Granadure."

"Do you think she'll come?"

"She'll come with me. She has to know how much danger she's in."

"If she flees to Granadure, she'll be abandoning her house. She'll be branded a traitor and could lose everything."

"No she won't, because in return, I'll help you plan and implement your revolution. We'll topple every other high house if we have to, but Alyth will join the revolution from the very start. She'll be seen as the truest patriot."

Connor considered that for a moment, then nodded." If we pull it off, your house could be positioned better than anyone."

"If we succeed, yes. If we fail, we're no worse off, are we?"

The proposal was reckless and foolish and dangerous. Those qualities had served him well during the Tir-raon, but could he really sneak back into Obrion all the way to Donleavy where the queen ruled in her unpredictable insanity? So many things could go wrong.

Then again, he needed Ivor. Kilian had told him to get the revolution off the ground. He might not have quite intended Connor take this particular initiative, but he had often said he appreciated creative thinking.

More than anything, what urged Connor to throw caution to the wind and agree to the daring plan was the look in Ivor's eyes. He was afraid for Alyth. Connor knew that fear all too well. It had eaten at him ever since Verena's injury and would never cease until she awoke. He could do nothing more to help Verena, but he could help Ivor save his fiancé.

He stood and extended a hand. "You have a deal, but we're going to need a third person along to make this work."

Ivor gripped his hand, looking relieved. "Who? Hamish?"

"No. Aifric."

1 8

STILL THINK THAT WAS A GOOD IDEA?

The great trading city of Crann in Obrion rivaled Altkalen for sheer size. Snow-capped houses reared three and four stories above many of the streets teeming with people. The busy crowds had churned the recent snows into slush.

Connor decided he didn't like Crann.

As he followed Ivor up a gently rising, cobbled street toward Lord Eoghan's palace, he grumbled silently to himself about their need to stop in Crann at all. Aifric, in her alternate persona as Mariora, had insisted. Mariora was a member of the Obrioner royal messenger service. She insisted she could get them into Donleavy and back out again before anyone noticed.

At first, the idea of stopping at Crann for supplies and appropriate disguises had seemed brilliant. They could easily blend into the population of the huge city without raising any alarms. Connor had felt eager for a chance to reconnect with the people of his homeland and just enjoy walking in secret among them.

Crann wasn't the happiest place to walk these days. The city fell within the realm controlled by the crown, and the powerful Lord Eoghan was one of King Turriff's cousins. That was the problem.

The population buzzed with worried rumors about Queen Dreokt and her ruthlessness. No one seemed sure if King Turriff was alive or dead, imprisoned or free. The doubts fueled the rumors.

What would the queen do next? Would she depose Eoghan like she had Turriff? Who would replace him? Would she use the huge army quartered just outside the city for the winter against the populace?

Those rumors heightened Connor's growing worry that their plan might be a terrible mistake. But as he trudged through the slushy streets and the chilly morning air after Ivor, he realized none of that was really what bothered him.

"Stop dawdling, boy," Ivor called back as they passed a group of wealthy merchants in fur coats.

Connor trotted a couple steps to close the distance to Ivor, who was now dressed like a nobleman in a calf-length fur coat made of rare golden nuall fur. Since he was looking for Alyth, a high lady, it only seemed right that his disguise reflect most of the reality of his position. Once he married her, he really would become a high lord, so pretending to already be one wasn't much of an exaggeration.

Once they passed the merchants and reached a rare stretch of empty street Connor said, "You don't have to lay it on so thick."

Ivor glanced winked. "Just getting used to the character."

"How about I get into character as a revolutionary and throw you into the dung heap behind that barn?" Connor grumbled.

"You're awful grumpy today. Are you feeling all right?"

"I'm fine," Connor snapped, hating that he couldn't seem to control his temper, but hating that question worse.

All his life, his mother had hounded him about being sick. He'd thought he'd left those worries behind, but during the trip into Obrion, both Ivor and Aifric had each asked him a dozen times if he was all right.

He wasn't all right, but that didn't mean he wanted them to bother him about it. He was far from okay, but he would deal with it. He had to. No one else could do it for him.

"You're not acting fine," Ivor said, concern evident in his voice. "We can't do this if you're not in control."

He gestured to the top of the hill, less than a hundred yards ahead. There, the shops and restaurants crowding both sides of the road gave way to a wide plaza. There they would enter a large, stone building with ornately carved columns along the front facade and attempt to board the speedcaravan.

Connor sighed, bottling up the irritation he felt at the badgering. Ivor was only trying to help. He didn't understand the Connor's history, and he couldn't help.

"I'll be fine. I promise. Just ignore me for a bit while I get my thoughts together."

Connor could tell he wanted to say more, and was grateful he didn't, but resumed his trek up the street. Connor followed behind, his eyes downcast, and not because he was supposed to be acting as Ivor's linn servant.

Porphyry. Ever since they'd crossed into Obrion, the need for it had intensified. He wasn't sure if it was because they passed through Dougal's realm and the secret quarry of the deadly stone, or if the distance from Verena and his worries about her were enough to fuel the beast to greater activity.

He'd fought the craving, but hadn't managed to suppress it as well as he had in the past. Both Aifric and Ivor knew about it, but their badgering only made things worse.

They couldn't help, and their repeated questions only reminded him that he was failing. That stoked his fears, which in turn magnified his problems. He needed to figure out how to control his desperate craving for more porphyry, or he was going to hurt someone.

Telling himself there was no more, no way to get any, no longer helped. It was like an angry voice in his head, whispering, begging, urging him to find a way to get more. His stomach ached and his head hurt almost constantly, but he hadn't told his companions.

He felt ashamed that he couldn't figure out how to beat it. He'd defeated Martys. Sure, his father had needed to hit him with his diorite hammer, quickened by Hamish, and blast him into the river to help him regain his senses, but he'd managed it.

Connor couldn't count on his dad to show up with that hammer again. He was Blood of the Tallan, stone's take it. He should be able to control himself.

As they entered the square, he forced himself to focus more on the moment. He would simply refuse to acknowledge the craving. Maybe it would give up. That tactic worked on his younger siblings sometimes.

The unusual emptiness of the square seemed all the more remarkably when compared to the rest of the busy city. The square was ringed by high-end shops and restaurants and even an inn that claimed accommodations fit for a high lord. The few patrons moved about nervously and made a point of not looking toward the speedcaravan station.

"Well, slipping inside ought to be easy," Ivor commented dryly as he led Connor across the square.

"No one wants to get anywhere near it," Connor agreed.

"Makes sense. If they go in there, they might end up on board, heading for Donleavy. Only fools or those unfortunate enough to have been summoned make that trip these days."

Aifric waited for them in the shadow of the entry portico. She was dressed in a bright blue uniform, trimmed in gold. She wore a leather satchel over one shoulder, similar to the satchel Verena always wore. This one was new, with a gold-trimmed emblem of the royal house on the outer flap. Seeing it reminded Connor of Verena, and he suddenly wished he had not left her.

"Any troubles?" Ivor asked softly when they ascended the stairs to join her.

"No. You?" She was wearing her Mariora personality, who spoke with a cultured, refined accent of Obrioner nobility.

"Just a grumpy servant," Ivor said with a smile.

Connor tried to smile too, but it felt more like a grimace. He interrupted Mariora before she could ask. "I'm fine."

She glanced at Ivor, who shrugged. "Hopefully the ride will give him a chance to center himself."

"I told you I'm fine," Connor said more loudly than he intended.

"Then act like it," Mariora said, raising one eyebrow as if inviting him to make another outburst. When he didn't, she said, "I've gotten us passage already. We can ride all the way up to Donleavy, and I doubt anyone else will come aboard."

Connor frowned. "I thought the plan was to disembark in Belmullet and either get horses or walk up Mount Raasay to Donleavy."

"It was, but from what I've gleaned from the officers working inside, it's highly unusual for anyone not going to Donlneavy to ride these days, so if we disembark early, we might attract the very attention we're trying to avoid."

"So should we just abandon this idea altogether?" Ivor asked. "We can take the Slide downriver to Belmullet easily enough."

"Sounds good to me," Connor agreed. He had introduced them to underwater Slide on the journey down from the upper Macantact, past Merkland, to the outskirts of Crann. Walking with water proved to be an excellent distraction. She seemed to enjoy his company, and her presence helped ease his ache for porphyry.

Mariora shook her head. "I've heard the roads are watched too. By taking the speedcaravan, we slip right through everyone and get to Donleavy fastest."

"But we don't actually want to meet the queen," Ivor reminded her.

"We won't. The terminal is in the lowest levels of the central palace. I've been there before. We can find Alyth and escape before anyone misses us, even if they note our arrival and expect us to present ourselves before the queen."

"It seems risky," Connor said. They weren't in Obrion to fight the queen, but to start a secret revolution. They weren't ready for open conflict.

Mariora chuckled. "Of course it's risky. We're trying to sneak into Donleavy, remember? Any way we do it will be risky, but I'm confident we can make this work."

Ivor glanced at Connor, who hesitated before nodding. If they had to do it, he'd prefer getting it over as fast as possible. Maybe when he returned to Altkalen, visiting Verena would help him control his wild craving better. If not, he might have to confide in Kilian and seek his help.

But first, he would help Ivor save his fiance. He couldn't imagine a better way to prove the queen wasn't all-powerful. Then they would start freeing Guardians.

Those thoughts helped him center his mind, and he felt more clear-headed than he had all day. So he said with more confidence, "Let's do it."

"On to Donleavy, then," Ivor said. He squared his shoulders and swept into the station, as if he owned it.

ASSASSIN-ASSISTED SELF-DELUSION

The marvels of the speedcaravan helped keep Connor distracted as the amazing craft slid southeast along the western bank of the Macantact. The river widened to more than half a mile after they passed the junction with the Lower Macantact, which flowed from the northwest.

Boats of all shapes and sizes plied the frigid waters under a steel-gray sky, while long merchant caravans of mule-drawn wagons crowded the highways on both sides. Mariora explained that a huge percentage of all goods transported through Obrion moved along that stretch between Crann and Belmullet.

It turned out to be a good thing they did not plan to disembark at Belmullet. A company of soldiers were stationed there to prevent anyone from bolting from the speedcaravan at that last stop. The fact that they made no move to disembark meant no one gave them anything more than a single, pitying look.

No other passengers embarked either, so they enjoyed the plush foreward compartment by themselves. Of course Ivor took the central, padded chair with its panoramic views of the scenery. Connor and Mariora were relegated to much simpler chairs to either side.

As the speedcaravan smoothly accelerated up the first foothill toward Mount Raasay, Connor turned to Mariora. "You said that as long as things hadn't completely changed, you were confident our plan would work. After Belmullet, I'm starting to think that maybe things have completely changed."

"I still think this is our best chance," Mariora said.

Ivor shrugged. "If I remember correctly, breaking things is your specialty. You broke the Carraig. I wonder if Donleavy will make as amazing a pile of rubble?"

The problem was, the Carraig had been destroyed fighting an elfonnel. Connor was not sure if it came to a fight that they would get the chance to break anything. So as the speedcaravan began to climb the mountain, he decided to spend some time planning out exactly what he would break first.

If he only had a moment, he'd have to make sure it counted.

The problem was, thinking of smashing things and remembering fighting that elfonnel brought his thoughts back around to porphyry and how amazing it felt to fight as a rampager. That unrivaled killing power was his, if he only dared take it again.

While Ivor and Mariora spent time discussing ways to avoid arousing suspicion when they arrived, Connor started to pace the plush compartment. He tried to fight down the craving, but this time he couldn't seem to focus on anything else.

Suddenly he needed porphyry. The gnawing hunger swept through him with an intensity he'd never felt before. He gasped, clutching at his stomach, forgetting where he stood and who he was, while a wave of rampager fury set his limbs quivering. He needed porphyry like he needed air or water or food. He began shuddering, his hands clenching without conscious control, and every joint ached with growing pain, as if trying to transform, but unable to do so.

Connor struggled to clear his thoughts, but his growing fear seemed to suck at his will. He couldn't lose control like this, couldn't fall to this addiction, couldn't admit that he was losing the fight.

He didn't have porphyry. That thought should help, but instead it triggered a low growl, deep in his throat. He began to feel panicked. He really was losing control. Was Martys right when he swore that taking porphyry would seal his fate too?

"Are you all right, Connor?" Mariora approached, her expression concerned as she shivered and changed back to Aifric, who placed a cool hand on his sweaty forehead.

"Not really," he admitted through gritted teeth and dropped back into his seat.

A trickle of healing warmth flowed into him from her hand, but it did little to alleviate the pain and aching need. Her expression turned more serious. "You're deteriorating faster than I expected."

"What can we do?" Connor asked desperately. "Should I try using my pendant?"

She shook her head. "Healing addictions is psychological as much as physical. Usually the trick is using the addictive substance to slowly wean people off of their dependence, but we can't do that with porphyry."

"We still don't have any," Ivor reminded them, looking worried.

"I need it, though," Connor panted, fighting a flash of rage at Ivor. Somehow he had to get his hands on some.

Then he got an idea. "Wait, Aifric, you said it's psychological too."

"Willpower and intent play a huge factor in successful recoveries."

"Maybe I can fool myself into thinking I have a little. That might buy me some time."

"How would you do that?" Ivor asked.

"You mean mirage," Aifric guessed, frowning.

He nodded enthusiastically. "I practiced it on myself at the border. I managed to trick myself into seeing Verena. I could make myself see porphyry. Maybe that would help."

Ivor shook his head. "Practicing self-delusion isn't often something I would recommend."

"It's a higher form of limestone power," Connor explained.

"Sounds like a higher form of idiocy," Ivor chuckled.

"I'll demonstrate it on you later."

"It's not a good idea, but it's better than my next best alternative," Aifric said after a moment's hesitation.

"I'm doing it," Connor told her.

"All right, but give me your other affinity stones first," Ivor said.

"Why?"

Aifric said, "Connor, you're suffering advanced addictive symptoms which often drive one to make rash decisions, and now you're planning to try tricking yourself into thinking you have porphyry. That's not exactly a recipe for peace and tranquility."

Connor didn't like the idea of giving up his affinity stones, but if handing them over got him closer to easing his suffering, it was a small price to pay. He tore the bag of stones off his belt and tossed it to Ivor, then removed his necklace, retaining only the limestone.

The other two watched closely as Connor focused on the limestone, trying to clear his mind and establish a strong connection with it. As soon as he felt it, he grabbed the light streaming past and twisted it. He didn't need chert to figure out his mental state or what he'd see when the light twisted the world out of focus.

There! Sitting on a shelf below the nearest side window rested a tiny bowl of purplish powder. Laughing with relief, Connor rushed over and snatched it up.

That was so easy. Why had he waited so long to get it?

Connor squeezed the powder, willing it to absorb, nearly over-whelmed by an ecstatic sense of anticipation. Finally he could again feel the glorious, unrivaled sense of power porphyry alone offered.

Instead of the hard, gritty grains biting into his skin as he expected, the porphyry squished between his fingers just like. . . .

Pudding.

The mirage burst and Connor found himself exultantly holding aloft a squashed handful of pudding he'd brought back from the food compart-ment after the last meal.

At some level he knew he'd intentionally tricked himself, but in his porphyry-fevered mind he'd succeeded better than he'd anticipated. The moment of shocked realization that he'd been duped triggered a violent rage. Connor lunged for the nearest chair, planning to use it to smash everything to pieces and vent his rage.

Ivor intercepted him, seizing him with granite-hardened strength. "Take it easy, Connor."

"Let me go!" Connor thrashed in his arms, helpless to break free, which only stoked his rage higher. He fought with all his might, but Ivor simply ducked his head a bit and held on.

"Connor!" Aifric shouted, stepping into his sight, one hand raised toward him.

Connor tried biting her fingers. She snatched them away with a yelp of surprise.

"I guess we proved self-delusion still isn't a smart life strategy," Ivor grunted as he fought to hold Connor back.

"Time for a different treatment," Aifric said calmly.

She slapped Connor hard across the face.

The unexpected sting knocked him out of his rage. "Ow!"

Ivor said, "You're lucky that's all she did. Biting a girl is always a bad idea."

"Not as bad as burning their hair." The memory of torching Shona's hair made Connor laugh. That helped him regain a measure of calm and he relaxed in Ivor's grip, panting for breath and wild-eyed.

Aifric said, "We might have to make a detour at Donleavy to find someone who can help."

Connor moaned, "There's no one who can help. Only Dougal. . . ."

He cut off as his fevered mind seized hold of the idea.

Ivor shook his head. "Oh, no. We are not hunting down High Lord Dougal."

"We can," Connor insisted, not even caring how desperate he sounded. "He's there. We'll be there. He knows where I can get more."

With a shiver of her features, Aifric shifted to the cultured tones of Mariora. "He's the queen's chief adviser."

Ivor said, "Going after Dougal is suicidal."

Connor wailed, "If I don't get more porphyry, it's going to kill me. Which would be worse?"

"Going after Dougal would get us and Alyth killed too."

"So you care about her more than me?" Connor accused.

"I'm not marrying you, Connor," Ivor said with a smile.

The attempt at humor only enraged Connor and he lunged against Ivor again, his vision coloring with a purple haze of impotent fury.

"This is not good," Mariora muttered. She switched back to Aifric. "Connor's condition is worse than I feared. We may need to secure him somewhere in the palace and go after Alyth alone."

"Leaving Connor unsupervised in Donleavy is a really bad idea," Ivor argued.

"We can't succeed with him acting like this."

"I'm fine," Connor insisted between panting breaths.

Ivor barked a laugh. "Look at you. You look like a wild animal."

"I'm fine!" he shouted, struggling uselessly again.

"We need to do something," Aifric insisted.

Ivor asked, "Do you have any ideas? Preferably before we arrive." She hesitated and Ivor said, "You do. Spit it out, Aifric."

Her features shifted slightly as she slipped into her Student Eighteen persona. "Aifric and I have been monitoring Connor's degradation. We hoped he wouldn't slip so far so fast. He should have maintained enough control until we returned to Altkalen."

"Deal with the now," Ivor urged. "Do you have an idea?"

She nodded, regarding Connor clinically, and he feared she'd suggest slicing his tendons to render him immobile and unable to cause much harm. Aifric could always heal him later, but the idea still terrified him. If Student Eighteen started slicing him with her knives, might she get a bit carried away?

She said, "It's a rather desperate idea, though."

Ivor chuckled. "Should fit the situation perfectly. The best I can come up with is throwing him out a window and leaving him out in the snow until we return. Is yours worse than that?"

"Well, when you put it that way, maybe we should consider it."

Connor insisted, "I'm fine. Stop talking about me like I'm not here."

"You're really not. Student Eighteen, what's your plan?"

"Simple. Connor in his current state is in no condition to infiltrate breakfast, let alone Donleavy."

"Agreed."

"So we need to give him another state."

That was an unusual statement, but it sounded better than carving him to pieces. "What are you talking about?"

She tapped her head. "The secret to the many different variations of me. I'm not crazy. We keep ourselves distinct and yet together through a technique that Mister Five developed, but which I perfected."

"You're suggesting I create another personality?" Connor asked.

"Nothing so drastic. Creating an entirely new person takes weeks of preparation. I'm suggesting a partial application of the same principles, just enough to help you change your mental state to block out the porphyry until you can get treatment."

"Self-delusion didn't work earlier. So you propose upping the insanity to Assassin-assisted self-delusion?" Ivor demanded.

"It's the best idea I've got," she retorted.

It didn't sound great to Connor either, but he needed something.

"How do you create new people to share your head without snapping your mind?"

Aifric sighed. "I suppose it was inevitable. Secrets just don't survive around you guys."

"Secrets and sweetbreads, two staples of our diet," Connor said, forcing himself to attempt a little humor. The conversation was intriguing enough that he was able to stay in control. Barely.

"Like I said, Mister Five pioneered the technique. He was the most skilled Mind Killer in the history of the Mhortair. He discovered many fascinating truths about the mind, including the fact that we only use a small fraction of our available mental capacity."

"Really?" Ivor asked.

She nodded. "Then he was assigned a very delicate mission that required a different set of affinities than he possessed. Instead of ceding the mission to another kill master, he figured out how to split his mind, creating a reflection of himself that lacked active affinities. When he transitioned into that mirrored mental state, he succeeded in establishing new affinities."

"If I didn't know you already, I wouldn't believe it," Ivor said.

Connor agreed.

"He was the first. He pushed the boundaries farther than anyone, but he did not achieve full personality split. The fact that he created mirrored images of his same self did allow him to establish different affinity sets and he actually managed to get both halves working together simultaneously for short periods of time."

"So he could use more affinities, as if he was Dawnus?" Ivor asked. Now he looked impressed.

She nodded again. "At Alasdair he used both soapstone and serpentinite at the same time, even though those affinities are established with different mirrored halves of his mind."

"That's why he was so dangerous," Connor muttered. He didn't feel bad about Mister Five's death at Queen Dreokt's hands. If she hadn't killed him, Connor had sworn to do so. Mister Five had nearly killed both Aifric and Verena, so his days were numbered, no matter how many ways he split himself.

"So what you do is different?" Ivor asked.

"It's the next logical step in the process. With his help, I managed to partition my mind, using those latent portions of my brain not already used. I create alternate people and give them life and space in those empty partitions."

"You're the first to manage it?" Connor asked.

Her expression turned grave. "So far, I'm the only person to succeed. Three others have tried. One broke her mind and died. All we can figure is she partitioned away the part she actually uses. The other two succeeded in splitting their minds, but got lost in the partitions. They sit like mindless, empty husks. Hopefully they'll find their ways out eventually."

"Um, I'm starting to think I don't want to experiment with breaking my mind apart," Connor said. Struggling with porphyry was hard, but at least he was still alive.

"That's why I'm not suggesting a full partition. I do think we can attempt the first stage of a mind-mirroring effect like Mister Five did, but not so drastic. Just enough to split away your porphyry affinity, but leave the rest intact."

"Really, I'm fine," Connor insisted. He gripped his hands together so they couldn't see them shaking. He was still sweating freely and his body ached as if he'd let Anika and Erich pummel him with a tree for an hour.

Ivor asked, "How likely is success?"

She said confidently, "I am the original me and I have seen the depth of Connor's affinity with chert."

The truth struck Connor like a bolt of lightning. Aifric was one of Student Eighteen's personalities. She wasn't a real person, well, not like everyone else. His good friend was in essence a figment of Student Eighteen's imagination.

Ever since he'd learned the truth about Student Eighteen's multiple personalities, he'd known she wasn't normal, but he'd never allowed himself to think through the ramifications of her condition to that point.

"So you weren't Aifric first?" Connor couldn't help asking.

Her features softened and she gave him her trademark Aifric smile. "I'm the first partition, Connor. I'm the first twin, so to speak."

Her features hardened again and Student Eighteen barked a short laugh. "First twin of what became a really large family. Connor, Aifric is just as real as I am. She's a full person. We just share the same head."

"Okay." That was mental. Literally. But it did still help him feel better.

She placed a comforting hand on his shoulder. "Trust us, Connor. Of everyone I know, you are best qualified to succeed. Let me help you."

Student Eighteen had sworn to protect him from all harm. He knew her resolve and could not imagine she would attempt anything that might destroy him. He wasn't sure he could trust anyone else so completely besides his parents. He would gladly give his life for Verena, but they were still working on absolute trust.

So he took a deep breath and nodded. "Okay, how do we do it?"

"Activate chert."

Connor took the little stone that she handed him and focused on it. The connection opened quickly, marked by that strange sound of rushing wind echoing through his mind.

He glanced at Ivor, who emitted a calm, greenish aura, suggesting he believed Student Eighteen. That was a good sign. If Ivor had seemed panicky, he might have second-guessed himself.

Student Eighteen motioned him to sit, then pulled her chair close in front of him until their knees touched. She met his gaze and her aura intensified into a bright, golden glow, almost as if she had ignited limestone under her skin like Saskia sometimes did.

"Focus on me. Open your mind and relax." Student Eighteen commanded in a firm but gentle voice.

Connor tried breathing deep and steady. That always helped him relax and focus better. Student Eighteen's glowing eyes mesmerized him, and the steady pulsing beat of her chert-enhanced mind meshed with the pulse of his own.

When she spoke again, her words seemed to sound directly inside of his head. "Good. The connection is strong. With both of us tapping chert and focusing on each other, the mental link becomes deeper than any other way. Now, I want you to think about porphyry."

Connor tensed and the link faded in strength. "I don't think that's a good idea."

"Concentrate," she urged. "Relax. While we're connected through chert, you should gain some insulation from the addictive impulses long enough for this to work. Now think about porphyry, how you established affinity with it, and all the memories of using it."

That was really easy once he started. Addiction-fueled porphyry rage wasn't fun, but it guaranteed really vivid memories.

So Connor allowed his thoughts to drift back to those moments. He thought back to the exciting moment of discovery when he found the bag of powdered stone in Professor Hector's secret apartment. He re-lived again the terrifying ecstasy of the first time he'd established affinity and absorbed it into his system. Again he reveled in its unrivaled strength.

He thought back to the training session with Ilse, how she'd helped him discover the secret to keeping his sanity while transformed, how the siblings had beaten him with that tree every time he failed. His breath came faster as he re-lived the glorious battle with the elfonnel, then the death battle against Martys. Again the unstoppable bloodlust flooded his heart and he yearned to taste the blood of his fallen enemies.

For a time, he lost track of where he was, of who he was as he sank deep into those memories of exultant horror, of glorious terror, and unbreakable violence.

Then the power of those memories seemed to fade. First the colors and scents drained away, then the images began to retreat like familiar sights slipping into a distant fog. The details blurred, then disappeared entirely. He was left standing in a mental fog, devoid of all thought, all emotion. Even the constant wind of chert through his mind seemed to fade.

Connor glanced around, suddenly chilled, but somehow not worried. He was locked into the gray, fog-filled expanse of his own mind.

Student Eighteen's voice called to him, echoing down from directly above. "Connor? Connor, can you hear me?"

"I can." His voice seemed to roll in endless echoes through him. It would be fun to test how long he could keep the echoes going.

Before he could, she said, "Close your eyes and will yourself to come awake."

When he did so, light seemed to explode into his eyes and he rocked back in his chair, blinking at the unexpected brilliance. For a second he felt dizzy and nearly toppled over, but Ivor's strong hand caught him.

Student Eighteen still sat close, facing him. She looked exhausted. Sweat streaked her brow and had dripped down her cheeks. Dark circles clung under her eyes, and she sagged where she sat.

"Are you all right?" Connor asked.

"I will recover," she said in a tired voice. "The question is, are you?"

Only then did Connor realize he was free of the raging need for porphyry. The absence of that hunger was like a heavy weight released from his heart. He felt alert and completely himself for the first time since the fight with Martys in Alasdair. He hadn't realized porphyry had affected him so much.

Connor laughed. "I feel amazing!"

"So it worked?" Ivor asked.

"I think so." He glanced at Student Eighteen. "What exactly did we do?"

"While you relived those memories, I directed them back into a different part of your mind. The process is sort of like emptying a cupboard in the kitchen and dumping everything into the barn."

Connor poked the side of his head. It didn't feel different. "So I partitioned my mind?"

"Nothing so dramatic. To manage a full partition, one of us would have to be ascended. No, I just helped you relocate those memories to a less immediate retrieval location. If you really focus on porphyry, you can access them again and re-establish your affinity. But if you're careful, you should be fine."

When he risked thinking of porphyry, he realized she was right. He found no clear memories, but sensed them buried deep, little more than hints of distant shapes in a thick fog. Something was there, but it was almost entirely invisible. He made a point of turning away.

"So could you use a similar approach to help people remove other painful memories?" Ivor asked thoughtfully. "I've known people who are all but crippled by painful memories or experiences. That trick could give them a new chance at life."

Student Eighteen's features shuddered and softened to Aifric's. "We should discuss the potential healing application when we have a little more time. It might help in the short term. The problem is that many who feel broken by their pasts refuse to let the past go, but choose to define themselves by it. Even more important than chert-assisted dulling of memories is the mental shift people need to undergo to release the past and embrace a future defined by who they are now instead of who they might have been."

"Perhaps helping reduce the strength of those memories could help them learn to change their focus," Ivor suggested.

Connor wanted to ask who he was thinking about. It seemed important enough that the person must be close to him.

But at that moment the speedcaravan rounded a long slope, and the city of Donleavy came into view. As they slid smoothly along the eastern reaches of the city, heading toward the magnificent palace and the long, streaming waterfall that plunged into the center of it, the three of them fell silent.

In a moment they would know if their mission had any chance of succeeding, or if their arrival at Donleavy would spark a fight they couldn't hope to win.

20

MIND OVER MATTER

When the speedcaravan came to a halt at the lower level of the palace, a squad of soldiers waited for them. Beside the captain stood an elderly fellow, dressed exactly like Aifric.

Ivor exited the speedcaravan first, but when the elderly courier spotted Mariora, he rushed forward, looking ecstatic.

"Mariora, what are you doing here? I haven't heard any reports of you in nearly a year."

Mariora saluted, then gave the man a quick hug. "It's good to be back. I was injured and out of commission for a while, and then working the outer realms."

"You picked a terrible time to return," the man said, leaning closer and speaking softly.

The captain of the guard saluted Ivor and said briskly, "State your name and your house."

Ivor gave the man a cold glare. "Since when do you give orders to a high lord?"

The man looked startled and snapped another hasty salute. "My apologies, my lord. Things are very tense right now and some of the old norms have been dropped until people pass the interviews."

Ivor huffed, "That's why things are so tense. We must maintain structure and discipline, or chaos lies at the door."

That was a pretty good line. Too bad Ivor wasn't a Sentry. He could have thrown out a bit of cryptic Sentry speak to top it off.

Ivor glanced dismissively at the guards arrayed behind the captain. "I know the way to the throne room. You and your men are dismissed."

The captain hesitated. "Our orders are to escort all new arrivals to their interviews. There have been a number of attempts to flee."

Ivor made a disgusted sound. "Fools and cowards. I have no time for either. Dismiss your men. I will not be escorted to the throne room like a criminal."

The captain looked like he planned to argue, but Mariora said, "I'll escort them."

"You need to be interviewed too."

"Then we accomplish two things at once."

Ivor did not wait for a response, but strode purposefully toward the huge staircase that spiraled up toward the main level of the palace. Mariora and Connor fell into step flanking him. Connor tried not to look nervous, but he already had a piece of marble under his tongue and a piece of quartzite wedged into his cheek. He'd downed a vial of soapstone before they stopped. With all the water nearby, he could make a spectacular mess in a matter of heartbeats.

Several of the soldiers reached for weapons, or swelled with granite strength, but the captain gestured them back. He rushed after Ivor and fell into step beside him. "I understand your point, my lord, but I have orders too. I will escort you personally. That should accomplish both of our objectives."

Ivor acknowledged the words with only a glance and a hint of a nod. They ascended the wide staircase without speaking, but paused at the main level to stare. Not even Ivor in his guise as a disgruntled high lord could ignore the fantastic sight of the waterfall thundering down into the rear of the enormous atrium, shielded by towering windows.

"I take it this is your first visit to the capital," the captain guessed.

"The first in some time."

Connor was glad no one asked him anything. He'd experienced many wonders in both Obrion and Granadure, but that huge, vaulted atrium with its waterfall plunging into the loch beneath them shook the building with its power. He touched soapstone and the falls glowed bright in his water senses. The air was laden with water, and the billowing clouds that rose up around the palace allowed him to feel it all and get an amazingly accurate picture of the entire structure in his mind.

The captain led them across the enormous atrium. They approached the third of the nine towers that supported the throne room high above and entered the staircase concealed inside. Connor's sense of wonder evaporated as he realized the captain intended to lead them directly to the queen.

As soon as they started to ascend and were clearly alone, Ivor paused and turned to the captain. "I think I owe you an apology, Captain. I'm rather in a hurry to see my fiance. Will you be so kind as to tell me where I can find High Lady Alyth?"

The captain's expression, which had begun to soften, shifted back into careful neutrality, but his eyes suddenly looked nervous.

"You know where she is, don't you?" Ivor demanded.

"I think we should speak about her after your interview."

Ivor's bulk didn't change, but he grabbed the captain and slammed him against the outer wall of the stairway. Connor couldn't tell if he was tapping granite, or just that worried for Alyth.

Flames danced in his eyes and his expression turned fierce. "You will tell me where she is right now."

The captain raised his hands in a placating gesture. "The interview process is merciless. I lost someone too."

Ivor growled and raised a fist to strike, but Connor grabbed his hand. "He's not the one to blame."

The captain looked from Connor to Ivor questioningly. "Since when does a servant speak that way to his lord?"

Connor gave the man an apologetic grin. "Like you said, some of the old norms no longer exist."

He curse-punched the man in the chin. The captain's head bounced off the wall and he crumpled into a heap.

Aifric checked him and gave Connor a disapproving frown. "You broke his jaw and possibly cracked his skull. I can stabilize him to ensure he recovers, but I would expect better control from you, Connor."

"Sorry," he quickly apologized. "But like he said, he has orders too. We need to make it clear that he did his best to follow them."

Ivor clenched his fists and asked angrily, "Now how am I supposed to find Alyth?"

"Leave that to me." Aifric shifted back to Mariora and disappeared down into the atrium, leaving Connor and Ivor in the stairway with the unconscious captain.

Connor took a moment to prop the man against the wall, with his hat down over his eyes, as if he was sleeping.

"That won't fool anyone for more than about a second," Ivor said.

Connor shrugged. "Did you see how people are acting? No one is looking at anyone. Everyone is terrified. They look like a bunch of linn trying not to be noticed by a taskmaster. The queen's got everyone terrified of being noticed. I doubt anyone will give this fellow more than a glance and then hurry past, convincing themselves that they saw nothing."

Mariora returned less than five minutes later. "I found her."

Ivor asked eagerly, "Is she all right?"

"I don't know yet. She's in the west palace, second floor. People I spoke to seemed nervous to say anything, although they seemed to know who I was talking about. The person who finally told me where to find her said only that she was receiving training for her new duties."

"That doesn't sound so bad," Connor offered.

Ivor said, "It doesn't exactly sound good either. High ladies are not known to receive new duties that require new training."

"There's one way to find out." Mariora led the way back to the atrium and across to one of the seven main corridors leading off into the various palaces.

After a moment she asked, "What is with all the eoin feathers?"

Connor had also noticed the feathers. A huge percentage of the people hurrying past wore eoin feathers, predominantly in their hats. Not even Crann had known about that new fashion. Honestly, it was ridiculous.

"I don't care. Let's just find Alyth and get out of here," Ivor hissed.

It took them almost half an hour to traipse through the enormous western palace, up to the second floor, and find the correct location. Every second seemed to hiss through Connor's mind like the sands of the timing clock in the Rhidorroch and his tension grew until simply walking with an unhurried stride took tremendous effort. They needed to grab Alyth and get out fast.

In her courier costume, it was not unusual for Mariora to seek out a particular person, but Connor also noted how nervous everyone looked when she mentioned Alyth. Luckily people seemed so intent on avoiding notice that no one challenged them.

They eventually ended up in a large, vaulted room, with a sign on the doorway stating that they were entering the "Worthy Servant Training Academy".

"This did not exist the last time I was here," Mariora said.

She led the way into the room. Dozens of people stood, sat in wooden chairs, or lay on simple beds along the walls. None of them spoke. They all seemed isolated, despite their proximity to one another. Several men and women wearing tan coats moved among them, but Connor couldn't tell what they were doing.

A big-boned, no-nonsense, hard-faced woman intercepted them near the entrance. The woman glanced at Ivor and Connor. "Are these new servants?"

Ivor huffed in his best offended noble tone. "Hardly. I require Lady Alyth."

Mariora added, "I have important documents for her."

The woman sighed, looking annoyed. "I doubt it. You think you're the first to come looking for a loved one, hoping the rumors weren't true? Take my advice, turn around right now, and forget all about her."

Ivor took one threatening step forward, his expression turning angry, but the woman raised a hand to forestall him. "Fine. Make it hard for yourself." Her expression softened. "I tried to warn you, but I should know better. Everyone has to see for themselves."

She gestured toward a small adjoining room. "You can wait in there. I will send her in. Don't break anything."

The three of them entered the small, empty anteroom. By the scars on the fine wooden walls and the splinters and bits of wood piled in the corners, Connor suspected the woman had good reason to tell people not to break things. He was starting to fear what they would find when they saw Alyth.

Ten minutes later, the door opened and a lovely young woman entered. Ivor, who had been waiting with growing impatience, rushed to her and swept her into his arms.

She did not react. She just stood there, arms at her side, an empty smile on her lips.

Ivor released her and gripped her shoulders. "Alyth? Don't you remember me?"

She made a little curtsy and said in a sweet voice, "How may I serve you, my lord?"

Ivor took a step back, but continued to hold her hands. He glanced at Mariora. "What's wrong with her?"

She switched to Student Eighteen. "Mental blocking, perhaps?"

She stepped forward and placed a hand against Alyth's temples. The young woman did not flinch, move away, or question the move. After a moment's concentration, Student Eighteen gasped and retreated, one hand going to her mouth.

"What is it?" Ivor demanded.

She shook her head, looking horrified. "She's gone."

"What do you mean?" Ivor was looking panicked, his voice rising in pitch. Connor had never seen him so rattled, not during any of the student battles, not when the elfonnel burst into the Carraig, and not even during the battle of Altkalen.

Student Eighteen gestured at Alyth. "Her mind. Her personality. Everything she was is gone. It's like her mind has been partitioned, but the part that included everything that used to be her was destroyed. All that's left is an empty shell, waiting for instruction."

"No," Ivor breathed, with tears glinting in his eyes.

"That's what she's doing here," Connor realized, horrified by the thought. "She's getting re-educated, becoming a 'worthy servant'." He gestured back toward the large room and the silent crowds there. "They're all being . . . rebuilt?"

"No," Ivor said again in a dazed-looking whisper, shaking his head in denial.

Student Eighteen said gently, "I believe Connor is right."

"No!" Ivor shouted. "There has to be something left. Maybe the rest of her is hidden away, like what you did with Connor's memories."

Student Eighteen shook her head. "I cannot see more. Connor might."

"But I'm new with chert," Connor protested. He had no desire to touch Alyth's mind and see what Student Eighteen had.

"You've ascended through the first threshold. Your natural ability already exceeds mine."

Ivor turned his anguished expression on Connor. "You have to try and see if you can find her."

He did not want to, but he could not deny Ivor. If Verena was the one with the broken mind, he would try anything and everything to rescue her. Wait, why hadn't he thought of that before he left Altkalen? Verena's lingering coma was a problem with her mind. With his new knowledge of chert, could he help her, find her trapped in there?

Could he help Alyth the same way? Was her problem like a waking coma? Suddenly eager, he approached Alyth, gripping his little piece of chert. She turned to him with a blank, friendly smile. It was deeply disturbing. Ivor had mentioned she had a sharp wit and a quick mind, but no sign of that remained. It had all been stripped away.

When he activated chert, his sense of dread deepened. The emotional beat from Alyth was almost non-existent, and her aura was weak and blank, like muddy cream. But Ivor hovered close, looking expectant, so Connor placed a hand on Alyth's head and tried to make a connection.

There was nothing there. Student Eighteen was right. Alyth's mind was an empty shell, waiting to be filled. She would take whatever instruction she received and do what she was ordered without question. Connor couldn't imagine Ivor settling for that. He doubted Ivor could instruct her how to be herself again.

Was that even possible?

Connor frowned and tried to focus deeper, to establish the kind of connection he'd felt with Student Eighteen on the train. Alyth did not resist and his thoughts touched hers with remarkable clarity, but it was like the clarity of a perfectly still loch at dawn. She was empty. He scoured the recesses of her mind, searching for any hidden compartments, any invisible barns full of the junk that used to be Alyth. He found nothing but a barren wasteland.

After a long moment, he dropped his hands, released chert, and simply stared into Alyth's friendly, empty eyes. What if he touched Verena's mind and found it broken too? What if her injury had left her a vacant shell like Alyth? The thought horrified him more than thinking she might simply fade away and die before waking up.

"What? Tell me what you felt?" Ivor demanded.

Connor turned to Ivor, at a complete loss for words, wondering how by the Tallan's name he could ever comfort his friend.

His expression told Ivor enough, and he growled, "No. I refuse to accept it."

Student Eighteen's features shivered and softened back to Aifric's. She gave Ivor a comforting hug.

A woman's voice spoke from behind them, by the door back to the larger room. "Young people are so full of drama. It is terribly annoying."

They spun toward the voice, and Connor's heart sank.

Queen Dreokt stood in the doorway, regarding them with a curious and annoyed expression.

21

DEFINITELY NOT A GOOD IDEA

For a second Connor froze.

Ivor did not.

He launched himself at the queen with a howl of animal rage, white-hot flames erupting from his open mouth. Water exploded out of a barrel on the far side of the room and leaped at her from that side. He had embraced both of his Dawnus tertiary powers in the blink of an eye, and no doubt he could have overwhelmed almost anyone in a couple of heartbeats.

He made it two steps.

Then he simply froze. Connor was just lifting his foot to follow Ivor. When retreat or fear didn't help, a suicide charge suddenly seemed like a good idea.

He never got the chance.

An invisible weight crashed down over his mind like a landslide. Every muscle suddenly locked up and refused to move. Worse, it crashed through his mind, scattering his thoughts, stealing away his will to fight, and leaving him standing placid and empty-headed.

Before he could even try to fight it, suddenly he could not remember why he wanted to resist. He watched the queen take a step into the room, and he knew he should feel something about her, but he was not sure what.

Ivor remained motionless, but his hands began to quiver just a little. He hissed, "You destroyed Alyth's mind."

The queen made a shushing sound. "Softly, my boy. I don't like the yelling."

Ivor stilled and spoke again, his voice soft, as if he had fallen half asleep. "I am going to rip out your heart and burn it to ash."

The queen gave Ivor an approving smile. "That's much better. We can discuss things like rational adults. I like your spirit, young man. You are one of the few I've met who shows real potential."

When she glanced at Connor, her expression turned disapproving. "I suppose it's a sign of how low our nation has fallen in my absence that people would look to you as some great treasure."

The insult sparked a moment of clarity and Connor said, "At least I'm not an old, unburied wreck that really needs to be buried deeper next time."

An invisible force struck Connor's mind, buckling his knees and driving him to the floor. He heard himself scream, but felt no pain. Again the heavy weight of her will smothered his conscious thinking, leaving him happily kneeling in front of the magnificent queen.

"That position suits you much better. I should reinstitute mandatory groveling for all of my servants."

Then she glanced at Aifric and her eyes narrowed in anger. "Did you think to lead this rabble into the heart of my power without any thought that I might assign other servants to watch for new arrivals besides that pack of brainless thugs?" The queen made no gesture, but Aifric simply collapsed at her feet. She fell in a limp pile of limbs.

Dead.

The queen spoke over her motionless body, her tone cold and regal. "No one misrepresents my authority or commits crimes in my domain."

Aifric was gone, executed in the blink of an eye.

The horror of seeing Aifric die helped Connor throw off the blanket of the queen's will. He leaped to his feet, tapped granite and lunged, one hand lashing out at her face, hoping to get at least one punch in.

Nope.

She raised one eyebrow in surprise and opened her mouth, but no words came out. Still, his fist stopped a fraction of an inch short of her face. Her will did not blanket his mind again, but his muscles remained frozen. He strained against the invisible bonds, but it was as if his muscles now obeyed a different mind.

Or a different voice.

Student Eighteen had once mentioned that serpentinite could be used as a weapon by ascended Petralists. Connor had a piece of serpentinite in his pocket. He concentrated on it, willing the affinity to open. It came easier when he held the stone in his hand, but desperation helped him make the connection anyway. His senses radiated outward and he became aware of a low-pitched sound emanating from the queen's partially-opened mouth. It resonated with the muscles of his body, locking them in place.

Connor wrenched at the sounds, hoping to redirect them back against the queen. If he could lock her muscles for a moment, perhaps they could escape.

It worked! The sounds deflected around him for a single glorious heartbeat. His muscles seemed to have built up a lot of energy while they were prevented from moving because his fist lashed out another inch and connected with her jaw.

It was not his best-ever curse punch, but it was driven by so much fear and horror it would have flattened anyone else. Punching the queen felt like punching the side of a mountain. Her jaw moved perhaps the width of one of her graying hairs.

She released serpentinite before he could wrench the sounds back around against her and simply grabbed him by his jacket and lifted him off the floor. Max-tapping granite, Connor beat at her arm to no effect. Her muscles did not swell, she did not transform into a granite-sculpted goddess like Shona or Anika would, but somehow she still completely ignored his futile strikes.

She pulled him a little closer and demanded, "You dare strike the royal person?"

With a negligent flip of her hand, she threw him across the room. He crashed into the wall so hard that he shattered the wooden sheathing. It rained down over him as he staggered to his feet. Behind the wood, the wall was made of solid stone.

Ivor abruptly took a staggering step toward Queen Dreokt, but she stilled him again with a flick of a finger, not even bothering to look at him.

Instead of chasing Connor, the queen gave him an approving nod. "Perhaps you are not a total loss after all. Young and foolish and inexperienced, but yes, there is potential there."

"Potential to crush your skull," he shouted, raising his fists, but completely at a loss for how to attack her.

"Why so combative? You're not the one foolish enough to fall in love with that unworthy servant." She glanced at Ivor.

The queen's abrupt changes in demeanor left Connor feeling unsettled, but one glance at the unmoving form of Aifric on the floor rekindled his rage. "You killed my friend," he shouted.

"You must learn to choose better friends." Her will touched Connor's mind again, but did not smother it like last time. Instead it simply slithered across his thoughts, and he realized with horror that she was reading them.

She laughed softly. "Of course I'm reading your mind, boy. The minds of all of my subjects are my property, as are their bodies, their bloodlines, and their lives." She gestured down at Aifric. "Those who offend me may suffer death. This courier you claim as a friend received a merciful, quick execution."

So had she killed her before . . . ? Connor cut off the thought before finishing it. He did not want the queen to know about Aifric's special abilities. It might not matter now that she was gone, but it felt like a final violation for the queen to understand fully the complex life she'd just snuffed out.

The queen gestured toward Alyth. "Others are simply misguided but still retain within them the potential to become worthy servants. Thus, this young woman can still serve me once she is reeducated."

"Reeducation?" Ivor exclaimed. He managed to take half a step toward the queen, his expression furious. "You wiped out her mind and everything that made her who she was."

"Of course I did. It was unworthy." She sounded surprised that he did not understand.

She stepped closer to him and touched his chin with her forefinger. He looked like he wanted to bite it, but she denied him the ability to move. "Then there are the rare individuals with real promise, like yourself, my dear Ivor. You are one who possesses a strong, nimble mind, who needs only to swear fealty to join the highest ranks of my servants,"

"I prefer killing you."

She chuckled. "You will come around in time, or if that stubborn will of yours proves too intractable, I will simply break it and use you anyway. Consider well your choices."

The queen turned back to Connor and considered him for a moment. "Wiping your mind would prove easier, but there are aspects to your affinities that might be dampened as a result. So the question is, how best to prepare you for worthy service?"

Her mind touched his again. Connor hated that she could so easily steal his thoughts. So he tapped chert. The pulse of her mind was like a deep, bass drum, washing over him like a flood tide. Her entire being glowed with a golden hue, like a distant sunrise burning through morning mist. He tried to focus his own thoughts and somehow push hers away. He was not sure what he was doing, or if it would help, but he had to do something.

She made a disgusted sound and stepped close, gripping his chin in her hand and tilting it up so she could look into his eyes. "I suppose it's a good sign that you've at least touched chert, but you are less than useless with it. You have no training whatsoever."

"Well why don't you teach me how to do it so you can see how it feels?"

She ignored the comment, but her thoughts again invaded his, brushing aside his weak attempt to protect himself, and churning through his mind like a housewife might whip cream into butter. Thoughts and memories whirled, too fast for him to grasp what she was doing.

She shook her head after a moment. "You have no idea what you're doing most of the time. You're like a child with a sword, but all you can think to do with it is slice apples."

"Sliced apples are great if you turn them into pies," Connor said. He had to say something, or the terror chilling him to the bone would freeze him solid and immovable.

Then she abruptly laughed. "Kilian, Master of the Arcane? What a foolish outlook you have on life."

He had to resist. If she was going to read his mind, maybe he could give her something unexpected to read.

Focusing his thoughts was like trying to lift the river barge onto the shore without the aid of granite, but he threw himself into the attempt with all his remaining willpower. It might be a foolish gesture, but it was all he could do, so he gave it everything he had. An image began to form in his mind with agonizing slowness, but he focused on it and willed it to completion.

He imagined the queen, rolled up in chains, lying in a giant pie plate, surrounded by apples and cinnamon. The upper crust was tucked around her like a blanket, and the entire construct was falling into the heart of a volcano.

The queen shook his chin, rattling him. "None of that foolishness, boy. You remind me of my wicked grandson."

She was talking about Evander. Connor felt a surge of triumph that he had at least managed to annoy her. That was more than his granite-hardened fist had done.

So he said, "The pie eaten in company of friends is most delicious, but the privy is best cleaned alone to avoid unnecessary splashing."

She shook him violently, lifting him off the ground so that his legs snapped back and forth and he had to max-tap granite to prevent his neck from snapping.

"You risk annoying me, boy." Her mind struck his again, harder, and that smothering blanket began to descend once more.

Connor had no idea if his mind would ever awaken again. He needed something more to break her hold, but nothing he tried had done more than waste a few seconds of her time. No, he could not fight her off with serpentinite or chert or granite.

He needed porphyry.

As his thoughts began to dull under the force of her will, Connor threw his consciousness into the shadowed corner of his mind where Mariora had helped him bury his memories of porphyry. She had warned him against seeking those memories, but porphyry insanity was preferable to mindless enslavement.

Connor found those memories and smashed their container apart. They erupted out and flooded his mind. He groaned with the need for porphyry, his muscles clenching, and his stomach cramping, as if he had not eaten for a week.

The queen gasped and slammed him against the wall again, so hard she would have shattered his skull if he had not already been max-tapping granite. The impact crumbled the wall, opening a gap between it and the next empty room.

But the queen's influence evaporated, leaving his mind awake.

As he struggled back to his feet, she snapped, "You fool. I thought I destroyed all knowledge of the animal rage. You have no idea how dangerous and unstable it is."

"I can handle it," Connor said, but his teeth were chattering with cold, and he felt an odd itchy feeling around his elbows and his little toes. What was that all about?

"Don't lie to me, child," Queen Dreokt ordered imperiously. "I was the first-ever Petralist to establish affinity through porphyry to the higher magnitudes of magic. It is simply too unstable, even though I was tuned to the correct frequency. You couldn't hope to survive extended exposure to it." Her expression darkened and she added in a voice as cold as death, "With that corruption in your system, you are unworthy."

Her right hand clenched into a fist.

If only he had porphyry. He didn't understand her rambling, but he would gladly transform and do battle with her as a rampager, even though he might never recover his humanity again. But he lacked porphyry, and she was about to kill him. He had to make some kind of last stand.

Connor tapped slate, which already rested in his boot. The gateway opened instantly. He was not near the ground, but he was standing in the shattered remnants of the stone wall and as his earth senses expanded and rippled out along it he found what he had hoped.

Just like the Carraig, that palace was built with pillars of power-grade granite that extended down into the earth beneath. Since he was already tapping granite, Connor's earth senses plunged down to those pillars and found earth waiting for him, a giant already quivering with anger. Earth gripped Connor, pouring strength into him, washing away the aches and the worst of the fear. He'd never felt Earth manifest to clearly to his mind, but it felt right and he didn't dare waste time wondering about it.

Earth was not enough, so Connor tapped both marble and soapstone. Water and Fire swept into his mind. Fire gripped his right hand, and white-hot flames appeared there. Water took his left, snatching liquid from the pools remaining from Ivor's failed attempt a moment ago and wrapping it around his left hand.

Queen Dreokt raised one eyebrow, but made no other move to block him.

Connor gladly took that bit of extra time to throw open the gateway to air. She laughed in his mind and flew circles around him. Wind rushed into the room from the cavernous chamber next door.

All together, Connor shouted the thought to his elemental companions and they linked arms, encircling him in their center. Fire and water, earth and air, all whipped their element around Connor in intertwined ropes.

Connor invited serpentinite to the party.

And he felt her take noticeable form for the first time. Like a beautiful young woman with thick locks of multi-colored hair cascading around her, past her waist. She threw her head back and sang, a hauntingly powerful sound and in his mind, placed her hands over his.

He had never walked with all five metamorphic stones before, but in that moment, they felt united, like long-beloved companions, not the squabbling children who couldn't play in the same sandbox. It was a marvelous moment, one he wished he could savor.

Instead he laughed with the wonder of it. He grasped that vibrant sound as it burst from his lips, amplified it, and bound it to the other elements circling him like a spherical shield. His mental companions nodded approval.

The queen might kill him now, but he was not about to make it easy for her.

Instead of ripping out his life, the queen gave him a thoughtful look, tapping her chin with one finger. "I see. You're a boy who only needs the right motivation. Perhaps I won't have to destroy your bloodline after all. No one understands what Petralist powers mean anymore, but perhaps once you are worthy we can begin reeducating everyone."

Connor didn't care why she was hesitating, didn't bother trying to come up with a reply to her lunatic statements. He flew at her, striking with every ounce of all of those elements combined.

At Altkalen, the whirling mix of four elements together had proven insurmountable to some of the strongest Petralists in the Obrioner army, had saved Connor's life, and enabled him to capture them.

The queen flicked out a hand, and the elements vanished out of Connor's mind, leaving him shockingly alone. His elemental assault deflected away, whipped around the room, and struck Connor in the back before he could stop them. The blow eclipsed the worst curse-punch he'd ever felt, and it drove Connor face first into the floor so hard that it cracked. The air whooshed out of him, and the queen snatched it to join the whirling elements circling over his head.

She tapped the side of her head with a wand of white-hot fire, her expression contemplative. She nodded once. "Yes. Definite potential. With the right motivation, you may be ready to serve me in the near future."

Connor leaped to his feet, but the words died on his lips. Her mind swatted his, scattering his thoughts again.

"Your first lesson is silence in the presence of your betters. How can you learn anything useful if you won't listen?"

Her eyes blazed with whirling elements and her entire body glowed with chert intensity, the golden light blinding his eyes and his mind. She spoke, her voice magnified somehow with serpentinite, with layers of sound woven around each other in mind-twisting patterns he could not hope to unravel. Her voice boomed in his mind like a thunderclap."

You will return to Granadure, my servant. Learn Kilian's plans and fears and walk in the counsel of my errant child. Enjoy the winter months in peace, convinced that all will be well. Then, at the first signs of spring thaws, you will murder every Builder and return to submit to me and embrace your destiny.

The words echoed through his mind over and over again, an avalanche of sound that squashed all other thought. Then the words wrapped his mind like serpents, slithering in deeper until they buried themselves deep into his mind.

Connor stood before the queen, trembling uncontrollably, unable to think, unable to process what was happening. A distant flicker of horror screamed from one dark corner, but evaporated a second later.

Queen Dreokt smiled at him then, and he felt unimaginable joy. His glorious queen approved of him!

She motioned him closer and kissed his forehead. The touch of her lips was like a lightning bolt across his mind. It slammed him off his feet and he struck the floor with brutal force.

As if from a great distance, he heard Queen Dreokt speaking to Ivor, but the words seemed to rush away before he could process them. He struggled to remember who he was or why he was so afraid. The queen approved, right? So what could he possibly be worried about?

Queen Dreokt swept out of the room a moment later, but paused in the doorway. "Leave my city at once. As a show of mercy, Alyth will lead you back to the speedcaravan. Should you attempt any additional treasonous actions, I will snuff out her life in front of your eyes." Then she gave them a warm smile. "Safe journey, boys."

Queen Dreokt wrapped the woven elements around herself, sat down on them like a floating chair, and whisked out of the room with as much grace as Verena on her best day in the Swift.

Her presence vanished from Connor's mind so abruptly, it left him feeling like a hollow shell. His thoughts faded and blackness settled over him.

A hand shaking him urgently awakened him some time later. He groaned, gripping his head in both hands. It hurt worse than any headache he'd ever felt. His body ached, as if a mountain had fallen on him while he slept.

"Connor, get up. Quick!"

He blinked open his eyes, groaning again when the lids felt like they were coated with sandpaper. It took a second for him to recognize the person leaning anxiously over him.

"Aifric!"

His worries and pains fled as he lunged up off the floor to hug her. She'd died. Hadn't she? The memory was sort of fuzzy.

She shook her head, her expression mournful. "Aifric is dead, Connor. Queen Dreokt killed her."

"But. . ." He recognized Mariora's voice.

"She snuffed out that part of our mind like a candle."

"How is it possible that any part of you is alive?" Connor asked.

"That's a great question. None of us have ever died before, and usually death is the result of catastrophic failure of the body, which would have killed us all." Her voice changed to Student Eighteen. "She struck the active portion of our mind, but did not investigate further."

Her voice changed again, to the self-confident swagger of Rith. "She's never dealt with anyone like us before."

Her voice changed again, becoming measured and studious, and Connor realize he had not met this aspect of her. "It is my supposition that perhaps the discovery of mind splitting and personality manipulation, discoveries which post-dated her extensive slumber, remain, for all the queen's mighty powers, unknown to her."

"That might give us an advantage," Student Eighteen said, reaching for one of her daggers. Her voice changed back to Mariora, and her movement changed to rubbing her chin. "But when she knows, she'll kill us all, body and mind together."

Connor's initial burst of joy at seeing at least part of her still alive was tempered now by wonder as he listened to her various personalities conferring. She had never done anything like that before, and he wondered if the trauma of one part of herself dying might have triggered it.

As the many people who were Aifric began conferring rapidly about potential uses for the advantage that a mind-split person might have against the queen, Connor interrupted. "So can you bring Aifric back?"

Student Eighteen said, "It's not clear. This is new territory. Perhaps it might be possible if another of the kill instructors was ascended sufficiently with chert to help us manage it." She switched back to Mariora. "In the meantime, we'll hold a memorial service for her."

Connor couldn't quite wrap his mind around that idea. He glanced around and frowned. The small room where he sat on the floor looked like a battlefield. One wall was broken, a part of the floor was cracked, and bits of broken furniture and stone littered the corners. Vague memories flitted around the corners of his conscious mind, but it hurt too much to think.

Then he spotted Ivor lying unmoving on his back. Fearful, Connor scurried over to him on hands and knees. Ivor's face was pale, his breathing shallow, his eyes closed, and his hands clutching the floor so hard his granite-hardened fingers had sunk into the stone.

Connor shook him. "Ivor? Can you hear me?"

Ivor gasped in a deep breath and sat up in one convulsive move. He shouted a wordless cry, his hands snapping out in front of him, one barely missing Connor's face.

"Whoa! It's me. Ivor, wake up!"

Connor shook him again, and Ivor sagged, groaning and holding his head. "Oh, I've never had such a headache."

"Tell me about it."

Mariora grunted. "Stop complaining. You didn't get part of yourself killed."

Ivor glanced at her in surprise. "Aifric?"

"She's dead. The rest of use are still here. For now."

Connor wanted to ask her more about that, but his head was really pounding. "What happened?"

Ivor looked toward the door, and Connor noticed Alyth for the first time, standing patiently there, waiting for them. The sight of her triggered a rush of memories and he gasped.

"Queen Dreokt!"

Ivor lunged to his feet, looking around, as if eager to confront the dread queen again. "Where'd she go?"

"What do you remember?" Mariora asked as she and Connor also rose. "Things are a bit fuzzy for me after she killed Aifric. Death has that effect, I guess."

"I remember Alyth's mind is broken," Connor said slowly, trying to put the pieces back together. "The queen came and she was going to kill us."

"Why didn't she?" Ivor asked, also frowning. His eyes kept returning to Alyth and his expression grief-stricken. Connor couldn't imagine how he'd handle it if Verena was the one whose mind was destroyed.

"I hate that woman," Ivor stated.

"I sort of remember something about her warning us to leave right away," Connor said. The words were like a distant dream.

Mariora nodded. "She did. She said Alyth will lead us out and not to linger."

"Why wouldn't she kill us, or wipe our minds?" Ivor wondered.

"She's insane. I'm just glad she's so crazy. Let's get out of here and get back to Kilian. Maybe he can help us figure out how to face her next time."

Mariora looked like she wanted to say more, and Connor didn't blame her. He felt a nagging worry that he was forgetting something important, but the harder he tried to remember it, the less real it felt. Maybe once they got some fresh air it would return to them.

Ivor walked over to where Alyth stood near the door waiting for them.

"If you will please follow me," she said, gesturing toward the open doorway.

Ivor shook his head and took her hand in his. "I know you don't understand me, but know that I think we could have made a happy life together." He leaned forward and kissed her left cheek. "And know that I will avenge you."

She gave him a dazzling smile, and for a second Connor hoped maybe Ivor had connected with some part of her that still clung to the depths of her soul. "I'm glad your stay here was pleasant. Now if you will follow me," she said in that same empty tone, dashing Connor's hopes.

"We can't leave yet," Mariora said. "I'm supposed to be dead, remember? The queen doesn't know we survived, but there's no way we'll make it back to the speedcaravan without someone noticing."

"We'll carry you," Ivor said.

She grimaced. "I've been carried over someone's shoulder before. It's not very comfortable, and we have a long way to walk."

"I think we can do better than that," Connor said.

She lay down again and pretended to be dead. She was very good at it. Connor rushed into the adjoining room and commandeered a couple of sheets and the side rails from a bed that one of the catatonic people waiting for their turn at reeducation was lying on. He and Ivor fashioned a stretcher and moved Mariora to it, then allowed Alyth to lead them out. Tapping a little granite, they easily carried the comatose Mariora back through the palace.

Connor tried not to think about Aifric's death. Seeing her lying there, knowing she was still breathing made her death seem less real, like the nightmarish memories of his confrontation with the queen. His friend Aifric was gone. No doubt the truth of her loss would hit him hard soon. He hoped he'd make it to the speedcaravan first.

Connor could scarce believe the queen would actually let them go. He sort of remembered her ordering them to leave, as if so unconcerned about any threat they might pose that she could fetch them whenever she chose. The thought irritated and terrified him in equal measure. She was so much more powerful than he'd imagined, even with all they'd heard about her. Still, what if she'd just been playing more mind games with them, extending that false hope just to snatch it away at the last minute? So he walked in fear, at every turn expecting to see her floating toward them on that throne of mixed elements, murder in her eyes.

He was even more shocked when they found Shona waiting for them near the top of the staircase leading down into the central palace. She was resplendent in a beautiful gown of blue and gold, with a ridiculous orange eoin feather sticking out of a wide-brimmed hat perched on her head.

She rushed up to them and exclaimed, "You idiots! Hurry, we need to talk."

22

DOING THE RIGHT THING SHOULD BE
EASY. RIGHT?

Shona, what are you doing here?" Connor demanded.

"Never mind that." She turned to Alyth and said, "Remain here. These guests need food. I will take care of it."

Alyth curtsied, then stood calmly, as if ready to wait all day.

Shona glanced down at Aifric's body, then placed a comforting hand on Connor's arm. "I'm sorry. I know she was a good friend."

"We're kind of busy," he told her, not wanting to discuss his complicated feelings about the loss of Aifric. Shona was not someone they could trust on a good day. Meeting her in Donleavy opened whole new realms of doubt as to her trustworthiness.

"You have time for this. Come." Shona led them down a side passage and into a long room with an arched ceiling and walls covered in beautiful paintings, with marble statues of lords and ladies interspersed between them. A small table piled with bread, fruits, and roasted beef stood in the center of the otherwise empty room.

Shona closed the door behind them and gestured at the table. "Eat something."

Connor and Ivor settled Aifric to the ground. Ivor crossed his arms and stared at Shona. "You're assuming we're hungry, and that we're foolish enough to take food prepared by your hand."

Shona gave him a disgusted look, hands on her hips. "Don't be daft, Ivor. I don't want you dead. Even if I did, I wouldn't be stupid enough to intercept someone the queen has ordered to leave. Countermanding any of her orders is tantamount to execution or mind wiping."

She held herself regally as she always did, but Connor knew her well enough to spot the signs of tension in her face and the undertone of fear in her voice. He still felt deeply shaken by their recent beating from the queen and by Aifric's death. He didn't have the emotional strength to withstand Shona's manipulations again.

He did have chert though, something he'd never enjoyed around her before. So he embraced the affinity, and thankfully it opened readily to his mind. When he focused on Shona, he felt fear rolling off her like a chill wind. She was holding a good facade of control over it, but he clearly sensed her terror. He hated how that still triggered a desire to help her, despite all she'd done to him.

"How long have you been here?" he asked, his voice a bit more brusque than he'd intended.

She gestured them again toward the table. "Eat something. Please. I told Alyth I was feeding you, so I need to. Otherwise the queen might glean that I lied."

"I'm not hungry," Ivor said flatly. "You saw Alyth."

Her expression turned pained and she placed a comforting hand on his arm. "Oh, Ivor, I wish you hadn't seen that, but you need to understand that almost everyone has suffered similar tragedies among their families or friends. Or worse. Please, I know it's hard, but please eat. Even just a bite."

Connor felt moved by her fear. With the aid of chert, he did not doubt her words. She was taking a real risk in speaking with them. So he led the way to the table and picked up an apple and managed to eat a few bites. Still scowling, Ivor sampled a piece of sliced ham.

Shona sighed with relief, then said, "You realize you're idiots, right?"

"I had to try to save her," Ivor said, glaring at her, as if eager to fight someone that he knew he could hurt.

She sighed again. "If you had arrived yesterday you might have managed it. The queen insists that everyone present themselves immediately. Not nearly enough of us survive the initial interview."

"How did you?" Connor could not imagine the queen did not recognize Shona's ambition and ruthlessness. Had she just caught the queen on a good day, or did the queen approve?

"Your aunt Ailsa helped me."

The idea of his aunt anywhere near the queen terrified him. "We need to get her out of here."

Shona shook her head. "I wouldn't worry about your aunt, Connor. She's even more clever than people at the Carraig ever knew. She taught me how to protect myself by filling my mind with thoughts the queen would approve of. If she has no reason to dig further, that's sometimes enough."

"So the queen interviewed Ailsa?"

"Ailsa is one of her favorite advisers now and she alone supplies the queen with all her power stone. The queen insists that Ailsa and I attend her every afternoon."

Shona shuddered, her expression reflecting her horror. The pulsing of her emotions grew colder. Connor could only imagine what it must be like to stand near the insane queen, watching her kill or brain wipe people that Shona might have known all her life. He did not believe he had the strength to handle that. Shona was many things, but weak was not one of them.

Ivor pressed his hands against his temples, for a second looking nearly overwhelmed by grief. "It's worse than I imagined. Is no one standing up to her?"

Shona barked a harsh laugh and Connor easily read the hopelessness in her eyes without needing chert. "Who could? At the first hint of a rebellious thought, she wipes peoples' minds or destroys them and casts them down into the waterfall."

"There has to be a way," Connor said. Sure, she'd just beaten them both with terrifying ease, but if he accepted that they had no chance against her, he'd lose all ability to act.

She shook her head vigorously and gripped his hands. "You can't think that, Connor. Not here, not now. You have to get away."

Her hands were warm on his, and as usual he caught the scent of roses wafting around her. Part of him wished he could comfort her, but he did not dare encourage her at all.

As if the same thought occurred to her, she leaned closer and lifted an arm to embrace him.

Connor hated to do it, but he stepped back and pushed her hand away, shaking his head. For a moment she looked utterly crushed, and he clearly felt her despair through the conduit of chert before he severed the connection. Her anguish almost made him relent.

"You don't know what it would mean to feel the touch of a true friend here," she whispered. She met his gaze, her big, hazel eyes wide and vulnerable. It was a look she had used on him more than once, and he hated that it still affected him so much.

"You know I can't, Shona."

She sighed, and turned to Ivor. "Do you hate me now too?"

"I hate that hat," he said with forced levity.

She chuckled, pulled it off, and grimaced at it. "It is hideous."

"What's with all the feathers?" Connor asked.

"One of the more ridiculous edicts from . . ." Shona's voice broke and she raised one quivering hand to her mouth. Connor had never seen her look so distraught, not even through the most intense fighting or Carraig intrigue. He was glad he had dropped chert. With that emotional connection in place, he doubted he could have held his ground against such an onslaught of her need.

Ivor wrapped her in his strong arms. She clung to him, and her shoulders vibrated a little as if she was suppressing sobs. Ivor held her, his eyes closed, his head resting on hers. For a moment they stood silent, simply taking comfort from each other.

Connor watched, torn. In a way it should have been him comforting Shona, but he could not. Not ever. She had made that impossible. He had to wonder if there was any way they could simply be friends, without all the layers of tension and all the baggage from the past.

Probably not.

After a moment the two released each other and Shona wiped at her eyes, even though no tears had actually slipped free. She kissed Ivor on the cheek. "Thank you. I needed that."

He sighed. "I did too. Did the queen destroy your father's mind too?"

She shook her head. "She needs him. He's her chief adviser. He knows too much about the kingdom, the politics, the economy, and everything else for her to waste."

High Lord Dougal was alive. The thought instantly triggered a wave of intense hunger that roared through Connor and made him groan. Dougal knew where he could get porphyry.

Before consciously deciding to, Connor grabbed Shona's arm. "You have to get me some more porphyry. He'll give it to you."

She looked shocked, and Ivor pulled Connor's arm from Shona's. "Get control of yourself, Connor. We're not out of danger yet. We have to leave."

"But I need some." Connor struggled against a mindless rage that urged him to attack Ivor. Every muscle quivered as he fought to maintain control.

"What's the matter with you?" Shona demanded.

Ivor said, "It's the porphyry. It's got a grip on his soul."

Connor begged, "Please, Shona. Get me some."

Shona shook her head. "He'd never give me any, and you know it. Even if he did, I don't think you can risk ever taking it again."

Connor spun away and swept an arm across the table, upending it and scattering food across the beautiful gallery. "If I don't get any, it'll kill me!"

Shona came to him and placed both hands on his shoulders, forcing him to look into her eyes. She spoke gently. "Connor, listen to me. The only way I could ever get my father to help you gain control over this would be if you came back to me, and you know it."

Ivor laughed. "You never give up, Shona. I like that about you."

Her closeness helped calm Connor, and that enraged him in a different way. Verena should be his protection against the rage of porphyry, not Shona.

He spoke with calm, deliberate words. "Shona, I have to make a choice. The choice I make will be final. I need you to respect that."

She hesitated, sliding her hands off his shoulder, a flicker of worry in her eyes. "Connor, I don't think you're in a position —"

Connor cut her off. "I am. And it's good that I can tell you directly.

Shona, I choose Verena. I have to. If she wakes up, I will do everything in my power to make her happy."

She impressed him by not crying, not shouting, not trying to manipulate him in any way. She only nodded. "I do respect you, Connor. And more than respect you." She hesitated before adding, "If for any reason things don't work out —"

He interrupted her again. "They will."

"Okay. But know I'm here," she said softly, an intimate whisper that conveyed the intense emotion reflected in her eyes. Her expression was a mixture of sorrow and obstinate hope.

He couldn't help it. He tapped chert again. She was far too good an actress for him to read her with any confidence. The conduit snapped into place between them, stronger than before, almost as if she was knowingly opening herself to it. His skin warmed from the connection and her emotions encircled him like an invisible caress.

She really did care. If she was faking that, she was fooling herself too because waves of intense emotion rose off of her like steam. Connor stumbled a step back from her and severed the connection to chert. He now wished he hadn't used it. Now he knew she did love him, or at least loved the idea of being with him. Hating her was so much easier when he'd convinced himself that she saw him only as a pawn to her plans. He'd thought that once he told her to her face that he chose Verena things would get simpler.

Nothing was ever simple with Shona.

She raised one eyebrow, studying his expression far too closely. He felt himself flushing, but couldn't afford to give her any false hope. He had to focus all his energy on Verena. So he said, "I know I promised to kiss you, and I've never gone back on my word before, but this time I have to."

That angered her, and she gave him that look that used a cow him. "You promised."

"And now I'm unpromising. Neither one of us can afford any weakness right now, and I cannot let anything stand between me and Verena."

Shona tapped granite, her body shifting into the perfect lines of a sculpted goddess, clearly visible even under the layers of her gorgeous dress. For a moment Connor thought she would strike him, but she only stomped away, muttering to herself.

He knew he shouldn't, but Connor tapped a bit of serpentinite. He snatched the little whispers that clung around her like mist and pulled them to him. They were so weak that several expired before he could listen, but he picked up a few words.

Some of the more colorful ones included, "Vixen. Wench. Inferior breeding. Eat her heart."

Ivor returned to Aifric's litter. "Thanks for the food and the chat, Shona. Don't lose hope. We'll find a way."

She released granite and turned back to them, not hiding her despair. "I can't see how."

Connor and Ivor lifted the stretcher. Ivor said, "There's always hope."

Shona's eyes shifted to Connor, her expression angry and sad at the same time. He should turn his back on her, sever all ties, but he simply couldn't leave her with that final insult. He would never submit to her again, but she too was caught in a horrible position and he couldn't leave her without a little encouragement.

"Stay close to Ailsa. She'll help."

23

WHEN FIGHTING IS THE ONLY WAY TO GET ALONG

Flying never felt so good.

Hamish couldn't stop grinning as he soared over the snowy Grandurian landscape in his new battle suit. The long flight down from Faulenrost toward Emmerich passed far too quickly as he flew through the bright blue winter sky, passed snow-capped mountains and wide, white valleys blanketed by evergreens.

The slightly bulkier design didn't impede movement as much as he had feared, and it fit him like a glove. The new helmet sealed better over the collar, blocking out the annoying, cold wind. Jean had augmented the face shield to improve his field of view and reduce fogging. She'd anticipated so many of the improvements he'd wanted to make, then added more that he never would have considered. She was simply amazing.

The bitter cold of the heights didn't bother him much. Jean and Dierk had designed ingenious, tiny leather tubes, treated with a new form of Althin waterproofing, and inserted them through all the limbs of his suit. When he flew, he could activate marble to heat the water between the layers of his armor and use a bit of quickened soapstone to pump the heated water through the suit. It kept him toasty warm.

Hamish flew over a final row of long hills and spotted the Emmerich township spread out in its flat plain, near the quarry. He tipped back into a reverse spin, exulting in the maneuverability of the suit. The multi-thruster design gave him so much more control, allowed him to turn tighter circles, and improved speed and efficiency. He was tempted to stay in the air until dark to play.

But when he came out of his fast loop, he activated the long-vision aspect of his visor and focused on the town, then frowned. Most of the townsfolk had gathered in the square, with the Alasdair refugees on one side of the enormous, intricate central fountain and the Emmerich locals on the other. The fountain was built with one wide lower bowl and several graceful, arcing posts rising to support nearly a dozen smaller bowls. In warmer weather, water shot in graceful arcs between them, but they all looked frozen now. The way the two groups were facing off did not look friendly.

As Hamish tipped forward into a fast dive, he wondered what could have gone wrong. When he'd left just a few days before, the two groups had been making great progress in integrating. If the two groups started fighting, they could unravel all their hard work.

He spotted Lord Wenzel and his family, along with Merten, the Emmerich Quader and his wife, Karola, in the center near the fountain, arguing with Hendry and Lilias. Nearby stood Stuart, thick arms crossed, looking determined. With growing dread, Hamish increased speed. The situation between Stuart and Stefanie had progressed faster than he'd feared. A common Obrioner showing interest in a noble Grandurian girl seemed so ridiculous most people would laugh it off.

Then again, Connor was linn, and Verena was nobility.

Hamish swooped down on the courtyard, triggering bursts of multi-colored fire to draw attention from the confrontation in the center of the square. At the last possible moment, he flipped in mid-air and slowed just in time to land close to Hendry.

With all eyes on him, Hamish pulled off his helmet and waved. "Hi! Thanks for assembling to welcome me back. What's for lunch?"

Hendry and Lilias looked amused, Wenzel and Karola looked amazed, Lady Theda smiled at Hamish in that motherly way she always did, and Lord Wenzel looked relieved by the interruption.

His son Torben looked annoyed. The burly cutter was dressed in a sleeveless leather vest, despite the cold, and he turned his scowl from Stuart to Hamish and said in Grandurian, "Don't interrupt, Builder."

"But you haven't started eating yet," Hamish pointed out.

"It's not lunch time," Torben snapped.

"Of course it is." Hamish pointed up at the sun standing directly overhead. He had timed his return perfectly to ensure he didn't miss a meal. "No wonder you look so grumpy. You must be starving."

With amusement in her voice, Lady Theda said, "Lunch will be served after we complete the business of the honor duel."

Hendry's expression turned annoyed. "With all due respect, your ladyship, we don't approve of our people fighting for fun."

"Is not fun," Torben said in barely-discernible Obrioner. "Is honor. Must fight for sister."

Hendry looked ready to argue further, but Hamish held up a hand to forestall him. "Have they explained what an honor duel means?"

"Not in any way that makes sense," Lilias said, then added, "No offense."

"It makes sense to us, and this is our town." Lord Wenzel looked irritated, and that was not good.

The union of the two groups was so new and so fragile, it could snap over any little misunderstanding. Honor duels were no little thing, and if the argument grew hot enough, Lord Wenzel might just kick out the refugees.

Hamish could not allow that to happen, so he raised calming hands. "Everyone please take a deep breath and relax for a second. This is a difference in culture. Lord Wenzel, will you allow me to try straightening out the misunderstanding?"

"If you can."

Hamish turned to Stuart, who hadn't seemed to pay much attention to the conversation at all, but stared at Stefanie with a look of stupid adoration on his face.

"Stuart!" Hamish called. "What is your intention toward Stefanie?"

"I don't answer to you," Stuart said defiantly.

Hamish sighed and gestured at the hundreds of villagers gathered on both sides of the square. "Look around, block-head. You've created a problem, so just answer the question unless you want to get thrown out of Emmerich for good."

Stuart glared but answered. "I love her." He cast the words at Hamish like a challenge. Torben's glare deepened and his fists clenched. He definitely planned to take up that challenge.

Hamish glanced at Stefanie. Generally in an honor duel, the girl was not supposed to interfere. She was staring at Stuart with the same empty-headed adoration. Hamish felt like asking Mhairi if she'd checked the girl for early-onset insanity.

"And do you welcome his courtship?" Hamish asked.

Stefanie blushed. The look was very appealing on her plump cheeks. "I do."Love is Really Blind.

Hamish turned to Lord Wenzel and Lady Theda. "You are willing to allow a courtship to proceed? He is not nobility."

Stuart opened his mouth to protest, but Hendry waved him to silence.

Lord Wenzel considered Stuart for a moment, and a frown tugged at his mouth before he concealed it. "The situation is unusual, but then again, so is our entire existence right now." He gestured from his people to the Alasdairians. "Stuart is a cutter, and it is not unknown for such a courtship to occur in Granadure. I don't like it, but I might consider it. However, that makes the honor duel all the more important."

Lady Theda added, "In this time of strife, demonstrating that our two nations can indeed learn to live in peace together is critically important. Lady Verena has accepted courtship from an Obrioner commoner. We cannot ignore that precedent."

Hamish only hoped Verena awoke soon, and that she and Connor reconciled. No one else needed to know their relationship was struggling.

So he nodded. "Then the next step is the honor duel, and Torben it seems clear that you're willing to fulfill your duty as brother?"

"Eager to serve," he declared, not taking his eyes off Stuart.

Hamish turned back to Hendry and Lilias. "The honor duel is an important Grandurian tradition."

"It's barbaric," Lilias said softly, frowning at Torben. "Why is it so important to try beating up a boy whose only fault is falling in love?"

Well, Stuart had a lot of faults, but none of those were important at the moment.

"The process demonstrates that the family takes the safety of their daughters seriously, and it helps prevent suitors who might not be sincere. Many times the honor duel is little more than a formality."

He glanced from Stuart to Torben and added, "Although sometimes by necessity the duel is more intense."

"What necessity?" Hendry asked.

"Think about it. An Obrioner commoner has stated a public intention of courting a Grandurian noble. They may not be high nobles, but what if he even joked about courting Moira? In Obrion he could be made daor, whipped, or even executed. Here all he has to do is face a potential beating, and he gets to defend himself."

"Well, when you put it that way—" Hendry began.

Lilias exclaimed, "Hendry!"

Stuart stepped a bit closer. "Doesn't really matter what you all think. It's my choice."

"Have a care, young man," she warned. "My husband might not be nobility, but you owe him respect for all he's done for you and this town."

Stuart looked appropriately contrite. "Sorry, Lilias. I only meant I appreciate your concern, but it's just a fist fight. I'm willing to take the risk for Stefanie."

Hamish said, "You can also think of this as a practice event. Once Verena wakes up, Connor will face an honor duel of his own."

"And if you'll let Connor do it, don't tell me I can't," Stuart said.

Lilias sighed. "Only a fool would try to step between Connor and our dear, sweet Verena." She fixed Stuart with a worried look. "Do be careful."

Wow. Hamish hadn't expected that to work.

They explained the situation to the rest of the townsfolk, and most of them looked eager to witness the duel. Hamish wasn't sure if they supported Stuart's ambitious courtship, or if they just wanted to see a fight, but the mood in the square changed to unified anticipation for the duel.

As soon as everyone was ready, Lord Wenzel called Stuart and Torben to face each other in front of him. Stefanie joined them, facing her father, with her suitor on her right side and her brother on her left. Lord

Wenzel placed a hand on each of their shoulders and spoke loudly in Grandurian.

"We all are witnesses today of this momentous event, this public honor duel for my lovely daughter, Stefanie. All young ladies deserve to enjoy the committed protection of family in defending their virtue and honor, and today Torben stands as your protector and your designated champion."

Torben raised his right fist high to enthusiastic cheering from all the Emmerich locals. Lord Wenzel repeated the same words in Obrioner, eliciting a much less enthusiastic response.

Then Lord Wenzel turned his gaze on Stuart. "Honorable love is the pursuit of every steadfast heart. You have chosen to declare to the world your intentions to court my daughter, and you are willing to fight for the right to spend time with her, to protect her virtue at all times, and to defend her from all harm. Do you so swear, and will you accept this duty today?"

"I do," Stuart declared, raising his fist in imitation of Torben.

The Grandurians cheered his resolve although less loudly than they had cheered Torben. Even before Lord Wenzel completed repeating his remarks in Obrioner, the Alasdairians began wildly cheering Stuart.

Hamish had never seen an actual honor duel, although he'd heard much about them. He found it funny that Stuart was charged with protecting Stefanie. As a Rumbler, she could easily beat up both him and Torben together.

Hamish hoped neither of the combatants got hurt too badly. That could overwhelm the good will sweeping the town. The two men glared at each other, making it clear neither would relent easily. Torben was the picture of Grandurian might, well-muscled, blonde, bright blue eyes, and chiseled good looks. Stuart was a little bigger, a little meatier, and a lot uglier. The two could easily hurt each other if the fight got too intense.

"Then I command you both to fight honorably and cleanly. The match will be decided if one of you can no longer continue, or if you signal surrender by raising a hand with fingers outspread. Do you understand?"

When both men nodded agreement, he gestured Stefanie back, then retreated ten steps and said loudly, "Let the duel begin!"

The two lunged at each other amid shouts of encouragement from all sides that echoed back and forth across the square. They met in a flurry of meaty punches, beating on each other with more enthusiasm than skill. Both big men shrugged off blows that would have toppled smaller opponents, and Hamish's worry grew. They were fighting hard, with that wild look in their eyes that he'd seen far too often in real battles.

He'd grown up as friends with Stuart and rivals for Jean's affection. For much of the last couple years prior to the battles of Alasdair, he'd dreamed of pummeling Stuart the way Torben was. Now he was surprised to find himself rooting for Stuart, hoping he'd win the right to court Stefanie. Not only might their courtship help unite the towns, but Stuart really looked like he was in love, and Hamish would always root for love winning out in the end.

After the first wild flurry of punches, Stuart closed to grappling range and tried to tie up Torben's arms for a throw. The problem was, Torben had actually trained in combat. He easily reversed the hold and sent Stuart tumbling off his feet. He landed on his backside against the fountain amid a fresh wave of cheering from the Grandurians and shouts of encouragement from the Obrioners.

Stefanie circled the fighting, looking like she wanted to help Stuart. She cast an angry glare at her brother, but he ignored it. In that second, they reminded Hamish of Anika and Erich.

Stuart leaped back to his feet and tackled Torben. Cheering erupted from both sides as the men rolled over each other, pummeling and grappling. Neither gained advantage, so they rolled away from each other and returned to their feet.

Stuart charged again, but Torben slapped his punching fist to the side, twisting him, and giving himself a chance to slip around behind Stuart. In a flash, Torben wrapped powerful arms around Stuart's shoulders and neck in a hold that Hamish recognized.

His heart sank. That choke hold was hard to escape. He'd learned a couple tricks to get out of it, but doubted Stuart knew any of them. The fight would end with a loss for love. He'd have to make sure the Obrioners understood what that meant, particularly Stuart.

The two men swayed and staggered. Torben knew he held the advantage and said between panting breaths, "Surrender now. Extend hand or I choke to sleep."

"Never," Stuart swore, eliciting a round of appreciative cheering even from the Grandurians. Everyone loved determined love, and Stuart was gaining a lot of support.

He was still about to lose, though.

Stuart dropped to one knee. The abrupt move dragged Torben forward over him, and Stuart lunged back up with a mighty heave, throwing the two of them back. They crashed into the fountain so hard they smashed through the ice in the lower bowl. Torben lost his hold and staggered to his feet, spitting water and gasping from the cold. Hamish grimaced. That kind of shock could steal the breath away and leave a man cramped and unable to move.

Stuart erupted from the icy water beside Torben, his huge fist whipping up in a mighty uppercut that caught Torben in the jaw. Stefanie's defender flew up and back, right out of the fountain as he somersaulted over backward and landed on his head.

He did not move.

His mother rushed to his side. Lord Wenzel blinked a couple of times, obviously surprised and disappointed. But he recovered quickly, raised both fists into the air, and shouted, "Stuart wins!"

The square erupted into wild cheering as everyone rushed to congratulate Stuart. He stumbled out of the fountain, soaking wet and shaking, but grinning like a fool. Stefanie threw her arms around him and kissed him squarely on the lips.

Stuart's eyes widened and he looked like he might fall right back into the fountain. Stefanie caught him and easily lifted him off the ground, carrying him through the throngs of people who swarmed them with shouted congratulations.

Hamish laughed and clapped. The fight had been close enough that the Grandurians would not begrudge Stuart courting their lord's daughter. Torben had defended Stefanie's honor with sufficient intensity to satisfy everyone, but love had still carried the day.

He pushed through the crowds to Lord Wenzel and Lady Theda, who knelt on either side of Torben. He was sitting up, with Mhairi checking him for concussion. Her gaggle of healer students clustered close, watching her every move with rapt attention.

"He'll be fine," Mhairi pronounced. "A couple of cracked teeth that might have to be pulled, but he's as thick a blockhead as Stuart."

Lady Theda said, "Leave the teeth, We'll summon a Healer to tend them."

Hamish breathed a sigh of relief. Things might just turn out all right.

Lord Wenzel cast a final worried glance toward Stuart and his daughter at the center of the throng, then shrugged.

When they leveraged Torben to a sitting position, Hamish clapped him on the shoulder. "You fought well."

"He fought better," Torben grinned. His teeth looked slightly twisted as well as cracked, but he seemed remarkably happy. "Stuart is worthy to court Stefanie."

"Then it is time to celebrate," Lord Wenzel said loudly to more cheering.

Hamish rubbed his hands together in anticipation. He had indeed timed his return perfectly. Lunch was shaping up to be epic.

2 4

GRACE UNDER PRESSURE

Shona climbed the long, winding stair toward the throne room to attend afternoon court, but her mind was unfocused and whirling. The added fear of knowing that she would soon stand in the presence of Queen Dreokt, but without her normal shield of careful calm served to escalate her anger at Connor to an even higher level. Blinking back tears, Shona cursed him for being such a grouted block-head.

He had no idea what she was going through or the constant terror she lived in. She couldn't even share her fears openly with her father. He was committed so wholeheartedly to the queen's service, Shona was starting to wonder if the she'd tampered with his amazing brain too.

"Connor, this is no time for your stupidity," she muttered to herself as she stomped up the stairs. Even though the queen had beaten both Connor and Ivor together, she couldn't help but believe that when Connor came to his senses and returned to her, together they could find a way to set things right.

It was all Verena's fault.

The vile wench Builder must have questionable heritage in her line. She'd addled Connor's brain beyond what Shona had ever imagined possible. Yes, she had made mistakes shepherding him toward his destiny, but Verena was nothing less than the most dangerous enemy of Obrion alive.

Shona decided to send a coded message via the listening posts to Craigroy in Merkland. If he really did have someone embedded in Granadure with access to the comatose Verena, he needed to call upon that person now. Shona could no longer wait for Verena to die on her own. The accursed woman had shown too many times that she lacked the good grace to do what was right.

"You took a foolish risk, Lady Shona." Ailsa's voice surprised her out of her reverie. Connor's aunt stood leaning against the outer wall of the stairway above, arms folded. She looked like someone who had been waiting for a while.

She did not need to explain what she was talking about. "I had to see him, had to glimpse a friendly face, someone not already bound to her will."

"How do you know they weren't bound? What if she altered their thinking, but in more subtle ways than usual?"

Shona gasped at the horrific idea. "Why would you suggest such a thing?"

"Because you need to think deeper if you hope to survive these trials," Ailsa said simply.

"Do you think she really might have done that?" Would that explain why Connor had acted so stupidly and flat-out rejected her? He had seemed unusually distant.

"I would have to speak with them at length to know for sure, but I suspect not."

"Why not?"

"It is not her way. I have yet to see Queen Dreokt choose subtlety."

"True, but Connor and Ivor are unusual cases. She might be trying something new."

"Perhaps, but that would suggest that she believes at some level that they represent real threats to her. I do not believe our queen sees anything as a threat."

"She let them go, though. She hasn't done that with anyone else."

"True. From the account I reviewed, she sees in them a potential use. If that is the case, then she freed them only because she does not yet feel they are ready to serve."

"That would mean she believes she can collect them again whenever she sees fit."

"There is much truth to that supposition."

Shona clutched her hands together to hide their shaking. "What are we going to do?" She felt such a depth of despair, it felt like she was falling into a bottomless abyss. All of her life she'd been raised and trained to always stay in control, always find a way to benefit from any situation, gain influence, and eventually accomplish her objectives. For all of her skills, all of her self-confidence, the queen had deprived her of any choice in her own fate.

She suddenly understood how Connor felt.

Shona couldn't hold back the tears. She covered her face with her hands and sobbed, not caring that Ailsa saw her weakness. She wasn't sure if she cried more for her own horrible condition or for what she'd done to Connor.

Instead of chiding her or reminding her that she had to be strong the way her father might, Ailsa stepped close and held her. Shona leaned against her and drew comfort as she cried.

If only her mother had been more like Ailsa. Her mother had never fully recovered from the failed birthing of Shona's younger brother. Always physically weak, her mother had withdrawn into herself, and Shona barely remembered her. When Shona was seven years old, her mother had decided to return to her family's estate in southern Obrion to see if the milder climate might cure her ailing health.

She had never returned. She died three years later.

Now Shona clung to Ailsa as she might have to a mother, and wished through her bitter tears that she'd known Ailsa sooner.

After a moment, she stepped back, and Ailsa handed her a handkerchief to wipe her face. "I'm sorry. I just couldn't hold it in any longer."

"I understand. Attending the queen every day could break the strongest among us."

"But not you."

"I am used to dealing with the vagaries in taste of my clients. The queen's issues deviate in magnitude more than in fundamental scope."

"I don't know if I can do it. I'm terrified she'll dig into my mind. Especially now."

"You must hold your thoughts like a shield like I taught you," Ailsa said gently but firmly. "I don't think I could find such a strong ally in all of Donleavy if you lose your nerve."

Shona smiled her thanks at the compliment but said, "You overestimate me. Can't you see the queen is more obviously insane, but what she's doing to us is no worse than we've done to our linn? I understand Connor now and why he had to fight so hard to break free." Fresh tears came to her eyes. "I forced him to run away by my very nature. I lost him when I could have had him. You should hate me. Why are you helping instead?"

Ailsa surprised her by giving her a warm, approving smile. "Because you are stronger than you think, Shona, and better than you were raised to be. Yes, you made some choices I disapprove of, and you need to let go of your lingering hopes to control my nephew."

Shona started to protest, but Ailsa held up a hand to calm her. "I find it encouraging that you can learn from your trials. Too many simply close their minds and bewail their fate. You will emerge stronger and wiser for your challenges."

Shona sniffed a couple of times and forced her emotions under control. She could not delay without risking annoying the queen. She shook her head slowly. "You speak as if there is any hope for any of us surviving this nightmare."

"There is always hope."

Shona clung to those words, holding them as an invisible lifeline. She would fight to survive, would face Connor again someday and apologize for what she had done to him. Perhaps then they could find a way to start over.

Ailsa cupped her face in her strong, calloused hands, pulled her head down a bit, and kissed her forehead. "Be strong, Shona."

Such simple words shouldn't help much in the face of Queen Dreokt's insanity, but somehow they did.

"At least you have a few extra minutes to prepare yourself today," Ailsa said.

"What are you talking about?" Shona gestured up the stairs, where light from the exit was shining into the stairwell. "We're almost there."

Ailsa shook her head. "You really have been distracted today. The queen has decreed that she will hold audience in a different location. It's a beautiful, sunny day, and is unusually warm outside. She will hold court on the loch."

"You mean at the loch?"

Ailsa shook her head and led the way down. "No. She distinctly said on the loch."

Shona shrugged. One more instance of the queen's erratic decision making process. Hopefully the queen would be distracted by the different venue and not pay her much attention. Shona needed a little time to compose herself.

When they reached the enormous main atrium room, Shona learned that the queen had also ordered the entire palace emptied. The exceptions allowing people to stand above her was rescinded for the day, so they joined tens of thousands of others hurrying to evacuate. As the flood of people swept out the lower exits and took the steep boulevards or long stairs down toward the lower levels of the city, Shona and Ailsa turned down a smaller stair that angled back under the lowest level of the palace where it extended more than a hundred yards out over the loch.

Shona had never seen the underside of the palace before. Thick stone pillars marched across the loch, supporting the massive palace, while dozens of boats and barges were docked along a series of long, stone wharves. By the piles of crates and bags and boxes, Shona guessed that much of the supplies required to run the enormous palace must arrive by boat every day. Now the entire wharf area was silent but for the creaking of hawsers and the gentle banging of boats against the padded sides of the wharves.

Deep shadows held sway down there, despite the bright sunlight streaming through the billowing mists across the rest of the loch. Shona immediately tapped her limestone, hanging on a heavy gold chain around her neck. She smiled as she connected as easy as touching her lifelong Boulder gift. As the stone blazed forth with brilliant, greenish light, she marveled anew.

She longed to learn the secret of how the queen bequeathed such marvelous new affinities. Only a handful of others had received similar gifts, and Shona had not found an excuse to speak with them about their experiences yet.

Other lords and ladies summoned to attend the queen began joining them or congregating on the opposite side of the loch. The mist-filled air was chilly with that wet cold that seemed to knife right through Shona's clothing. She wished she had thought to bring a thicker jacket.

Or better, if she was a Firetongue she could warm herself with marble. The thought of the queen noticing her for any reason that day made her tremble with fear, but she tried to bolster her courage with the hope that maybe the queen would notice her shivering and decide to grant her a tertiary affinity.

Her musings were cut short as a rush of air swept across the loch, whipping the previously smooth service into little waves. Queen Dreokt descended out of the sky, directly above the center of the loch, floating with regal grace that not even that infernal Builder Verena could hope to match in the skies.

All conversation ceased among the nobles gathered around the loch as the queen touched down upon the surface, and the entire loch immediately became as smooth as glass. Stragglers out of the palace who were not invited to attend the queen accelerated their pace, rushing down toward the lower level with terrified haste lest the queen decide their tardiness suggested they were unworthy.

Instead of snuffing out hundreds of lives, Queen Dreokt sat upon a glittering throne of water that rose from the loch. The water refracted the bright sunlight like faceted ice crystals.

She beckoned the assembled courtiers with a sweeping gesture, and her voice boomed loudly across the waters. "Come. Join me, those privileged to attend me today. I am in a fine mood, and I wish for my most worthy servants to stand with me."

Many hesitated. The waters were dark and cold, certainly just barely above freezing. If one fell in, they would die and sink to the depths long before they could swim out to the queen. Then again, how was that different than standing with her in the throne room where she could dissolve the floor and send them plummeting to their deaths?

Shona moved at the same time as Ailsa. Together they led the way down the last few steps to the stone walkway at the edge of the loch. Together they stepped off the dock, dropping about eight inches to the glassy smooth surface of the water.

They did not sink. The surface bowed slightly, like a piece of canvas stretched taut. It held their weight as they proceeded out onto the water. It was an impressive display of water mastery, but not unheard of. Shona only hoped walking on water was the scariest thing they had to deal with that day.

She caught sight of her father approaching from the opposite side of the loch, leading the lords and ladies from that side. Queen Dreokt smiled happily as her court joined her in the sunlight at the center of the lake. Invisible restraints held the billowing spray from the waterfall away, forming shimmering walls of mist about fifty feet away on all sides.

Without preamble, the queen declared, "Today the first interview is with a remarkable young woman who I hope will serve as a shining example of bravery and wisdom for all who live anywhere across this continent."

At her gesture, another gust of wind rippled across the lake, this one surprisingly warm. Shona had to wonder if she had also tapped marble to make it more comfortable.

Another figure descended on that wind, and as she settled below the obscuring mists, Shona was startled to recognize Padraigin.

The rare, Althin Dawnus, one of the contenders for Tir-raon champion during the last season, looked as beautiful and graceful as ever. Shona had not become good friends with Padraigin, since she like almost everyone else had resented the inclusion of a foreign Petralist as champion. However, she had secretly admired the courage and resourcefulness that Padraigin had shown in a competition where she faced universal opposition.

Shona heard soft trilling of invisible trumpets as Padraigin settled to the lake in front of the queen. That was one of Padraigin's signature and unusual abilities with quartzite, but Shona had never seen her fly. Had the queen taught her the trick, or had Dreokt herself orchestrated the grand entrance as a way to reinforce her words?

Either way, Shona welcomed Padraigin's arrival with far more enthusiasm than she usually allowed herself to feel at the commencement of any interview. The queen already seemed predisposed to approve of Padraigin, and Shona was eager to speak with her after that session of court. The thought of having another friend and confidant there in Donleavy encouraged her tremendously. That's exactly what she needed to regain her emotional footing.

Queen Dreokt greeted Padraigin with a smile. "You do yourself and your new house much honor by swearing fealty to Obrion and choosing the way of wisdom."

"Thank you, Your Majesty." Padraigin's cultured voice held only a hint of Althin accent.

Shona had not truly believed that Padraigin would keep to the agreement that allowed her to compete in the Tir-raon. Padraigin had sworn to marry into House Pilib, abandon allegiance to Althing, and commit to raising any offspring as Obrioners. She had done everything she promised to do, and Shona had heard that her house already considered her their finest Petralist jewel. With her powerful gift, they clearly hoped for remarkably powerful Petralist offspring.

Queen Dreokt leaned forward slightly, her eyes fixed on Padraigin, no doubt touching her mind. Shona hoped she would be content with a quick scan and confirm Padraigin as a worthy servants. Padraigin stood calmly and confidently faced the queen, looking far more composed than most.

The queen suddenly gasped, her smile evaporating, and her benevolent expression turning in half a heartbeat to one of outrage. "You deceitful traitor!"

Shona gasped, as did many of those assembled, all retreating a hurried step. They'd all seen enough interviews to know what was coming next. Shona wanted to scream with disappointment and horror. She couldn't bear to lose another friend. Would Queen Dreokt mind-wipe Padraigin or simply plunge her into the depths of the loch and seal her underwater forever?

Padraigin looked more resigned than terrified. She sighed and shifted into a more aggressive stance. "I had hoped to enjoy a few more days here before this moment, but no soul who enjoys freedom could ever submit to your slavery without challenge."

Fires erupted in the queen's eyes and she snarled, "You petulant, stupid girl. I planned to raise you to greatness, to walk hand-in-hand with you to lead your wayward nation back to the fold of my protection."

Padraigin gave the queen a look of disgust. "You are a fallen woman, a blight on the honor of all nobility and Petralists. I defy you, and I guarantee your reign of terror will end soon."

Shocked gasps echoed across the loch. Shona expected the queen to tear Padraigin to ribbons. She wanted to scream at the idiot girl, but it was far too late.

Queen Dreokt laughed delightedly, as if Padraigin was her favorite niece and had said something particularly endearing. Despite being conditioned to the Queen's erratic mood swings, Shona still felt startled.

So did Padraigin. The queen said, "My dear girl, you could have become such a worthy servant. Your bravery inspires me, even though you are sworn to such a foolish cause. Nevertheless, I respect your audacity, and I will grant what you so clearly desire. I will allow you to face me in a duel to the death."

Queen Dreokt gestured at Ailsa. "Ensure that this young lady has all the power stone she requires."

As Ailsa moved to Padraigin's side, Shona felt a powerful urge to join them, but she did not dare. She already risked the queen's wrath and could not bring more attention to herself. She hated her cowardice, hated how much Padraigin's defiance inspired her, and hated that such a remarkable person would be executed just for thinking differently.

Padraigin glanced at her and winked. That left Shona even more unsettled. Did Padraigin know something, some secret that might turn the tide in her favor? Did anyone else know it? Or if Padraigin fell, would it be lost forever with her?

Padraigin said, "I accept your challenge."

The queen laughed delightedly, and the laughter spread to the rest of the court. It was so ridiculous for Padraigin to act like an equal, as if she had any hope, but Padraigin faced the new mockery with the same calm that she had at the Carraig.

She spoke again. "I confess that the location leaves me at a distinct disadvantage. I request that we retire to the bank so that I may use my full range of affinities."

Again Shona was stunned by Padraigin's audacity. The queen did not look offended, but shook her head. "The bank is all dark and dreary today. I prefer you meet your fate in the sunlight."

The waters beneath Padraigin suddenly boiled and bubbled and spurted all around her. Padraigin's expression turned fearful for the first time. Shona wondered if the queen would end the dual even before it started. That seemed disingenuous, but who would challenge her on it?

Seconds later, the watery spray dissipated, revealing that Padraigin stood upon a column of earth, more than ten feet in diameter. The queen must of pulled it up from beneath the loch.

Queen Dreokt made a bored wave of her hand from where she sat. "Show me what the jewel of a high house can do."

The ground to either side of Padraigin erupted. Spears of earth shot toward the queen, but they exploded to dust that blew away in a gust of wind.

Before Padraigin could try again, the earth buckled underneath her, tumbling her across the surface of the water as if it was ice. She rolled to her feet, tapped basalt, and shot toward the queen in a fully fracked sprint. A dagger appeared in her hand.

It was a laughable attempt, but Padraigin looked sincere. Invisible trumpets blared and drums boomed in Padraigin's wake as she closed on the queen.

The queen made no move, did not rise to meet her, but allowed Padraigin to close on her. With a shout of victory, Padraigin slashed with her dagger as she flashed past the queen.

Her blade shattered, as if the air had turned to steel. Even as Padraigin tried coming around for another pass, a cyclone howled down from above. The dark gray air shrieked like the combined death cries of all of the queen's victims as it tore Padraigin's feet out from under her. She fell, but the winds caught her, lifting her into the air, stretching her limbs spread-eagled as if the air currents were grasping fingers. The trumpeting horns ceased, and Padraigin opened her mouth to scream.

A gust of wind tore down her throat. Air filled her lungs to bursting, and more air poured in after. Padraigin thrashed helplessly, her expression now terrified. Her eyes flickered to Shona, and Shona read the truth there.

Padraigin was about to die. She had not learned any secret, but had merely dared become a martyr.

More air clawed into Padraigin's mouth. Her body swelled, her ribs cracking outward, her entire body looking like it was about to burst.

Then with a surprisingly gentle sigh, the air whisked out again, taking her last breath with it. A deep calm settled over the loch, so deep Shona felt like she could hear the racing heartbeats of the people around her.

Padraigin fell dead and lifeless to the surface of the water.

The queen drummed her fingers on the bright, icy surface of the arm of her throne, looking disappointed. "The world has indeed fallen while I slept. Is there nowhere to find worthy servants any more?"

Padraigin slid beneath the surface of the water without a ripple, and it sealed behind her, as if she had never been.

Queen Dreokt turned to Shona and beckoned her closer. "My dear child, it's time we have a little chat."

25

AN UNEXPECTED JOURNEY

Shona stumbled forward and nearly fell to her knees as she curtsied before Queen Dreokt. Her heart raced so fast it felt on the verge of leaping right out of her chest. She found it hard to breathe, and her limbs quivered with terror. The memory of Padraigin hanging helpless in the queen's power kept playing through her mind, and she felt like she was about to be sick.

No. She refused to collapse into a heap like some commoner. Could she, a high lady of Obrion face her fate with less dignity than Padraigin had? Forcing herself to take a deep breath, she rose and met the queen's penetrating gaze.

Queen Dreokt gave her the barest of approving nods. "My dear Shona, I should not feel surprised by your creativity nor by your courage in daring my wrath by intercepting those foolish boys."

"Please accept my apology if I in any way offended you, my queen. It was not my intention." She felt a thrill of pride that her voice did not shake.

Queen Dreokt's mind slithered across Shona's thoughts in a now-familiar touch, but this time it lingered longer than it had in the past. Her influence crawled into Shona's mind, digging beneath her scattered, unfocused surface thoughts.

Her heart began to race again, but she refused to even think about her screaming terror, or the desperate desire to flee. Images began flashing behind her eyes.

Memories.

Shona couldn't suppress a gasp as the queen's glowing eyes seemed to consume her vision. Her face became super-imposed over the memories flashing quickly past. After several seconds, one image rose above the others and hung in her mind, unmoving.

Connor.

Queen Dreokt rose and approached. Shona did not dare move, did not dare even wonder what form her fate would take. She forced herself to stand erect, outwardly calm, even though in her mind she stared at Connor's face. She couldn't even let herself wish to be with him one more time.

The queen paced around her and the silent scrutiny ratcheted up Shona's fear.

Then abruptly, Queen Dreokt grinned, looking pleased, as if she'd just learned a wonderful secret. "You are even more interesting than I thought, child."

She settled back to her icy throne and her influence evaporated from Shona's mind. Shona remained rooted in place, not sure what had just happened, or whether or not she was in trouble.

"Oh, relax, child," the queen said, making a shooing gesture. "All that formality rankles sometimes."

Shona tried to relax, but what did the queen want her to do? She couldn't just sprawl on the surface of the water. The thought of looking down into those dark blue depths and maybe spotting Padraigin's body floating beneath the surface sent a fresh shudder of horror creeping up her spine.

"Patronage is such a silly thing, but I can see the reasons why it was implemented. Clever, really. The commoners are kept in line but can still be harvested for powerful gifts. That is one way to build better Petralists, I suppose. With what knowledge remained available, it does make sense. Perhaps I should have shared more." She laughed, as if finding that extremely funny.

"Yes, Your Majesty," Shona said, but the queen seemed to have spoken to herself, as if she had entirely forgotten Shona was there. The words encouraged her. Maybe somehow she would survive after all.

As her fear ebbed just a bit, she started wondering what the queen meant. What other information had been lost? What other ways might there be to build better Petralists?

Queen Dreokt's gaze snapped to Shona and their piercing intensity took her breath away as always. "You were the boy Connor's patron. You held sway over his life, planned to marry and control his gift."

She spoke with no trace of question in her tone, but Shona still felt obligated to nod. "Yes, my queen."

"Yes, he has potential but needs much guidance. Needs molding to become a worthy servant." She nodded her head, as if reaching a decision, and declared, "I approve. You shall have Connor. He is your duty, yours to mold and present as a worthy servant."

"Thank you," Shona said, curtsying again, trying not to show her confusion. "But he is gone, and he is promised to another." The words seemed to cling to her mouth like molten caramel and she barely got them out.

"Posh. I saw the strumpet he claims to love. His mind was sodden with her, but she is a Builder and must be executed. I'll bring the foolish lands back to heel as I did before. Then you shall have him and you shall prepare him."

Maybe the queen wasn't so bad, after all. Could she really remove Verena and give Shona another chance to win Connor's heart? She felt confident she could win him back, heart and soul, if given but a little time. Thinking about Connor helped her not think about Padraigin or about the constant terror she lived in. With Connor, maybe she could find a way to be happy.

The queen's other words finally registered and Shona dared ask, "Please forgive my ignorance, but will you please explain, my queen? You said you brought the lands to the north to heel in the past. I thought they were always part of the Obrioner empire."

Queen Dreokt laughed heartily. "Such foolish thoughts cling to this land. It's like everyone reverted to helpless children while I slept. Of course these lands were not all united. My husband and I took them all when we arrived. We introduced Petralist powers, founded the first quarries even as we took Obrion as our home and conquered the other foolish nations that clung to this disappointing little continent like barbarians."

She rose and finished in an angry shout, one fist half-raised, with flames and water dancing around it. "We brought peace to the entire land, raised them to greatness, and how do they repay me? They revolt and forget everything!"

Shona took a fearful step back and stammered, "Please forgive me. I didn't know."

The queen's rage evaporated as quickly as it arrived and she waved off Shona's apology and resumed her seat. "Of course you couldn't know, child. The only people who knew were dead or sleeping."

Shona wanted to ask for more details, but didn't dare. Sleeping? In that one brief ranting monologue, the queen had offered unprecedented glimpses into the nation's history. She knew so much, but could Shona get her to share more without triggering a new rage?

"I wonder if Kilian knew any of the history," she ventured.

Queen Dreokt huffed derisively. "My son is such a wastrel and a rebellious young man. I shouldn't be surprised he let things get so bad."

Shona blinked, the only outward sign she allowed herself to express her surprise. She knew Kilian was old, but hadn't known the true extent of his history. Connor must know, but he had withheld the information.

The queen's expression turned thoughtful. "I'll have to bring Kilian to task for his many crimes, but this land has fallen to squalor. Are there no worthy servants?" Her voice trailed off and she abruptly rose and focused on Shona.

"My child, go fetch some warm travel clothes. You and I are going on a journey."

"I'm honored," Shona managed, even though the thought of enduring any journey in the queen's presence terrified her.

Her father took a step closer and bowed low. Shona had completely forgotten that he stood close by the entire time. "May I inquire as to your destination, my liege?"

"That is my business. You're in charge while we're gone. This nation has fallen into disrepair, and I am wearied by the ignorance and weakness of my Petralists. Your daughter will come help me change that."

High Lord Dougal gave Shona a proud smile, but she wanted to protest. Did the queen plan to go after Connor so soon? Would she dare chase him and Kilian into the heart of Granadure?

Would she finally rid the world of that harlot, Verena?

Shona made a deep curtsy. "I am yours to command, my queen."

26

ONLY TRUE FRIENDS WILL BEAT YOU
SENSELESS

The sleek underwater Slide slipped like a wraith up the Macantact River, a part of Connor, like an extra watery limb. Every gleaming inch felt like an extension of his skin. Immersing himself so deep into water that he felt more part of the river than one of the people riding in comfortable chairs on the deck helped him escape the maddening hunger for porphyry. Water walked close by his side, her arm around his waist, her presence supportive and comforting.

Leaving Donleavy had taken every bit of self-control he could scrounge up, assisted by a healthy dose of empathy from Student Eighteen. They hadn't dared pause long enough for her to try burying his porphyry memories while they still lingered in the capital.

The trip down the mountain in the speedcaravan went blessedly fast and uneventfully, even though every compartment was packed with nobility and couriers who had found valid excuses to escape the city. Many others had watched the speedcaravan pull away from the terminal with longing glances.

Once they escaped the outskirts of Belmullet, Connor had formed another Slide and drew them under the protective blanket of the river. They had barely surfaced in the past two days, pushing on past Crann toward Merkland. Connor was beginning to dread the end of their trip when they would leave the river and he'd need to return to himself and the pangs of porphyry withdrawal.

Ivor seemed content to travel in silence. He had passed the time brooding, no doubt thinking of Alyth. Connor could not imagine him wallowing in misery, though. Ivor would also be searching his memory for clues that might identify a weakness they could exploit against the queen.

Connor had tried to do the same, but had found little to feel encouraged about. He and Ivor together could wield enough power to intimidate most armies, but the queen had toyed with them like new pets. Worse, his fuzzy memory of the final moment before the queen inexplicably left them still hadn't clarified. How had they driven her away?

It seemed beyond reason that she she considered them such minimal threats that she'd simply decided not to kill them. Then again, she'd proven she was well and truly cracked. When he tried discussing the question, Ivor confirmed his memories were fuzzy too, but didn't want to talk about it. Connor hoped Kilian had some ideas, because they needed some badly.

Student Eighteen spent the bulk of the journey in busy conversation with herself. Sometimes her words became audible, and it was fascinating to glimpse how the many women sharing her head managed to get along. They were all very different, and Connor was glad they found ways to coexist. If she suffered an internal revolution and started pummeling herself, Connor was not sure what they could do to help. Even tying her up wouldn't stop the fighting inside her head.

Could one personality kill another, like the queen had done to poor Aifric? Connor shuddered at the thought.

"We should stop in Merkland," Ivor said abruptly, breaking the long silence.

"I'm not sure that's a great idea," Connor said.

"We need to speak with Rory. The queen is consolidating her power far too quickly. It's past time to get our revolution moving."

Student Eighteen asked, "So you want to start with the commanding general of one of the most powerful armies in Obrion?"

Ivor nodded. "Rory needs to know. We don't have time to creep around in the shadows. If we delay, the queen will beat the entire nation into submission and lock it down so tight we'll have no chance of opposing her. We'll be playing a defensive war from day one, and that's no way to win."

Connor said, "There has to be a way to counter her. When we find it, we need to be ready to strike. We're going to need an army for that."

Student Eighteen asked, "So how do you propose we enter the city? I can slip in undetected, but you two are not exactly stealthy."

Connor said, "I say we walk in through the main gate."

He expected Ivor to complain about how stupid that idea was, but Ivor only grunted and returned to his brooding. That said plenty about the state of his mind. He really was in deep mourning for Alyth.

Connor wasn't sure how to comfort him, and thinking of Alyth's broken mind got him thinking again how dangerously similar Verena's condition might be. The very first thing he'd do when they returned to Altkalen would be to try reaching her with chert.

He surfaced the Slide a couple miles south of Merkland, just as afternoon was fading into twilight. As soon as they reached the road, Student

Eighteen saluted, then trotted away. She seemed to melt into the early evening shadows. Connor did not worry about her. She'd show up if they needed her, and no doubt she would pick up at least as much information as they did.

Snow blanketed the area in pristine white. As they followed the wide road north, along the river, beside the speedcaravan track, Connor surveyed the flat-topped bluff of Merkland that rose steeply above the countryside along the western flank of the river. Even in the shadows, the famous, towering, white-granite walls of the city seemed to glow.

He caught glimpses of figures moving along the battlements, the soldiers looking tiny in the distance until he tapped quartzite to improve his vision. The guards looked alert, but bored. Good. That would reduce the level of scrutiny they'd receive as they entered. Connor didn't feel like fighting an army. He just wanted dinner, a warm fire, and a chance to chat with Rory, and hopefully Tomas and Cameron. Their easy banter would help tremendously.

A sizable township clustered along the eastern banks of the river, directly across from the main city. Connor hadn't paid it much attention before, but as he and Ivor approached, he studied it. Many piers extended into the river, with barges and boats of all sizes tied up with frost-coated hawsers. Even a few large ships, complete with furled sails, banged softly against their protective leather moorings. Many long warehouses fronted the river, with rows of multi-story dwellings clustered close together behind them.

It made sense to keep workers and merchants involved in the busy river trade closer to the river. That saved the need to transport everything around to one of the gates on the opposite sides of the city. The bluff rearing high above the river denied all direct access from that side.

A chill breeze blew south from the Maclaclan Mountains, and Connor glanced in that direction, as if he could see all the way to the towering, broken peak of Mount Macduib. If he max-tapped basalt, he could reach Verena before morning.

The temptation was nearly overpowering, but he reined it in. Spreading the truth about patronage was his duty and he was eager to finally share the truth with Rory.

Just south of the high-walled city, the road split. To the right, it crossed a wide, stone bridge across the Macantact to the township. To the left, it curved around the flank of the city toward the nearest of several huge gates set into the immense outer wall.

The speedcaravan track continued straight, rising on an elevated ramp over the road, then higher still, all the way to the top of the bluff. It plunged through a tunnel in the wall, currently closed with a heavy iron portcullis.

As Connor circled around the city with Ivor, he studied those famous white walls of Alasdair granite. They formed an octagonal shape, with massive gates set into the sections facing the eastern and northern sides where the ground rose to meet the bluff.

Ivor nodded to the first gate, already closed for the evening. "That's the Army Gate. Barracks and officer's quarters are concentrated in that quadrant of the city."

"How do you know that?" Connor had glimpsed Merkland from afar several times, but knew little about his own high lord's capital.

Ivor shook his head. "Never ceases to amaze me how little you know. In my years prepping for the Tir-raon, I studied all the realms. We spent weeks on Merkland and High Lord Dougal."

"So tell me about the city," Connor urged, happy to see his friend willing to talk, although it rankled to think Ivor knew more it than he did.

"Did you know the North Gate is also known as the Trade Gate because it's closest to the north bridge that connects to the other side of the township?"

"I didn't."

"That quadrant of the city holds more warehouses, markets, mansions of wealthier merchants, and the guild halls. Then there's the northwestern Farmer's Gate. It leads to the market square and a quadrant of tenement buildings for workers and craftsmen. Not an area I plan to spend much time."

"Until I left Alasdair, I probably would have thought it grand," Connor said.

"I doubt it. In Alasdair you had space, clean homes, and adequate streets."

"I'll take your word for it."

"That leaves the West Gate, often called the Curadh Gate." Ivor pointed ahead to the huge gate in the next section of wall. It was still open, flanked by a dozen tall lantern poles and many torches along the wall and the gatehouse just inside. Despite the hour, steady traffic continued. People bundled against the cold hurried in and out, on foot, mounted, or riding wagons and carriages.

"That's the main avenue leading past the higher-end markets and residences of all the minor lords and ladies. Leads to the main city square which is flanked by the mansions of more important lords and the city administration offices. The palace takes up the entire eastern quadrant."

"How do you want to do this?" Connor asked, suddenly second-guessing his plan. Merkland at a distance was a striking sight. Merkland up close was intimidating.

Ivor grinned. "Too late to change course now."

He led the way, marching purposefully to the Curadh Gate and the guards stationed there inspecting everyone who entered. The hard-packed earthen road transitioned to paving stones at the gate, and Connor caught a whiff of fresh-baked bread. The smell set his stomach rumbling.

Dinner definitely needed to play a big part in their meeting with Rory.

A big, grizzled guard, his face red from the cold, glanced at them as they approached. Then he looked again, a disbelieving grin spreading across his face. "Commander Ivor?"

"At ease, soldier," Ivor said calmly.

The man snapped a salute. "Yes, sir. But, sir, I heard you were lost at Altkalen."

"It's been a long journey home. I need to speak with General Rory."

"Yes, sir!"

Ivor glanced at Connor and allowed a little smile to tug up the corner of his mouth. "It's good to be recognized."

"I'm glad they recognized you and not me." Connor had stood against the men of Obrion during the invasion. If they remembered him, things might get ugly.

The guard ushered them through the gate, shouting to his companions that Commander Ivor had returned. They quickly took up the cry, many of them rushing to congratulate him on his safe return. The crowd grew quickly until over a hundred soldiers packed the road between a couple of stone-walled buildings, effectively penning them in. Connor kept his head down and tried to act like nothing more than a simple traveling companion.

Of course everyone asked what happened, and although Ivor kept his comments brief, they cheered to hear he'd escaped the evil Grandurians. As they slowly made their way up the packed boulevard, throngs of people poured into the streets to cheer. Eventually Ivor convinced a captain that a military escort to the general would help a lot.

It did. Their progress accelerated as the soldiers formed up and ordered everyone to make way.

"This won't exactly be a low-key meeting," Ivor muttered to Connor as he waved to the cheering townsfolk who seemed eager for something to celebrate.

"It'll get Rory's attention, for sure." Maybe such a grand entrance wasn't smart, but Connor had learned that if they couldn't do something smart, they might as well do something stupid with as much flair as possible. Sometimes it worked.

Tomas and Cameron met them at the point where the wide avenue emptied into an enormous square facing an inner wall and the majestic, many-tiered bulk of High Lord Dougal's main palace. They saluted Ivor, then glanced at each other before approaching Connor.

Tomas chuckled as he pounded Connor on the back. "Welcome back, lad. We weren't sure if we should salute you or put you in the stocks."

Cameron pounded Connor in turn and added, "But we decided it's too cold to wreck the palace tonight. Can you at least wait until our shift ends?"

"It's good to see you two," Connor told them honestly. "I promise not to break anything as long as I get a hot dinner."

"Done!" They said in unison. Tomas added, "You've lost your touch, Connor. You could have bartered for a whole lot more than one dinner."

"Don't give him ideas," Cameron hissed. "He took the whole army last time we encouraged him."

"But captain was only captain then. Now he's general."

"Bigger title means bigger army to steal, muffin-for-brains," Cameron said, as if that was obvious.

Connor smiled. Their easygoing, irreverent presence always helped him relax. His many troubles seemed a little less terrible when he could laugh at them with the unflappable duo. Then again, their comments were starting to make other nearby soldiers seem nervous. Some of them started casting worried glances at Connor, as if he really might pull an elfonnel out of his shorts.

"I'm not planning to steal another army on this trip," Connor assured them.

Tomas thumbed his nose and gave Connor a knowing wink. "A reconnoitering mission, eh?"

"And you said he couldn't be taught new tricks," Cameron added.

"He can. You can't. You still think smiling at a lady with that ugly face is a good idea."

"Last time I talked with Connor's girl, Verena, she didn't even flinch."

"She's in a coma. Delayed reaction."

They fell to bickering and calling each other increasingly colorful names as they escorted Connor and Ivor across the square, through the inner gate, and into the palace's main entrance. Connor had seen many impressive palaces, and Dougal's rivaled the best of them. The central palace reared five stories above the inner court, lined with marble columns, with tall windows between them.

The doors opened into an enormous, vaulted great hall, with walls trimmed in gold, silver, and Dougal's colors of blue and green. Word of Ivor's return had preceded them and the halls were lined with people, both noble and linn, soldiers and servants, all excitedly welcoming him home.

While Ivor paused to wave, Connor scanned the area. He didn't see anything threatening. The people looked genuinely happy to greet Ivor. As usual, he'd captured the hearts of his forces.

A grand staircase rose to the third level above them, while huge hallways led into the northern and southern wings. Connor caught glimpses of beautiful statues and paintings lining the halls behind the crowds, while a chandelier hung over the stairway, blazing with enough light to make it feel like midday. Its glittering crystals seemed to magnify the light source, which had to be generated by a Solas.

The palace was comfortably warm, but Connor spotted only a few heat braziers. Dougal must have a Firetongue on staff responsible for keeping the temperature comfortable. He wondered how often things got accidentally burned. He couldn't think of a single Firetongue he'd met who would enjoy such a mundane duty without going a little wild.

Ivor grumbled at Tomas, "Did you two bring us through here just to parade us around? I bet Rory's really waiting in the military command building."

Connor had assumed the military command would reside in the central palace.

Tomas said, "Usually he'd be there, but he should be wrapping up a meeting with the lesser nobles, and he's got another meeting with Lord Nevan in a few minutes."

Cameron grimaced and rubbed one temple. "By the Tallan's bad memory, never imagined we'd have to keep track of so many meetings. So much thinking dulls the reflexes."

Tomas nodded agreement. "Good thing we work together. We can share the load, keep from overloading the brain muscles."

They eventually led Connor and Ivor to a spacious room on the fourth floor. Limestone lanterns hung on the tapestry-lined walls, while a long, gleaming wooden table occupied most of the floor space. Two dozen velvet-padded chairs stood in formation around the table, with General Rory alone sitting at the head.

The sight of Rory triggered a smile and a flood of memories. He'd helped teach Connor his first lessons about his affinity, battlefield strategy, and fighting. Rory was a good man, a treasured friend, and hopefully soon, a key player in their revolution.

Rory rose, his hard, craggy face actually cracking into a smile.

Ivor saluted. "Returning from duty, General."

Rory returned the salute. "How did you get out of Granadure? And where are the rest of my troops?"

"It's just me for today, but the rest will be coming soon, I wager."

Rory shook hands with Ivor, then with Connor. "I can't imagine you two simply sneaking out of Altkalen, but if you had leveled the city, you would've brought everyone else with you."

"We're sort of on a secret mission," Connor said.

Rory raised an eyebrow. "Working together?"

Ivor shrugged. "There's a peace accord in place, so why not?"

Rory gestured them to take seats. "So if you're on a secret mission, why create such an uproar here in Merkland?"

No sense using a little hammer when a big one could do the job faster. They had left subtlety behind in the queen's palace, so Connor said, "It's more fun to start a revolution with a bang."

"A revolution? Are you here to destroy Merkland, then?" Rory didn't show any outward concern, but Tomas and Cameron exchanged knowing glances and made several gestures between them. Connor figured they were betting on how much destruction he'd cause.

Ivor shook his head. "This is more of a recruiting stop, you might say."

Rory gestured Tomas and Cameron from the room. They left reluctantly and Connor wondered why he bothered. Rory could never hide anything from them, and he'd need them on his side, but he'd figure that out soon enough.

After the door closed behind them, Rory said, "We've had that discussion."

"Not like this. Last time, you were under orders to invade Granadure. You were a captain, not a commanding general."

Rory chuckled. "I don't think I've ever heard of a commanding general defecting to the other side."

Ivor said, "More like defecting to the same side. We're on our way back from Donleavy."

That cracked his calm. "Are you boys mad? Reports suggest the queen is wreaking havoc among the nobility worse than any Grandurian army ever did."

Connor grimaced. "It's even worse than you've heard. If we give her much time, she'll either kill or mind-wipe everyone and lock the entire nation under her thumb."

He and Ivor spent a few minutes relating to Rory what they had experienced in Donleavy, how the queen mind-wiped her own people, her crazy insanity, and the warnings from Shona.

"At least Lady Shona is okay," Rory said, looking relieved.

"Too many others aren't. That's why we're here. Rory, you need to understand what you're fighting for," Ivor said angrily, gesturing to Connor. It was time to throw every stone on the table.

Connor said, "Rory, patronage is a lie. There is no curse, there are no unclaimed, and Guardians are enslaved by the nobility."

Rory rocked back in his chair as if struck, and looked like he didn't believe it. Connor did not blame him. The lie was so massive it defied understanding. It defined the lives of Guardians. Without it, the entire framework that they lived within evaporated.

Ivor said, "He's right, Rory. You saw Connor turn unclaimed at the Carraig."

"I saw something," Rory admitted slowly.

Connor said, "What you saw is what we now call rampagers. It has nothing to do with patronage, but everything to do with a secret power stone called porphyry."

As soon as he said it, the maddening, addiction-driven hunger seized hold of his mind and Connor groaned under a wave of agony that seared through his midsection. His muscles clenched and unreasoning rage swept through him. Before he realized what he was doing, he snatched up his chair and lifted it high to smash over the table.

Ivor grabbed the chair and said in an irritatingly soothing voice, "Connor, fight it. Stay in control."

For a moment they wrestled over the chair. Rory looked shocked. The initial wave of raging need subsided after another moment and Connor released the chair and staggered back. He was sweating heavily and breathing hard. His vision had gone blurry, and it was hard to think straight.

"Sorry," he stammered as he dropped into a chair with Ivor's help.

"What just happened?" Rory asked, his tone concerned.

Ivor said, "Porphyry. Connor's only used it a couple of times, but it's extremely addictive." He placed a comforting hand on Connor's shoulder. "We need to get you back to Kilian fast. Hopefully he'll know what to do."

Connor looked up and met Rory's concerned gaze. "It's real, Rory. Only the heads of houses know the secret that patronage is a lie, but only Dougal knows about porphyry. He spent years secretly building up an army of rampagers. We destroyed the last of them in Alasdair just before the earthquake."

"How—" Rory began, but the door opened and a grizzled, elderly man strode into the room.

Rory was supposed to be meeting with Lord Nevan, but this fellow was not Nevan. His gray hair was a little longer than military standard and his black eyes seemed shrouded in flickering shadows. Connor realized he must be a Pathfinder. He did not look surprised to see them, nor did he look concerned that he had just barged in on the commanding general.

Had he heard their conversation?

Rory didn't bother hiding his annoyance. "What do you want, Craigroy?"

The newcomer pointed at Connor. "I want him, of course. His service to our high lord is past due, and I am here to collect him."

Connor welcomed any challenge that helped take his mind off porphyry. He rose slowly, hating his quivering muscles and shaking hands. "You're either remarkably optimistic, or remarkably stupid. Doesn't really matter which. I'm planning on killing High Lord Dougal, not serving him."

Rory said, "Connor, this is Craigroy, head of High Lord Dougal's intelligence network. He thinks highly of himself, but has never interrupted one of my meetings before.

Craigroy gave Rory a confident smile. "You command the army, General. I do not report to you."

"And I don't live in your dark webs of intrigue," Rory said, his expression unfriendly. "I thought we agreed to stay out of each other's business."

"Until now, our business has not overlapped." Craigroy swept his dark-eyed gaze over Connor and smiled again. "I heard you're brave, and

I applaud your resilience. Most people I've known who've fallen under the grip of porphyry would've been reduced to blubbering, pathetic wrecks by now. They were some of the mightiest Petralists in the kingdom, but no one beats porphyry."

"That's why there are so few Agor," Connor guessed with sudden understanding. "Dougal took all the children with the most powerful gifts from birth. That's where he got his rampagers, like my uncle."

Craigroy nodded. "It's refreshing to find a servant who can think once in a while."

He noted Rory's surprised expression and said, "Yes, I'm afraid what they revealed to you is true. Connor will keep the secret once I take him into service. You and Commander Ivor are bound by your oaths to our mutual high lord, and I expect you to maintain the secret for national security reasons."

Connor took an angry step toward the irritating old man, embracing the rage still thundering through him. "I told you I'm not serving you. Since you seem to think you represent Dougal, I'm thinking you deserve the same treatment."

Ivor looked ready to help, but Craigroy did not look nervous. He simply held up his left hand and opened his fist, revealing what he'd held clenched inside.

Porphyry.

Half a dozen tiny grains of the purplish powder glinted in the lantern light. They seemed to seize Connor's mind and he howled like an animal and leaped forward to snatch them up.

Craigroy pulled his fist behind his back and cried, "Stop!"

Connor paused a quivering stride away, hands outstretched, barely restraining the urge to rip the man apart. He could, but that might scatter the precious porphyry. He couldn't risk it. Not yet.

Craigroy said in a commanding tone, "I will give this to you, boy, but not until you drop to your knees and swear fealty to High Lord Dougal. Then you get enough every day to keep the beast under control."

Connor seized him by the throat and tapped granite. He gloried in the itchy-crawly feeling of his curse blossoming out through his body and strengthening his muscles. It paled in comparison to the ultimate glory of rampager power, but it was more than enough to crush out the life of the man keeping that powder from him.

Connor hissed, "You fool. I'll just take it from your dead fingers."

Craigroy's eyes bulged and he pried uselessly against Connor's stone-hardened grip. Fear glinted in his eyes, but he managed to croak, "Think, boy. What I have is barely a taste, not even enough to quell the pain tormenting you for a day. If you kill me, you'll never find more, and you'll die in more pain than anyone you've ever known."

Connor wanted to crush him, rip his head right off. His lips curled back into a snarl and his arm shook with the need to vent his fury, but he hesitated. A tiny flicker of reason held him in check.

Craigroy was right. He needed more.

"Kill him," Ivor said, his tone cold. He had circled around them and now stood between Craigroy and the door.

Connor couldn't take the chance. He dropped the man and retreated a pace, breathing fast, eyes glued to Craigroy's hand as it came back into view and lifted slowly toward him.

Ivor took a step forward, but Connor hissed, "Stay back!"

"But—"

"I'll deal with this," Connor snarled, his voice shaking with rage. Ivor looked torn, but hesitated, so Connor focused on Craigroy and begged, "Give it to me."

"Kneel," Craigroy commanded, looking absolutely confident that he now owned Connor.

Connor laughed. The sound came out hysterical and high-pitched, and it visibly rattled Craigroy. His confident expression wavered, but he commanded again, "Kneel!"

The need for the porphyry was like a living thing ripping at Connor's innards. He couldn't endure it long. The thought of leaving now, of facing the long journey back into Granadure with no hope whatsoever of quenching his need made him want to whimper like a chained animal. No, he couldn't just leave.

He'd take all of Craigroy's stash with him. "You forget who you're dealing with. I have ways of making you tell me what I want to know." He did, right? Thinking through the haze of porphyry need was like running fracked through a fog. He couldn't quite see what he was doing.

Was he planning to pretend to swear fealty? He could leave once he got more. No, somehow he sensed that once he took another full measure of porphyry he'd never again muster the willpower to deny that need. If he surrendered now, he was accepting a chain he could never break.

There was something he could do, some other affinity he could use? But he didn't want to use anything but porphyry.

Craigroy must have sensed his confusion because his smile returned and he opened his mouth to speak.

Ivor didn't give him the chance. He calmly slugged Craigroy in the side of the head. Craigroy never saw it coming, and the granite-enhanced blow threw him off his feet, across the room, and into the wood-paneled wall.

The tiny grains of porphyry went flying.

Connor caught sight of them for a second, glittering in the lantern light as they sprayed across the room. He shouted with despair and lunged after them.

Ivor intercepted him with a much harder curse-punch. He caught

Connor in the stomach and the blow lifted him off his feet. Air exploded from his lungs, and his innards burned for a new reason.

Ivor helped him straighten up.

He coughed, "Why?"

Ivor winked. "Just returning a favor."

He curse-punched Connor in the chin.

All the lights went out.

27

AN UNWORTHY SERVANT

With a remarkably soft rush of air, Shona touched down slightly behind Queen Dreokt. The rich, frozen soil of southern Obrion stretched away in every direction, cluttered with rotting, broken stalks of grain from the recent harvest. They had crossed half the kingdom, supported only by a warm cushion of air, as fast as Connor might hope to fly in one of those infernal Builder flying machines.

They'd flown so far, so fast, for this?

Shona glanced around in confusion at the boring farmlands, empty of any sort of human habitation. She'd never visited the vast fields of High Lord Lenox's agriculture-heavy realm before. Now that she saw it, she was happy she'd never wasted the time. She couldn't see any mountains, saw no rocks at all. How did people live in places like that? Why had Queen Dreokt brought them there?

Shona glanced at the queen, who was dressed for travel in a purple skirt, split for riding, a snow-white linen blouse, and a leather jacket with ornate, golden filigree worked all over. Shona had opted to wear her battle leathers. She had no idea where they were going or what they might be doing, and she refused to enter a potential battlefield unprepared.

That desolate field was no battlefield.

She couldn't even see anyone who might have witnessed their unique form of arrival. Shona had always thought Petralist flight was virtually impossible. It wasn't impossible for Queen Dreokt. She wielded the unruly currents of air as easily as Shona might throw Verena off a cliff using granite. Air had held them aloft, as if sitting together on an invisible couch as it hurtled through the air, protected in a bubble of warmth and calm.

During the journey, Queen Dreokt had acted downright bored and spent the time asking Shona about the various realms and the high lords and ladies who ruled them. Shona doubted she was actually interested in the information, which she had probably already pulled directly from Shona's mind, the mind of her father, and others in Donleavy. That meant she was interested in Shona's interpretation of the current political situation and the families that ruled across the kingdom.

She had silently thanked her father for educating her so thoroughly in politics, intrigue, and the complex economics that supported the many semi-independent realms that made up Obrion. She had no idea what the queen thought of her answers and analysis, but she did not strike Shona down for making a wrong answer. That suggested she might be doing all right.

It was by far the longest period of time that Shona had ever seen the queen not flip abruptly between widely different emotional states. Perhaps after so many years of slumber the queen needed a little more alone time to gather her thoughts and grow accustomed to returning to humanity.

Queen Dreokt turned to look back at her. "You may have a point, child, but do you really think it wise to try analyzing my psychological state?"

The queen's unexpected question caught Shona by surprise and she started, retreating half a step and tapping granite before catching herself.

Queen Dreokt gave her an approving nod. "Good defensive reflexes, suggesting a strong survival instinct. Very appropriate for one in your position."

"Thank you, Your Majesty," Shona said, feeling weak with relief.

Queen Dreokt looked satisfied as she paced around the empty field. A chill breeze crept along the hardened furrows of soil, carrying a faint scent of dry plants. The queen stopped after a few steps and stretched forth a hand. The earth beneath it rose in a delicate column. She grasped it and her expression turned thoughtful.

Shona wondered what they were doing in that barren valley. Queen Dreokt had spoken of the need for worthy servants, but not even the farmers lived within sight of that remote field.

"Youth are so impatient. You will learn something today, girl. I seek an ancient servant who has slumbered with the elements for a very long time."

"An elfonnel?" Shona asked nervously as she glanced around at the empty landscape. Her memories of elfonnel were among the most terrifying of her life. Her father might have mastered the trick to controlling them at least part of the time, but Shona lacked that knowledge.

"Have no fear, child. We are in no danger," the queen said, her voice distracted.

"I've heard theories that slumbering elfonnel generate power stone, that's why they've been found at quarries," Shona dared say. She didn't want to interrupt or anger the queen, but if they were seeking elfonnel, maybe the question would help the queen realize she'd come to the wrong place.

"They do, but we seek a special case."

That shouldn't have surprised Shona. Information that quarries might shelter long-slumbering elfonnel was a remarkable discovery, but the queen was already moving past that to a special case. She suppressed a flash of irritation. The woman possessed so much knowledge that Shona yearned to know. That knowledge might help her understand her liege and her place with the woman better. It might help her survive a little longer too.

"There's really an elfonnel hidden beneath a farm field?"

"Indeed. Tristan was one of my first and greatest servants, a brilliant researcher who assisted in our first grand discoveries in harvesting magic." A little smile played across her lips. "Dear Tristan was one of my husband's closest friends. Those two worked miracles together in the early days of our work."

Shona listened in rapt attention, silently willing the queen to reveal more about those early days, how they first learned to tap Petralist powers, and where they came from.

But the moment passed and the queen's smile vanished. "I sent him to slumber with the elements when we first arrived in this backwater continent. His unique gifts made him the ideal candidate. This location conceals a nexus of magic deep within the earth and his presence served to disrupt the flow of energy through these lands."

She giggled to herself, like a little girl hiding in the cupboard with a jar of fresh-baked cookies. "That's the key. The disrupted energy scatters and settles into the stones. Only then can we harvest the power, distilled to its lowest frequency, through the stones to fuel our affinities."

"How is it that no one else knows this?" Shona breathed. The magnitude of that short explanation boggled the mind. So much history had been lost.

Queen Dreokt chuckled. "Most people can't remember what they had for dinner a week ago. How do you expect them to remember deeper truths?"

"But why has no one thought to explore such a nexus of power?"

"No one knows about it. Only one attuned to a higher frequency can sense it."

"I don't understand," Shona admitted, feeling frustrated by the unusual sense of ignorance.

"Of course you don't," the queen's laughter vanished and her tone turned deadly serious. "And you won't. Not until you prove that you can guard well the treasure of information I just entrusted to you."

"I'll guard it with my life," Shona insisted quickly, hating the rush of fear she felt. Hating more that the queen had shaken off those old memories so quickly.

"See that you do. One secret is more than enough of a trial for an ambitious young woman like yourself." Her expression turned kind and motherly. "Show yourself worthy and perhaps I will speak more on the matter. My old memories are still fuddled from the long sleep, so I find it helpful to talk through these things."

"I am honored to offer any service I can," Shona said, eager to hear more.

Again the queen's mood shifted back to deadly sincerity. "Should you betray my trust, I will wipe your memories of this conversation and take away that which you hold most dear."

"Connor?" Shona gasped. The thought of losing him again shook her deeply, especially since she honestly believed the queen intended to kill Verena and give him to her.

Queen Dreokt snorted in disgust. "Think deeper, child. Men can be replaced. I speak of your affinities."

Shona opened her mouth in silent protest, but couldn't find the words to express the horror she felt at the thought of losing her precious affinities. They defined her, played a crucial role in who she was and who she planned to become. Losing them would make her so . . . common.

The queen watched her carefully. "I see you understand."

"May I ask how you can affect the affinities of others?" Shona ventured.

Queen Dreokt laughed with delight. "Oh, you are indeed a treasure, girl. Such ambition in one so young warms my soul." Her smile vanished again and she said. "Enough prattling. I've found him."

The slender pillar of earth connecting her hand to the ground dissolved and the queen threw her arms out wide. Orange flames erupted around her left hand, while bubbling streamers of water materialized around her right. The two streams of elements arced over her head, twining together into a glittering rope. That arc of twined elements flowed with intricate patterns that moved along its length. A subtle scent of baked sunflower seeds mixed with the smell of sun-warmed stone right after a brief summer shower.

"Tristan. Tristan. Tristan. Awake and come forth." The queen spoke softly, but the words somehow echoed around the empty field, growing in strength until her voice boomed like rolling thunder.

"Tristan! Tristan! Tristan! Awake!"

Shona covered her ears with her hands, but that did little to silence the still-growing crescendo that hammered at her mind until the words seemed to shout inside her thoughts rather than merely pummel her ears from the outside.

Abruptly the queen clapped her hands together, sending the arcing rope of water and fire, with their intricate symbols, shooting into the air.

The elements then plunged down into the earth, driving deep, like a spear piercing water toward the heart of an unsuspecting fish.

As soon as that spear of water and fire disappeared into the ground, the sounds ceased, leaving the land huddled in a deep, expectant calm. Queen Dreokt cocked her head to one side, as if listening, but Shona heard nothing. She wanted to ask what was happening, but didn't dare make a sound.

"Tristan," Queen Dreokt whispered and extended a hand.

The ground in front of her exploded. Earth erupted in every direction and pelted Shona so hard she staggered. She spat out a clump of earth, but the taste of the rich soil clung to her mouth.

She didn't have time to spit again. A geyser of white-hot flame burst up from underground, instantly turning the air searing hot and nearly blinding Shona. She stumbled farther back, raising her hands to shield her face from the light and the heat.

Queen Dreokt did not move, did not seem affected by the unexpected onslaught of elements. She waited as the flames soared over a hundred feet in the air and the sound grew from a nerve-tingling roar to a whistling scream that set Shona's hair standing on end. The air smelled charred and somehow old.

The flames curled back upon themselves and plunged down toward Queen Dreokt. The leading edge of the fire transformed into the rough shape of a demon-like head, complete with horns, fangs, and slitted, crimson eyes.

Shona's fear escalated into full-blown terror. This was an elfonnel. Fire-bound. And it didn't look happy.

Queen Dreokt spread her arms and laughed, as if she planned to embrace a long-lost friend.

The elfonnel opened its enormous mouth wide, the flames expanding until its head was over a dozen feet in diameter. Shona dove away as that enormous maw gaped wide and plunged down over the queen. Flames swept out in every direction, whipping past Shona with the scent of rotten eggs and burned toast. She shrieked and clutched her hair. She'd experienced getting her hair burned more than once, usually Connor's fault, and hated to think of it happening again.

Luckily the flames ignored her hair and instead flowed into the constantly shifting form of the elfonnel's body. For a second it looked roughly humanoid, then morphed into a four-legged monster.

Shona huddled at its feet, eyes glued to where its face still pressed down to the earth. Could it have really killed the queen like that? If it was eating her, it would kill Shona next. She felt surprised to realize she'd lived in such a constant fear of death that after the initial fear of the elfonnel, her terror actually subsided, replaced by growing curiosity.

"Are you all right, Your Majesty?" Shona shouted over the loud crackling of flames.

The elfonnel lifted its head, which transformed into the shape of a nuall hunting cat. Queen Dreokt stood exactly where Shona had last seen her. She looked undamaged, not even singed by the flames, although tears glistened on her cheeks. She petted the elfonnel's smaller head and sighed, then beckoned Shonoa closer.

Shona rose and hesitantly obeyed. Standing so close, she expected to feel overwhelmed by the heat, the sound, and the stench, but she instead stepped into a pocket of clean, calm air that wrapped the queen like a protective bubble.

"Is this Tristan?" Shona asked, her parched throat making her voice rough.

Queen Dreokt sighed. "Alas, poor Tristan has slumbered too long. That which connected him to his mortal self is gone. He cannot return." She leaned her forehead against the elfonnel's head, and its body shrank to the size of a horse, but still in the shape of a nuall. It purred and nuzzled her, as if seeking to comfort her.

The sight unnerved Shona. The queen really was the master of the elements.

"I fear there are no worthy servants left, none who would answer my call," Queen Dreokt said softly. She gripped the elfonnel's face, unaffected by the flames and looked into its crimson eyes. "Show me the others."

It lunged forward, its face flattening as it wrapped around her head.

Shona gasped and stumbled back, but the queen did not move, did not struggle as the flames wrapping her head shifted from crimson to blue. Heat intensified around their protective bubble, and Shona crept closer to the strange sight. If she accidentally stepped outside that sphere, she'd melt away before she could return.

Queen Dreokt abruptly threw her hands out wide, throwing the elfonnel away. Her expression had turned exultant, and she laughed in triumph. "Harley! One servant yet remains who may do my bidding!"

She laughed again and shooed the elfonnel away. "Return to your slumber, Tristan. Guard well your charge. I may call upon you to assist when I move against Kilian, but for now, remain concealed here."

The elfonnel swept up into the sky again, then plunged back into the earth, leaving only a charred hole in the ground to mark the spot. The field was blackened, but no doubt after the next snowfall, all trace of the encounter would be erased.

Queen Dreokt turned to Shona with a smile. "Come, my child. We have another stop to make."

Before Shona could reply, a gust of air swept out of the clear, blue sky and drew them gently off the ground.

PERHAPS THE FREAKIEST PLACE TO EVER WAKE UP

Connor awoke in darkness with a pounding headache and a raging fury. He tried lunging to his feet, but managed nothing more than to rattle the thick chains that bound him on his back. He lay in complete darkness on a hard bed. Maybe a board. When he tried rolling to test the limit of the chains, he bumped into wooden walls close beside him on both sides.

He was in a box.

Was it a coffin?

Had Rory deemed him a threat like all unclaimed and sentenced him to be buried alive?

Fear helped him collar a new rush of anger. It was hard to think rationally through the porphyry withdrawal madness, but he had to. If he was about to be buried alive with no power stones, he needed to figure out something to do.

He had to break free. Connor struggled harder, heaving at the steel links, trying to draw upon his granite strength, but found nothing. In fact, his muscles felt weak and lethargic. After a moment he realized he had slept with active granite in his system. He had not purged, so he was suffering untapped reversal sickness, which could debilitate him for a full day.

He did not plan to wait that long. His memories sharpened through the red haze of fury and he remembered Craigroy and the porphyry powder. He needed to get free, track that man down, and take that powder.

Struggling against the chains was useless in his current condition, so he shouted and cursed as he weakly rocked side to side. The box rocked a bit with him. That was surprising, and maybe hopeful. He wasn't interred already, but was he being carried to the burial site?

"Hey! I'm alive. Let me out of here!" he shouted, but received no answer.

He'd faced the possibility of death by burial by Sentries, but this was somehow worse. He wasn't in battle, wasn't pitting his affinity strength against another. He was powerless, a helpless victim. The thought enraged him. He had to think of something.

Sandstone. The sculpted sandstone pendant that he always wore around his neck could help.

It was gone.

That fueled another fit of rage, and he rattled the chains and screamed in fury.

Without warning, whoever was carrying the box dropped it. It fell three feet with a crash. Landing on those thick chain links hurt.

He grunted with pain, kicked his feet angrily against the bottom, and shouted, "Tallan curse you, I'll rip out your heart if you don't let me out!"

The top of the box flipped open, spilling fresh, cold air and brilliant sunshine inside and temporarily blinding him. He blinked up at two silhouetted figures who leaned in over him. It took a few seconds to recognize Ivor and Aifric, both wearing Boulder battle leathers.

"Welcome back to the land of the living," Ivor said with a smile.

"Student Eighteen said you were going to be all right, but she figures anyone she hasn't stabbed through the heart isn't dead enough," she said, in a deeper voice than Connor had ever heard her use.

When he spoke, his own voice rasped with thirst. "Please get me out of here."

Ivor shook his head, instead extended a canteen and helped Connor drink. "I don't think so. I can't trust you."

Connor snapped, "I'm in control. I just need some more porphyry from Craigroy. Help me track him down."

The unknown personality that was speaking through Student Eighteen's voice shook her head. "That sneaky Tallan-cursed devil fled before we even left Merkland. We're almost to the pass now."

"What? You let him get away?" Connor exclaimed, again struggling uselessly to free himself. "We have to go back. And who are you right now, anyway?"

"I'm Tresta. Best Boulder in High Lord Feichin's army."

That sounded about right. Aifric didn't waste time on humble or unremarkable personalities. He wanted to ask what mission she'd been created for.

Ivor said, "Rory insisted I let Craigroy go instead of killing him. I still think that would have been wiser, but not on your life are you returning to Merkland. I don't think you could withstand Craigroy's offer again. He almost owned you."

Tresta gave him a disgusted look. "Weak."

Connor felt too grumpy to listen to part of Aifric's fractured personality belittle him. "Really, I'm fine." It was an effort to keep his voice calm, but he managed it. He needed to escape that coffin. It really made him nervous. And knowing that porphyry was out of reach helped a little too.

Ivor and Tresta exchanged a glance and she nodded. "Mariora suggests it's worth the risk, and it would be unfortunate if we had to return this sorry excuse for a hero to Kilian in a box."

"What did I do to upset you?" Connor asked as Ivor produced a key and reached into the box to unlock his chains. He'd managed to get along with most of Aifric's personalities. With Aifric dead, it bothered him to think any of the rest of her didn't like him.

Tresta shrugged. "You showed weakness in the face of an enemy. Can't tolerate that or discipline goes out the window."

Her face shuddered slightly and she shifted to Student Eighteen's voice. "Aifric's loss is affecting us more than I care to admit. Tresta's anger is only partially directed at you."

She shuddered again, switching back to Tresta. "Aint my fault he's weak. I've seen comrades die before. I can handle it."

"You've never had one die inside your head, though," Connor said.

She snorted. "Worry about your own failures, weakling."

"There were some extenuating circumstances," Ivor offered as he helped Connor stand.

Tresta grunted, not looking impressed. "When it's difficult is exactly when you need to be strong."

Connor stumbled out of the box, hating how weak he felt. "It's easy to judge when you've never felt that crazy porphyry addiction rage."

Tresta placed hands on her leather-clad hips and gave him a hard look. "So you were tempted? So you felt angry? Who cares? You decide what you do. You can be strong if you really want to. Aifric once explained that the key to overcoming any addiction is to be strong and to swear an unbreakable oath never to give in."

"This is different," Connor insisted. He glanced at Ivor. "Where are my power stones?"

Ivor handed him his worn sandstone pendant, but nothing else. "I think I'll hold onto the rest for a while. Like you held onto mine."

That was super annoying, but Connor did need sandstone first, so he accepted the pendant from Ivor. Its warm healing power eased his post-granite exhaustion until he almost felt normal again. Then he glanced at Ivor and accused, "You sucker-punched me."

Ivor grinned, not even pretending to feel bad. "You did the same for me at Altkalen when I was on the verge of doing something suicidal. Just returning the favor."

Connor was not in the mood for gracious acceptance so he muttered, "I still don't appreciate it."

"You will."

He glanced around. They were standing on the high mountain plateau that led up to the broken peak of Drumwhindle Pass. Thick snow covered the ground and their trail back south toward Merkland was clearly visible where Ivor had plowed the way. It looked to be about noon, and the sun broke through the heavy cloud cover enough to set the snow sparkling and make Connor wish he had his darkened goggles.

Near the northern edge of the plateau, right on the point where it met the narrow causeway that led across a deep chasm to the pass, a tiny garrison of soldiers was camped. Their heavy winter tents were half buried in snow, although a much larger earthen building rose three or four stories out of the center of camp.

Ivor noted his gaze. "We shouldn't get any trouble from them. The peace treaty is signed after all, but Rory also gave us some official documents authorizing us to pass into Granadure."

"Good. Let's get going." Connor felt ashamed of his weakness in almost surrendering to Craigroy. Tresta's words were still ringing in his mind. He wished he could speak with Aifric about his problem, but maybe he could find time to visit old Mhairi. He could not keep going on like this.

First, he had to go check on Verena.

29

ONE WORTHY SERVANT

After flying beside Queen Dreokt for so long, Shona caught herself relaxing. It began to almost feel natural to hurtle over the wintry landscape in that protective bubble of warm air. She had to wonder if she was just numb from the emotional highs and lows that she'd suffered in recent days, or if she really was adapting to her insane new reality.

Hopefully it was adaptation and not impending emotional breakdown. She doubted the queen would consider her worthy if she couldn't stay in control.

Queen Dreokt, who had remained silent ever since they departed Tristan's elfonnel, glanced at Shona and said simply, "No. I would not."

Shona gulped and clenched her hands to conceal their shaking as a new wave of icy fear filled her. She'd allowed her thoughts to wander far afield in that extended silence.

"Do all young people worry so much and let their thoughts flit about like butterflies?" Queen Dreokt asked, her expression honestly curious. "I barely remember my own youth and my oldest memories are the fuzziest."

"I like to think I do better than most," Shona admitted. Lying to the queen was impossible, so trying to assume false modesty would be stupid. No doubt the queen already knew the answer.

"I am not reading you deeply, child. It's just, young people think so loudly, it's impossible to shut you out entirely unless I drop my affinity altogether. That is something I rarely do."

"You keep your affinities active all the time?" Shona dared ask, astounded by the revelation. She'd never imagined tapping granite constantly. She would burn through far too much precious powder for no reason, and she wasn't sure what such extended exposure would do to her.

Queen Dreokt nodded. "At my threshold, I require very little stone to establish an affinity, and I can maintain that connection without consuming any additional stone."

"How is that possible?" Shona asked, encouraged by the queen's answer.

"It is the state I sought from the first day we discovered how to tap the world's magic through stones. They are but the filters that allow our untuned, weak physiques to make our first clumsy affinities possible. But they are not the source of our power. I've tuned myself to both of the lowest frequencies so I almost don't need the stones any more."

She spoke softly, looking out over the cold afternoon, her gaze unfocused, as if she was lost in one of those old, fuzzy memories. Shona wanted to ask a thousand questions about how they figured out how to create power stones and affinities, what threshold the queen has ascended through, and what she meant by different frequencies.

She hesitated, hoping the queen would continue her soft monologue, but she fell silent. Shona considered the many questions she might pose, but what if she only got one more? She should ask the most important question she could think of.

So Shona asked, "Might I inquire, Your Majesty, if there is a technique I can employ to facilitate establishing a tertiary affinity?"

Queen Dreokt abruptly laughed, as if Shona had said something particularly funny. She gave Shona a warm smile and said, "Of course there is."

Before Shona could ask for more details, their cushion of air began descending sharply. Shona clutched at the invisible cushion out of pure reflex, but felt nothing to grab hold of. They were crossing a row of low, craggy hills and she caught sight of a ribbon of deep blue on the eastern horizon. It took a few seconds to realize she was seeing the distant Sea of Olcan.

As soon as she recognized it, she noted a faint smell of salt on the air. They banked around another hill and a long, low valley opened beneath them. A wide, open pit gaped in the ground near the northern end of the valley, close to where they'd crossed the row of hills. It was a large quarry, dug more than seven levels into the rocky ground.

Immense, circular tiers descended in ever-narrowing bands for over two hundred feet into solid rock. The center of the quarry was obscured by an oblong loch of motionless, green waters. A nearby township filling the land to the south.

Shona felt pretty sure they'd crossed into High Lord Pilib's realm. That was the house the late Padraigin had married into. House Pilib, which was really two high families merged together, was officially responsible for limestone and sandstone. They had several other excellent quarries too, and it looked like the queen was heading toward a slate quarry. That meant they'd traveled to Delabole.

Delabole produced top-rate slate, but was often considered lesser than the power stone quarried by House Berach, which was officially responsible for slate. House Pilib had always resented that slight. Did any of that factor into the queen's decision to visit there, or did it reflect somehow on Padraigin's recent death?

Shona had never visited the Delabole quarry, and she worried what they'd find there. The queen had seemed excited about what she'd learned from Tristan's elfonnel, but Shona had no idea if Harley was a person, another elfonnel, or something entirely different.

Together they touched down on the edge of the highest level of the quarry, on the northeast rim, not far from where a bluff rose steeply above the valley. All the cutters and workers had stopped to stare at their arrival. They wouldn't recognize their queen, but they'd understand powerful Petralists had arrived.

Queen Dreokt spoke, her voice magnified many times. "Leave this place immediately."

The cutters scrambled to obey. Linn workers were accustomed to obeying without question, and they'd be motivated not to anger ladies who could fly.

Even as they fled, the queen closed her eyes and raised her left hand, fingers outspread, as if preparing to lift something off the ground. Shona tensed. The queen was definitely planning to summon something again

Shona listened intently, but heard nothing. It might be wise to retreat, but to where? She felt a slight vibration through her boots, and suspected the queen tapping slate.

With the queen distracted again, perhaps she would answer Shona's last question. She'd seemed amused by it, and Shona desperately wanted to know the answer. Although max-tapping granite was an unrivaled joy, a high lady like herself with only a primary affinity was considered stunted.

Becoming a Solas raised her personal station significantly. Acquiring a tertiary would establish her as an elite Petralist, able to stand tall in any company, even without the benefit of her father's wealth and station.

So she dared to speak. "Your Majesty, I would love to assist you today. Is there any way you could teach me—"

"Stop your prattling when I'm working," the queen hissed, and the ground under Shona's feet buckled.

She squawked with surprise, limbs flailing, but failed to keep her feet. She fell forward and the ground pushed her farther, tumbling her right over the edge.

Shona tapped granite before slamming into the next narrow step of the quarry and bounced right over. In quick succession she tumbled down all the way to the third-lowest tier with jarring impacts.

Protected by granite, the fall hadn't hurt, but she still trembled with fear as she rolled back to her feet to look up at the still unmoving queen. Dreokt had made no other move, no other sign of displeasure, but she'd made it clear that Shona had overstepped her place. Would the queen simply obliterate her there in the quarry? Or would she wipe her mind and re-educate her?

She dare not run, dare not speak again out of turn, but was forced to wait in dreadful, expectant silence. Half a minute elapsed, with her heart racing, her muscles quivering with the need to move. She held perfectly still.

Then the queen's voice boomed across the quarry, imbued with supernatural depth and power, just like when she summoned Tristan. "Harley. Harley, come forth. Arise and resume your position by my side."

Shona tensed against the expected rise of another monster. Tristan's raw, elemental power had rattled her. She wanted nothing more than a quiet day or two somewhere far away.

The ground began to shake. Loose stones rattled and dust floated into the air, creating a dark, obscuring cloud. A stronger tremor shook the quarry and must have spread to the town beyond. Screams of fear echoed across the valley, giving voice to Shona's terror in a way she could not allow herself to.

Then the stone all across the quarry began to crack. Enormous blocks sundered with explosive reports. Cracks spread like the stone had turned to thin ice during a spring thaw. The continuous rolling thunder of the shifting rock echoed back and forth and pounded against Shona's granite-hardened skin with physical weight that smelled of broken stone.

The waters of the little loch at the bottom of the quarry erupted in a mighty spray of water and stone. Smaller chunks flew hundreds of feet into the air, and a wave of obscuring, muddy mist billowed over Shona as rocks tumbled back to the ground all around her. She shouted with fear, max-tapping granite and crouching in a ball, with her hands over her head.

The sound was deafening, the muddy mist choking, the darkness complete. The solid stone underfoot cracked and shook with brutal impacts of rocks crashing into the ground all around her. Shona screamed in fear and clutched the piece of limestone that she kept on a chain at her throat. It blazed forth with brilliant light that reflected back off the dirty mist, illuminating little and only serving to blind her further. She reduced the brilliance and focused on the little glowing stone as she fearfully waited for the avalanche to subside.

If one of those blocks struck her, would she shatter and die immediately? If she was only badly wounded, would the queen heal her, or leave her to die? She hated feeling helpless, but at the same time, the obscuring darkness and blanket of overwhelming sound insulated her from everyone, everything. It was as if she was alone in the world for a moment.

So she let herself scream out her fear and terror, allowed the tears to flow unchecked and sobs to wrack her frame as she huddled in the darkness, shaken by thunder, perhaps about to die. She gave vent to all the emotions she'd been suppressing, from the agony of Connor's rejection to the horror of Padraigin's brutal death, to the constant, exhausting fear that had become her constant companion while attending the queen.

It seemed to take forever for the elements to subside, but Shona didn't care. She let herself vent all her emotion, and as silence began to finally creep back over the quarry, she drew it into her own heart. She felt empty and calm for the first time since arriving in Donleavy, and she silently thanked the queen for that unexpected boon.

The silence seeming all the heavier after the tumultuous noise. Shona stood, feeling more in control and refreshed than she had in ages. She was covered in mud and flakes of stone. She must look like a piece of living piece of stone herself, rising from the rubble of the quarry to take new life.

Rocks and debris ringed her in unbroken piles nearly ten feet high. Some of the blocks were as big as wagons. How had she survived without getting flattened?

Queen Dreokt must have saved her life. Relief was a strange feeling in the presence of the queen, but Shona embraced it, filled her mind with gratitude in case the queen decided to read her thoughts again.

Reducing her tap rate, she scrambled to the top of the nearest boulder to see what was going on. The queen no longer stood at the lip of the quarry. Shona slowly turned a circle, peering through the still-settling gloom until she spotted her. Queen Dreokt had traveled down to where the loch had erupted. The waters were gone, replaced by smooth, gray stone.

The queen stood there, petting an elfonnel.

Unlike the other earthbound elfonnel Shona had seen, this one looked like a giant bear, complete with shaggy fur and an enormous head, with jaws that looked like they could crush mountains. The monster was crouched in front of the queen, its massive head bowed until she could reach it. Its enormous bulk filled half the quarry, but the queen stroked it calmly, as if she were petting a household cat.

Shona gasped in wonder, despite having witnessed how easily the queen maintained control over Tristan. The queen really was the master of the elements and the monsters who served as living manifestations of their power.

Queen Dreokt's voice sliced across the silent quarry. She spoke in normal tones, but they reverberated through Shona like an earthquake through the air. "It gladdens my heart to know you still live, my old friend. I need your services again. Awake! Return to mortal form, shake off those elements, and rise again. We have work to do."

The giant bear's fur began to rustle, as if an enormous wind was blowing through it. A mini-tornado formed around the monster, sucking dirt and debris off the ground and momentarily obscuring it from view.

Then the wind scattered, whistling away in every direction. In the place of the monster stood a tall, broad-shouldered woman. She was thick of limb, with a strong jaw, and shaggy black hair hanging down to her shoulders that strongly resembled the mane of a bear. She wore a heavy, black leather jacket over a black, silk blouse, and brown, linen trousers instead of a skirt.

The woman threw back her head and howled, a sound far too powerful to have come from human lungs. The sound grew until the entire quarry shook again and little rocks skipped around everywhere. Then the sound disappeared, snuffed out in a single heartbeat, and the woman dropped to one knee, pressing her face to the queen's hand.

"I'm really back. I live to serve you, my Queen. Thank you for waking me."

Queen Dreokt placed a hand on the woman's head in blessing. "Harley, why did you choose the long sleep after I failed to shake off the elements? You could have taken the kingdom." Her tone was calm, but Shona sensed an unspoken threat. Was the queen pleased or angry that this woman had not become queen?

Harley said simply, "I could have. I considered it, but this nation needs you. I dared hope you would return, and I realized you would need me when you did. The only way to ensure I could again serve you was to risk the long sleep and hope this day came."

Queen Dreokt pulled Harley to her feet and embraced her. "I am so happy you did."

"As am I, my liege."

Shona scrambled out of the pile of debris and dared step to the edge of the level where she stood. Who was that elfonnel woman? She must have also lived through the Tallan wars, had probably slept for the last three centuries like her queen. Did that mean she was just as insane, just as overpowering?

Queen Dreokt pushed Harley back to arm's length, her tone turning businesslike. "You've slept long enough and I face a drought of worthy servants. The price of our last conflict was dear, and I'm afraid we have few resources to work with in rebuilding our empire."

Harley did not turn in Shona's direction but said, "There is one who dares eavesdrop on your conversations, my queen. Shall I eliminate her?"

The ground under Shona's feet rippled, as if she was standing on a thin crust above a bottomless deep, and she held her breath in new fear. The woman was powerful enough to raise an elfonnel and return. If she decided to kill Shona, there was absolutely nothing Shona could do about it.

The queen shook her head. "She is one of the few who shows potential, with the proper training."

The stone beneath her feet flowed up and sealed around Shona's feet. She squawked with surprise before clamping her lips together. Her stone-encased feet dragged her over the edge and down toward the queen. Rubble flowed out of her way as she accelerated toward them.

Neither woman looked surprised by the amazing feat. Most Sentries could slide across earth, but not solid stone. Apparently Harley could manipulate the stone as easily as Queen Dreokt herself. Shona tried to regain her composure by the time she reached them.

The queen spoke again. "Harley, your homecoming party will have to wait. I have a task for you to perform, and this child will act as your guide."

Harley cast a dismissive glance at Shona. "I hardly need such a guide."

"The nation has changed and degraded substantially since you last walked these lands. This girl knows the situation, who are allies, and who are expendable."

Harley did not look pleased but did not argue further. The queen added, "Return to Stornoway. Your old love lurks there in the ruins, making a nuisance of himself as always, no doubt."

Harley frowned. "The fool still lives?"

"It appears so. I can no longer afford his childish vacillating. Recruit him and secure his oath."

"He could prove a powerful ally, but ever has he resisted committing."

"That time is past. Secure my grandson's oath. I cannot waste the time to attend to him myself, and I have not the patience for his foolish games. I fear I would destroy him without giving him enough time to come to his senses. Perhaps you can do better."

"I swear it will be done," Harley promised.

"Do so, or remove his head and bring it to me."

Harley nodded and made more of a bow than a curtsy.

Only then did Queen Dreokt look at Shona. "You have much to learn, child. Harley will serve as your guide as much as you will serve as hers. Attend her words carefully and she can help accelerate your learning."

"Thank you, Your Majesty." Shona wasn't sure what else to say, wasn't sure what type of learning the queen intended.

Harley considered Shona more closely, pursing her lips in thought. "It's been a long time since I took an apprentice under my wing. What is your tertiary, girl?"

"I don't have one yet," Shona admitted, dropping her gaze in embarrassment.

Harley barked a laugh and turned an incredulous look on the queen. "This is what you consider a promising student?"

"She has the potential, if prepared properly," Queen Dreokt said simply, and her words sparked a ray of new hope in Shona's heart. Could she really gain an tertiary affinity?

"We shall see. What do you call yourself, girl?"

"I am Shona, daughter of High Lord Dougal," Shona declared, feeling a bit more confident.

"Well, we'll see if we can make something useful out of you. Come on, then."

The ground rumbled beneath their feet and Shona tensed. A pair of narrow earthen seats rose from the stones. They were strikingly similar to the unique chair Evander liked to use.

Queen Dreokt shook her head slowly. "Still afraid of heights?"

Harley scowled. "I prefer the stability of earth, that's all."

"You and your soft ride," the queen chided gently, a little smile on her lips. "Fine. Be off with you."

Harley swung a leg over one narrow seat, straddling it, and leaned back against the backrest, propped her feet onto the stirrups, and grasped the handles that extended out in front, then gestured Shona to do the same. The strange seat looked uncomfortable and Shona resigned herself to a difficult journey. She was surprised to find the position actually felt remarkably good.

The two seats accelerated across the solid stone of the quarry, straight toward the northern cliff. Without slowing, they angled back sharply and ascended. Shona grinned at the wonder of it. These powerful, ancient Petralists might be deadly dangerous, but they weren't boring.

She wasn't sure what that cryptic conversation between Dreokt and Harley meant, but she hoped it suggested they planned to teach her more of the ancient secrets, and perhaps help her unlock a coveted tertiary affinity.

If they did, Shona would owe allegiance out of loyalty and gratitude more than fear. Did the queen understand how much more powerfully she'd own Shona at that point?

Was she willing to commit so wholeheartedly to the queen's service?

Did she have a choice?

The queen called after them. "Today our home lies in ruin. They call the place the Carraig now."

Shona's smile evaporated and she barely stifled a gasp. Her hands shook on the handles as she realized what Harley intended. The magnitude of the looming confrontation paralyzed Shona with terror.

She meant to challenge Evander.

WHEN THE SOLUTION MIGHT JUST BE
WORSE THAN THE PROBLEM

Verena still slept.

Connor went straight to her room when they reached Altkalen after a quick flight up from the border on the courier windrider. She looked unchanged, but just sitting beside her and holding her hand cheered him. He told her about everything he had experienced with Ivor and Student Eighteen in the past days.

He spoke freely of how much Aifric's death impacted him, of his feelings of sorrow, and guilt that he couldn't save her. Worse, he had invited her to join them, so her death was at least partially his fault. Speaking of it to the silent, unmoving Verena still helped a lot. As he related the misadventure, he realized it was a miracle that any of them had survived. He still didn't remember the last bit of what the queen had said to him, but that didn't matter. What mattered was that he had no idea how to deal with her. The challenge seemed impossible.

After double-checking that they were really alone and no one was eavesdropping, Connor told her about the struggles he was having with porphyry. He wished she could hear and understand him. One smile from her, one word of love and encouragement would strengthen him more than anything else he could imagine. When he related Tresta's words, he paused to consider them again.

She was right. She had to be. If he admitted there was nothing he could do, it was only a matter of time before he crawled back to Craigroy. He'd have no other option than to lick the man's feet, swear fealty to a life of slavery, and seal his fate.

Connor took Verena's warm little hand in both of his and made his choice.

"Verena, I swear on my love for you that I will stay strong. I will not give in, no matter how much it hurts. I will find a way to overcome this thing." He paused for a moment, simply looking at her, wishing for the millionth time that her eyes would flutter open and she would give him that special smile she reserved for him alone.

"If this addiction kills me, know that I refused to give in. If I surrender to it, I could hurt you, and I refuse to do that. Verena, know that . . ." his voice trailed off. He could not bring himself to speak aloud the fear that he would never get to speak with her again.

Instead, he reached for his little piece of chert. Very little remained, but hopefully it would be enough. Connor took a deep, slow breath, focusing on the little stone. Thankfully, the affinity came quickly.

He focused on Verena. He wanted desperately to feel some confirmation from her that that she was in there, just waiting to awaken. He paused for a moment, though, afraid that he mind find her an empty shell, stripped of her mind by the accident the way Alyth was stripped away by the queen's brutal mind-wiping.

"Stop being a grout-for-brains," he chided himself. He couldn't let fear control him. He had to know.

As he gazed at Verena's peacefully slumbering face, his skin did not turn warm or cool, and he felt no distant whispers suggesting she was thinking. Fighting back the rising worry, Connor again took her hand and embraced chert, trying to reach that state of mental linking he had with Student Eighteen.

For a long moment, he felt nothing while his fears grew and tears threatened to flow freely.

There! He felt something.

Connor scooted closer, leaning over the bed to press his face to Verena's hand as he sought for that distant whisper. Hope sang in his heart and he found it hard to breath as he desperately tried to connect with Verena's mind.

A breathless moment later, he felt it again. Distant and weak, more an echo of a whisper than a real sound. Still, it was something!

Focusing on that weak, distant whisper, Connor tapped sandstone. *Verena, if you can hear me, know that I love you. I'm here, and I know you can wake up. Please, Verena. Come back.*

As he cast the words across the feeble link to Verena, he poured a flood of healing power down the conduit. He wasn't sure exactly how he did it, or why he even attempted such a thing, but it felt like somehow he was sending healing directly into her thoughts.

His pendant was looking decidedly worn. Maybe he should save its unrivaled power for the looming battles with the queen and her armies. No, Connor would face a thousand battles with no sandstone if by using it he could help Verena.

He felt no response from her, and that tenuous connection to her distant thoughts faded a moment later. As Connor sat back and released her hand, he couldn't help grinning with foolish, exultant joy. He'd felt something. She was in there, still alive, still recovering. She would wake up. He had to believe that, and he hoped that his visit had somehow helped.

Eventually he stood, trying to fix every aspect of that moment in his mind. He would use that image as a shield against the difficult times that would surely come.

But if he hoped to win against the insidious addiction of porphyry, he needed more than that. So he went looking for Kilian.

It took a while, but he finally tracked Kilian down in a huge, comfortably appointed apartment high up one of the citadel's many towers. A servant ushered him into the large sitting room, with panoramic views across the citadel and out over the river and the city beyond. Kilian sat sprawled in an overstuffed chair, reading a long scroll. He gestured Connor to sit and ordered some drinks and food. Then he rolled the scroll with an abrupt flip of his wrist and gave Connor a long, hard look.

"You really are an idiotic child."

He spoke the sentence as a simple statement of fact. The declaration stung Connor deeply. He wanted to argue, wanted to share all the justifications for the risks they took, but he suspected Kilian had already debriefed Ivor.

"Is Ivor a prisoner again?"

"He should be. He acted as foolishly as you, but his ideas about spreading the revolution in Obrion are right on the mark. I think he learned an important lesson, and we need him."

He did not ask if Connor had learned a similar lesson, or if he ever would, but the question hung in the air between them.

"I need help," Connor said. Admitting that out loud to Kilian was extremely hard, but he was immediately grateful that he had.

"Perhaps there might be hope for you yet."

Connor chuckled. "That's just what your mother said."

Kilian shook his head in disbelief. "You have no comprehension even after what you saw of her how miraculous it is that she let you go."

"I know. I think she hit me pretty hard because I don't really remember what she said before she left. Something about collecting us later."

"You're lucky she's so overconfident. When Student Eighteen gets her chert affinity stabilized, I plan to have her scan you thoroughly."

That surprised Connor. "She didn't say she was having problems with chert."

"She didn't want to worry you. Besides, she's not thinking as clearly as she usually does. Aifric's death has destabilized the delicate balance she maintained in that unique mind of hers. I don't think she understood how extensive the trauma to the rest of her was until she arrived here."

"Will she be all right?" Connor asked, full of new worry. The thought that she might suffer lingering problems added another layer to the guilt he was already struggling with.

"I hope so. She's the only one who can scan your mind. It's possible my mother might have tampered with you."

Connor had not considered such a horrible possibility. "Could she do that?"

"You saw her wipe minds. That's a very heavy-handed technique, but heavy-handed has always been her default approach to problems. From all the reports I received, she's only gotten worse. So I'm hopeful she actually left your mind intact. Otherwise I would have to take steps to protect us against you."

That did not sound good. He spoke matter-of-factly and Connor did not doubt that if he decided that Connor was more of a threat than an ally, he would not hesitate to strike him down.

Some days he wished for simpler friends.

Kilian added in a grave tone, "But if you remember anything else, anything at all, about your interaction with her, you must tell me immediately. Dealing with my mother is deadly. We cannot hold secrets from each other."

He did not activate fire or water in his eyes, but his gaze still seemed to burn. Connor quickly nodded agreement, but was tempted to ask Kilian to share all of his other secrets, just to start out even. That might take a month though, and Connor doubted they had that much time or that Kilian would share so much so quickly. Connor had learned enough from Kilian to know that he shared what he felt they needed to know, and no more.

He toyed with the idea of tapping chert, but decided trying to pry into Kilian's mind would be singularly stupid, even for him.

"Did Ivor tell you about Craigroy and the porphyry?" Connor asked instead.

Kilian nodded. "He saved your life. Craigroy is a devious man, the head of High Lord Dougal's spy network. We'll have to deal with him eventually."

"Next time I'll be better prepared," Connor promised. When Kilian raised his eyebrow in question, Connor told him what Tresta had said and the oath he swore to Verena.

"That's a good start," Kilian acknowledged. "Taking responsibility for your condition is an important step, but I've found that more active measures are sometimes required."

"Like killing Craigroy?"

"Eventually."

It pained Connor to admit he couldn't beat this on his own, but the risks were too great not to. "Is there something else we can do? I need help."

Kilian gave Connor an encouraging smile. "I'm glad you asked.

Knowing you have support will help bolster your courage. And yes, I know a way to help you deal with those addiction cravings when they grow severe. I think your need outweighs the very real risks."

Kilian loved talking about risks, and those conversations always ended up proving most interesting.

"I'm willing to try just about anything," Connor admitted. He wished the solution included throwing Mattias out windows. He would happily make that part of his daily routine.

Kilian smiled that roguish smile of his and rose. "Come with me then. I'm going to teach you how to use diorite."

31

SWALLOW THE SNAKE

Kilian led Connor on a fracked basalt run southwest. Snow lay heavy on the land there, masking the unstable landscape with a docile, pretty blanket. Kilian, Anton, Saskia, had led a team of powerful Petralists to carefully soothe the elements and direct their energies away from the city, but Connor wondered if that would really work.

Kilian finally stopped in an area that did not look so calm. A bowl-shaped depression, about a hundred yards across, had sunk into the plain. The ground there was a patchwork of snowdrifts and open fissure oozing slow streams of molten lava. The scent of superheated rocks hung heavy in the air, along with whiffs of the rotten-egg stench of sulfur. Luckily the wind was blowing most of the stench away to the south.

"Do you think it's wise to train with diorite in an area like this?" Connor asked.

"This is the perfect place. You can't hurt anything here, and the subterranean vent that runs under this area needs to be collapsed anyway."

"Oh. In that case, I hope you brought a lot of diorite."

"First, you need to understand the danger. Most Petralists who've tried to establish affinity with diorite ended up blowing themselves to pieces."

Connor had felt the explosive, lightning-like power of diorite when he had wielded his father's hammer. Diorite represented a unique and terrifying danger, so naturally he couldn't wait to give it a try.

"That's where blind coal comes in, right?" Connor asked.

Kilian nodded and extracted a worn, ornate little box out of his jacket pocket. The ebony coloring seemed faded from years of use. The brightly painted scene on the lid looked like a cityscape, but time had worn it down to little more than a shadowy hint of its previous luster.

Kilian opened the box and extracted a couple pieces of blind coal. Connor recognized the metallic-looking rock. Kilian handed him a piece, and Connor ran his hands over its smooth, slippery surface. It did not dirty his fingers, and its near-metallic sheen had a brownish tint.

"Blind coal is the key. We don't have a lot of it, and it expires very quickly. Keep that in mind when you use it. Blind coal and diorite are a combination reserved only for desperate situations."

Connor was liking the lesson more and more already. Verena had told him of the time Kilian had used that deadly combination in his fight against the rampagers, and he wished that he had seen that. She had also used it to plunge herself and Hamish right through a giant boulder falling on them from when Anton brought down that mountain. He still did not understand how they somehow slipped right through the boulder, but she had shared her terror of that moment and how the blind coal had nearly run out before they had escaped the far side.

"This is a sedimentary stone, so establishing affinity is done by simply holding it," Kilian said.

Connor focused on the stone, savoring its slippery feel, and willing a connection. Limestone had given him some trouble, but he'd managed chert pretty well. He hoped that meant that now that he was ascended it would prove even easier to establish new affinities.

It took a few minutes of silent concentration but suddenly he felt it. A prickling feeling crawled up his skin, almost as if an invisible snake was slithering just above the hairs of his skin, close enough that he could feel something, but not quite touching.

He loved it.

"I feel it!"

Connor willed the feeling to spread, and it slithered up his arms and spread across his torso. He grinned.

Instead of answering, Kilian lunged and threw a fast punch at Connor's face. The blow caught Connor completely by surprise, but instead of plastering his nose to his cheekbone, Kilian's fist somehow missed. It slipped close by, sliding along the back of that invisible snake wrapping Connor in its protective coils.

Connor laughed. "That's amazing."

Kilian grinned but said, "Release it, or you'll burn through that entire stone before we get to practice with diorite."

Reluctantly, Connor broke the connection and let the invisible snake fade away. He wondered if Shona was afraid of snakes. A lot of girls were. If only he could wrap her in those invisible, slithering coils. He'd love to hear her shriek.

In that brief moment of use, the little stone in his hand had shrunk by almost a third. He knew that blind coal exhausted itself quickly, but that still surprised him. "I see what you mean. You'd have to carry a piece as big as a house on your back to use it much in battle."

"Use your other stones in battle. This stone you use only at the utter-most need."

"Like escaping from your mother."

"Even blind coal won't protect you from her for long, but it might make the difference between life and death. More importantly for today, it allows you to tap diorite."

He extracted from his other jacket pocket a small leather pouch. He pried it open and showed Connor the glittering, black and white crystals. Connor reached for it, but Kilian pulled the bag away.

"Not so fast. Let me explain before you blow yourself up."

Connor forced himself to wait, although he was eager to learn the secret. He couldn't wait to show Hamish that he could blow things up as well as Builders could.

"Diorite is absorbed like other primary affinity stones, but you cannot tap it unless you have blind coal equipped first and bound to your bones."

"You can focus blind coal internally?"

"No. Well, it's possible but internal-focused blind coal would kill you. Applied internally, blind coal creates enormous friction resistance in every bodily system and would tear you apart. Never attempt it."

"So how do you bind it to your bones?"

"You have to activate the external slipperiness of it, but then swallow it."

Connor frowned. "Then you're using it internally."

Kilian chuckled. "Actually, you're not. It's a fine distinction, but a crit-ically important one. You're tapping the external power of blind coal, but then ingesting it. It works, or I'd be dead."

"How did you figure that out?" That was some of the best circular reasoning Connor had ever heard. Kilian must have gotten away with so much as a kid. Actually, Connor couldn't quite imagine Kilian as a child. When he tried, all he saw in his mind was a half-sized Kilian who looked exactly as he did now.

"I had some creative moments in my youth."

"So, do other stones have other internal or external applications I don't know about?"

"Excellent question. Most stones do have both, although some cannot be tapped until you ascend various thresholds. In most cases, the internal and external applications produce opposite results, like we've just discussed with blind coal. We'll need to find time to sit down and discuss the others."

So much for open and immediate access to all secrets. Connor decided to start counting how many times Kilian said there were things he needed to know, but later.

He wanted to ask more questions, but Kilian said, "On to practice. Tap blind coal again. Then swallow it."

That was such a weird idea, Connor eagerly attempted it. Blind coal seemed to like him a lot better than limestone, and it activated immediately. He grinned again at the odd sensation of the invisible snake coils wrapping him in their protective embrace.

The problem came when he tried to force that snake in through his skin to bind it to his bones like Kilian wanted him to. It just wouldn't work. It easily flowed all over, but refused to plunge down through his skin. That was frustrating. With sandstone, the healing power flowed into him without hesitation.

Then he got the brilliant idea to imagine swallowing a live snake whole.

The sensation of that invisible snake slithering down his throat nearly made him gag, and he turned away from Kilian to avoid puking on him. He closed his eyes and tried to breathe shallow, but the rotten-egg stench of that area only turned his stomach even more.

"What's the matter?" Kilian asked.

Connor waved him back. "I'm okay. It's just, swallowing snakes was never a particular talent of mine."

Kilian grimaced. "Connor, I know I told you to visualize as much as possible when you work with stones, but where did you get swallowing snakes?"

He didn't respond. The snake had reached his stomach, and it seemed happy to take up residence in his innards. The slithery feeling of snakes sliding through his muscles and wrapping his bones with a protective, slippery layer left him feeling queasy.

"You look green," Kilian chuckled.

"Good thing I didn't eat more of those snacks you ordered in. Next time I challenge Hamish for the vomit distance record, I plan to tap blind coal. He won't know what hit him."

"You throw up on each other?"

"Just a figure of speech." Actually, they had thrown up on each other once. No, twice. Well, a few times, but always for good reasons. Hadn't Kilian ever had a best friend?

"You've got it bonded internally?" Kilian asked. When Connor nodded he asked, "Are you sure?"

"I'm sure."

Kilian eyed him closely. "Make sure you are. I don't feel like anyone blowing up so close to me. It's messy."

"I don't plan to die today. When we blow things up, do we have to punch them, or can we blow up things from a distance?"

"Usually I punch things. It may be possible to eject the explosion and focus it at a distant target, but I've never tried that," Kilian admitted.

Connor grinned. Explosive vomit. He'd have to test that with Hamish. Hamish was perhaps the only person he knew who could appreciate a higher form of vomiting.

Kilian shook his head, looking resigned, as if he'd again somehow read

Connor's thoughts, disapproved, but realized there was no way he could prevent Connor from testing out the theory. For a second he looked like maybe he was regretting the decision to share the secret.

But all he said was, "Focus now. When applied internally, blind coal will last a bit longer, but not by much. We don't have a lot of time, so purge and see if you can establish affinity with diorite."

Connor purged the last of his basalt and eagerly thrust his hand into the bag of diorite when Kilian extended it to him.

"Only a small portion for the first attempt," Kilian warned.

Connor focused on the powder and willed it into him. He doubted he'd survive a tiny portion if he got it wrong, so he planned to absorb a good-sized dose. If he was going to die, he planned to make it spectacular.

He didn't plan on dying, though. A sense of eager anticipation filled him with energy, almost as if he was tapping basalt again. Diorite seemed to understand his purpose with blind coal applied to his skeleton, and it must have approved because it took less than a minute for the connection to solidify.

A tingling rush rippled up his arm and coursed through his body. He gasped and rocked back, his muscles locking in a spasm as diorite raced through him. If he could close his eyes and peer inside of himself, he bet he'd see the diorite like miniature lightning bolts shooting up and down his veins.

"Whoa! I feel it," he exclaimed. Diorite filled him with a different kind of energy than any other power stone. Basalt made him want to run, granite made him want to curse-punch things, and slate imbued the strength of the mountain.

Diorite wanted to erupt.

It was like a volcano building in his gut, a hot pressure to explode. Even though he wasn't tapping it, the force built with alarming speed.

Kilian said, "Don't hold it in too long. It takes time to get used to it, but at first it'll cause internal damage if you try to hold diorite back."

That would have been good to know before they started. "What do I do?"

Kilian gestured at the snowy ground underfoot. "Hit something. Will it out through your fist."

Perfect. Breaking things was his specialty, after all.

The surging need to erupt swelled to an unstoppable wave, as if the diorite heard Kilian and was eager to obey. Riding that inner swell of destruction, Connor whooped and leaped high, landing fist-first and driving his hand through the snow, all the way to the hard stone underneath. He shouted again as he struck and willed the explosive might out through his hand.

The explosion started in the pit of his stomach.

It filled him in a flash and would have ripped him asunder if not for the protective layer of blind coal. Instead it seemed to condense along his skeleton, roll up his bones, and drive out to his hand.

All that happened in the fraction of a second right before his hand struck the stone. When his knuckles connected, all the concentrated explosive power erupted with a blinding flash. It emptied out of him in an eyeblink and created an inner void that threatened to suck all his insides out through his hand too.

Again the blind coal saved his life, but the diorite explosion drained away his strength, his eager excitement, and all the rest of his emotions.

That left him in a state of absolute calm as stone exploded under his hand and snow flashed to billowing steam around him. The ground shook and geysers of lava spurted from several nearby fissures. Connor stood in the center of the storm, unscathed and unaffected.

He stared at his fist. Remarkably it hadn't vaporized, but he felt completely drained in every conceivable way.

"Not bad," Kilian laughed, clapping several times.

Connor's legs gave out and he plopped onto his backside, right into a muddy puddle. He was too tired to tap soapstone and will the water away. His eyelids drooped and every muscle seemed to want to sleep.

His mind was awake, though, and his thoughts raced. How had Kilian fought those rampagers? Verena had said he moved with unbelievable speed, triggering a rapid series of explosive punches. There had to be more to mastering diorite.

"What happened?" His voice sounded tired and distant.

"You're not dead," Kilian laughed.

"But I'm exhausted."

"It takes some time to understand how to focus the blast properly."

"Teach me."

"I think you've had enough for today."

Connor started to protest, but Kilian placed a reassuring hand on his shoulder. "I promise to practice with you again. Hopefully often. We don't have large quantities of blind coal or diorite, but we have enough, and you need to master this skill before we leave Altkalen. The first couple of times are difficult and you need time to internalize what diorite does to you, or you could still kill yourself."

"Dying would be bad," Connor admitted, hating how his tongue slurred the words.

Kilian's expression turned more serious. "Have you noticed how diorite drained you internally, not just sapped your strength?"

Connor nodded. "I feel numb."

"Not even a little porphyry addiction-fueled rage?"

"No. It's gone." For the first time in a long time, he felt completely free of the porphyry hunger.

"That aspect of diorite bothered me at first, but in your case, it's a boon. Diorite pulls it all away, consumes all of your emotion like a cleansing fire. Blind coal keeps you alive, but it can't prevent all of the side-effects. You'll enjoy an exceptionally calm state for at least several hours, and I suspect it'll take days for porphyry to drive you to distraction again."

"This is amazing," Connor laughed softly, but his joy felt weak. He'd take it.

Kilian hauled Connor to his feet, lifted them on a pillar of snow, and slid across the plain, back toward Altkalen. Connor was grateful he didn't insist they run. Connor could barely stand, although as they accelerated across the plain, the cool breeze helped wake him up a little. He swore to master diorite in the next practice session.

Then he'd figure out how to vomit explosions.

Let Hamish try matching that.

32

─────

TEMPORARY GREATNESS

Shona gratefully climbed off her earthen seat, stretched, and stomped around to get blood flowing through her chilled limbs again. As comfortable as the ride might be, it was still an unfamiliar position, and they'd traveled hard for the past two days up the length of Obrion. The brief rest stops for food and sleep hadn't lasted nearly long enough, and she felt cold, dirty, tired, and grumpy.

Harley lacked a marble affinity, so she hadn't been able to shelter them as effectively from the cold. She did somehow slide them across the landscape through a continual calm, despite the speed of their passage. If Shona had been forced to suffer an icy wind too, she might have frozen solid. Harley seemed immune to the cold, but Shona had purchased additional winter clothing at their first stop.

She still felt a sense of homecoming as she stared down at the distant Carraig from the flank of Mount Murdo. The Carraig had served as one of only two places she considered home, and as she looked down upon it, she wished suddenly that she could return to the simpler life of a student. The gealls and intrigue and stress of classes and position in the Tir-raon had seemed so all-consuming at the time. Now she thought back to those days with nostalgic longing. Death didn't stalk the land then like it did now.

Harley was not a chatty companion, but had ridden with her face set and determined. Shona had yearned to ask many questions, but had not dared start the conversation, not after the casual beating the queen had delivered the last time she spoke out of turn. Maybe Harley needed some alone time to organize her thoughts after her long sleep. Shona forced herself to wait until Harley explained what the queen had meant when she said Harley would train her.

So she was surprised when Harley asked, "That pitiful hamlet is how they've rebuilt Stornoway?"

No one had ever described the Carraig as pitiful before. It might not be as expansive as Donleavy or Crann, but the many lofty palaces of the inner city impressed even high lords and ladies when they visited. At the moment it looked far less majestic than normal, with so many palaces reduced to rubble and others clearly undergoing renovations.

A blanket of snow covered everything, softening the marks of damage from the elfonnel attack. The eastern plain had been rolled back, revealing the underground ruin of the ancient city. That must be part of Stornoway, although Shona had never heard the name before. She wondered how such an important truth could be so thoroughly concealed.

She felt a need to defend the Carraig. "It doesn't usually look so rough. It's the school of the Petralists."

Harley grunted with another frown. "Dogs fighting over the scraps discarded by their betters. What is your affinity, girl?"

She started to say Boulder but remembered just in time and declared proudly, "I'm a Solas."

Harley barked a humorless laugh. "And what are other affinities called?"

Shona quickly ran down the list of Petralist powers then asked, "Have the names changed since your day?"

"We spent little time making up titles to celebrate mediocrity."

The woman's determined disdain was so irritating, Shona snapped, "We may not enjoy as many powerful Petralists as you did in the past, but we're doing the best we can. We've had to rebuild a nation that you broke and left desolate."

Instead of splattering her into oblivion, Harley chuckled. "Finally, a spark of courage. I was starting to wonder what my lady queen saw in you. Perhaps there is hope."

Shona understood goading and testing, although she wasn't usually the one on the receiving end. So she stood a bit taller and reminded herself she was a high lady. She did not need to cower before this newcomer.

She gestured toward the ruin on the eastern plain. "What was Stornoway like?"

Harley's expression softened and her tone turned wistful. "It was the crown of this backward land. When we arrived, Obrion was little more than tribes of ignorant peasants scratching out a basic living. We brought glory to this land, united the kingdoms, and launched the Age of Discovery. It was a glorious time, and Stornoway was the center of all learning and all power. Those were remarkable days."

Shona wanted to ask about where they'd come from, what land had birthed such mighty Petralists? What was that nation like? Why had Dreokt and Harley come if it was so wonderful?

But Harley frowned down at the Carraig. "Now this poor excuse for a city perches on the bones of our ruin. If you had seen Stornoway, seen what real Petralists could do, you would understand my disdain."

"So much has been lost since the Tallan Wars."

Harley barked another laugh, looking incredulous. "Tallan Wars? That's what they call the insurrection now?"

When Shona nodded, Harley's expression darkened. "More has been lost than you know. Our city shattered, our nation broken apart, all of my family and friends killed or turned traitor. Then my lady queen herself fell into the great sleep."

She gestured at the Carraig again with one clenched fist. "I was the senior Petralist after that. I could have taken the reins, could have taken the war to its uttermost end, but what was winning without true victory? No, I too chose to embrace the long sleep, awaiting the day that my lady queen would again rise to power so that I could serve her and help restore the glory of her rule."

Shona hadn't expected to feel impressed by Harley, but she doubted she would ever choose centuries-long hibernation for the distant chance that perhaps one day her liege would again arise. No, she would have taken power and orchestrated her own victory. She was a leader. Harley was a follower. Hopefully she was also a teacher.

Harley swung back onto her earthen seat and her determined expression returned. "Any who oppose us will be destroyed."

Shona scanned the distant Carraig again and frowned. It looked like an unusually large number of people were swarming the streets, but the distance was so great she couldn't see what they were doing. "Do you see the people?"

Harley nodded and her eyes hardened to the faceted crystal of a Pathfinder. "They are fleeing the city."

"Evander must have sensed our approach," Shona guessed.

Harley didn't look pleased by that. Shona wondered if she'd been shielding.

"The boy was always exceptionally gifted. Today let us hope he chooses wisdom instead of folly."

"Maybe I should wait here," Shona suggested. Waiting in Donleavy would be even better, but several miles away from the impending conflict might offer her a chance of escape at least.

Harley hesitated, then nodded. "Perhaps you should remain at a distance."

Shona breathed a sigh of relief, barely believing her good luck. Harley dashed her hopes all too soon, however.

"But the queen ordered you to witness, and so you shall."

"I thought you just said I should remain at a distance."

"If you'll shut up for a minute, I can begin to teach you deeper truths."

Shona snapped her mouth shut, and Harley nodded approval.

"Standing at my side will likely prove fatal. The queen has expressed interest in keeping you alive, at least for now, so that course is perhaps not wise. I will secure you in position to observe and witness."

"How do you propose to do that?" Shona asked cautiously.

"First, I will loan you the power of quartzite."

"That's impossible. I'm a Solas." Shona blurted. Unless Harley knew the queen's secret to helping others establish new affinities.

"Even before I embraced the long sleep, this secret was known to few."

Harley concentrated and lifted a hand to her eyes. She bowed forward into her hand, as if praying, or seriously pained. When she lowered her hand, she held a soft, white powder.

"Is that lamacal?" Shona asked.

Harley nodded. "From purging quartzite out of my eyes."

Shona grimaced at the thought of purging through her eyes. She hadn't even known that was possible, or that one could even purge tertiary powers. She'd only ever known anyone to purge primaries. Her frown deepened when Harley extended the handful of waste powder toward her.

"You want me to dispose of that for you?"

"Swallow it."

"No one uses lamacal," Shona said, not bothering to hide her disgust.

"And few who try could make it work." Harley kept her hand extended, proffering the powder, so Shona took it. Harley added, "I know the secret to purging tertiary powers in a way that allows others to tap that same power, even if they lack the affinity."

Shona gasped, astounded by the idea. "You can loan your affinities?"

"That is an apt description. We discovered the potential in lamacal during the early days when we were still developing the earliest Petralist power stones."

"How . . ." Shona began, not sure how to even ask about that. It still amazed her to think there were no Petralists before Queen Dreokt's and Harley's generation.

"That is not today's lesson. Swallow it, quickly," Harley barked.

The thought of swallowing waste powder still disgusted Shona, but if it really could grant her the power of a Pathfinder, even temporarily, she would attempt it.

The white powder tasted somehow colorful, as if Harley had concentrated the view of a rainbow into it. Shona shoved it into her mouth, but it was rather dry and she nearly coughed and sprayed it away. She bit back the cough and snatched her water canteen. Three long gulps, and she choked it all down.

"Now, tap it to your eyes," Harley ordered.

Shona concentrated. Her familiar granite power radiated through her entire being. Her new limestone affinity sparkled in her mind too, but now there was also something new. A liquid feeling of warmth flowed up from her stomach and pooled in the center of her head, behind her eyes.

She tapped it.

It rolled forward and touched her eyes.

Shona gasped at an unexpected stab of pain and clutched her face. Her eyes felt hard, like faceted crystal.

She blinked them open and looked around, mouth agape in wonder. The world looked somehow deeper, colors more vibrant, as if painted with a thicker brush. When she looked down at the majestic towers of the Carraig, her vision swooped over them in a stomach-twisting way that nearly plopped her onto her backside.

She gasped in amazement as her gaze swept over the soaring towers and beautiful palaces, as if she stood mere feet from them instead of miles.

"How is it possible?" she breathed.

"With knowledge. All things can be learned, but most lack the will and drive to attain the knowledge that matters most."

Shona blinked, snapping her gaze back to Harley. "I have the will. Teach me how to attain greater power."

Harley nodded in approval. "Potential indeed. If you survive today, we will begin your education in earnest."

The two of them returned to their earthen seats and accelerated down the slope toward the eastern side of the great outer wall. Shona's nervousness returned and grew with every passing moment.

She could watch the confrontation with Pathfinder eyes, but she'd die just as dead if Harley or Evander decided to squash her.

Harley intended to challenge Evander in the heart of his home. An elfonnel had attempted to do that recently, and it had died. Connor might not be there to help fight it again, but somehow she suspected she had not seen the full extent of the powers Evander might be able to bring to bear in a fight for his life.

She really was not looking forward to experiencing those up close.

33

THIS RELATIONSHIP IS DOOMED

As Shona and Harley sped toward the outer wall where it looped around the long plain of the ruined Stornoway, the wall simply split like an enormous gate. They sped through without slowing, and it closed behind and sealed perfectly, leaving no trace that it had ever parted.

Shona expected Harley to head for the inner city, but she maintained course directly for the Stornoway ruins. She didn't slow until they reached the edge of the pit that held the ruins nestled below the level of the surrounding land.

The rolling hills of the plain had once concealed the sunken ruin, but had been ripped away by the elfonnel. Now that the secret was revealed, it appeared Evander planned to keep the ruins exposed.

"Keep watch. You will report all you see to the queen," Harley ordered.

"From here?"

Harley did not answer, did not even look at her, but a powerful wind suddenly plunged down from the heights and seized Shona. She squawked in surprise as it lifted her off her seat. She snatched for the handles to hold on, but they disintegrated back into the ground.

"Relax. Panicky children annoy me," Harley snapped.

Shona forced herself to stop struggling as the air carried her higher, then higher still. Most Pathfinders lacked much control over elemental air, and Harley lacked the effortless finesse of the queen, but the whistling wind carried Shona two hundred feet into the air without dropping her.

Then it split around her, whistling past, but leaving her standing in a bubble of calm at its center. It lacked the cushioned seats the queen had fashioned on their long flight down to Delabole, but it felt remarkably stable.

If Harley had also granted her external quartzite power over elemental air, she would have willed her observation bubble higher. She could watch the confrontation just as easily half a mile up.

Harley accelerated again, sliding right down the wall of the pit, then along one of the ruined boulevards. Shona studied the ruin as Harley rode through it. The broken buildings and disintegrating palaces hinted at a glorious past. Looking at them saddened her. It was like staring at a corpse in a recently opened grave.

Her bubble drifted slowly after Harley, who rode into the center of the ruin where the devastation seemed less complete. Some paving stones remained in place and some of the buildings retained stronger vestiges of their original purposes. Harley stopped in an enormous, paved plaza near a huge, many-tiered fountain. It had been carved by a master and even though it had languished for centuries underground, with some careful restoration, it could rival the best fountains in the Carraig's inner city. The levels included fantastic animals and warriors still watching over the plaza in eternal vigil.

Harley dismounted and her chair melted into the ground. She glanced around, looking unimpressed by the amazing ruin.

Then Evander rose out of the ground ten feet away from her.

There was no geyser of earth to dramatize the entrance. The paving stones simply flowed apart, then returned to their previous positions under his feet. He towered over Harley, gigantic in his usual long, leather jacket. His mahogany skin seemed shadowed under his black hair and beard.

Harley rushed Evander without a word of preamble. Shona tensed. The insane, ancient woman really did intend to attack him.

She didn't attack.

She threw her arms around his neck and kissed him tenderly on the lips.

Shona gaped, more surprised by that than any of the wondrous higher powers she'd glimpsed from Harley and the queen. The giant Evander seemed more like a moving mountain than man. She'd never imagined anyone actually kissing him.

He returned the embrace, his huge arms swallowing her up. They kissed for a long moment before Harley retreated a step. The ground lifted her enough to stand eye to eye with him. She might care for him, but she didn't seem to like looking up to anyone.

Harley spoke, her voice enthusiastic. "I'm back, lover. I can hardly believe you're still lurking around."

Shona still couldn't read Evander's expression. She crouched on her cushion of air high above, straining to listen. Her quartzite power responded by flowing into her ears. They elongated and she suppressed a giggle as they flexed and rotated. Sounds rushed in. Wind roared through her head, as if it had gotten trapped between her ears. She forced it out but was momentarily overwhelmed by a flood of sounds.

Thankfully the school wasn't packed with loud, chatty students and its regular bustle of activity. She wasn't sure she could have survived that. Even though the Carraig was all but empty of people, it was not empty of sound. The stone gargoyles perched on every peak of every palace caught the wind and transformed it into hauntingly beautiful music that rang in her ears. She could have listened all day long. If she wasn't observing such an epic meeting, she'd easily get distracted by the sounds.

But Evander's voice cut through it all. "Winds of winter alone touch the peak of the snow-capped mountain under the silver light of the new moon."

Poetic, but it didn't seem equal to his normally indecipherable Sentry speak.

Harley smiled. "I remember when you first said that to me."

Shona shuddered, trying to imagine what a date with the confusing giant must have been like. What would possess Harley to date the man? What would possess him to date her?

"Time alone wears down unyielding stone, but the determined heart can never be broken."

Harley's smile faltered. "You know your grandmother is back. She has retaken her throne and she summons you to join her. Don't pretend you don't understand why I'm here."

"The sun rises without fail, despite obscuring storm clouds, but the blind man never sees the light," Evander said, his expression remaining unreadable, his stance unchanging. Shona had no idea what he meant. She only hoped they kept talking.

"You know that's just as annoying as when you were a child." Harley touched his face with one hand. "Please, Evander. Come with me. Swear fealty to our rightful and only queen and we can unite in love and conquest. Together we can sweep away any opposition from this weak, leaderless world."

She was right. With Evander by her side, Harley could lay waste to Granadure and the Arishat League both. Shona doubted Kilian and Connor and all the mechanicals those infernal Builders could devise would more than slow them.

She held her breath, waiting for Evander to answer. She was surprised to realize she hoped he turned Harley down. Why would she hope that? Those two represented all the army Queen Dreokt would need at her back to secure a granite-hardened hand over the entire continent. She could force peace upon everyone, stop the war.

Remove any free thought.

Evander gently reached up and pulled Harley's hand from his face. He looked a little sad. "Dross is impossible to separate from silver until plunged into the refiner's fire. And lies, though sweet as honey on the tongue, plunge the fool into darkness."

Harley shook her head slowly, looking disappointed, and retreated a step. "You rejected me once, foolish boy. Don't dare my wrath by doing it again. Drop your annoying rhyme and join me, or face the consequences." All traces of friendliness had vanished from her tone.

"The pedra thinks itself invincible until taken by the hunter's arrow."

She sighed, her expression hardening. "Then you will die."

He punched her in the sternum.

The blow came without warning, just a straight jab, erupting outward faster than such an enormous man should be able to move. Anyone else struck like that would have crumpled into little pieces and died.

Harley rocked back slightly and laughed. "Boy, I'm going to beat you to death."

She lunged, driving fists into his giant torso, as if expecting to actually hurt the huge man. With Shona's enhanced vision, she clearly saw how they struck hard enough to compress his leather jacket into his ribs harder than any punch from a max-tapped Boulder.

Evander ignored her fists and clobbered her jaw with his left forearm. That actually sent her tumbling. The ground caught her and threw her back at him like a javelin from a ballista.

She plowed into him and laughed as the two of them crashed to the earth together. They pummeled each other with brutal blows that would have shattered any regular Boulder. They shrugged off the hits as the ground shifted under them, righting them and allowing them to keep fighting without interruption.

Harley grinned as she fought. Evander looked almost bored. They could have smashed through an entire company of Fast Rollers, but looked like they were still just warming up.

Shona suddenly felt like she was hovering way too close.

The ground swayed and bubbled around them, and Shona's enhanced ears heard the groaning and creaking of the earth. The real contest was transpiring there, beyond her senses.

After several seconds they both rose onto columns of earth that moved with their fighting, twining around each other. The two combatants continued to hammer unproductively at each other as their earthen columns swayed and twisted. The earth creaked, and it looked like they were trying to strangle each other's access to earth.

After a moment, Evander managed it. His earthen column swept him in a full, looping somersault, wrapping Harley's column and shearing it off.

She fell, and Evander swept earth around her, clearly trying to envelop her and maybe suffocate her. She burst free and tumbled away, bouncing across the paved plaza. She leaped back to her feet, no longer laughing. She looked annoyed as she ripped the exquisite fountain out of the ground and threw it at Evander, who was already chasing her, still attached to his amazingly flexible, earthen umbilical.

The fountain shattered in mid-air, the stone splitting around him as if it struck an invisible barrier. He declared, "The proud are blind with eyes wide open, and death stalks those who ignore truth that might save them like a lifeline in turbulent waters."

Harley glared. "I told you to stop that. At least honor me with straight talk before you die."

"The whisper of wind across the face of the lilies carries more weight than the screaming breath through angry lips."

Shona had to admit, that was a pretty good insult. She wondered if he stayed up late at night preparing phrases, or if he just invented them on the fly.

Harley ripped the facade off of the nearest palace. Shona gaped as a fifty-foot-square section pulled free. It didn't collapse under its own weight like it should, nor did it squash her, but she heaved it at him like a thrown hammer.

Evander had dropped to the plaza, and he walked right through the thrown wall, splitting it without even raising a hand. The broken sections crashed to the ground, but did not shatter. Instead they flowed back into position and reattached themselves to the palace they'd just been ripped from. Within seconds, Shona couldn't see any marks from Harley's damage.

Harley laughed. "You actually care about this old ruin?"

Evander advanced, looking angry for the first time. "The lord of the manor casts aside food without thought, while the beggar yearns only for a kind hand to feed him."

Harley looked disgusted. "I bet you even worry about what happens to those squatters who live on the ruins of their betters." Her smile returned, looking predatory. "I think I'll go say hello."

34

HOW FAR WOULD YOU GO TO MAKE A POINT?

Harley shot away across the ground and up onto the solid earth near the Sculpture house. Evander rushed after, but dozens of spears of earth erupted out of the ground all around him, slowing him for a precious second.

Shona pounded a fist against the soft but unyielding floor of her floating observation post and shouted, "Don't wreck the city! Not again."

Her voice sounded weak, and she doubted they heard. She needed to figure out how to apply the quartzite to her voice. It didn't flow there as readily as it did to her eyes and ears.

Harley slid past the Rhiddoroch, where Frazier stood defiantly on the wall, a gleaming sword in hand, shouting curses. She ignored him and swept past toward the inner city.

Evander ripped out the eastern wall of the Rhiddoroch and hurled it at her. It shattered around her, but she didn't slow.

"Not again!" Frazier shrieked and threw down his sword in frustration. "I quit!"

He stomped away toward the outer stairs. Shona hoped he kept walking. Most of the people had already evacuated, but she was starting to fear they might not have escaped to a safe distance yet.

Harley was already closing on the eastern formal gardens, just outside the inner-city wall. Evander was sliding after her, closing the distance, but she had too great a lead. Shona didn't want to watch how much Harley could destroy before Evander intercepted her, but couldn't look away.

Then movement on the nearest palace caught her attention and she glanced up, then blinked in surprise.

The gargoyles that clung to the eaves of the palace were crawling out of their posts. Shona blinked, rubbed her faceted eyes, and looked again. She wasn't imagining it. Those ornamental heads were attached to huge, monstrous bodies that had crouched concealed under the roofs all those years. They galloped down the walls like horizontal surfaces, gigantic bodies the size of horses flexing like living stone.

And there were lots of them.

Some were more feline or wolfish, while others were roughly humanoid, but their heads were wide and complex, their granite profiles ornate.

Harley caught sight of them too, and she paused in surprise and glanced back at Evander. For a second, she might have even looked impressed. She swept a hand toward the nearest gargoyles as they leaped the inner-city wall. Waves of earth swept them away.

Two of them shattered against the wall, but within seconds, the rest of them clawed their way out of the earth and resumed the charge.

More gargoyles galloped through the main inner gate, running away from the fight. Each carried one or two people in their gnarled, stone hands or paws. Those must be the people too proud, too stubborn, or too stupid to have fled earlier. The gargoyles raced with amazing speed out to the western gate in the outer wall, tossed the people to the ground, and returned for more.

But dozens more gargoyles swarmed Harley. Shona expected her to simply obliterate them all, but her defenses seemed less effective. Perhaps Evander was blocking or diverting it somehow.

Shona gaped anew at the spectacle. Each gargoyle rivaled the great stone pedra for sheer mass. That summoned monster had challenged the entire might of Rory's initial command, delaying their attack on Ilse. Kilian and Ilse together had summoned that pedra and it had tested their limits.

Now dozens of gargoyles swarmed right through Harley's defenses. Many were swept away by waves of earth, but some clawed back to the surface after several seconds. Gaping holes yawed open under others and the sides of those pits smashed shut around them.

Some shattered into whirlwinds of broken stone that wailed their final death cries, while others broke into piles of dark earth. The effort to summon so many should have killed Evander or left him comatose with exhaustion. At minimum, the distraction of managing so many summoned creatures should have left him standing helplessly with a vacant-eyed stare.

He was standing still, but not idle. His hands were raised to shoulder height, cupped inward around a globe of intense amber light. He slowly pressed his hands together, shoulders hunched with the effort to compress the light. He completely ignored the raging battle between Harley and the swarm of gargoyles.

At least ten gargoyles reached her and attacked with granite claws. Harley lunged to meet them, cursing loudly in a language Shona didn't know. It was far more musical than either Obrioner or Grandurian, and those beautiful sounds didn't fit the brutal moment.

Harley caught the first gargoyle, a beast with a short, but thick torso, but with enormously muscled arms. She shattered its wide fists, then ripped its head apart with a single mighty heave of her shoulders. The impressive move shocked Shona. How strong was that woman?

It took a couple seconds too long, though. The other gargoyles swarmed over her, raking her with deadly claws that tore horrible gashes across her face and torso. Blood sprayed from the ghastly wounds, but she did not cry out, did not even seem to feel them, and the wounds healed as fast as they appeared. Harley methodically dealt with each monster, tearing them apart, shattering skulls and ripping off stone limbs in a mind-boggling display of raw ferocity and brutal strength.

Shona had seen some miraculous healings, particularly from Connor and his sculpted sandstone pendant, but she'd never witnessed anything like that.

It took only seconds for Harley to smash apart the amazing gargoyle army. Shona hated to think what would happen to any human army that challenged her. Even the mightiest Petralists would have fallen to her seemingly unstoppable strength.

Harley stomped on a few fragments of broken gargoyles and shouted with victory. Then she blew out a breath and turned toward Evander. Her voice echoed clearly up to Shona.

"You annoying, little fool! I'm going . . . wait!"

She raised a hand defensively, for the first time looking afraid.

Evander had condensed the light into a narrow beam, thinner than his finger. It blazed with blinding intensity, bathing his face in its pure, amber glow.

Evander released it.

That narrow beam of light shot across the distance to Harley in less than an eyeblink, leaving an afterimage hanging in Shona's enhanced sight. The spear of light easily drilled right through a defensive wall of earth Harley began to raise around herself. It plunged into her chest and erupted out her back in a horrible spray of blood and gore, as if it abruptly widened inside of her.

Harley's entire body convulsed under the impact, as if struck by the force of a landslide. She screamed and fell to her knees, convulsing, vomiting blood. Her eyes stared wide with shock and she seemed to have lost her strength.

Shona gasped. Had he really done it? Was she witnessing Evander kill Harley with a power Shona had never seen before, never imagined possible? He'd used light. Like a Solas.

Could she do the same?

The thought terrified and excited her in equal measure. If only she could learn that technique, she could defend herself from anyone, maybe even the queen herself.

Evander looked exhausted, but stumbled toward Harley, drawing a short-handled hatchet from a deep pocket of his coat. Shona had never seen Evander bother drawing a weapon before, had never imagined a time when he might need more than his incredible earth powers or super-human strength.

Hadn't he killed Harley already? Did he plan to remove her head, just to be sure?

Harley had toppled to the ground, eyes closed, not seeming to breathe. A cloud of dust shuddered off the ground, momentarily obscuring her.

Evander broke into a charge, hatchet raised. He leaped the last ten feet, fully extended, bringing the hatchet down in a mighty blow that would have probably cut all the way through a mountain.

Harley caught it.

Her hands erupted from the mist and met his on the handle of the hatchet, stopping it dead. Evander crashed down over her and the two tumbled together, the hatchet flying from their hands as they beat on each other in renewed fury.

Then Evander somersaulted off Harley. Shona blinked in astonishment, not daring to believe her quartzite-enhanced eyes.

Harley rose to her feet, looking whole and healed, and extremely angry. She stalked after Evander and demanded, "Did you think that abomination of yours could kill me? Fool! I'm the greatest Healer who ever lived. I invented sandstone healing!"

He lunged to his feet and struck at her, but she caught his hands and spun, yanking him right off his feet.

She threw him.

Shona expected the giant to topple back to the ground, but he kept ascending, limbs flailing, as if he weighed nothing at all. A roaring wind rushed in around him and threw him higher still. He soared away, flying faster and faster, tumbling wildly, his great coat billowing around him like ineffectual wings.

He soared all the way to Mount Murdo, halfway up the mountain. The wind carried him at least three miles and Shona winced at the impact. He struck so hard he drilled deep into the solid rock of the mountain.

She glanced down at Harley again, who stood with hands on hips, head tilted up toward her. "That's how you deal with annoying men."

Maybe she'd loan Shona that incredible strength long enough for her to throw Verena into a mountain like that?

A distant crack, like a dozen thunderbolts together violently shook the air over the Carraig and sent Shona's observation bubble sliding south-east. She turned back to Mount Murdo and suddenly wished she could fly several miles higher.

One entire shoulder of the mountain had broken free. Instead of avalanching down the steep slopes, it was soaring through the air toward Shona.

Evander was riding it.

She rubbed her crystal-hardened eyes, but the view didn't change.

"We are so grouted," she mumbled, borrowing one of Connor's favorite phrases.

As the gigantic piece of mountain neared, it looked as big as the entire inner city. Harley had thrown Evander several miles. He was throwing a mountain back at her.

It lost altitude as it neared, and Shona breathed a sigh of relief when she realized it would miss her. It swept past, with the furious Evander riding on top, his gaze fixed on Harley. Wind raced around the flying mountain in a howling whirlwind that sent Shona floating even farther to the southeast. She silently encouraged it.

Harley didn't flee. She erupted off the ground to meet Evander's new attack, sweeping most of the ruined ancient city along with her in a gigantic, earthen tidal wave.

The two colossal forces smashed together in an explosion of earth and stone that erupted in every direction. The shockwave triggered several avalanches on Mount Murdo. The concussion also knocked Shona from her feet and whisked her observation pocket away like a bubble on the Macantact. Debris whistled past and she instinctively tapped granite. Rubble struck with jarring force, accelerating her journey away from the epicenter of the epic battle.

For a moment she lost sight of Harley, Evander, and most of the Carraig under the clouds of debris and dust. Wind whistled in from every direction, creating merry dust devils that spun away in chaotic patterns as the heavier debris cascaded down over the shattered plain.

The plain was gone, as was the Sculpture house, the Rhiddoroch, and the eastern side of the inner-city wall. Several palaces on that side of the city had collapsed under the onslaught, the thunder of their implosions lost amid the booming shockwaves of the mid-air collision of two mini-mountains. The air was heavy with earth, but smelled charred, like stone struck by a heavy hammer.

Then the debris stopped falling.

It just hung there in the air, a wall of earth and air a quarter of a mile high and more than a mile thick in every direction. Shona spotted movement in the center of it. Evander and Harley hung in the center, again pummeling each other with unrestrained fury.

Always when Sentries clashed, much of the battle happened under-ground, visible to the rest of the world only as trembling ripples or occasional geysers in the earth. This time, surrounded by the elements, that aspect of the battle raged around them in its full, terrifying glory.

As the two mighty Petralists fought, earth and air swirled together and clashed in a growing cyclone of destruction. Invisible currents of their will threw the elements at each other. They formed enormous fists and spears on every side, slashing and stabbing. The battle raged with such speed and ferocity that Shona could barely follow it.

Her bubble continued drifting south, away from the fight. It also ascended, keeping her just above the combatants. Was that simple happenstance, or was Harley somehow still controlling it? How could she spare any attention for Shona and still fight that incredible duel.

Shona only wished she could accelerate. Even with her enhanced vision, the two combatants often appeared as little more than ghostly figures caught in battle rage that might never end. She was starting to wonder if either of them could ever find critical advantage over the other? Would one of them die, or both of them? Or would they stay up there forever, battling for all time?

The aerial battle drifted slowly toward the inner city, like a shadow of doom that blocked out the sun and all hope of salvation. Billowing clouds of mixed earth and air first caressed the battered palaces and chipped towers, then began clawing at them.

Harley's voice echoed past on the wind. "Today you die, and this entire city will serve as your coffin."

Something new rippled through the whirlwind, and Shona frowned as she tried to make it out. The fighting continued, clashing and smashing elements in an eye-twisting, chaotic confrontation that boomed with deafening thunderclaps as tons of elements smashed into each other over and over again.

But now a new wind rushed out of the center, toward the city, bearing with it a storm of brown dust. It looked different than the dark earth and decaying rubble of the rest of the fight. That brown wind engulfed one of the nearest towers, a majestic building with delicate lines that had once been sheathed in pure basalt.

At the wind's touch, the outer facade of the building simply disintegrated. The wind was like a scouring sandstorm that seemed to melt the structure as fast as a hot wind might melt a dusting of snow.

Within seconds the elegant tower collapsed, the pieces disintegrating further even as they fell to the ground. Waves of new dust rose into the whirlwind, reinforcing it and adding to its might as it swept on to the next tower.

Shona decided she needed to flee. That had to be another higher power that she'd never heard of. How many deadly powers did those two possess? Might they unleash something that would catch her in its grip too? She was only a mile away from the edge of the gigantic battle, but it felt far too close. She beat against her imprisoning air, but found no purchase against it. Evander and Harley were going to destroy the Carraig and she didn't want to become another casualty.

Trying to control her rising fear, she settled to a cross-legged position to watch the titanic duel. They still battled in the heart of the raging elements, but the sandstorm had rebounded back against an invisible barrier.

Evander's voice rose above the constant booming clash of the ongoing struggle. "The simple crab tears down any who try to climb above them and escape the trap, but—"

His words were cut off by a stiff uppercut from Harley that would have ripped the head off of any other man. "Oh, shut up."

The fighting actually intensified, a swirling maelstrom of mixed earth and air that smashed and collided in terrifying intensity that spread out farther and drifted far too close to Shona. She silently hoped the whistling, gusting wind would carry her away faster, but it rushed in from every direction, canceling out any progress she might otherwise have made.

With a heart-stopping groan, an enormous section of ground erupted upward out of the inner city, ripping up through one of the school governing offices as it swept into the air and smashed into the two combatants. Shona couldn't tell which of them pulled it into the fight, couldn't see that it made any difference. That new chunk of earth simply dissolved and joined the murky tumult.

More sections of ground erupted upward, as if the natural laws became broken over the Carraig. Shona could no longer see the two combatants in the center of the storm as it intensified and darkened around them. The wind turned colder, carrying with it the scent of ice-covered peaks.

She glanced at Mount Murdo and gasped as streamers of earth ripped free of the mountain and rushed in to add to the bulk of the aerial battlefield.

How much could the two of them support? Would they rip off the entire mountaintop, strip the Carraig to the roots of the mountain and use all of it to continue fighting?

Without warning, everything stopped.

The sound faded away to distant echoes as all the swirling, smashing elements ceased all movement, as if frozen solid. The air shook with a silent thunderclap.

Shona looked around, wondering what new devilry the two combatants had unleashed, but nothing moved. Even a palace had stopped in mid-fall. For five long heartbeats, the area remained absolutely still, as if the fight had broken time too.

Then everything fell. The rumbling impact built upon itself, creating a rolling crescendo that shook Shona to her bones as the elements smashed down over the inner city in an avalanche of destruction. Palaces shattered, streets filled with earth, and within seconds, the entire inner city lay in ruins, buried and consumed by the disaster.

Dust billowed up around the destruction, concealing it from view. The air smelled tired and thin.

Then Shona felt a warm breeze. The change from the icy cold air of those heights startled her and she glanced around for the source.

That's when the top of Mount Murdo exploded.

The eruption came with the grandfather of all thunderclaps. It shattered the air and would have shattered her head if she'd been applying quartzite to her ears. She still screamed and clapped hands to her ears as the thunderclap and tornado-strength winds shredded her protective bubble. She plummeted into the murky cloud concealing the earth.

Shona max-tapped granite as she fell, but didn't look down. She couldn't take her eyes off of the gigantic explosion of stone and fire and ash as the mountain blew itself apart. The eruption made Evander and Harley's duel seem a paltry, childish thing.

Crimson lava sprayed out the broken mountaintop in a deadly fountain at least half a mile high. Shona struck soft earth and plunged several feet into it just before a shockwave of superheated air blasted past, scouring the ground and sucking the air from her lungs.

She buried her face in the protective earth, holding her breath and clenching her eyes against the searing heat that charred her exposed skin, despite the protection of granite. Her battle leathers smoked and melted to her, and she refused to think about what was happening to her hair.

If she hadn't fallen when she did, that wind would have killed her. Even several feet underground, she felt scoured raw and terrified.

After the initial blast, she managed to suck in a lungful of rank, sulfur-laden air that stank like the earth's innards. Gasping, Shona clawed her way back to the surface and risked peeking out.

What remained of the peak of Mount Murdo was obscured by the mushrooming cloud of destruction, which glowed a sinister orange from the lava still erupting through its heart. The scarred landscape around her was shrouded in dust. The desolate scene was drained of color, like a funeral pyre. No trace of the beautiful Carraig remained. The countryside was scoured completely of all life.

Then Evander erupted out of the earth nearby and staggered to his feet. His clothing was shredded, his face bloody, and he swayed like a drunkard. Shona felt only relief at seeing another living soul.

Seconds later, Harley burst into view in a spray of dirt, clawing her way to the surface. She looked filthy and exhausted. And terrified.

Evander pointed at the mountain ripping itself apart in the murk above them. He shouted, his voice hoarse, tinged with fear. "You arrogant fool! You broke the root of the mountain. The elements are enraged, just like at the border. Do you again plan to destroy everything that you cannot conquer?"

Harley cringed, and her gaze lingered on the eruption. She grimaced, rubbed her hands across her face, then glared at Evander. "At least I got you speaking normal."

"What will my insane grandmother say when Donleavy shakes itself to pieces around her ears? She can't be queen of a broken kingdom."

"You always focus on the negative," Harley snapped.

"How is this not negative?" Evander exclaimed.

She opened her mouth, but for a moment looked unsure what to say. Her gaze flickered back to the eruption and her shoulders sagged. "Maybe we did draw too deep, but between us, the queen and I can save Donleavy." She spoke forcefully, as if trying to convince herself.

That made Shona feel even more terrified. She'd just witnessed the two of them sling elements around in ways she never would have believed possible. She barely accepted what she'd witnessed. And yet, now they looked frightened. What had they broken? What consequences would the nation face?

"Saving has never been your strength," Evander pointed out.

"But killing you will be my pleasure. Next time we meet."

Harley turned and stalked away. Evander took a step after her, but the ground shook across the devastated land, bucking and rippling like waves in a tempest. At first Shona thought they were joining in battle once more, but both Harley and Evander staggered. That seemed to make up his mind, and he turned and hurried in the opposite direction.

Shona scrambled out of her hole and rushed to Harley, tripping several times on the rolling ground. Harley fell to one knee, and that frightened Shona more than anything.

"Can't you stop it?" she cried.

"Oh, you survived." Harley sounded surprised and distracted.

"What's happening?" Shona demanded, restraining the urge to slap the woman to get her to focus.

"The elements rebelled. We drew too deep and triggered an adverse reaction."

"This is more than an adverse reaction. This is a disaster!" Shona shrieked.

Harley scowled at her. "The borderlands are unstable, but this area felt secure. I hadn't expected the fault lines to connect so closely, but that instability transferred here too."

"You can't stop it?"

She shook her head. "Not here. Not yet. The eruption must run its course. Not even my lady queen could stop that, but together we should be able to shield Donleavy. Come girl, we have to leave."

Instead of summoning one of her sliding chairs, she glanced up into the sky. "The air is unstable, but the earth is rejecting all control. I hate flying, but I don't see any choice."

Shona started to protest, but a whirlwind rushed out of the turbulent sky and caught them both into the air. Shona started spinning, but Harley grabbed her arm. She ended up backward, facing over the destruction of the Carraig. The land looked broken, as if a crazy farmer had taken the world's biggest hoe to the entire plain and hacked it to soft, broken earth.

The flight was rocky, the unstable air pitching and spinning them about as they ascended. Harley grimaced and looked like she might get sick. Shona didn't think she could feel any sicker.

Looking back, she caught a final glimpse of the broken lands where the Carraig had stood. The billowing clouds of dust parted for a moment and she noticed a geyser of earth in the center of the devastation.

A long, metal building, like the vault of the Sculpture House, rose to the surface, with Evander holding onto the end. He heaved the heavy structure, which must have weighed several tons, onto his back and shot away over the broken lands, heading southwest, around the erupting mountain.

She felt relieved he wasn't chasing them.

FRIENDS IN HIGH PLACES

Jean stood on a catwalk ten feet up one of the walls of the barn workroom in Faulenrost. That vantage gave her an excellent view of the test Dierk was conducting in one of the workspaces below.

Two prototype armor plates were secured to a heavy work table on a framework that mimicked the planned skeleton of the spherical armor they were building for Hamish. Dierk gave a signal, and those plates rotated apart, allowing a spinning drill to extend up between them for more than a foot.

The fast-spinning drill made barely any noise, propelled by quartzite, basalt, and some complex gearing. It was one of the new components that could act as both tool and weapon, depending on the need.

Jean clapped as Dierk raised his hands in victory. "Well done!"

She scrambled down to the work floor to join him and his team, who were congratulating themselves on the successful test. Dierk grinned at her, looking like his old, happy self. The dark anger that had been clouding his features so much in recent days couldn't compete with the thrill of new inventions.

The day before, they'd worked through a five-hour brainstorming session about how to actually start attempting to make the ambitious project. She wished Hamish hadn't left for Altkalen after that. He would have loved to see this test.

She also needed his amazing flashes of Builder inventiveness in their work developing close-vision goggles. She'd hoped adapting the long-vision goggles to magnifying tiny objects would prove simple, but they'd run into unexpected issues. The technique wasn't quite the same. He'd developed the first long-vision goggles. Hopefully he could help her get the new ones figured out. She couldn't wait to invite Karlmann to peer down at disease and see what it really looked like.

Bruno came around a line of high shelves that blocked Dierk's group from the next work area where carpenters were assembling a one-tenth scale model of the spherical armor.

"Another success." Bruno smiled, his teeth flashing white against his dark, tanned skin. "Amazing how much work we've accomplished in a single morning."

"I know. When we get our teams focused, they really focus. I'm glad we had so many new people looking for projects."

They had assigned every available person, and even pulled people from other projects to work on the huge armor. The project was big in scope and huge in complexity. Not only did they have to develop the shell, but had to pack the sphere with new mechanicals. The complexity was scary and exciting. Luckily, several other Builders had returned from Altkalen recently, drawn by the news of functioning workrooms. They eagerly dove into the new project.

"Is big complex, but big win," Bruno said, switching to Obrioner. He was trying to learn her language as hard as she was trying to learn his, so they took turns practicing.

Jean's smile faded. "I honestly believe we'll make it work, but I worry about how much power stone it'll consume."

Bruno shrugged. "Is big huge. Need mighty fire to make move."

Jean shook her head. "There has to be a way to harness the raw power more efficiently. All our progress with pulleys and gears prove it's possible to take a little force and make it bigger."

Bruno nodded, his brows creasing in thought. "Pulley and gear good for some things, but no can make fire burn hotter."

Jean paced away, hands dipping into a pocket for her notebook. The many concepts they were studying were fascinating, and she felt a burning conviction that they would continue discovering important breakthroughs. She hated how rushed everything felt, though. They needed months to study and experiment, but they only had days.

"What are think?" Bruno asked.

She blew out an exasperated breath. "There has to be a way. I know it. With the information about the speedcaravan, I feel like there are concepts right there under our noses that we should be seeing. Even a little fire produces a lot of force. We should be able to take that, control it, and magnify . . ."

She trailed off as an idea struck with the force of pure inspiration. She gripped Bruno's enormous hands in hers. "I think I have an idea how to make this work!"

"How?"

She pointed at the drill that Dierk and his team were gathered around. "We already know how to use air or fire to generate force, but we aren't harnessing it tightly enough. What if we generate a little fire, but seal it in a tiny chamber, sort of like the smashpacker? Every bit of force could get harnessed to drive gears that could then magnify and disperse it."

He started asking another question, but she interrupted. "Sorry. Give me a second." She flipped open her notebook and began writing furiously, trying to get her thoughts down before they faded. Bruno had worked with her long enough to recognize those moments and he stood patiently, waiting for the flurry of creativity to ease.

"You're looking very productive."

Jean glanced up to see Danhildur, the leader of the brilliant Althin delegation, approaching. The mature woman had streaks of gray in her blond hair, and smile lines around her mouth and eyes. The Althin team had also received supplies and a dozen additional scientists recently, and they all eagerly jumped in to help.

Jean liked Danhildur and she suspected that was one reason the woman was chosen to lead the delegation. Most of the Althin scientists were so focused on research that they didn't bother integrating socially.

Jean explained, "I just had a great idea about better harnessing the force of our power stones. How about you?"

"I look forward to seeing your notes. We are making steady progress in exploring and documenting fields of science and mathematics to support our mechanical building work. The mechanicals teams are thrilled by all they are learning about mechanicals."

No doubt they were also eagerly sending reports back to the Arishat League. If the queen didn't represent such an immediate and over-whelming threat, Jean would feel concerned about the amount of intelligence they were gathering, but she pushed those worries out of her mind. War with the Arishat League seemed less likely than Hamish going on a hunger strike. They needed each other too much.

She definitely needed them. They shared her love of learning and inventing, but they enjoyed a deeper education and even more experience with rigorous testing models, required by their often dangerous work with chemical weapons.

Danhildur held up a fresh set of plans for the armor. Her team included a talented draftsman who had taken their crude initial sketches and developed them into a full-blown set of plans. Those plans were getting updated hourly as the teams dove into the project, established workable test models, and teased out greater details required for the finished product.

Danhildur spoke both Obrioner and Grandurian with barely a trace of an Althin accent. "This armor will change the nature of battle."

"I hope so."

"Think what we could do with twenty of these. Not even a united Obrion would easily invade then."

"Let's focus on making just one for now." Jean didn't need to create an army of Builder-powered, giant, armored suits. They lacked the

Builders to drive them, anyway. She had not yet shared with Danhildur the secret of the keystone that allowed non-Builders to power mechanicals, and she did not plan to until she better understood the Althins and their ultimate objectives.

"Two of my researchers are creating a plan to include some of our best weapons in this armor. If your man plans to help fight the great queen, he will need every advantage."

"What weapons? Like the mega-stench?" Jean would not refuse any help, but she would not send Hamish into battle with weapons she did not fully understand.

Danhildur shook her head. "We have not yet replenished that supply, but we have other chemicals that could potentially disable even the queen."

"We'll have to review them and test them to make sure they won't hurt Hamish."

Danhildur hesitated, just for a second, but Jean noted it. "I will arrange a series of demonstrations as we prepare the first prototype for testing."

"Good, and please send me the details of those weapons so I can study them in advance."

Again a slight hesitation before she said, "I will see it done."

The Althins would need to learn to share and to trust Jean as much as she was trusting them. So she added, "Thank you. I appreciate all the hard work you and your team are doing. We're building the foundation of a unique school and new international cooperation. I'm glad you understand the importance of sharing information openly."

Jean held her gaze and read in her eyes that she understood they needed to give as much as they received for the partnership to work.

Danhildur nodded in an almost-bow and gave her an approving smile. "When we first arrived, I had reservations about how well a country healer could lead this ambitious endeavor, but I believe your leaders made an excellent choice in picking you."

Jean flashed a smile. "I picked me. They were smart enough to get out of my way."

Danhildur laughed and returned to her team. Jean watched her go, feeling optimistic that they could make this situation work.

Hamish's life depended on it.

Gisela rushed up, looking flustered. "Jean, I have receiving alarming news."

"Is Hamish all right?"

"I have hearing nothing about Hamish." Gisela pulled her aside, even though the banging and clanging and shouting of the work crews drowned out their words. "Lord Eberhard has receiving word from Lord Mattias ordering that we stopping all work here and relocating to Edderitz."

"What?" Jean exclaimed.

"He has ordering that we build New Schwinkendorf on lands he is owning, near one of his palaces."

For several seconds, she was not sure how to respond as her mind raced with the ramifications of that order. The New Schwinkendorf rebuilding effort out on the valley floor was progressing rapidly, despite the cold weather. Already the framework of the central hall was nearly complete and the outer shell should be done within a week. It made no sense to throw away all that work.

Then there was the tremendous progress they were making on the huge armored sphere, and the school planning. All of that work would be paralyzed for weeks to move everything to Edderitz. Why would Kilian . .
.

Jean's eyes narrowed and she asked, "You said this order came from Mattias, not Kilian?"

Gisela nodded.

Now it made perfect sense. "Has Verena awakened yet?"

"Not that we are having received word."

"We're not going anywhere. Come with me."

She marched out of the workroom, through the cold streets of Faulenrost, to Lord Eberhard's manor. The house guard escorted her immediately to his private study, a modest room that felt snug and tidy with its large bookshelf, thick rugs on the hardwood floor, and four comfortable chairs arranged in front of the fireplace full of glowing coals. Lord Eberhard sat near the window behind his paper-strewn desk, holding an open scroll of parchment in his left hand.

He waved Jean in with a smile. "You arrived even faster than I anticipated. Thank you, Gisela."

She curtsied and left the room. Lord Eberhard came around the desk and gestured Jean to take one of the seats near the fireplace. He handed the scroll to her and she scanned its contents. She was learning Grandurian quickly, but struggled with the formal, flowery wording.

Lord Eberhard translated for her. "Mattias spends a great deal of time congratulating me and my people on our efforts to help the refugees from Schwinkendorf. Then he simply orders everyone and everything tied to the Builder compound transported to one of his estates outside of Edderitz."

He gestured at the bottom section, packed with crests and insignia. "He included every official seal he could get his hands on." He looked amused. "I suppose he's trying a shock and awe tactic like the Crushers might attempt in battle."

"But does he have the authority to do this?" Jean asked. She doubted it, but she was not nobility, wasn't even Grandurian, so she had to tread carefully.

Lord Eberhard dropped into another chair and chuckled. "Authority to relocate an entire township, particularly the one that houses the Builders? Of course not. Only a direct order from the monarchy or the central high command during a time of war carries that kind of authority."

"Or Kilian."

"Yes, but Kilian does not meddle in such things often."

"He has taken a personal interest in the development of the Builder school, rebuilding of New Schwinkendorf, and resumption of mechanical production."

"That is true," he said with a smile. "And of course, we cannot ignore the wishes of the Hero of Schwinkendorf, can we?"

Jean grinned. "Can you ignore the order, then?"

He hesitated. "I cannot simply ignore it. Mattias enjoys very good connections, including the patronage of the crown prince himself. No, we must tread carefully or he might attempt to leverage those connections. We would have to obey then."

"But he hasn't done it yet. He must know that he might be refused. He must think it better to try moving everything quietly, then ask for forgiveness later."

"Why do it at all?" Lord Eberhard asked.

"He's trying to position himself so Verena has no choice but to accept his suit when she awakens. If New Schwinkendorf and all mechanical research is established on his estates, she'll have to live right next to him anyway. What's more logical than resuming their courtship?"

"I thought Lady Verena had chosen your friend Connor."

"She has, and she will, but there were some complications. No doubt Mattias will try to ban Connor from seeing her long enough to capitalize on those complications and secure her to him."

Lord Eberhard's expression hardened. "Verena is very popular here. I would feel honor bound to resist efforts to manipulate her into an alliance against her will."

"I hoped you'd see it that way. What if you responded by saying you're happy to help Mattias in any effort he's been ordered to undertake. In fact, you plan to immediately write to Kilian to ask for guidance on transitioning production from here to the new location near Edderitz?"

He laughed. "I like it. And of course, I'll have to send a delegation to that property to plan the layout of the community. I'll even ask for a sizable advance sum of money to purchase supplies to position to help speed up the process. We could optimistically begin the effort within three months of receiving those funds."

Jean grinned. "Plenty of time for Kilian to block the whole thing. I do hope Mattias is desperate enough to send the money before the plans get canceled."

Lord Eberhard's smile widened. "We'd have to dedicate those funds to the rebuilding effort. Probably even name one of the buildings in his honor."

"I'd feel obligated to send him a thank you letter, signed by all of us for his generous patronage," Jean said.

They rose and he bowed over her hand. "Keep up the good work, Lady Jean. I will keep Mattias at bay."

Only after she left did she realize what he'd called her. Was he just being polite, or did the crafty Lord Eberhard actually plan to raise her to Grandurian nobility?

If it helped her watch over her friends, she'd eagerly accept.

36

IS THAT HOPE, OR INDIGESTION?

Shona walked slightly behind Harley as the two approached the queen on her throne in Donleavy. Shona would have looked elegant in her sky-blue satin dress if not for her badly burned hair. She felt immensely self-conscious under the scrutiny of every eye as they traversed the packed throne room.

Her wide-brimmed hat with its ridiculous eoin feather would have helped mask her shameful hair, but the queen had passed a new edict that very morning that all hats must be removed in her presence.

Harley wore a set of Boulder battle leathers, but had added a bright blue cape that flared as she walked. The queen was already scowling, and Shona schooled her expression to careful neutrality. Luckily Harley led the way and would therefore hopefully receive the brunt of the queen's wrath.

Would the leftover anger still prove fatal?

She glanced at her father, who stood at the queen's right hand, up on the dais. He looked confident, and Shona had heard reports that the queen had praised him highly for how well he maintained order in her absence. Could his good standing help Shona if the audience went poorly? Would he even dare try to help?

Ailsa stood on the other side of the queen, near the dais, slightly farther back. Shona met her gaze momentarily, and Ailsa gave her a quick, encouraging smile. Knowing that Ailsa was there, offering her silent support, helped a little.

"How could you make such a stupid blunder?" Queen Dreokt snapped even before Harley and Shona stopped before her. Shona curtsied deeply, while Harley brought a fist to her heart and bowed her head in a strange type of salute.

Harley faced the queen with none of the cowering terror of most of the nobility. She did look contrite and had mentioned on the wild flight over the mountains from the Carraig that she hated letting down her liege.

"Evander rejected your offer." That generated a ripple of nervous whispers. People who knew about Evander feared him. "He has grown stronger during our long sleep. Our duel laid waste to the Carraig and in the heat of battle, we both drew too deep from the elements. I still did not expect the backlash that we triggered. The connection to the unstable border must be stronger than it used to be."

"Of course it is," the queen snapped, ignoring the fresh wave of rippling whispers. "You should have considered the possibility."

Shona couldn't turn around and study the crowd, but the glimpses she caught with subtle shifts of her head showed worry and horror at the news. The Carraig was a vital city, but Harley just reported its destruction as casually as one might discuss weeding a garden.

The queen rose, and most of those assembled took a fearful step back. Some of her executions grew quite messy, and more than once innocents were injured or even killed just by standing too close.

Harley bowed her head in the deepest display of humility Shona had seen from the woman. "I returned immediately to assist in protecting Donleavy from the elemental backlash."

Queen Dreokt swayed forward, one hand rising toward Harley, her expression a mask of rage. Shona tensed for the deadly blow, hoping the queen didn't kill her too.

It never came. Amazingly, the queen stopped, her hand half-extended toward Harley. Her fingers shook, as if the queen had to fight her own instinct to destroy, but the hesitation only lasted for a second.

Then she let her hand drop and took a long, slow breath. Her expression softened from a killing rage to stern disapproval. "So the foolish boy escaped?"

"For now."

"I am severely disappointed in you," the queen declared, with sparks of fire dancing in her eyes.

This was usually the point when the queen executed whoever had displeased her. Shona was tempted to sidle farther away.

Her heart nearly stopped in her chest when the queen turned her angry glare on her. "Tell me what you witnessed."

Stumbling a little over the words, Shona summarized the confrontation with Evander. She left out the details of the conversation. She wasn't sure if Harley wanted the entire court knowing she and Evander had once dated, or that she had offered to resume their relationship when he returned to the queen's service.

She couldn't help mentioning the wonder of Harley's gift of quartzite senses. That generated waves of murmured interest from the assembled crowd, and her father looked pleased. His proud smile faded a bit when she mentioned that those Pathfinder powers were only a temporary gift.

She looked forward to discussing the experience with him. Could they somehow figure out how to replicate that gift? Might that help them discover the secret to unlocking additional Petralist powers?

Shona's description of the epic duel between Harley and Evander drew gasps of awe from every side, but the queen listened in silence. Only when Shona mentioned her final glimpse of Evander traveling away, with that huge vault on his back did the queen speak.

"What has that boy been collecting?" she asked with furrowed brow.

"He always loved researching and delving into old secrets," Harley said, not looking pleased by those memories.

"Indeed, and he's had too long to root around in the bones of Stornoway."

The queen gave Shona an approving smile. "You served well, my dear, and all worthy service earns rewards."

She beckoned Shona closer. Shona approached carefully, hoping the queen didn't suffer a sudden mood reversal. Queen Dreokt stepped to the edge of the dais, took Shona's face in her hands and kissed her on the forehead.

When the queen released her, Shona's scalp began to itch, but she refused to scratch and draw attention to her burned, patchy hair. Gasps of wonder filled the hall, and she risked glancing around. The men looked impressed, while the gathered women looked thunderstruck. One of them patted her own hair.

She could no longer resist, but lifted one hand to her itching scalp. Instead of rough, burned hair, she felt silky smooth locks. Astonished, she pulled her hair forward over her shoulder and was stunned to see thick, golden waves cascading almost down to her elbow. The queen had gifted her a glorious new head of hair.

Shona turned to the queen, who watched her with a little smile on her lips. Shona dropped into a deep curtsy, loving how her beautiful, heavy hair fell around her face. "Thank you, Your Majesty! This is a wondrous gift."

Harley grunted. "It's a simple thing." She glanced at the queen and added in a softer tone, "But wondrous, as you say."

"I will deal with the traitor Evander soon enough, but the elemental instability is an immediate and pressing concern. We cannot risk further destabilization." The queen spoke in a ringing tone. "Therefore, as of this moment, all tertiary Petralists must cease all slate or marble activities unless granted specific permission by myself or Harley."

Most of the gathered nobles looked as shocked as Shona felt. Those were the two most powerful battle stones. Terminating use of slate and marble effectively shackled the army's greatest weapons. Shona had seen the destruction of the Carraig, so she supported the plan one hundred percent.

"Dougal, see that the edict is communicated to all corners of the realm. We must exercise great care until this elemental threat is contained and reversed." Then she waved a hand and shouted, "Begone. Everyone out. Only my chief advisers remain. I want to counsel in private."

People flooded toward the exit, eager to escape her presence. In moments, only Shona, her father, Harley, and Ailsa remained, along with the royal family, patiently waiting behind the throne for any orders.

Queen Dreokt paced away, then returned to Harley. "I expected better of you, my dear."

"As did I," Harley admitted.

"You've placed us in a dangerous position. You of all people know the risks. We cannot allow the elements to reject our control, not again."

"We have time," Harley insisted.

Shona wanted to ask what they were talking about, but didn't dare open her mouth. The queen looked distracted, and she'd learned the hard way that interrupting brought painful consequences.

Then again, maybe the queen would decide to speak with her in more depth later. Shona would welcome the chance to serve as the queen's sounding board again. Such proximity brought risk, but she would accept them for a chance to learn more of the deeper truths. She was quickly coming to realize that access to that knowledge would determine how far one could rise in the queen's court, and perhaps factor in to how long they lived.

"We'll have to remove him before he can cause any mischief," the queen said, switching gears back to Evander.

"I'll see to it at once."

Queen Dreokt shook her head. "No. I have another job for you."

She made a dismissive gesture. "The rest of you leave us. Harley and I must confer alone."

Shona's father insisted on waiting just outside the throne room. He seemed terrified to allow any space between himself and the queen. Shona wondered if he worried another might try to slip into his spot. She doubted anyone was brave enough to make the attempt, even if they were ambitious enough to seek the opportunity.

"I'll speak with you soon," he promised her and kissed her forehead. "Well done, my dear."

"Thank you, father."

Shona descended one of the long stairways leading back down to the central palace. Ailsa had paused on the stairs to walk with her.

"It sounds like you were lucky to survive."

"Most of it was terrifying."

"I find it interesting that she did not punish Harley for such a failure."

Shona nodded. "She needs her. Harley is one of her strongest supporters from her first reign. I think it would take a lot for her to actually punish her."

Ailsa nodded, thoughtful. "That suggests that perhaps she does not consider her reign as secure as she would like us to believe."

"I can't imagine anyone challenging her," Shona said, careful to keep her tone neutral and not share how much she'd love to see the queen removed. Life was simply too unstable around her.

"Perhaps. And yet if she felt secure in her power, why hasn't she simply flown north to Granadure and taken the royal family there like she did here?"

Shona stopped, one hand on the rail, the other going to her mouth as the horror of that idea stunned her. "She could, couldn't she?"

"Perhaps. But she hasn't." Ailsa let her think about that for a moment. As they resumed their descent, Ailsa added, "What do you think she meant by that comment about not allowing the elements to reject her control again?"

"Not sure. I was wondering about it."

"I suspect it might be important. Pay attention and perhaps you'll discover more."

"I will, but do you think it could actually help?" Shona glanced around to make sure they were alone, wishing for her Pathfinder hearing to double-check the rest of the stairway, then added in a whisper. "You talked about hope, but now with Harley returned from the long sleep, it's impossible."

"Nothing is impossible, just sometimes harder than we can manage," Ailsa said with that indomitable look in her eye.

"You didn't see her fighting Evander. He helped Connor defeat that elfonnel, but he barely held his own against her."

"And yet he survived and managed to salvage important information from the ruin of Stornoway."

"How do you know it was important?"

"In the midst of that catastrophe, he risked using earth one final time to pull that vault to the surface and carry it away. I guarantee whatever it held is important. I just need to find a way to learn what was in there."

"Share it with me when you do."

37

NOTHING LIKE A ROAD TRIP TO EASE TENSION

Connor sat at Verena's bedside on a little wooden stool pulled close. He'd spent an hour beside her every day since returning to Altkalen. Even though Abigail, the Healer, insisted Verena did not need any more healing magic, he'd continued his attempts to reach her through chert and sandstone. If she didn't need help, she would have woken up.

He'd grown used to her new hair color, which hadn't changed, even when he applied a bit of healing magic to it. He barely noticed the time flying past as he immersed himself in chert and sandstone. His mind rode along with the comforting warmth of the healing magic as it flowed into her, and he tried to link it to the occasional weak pulses of distant murmuring he sensed through chert. They still weren't as strong as any wakeful person he'd sensed, but they seemed to be growing in regularity. He took that as a good sign and clung to the fragile hope that he was somehow helping.

The regular immersion in the two stones helped strengthen his connection to both of them. With the aid of the sandstone pendant, he'd always enjoyed a strong connection to that affinity, but previously the pendant had done most of the work, sweeping his senses along with it as it healed. Applying only a tiny trickle of healing to only the points it was most needed dramatically improved his sensitivity. Thankfully Student Eighteen was willing to share more of her tiny hoard of chert.

He came to know Verena on an entirely different level. With one touch of healing magic, he could tell how she was doing physically. He knew how her internal systems worked, and he marveled at how strong and healthy every other part of her was. Only her mind resisted his efforts.

Connor worked every day to tease out a connection to her flighty, weak thought patterns. He still sensed no emotions emanating from her, but several times briefly felt a tighter connection, a whisper of a link, like a gossamer thread to her mind. At each of those moments, he pushed a trickle of healing power across the link, willing her to receive it.

The work was delicate and surprisingly exhausting. He ended each session feeling like he'd run for miles without basalt. He began to worry he might exhaust the pendant before fully healing her. It had seen him through many adventures and saved many lives. He dreaded losing it, and needed to find a way to contact his aunt Ailsa. Could she supply a replacement somehow?

When Verena's thoughts seemed quiet and unreachable, he talked. Abigail had suggested that the sound of his voice might help, so he spent the time reviewing what he learned from Kilian in their daily training practices and his worry that they might never find a way to defeat the dread queen.

Speaking with Verena helped keep the maddening hunger for porphyry at bay. The first couple of days after diorite burned it out of his system, he'd felt great, but it had begun creeping back into his thoughts. He found himself dwelling on those moments of porphyry glory with renewed longing.

He tried blocking those thoughts, pushing them away, refusing to give in to the soft tugging at his will. He'd slipped far too close to the edge of control in Merkland and he knew better. The oath he'd made to Verena helped, as did the daily talk. If the craving grew much more, he'd ask Kilian for another chance to practice with diorite.

Now he looked down on her slumbering form and studied the contours of her lovely face. He'd long since memorized every curve of her cheek and how every lock of her hair caressed her skin.

Connor leaned over and kissed her forehead, then whispered, "I know you're in there, Verena. You're strong. You will find a way to solve this puzzle, and I'll be here when you wake up. No matter how long it takes."

Verena's mouth fell open into a soft snore.

Connor leaped to his feet, shouting for Abigail. She rushed in, her blue eyes seeming to glow as she shouldered Connor aside to place a hand on Verena's head.

"What happened?" she demanded.

"She snored," Connor said excitedly, keeping his eyes glued on Verena, expecting to see her eyelids flutter open any second.

Abigail dropped her hand, rounded on him, and asked very slowly in a deceptively soft voice, "She snored?"

"Right after I spoke to her. I think she's waking up."

"Tallan . . . preserve me from fools," the woman muttered. She closed her eyes for a second and took a deep breath. When she opened them, her gaze was once more kind. "People snore when they sleep. It doesn't mean anything."

"But she's never done that before," Connor protested. He refused to believe she hadn't made the sound in response to his voice. "She was trying to tell me something."

"If anything, it was a plea for some blessed silence."

"But you said the sound of my voice might help."

"And it might, but monologues are always annoying. Try pausing for breath once in a while at least."

"Have you been listening?" Connor asked, suddenly feeling self-conscious.

Thankfully the woman shook her head. "I just hear the drone of your voice, not the words." She patted his hand gently. "No doubt she appreciates your dedication, but I've heard her snore. Not often, but occasionally. I tell you young man, it means nothing."

"It did this time," he insisted.

She gave him an understanding smile and gestured him out of the room. "Maybe it did, but a message just arrived for you bearing Lady Marshal Saskia's seal. It's on the desk in the other room."

Surprised, he followed her into the sitting room where a scroll sat on the table, sealed with teal-colored wax, stamped with an image of a Sapper tower standing before a rising sun. He broke the seal and scanned the short letter. "I'm summoned to the council chamber immediately."

"Then you'd best be off. They don't like to be kept waiting," Abigail said, shooing him from the room. "I'll double check Verena, just to be sure nothing has changed."

He thanked her and jogged toward the distant council chamber, wondering about the summons. Had the war started again? More likely, the queen had done something barbaric, but to who? He hadn't been invited to any official meetings since the battle weeks before. He thought Saskia and Mattias were pretending he wasn't around.

When he reached the hall outside the ornate double doors to the council chamber, the guards admitted him immediately. The magnificent room awed him as much as it had the first time. It ran a solid hundred yards over warm golden oak floors. Connor had to wonder how far he could slide on that enormous, polished surface if he got a good running start.

A long mahogany table lorded over the center of the room. He bet fifty people could easily fit on each long side, plus another five at the ends. The ten council members sat in their throne-like chairs, along with Ivor and Student Eighteen. Saskia and Mattias sat at the head of the table, while Kilian and General Wolfram occupied the far end. Identical short stacks of parchment were positioned in front of each person. More papers sat in front of two unoccupied chairs, near the foot of the table, next to Ivor.

As Connor approached, he glanced at the high, arched ceiling and tall row of windows that marched down the left-hand wall and bathed the room in bright afternoon sunshine. Instead of baskets of flowers at every column, today they held evergreen boughs that filled the chamber with a soft, pleasant scent.

Every eye turned to watch him approach so Connor waved. "Hello everyone. Sorry I'm late."

"Welcome, Connor," Sakia said formally, gesturing him toward the table. Mattias kept his expression neutral.

Connor scanned the group, wishing he could remember the names of all of the councilors. He did remember the council leaders, who sat closest to Saskia and Mattias.

Lord Pankraz, commander of the city watch, sat on the left side next to crafty old Ulrich, the architect of the city's successful battle plan and voice of the trading houses. Liane, the elegantly dressed matron of the seamstress guild, sat on the right next to jolly Hette, the plump leader of the culinary guilds. Connor hoped she'd brought lots of treats concealed under the billowing folds of her dress like last time.

Connor barely reached his seat before the door opened again and Hamish strode through. He was wearing a new Builder battle suit. Iw as slightly bulkier, and sported an impressive outer layer of leather and steel. Seeing his best friend thrilled Connor, and he jumped back out of his seat to go greet him.

With his helmet tucked under his arm, Hamish waved to Connor as he strode into the room, then grinned at the rest of the assembly. "I heard we're meeting over cake."

"Soon," Hette promised with a laugh.

"Welcome, Builder," Saskia said in the same formal tones she'd used to greet Connor.

Connor gripped Hamish's hand and punched his shoulder. With that suit on, he doubted Hamish even felt it. "I thought you were with Jean."

"Got summoned back. Barely flew in. Couldn't leave you to have all the fun, and eat all of Hette's cakes."

"That new suit looks amazing."

Hamish's grin widened. "It works even better. Wait till I show you what it can do."

Wait till Connor showed him he could vomit explosions.

Kilian gestured them to take their seats, then spoke. "Now that we're all here, let's focus on the business at hand. You all have in front of you the most recent report from our best asset in Donleavy. I recommend you study it in detail at your leisure, but for now I will summarize."

He must be speaking of Aunt Ailsa. Connor couldn't imagine anyone positioned more perfectly, or more dangerously.

Kilian continued. "Queen Dreokt is rapidly consolidating her reign. She will soon represent a direct threat to all of us."

Old Ulrich spoke. "I wish she would take her time. Sounds like she's wreaking more havoc among her own lords than we ever could."

"She is bludgeoning them into total obedience. We need to make some decisions immediately if we hope to counter her growing power before she launches a new invasion."

Mattias, who was looking grumpy but trying to hide it asked, "We have a little time, surely. She can't hope to invade before spring."

Kilian shook his head. "An army like the last invasion would struggle to launch a winter assault, but there is nothing preventing her from deciding to travel north and dethrone our own king like she did Turriff."

"Alone?" Mattias exclaimed, not trying to hide his disbelief.

Kilian said calmly, "If she chose, she could. This latest report states that she has raised one of her most powerful supporters from a centuries-long elfonnel slumber. I knew Harley. She is one of the original Petralists, a Dawnus of incredible power. Our contact reports that she challenged Evander. Although they both survived the ordeal, it grew so fierce that they further triggered elemental instability through much of Obrion and destroyed the entire Carraig."

"Oh, no," Connor breathed. He'd loved the many-spired inner city, and he still thought of the Sculpture house as a home.

"You did wreck things pretty thoroughly before you left," Hamish pointed out.

"But I'd hoped they could rebuild." No one would ever get to run the Rhidorroch again. That thought saddened and enraged him at the same time.

General Wolfram said, "I've received reports from Sappers that the broken lands north of Harz have worsened as a result of that calamity."

Saskia said, "I had been thinking we were getting things under control, but the ground is wilder than ever."

That surprised Connor. He hadn't walked with slate in a few days. He reminded himself he couldn't afford to not know what was going on.

Kilian glanced around the table, holding each eye in turn. "The entire continent could destabilize if we're not careful. That could lead to catastrophic destruction that could lay waste to every major city."

Connor exchanged a worried look with Hamish, who was holding a half-eaten pastry partway to his mouth. Where had he gotten that?

"What can we do?" Ulrich asked, and several of the others echoed similar questions.

"Effective immediately, we must order cessation of all slate and marble affinities. No Sapper or Firetongue can utilize their tertiary powers for the foreseeable future."

That generated a round of angry responses. Saskia looked furious at the thought of shackling her greatest power. She rose to her feet and declared,

"There once was a fool so complete,
He threw himself at his enemy's feet.

Afraid to still fight, he ignored what was right,
And accepted eternal defeat."

Connor grimaced. Saskia usually only slipped into her limerick Sentry-speak when she wanted to tease someone, or when she was angry. Most of the assembled looked like they agreed with her. Connor did not want to lose two of his powerful battle stones, but neither did he want to try living on a continent that decided to tear itself apart beneath them.

Kilian did not look surprised by the outburst. "I understand your concerns, but in this report, our spy relates that the queen herself issued the exact same decree across Obrion. If the elements have revolted enough to scare her into caution, we should feel terrified."

That mollified their anger a bit, and Wolfram spoke into the calm. "Timing couldn't be worse. I received word just an hour ago from General Rory. He's hearing rumors that the entire army wintering at Crann may be mobilized and sent to Merkland."

"Why would Rory tell you that?" Mattias demanded.

Connor said casually, "Oh, didn't you hear? Ivor and I stopped by after we visited Donleavy and recruited Rory to the revolution."

"What revolution?" Ulrich asked, looking surprised.

Ivor said, "Like Kilian said, the queen is consolidating her power too quickly. Rory and I will start a revolution right under the queen's nose. If that doesn't disrupt her plans for a while, I'm not sure what will."

"And Rory agreed?" Ulrich asked.

"Well, we got interrupted before getting into the specifics, but the conversation was definitely moving in that direction."

"Why would Rory start a revolution now? He's a commanding general," Mattias asked.

Connor decided they all needed to understand the truth as much as the Obrioner Guardians did. "Because we've proven that Patronage is a lie, and when we spread that truth, it will destroy the stranglehold that the high houses have over Guardians. With the queen tightening her grip over everyone, revolution is a logical next step."

The gathered company instantly grasped the immense ramifications of what he was saying, and they broke into excited discussions.

"You really proved the lie?" Mattias asked, looking like he didn't believe it.

"Conclusively," Kilian confirmed. "The revolution spearheaded by Ivor and Rory will be part of our first-phase response to the new threats in Obrion, but we must do much more. I have been in contact with Prince Theodor and he has authorized a delegation to Althing to formalize a joint defense agreement with the Arishat League and begin drafting battle plans."

"Battle plans for what?" Ulrich asked.

General Wolfram said, "For potential invasion of Obrion to defeat Queen Dreokt, of course."

A somber silence settled over the crowd as they digested that. It was one thing to plan a brilliant defense of one's home, but an entirely different thing to undertake invading Obrion.

Kilian said, "We cannot delay. This embassy is critical, but I myself cannot go. I plan to return to the border to set wards to notify me if my mother or Harley, or both, decide to head north."

"You can't stop them," Connor warned.

Kilian might be the master of the arcane, but his mother had talked about him like a petulant child. He had failed to destroy her when she first rose from the long sleep. Now she was strong, and if Harley was strong enough to fight Evander to a draw, the two of them together could destroy every army Granadure threw at them.

Connor didn't like feeling small or weak or helpless. He knew the feeling all too well from growing up as a sickly linn in Alasdair, but he'd never expected to feel that way again. The thought of facing Queen Dreokt again made feeling that way all too easy.

Kilian only gave him that roguish smile. "Perhaps not, but with a little luck I could delay them a little. My next duty will be to return to Edderitz. If my mother or Harley do cross the border, their target will be the royal family. I'll work with them to set up a defensive plan."

He scanned the somber gathering. "War is coming. A war to make the last incursion by High Lord Dougal feel like a minor clash from the vanguard. We must act quickly, or we may never get the chance to act at all."

Mattias said, "Then I will go to Althing. I have the prince's authorization already. I have the authority to negotiate the agreement."

That surprised Connor. Mattias had seemed intent on staying close beside Verena until she awoke.

"You're probably the best choice," Kilian agreed.

"I think Connor should come with me," Mattias said, looking right at Connor, as if daring him to refuse.

Well, that explained it. If Mattias had to leave, he didn't want Connor to enjoy sole access to Verena if she awoke during his trip.

Saskia said, "You must go, Connor. You're Blood of the Tallan. Your presence will lend additional weight to the negotiations."

Connor tried to refuse, but Saskia supported the idea with such enthusiasm that the rest of the council soon clamored for him to go. He'd just returned from a long trip. The last thing he wanted to do was leave Verena again. He'd love to visit Althing, but with Verena at his side.

"I think you should go," Kilian said finally. "We need this alliance. You've seen my mother and lived to tell the tale. Few can say that."

That plea effectively ended the discussion. Connor wondered if Kilian might have other reasons for wanting to send him halfway across the continent when they really needed to continue his training, but Kilian did not elaborate. Connor could not think of a good enough reason to deny him.

"I will join you too," General Wolfram offered.

Mattias looked pleased by the offer. "I gladly accept. They know you and respect you."

"And I think I should go too," Hamish said, breaking his long silence. He'd spent the bulk of the meeting listening and jotting notes on a small notebook that looked like a half-sized version of one of Jean's.

Mattias frowned. "I think we have enough. Your place is with the other Builders."

Hamish shook his head. "Like Kilian said, we need to reinforce the urgency of the moment."

Connor added, "Hamish is one of the lead Builders. I'm sure the Althins will love meeting him."

Mattias didn't have a good argument, so Hamish's appointment to the team was quickly confirmed. They also decided to pick up Gisela from Faulenrost, along with some mechanicals to offer as gifts to the Arishat League leadership. Student Eighteen volunteered to round out the company.

"Are you sure that's wise?" Saskia asked.

She grinned. "Don't worry about me. I love Dagmanson. I once spent three months there doing research in the vaults. My contacts might prove useful."

Connor grinned, looking forward to meeting another of her personalities.

IMPORTANT PEOPLE FLY FIRST CLASS

As they banked over Schwinkendorf valley on their descent toward Faulenrost, Connor pressed his nose against the shimmering shieldstone canopy that protected the long windrider from the icy wind.

Without warning, the barrier disappeared, and Connor lurched forward, nearly tipping over the railing. He glanced at Hamish, who sat next to him on the high pilot bench in his flying suit. "Warn me next time." He was tempted to punch him on the shoulder, but he'd have to tap granite in order for Hamish to feel it.

Hamish laughed as freezing air sucked away the warmth. "I thought you were eager to land."

"Not that eager."

"Don't be so timid." Hamish leaped over the front railing and plunged down out of sight.

Connor laughed. Mattias, who sat on the opposite end of the pilot bench scowled. Such a bright guy should have gotten used to the stunt by now. Hamish had jumped out several times on their trip south.

Each time he spent a few minutes performing aerial acrobatics, insisting that he had to calibrate every component of his new suit. Connor could read his friend too well, though. Hamish should have thought about how slow the return trip would be when he decided to leave the Storm in Faulenrost.

Connor studied the valley below. The destruction of the Builder compound had been cleared and New Schwinkendorf was already laid out in the snow, with several buildings under construction. The framework of one huge, multi-story edifice was complete and the outer sheathing and roofing were being added. It swarmed with workmen like an anthill.

Hamish swooped out from under the wagon near Connor and leaned on the rail from the outside. He pushed up the visor of his helmet and pointed at the ongoing construction. "More people keep returning, and literal tons of supplies have rolled in. This will be the fastest rebuilding in Grandurian history."

"They've made a terrible mistake, though."

"What do you mean? It's going to be amazing."

"It's too neat." Connor gestured at the orderly streets marked onto the snowy plain. "The old Schwinkendorf was like some untidy giant who liked hoarding buildings."

Hamish laughed. "I'll miss that part, but do you honestly think Jean would allow anything that chaotic to be constructed when she had a say in it?"

"Good point."

Student Eighteen, who sat on one of the benches behind them with Wolfram said, "Hamish, do you plan to fly right over Faulenrost?"

They'd almost reached the picturesque town, nestled in the hills to the east of the valley.

"Oh, right." Hamish performed a double backflip up and over the wagon and landed perfectly on the high pilot bench. Grasping the control rods, he pivoted the wagon and settled it to the landing field just outside of town, next to an older windrider that looked battered from heavy use.

A small crowd was already gathered. Jean stood at the front, wearing a long, fur-lined coat, but no hat. Her thick, blond braid blew in the wind from the thrusters.

Hamish leaped out, soared across to Jean, and caught her off her feet. The two ascended a dozen feet, twirling slowly together and laughing.

While most of the crowd watched the happy couple, Gisela and Dierk approached and greeted Connor warmly, then Student Eighteen and Wolfram. They somehow missed Mattias, who stood slightly apart, but instead turned back to Connor and enthusiastically started talking about the rebuilding efforts and mechanicals production.

Hamish and Jean landed nearby. They both looked jubilant, and Connor loved seeing them together.

He hugged Jean. "I'm impressed. You haven't wasted any time."

Jean beamed. "We have a lot to do, but we have a lot of help. Lord Eberhard purchased a large shipment of additional supplies out of his own coffers to help speed up the work. In the past three days we've increased efforts by nearly a third."

"Are you sure?" Mattias asked. He'd remained slightly apart as the friends all reunited. He looked troubled instead of pleased. That didn't make much sense. Mattias was an outspoken supporter of Builders.

Jean nodded. "Indeed we are. Have you not received Lord Eberhard's reply to your command to cease production and move New Schwinkendorf to your estates near Edderitz?"

"What?" Connor and Hamish exclaimed together.

"How do you know about that?" Mattias demanded, sounding affronted.

"I consult with Lord Eberhard on a daily basis. He proclaimed me the hero of Schwinkendorf and he takes titles very seriously. I chair the committees responsible for rebuilding efforts, the Builder workroom reconstruction, and the school."

She spoke calmly, but she stood unafraid before Mattias, chin up, with a hint of anger in her eyes.

Mattias scowled. "Congratulations, but I suspect he may have over-stepped his authority."

Jean stepped closer and she gave him that look she usually reserved for Hamish and Connor when they did something particularly stupid. "As have you, Lord Mattias. I've sent word to Kilian asking for direction on how best to wind down production here in the event that a move is indeed required, but nothing will change until he replies."

"You did what?" Mattias looked a little sick.

So much for letting the best man win Verena. Connor seethed at Mattias's underhanded actions.

Jean continued, "I am doing exactly what Kilian authorized me to do. Our work here is vital. Do not attempt to undermine it for personal gain. I will not allow it."

Mattias's surprise was quickly turning to anger. "Have a care how you speak to me, girl. You are nothing but a commoner, a foreigner. I am a lord of Granadure."

Hamish balled his hands into fists, his expression furious, but Connor stepped between him and Mattias. "I don't care who you are. If you ever speak disrespectfully to Jean again, I'll call you out."

"You'll what?"

Hamish said coldly, "Means he'll beat that pretty smile off your face, but only if you accept his challenge before mine."

General Wolfram stepped between them, hands raised in a placating gesture. "Easy now, boys. We're all allies. Let us not begin our mission together with infighting."

"I agree completely," Mattias said, sniffing airily at them. "I apologize for growing irritated. I suspect we're dealing with a challenge of translation."

"Oh, I think I made myself quite clear," Jean said. Then she gave him a graceful curtsy and added, "I'm sure Lord Eberhard will be happy to meet with you in his manor and answer any questions you may have."

Mattias clearly recognized that he was being dismissed, and just as clearly didn't like that an Obrioner commoner was doing the dismissing. Making an issue of it would only make him look like an even greater fool, so he stomped away without another word.

Hamish swept Jean into a fierce hug. "You're amazing, you know that?"

"How can I forget? You tell me all the time."

"I should pound him," Hamish said.

"No, you shouldn't," General Wolfram said sternly.

"He does deserve it," Connor said.

Wolfram hesitated long enough to show he agreed before saying, "Pounding Lord Mattias will accomplish nothing but place you in his power. He is a good man at heart, but he's facing a situation he is not well equipped to handle."

Jean said, "He's not acting like a good man. Even though he's losing Verena to Connor, he shouldn't discard his honor."

Connor agreed. "He made a pact with me to accept Verena's will when she awakens and chooses one of us, but he's trying very hard to circumvent that agreement and force her hand."

Wolfram said, "Not the most honorable action, but consider why he feels the need to attempt such tactics. Which army must use deceit and trickery?"

"The one that wants to win," Hamish said.

Jean said, "The weaker, of course. The stronger army holds the advantage." She placed a hand on Connor's arm and gave him an encouraging smile. "Verena loves you, Connor. Even Mattias knows it."

"Mattias is a man used to getting what he wants so it's hard to admit he might lose something he feels is important. It's even harder when he's made a public claim." Wolfram said gravely. "Don't let him get away with his tricks, but don't condemn him."

Connor preferred simply hating Mattias and looking for his chance to punch him through a window. There had to be a way to make that dream come true without undermining his position or his access to Verena.

Until he figured it out, he'd play along. "Fine. Let's change the subject. Jean, we're heading for Althing on a special mission from the crown prince. Gisela, we'd like you to join us."

"Of course," Gisela said immediately, but then hesitated and glanced at Jean.

She gave Gisela an encouraging nod. "You have to go. We'll manage without you for a little while. Don't worry. I wish I could go with you."

"You should," Hamish said.

Jean shook her head. "Someday, but there is simply too much to do. If both Gisela and I leave at the same time, too many aspects of our work would probably grind to a halt. You'll just have to take me back there for another visit in the springtime."

"Is much loveliest in the spring," Gisela said.

Hamish sighed. "I figured you'd say that. Springtime for sure, then. We're going to grab a few mechanicals as gifts to help secure a military alliance."

"We don't have a lot," Jean warned.

"Can we round up three or four healthbeds, a few pairs of blind coal gauntlets, and maybe a couple speedslings with two or three full rearmings each?"

Connor figured that if negotiations went unexpectedly sour, those mechanicals would still come in handy.

"I think we can do that, but it'll be a tight fit."

"The Storm can handle it," Hamish said.

Jean shook her head. "You won't be taking the Storm. I need it for research."

"But we can't fly all the way to Althing in that creaky, slow, old windrider," Hamish complained.

"Of course you can't." Jean gave him a dazzling smile. "For a royal delegation, you must have the best. Come on, it's finished."

"What's finished?" Connor asked as they all trooped after her to a warehouse near a huge barn on the outskirts of town. The barn was one of the new Builder workshops, with people working on five different types of mechanicals, surrounded by crates of power stone and piles of supplies.

Jean gestured for Connor and Hamish to pull aside the long, sliding door of the warehouse, then led them into the dim interior. Hamish activated a brightly glowing limestone before Connor could.

A sleek new craft, about the same size as the Storm, crouched on the floor, as if barely restraining the urge to leap into the sky. Connor had always thought the Storm a marvel, but this new craft made the Storm look like a clunky, ugly brother.

The new craft had gracefully tapered lines, its body more like a fat falcon than a box like all the other flyers. Two stubby wings protruded from the sides, adding to the image of a bird poised for take-off.

Hamish whistled softly and slid a hand down one smooth side. "You built our new prototype. It's even more amazing than I imagined. This is so much more than our rough drafts suggested."

"Thank the new school," Jean said proudly. "We aren't actually teaching many classes yet. We're too busy doing research and documenting foundational principles. We made this a major focus of our initial efforts."

"She's beautiful," Hamish whispered.

"We dubbed her the Hawk."

"It's perfect," Connor said, and the others all nodded.

"I'd hoped you'd like it. It's almost as fast as the Storm, but uses a fraction of the power stone to reach top speed, and it's far more maneuverable. It banks like a bird."

The inside was configured much like the Storm, with three rows of three seats near the front and a wagon-like bed in the back for supplies. The seats were padded and looked a lot more comfortable, though.

Several additional storage compartments fit seamlessly into the curving underside and included access panels from within the passenger compartment. A skeletal framework enclosed the passenger space, with wide, curving window openings between.

Jean showed them where quartzite stones, cut to geometric patterns, were already embedded in that framework. "These shieldstones are cut to generate overlapping shields to form a protective dome against the elements. The shapes are similar to the ones in your helmet, Hamish. They produce stronger shields but consume less power. Should make the trip comfortable."

Hamish pointed to a couple of small metal stoves bolted to the floor. "I'm glad you copied my heating idea."

"No reason not to stay warm," Jean agreed.

She briefly summarized the Hawk's armaments. The sleek body was made of armored steel for defense. Two oversized speedslings were concealed in the belly, with quartzite-operated doors that swung aside when they spun up. Puking Dooms that blasted intense flames were built into the underside, while eight large diorite-tipped missiles were recessed into the wings.

"We're looking into more powerful armaments, but these were the best we could do on short notice."

Hamish laughed and kissed her. "You did all this on short notice? I can't wait to see what you can do with all the time in the world."

"Me too," she grinned.

"Let's pack up everything we need tonight so we can get an early start in the morning," Wolfram suggested.

"I'm still working on that flash cooker of yours, and hope to install it for in-flight food. In the meantime, we built an enhanced smashpacker so you'll have plenty of cubed meals," Jean said.

Hamish sighed, looking so happy he seemed to struggle to find words. So he just took her hand and said, "Why don't the rest of you see about those mechanicals? We'll catch up."

As Connor and the others headed for the nearby workroom, Hamish lifted Jean into the air with a whoosh of thrusters. Their laughter seemed to hang around the warehouse a long time after they disappeared into the bright blue sky.

39

GAFFER-KICKED-YA

The Hawk took to the skies like a true bird of prey. Hamish loved flying it nearly as much as he did his own battle suit. The Storm was fast, but it turned like a brick. The Hawk banked at speed with beautiful grace, and Hamish laughed as he pushed it to the limits.

"I think I will being sick," Gisela moaned from the middle seat behind him.

Hamish had forgotten anyone else rode in the amazing craft with him. He glanced back and noticed that Wolfram clutched the rail beside his seat in a white-knuckled grip and Mattias looked like maybe he'd already thrown up into his shirt.

Connor, who sat beside Hamish in the front row was grinning with the thrill of the intense flight. Hamish knew he could count on Connor to keep up, no matter how wild the ride got. Student Eighteen sat alone in the back row and she gave him a jaunty wave, looking like she was also enjoying herself.

"Sorry," Hamish said as he leveled out the Hawk and slowed. He dropped one of the shields from a back window to let in some fresh air, which seemed to help.

"Are you trying to kill us all?" Mattias demanded.

"I need to get a sense for how she flies. Otherwise we might run into trouble if we hit rough air."

"We've hit rough air," Wolfram groaned, rubbing his temples.

Student Eighteen's face shivered a bit, a telltale sign she was shifting personalities. She spoke in her Rith voice, "Buck up, old man. That ride was the closest thing to real speed I've seen any non-Strider manage. Well done, Builder."

"She's amazing though, isn't she?" Hamish grinned.

"Amazing but a little too spiriting for me," Gisela said. She unbuckled her restraint, rose from her seat, and went to the open window to better savor the cold, rushing air.

Hamish didn't understand why flying, spinning, and turning affected so many people so adversely. "Well, it's smooth sailing from here to Emmerich Quarry."

After a good night's sleep, they had tarried in Faulenrost through the morning, detained by Lord Eberhard, who had insisted on celebrating their arrival with a town-wide breakfast feast. He'd made a passionate speech, thanking Lord Mattias on behalf of the crown prince for the generous support they'd received for the rebuilding effort.

The townsfolk had cheered wildly, and Mattias had seemed taken aback by their enthusiasm. Hamish imagined he'd seen a flicker of guilt in his expression for having tried to steal away the entire town of New Schwinkendorf. Hopefully Mattias would drop his foolish plan.

Hamish hadn't been in a rush to leave and had found reasons to delay their departure until almost noon. He and Jean had spent the time together, reviewing mechanicals production and discussing plans for the immense outer armor her teams were building. They'd made tremendous progress, and even though he knew Jean better than anyone except maybe her grandmother, he still felt awed by how much she'd accomplished.

"We'll overnight in Emmerich and get an early start tomorrow," Mattias said. "Can we make it all the way to Althing in one day?"

"Probably two, if the winds continue as good as they have been," Hamish guessed. He'd never traveled that far east, but he'd studied some good maps of the continent before leaving Altkalen.

Once everyone felt settled again, Hamish restored the shielding over the back window and accelerated smoothly south. The little wings stabilized flight incredibly well. They should have added wings sooner, and he bet the Storm would have a pair by the time they returned.

By midafternoon they soared over a long row of high hills and caught sight of Emmerich valley. The town spread out to the south of the quarry, windows glinting in the afternoon sunlight. Hamish pointed. "There it is."

He studied the distant town, increasing the magnification factor of his long-vision goggles. Then he got a great idea and activated a second aspect to the quartzite embedded in the pillars supporting their roof. The nearly transparent shield of the front window shimmered, then the landscape seemed to rush toward them.

"What's happening?" General Wolfram asked, sounding a bit shaken.

"I set the front window to act like a giant long-vision goggle." The view zoomed in on the town and the crowds of people already pointing up in their direction.

"Excellent," Student Eighteen said.

Hamish set down in the center of town, not far from the fountain where Stuart had won his honor duel. The Alasdairians nearly swarmed them under with their enthusiasm, although many of them berated Hamish for failing to bring Jean along too. He finally earned some respite by promising to bring her for sure the next time.

He grinned as his family encircled him, siblings clamoring for rides with him on his new suit. His mother hugged him fiercely, and his father clapped him proudly on the shoulder.

"How is lovely Jean?" his mother asked.

"Taking over the world, one city at a time."

Mattias stood close enough to hear, and he frowned. Hamish grinned at him, hoping the man was foolish enough to push Jean again. No doubt his estates were opulent. She'd look good as their new lady.

Of course Lord Wenzel declared a feast. He was a good man. Hamish grinned when he noticed how the different dishes from both countries were passed around freely across both groups. Instead of sitting strictly in their town groups, they were beginning to intermingle more too. It seemed that working together daily had helped ease tensions far more quickly than he'd feared.

Just as important, both towns embraced Stuart's courtship of Stefanie. The unusual relationship seemed to have come to symbolize the union of these peoples from different lands into one community. Hamish hoped the goodwill continued. They would need examples like Emmerich to help demonstrate to others that coexistence was possible.

Hamish ate enthusiastically. He was looking forward to trying Althin food, but the best way to gauge its quality was to bring a fresh memory of all the best from both Obrion and Granadure with him. So he pushed himself to the bursting point. For pure research.

At one point, he noticed Connor walking in the back of the room with Mhairi. She placed a hand on his shoulder and spoke earnestly for several minutes.

Hamish appreciated Connor's thoughtfulness. By keeping Mhairi so distracted, he guaranteed she'd forget to give Hamish any of the nasty tonics she no doubt had prepared to test his courage in order to prove him worthy of Jean.

Tomorrow was plenty early for that challenge. Hopefully a tomorrow that never became today.

The evening passed far too quickly. The feast lasted for hours and transitioned somehow to dancing that lasted into the night. Hamish enjoyed catching up with his family and friends. They were beginning to see Emmerich as their home, and he loved how quickly they were recovering from the traumatic loss of Alasdair. Knowing they were well helped him focus on the upcoming mission.

They managed an early start from Emmerich. Lord Wenzel wanted to get his workers out into the quarry without delay to work on their backlog of missed quotas. So he fed them a quick breakfast and ushered them to the Hawk.

As they prepared to leave, Connor's mother approached him and Hamish. She spoke in a conspiratorial whisper. "I've heard the Althins make wonderful winter socks with their special strains of wool. If you can get your hands on some while you're there, I'd appreciate it. I want a surprise gift for your father for the winter solstice festival."

Hamish grinned as Connor promised her he'd make sure to keep his eyes out for the special wool. Hamish never would have planned a surprise sock gift. He and Connor had pranked so many people by dropping little surprises into their boots that socks weren't high on his gifts-that-make-people-smile list.

When they climbed into the Hawk, Connor's younger brother Wallace shouted, "Bring me a baby seal from the fjords!"

"Do they have fjords in Althing?" Connor asked as Hamish activated thrusters to lift them gently into the air.

Gisela nodded. "How did Wallace learning about that?"

Hamish smoothly accelerated into the sky and banked to the east. "Wallace always wanted a pedra. I bet your mother searched everywhere for less lethal ideas. Seals would be just the thing."

"Unless he tried to ride it underwater," Wolfram said with a smile.

"Don't ever give him that idea," Connor warned.

They rose high into the early morning sky and pointed toward the rising sun. Hamish found an eager tailwind that threw them across the landscape at tremendous speed. Without the shielding over the windows to block out the howling wind, and the marble heaters fighting back the bitter cold, they would have suffered a miserable journey.

Hamish leaned back in his comfortable chair, with his feet up on the front window sill and sighed as he studied the landscape flowing past, thousands of feet below. "I never thought I'd say I preferred flying any way except in my suit, but I have to admit this is pretty nice."

After an hour of cruising, with the peaks of the Abwehr Mountains marching along the horizon to their right, Connor asked, "Gisela, can you tell us about Dagmanson?"

Gisela, who seemed to be a nervous flyer, seemed eager to talk. "Althing is much sparselier populated, especially compared to Ravinder or Sehrazad, but we are having beautiful, wild countryside."

She explained that the center of the country did produce bountiful crops, and their rocky coastline along the Sea of Olcan offered excellent fishing and trade routes with the rest of the continent.

"Dagmanson is being the jewel of our nation. More than a quarter of all Althins are living there. It lies to the east, protected by the Kalfafell mountains that form the border between Althing and Granadure. It also is serving as the seat of the Arishat League for over two centuries."

"What do you call those mountains in Granadure?" Connor asked.

"We just use the Althin name," Wolfram said.

Hamish frowned. "But why did you rename the Maclachlans the Abwehr mountains and change Mount Macduib to Osterwald?"

Wolfram shrugged. "We haven't fought as much with the Althins."

Hamish chuckled. "Really? You changed the names just out of spite?"

Mattias actually smiled. "Something like that. Think about it. When you grew up thinking Granadure was evil, would you have wanted to use our names?"

Hamish shook his head. "Of course not, but not because we hated you. Our names are just better."

Before they could get that argument heated up properly, Connor interrupted. "I don't understand how Althing can be bigger than Obrion and Granadure combined."

Hamish also found that odd.

"You'll seeing once we cross the Kalfafell," Gisela promised. "Dagmanson has building in a spur of the mountains that running east, called the Skaftafell."

Hamish loved how the foreign words flowed off her tongue with a grace he could never manage, but Connor grimaced. "Your names are so weird."

Wolfram muttered, "Says a man from a nation that named the Drumwhindle Pass and Mount Macduib." He pronounced it mac-dweeb.

"Well, when you say it like that, it does sound pretty bad," Connor admitted.

Gisela explained how Dagmanson stood at the head of the Three Sisters, great rivers that formed the backbone of the nation. They brought life, trade, and travel across a land that would surely fall barren without them.

The first was the deep Saol river, which flowed southwest and eventually formed the border between Althing and Obrion. It served as an important trading waterway between them all the way from Trodaire to the twin trading centers of Freastal and Deifur. There it melded into the mighty Macantact in the final stretch of its miles-wide journey out to the sea. At the mouth of the Macantact stood the cities of Fossholl on the northern Althing side and Cromarty on the southern Obrioner side.

"I've barely ever heard of those," Connor said, and Hamish nodded agreement.

"How can you not knowing such important cities of your own nation?" Gisela asked.

Connor shrugged. "In Alasdair, we didn't know much about anything but cutting granite. Seems like whenever I think I'm starting to get a feel for things, I learn about so many more places I never knew I needed to know."

Wolfram said, "Don't feel bad. With how the different high houses of Obrion squabble for power and influence, fewer travel widely in Obrion than in most of the rest of the continent. You've already seen more than most."

Hamish loved learning about the wider world and asked, "Tell us more about those three rivers."

Gisela said, "The second sister is the Bergrin. It is flowing south through the fertile plains of central Althing. The last is the Enok. It is the littler sister that does racing southeast to plunging into the icy fjord of Finnlauger."

Mattias said, "Althing is big, but the land is harsh. That's one of the reasons they ended up with so much after the Tallan Wars."

"And good treaties," Gisela said.

Mattias nodded. "What's the term you Althins always use? Good treaties are the lifeblood of the nation?"

"Very good," Gisela said.

He said, "That's probably the most important thing to know about Althing. I'd wager it's got more politicians than every other nation combined."

"We must having many treaties to keeping order with all nations of the Arishat League," Gisela protested.

"And then some. I believe your parliament seeks to win over the entire world by sheer weight of signed formal papers," Mattias chuckled.

Student Eighteen, who had sat silently listening for most of the journey suddenly laughed, a more girlish sound than Connor had ever heard from her. "He has making a valid point. Althing has gaining advantaging over other Arishat nations by cleverly treaties." She spoke in a high-pitched, girlish voice with a strong Althin accent.

"Have we now meeting a new person in your head?" Gisela seemed happy to turn the conversation in a new direction.

She actually flushed and looked around the group, a nervous little smile on her lips. "I am pleasing to meeting you all. I am Eystri."

Gisela gaped. "I have hearing of you if you are being the same Eystri who did suggesting the new cataloging system for ancient artifacts for quicklier sorting."

Eystri's flush deepened and she dropped her gaze and said in a soft voice. "I had much helping from many peoples."

Connor grinned. "Pleased to meet you, Eystri."

Hamish added, "Tell us about yourself."

She again dropped her eyes and spoke toward her hands, which were clasped together in her lap. "I did growing up in the port city of Grafarkirkja, at the mouth of the Bergrin."

Hamish barked a laugh. "You lived in Gaffer-kicked-ya? I've got to send old Mhairi down there. Do they have an annual kicking competition for elderly? She'd win ultimate champion for sure!"

Connor laughed with him, and even General Wolfram cracked a smile. Mattias tried to look like the humor was beneath him, but he probably just didn't get the joke. Gisela sniffed, clearly not appreciating the jab at her homeland's strange names, and Eystri turned bright red. "Oh, no. We having too many respecting the elders for kicking."

"It's all right, Eystri," Connor told her in a comforting voice.

Hamish marveled at how different she was from the other strong, confident personalities living in that head. No wonder they hadn't met her before. She must spend most of her time hiding in there.

Hamish said, "We heard that you spent a few months in the vault. I take it that's some kind of library, right?"

Gisela looked shocked and Eystri's shy gaze snapped up to meet his. She sat straight and in a deeply offended tone declared, "The vault is being nothing less than the finest library and housing the most informations than anywhere in the world."

General Wolfram said, "From what I've heard, that's the one place built like a fortress, with a substantial guard on permanent duty."

"Information is the most vitalest things," Gisela declared, and Eystri nodded solemn agreement.

Wolfram said, "Indeed. With the vault intact, your research secrets secure, and your treaties protected, you don't need much of a standing army. Your treaties require the other nations of the Arishat to supply most of the soldiers and shoulder the immense financial burden of maintaining all your troops."

"We all focusing on our strengths," Gisela said a bit sharply. "Althing has developing the best scientists and researchers of all the continent."

"And you now have researchers assisting Jean," Hamish pointed out. "How much are they reporting back home?"

Gisela looked surprised by the question. "Every things, of course. We can protecting the information best and assigning large teams of additional researchers to reviewing it for accuracy."

Connor said, "No doubt your research teams feel the need to build replicas of everything they can. Just to prove the concepts, right?"

Gisela nodded. "We can having no Builders so we cannot operating mechanicals, but we can helping in every other way."

Hamish exchanged a look with Connor, who nodded in silent agreement. Neither of them would discuss the keystone with the Althins. It sounded like Jean hadn't shared that secret yet, and he hoped she kept it from them as long as possible. Once they learned about the existence of the keystone, no doubt they would find ways to obtain some of them, thus gaining the ability to activate at least some mechanicals.

The Althins were important allies, but he reminded himself to tread cautiously. The Althins would negotiate with their own best interests in mind. They needed to do the same.

He was starting to think the visit might turn out far more interesting than he'd first expected.

40

WHAT WOULD YOU DO WITH A PERFECT MEMORY?

They reached the high range of the Kalfafell mountains on the eastern border of Granadure by nightfall. The sun set behind them in a blaze of orange and red. The weather remained clear and cold, and when Connor placed his hand against the gently pulsing shield forming the side window, he could feel a hint of the brutal cold seeping through. Thankfully the little bits of active marble kept the cockpit comfortable.

Camping on the cold, snow-covered mountainside didn't look very appealing, so they decided to fly through the night and arrive at Dagmanson that much earlier the next day. The little wagon bed in the back was stuffed to overflowing with mechanicals and supplies, so it took a few minutes to prep the cabin for sleep.

Luckily, the armrests for their seats were removable, transforming the three rows of seats into narrow, but functional beds. Gisela and Eystri got two of them, and since Wolfram was the eldest, he scored the third. Connor and Mattias slept on the floor between rows, and Hamish floated up to the ceiling in his suit.

It wasn't exactly comfortable, but they'd brought enough bedding that it wasn't exactly uncomfortable either.

Hamish and Mattias apparently challenged each other to a snoring competition, and for a while the little cabin vibrated with their throat-rattling sounds. Connor pushed his blankets off with a groan and sat up, planning to fill Hamish's suit with warm water.

Eystri was lying on the nearest bed of seats with her hands pressed over her ears. She glanced at Connor and whispered, "We have never hearing Hamish snore like this."

"I wonder if it's the altitude," Connor suggested. "Verena said something about the air being thinner up here, so maybe it can't contain the sounds as well. I think I'll tie their mouths shut."

"We are having a better idea," she said and timidly handed him a tiny piece of serpentinite. Her features shivered and her voice shifted to Student Eighteen. "Watch and learn."

He still liked his idea, but took the stone and connected with serpentinite. Immediately, the loud snoring became visible as brightly colored streams issuing from both of their mouths. The sounds bounced all around the little cabin and seemed to take far too long to fade away.

Student Eighteen seized those streamers of sound and pointed them between Hamish and Mattias, as if fired from invisible bows. The rest of the cabin faded to blessed quiet as she somehow wrapped an insulating layer around them to keep the sounds from escaping that narrow conduit.

With all that sound directed between them, Mattias grunted and grimaced in his sleep, then rolled over and stopped snoring. Hamish coughed a couple of times, then he too fell silent.

"How did you insulate the sounds like that?" Connor whispered.

"It's a—" Student Eighteen winced and rubbed her temple. When she spoke again, her voice had shifted to the gruff tones of Tresta.

She hissed, "Hold the line. That wall's critical."

Back to Student Eighteen. "I know. Who do you think created it?"

Tresta responded, "Then stop whining and do what needs to be done."

Rith's fast, cocky voice jumped into the conversation. "We can't outrun it. We need help. Just tell him."

Student Eighteen shuddered, clutching her head, her lips moving but the sounds so weak they looked like pale, smoky whispers to his serpentinite-enhanced eyes. Again Connor was struck by how much he missed Aifric. So many different women resided in that head, but that face would always be Aifric to him. He'd tried to bury his grief at her death, could easily imagine Aifric was still somewhere in that head when he talked with Student Eighteen, but now in the quiet, dim cabin, he felt overwhelmed by grief and guilt.

So he couldn't help himself. He tugged those whispered sounds to him. It was like that moment right after Aifric died when she'd momentarily lost her ability to shield her internal dialogue from the outside world.

He couldn't keep up with the many different personalities as they argued rapidly together. Worse, about half of her words were so soft, they faded away before he could snatch them. What he did hear made him suddenly worried. She seemed to be arguing amongst herself about some kind of internal damage she'd suffered when Aifric died. It sounded like it was threatening to spread, like a disease of the mind.

Kilian had suggested that she'd suffered more trauma from Aifric's death than she'd admitted. She hadn't spoken of it, and Connor hadn't brought it up. He'd told himself it was because he wanted to give her time to mourn, but the truth was, he was scared to. He wasn't sure he could bear the thought of her dying inside any more. Would she blame him for her pain?

"Are you all right?" he finally interrupted.

"We're fine," she answered, her voice somehow carrying the sounds of several of her personalities at the same time.

"It didn't sound like you're fine," Connor insisted.

She took a deep breath, then spoke as Student Eighteen. "We need some time, Connor. Aifric's death unsettled our internal balance. We just need to figure out how to restore it."

"Can I do anything to help?"

"Yes. Don't say anything to anyone else about it."

"But—"

She fixed her steady gaze on him. "Connor, give us some time. I'll let you know if there's anything else you can do."

"Promise?"

"I promise."

She lay down and turned away. Connor reluctantly returned to his blanket. He worried about her for a long time before the soft humming of the window shields finally lulled him to sleep.

By morning, they'd soared over the craggy peaks of the Kalfafell, which formed an impressive natural barrier against anyone not flying. The land to the east settled into rolling hills, covered in dense forests of mixed hardwoods and pine. They found a wide river flowing out of the northeast and Gisela confirmed it was the Saol.

Turning upriver, they followed the Saol through much of the rest of the day, passing mile after mile of heavy forests, followed by wide open lands that Gisela said were either farmlands or grazing lands for cattle or the famous Althing sheep.

"My mother said Althin wool is supposed to be pretty good," Connor offered.

"Best in the entirely world," Eystri confirmed in her timid voice. She showed no sign of any lingering issues from her late-night argument with herself. He wanted to ask her how she was doing, but couldn't in front of the others.

Mattias said, "The crown prince insists on using Grindavik wool in winter uniforms."

Gisela said, "He has being very wise. Grindavik wool is one of the best varieties."

"What makes it special?" Hamish asked.

Eystri answered, speaking as if reciting a written description. "Grindavik wool is unusually dense, making it exceptionally warm and weather proof, but still lighter than most other wool."

"What happened to your accent?" Connor asked, wondering if she was slipping a different personality into the conversation.

Eystri flushed, looking down and making a bobbing motion with her head. "I have many sorrowing. That was part of a report I have reading once in the vault."

"You memorized a report on wool strains?" Hamish asked, sounding impressed and confused at the same time.

"I have developing ability for remembering every things I have reading," Eystri explained.

"Wow. How many sweetbread recipes have you memorized?" Hamish asked.

"Sixty-three," she answered without hesitation.

Hamish twisted in his seat to face her, his expression amazed. "You have to write all those down for me."

Eystri gave him a shy smile and agreed. That was an incredible ability, although Gisela suddenly looked a bit uneasy. Maybe she worried about how much access Eystri had gained in the vault. How many precious documents had she seen?

If she could indeed remember everything she ever read, there was nothing preventing her from making copies. Connor bet there were secrets in the vault that some people would pay dearly for. Was that why Aifric had developed Eystri in the first place?

Half an hour later, Gisela pointed toward the north where several mountains extended east out of the unbroken Kalfafell range. "That is the Skaftafell spur. Dagmanson lies at the easternly edge.

An hour later they soared over the last row of round-topped foothills and gained their first good look at Dagmanson. Connor whistled softly as Hamish slowed the Hawk so they could stare.

Dagmanson sprawled across a wide valley nestled beneath sweeping arms of the mountain, covering several miles and creeping right up onto the slopes. A long, oval-shaped lake started right at the base of the mountain where the head waters of the Saol burst out through a cliff in a turbulent waterfall. The lake ran south for over three miles and had to be over a mile wide at the center. It fed the Three Sisters, which all started there.

Boats of all shapes and sizes plied all three rivers and crowded the southern half of the lake. From tiny rowboats and skiffs to wide, low barges piled with goods, to many-masted sailing ships. The three rivers diverged immediately, with city built close along their steep, stone banks.

Hamish again activated the long-vision aspect of the front window so they could study the distant view. The lowest reaches of the city, all along the banks of the rivers and the lake, were constructed of wood. Tight-packed, three-story buildings huddled close around warrens of narrow streets in several dense communities pressing toward the waters. Those were probably the tenements of workers and the lower classes. Other areas enjoyed wider streets crowded with shoppers. Long caravans of wagons trundled between the many docks and long, low warehouses.

Farther from the rivers, the streets widened even more, with larger buildings flanking them. With steeply-pitched roofs, most were constructed of wood and painted in bright colors. Blues and yellows and reds seemed preferred, but Connor spotted greens, oranges interspersed between them.

The northern banks of the lake were far more ornate, with tree-lined avenues snow-covered parks, complete with geometric-patterned hedges. Enormous stone buildings rose in stately majesty there, reminding Connor of the Carraig, with their fluted stone columns, ornate carvings, and many statues and frozen fountains.

"What are those huge buildings on the north sides of the lake?" Connor asked as everyone studied the enormous, sprawling city.

"Government offices, embassies, and the parliament house." Gisela gestured toward a gleaming palace of light gray stone built atop a low hill on the north-eastern bank of the lake. "There is lying the residences of the monarchy."

"So who lives in the palaces on the hills?" Hamish asked.

Connor hadn't even noticed those yet. Dozens of opulent mansions dotted the hills rising on the northeast and northwest sides of town, flanking the steep cliff of the mountain that reared high above the city.

"The noble classes, families of the parliament, and notable government officials mostly."

"There are a lot of them," Connor noted.

Mattias said, "Like I told you. Althing's number one product is politicians."

Eystri rose and pointed with a trembling finger, looking excited. "There, on the west side of the parliament hall, is the vault."

Connor spotted the parliament, a long building facing a park that ran along the northwest side of the river. At least fifty stone pillars supported an ornate balcony that ran along the fourth floor. It looked self-important and pompous enough to house a parliament. The vault was a huge, five-story building of heavy, black stone just to the west. Unlike other buildings in the area, it was surrounded by a thick stone wall, complete with portcullis on the gates and soldiers prowling the parapets and grounds.

"Where to?" Hamish asked as they approached the lake.

"Please to taking us across Dagmanson Lake and landing in front of the parliament building," Gisela said. "My mother and the rest of the sitting councilors of the Logretta will sending delegates. We will arranging to presenting before the Lawgiver."

She had explained during the trip that the Logretta was the parliament, the legislative branch of the government, and the body that held the real power. The monarchy was more a figurehead, but the lawgiver, the president of the Logretta, held far more influence.

"Is Hannes still the lawgiver?" Mattias asked.

Gisela nodded. "He has being the lawgiver for thirty-eight years, the longest of any in our history."

"So he's really old?" Hamish asked. She nodded and he said, "Probably likes soft breads, fresh from the oven."

"I am sure I do not knowing." She seemed scandalized to consider what the lawgiver ate.

"Depends on how well he's kept his teeth, unless he's got special ones manufactured for meals."

"Please don't make that a topic of conversation," Mattias said in a pained voice.

"Of course not. I've never asked you about your teeth, even though you go around glowing them at everyone, as if begging someone to ask if they're fake."

"My teeth are not fake," Mattias declared.

"If you say so."

Mattias half raised a hand toward his mouth, frowning at Hamish's back. Connor stifled a chuckle.

Many heads turned and fingers pointed in their direction as they crossed the city. Connor wondered if any of the Grandurian windriders had ever been sent to Althing before. By the way people were gawking and shouting, he doubted it.

Hamish took his time landing on the expansive, snow-covered lawns outside of the enormous Logretta building. A crowd scrambled to meet them, including at least a dozen soldiers.

The soldiers didn't look like locals. Most Althins were fair skinned, with brown or blond hair, often with blue eyes. Those soldiers were tall, wide of shoulder, with dark hair and swarthy skin. They wore plate armor over thick, fur-lined leathers, and fur-trimmed helmets. They carried their swords, axes, and polearms like they knew how to use them.

Wolfram noticed them too. "Varvakins. They provide most of the security for Dagmanson."

Connor had never met a Varkakin. He hoped his first experience with them didn't involve denting all those pretty helmets.

Crisp, cold air rushed into the cabin as soon as Hamish dropped the shielding. Connor shivered, despite the fur coat he had just donned. Dagmanson was colder than Altkalen.

Gisela stepped out of the Hawk first, and timid Eystri surprised Connor by rushing to join her.

The many civilians stared wide-eyed at the Hawk and its passengers. The soldiers pushed to the front, their captain a grizzled veteran who looked tough enough that he might not need a granite affinity to enjoy bash fighting. Gisela had said the Arishat League countries enjoyed few Petralists, but Connor decided not to make assumptions.

The captain barked something in a harsh language that Connor didn't understand, his hand on the pommel of his sword. Gisela replied in what

Connor had to assume was the same language, but it flowed with beautiful sounds that rolled off her tongue, punctuated by rolling R's and strong K's.

The captain switched to Obrioner. "Name business and intent." He spoke with a deep accent, and the syllables seemed longer and slower and meaner.

"Oh, put that away, Captain." A middle-aged woman in a long, fur coat pushed through the crowd. Her head was bare, her thick brown hair tied back in a bun. She spoke with authority and almost no accent, and others in the crowd made way for her.

Gisela grinned and rushed toward her. The captain moved to intercept her, but the other woman snapped, "I told you to stand down. That is my daughter."

She and Gisela embraced warmly and the sense of potential violence that had hovered around the soldiers subsided. Gisela towed her mother to the where the rest of them waited beside the Hawk.

"This is my mother, Briet, senior counselor of the Logretta. Mother, these are my companions." She introduced them all in turn.

Briet greeted Lord Mattias and General Wolfram with warm dignity. "I heard rumor that Crown Prince Theodor was planning to send an embassy, but had not expected you so soon or for you to arrive in such a startling manner."

"You are well informed," Mattias said smoothly, with just a hint of glow in his teeth. "The decision to send a delegation was made only days ago."

Connor wondered how she knew anything about it. They clearly didn't have access to fast flying craft like the Hawk. Did they have a listening post like the ones Shona had told him about in Obrion, leftovers from the Age of Discovery?

"Allies should work as hard as possible to understand each other."

And no doubt, she worked twice as hard to spy on her enemies.

Surprisingly, Briet grabbed Eystri's hands and hugged her. "Eystri, dear! Where have you been, and how did you join up with this group?"

Eystri smiled warmly at her. "I have being doing much researches."

"You were never a field researcher," Briet noted, studying Eystri more closely.

"My studies of the Blood of the Tallan have leading me to Obrion and Granadure, to the inheritor of the bloodlines." Eystri gestured to Connor.

Briet inhaled sharply as her eyes settled on Connor. "You're not Grandurian."

Connor made a formal bow the way Aunt Ailsa had taught him. "Like Eystri said. Blood of the Tallan in the flesh. Figured I'd come along for the ride."

Briet gripped his hands excitedly. "Welcome. Welcome all of you." She surprised him again by giving him a quick hug. While she did so, she whispered softly into his ear. "Ailsa told me much about you, but said nothing about this visit. Her reports about the queen are disturbing."

"She's worse in person."

Briet pulled back, looking astonished. "You've met Queen Dreokt?"

"Cracking mad as a blind pedra hunter."

Briet gestured them all to follow her. "Come. We have much to discuss."

As they followed her toward the Logretta, she ordered the captain to keep people back from the Hawk, then turned to Hamish without breaking stride. "I apologize for not waiting to be introduced. You must be Hamish, the first Obrioner Builder."

"How'd you know that?" Hamish asked, sounding surprised and proud at the same time.

She gestured toward his suit. "I've heard of your fantastic research exploits and unprecedented battle prowess."

Hamish walked a little taller. "If you know so much, what's my favorite food?"

Briet smiled. "From what I've heard, you prefer quantity above all else."

"I think we're going to get along just fine," Hamish said with a smile.

41

NEW FRIENDS, NEW BAGGAGE

The inside of the Logretta building was just as grand as the exterior suggested. They followed a wide, marble-tiled hall with twelve-foot ceilings. Paintings, statues, and ornate woodwork trimmed in gold leaf seemed to be everywhere. It was surprisingly warm too, although Connor spotted no fireplaces.

"How do you keep it so warm?" he asked Briet, who led the group, flanked by Wolfram and Mattias.

"This area is much like Altkalen, with many hot springs. All of our heating needs are supplied by the mountain itself. We harness the hot water and use it to heat the flooring, which in turn heats everything else."

Connor pressed a hand to the tiled floor and it was indeed warm to the touch instead of icy cold like it should be.

Hamish said, "Clever. Do you eat a lot of soups too?"

Briet smiled. "Some days nothing will do like a good soup."

The halls were crowded with well-dressed men and women of such varied appearance and dress that they had to be from different countries. Many cast interested glances at them, but Briet did not stop to chat.

Connor easily picked out the fair-skinned Althins in their colorful, woolen clothing. Now that he knew what Varvakins looked like, he also easily picked them out of the crowd. The diplomats didn't wear armor, but every Varvakin he saw proudly wore on their left breast an insignia of a pair of golden eagles, clasping in their claws a sword and a bolt of lightning.

He picked out a number of Grandurians, and even several who looked like Obrioner nobles. Other darker-skinned people wore flowing robes and strange turbans instead of hats. The men wore long, curving scimitars on wide, cloth belts. The women concealed their faces behind gauzy veils that gave them an exotic, mysterious air.

Eystri noted his gaze and said, "Those are Sehrazad. Not so many remaining through the winters. They have suffering so very cold in the winters."

Hamish said, "So those blokes with the vests and jackets, and the women wearing the sensible shoes are from Ravinder?"

Connor hadn't noticed the shoes, but he had spotted a group who seemed to like smiling more than everyone else. The men wore pastel-colored vests buttoned over white shirts and open, long jackets of oiled leather or dark wool over it all. The women with them wore modest dresses with far less jewelry and ornamentation than many of the other ladies.

"Correct. The Ravinders are mostly farmers, and all are being so very friendly."

Gisela had once explained a little about the various nations. She'd also mentioned Ravinder was very peaceful. They specialized in agriculture and supplied large portions of everyone's foodstuffs, even Obrion.

Student Eighteen had mentioned that her homeland was concealed in Ravinder, though. If anyone tried invading, they'd have a host of angry assassins descending on them in vengeful fury. Not a wise move.

Briet led them into a spacious conference room on the ground floor, with a massive table surrounded by forty chairs. She gestured them to seats. "This late in the day, we will most likely need to postpone a formal welcoming banquet until tomorrow. I will send for some light refreshments for now. No doubt Hannes the lawgiver will wish to meet you later. If we're lucky, he'll be able to join us at my manor to dine this evening."

"We appreciate your thoughtfulness," Mattias said. He looked a lot more comfortable in the role of delegation leader than he had riding in the Hawk.

Connor was happy to let him deal with all the formal chatter. He'd seen enough of that at the Carraig to prefer sitting out of the circle of attention. He could study what was said better that way. Politicians loved double meanings almost as much as Sentries, but without quite as much style.

Briet sent messengers to summon other council members to meet with them, along with senior military officers. "I'll make introductions, although I recommend we limit our discussions to preliminary topics for today. We can delve deeper into the specifics of your proposed treaty tomorrow."

No doubt she wanted time to speak with Gisela in private and learn more about their objectives. Although Mattias must have understood that, he nodded politely. "Exactly what I was thinking, my lady."

Connor dreaded the idea of days of political speak, the intricate dance of words that they'd weave together as the basis for their treaty. Every word could prove important, and those kind of negotiations were as exhausting in their own way as bash fighting, but not nearly as much fun.

While they waited, he said, "Lady Briet, thanks again for the chemicals you provided to Gisela. They helped a lot at the battle of Altkalen."

Hamish added, "The mega-stench was a life-changing experience."

"You smelled it?" She looked astonished. Maybe the many accounts she no doubt received from all of her spies in Altkalen hadn't been quite so complete after all.

Hamish nodded, a look of awe on his face. "I didn't even get a full measure of it, but still emptied my guts all over myself. There's nothing like it in the world. I started milking skunks after that. Initial battlefield tests were promising, but milked-skunk stench is just not epic enough to compete with your mega stench."

"Milking skunks?" Briet asked with that surprised look so many people often wore around Hamish. "I can't say I've heard our researchers ever tried that."

"Gotta have the right kind of suit. They get testy, and sometimes you have to stand in a hot fire for a while to get properly clean. I'd be happy to give your research teams some pointers."

"Thank you," she said, but her enthusiasm seemed forced.

Now that Hamish got her distracted, Connor asked, "How do you think your Arishat armies can help stop that raving lunatic, Queen Dreokt, if Obrion invades?"

Briet looked surprised by the straight-forward question and Mattias gave Connor an angry glare. "That's one of the points we need to negotiate. Weren't you listening?"

"Just making conversation. You've probably got some other impressive chemicals to help. Hopefully they can disrupt armies as well as the mega-stench and the pedra's spittle, but those were mostly distraction weapons. They didn't stop Petralists for long. I'm hoping you have some that can cause more direct damage."

"We mostly wish to be left alone," Briet said, once again calm and collected.

Connor shook his head. "Too late for that. When Obrion comes, they'll hit hard and we've got to be ready to hit harder or the queen will destroy everything."

"You've met her and survived. Tell me," Briet asked.

Connor thought back to that terrifying day and shuddered. "She has a sense of absolute self-confidence. She simply walked into the room and took over." He described how she smothered free thought, how she stole their will to fight, and how she shrugged off the few brutal punches he'd managed, as if they were laughably weak

He didn't tell her everything, didn't mention that their courier guide was another of Eystri's personalities, or that Aifric died in the encounter. He left out everything about Shona too, as well as any reference to his porphyry addiction. As he spoke, Briet's concern grew to open fear.

"How did you escape?" she asked.

He hated that he still didn't quite remember, so he said, "She let us go. Told us she figured she might find use for us sometime later and that she'd come collect us when she was ready."

Connor shivered as he remembered that sense of complete helplessness. Everyone looked at him as something special because of his affinities, but he now knew the truth. He barely understood how to tap his powers and he stood absolutely zero chance against Queen Dreokt. He honestly could not imagine how they were going to stop her.

So he added, "While you're negotiating, remember what the stakes are. The queen is an entirely new threat. She will laugh at powers we used to think were amazing. If she decides to attack your country, you have to be ready to hit her with everything you've got. I hope you've got a lot more than we've seen so far because it won't be nearly enough."

"Thank you for your honest assessment," she managed weakly, looking a bit sick.

General Wolfram's brows were furrowed in thought, and he idly stroked his long mustaches. Mattias was glaring again, but Connor wasn't sure why. Had Mattias hoped to use some of that information to somehow leverage their position in the negotiations? Maybe he felt jealous that Connor had stolen so much attention away from him.

Connor didn't care. He needed to know the Arishat League could help. They needed to offer something big or the entire delegation might prove a colossal waste of time. He'd prefer heading back to Altkalen and Verena if that was the case.

Briet took a deep breath and said, "We do have additional chemicals that should help. Our allies in the Arishat League have their own unique strengths too. I'm glad you all came. We will convene a wider council than I had at first planned, one tasked with developing detailed battle strategies to deal with the evolving and escalating nature of the threat we all face."

That was a pretty speech and it seemed to please Mattias and Wolfram. Connor hoped it produced some usable results.

The door to the chamber banged open and a uniformed officer rushed in, looking flustered. He was apparently not one of the people Briet was expecting because her expression turned concerned.

"What is going on?" she demanded.

The man slid to a stop and threw a quick salute then reported in a breathless voice, "My lady, we just received reports that the entire border town of Hafnir was just destroyed."

Briet maintained her composure remarkably well, but Connor felt a cold chill wrapping around his heart. Briet said, "I need more details."

"We have few. The listening post managed to send out a brief message, but it got cut off before completion." He handed her a piece of paper.

She scanned it, her brows furrowing. "This does not make sense. How can a single person lay waste to an entire town? And what does this mean, 'She rode up to town on an earthen seat'?"

The soldier said, "We don't know yet. There were no active threats in the area before this, and we've sent a column of cavalry south to investigate."

Connor said urgently, "Call them back, or they'll just die."

"Do you know something of this attack?" Briet demanded suspiciously.

"No, but we recently received word about an extremely powerful Petralist that Queen Dreokt raised from a long elfonnel sleep. Her name is Harley and she apparently battled Evander at the Carraig until they destroyed it completely and destabilized the area."

"Tallan preserve us," Briet muttered, color draining from her face.

"Do you really think she'd attack Althing first?" Wolfram asked, an actual frown on his usually impassive face.

"We had expected her to attack Granadure. That's why Kilian was preparing a response at the border to intercept and slow her down as long as possible."

Briet gripped the table with a shaking hand. "Kilian expected to do no more than slow her down?"

"Against Harley alone, he might do better than that, but we feared Queen Dreokt might decide to slip into Granadure and brain-wipe the royal family like she had in Obrion," Connor said.

That didn't seem to help her feel much better. She looked around the table and said in a small, terrified voice. "What are we going to do?"

Wolfram said, "We don't have time to send for aid from Granadure."

Mattias cursed. "I wish we'd brought Ilse and Lukas and the Crushers along."

Connor said, "General Wolfram is right. There's no time for any of that. Lady Briet, what kind of armies do you have available?"

"Not much locally. The Varvakins are preparing a large force, but they won't arrive until spring. Our biggest standing army is gathering in Ravinder. Attacking from their capital of Maninder along the great west road into central Obrion seemed the best counter-attack option. Our local forces are spread between all of our cities for winter."

That was even worse than he'd feared. They'd never manage to treaty Harley to death. They might have to resort to dropping the vault on her head, but he doubted even that would do more than slow her.

He exchanged a worried glance with Hamish. "Briet, you've got to assemble every bit of military might you have available. Break out your best chemicals and get whatever forces you can get your hands on moving. We have to stop her before she reaches this city."

"Do you think she'd really destroy all of Dagmanson?" Mattias asked, looking horrified.

Briet answered in a shaky voice. "We have to assume she would.

Althing is the head of the Arishat League, and Dagmanson is the heart of Althing. If this Harley is as powerful as you claim, she could bring the mountain down on top of us and crush the city to powder. With that one blow, she'd destabilize the entire league and effectively decapitate its leadership."

She rose to her feet. "Is the council summoned?"

The messenger nodded. "The lawgiver ordered all to assemble in thirty minutes."

"Send every senior military leader to the meeting and on my authority sound the general alarm. Dispatch messages to every city within two days' march to send all available troops immediately. We'll send additional orders after the meeting."

The officer saluted again and rushed from the room. Briet looked concerned but determined. "I am afraid our negotiations must wait until we know for sure if we'll still have a nation in a week. You are all welcome to return to Granadure in the meantime."

Mattias shook his head. "We came here looking for a way to help each other. We'll help defend your home. We offer any aid we can."

She took his proffered hand gratefully and Connor felt proud of Mattias, a feeling he really hated to acknowledge.

Then Mattias turned to Connor and said, "You realize you'll have to fight her, right?"

4 2

A BATH DISTRACTS SOME WOMEN MORE THAN OTHERS

The next couple of days passed way too fast. The Logretta declared a martial emergency. That got things moving fast, with the scattered components of the army scrambling to assemble and march south to intercept Harley.

Connor didn't see much of that part of the mobilization. He and Hamish and Gisela spent the majority of those two days in the Hawk, flying southwest along the length of the Saol. They stopped at every fishing village, town, and hamlet, warning the people of the approaching danger and delivering the lawgiver's decree of immediate evacuation.

Mid-winter was a terrible time to evacuate, but the alternative would be worse. Many farmers and shepherds simply drove their herds higher into the mountains since chances of Harley hunting down solitary shepherds was slim.

They ventured south far enough to spot her in the distance, sliding upriver on her peculiar earthen seat. It resembled the one that Evander always rode.

She looked bored.

Hamish spotted it too. "Doesn't seem to be in much of a hurry."

"She could easily double that speed," Connor said with a frown.

Gisela frowned too. "Why would she choosing to invading slowly?"

"Maybe she wants to make sure the army has enough time to assemble," Hamish said bleakly. "That way she could wreck them all in one battle."

"When did you become such an optimist?" Connor asked, but he feared Hamish was right. If that really was part of her mission, success would add one more layer to the psychological blow her single-person invasion of Althing would deliver to everyone planning to oppose the queen.

The scariest part of that thought was that she might just succeed.

Hamish shrugged. "Anyone who can fight Evander to a standstill is someone I'm afraid of. Stew the Tallan's socks and feed them to a parrot, but I wish my armored shell was ready. Then we could take the fight to her."

"Stew his socks?" Gisela asked with a frown. "I have not hearing that one before."

"I'm trying to broaden my horizons now that we've traveled halfway across the continent. Your mother said sometimes you like a good stew, so it seemed appropriate."

The air suddenly bucked them sideways into a vicious spin, and a vortex of wind howled around them, wrenching the Hawk over and threatening to cast them right out of the sky. Gisela screamed, Connor shouted, and Hamish laughed.

As Hamish fought to adjust thrusters and call for more power from the nimble craft, Connor shoved a piece of quartzite into his mouth. Imagining the gateway to air, he pushed his thoughts through. Air greeted him with a mischievous laugh that echoed through the howling wind.

He sensed her flying nearby, hands clasped with Harley. Together they drove the winds like one might whip horses. Connor called for air, tried to pull her away from Harley to give Hamish time to stabilize the Hawk and get them out of there.

It felt like tugging against a hurricane.

Harley's will slapped his questing fingers of thought aside with a decidedly offhand flick, as if brushing a mosquito from her face. Air obeyed her with none of her usual flighty distraction. Connor had never sensed anyone command such obedience. After his ascension, air had responded better, but still teased and flitted away more often than not. She did not seem capable of ignoring Harley.

The Hawk nosedived and began to spin, faster and faster as a howling wind tunnel solidified around them. The noise was like a waterfall crashing over rocks, and the air turned bitterly cold. Gisela screamed and reached the stomach-lurch point, spraying her last meal all across the cabin.

The stench made Connor gag, but he fought down his own vomit. This was not the right time to initiate a puking contest.

"I can't pull out," Hamish shouted as he flicked hands across the various controls. "Can't you do something?"

"Working on it!" Connor closed his eyes and lunged against Harley's will, reaching for Air's hand. He only needed to touch it for a moment.

Harley's voice drifted up to him from far below. "Little Petralist. You're a child pushing stick boats in a puddle when you need to launch battleships across the mighty seas." She laughed. "My lady queen suggested you might prove useful, but is this the best you can do?"

How did she recognize him? Could she read that much about him in their contest of wills. Her scornful tone angered him and he redoubled his effort, but she scattered his will like an eagle diving through a flock of sparrows. She was simply too strong. He sensed air flowing him a kiss and waving good-bye.

So he also tapped soapstone. The gateway opened easily and she slipped her hand into his without hesitation, bolstering his confidence with her sure touch. The fast-spinning air was condensing the water that had hung lazily in it, forming sheets of rain all around the Hawk. The distant Saol river was like a ribbon of light, running along the ground.

Harley spoke again. "Poor child. Die knowing you are unworthy of my lady's favor."

"Old ladies should get off their rocking chairs and out of the rain," he shot back.

Connor yanked on the distant waters of the Saol, creating a ten-foot wave that leaped the bank and side-swiped Harley, spinning her earthen craft and nearly toppling her off.

She reacted quickly, regaining her balance and deflecting the water away with a curved wall of earth. She was fast, but predictable. That was exactly the move an earth-focused Sentry would do to protect her connection to earth before the ground grew too muddy and weakened her connection.

That moment of distraction was all he needed. Connor seized those sheets of water around the Hawk, squeezed them together and cast it at her like a watery lightning bolt.

Harley never saw it coming.

The watery spear struck like an epic curse-punch from the Tallan himself. It catapulted her off her chair and most likely shattered bones in her chest.

That impact would have killed most Sentries and probably would have disabled Anton. He liked to think it might have even rattled Evander for a few seconds. Harley reacted far faster than Connor hoped, wrapping herself in a protective blanket of earth and sliding farther from the river like a fat, muddy tick.

Hamish shouted in triumph and the Hawk leveled out, shooting through the funnel cloud. They had fallen perilously close to the earth and for a second Connor feared they'd crash anyway.

Hamish increased thrust from the forward thrusters and triggered all the puking dooms. Fire erupted from the blocks of marble placed along the bottom of the craft, and the upforce drilled Connor into his seat as if a blanket weighing a ton had just dropped over him. Gisela groaned and passed out. She flopped sideways and would have fallen to the deck if not for the restraining straps holding her into her seat.

The Hawk leveled out so close to the ground that snow flashed to water directly below them, whisked into the air by the wind of their passage. Their dive tripled their speed though and Hamish pulled up just enough so they shot across tree tops faster than Connor's max-tapped sprint. Hamish whooped again as he banked the Hawk higher and climbed back into the sky, trading speed for altitude and racing north, away from danger.

"What did you do?" Hamish asked as Connor shook Gisela awake. She looked sick and wept with relief when she realized they hadn't died.

"She was too strong in the air, so I hit her with water. I hit her hard. Would've killed most people."

"Think she can heal?" Hamish asked.

"Probably. From Ailsa's report, she must have sandstone or she wouldn't have recovered from fighting Evander so fast."

Gisela moaned and rubbed her temples. "We should not having gone so close."

Hamish gave her a cocky grin. "Nonsense. We learned something about her."

"What?" Gisela asked.

"She's willing to give us time to get ready to face her. She's overconfident, and baths distract her more than most women."

"How will that helping?" Gisela asked.

Hamish shrugged, dropped the shielding over the windows and gestured at the vomit-splattered cabin. "I have no idea yet, but speaking of baths?"

Connor said, "Hold your breath."

Gisela sucked in a deep breath, clutching her seat, as if expecting him to plunge them underwater. Instead, Connor drew only a little water from the air, forming it into a soft mist that he billowed through the cabin, gently scrubbing away dirt and vomit and carrying it out through the windows.

"That is it?" Gisela asked.

"I could fill the entire cabin with water if you want."

"No. That was very excellent," she assured him quickly.

"Sometimes it's not how much power you bring to bear, but how you apply it," Connor said with a grin, quoting one of his favorite sayings from Kilian.

Hamish grimaced as he restored the shielding windows and accelerated. "I hope so, because Harley's got more power. If we can't figure out how to trip her up, we'll be the ones getting cleaned out for good."

43

SHUFFA GOOFA MIFFA

The only large city on the Saol south of Dagmanson was Raufarhofn, about fifty miles upriver from where Harley had almost knocked the Hawk from the sky. The Althin commanders chose it as the place for their armies to make their stand the next day.

If things went poorly, they could still attempt to regroup outside of Dagmanson, but the capital was already being evacuated as a precaution. Every boat had been commandeered for the effort and they sailed south by the hundreds down the Bergrin and the Enok.

Connor decided that was a good idea as he surveyed the tiny army assembled to stop one of the most powerful Petralists on the continent.

Raufarhofn was a prosperous, quiet town, with orderly streets that Jean would have loved. Their major products were salted fish and Grindavik wool. The town sprawled across both banks of the river, with farms extending west toward the Kalfafell mountains. Miles of grazing lands spread across the lowlands to the east. The population had evacuated and the shepherds had driven their flocks away.

The bulk of the army consisted of about ten thousand men. Half looked like professional soldiers while the rest were drafted from militia and police across the nation. They were formed up in ranks just south of town. They'd accomplish little more than give Harley something to use to fill a big mass grave.

Looking at them, Connor wished for his Carraig army. With that little force of Petralists, he'd accomplished the seemingly impossible and defeated the student armies of the other champions. Later, with all those armies combined, they'd fought an elfonnel. Some of his student soldiers had died, though, and all accounts suggested Harley was even more dangerous than an elfonnel.

He wished he'd taken a little more time to say good-bye to Verena. As much as he despised Mattias for meddling with her, Connor had to admit Mattias's assessment was right. He was going to have to take the lead against Harley.

He was so grouted. Evander usually terrified him, and Harley had fought him to a standstill. Queen Dreokt had toyed with Connor like a little child, and that failed mission eroded his confidence. He needed to stop Harley, but so far he hadn't figured out a good strategy.

He'd even tapped obsidian. He borrowed a little from Student Eighteen and used it to accelerate his thinking. One thing became abundantly clear. He could not hope to fight toe to toe with her, slugging it out with elemental power. She was so much more experienced, so much more powerful in earth and air. Just like at the Carraig, he needed to fight smarter. Luckily, he'd shown that he performed best under pressure, and the ideas were starting to form.

They just needed to form faster.

It might be easier if he commanded the army, but he was a foreigner. Mattias had refused to propose the idea when Connor suggested it. They didn't have the proper treaties in place.

So he scanned the pitiful army with growing concern. The other groups assembled to fight were the ones who offered what little hope could be dredged out from under the ice and snow.

Several companies of Althin researchers were assembled on the west bank, each with wagons full of chemical weapons. They remained well outside of town, up on the only meaningful hill on that bank. They busied themselves assembling long-armed catapults that Gisela called trebuchet.

Mattias had explained that the chemical research facilities were located twenty miles outside of Dagmanson, around the far side of one of the lower mountains to prevent accidental catastrophes. Transporting those dangerous materials down to Raufarhofn had been a huge logistical challenge.

Connor hoped the winds continued to blow south, and decided he'd do his best to help keep them pointed in that direction when those chemicals were launched. He stood on the east bank, on an earthen lookout tower he'd slowly erected, being careful not to draw deep from the earth and risk triggering a backlash. The ground felt pretty stable, but he could feel the unsettled quivering of the elements to the west at the outer limits of his senses. It wouldn't take much to spread that unrest into Althing.

He spent ten whole minutes building the most extensive shielding he'd ever attempted around the base of his tower. The few Petralists in Althing were clustered around the central command, about fifty yards closer to the city. At least one of them was a Sentry and they raised a careful tower similar to his. When he probed in that direction, their shielding proved pretty solid.

He hoped they could keep Harley at bay with the Arishat's creative attacks. If she decided to strike hard through the earth, none of the shields would hold for long.

Mattias and Wolfram stood with Briet on that command tower, along with the other military commanders and two other senior counselors Connor hadn't met yet. He'd expected to get invited to join them, but had been asked to station himself a little farther away. He wondered if they feared Harley might target him as the most dangerous threat and therefore didn't want to stand too close.

If Harley killed him, they'd join him all too soon. That was a depressing thought. It drove home how desperate their position really was. They were facing one of the strongest Petralists alive, with barely a token force, cobbled together in the middle of winter at the last minute. Chances of success were dismal at best.

If only he had a little porphyry.

The thought triggered the strongest wave of craving for the deadly powder that he'd felt since using diorite outside of Altkalen. Connor's fists clenched as a wave of need burned through him and set his teeth grinding against the urge to growl. He should banish the thought instantly, knew better than to give that need any root in his heart, but he hesitated.

Porphyry did offer perhaps their best chance of survival. For one dark moment, he allowed himself to consider the idea. He'd dared porphyry twice, and twice it had helped him survive battles that would have killed him. If he did have some, would he dare try it again, despite knowing he might die a frothing, insane rage monster as a result?

Luckily he didn't have any, so it was a moot point. He fought down the craving by studying the other components of the army. There weren't many.

A company of heavily armed and armored Varvakins stood at attention south of the command tower. Half a hundred scimitar-wielding Sehrazad raiders waited on horseback a little farther back, huddling in their saddles in the cold.

Connor couldn't imagine a cavalry charge accomplishing much. He thought back to the battles of Alasdair when Ilse had frozen the slope to disable all the horses of Carbrey's cavalry. Harley would probably just dump them all into a pit and smother them.

Another company of Varvakins stood at the vanguard of the army. They were a strange sight. Every one was fully sheathed in gleaming plate armor, but they only carried long, steel spears for weapons. Stranger than that, they were all bound together with lengths of gleaming steel chain.

Connor lifted a speakstone Hamish had paired that morning. General Wolfram carried its partner. "General, why are those Varvakins chained together?"

"Necessary to launch a special attack they've only recently developed. Lady Briet said it's never been used before. It has something to do with that huge energy storage tank they set up in town and the contraption they placed into the river."

"The one that looked like a water wheel?"

"Indeed. Somehow captures energy from the waters. Eystri said it's something like bottled lightning."

"Water doesn't generate lightning."

"Apparently they've figured out a way. They've got a specially coated wire running to the energy storage tank from the river, and more extending to that company of soldiers. From what I understand, if they can strike Harley with those spears, they should be able to hit her with that captured lightning."

That sounded pretty good. Connor had been wishing for his father's Ashlar hammer. If he had to fight Harley close up and personal, he'd love to smash her in the face with that lightning-like diorite power that had blown the mountain above Lord Gavin's manor. That might dent her confidence, and her face.

"Won't they get killed too?" he asked.

"Apparently not. Something about all that steel encasing them sheds the jolt and simply passes it down the line."

That must be why they were chained. The steel chain must pass it along too. The idea was fascinating, and he hoped he'd get to witness what it did to Harley.

The Hawk plunged out of the early morning clouds, flared danger-ously close to the ground, and settled gently to the snowy grasses. Hamish climbed out and jogged over to Connor, bearing an enormous tray crammed with four cakes, a dozen sweetbreads, and a huge bag of cookies.

"Where'd you get that?" Connor asked.

"The baker in town was panicking, so I offered to help rescue extra stock."

"Did they know that meant you'd eat it?"

Hamish shrugged. "Confiscated for the war effort. This is my thinking food." He shoved two cookies into his mouth, then mumbled, "Shuffa goofa miffa."

"Well I'm not going to find milk for you. I can't believe you forgot it."

Hamish swallowed and sighed with exaggerated suffering. "The sacri-fices we make."

Connor smiled, glad that Hamish hadn't let the stress of the day rob his appetite. Connor couldn't enjoy food at the moment, but he could enjoy watching Hamish enjoy it. Watching Hamish polish off several cookies actually helped settle Connor's nerves.

Hamish grinned after swallowing one particularly huge mouthful. "You know, I love the name of this town. I hope we can save it."

"Raufarhofn?"

Hamish grinned. "Sounds like that skin disease old gaffer Clifden tried to convince Mhairi he suffered from that time he tried courting her."

Connor couldn't help laughing. Clifden must have addled his brain with a particularly bad batch of his local brew to think he had any chance with old Mhairi. She'd given him such a vile tonic, he'd looked green for a month.

"What did you see?" he asked his friend, who had been out scouting for Harley's approach. Carefully.

"She's coming, all right. Seems to know we're here. She sped up while we were watching and made what had to be an ancient obscene gesture."

"Really?"

"I'll show you later. Maybe use it on Mattias and ask him if he's ever seen it before. I love historical research sometimes. How's the army?"

Connor grimaced. "Remember at Altkalen when we were worried we were underpowered with several thousand Petralists? We had no idea how good we had it."

"The Varvakins look optimistic," Hamish said, nodding toward the chain-linked, steel-clad warriors.

Connor explained about them, then pointed out the Althin researchers on their hilltop across the river. "Those two groups are our best bet."

"What about that lot hiding behind town?" Hamish asked, pointing with a cookie.

Gisela had mentioned that those soldiers with the strange, conical helmets were from Tabnit. They had erected a long, open-topped tent on the northern end of town, opposite from where the rest of the army gathered, and busied themselves inside. Gisela didn't know the details of their planned contribution to the battle, and Eystri had headed over there to investigate. Connor hated not knowing the details of the plan. How was he supposed to help if he didn't know exactly what was going to happen?

When he'd asked, Briet had admitted they were still working on it. She'd also tried to get him to sign some kind of 'I-won't-betray-you-during-the-battle' agreement, but he'd laughed at the suggestion. He was planning to risk his life to help them. The least they could do was show him a little trust in return.

"Did you get a look inside the tent as you flew over?" Connor asked.

"Of course. Didn't make a lot of sense, though. They've got three enormous, steel tubes in there, like the front end of Dierk's thump driver, but without the catapult arms to throw anything. I saw a stack of big round iron balls that have to be some kind of projectile."

"Gisela once said something about Tabnit, remember? That they've got some kind of sand, wasn't it?"

Hamish nodded, then snapped his fingers. "Angry black sand. Sounded a lot like diorite."

"Hopefully we'll get a chance to see how it works. Long-range attacks are a really good idea, but only if Harley doesn't see them coming."

"Can you do something to distract her again?"

"I'll try." He really wished he had his armor, but he'd left it at Altkalen. He hadn't expected to be going to battle in Althing. It might not help much against Harley, but he always felt more confident with it on. Besides, Verena had gifted that armor to him, and wearing it helped him feel closer to her.

A horn sounded, three notes that pierced the chill morning air and hung over the town for a long time. It was the signal.

Harley had arrived.

44

DESPERATE TIMES, STUPID IDEAS

Harley slid around a bend in the road, about two miles downstream, riding that peculiar earthen seat of hers.

General Wolfram spoke through the speakstone in Connor's hand. "The best range for the Althin chemical attacks and the Tabnit fire tubes are about half a mile. Can you do something to distract her at about that point?"

"Of course," Connor said confidently, but inside he felt cold as he tried to figure out how to do that without getting obliterated.

Hamish swallowed another cookie and nodded back toward the Hawk. "If you get into trouble, I'll hit her with those diorite missiles. They're several times larger than regular ones. Should pack enough punch to bother her for a few seconds."

"Thanks." Connor's throat was dry and his voice sounded nervous even to him.

Hamish offered him a cookie, but that wasn't what he needed. He settled his earthen tower back to the ground, and Hamish jogged with his tray of sweets back toward the Hawk. Connor then popped a little piece of marble into his mouth and wedged it under his tongue. As soon as he sucked on it, spicy flavor exploded into his mouth and he breathed deep, savoring it.

If marble could just taste like that all the time, he'd use it a lot more often. All too soon the spice faded to a dull burning sensation, but he kept sucking, filling himself with the intensifying burn. He needed that rather crazed intensity to dare heading down that road to face Harley.

The thought of heading into battle without granite itching along his skin scared him more than he cared to admit, but he needed the accelerated reflexes of obsidian. So he absorbed a small portion, just enough for a few minutes quick thinking. He could purge that much pretty fast and switch to granite, if needed.

As soon as he tapped obsidian, his thoughts sped up and the sound of Verena's silvery laughter played in his mind. He smiled and breathed deep, savoring the sound and using it to help him settle into battle calm.

He'd already swallowed a soapstone mixture and had wafers of slate in both boots. He now wedged a bit of quartzite into his cheek. He had some serpentinite in his pocket. He touched it, and the area lit up with the bright lights of sounds. He easily tracked hushed conversations, the clinking of armor and weapons and creaking of trebuchets being cranked back.

He spoke and imbued the sound with extra energy. "Harley, stop now, or I'll be forced to destroy you." He cast the sounds across the valley to Harley. This way she alone could enjoy the ridiculous boast.

She laughed and her voice boomed over the valley, enhanced by quartzite. "I see you're determined to die today. I applaud your bravery, but pity your stupidity. Swear fealty to Queen Dreokt now and you will be pardoned and welcomed home."

Briet's voice boomed back, magnified by one of only two Pathfinders native to Althing. "We are a free people and we will fight for our freedom. Begone, vassal of evil."

Ooh, that was a really good insult.

Connor tapped slate. Earth opened to his affinity senses and he felt Earth standing beneath him, seeming distracted. Immediately, he felt Harley's strike surging through the ground toward the command tower, like an underground spear. He couldn't hope to stop it, but did manage to strike a glancing blow against it with his own slate senses. The attack deflected to the west and struck a large storehouse on the edge of town.

The storehouse shattered, showering broken bits of timber and bales of wool that had been stored inside all across the town.

Harley was still advancing, but was still over a mile distant. If she continued to press the attack from that distance, she'd destroy them all before they ever got the chance to strike back.

Connor summoned his own narrow earthen chair, swung astride it, and willed himself south to meet her. The ride was more comfortable than it looked. With his feet propped on little stirrups and his hands gripping the bars extending from the front, he figured he could easily ride like that for hours.

As he slid past the nervous army, they cheered loudly and he raised a hand in salute. Their support bolstered his confidence, although they'd probably cheer anyone dumb enough to step out alone against Harley.

Connor pulsed his earth senses outward, mapping the ground in his mind and trying to sense Harley's intentions. She did not strike again, but he felt her presence in the ground, like a thunderstorm approaching with relentless and unstoppable might.

Connor slid out onto the road, but kept his pace slow. He didn't want to meet her before she closed the distance to that last half mile. She spotted him and her voice boomed out again, this time sounding angry.

"You dare assume you're worthy of using my ride, pup?"

He'd hoped to distract, not anger her. Oops. He tapped quartzite to his throat and responded with his own booming voice. "Who says it's your ride? Evander uses this all the time."

"I invented it. I once made the mistake of allowing him to borrow the idea and now he seems to think he has a right to it. You never even bothered to ask."

She had accelerated while he slowed. Let her think he was afraid of her. He was, but that wasn't the point. She reached the half mile point, about a hundred yards from him. That was close enough. Probably too close, if the Althins planned to launch another mega stench.

So Connor tapped soapstone and marble together. The elements responded immediately, like old friends flanking him. Water slipped her hand into his, while fire paced around them, laughing maniacally.

As soon as he called upon them, Water yanked a section of the river right over the bank. Fire threw back his head in glee, and fire exploded out of thin air all around Connor. He wrapped the elements together and rose on a twined column of burning water.

As he hoped, Harley stopped, even though she didn't exactly look impressed. Immediately, three of the Althin trebuchets fired. Instead of launching rocks like most catapults, or even the ceramic pots full of explosives like the Builders used, they launched cylindrical steel drums.

To keep Harley distracted, Connor formed gigantic arms of twined elements and struck at her. She raised a protective wall, just as he'd hoped, and his attack did little more than leave a patchwork of charred and muddy streaks across the barrier. He didn't whip the elements up over the top because he wanted her blind, but not protected from above.

For a second it looked like the plan would work, but then the earthen barrier rolled back over her, forming a full protective sphere.

"Tallan spit in her eyes," Connor exclaimed.

The steel barrels struck. The researchers were good at calibrating distances because although the first one struck to the right, the other two hit Harley's defensive sphere dead center.

They all exploded with amazing intensity. Whatever those barrels contained, it liked to blow up big, as big as quickened diorite. The violent explosions shook the valley with thunder, and crimson flames billowed all around Harley's protective earth.

The blasts tore through the defensive wall, shredding it and hurling Harley out the back side. She tumbled, bounced once, but on the second bounce, she slid abruptly to a stop. She must have reconnected with slate and bled away the force of the impact.

Her leather jacket was singed, and she looked battered, but as he focused quartzite-enhanced vision on her face, his heart skipped a beat in renewed fear.

She looked really angry.

Harley rose to her feet, showing no lingering effects of the brutal explosion. Connor wasn't about to give her time to recover. He seized the still-billowing flames, raised them high and condensed them into spears of fire like the ones he'd used to incinerate General Carbrey. That memory still haunted him sometimes, but the plan worked once. It'd work again.

Harley raised another protective sphere of earth around herself as he drove those spears of fire at her. His fire plunged down into her earthen defense, driving in several inches, but then sheared off.

It wasn't a single sphere at all, but several layers, built atop each other, and the inner layers were spinning in different directions. The movement easily deflected his fires.

"No fair," Connor grumbled. Harley couldn't both be so much stronger and so clever.

The ground rippled beneath him, but standing atop his mixed water and fire, he couldn't feel what Harley was attempting.

He saw it though.

Three seconds later, the ground buckled under the Althin researchers, smashing the careful stacks of steel drums together.

One of them ruptured.

The explosion ripped through the Althin company, triggering the other barrels, resulting in an enormous fireball. It consumed the entire hilltop with a thunderclap that set the Sehrazad horses on the opposite side of the river screaming and bucking in terror.

Connor pulled the flames away as fast as possible, but it wasn't fast enough. The initial shockwave from those explosions had shattered the trebuchets and scattered people and equipment in every direction. Many of the Althin researchers lay unmoving, broken by the explosion. Others twitched or screamed once he pulled the flames away.

Connor turned back to Harley, his fears fading under a wave of anger. He pulled all that fire across the valley and wrapped it around Harley's defensive sphere, shearing it off the ground to separate her from her element. He'd incinerate her defenses, no matter how many layers of spinning earth she constructed. She'd see how well she liked getting burned, or at least suffocated.

The earth blackened and smoked, and he drove the fires in harder, whipping them around the sphere in a whirlwind of flames that tore at the outer layers. He only needed a little time, and he'd destroy her.

Behind him, the Varvakins broke into a charge, shouting their battle cries, steel spears raised, chains clanking. A little lightning might help a lot. He vowed to keep her busy until they could strike.

The front of the sphere erupted outward and Harley charged out through his flames. Only, Harley now stood at least twelve feet tall, her torso eight feet thick, with limbs nearly half that diameter. She'd wrapped herself in layers of earth, forming an elemental battle suit like nothing he'd ever seen before.

"I hate you," he muttered.

Connor struck again with fire, but it only charred the outer skin of her suit. He tried seizing her limbs with the flames to restrain her, but fingers of earth erupted all around her, shearing off his fiery ropes and rendering his attempt useless.

Her voice echoed out of the suit. "Not a bad try, pup, but I was the general of the queen's own battle maidens. I've survived dozens of battles against Petralists who actually knew how to use their powers."

Her laugh chilled him.

So he yanked waters out of the river and clobbered her with a huge wave, hoping to send her tumbling back and win some time to figure out what to do next.

Just before the water hit, her legs fused to the road, locking her in place. His wave struck with tremendous force, but it barely rocked her a little to the side. Growling with frustration, Connor struck again and again, rocking her side to side, blasting apart the roadway, and churning the earth there into mud.

Harley maintained her connection to the earth, refreshing it as fast as he tore it away. Connor wasn't sure if the queen's edict against using much earth elemental powers extended into Althing, but he didn't want to give her time to decide that destabilizing the area fit into her plans.

So even as he kept bashing at her suit from every side with water, he pulled the waters away from the top and drove all that fire he had hanging around down into it with all his might, spearing deep into the suit.

He hit something solid, something human. He felt the connection for the briefest instant before the earthen suit exploded in every direction. It shredded his water and scattered his fire, revealing Harley standing on a patch of dry ground, fury boiling off of her like invisible fire.

Her face bore a wicked burn mark, right down her forehead, between the eyes. He'd missed her skull and brain by inches. Even as their eyes met, her red, blistered skin healed, returning to perfect health.

Angry Harley was even scarier than earth-giant Harley. This close, he got a great look at her. She was tall and muscular for a woman, with a blocky face and unruly black hair that fell to her shoulders. She wore a long, black leather jacket that reminded him of Evander. He was surprised to note she wore a pink silk blouse underneath.

"If you hold still, I'll finish you off quick. Less pain and a lot less mess that way," Connor told her conversationally, trying his best to appear calm.

Harley stalked forward, fingers curled like claws. "You've officially annoyed me, pup."

She still didn't unleash the full might of her earth powers on him, but as she walked, the soles of her boots began to extend. First growing to high clogs, then long, earthen stilts. She clearly planned to rise up to catch him on his elemental pillar.

As if he'd just stand there and wait for her.

Actually, he did wait a bit to give a little more time to the charging ranks of clanking Varvakins, with their coated cable snaking back toward their power station. She cast only a single, disdainful glance in their direction, then ignored them.

Someone who just woke up from a three-centuries nap should consider that maybe progress was made in their absence. Connor was happy that in her arrogance she didn't seem to consider the possibility.

That didn't mean she wouldn't scatter them like pesky flies, though. Connor needed to hit her hard enough to give them a chance, but he didn't dare to leap into close physical combat with her.

She didn't know that, though.

His obsidian-fueled thoughts finally caught hold of a brilliant idea and whipped it into a plan by the time she took one long, lumbering stride and rose to six feet above the ground. She was barely fifty yards away and approaching fast, while the Varvakins were already beginning to swarm past him from the other side.

Connor tapped limestone.

He gave the light streaming past a savage twist and tapped chert at the same time. Riding that obsidian-fueled moment of inspiration, it seemed obvious that he should push toward her what he wanted her to see. Harley's emotional state was easy to read. His skin prickled with angry heat, although the pulsing sense of her thoughts seemed far too calculating and calm.

Time to rattle her.

Connor threw himself high into the air, launching off his twined elements. What everyone else saw was him lunging forward, propelled by his twined elements, fist cocked to deliver a hammer-strike.

The Varvakins cheered, and Harley actually looked startled. She surged up to meet him, looking eager to pummel him in the face and prove herself stronger.

Instead, Connor swept his elements across her earthen stilt legs, slashing them apart in a dozen places. They shattered and Harley cursed in surprise and fury as she dropped like a stone to the ground.

Shouting war cries in their harsh language, the soldiers lunged, steel spears stabbing to meet her. She hit the ground a second before they pierced her.

That was at least a second too long.

Earth erupted upward and deflected the spears away.

Blue-white lightning erupted from the spears. It scattered across the earthen barrier, blackening it and sizzling like a hundred sausages flash-frying in half an eyeblink. Intense heat radiated off the lightning and Connor grabbed it, adding it to his flames, which intensified to white.

As impressive as the lightning looked, it did not penetrate the earth to Harley. She looked briefly surprised, then just annoyed. Fingers of earth snatched spears away from the soldiers, spun them around, and stabbed them back with terrific force.

Their armor was thick, and most of the spears deflected off. A couple punched through, though, and the soldiers screamed as lightning charbroiled them inside their suits.

The earth erupted under the soldiers, tossing them aside before Connor could help. The stench of charred earth and burned bodies rose all around him in a sickening cloud, which dissipated a second later under a gust of wind.

Hovering in the air under a huge canopy of fire that provided enough lift to keep him aloft, Connor drove more of his fires down against Harley again, but her protective suit reformed, deflecting it away. The helmet hardened into solid stone. Connor couldn't do that, not yet. In her element, Harley commanded powers that Connor couldn't even imagine yet.

His mirage faded, and Harley turned her stone head up toward him. Just in time for Hamish to unleash all eight missiles from the Hawk as he swept in from above. Propelled by quartzite, they jumped across the distance and struck Harley's huge earthen torso, exploding with enough power to send the Varkakins tumbling back to the ground.

Harley leaped through the explosion, her suit charred but not seriously damaged. Stones the size of horses erupted out of the ground at the Hawk, but Hamish seemed to be expecting that. The puking dooms erupted, shooting him skyward, and he banked away to safety.

Connor needed space to figure out what to do next. Everything they'd tried had failed, their initial attack was broken, and if he lingered, she'd tear him apart. So as he transformed his fiery canopy into wings to bank away around the town, he tapped serpentinite, drew deep from the stone, and threw a barrage of high-pitched, screeching sound at her. He imagined all the most annoying, cringe-worthy sounds he'd ever heard, magnified them a hundred-fold, and beat at her with them.

Student Eighteen had said that serpentinite could transform sounds into weapons once one ascended with the stone. He didn't know how to do that yet, but the sound barrage did have an impact.

It enraged her.

Harley gripped her stone head with giant hands, and earth flowed up out of the ground to reinforce it, turning her head into a huge ball, wider than her shoulders. It made her giant look goofy, but must have protected her ears because she raised an angry fist after him.

The air bucked all around him, currents screaming in from every side as she struck after him with her other elemental power. Connor tapped quartzite and tried to fight for control, at least around himself, but Air had a new master, and winds ripped away his fiery wings and began tumbling him around.

Connor felt panic building as he tried to right himself. He didn't have time to purge obsidian and absorb granite before crashing. She was going to splatter him against the buildings of Raufarhofn.

He caught a brief glimpse of the Varvakin knights fleeing from her, their cable shredded. She didn't even bother to look at them, but was focused on crushing Connor.

Connor called to Air and tried to draw water out of the air to help shield himself, but Harley overwhelmed his feeble attempts. Air suddenly grabbed his hand, but only to yank him around, spinning him even faster. He wasn't sure if he'd reach the stomach-lurch point first, or if he'd simply pass out. He was plunging down toward the city far too fast.

He was going to die.

In that moment, the Tabnit soldiers joined the fray. Their three long metal tubes belched thunder and flame. Projectiles half as tall as Connor erupted from the raised mouths of the steel tubes, already flying at tremendous speeds. They whooshed dangerously close past Connor, and he urged them on with all his fading hope.

The missiles struck true. Two fell to either side of Harley, while the third struck her giant in the chest. They exploded with enough force to shatter the front of her suit, rip giant holes in the ground, and send Harley tumbling out the back.

Her control over the air faltered, and Connor seized Air with all his affinity strength. She didn't fight him, and through that connection, he yanked on the wild currents. He managed to deflect his course enough to plunge down into the icy river instead of shattering himself against the cobblestone streets.

The shock of the cold water nearly made him gag and inhale a mouthful of water, but Connor was now in his element. Water embraced him and pushed him back to the surface. Connor rose, completely dry, on a pillar of water. Relieved, Connor wasted a couple of precious seconds simply breathing and accepting the fact that he still lived.

By the time he turned back toward Harley, she'd already risen an impenetrable bunker of earth around herself.

"She's not moving," Wolfram said through the speakstone still tucked into Connor's belt. He started in surprise, amazed that he hadn't lost the little stone.

"Those explosions hit hard. She might be wounded. Hit her again," he urged as he swept toward the bank.

"It'll take half a minute to reload."

Connor's brief flash of hope melted away. "She'll be back to full strength before then."

"Can you slow her?" Wolfram asked.

"I haven't been able to manage much yet. I'm trying to figure out a better plan."

He didn't dare return to the air or step onto earth. That left only one option.

Time to take things up another notch. Maybe he could irritate her enough to make a mistake. Connor turned back to Water and yanked on the river, diverting the entire flow over the bank and smashing it into Harley's earthen bunker.

More earth rose around her, thickening her defenses, but she could have managed so much more. Maybe she really was worried about further destabilizing the area. If she hesitated long enough, he might manage to get to her.

So Connor rose on a slender pedestal of water over the river beside the town. He twisted the waters into a huge whirlpool, centered over her bunker, and drove the spinning waters down into the ground around her. He wanted to uproot her and lift her away from the earth. He'd destroyed an elfonnel once he got it separated from the ground. He could do the same to her.

The problem was, the bunker was surrounded by tons of earth and it would take far too long to tear through enough of it to matter.

He didn't have that much time.

Enormous missiles of muddy earth erupted out of the ground outside of his whirlpool. The size of oxen, dozens of them soared north toward the gathered army and the town.

Soldiers scattered, and Connor diverted waters to slap the missiles out of the air. They struck fields and river with muddy splats or impressive geysers. He managed to catch them all, but the distraction cost him too much time. Harley's bunker sank all the way into the earth.

That couldn't be good.

Connor hated landing, stepping into the element of her power, but he had to know what she was doing. So he released the waters to return to the riverbed and threw himself across the town, dragging enough water with him to form a soft cushion to land on. Hopefully that would help insulate him from her earth senses too. As soon as he touched down, he connected with earth and cast his senses in every direction.

Earth felt a bit grumpy to his slate senses. Connor hoped he didn't get angry. Harley wasn't even trying to hide. She had slid back to the road. As soon as he touched her with earth senses, she rose to the surface, still encased in her earthen suit.

She laughed, her quartzite-enhanced voice booming again over the valley. "Creativity, halfway decent teamwork, and some new inventions. Well done, little people. What else have you got for me?"

She made a dismissive gesture and sat back on a giant earthen chair that rose to support her. "I'll give you a few minutes to prepare a second attack. Impress me again and I might even let some of you live for re-education."

Hamish landed nearby and jumped out, looking as worried as Connor felt. He jogged over, not even bothering to bring his tray of sweets. "Did you see that? I hit her with every missile and it did nothing!"

"We hit her with a lot of things that would've killed anyone else ten times over, and she's taking a nap."

"Got any new ideas?" Hamish asked hopefully.

"Not yet."

"If you need thinking food, I've still got a cake in the Hawk."

"No, thanks." He was too nervous, too scared to eat. How could they stop her? If they failed, she'd march through them and destroy Dagmanson, burying it under tons of earth and stone like the queen had done to Alasdair.

"I think I hate that woman," Hamish decided, frowning in her direction.

"I wish Kilian was here," Connor admitted. As much as they needed his unmatched Dawnus powers, his very presence would have bolstered Connor's confidence. Kilian always seemed to know what to do, but ever since the queen had treated Connor and Ivor like amusing pets, he'd begun doubting himself.

Did he really think he could beat Harley? She was an ancient Dawnus, one of the strongest Petralists of all times. What could he do against that?

Hamish ran back to the Hawk and fetched a tray of cookies. He began shoving them into his mouth and gulping them down.

"Ideas?" Connor pleaded as Hamish returned.

"Not yet, but I'm working on it." Hamish took another huge bite and chewed fast. Connor usually agreed with the sugar-induced inspiration approach, but couldn't make himself embrace it today.

What was wrong with him?

He considered the question as Harley put her feet up. It was hard to tell, but he wondered if she was actually dozing off.

Connor glanced at the central command tower, but everyone there was looking at him. He didn't need quartzite vision to read their fear. They were completely stumped. The lord of Raufarhofn who stood with them was gesturing wildly, trying to convince them to act, to do something, anything to protect his city.

Across the river, the Althin researchers who hadn't died in that earlier explosion had managed to right one trebuchet and were cranking back the long catapult arm. Maybe they had something still to try, but could it do more than their earlier, failed attempt?

Hamish had closed his eyes and begun to chew much more slowly, a sign that he'd reached sugar saturation. He mumbled to himself, "Raufarhofn. Roffer-hoffin. Rotter-coffin."

Then his eyes popped open and he got that surprised look that signaled fresh inspiration. "Can you fill her ears with water?"

"Um, maybe. Why?"

"Remember that time when my sister Neilina got really sick a couple years ago? Even Mhairi looked worried for a couple days before she got it turned around."

Connor nodded. Mhairi was a brilliant healer, but not even she could save everyone. Children seemed particularly susceptible to strange illnesses that could claim their lives before she could identify and treat the disease. Neilina had nearly died.

"A couple days after she started recovering, all of a sudden she couldn't walk straight. Kept toppling over without any reason. My mom thought she was having a relapse, but when Mhairi checked her out, she said it wasn't a big deal. Neilina had fluid build-up in her ears."

He spoke the last like it was important, but Connor shrugged, not understanding. "So?"

Hamish pointed a cookie at him to drive home the point. "So, she said that it caused a pressure problem in the inner ear." He paused and frowned. "That's so strange. I never even knew we had an inner ear. What does it listen to, and why can't we hear what it picks up? I bet it hears everything that goes on in there, like the dripping of snot when we get sick, or the sounds of thinking really hard."

"Hamish, do you have a point?" Connor interrupted. The questions were good ones, but they really didn't have time to digress that far.

"Oh yeah. Mhairi said that pressure problems with the inner ear mess up people's balance."

"There's got to be more to it than that. If I filled Harley's ears with water, she could just tip her head and dump it all out."

Hamish shook his head. "I don't think so. The inner ear hides deeper inside your head. I think there's something usually blocking it. Mhairi mentioned some kind of drum, but that didn't make sense to me."

Connor considered that. He felt sure he could hit Harley with water and shove some into her ears, but it sounded like he needed to do more than that.

"Let me check your head." He reached for Hamish.

Hamish's eyes widened and he looked excited by the idea. "Are you going to test making me trip all over the place?"

"Maybe. First I want to see if I can figure out what the inner ear feels like."

He grabbed Hamish's head and drew from the sandstone pendant hanging on its chain inside his shirt. Liquid healing rolled into him, warming him and easing his fears as it infused him with vibrant health. He directed it into Hamish's head and let his thoughts slip along for the ride.

He'd used the method to explore injuries many times and had learned tremendous amounts about the human anatomy. The head was squirrelly, though. He'd spent so much time in Verena's head, but hadn't bothered to check her ears.

Connor pushed healing power into Hamish's ears and studied them. The outer ear was about what he expected, with the little canal leading into the head. Then some kind of membrane blocked it. Maybe that was the drum Mhairi had mentioned?

Hamish shivered. "It kind of tickles."

"Ears are strange," Connor muttered as he studied the little cavity behind the drum and the tiny bones and weird handle-like extension that connected it to a strange, spiral-shaped organ deeper inside. There was fluid in part of it. Was that where he'd need to increase the pressure, or should he fill the entire cavity?

Probably both, just to be safe.

When he released Hamish, his friend grinned. "My head never felt so good, like I could run into walls and not even feel it. What did you figure out?"

"It might work, but I'd have to get my hands on her for a few seconds."

Hamish grimaced. "Not our best option, then."

"Probably not, but something to keep in mind."

"Maybe I can come up with some kind of mechanical to help with that next time we need it."

"If we get a next time?"

The speakstone at his belt spoke. Wolfram said, "I doubt she'll give us much more time. The Althins have another chemical that survived that explosion, but I'm not confident it'll do much. They hadn't invented things with the goal of dissolving several feet of stone and earth."

"That suit of hers is super annoying," Connor admitted.

He studied Harley through Pathfinder eyes, trying to calm his fear and see her as a battlefield challenge, like the Carraig battles. If they survived the day, he needed to try that earthen suit idea. Could he do it?

Could he do it now? Could he master the concept well enough to challenge her to a duel, get close enough to grab her and fill he ears with water?

That sounded suicidal.

Hamish mumbled around a cookie, his eyes still closed. "Tallan take it and smoke fish with it, but that woman's got impressive armor. I don't think we can beat her until we figure out a way to strip it off."

He was right. They had to get Harley out of that armor. Then maybe one of the creative chemical or lightning attacks could finally hurt her.

General Wolfram must have heard that because he spoke again. "How do you propose we get her out? Connor, can you separate her from earth long enough to strip it away?"

"I haven't managed it yet. She clings to the ground like a tick. She hasn't drawn deep from the earth yet, but she might decide to try and that might destabilize this area like what happened at Harz."

Hamish said, "Well, I guess that means you have to get her to drop it voluntarily."

"How do you propose we do that?" Wolfram asked.

"Not we. Connor."

That's what Connor had feared he might say. He considered possible attack plans, but discarded every one of them. Finally he settled on the only one that might help. It might also obliterate him.

"Come on, Connor," Hamish urged. "You're the clever battlefield guy. You've got to have something."

Connor nodded slowly. "I do."

"Really?" Wolfram sounded surprised.

"I need to ascend the second threshold."

45

WHOSE STUPID IDEA WAS THAT?

Wolfram rushed up to Connor, looking more worried than Connor had ever seen. Eystri followed close behind, and she looked like she was contemplating transitioning to Student Eighteen to check him for mental collapse.

For his part, Hamish only took another huge bite of cake, his eyes half-closed, a look of rapture on his face. Connor wasn't sure he heard anything they said any more. Maybe he'd decided his best defense against the looming defeat was to eat himself into a coma and hope Harley would ignore him.

"Are you cracked?" Eystri demanded, her face flushed and her eyes flashing with unusual passion.

"The way I see it, Harley is simply more powerful. She has access to abilities that we just can't match," Connor said.

Wolfram said, "Agreed. Are you thinking that committing a spectacular enough suicide might impress her enough to leave?"

"I doubt it. Dying never seems to work out for me. I can't stop her unless I have access to the same amount of power."

"You are forgetting the facts that she has getting centuries of experience and you will having about fifteen seconds," Eystri pointed out.

Hamish shook himself out of his sugar stupor and said, "The situation sounds hopeless when you describe it with that attitude."

She glared at him. "So you are thinking it's a good idea?"

"Actually, I do."

He really had slipped beyond rational thought. It was a terrible, insane, desperate idea.

Wolfram asked, "Why would you say that?"

"Because none of us can come up with anything better, and he's right. Without a lot more power, we're doomed. So we either quit and go find the best seats to watch Dagmanson get buried under a falling mountain, or we dig in our heels and try something crazy."

"I watched Alasdair die. I won't watch another city get buried like that," Connor stated. He trembled with fear inside, but that single thought helped stiffen his resolve.

"Kilian said not to do it," Wolfram reminded him.

"He said ascending again is dangerous. He said don't do it anywhere near Dougal. Dougal's not here, and I don't think Harley's got the same mind controlling power. I think she's even more dangerous than anything the threshold might throw at me."

When Wolfram couldn't come up with an argument to that, Eystri shivered visibly, then spoke in Student Eighteen's voice. "We can't think of a better idea either, but we don't like it. If she can somehow turn you after ascending, I'll have to kill you."

Connor smiled. "Thanks. You have no idea how comforting it is to hear a trusted friend promise to kill me again if my choices turn out badly."

"Even if she doesn't get to kill you, Verena will probably punch you in the face once she hears about this," Hamish offered.

Connor welcomed the day when Verena recovered enough to do that.

Harley stirred in her chair half a mile away and her quartzite-enhanced voice boomed across the valley again. "I'm getting bored. Do you really have nothing else?"

Connor gestured toward the Hawk. "Hamish, go! My sculpted stones are in the compartment under the second row. Bring me marble."

Wolfram stroked his long mustaches. "I've heard the marble threshold is particularly difficult. If you hesitate or fail to push through the burn, it'll incinerate you."

"Then spread my ashes over the ruins of Alasdair, if you make it that far."

Connor tapped quartzite to his voice and boomed back at Harley. "Relax. We're preparing some arsenic-laced refreshments."

Harley rose and laughed. Her earthen chair melted away and she stretched her enormous earthen arms wide. "I admit I'm disappointed."

"You haven't even tried them yet," Connor said.

As if on cue, the Tabnit fire tubes belched and thundered, flinging another volley of projectiles. These looked different, more silvery than the last.

Harley slid to her left, and the projectiles missed by several yards. They exploded, but without the enormous blasts of the last ones. Instead, amber-colored liquid splashed out in every direction. She still stood well inside the blast radius and ended up covered from head to toe.

She started to laugh.

Wolfram said, "They mentioned they might try this. Would you be so kind as to ignite that liquid, Connor?"

"My pleasure." He created a spark in front of Harley's face.

The liquid ignited like lantern oil. Thick flames rolled over Harley, billowing black smoke, temporarily obscuring her from view. She stepped through the smokescreen, with fire burning fiercely all over her, making her look like a fire elemental.

Earth flowed up to smother the flames, but a second later new smoke began seeping out and the flames ate through.

"It burns through earth?" Connor had never heard about anything that could do that.

"They call it the Fires of Olcan. Water can't extinguish it. It can't be smothered. It continues to burn until all the fuel is gone."

Harley seemed just as surprised. More earth flowed up around her form, but then she began beating on her chest, as if trying to put out the flames.

"Abandon your suit," Wolfram whispered, hands clenched, leaning forward as if he could command Harley by force of will alone.

She didn't abandon the suit, but it did suddenly shrink, most of the layers melting away, taking the still-burning liquid with it.

Close enough. Connor yanked on the river and struck with concentrated blasts of water aimed at Harley's feet. They struck with enough force to stagger her back, but couldn't quite trip her. He kept the water pouring in, scouring away the earth, trying to break her contact.

For a second, it looked like it might work. The ground under her feet ripped away under the focused water barrage, but then more earth flowed up, buttressing her feet. Three low, earthen walls rose between her and the water assault, deflecting it away.

Wolfram muttered a curse. "So close."

Hamish ran up, holding the exquisite, sculpted marble, shaped like a woman wreathed in flames.

Connor took it and said, "Not close enough."

As soon as his fingers closed around the stone, fire erupted out of thin air around him, ringing him with orange and crimson flames. The others cried out in surprise and retreated.

He wanted to apologize, but couldn't make the words come. Fire seemed to fill his veins, his lungs, and his vision. Everywhere he looked he saw a world on fire. Heat shimmered in his vision and his worries were immolated under a rush of marble-induced euphoria.

Fire roiled through him, not burning his flesh, but burning away hesitation. Fire appeared in front of him, like a wildly laughing youth. Connor laughed with him, and Fire grabbed him, lifting him off the ground.

Connor had never felt so wildly and completely *alive*. He drank in the power of the marble statue, far beyond the point he'd ever tried before. The burn intensified until he no longer felt it, couldn't taste anything. Flames roared through his ears like continuous, rolling thunder, and Fire leaped about him, laughing harder still, eager to consume anything he focused on.

He focused on Harley. She had noticed his fiery pillar and stood watching him, one enormous hand on her hip, stone head cocked, as if intrigued.

In a moment, she'd fear him.

Connor threw aside all restraint and gestured Fire closer.

Fire's eyes burned white-hot, and he spoke for Connor's ears alone. *The threshold is the ultimate purifier! You can't stop the burn once it starts.*

"Do it!" Connor shouted.

So be it. Fire stopped laughing. He reared back and lunged, his form condensing into a blistering-hot spear that plunged down Connor's throat.

Fire erupted through Connor, infusing his entire being. He became one with the flames. He was fire.

A wild hunger consumed him, an intense, insatiable need to feed, to consume everything. The flames around him intensified from crimson to white, and then to blue. He floated higher and the air around him crackled with pure heat.

Fire raced through his veins like a molten bloodstream, and in that moment he felt pain. Connor convulsed under the searing heat that seemed to be burning away everything that defined him. His flesh seemed to be melting from the inside, but Fire also stripped away his thoughts, his fears, and his hopes, until all that remained was the innermost core of his identity, his will to live and to fight to the last breath.

Fire consumed.

Fire purified.

Connor sensed the threshold, looming just above him as the water threshold had done. It felt like a gateway of living flames that would melt away the last of what made him Connor if he dared leap up through it.

If he hesitated, it would consume him anyway.

So Connor leaped.

Screaming with the need to survive, to win, to return to Verena, he shot up through the threshold like a comet.

For a second, all he felt was searing heat and blinding pain. It scattered his thoughts then burned them to ash. He saw only the intense blue flames, heard only the thunderous roar, smelled smoke that just might be the last of him floating away on the wind.

Then his thoughts snapped back into place, his vision cleared, and feeling returned like a splash of icy water across his skin.

Connor stood two hundred feet above the ground, encircled in fires so hot that down on the ground people were retreating, hands shielding their faces. The charred ground far beneath him looked melted. When he glanced down at himself, he was amazed to find he hadn't melted away with it.

Connor looked out across the valley and everything glowed in his elemental senses. The flames ringing him were like extensions of his mind. They no longer hurt, but still filled him with wild, enthusiastic energy. Fire stood in the air beside him and saluted.

Welcome, brother.

Without conscious thought, he tapped soapstone too. She appeared beside Fire and gave Connor an approving smile. Then she embraced Fire.

Laughing, Fire hugged her back, and for the first time, they did not fight, but embraced like long-lost lovers. Connor felt moved to witness the elements reconciled. He hadn't expected that, but it must be tied to his ascension.

Together, Water and Fire gripped Connor's arms. The river glowed in his sight, as did every living person. When he focused on Hamish far below, he could sense the blood flowing through his veins. Unlike his rampager sight that seemed capable of looking into flesh for the lifeblood beneath, Connor sensed the water within that liquid.

He could take it.

Just as he could pull water out of thin air, somehow he sensed he could yank the water right out of a person's blood. That thought disturbed him so much that he looked away.

He tapped slate. Even though he hovered so high over the earth, he sensed Earth in the distance, felt him raise a hand in salute and share his strength.

Amazed, Connor tapped quartzite. She appeared nearby and blew him a kiss, looking far less flighty than he'd ever seen her. Strands of her hair blew to him, and when they touched him, all the nearby air currents became visible to his air senses.

When he called one to him, it responded instantly, with none of its normal hesitation. He wrapped it around himself, flaring his fires brighter and helping support his weight.

Connor laughed with wonder. The elements felt more real, more like dear friends than ever. He'd survived, and the ascension had affected all of his affinities far more than the first. He was fire, but he was also water, earth, and air.

Before he could reach for serpentinite to see if he'd gained greater connection to sound too, his strength abruptly fled. Just like that moment after ascending through soapstone, he exceeded his strength and exhaustion crashed in over him.

The elements faded from his sight. Water left last of all, and her expression looked somehow sorrowful. The fires ringing him winked out, and the current he'd wrapped around himself whistled away, as if laughing. Connor grabbed for them, cursing himself for having forgotten that dangerous, momentary weakness that came with ascension. For a second he connected with them again.

They felt wrong.

As Fire, Water, Air, and Earth appeared in front of him, Connor saw that the power that gave them life did not emanate from within them. Instead, they stood within a vast current of energy. Some of it funneled through them, using them like a conduit and giving them life. He tried to understand the shocking revelation, but it faded from his mind, and that current of power split into distinct waves.

One was red. It rolled across the landscape like shimmering tides from an invisible ocean. Those waves flowed through the elements and connected them to him through his affinity senses. That connection allowed him to tap that power.

But the second set of waves was green. It had higher crests, packed tighter together, driven by a stronger and faster current. They flowed over the landscape beside the the red waves, but didn't seem to quite touch. It was as if he was peering through two different windows at the same time and each showed a slightly distorted view.

To Connor's new sight, it seemed the elements standing before him donned billowing robes of intermingled red and green power. The different colored magic swirled around each other, and where they touched, they sparked and hissed. The elemental figures grimaced, as if in pain.

Connor had never imagined the elements might feel pain. He reached for them, but that swirling, sparkling mixture of red and green power covered their hands too. For a second, he felt a jolt of jarring energy, then his grip slipped through theirs, not quite gaining purchase. It was like trying to swim through the frothing, bubbling Upper Wick, finding nothing but insubstantial bubbles, unable to support his weight.

Connor struggled to understand what he was sensing, confused and afraid. He'd ascended to gain access to greater power, but his affinities felt unstable, on the point of breaking.

Harley was going to kill him.

He tried again, grabbing hold of their hands with all his strength. The connection jolted him like a blast from the Varvakin lightning spears as red and green waves of power smashed into his mind with churning discord. The two conflicting waves interfered with each other, shaking his connection and making it blurry, as if he were trying to study the stars by reflection off a choppy loch.

He couldn't maintain the connection. Air yanked her hand away and fled. Earth scowled, then sank out of sight. Fire erupted into sparks that cascaded in every direction. Water hesitated for a second, her expression pained, before she broke the connection and dived into the river without a ripple.

Connor felt completely alone, void. His thoughts faded to black, and the mighty flames that had been holding him aloft vanished, like candles snuffed out by a single breath. He plummeted toward the earth, unable to move, unable to feel any of his affinities, unable to rescue himself.

The ground rushed up and all he could think about was how stupid it would be to die like that, the moment after he touched such unrivaled power.

He should have figured out how to handle those strange waves. Kilian had warned him of great dangers in ascending. If only he'd explained more.

That was at least twice Kilian withheld information he should have shared. Connor had expected to live long enough to see that number rise a lot higher. He felt a bitter sense of disappointment about that as the ground rushed up to splatter him.

Tresta caught him.

Her body sculpted like stone, she snatched him out of the air, spinning him to transition some of his momentum and cushioning the fall. The two of them spun so many times that Connor retched, spraying his last meal a really impressive distance.

Tresta placed him on the ground and shivered. Her body shifted back to normal, and lamacal appeared at the base of her throat. She leaned close and spoke in her Eystri voice.

"I cannot believing I had to getting Tresta's help to be saving you. No one here has ever seeing her. Hopefully they won't asking too many questions, or I might not being able to ever returning."

Connor tried to thank her, but his mouth wasn't working. Nothing was. His muscles seemed frozen and as unresponsive as the elements. He lay prone, so weak it was a wonder his body didn't just implode.

Healing warmth flooded through him, helping ease his exhaustion and pushing back the welcome blackness of sleep right when it was looking so tempting. Now that he could feel his muscles again, they started to complain. Loudly.

"Ow," he whispered.

"I'm impressed you survived," she said in a noticeable Grandurian accent as she scanned him for injuries. "You're remarkably whole, but everything feels thin, as if you were burning from the inside, but without actually charring the flesh. It'll take some time and probably lots of food to restore what you lost."

As his mind cleared, he realized she was healing him. Hope helped burn away his lingering exhaustion. "Aifric?"

She shook her head. "Possible brain trauma. Will have to monitor carefully."

Her voice wasn't Aifric's, but he asked, "Then how are you healing me?"

She flashed a warm smile, but it seemed cockier than Aifric's. I'm Isabell. We haven't met yet."

"Oh. Nice to meet you," he managed, trying to hide his bitter disappointment. It seemed somehow wrong that Student Eighteen might have invented another healer. Her voice was strong, but lacked the compassionate warmth of Aifric's. Knowing that Isabell could step in and help instead seemed to cheapen Aifric's death somehow.

At some level, he knew that was stupid, but he couldn't make himself not feel it.

"I told you he wasn't ready to meet her," she said in her Student Eighteen voice.

"I had no choice," she responded as Isabell.

"Don't telling him about your crimes," Eystri added.

Again her voice fell to an inaudible whisper as her lips moved rapidly in another inner conference. Connor lacked the willpower to eavesdrop again. He should worry for her health, but he just couldn't focus on anything other than trying to stay awake.

"Help me up," he said weakly, interrupting her argument just as Hamish and Wolfram rushed over. Briet and the high command were all watching from their tower, and Gisela was nearby, scribbling furious notes on a little notebook exactly like one of Jean's.

"Did it work?" Hamish asked, dropping to his knees beside Connor.

"I think so. Maybe." He glanced at his hand where he'd held the marble sculpture. All that remained were stone flakes. He'd consumed the entire thing.

"Did you learn anything?" Wolfram asked. He glanced back toward Harley, who was marching north toward the army, as if planning to crush every single one of them with her giant earthen hands.

"Give me a second. I crashed, just like after the first threshold."

"You were weakly for a couple days after that," Eystri reminded him.

"I don't have time for that today. Give me a little obsidian."

She produced a small pouch and he shoved fingers inside and absorbed a little. He really needed to start carrying some with him, now that the threat of Dougal attacking his mind wasn't so immediate.

The obsidian rippled up his arm to his heart and mind, and Verena's clear laughter sounded in his thoughts. He smiled, suddenly feeling more revived than Isabell's sandstone could ever manage. His thoughts accelerated and new ideas flooded his mind.

He needed to focus on Harley, tease out a plan to stop her. His primary affinities still seemed to work, but when he attempted to tap his elemental tertiaries again, he again he felt the confusing split of affinity power in his mind. He frowned, confused and immensely annoyed. He wanted more power, not weird power.

When he focused on the elements, he again saw them standing in his mind, wearing those coats of mixed, clashing power sources. When he tried to touch them, again the two frequencies interfered with each other, severing his connection.

He sensed that if he could tap both of them together, somehow smooth out the interference, he could tap enough power to challenge even the queen, but he didn't know how to do it. The red and green waves bucked and crashed against each other, like snarling dogs battling for dominance, but neither gaining an advantage. All they managed to do was prevent any useful connection. Even his connection with obsidian began to flicker.

He forced himself to face the fact that his tertiary affinities were somehow unstable. Not dying was still the priority, but how could he face Harley without his tertiary affinities?

As he tapped obsidian deeper, that affinity too faded away. It didn't seem as affected by the conflicting waves of power, but neither was it immune. Would his other affinities also abandon him? The thought terrified him and made it really hard to think about anything else.

"What in the Tallan's twisted memory is going on?" he growled.

"What is it?" Hamish asked, while Eystri hovered nearby, twisting her hands together nervously.

"There's something wrong with my affinities."

"You broke them?" Hamish gasped.

"No. There's just something different. I don't understand."

Eystri wrung her hands tighter, looking terrified. "I knew it was a badly idea. Kilian said not to, but you had to disobeying again. This is most terrible."

"Calm down. It's not all bad." He wasn't sure yet how it wasn't, but refused to accept that he might be powerless.

He tested his footing by trying to take a step. He wobbled a bit, but managed to not collapse. He felt as weak as a kitten, but decided he could be a fierce kitten. Harley was barely a quarter mile away and the main army had wisely turned and fled. Soldiers poured through town, not even pretending they weren't panicking.

The high command tower settled to the ground and the entire group rushed over. They looked desperate.

He didn't have the strength to withstand their barrage of questions. He tried sandstone and felt a surge of relief when he connected with it. Healing power thundered into him, more powerful than he'd ever felt before.

Connor rocked back and would have fallen if not for the supporting hands of Hamish and Wolfram. Healing blasted aside his pains and weakness and for the moment restored his sense of health.

"Wow! Sandstone is a lot stronger," he laughed.

"Will that help?" Wolfram asked.

"It's helping me now."

Hamish handed him a cookie. "Good. Eat this."

Connor shoved it into his mouth as the senior command all rushed up, breathless and panicked. The lord of Raufarhofn was a thickset Althin who wore his light brown hair long and braided. He carried a thick-bladed ax and walked like a warrior instead of a pampered lordling. Connor immediately liked him.

Briet spoke for them. "What happened? Can you fight? Do you have any ideas?"

"I'm working on it," he said around the cookie.

The lord of Raufarhofn muttered to one of the generals, "I expected something a bits more impressively."

"Says the guy who didn't even bring me any milk," Connor said.

The fellow chuckled, but then glanced back at his city and his expression fell. "Please helping our city. What can we doing?"

Connor still didn't have an answer, but he couldn't bear to say that. So he looked out at Harley, who was nearly level with their position, marching toward the main gates and the fleeing army.

She made a waving gesture toward the town with one hand, an evil smile spreading on her huge stone skull. A wave of what looked like brown sand materialized in front of her and swept toward the city.

"What is that?" Hamish asked, snapping down his visor to activate his long-vision goggles.

Connor tried to tap quartzite, but couldn't even get a glimmer out of it. Suppressing a curse of frustration he asked, "What does it look like?"

"Like sand, actually." Hamish glanced at him and shrugged. "Have you ever seen something like that?"

"No." Everyone else looked equally confused.

Five seconds later the strange billowing cloud of sand struck a small military outpost next to the gate where merchants registered their loads and paid the local tax. The sand enveloped the building and it started to melt.

The walls crumbled, wood and bricks cascading down and disintegrating even as they fell. In seconds the entire structure was reduced to a pile of sand. An invisible wind swept it all up into the air, adding to the cloud already billowing out to the next building.

Great. A whole new level of destruction, right when Connor's own strength was weakened. Kilian had said something about an opposite, destructive power of sandstone. That must be what he was seeing.

"Do you know what she is doing?" Briet asked.

"Something bad."

Connor realized then that he could feel it, like a sandstorm in his mind. It was growing and spreading as Harley sauntered toward town, punching a swath of destruction through the city ahead of her. He was already tapping sandstone internally, and as he focused on her sandstorm cloud, it glowed softly to his sight.

He'd ascended the second threshold. Maybe he could now wield the sandstorm?

"Do something!" the lord of Raufarhofn cried.

Connor ignored him, raised one hand, and focused on the power of sandstone, willing it out, beyond himself. It took a few seconds to connect with sandstone externally instead of internally. The internal healing connection was so ingrained, but watching three shops melt under the growing sandstorm helped him focus.

Then he felt it, and the sandstorm cloud glowed bright gold in his sight. Connor threw out his affinity senses and tried to grab the sandstorm, to halt its progress or deflect it back against Harley.

The second he connected with it, the new hope that he could actually do something to stop Harley shattered. She held iron sway over the sandstorm. His affinity senses slid off without finding purchase, deflected with frustrating ease. Trying to stop that sandstorm was like throwing daisies in front of an avalanche. Harley's control felt as complete as when she walked the earth.

Harley paused and turned her huge stone head in his direction. She waved and her voice boomed loudly. "I'm impressed you're active so soon after the ascension, but sandstorm is *mine*."

"She's going to destroy everything," the lord of Raufarhofn wailed.

The sandstorm gathered speed, churning toward the center of town, chasing after the fleeing soldiers. Connor followed its eventual path and realized it would roll right over the Tabnit soldiers and their strange tube weapons.

Wolfram had recognized the danger, and was already dispatching a Wingrunner to warn the soldiers to flee, but they'd have to leave their marvelous weapons behind.

Connor despaired. They needed those weapons. They needed something, or Harley was going to casually destroy everything. It was so infuriating! He'd just ascended. After the first threshold, he'd seized new powers and destroyed an elfonnel. Shouldn't he be able to do something amazing now too?

He still couldn't establish a solid connection with his tertiary affinities. Sandstone responded better than ever, so maybe his primaries and secondaries still worked, except for maybe obsidian, but what could he do with those?

He needed Kilian, or Evander. Or both.

Then, as a huge inn near the center of town crumbled and dust billowed out, momentarily obscuring Harley and turning the scene a bit surreal, Connor gasped.

He turned to the others. "I've got an idea."

SOMETIMES IMAGINARY FRIENDS ARE
BETTER THAN REAL ONES

"Quick, man. Do it!" Briet cried and the others eagerly echoed her.

"I'll try to distract her again, hurt her maybe. Tell those Tabnit soldiers to hold their ground and send runners to the Althin trebuchet team. On my mark, hit her with anything you have left."

Mattias glared. "You overstep your authority, Connor. You don't command these armies."

Gisela cried, "Oh, shutting up. If Connor can doing this, we should listening."

Hamish added, "Crazy battlefield tactics are sort of his thing."

Briet exchanged glances with her generals then said, "We agree to obey your commands. Just tell us what you need."

That was more like it. Connor grinned as he tried to form his crazy ideas into a workable plan. He wished he had a moment to simply enjoy the moment. He'd officially taken command of the Arishat League armies. Of course, if he didn't do something fast, he'd be the commander who got to see Althing fall.

So Connor pulled out a piece of flint-like chert and tapped it. Immediately his skin prickled with cold drafts from everyone standing close around him. Fear, worry, and near-panic on the part of the lord of Raufarhofn poured off of them.

When he'd used chert in the past, he'd heard almost-whispers from the people around him, hints at their emotional states. Now as he scanned the group, their actual thoughts sounded loud and clear.

Loudest was the lord of Raufarhofn. *"Not the warehouses! The last cutting is still in there."*

Hamish was thinking, *"I hope Connor actually has a plan. He hasn't eaten nearly enough cookies for ideal inspiration triggering, but sometimes I worry he doesn't really understand the power of sugar."*

Briet was staring at Connor intently, but he read absolutely nothing from her. Her eyes flickered to the chert and he read understanding there. Did she know a trick for shielding her thoughts? He needed to ask Student Eighteen about that.

Eystri was carrying on a rapid-fire conversation in her mind, and Connor picked out a dozen voices all clamoring together. The individual words came too fast to understand.

Then Student Eighteen's voice sounded loud and clear. *Connor, it's considered rude to eavesdrop on your teacher's mind.*

Sorry. He changed focus.

Gisela was writing in her notebook, her thoughts orderly and excited. *"Blood of the Tallan tapped chert. A startled look on his face. Does he really have any idea what he's doing, or is it a symptom of the affinity?"*

He almost protested, but realized that would give away the fact that he was eavesdropping on her mind.

Wolfram and the military men were busy calculating losses, logistics, the best ways to get their forces away from Harley, how many soldiers might be called up to confront her before she reached Dagmanson, and if they were really willing to sacrifice thousands of lives to save the city.

That reminded Connor of his real purpose, and he again focused on Harley. She'd progressed three streets into the city, leaving a wide path of destruction around her. In that twelve-foot tall earthen battle suit she was easy to spot.

The distance made it harder to read her, but as she stepped past a building and came into clearer view, he felt her.

Intense heat radiated off her. She was enjoying herself. No, it was more than that. She loved destruction, battle, proving that she was the most powerful. She enjoyed toying with them, teasing them, then destroying them once she'd bled out all the fun.

She must also have training in protecting her mind, but snippets of her thoughts filtered through. She didn't consider anything or anyone arrayed against her a serious threat. Only two beings might challenge her.

Perfect. That bit of knowledge was the last piece Connor needed to launch his assault. He gripped limestone in his other hand and called upon it.

Hamish said, "Light? Do you really think that'll help?"

He was thinking, *"I can get limestone to glow twice as bright as Connor. We should have a light duel. That would be so much fun. Winner gets the other's dessert for a week."*

That was a great idea. Later. Connor focused on the light streaming through town in front of Harley. Smoke and billowing sand cast excellent shadows that gave him plenty of material to work with.

But first he focused on her again with chert, closed his eyes, and willed the connection to solidify. It remained tenuous, but he only needed to send thoughts back to her.

There. It snapped into place for a second, just long enough for him to send a gentle, whispered thought.

"What if they've been distracting me, just long enough to call for aid?"

He dropped the connection and reached out through limestone and gave the air near her a mighty twist.

"Kilian!" Hamish shouted with jubilant surprise. "When did he get here?"

Connor almost dropped his affinities. He wasn't supposed to be fooling Hamish. But then the others started exclaiming too, and Connor himself saw first Kilian, then Evander step out of the shadows in front of Harley.

The mirage looked amazingly substantial, and it felt solid in his mind, as if he actually controlled those false images. Maybe he'd just discovered a new ability unlocked by his ascension. Finally, something good from all that pain.

She paused at the sight of the two illusions, her bored confidence replaced by battle-ready tension. She crouched in a battle stance, looking shocked right through her stone head.

Connor wished he could tap serpentinite, but all the tertiaries were still eluding him. If he could generate their voices, those illusions would be really believable.

"I need a Longseer," he ordered.

One of them hovered close, attending the generals. Connor wanted to tell everyone the truth, but what if Harley was tapping quartzite? She could hear the explanation and realize what was going on.

So he only said, "Please apply quartzite to my voice."

He felt it tingling along his throat and shouted with a booming voice, "Kilian! Evander! Thank you for coming, but I don't think we need you after all. She's pretty useless."

"What are you doing, you fool!" Mattias shouted, echoed by just about everyone else.

Connor made the Kilian illusion gave Harley a roguish salute, then turn and start walking away. She looked baffled. Connor sent the Evander illusion circling around her, walking toward the south end of town. Harley turned to follow him, but kept glancing back at Kilian, as if expecting them to attack at any second.

Connor made a slashing motion across his throat, indicating to the Longseer to stop enhancing his voice. As soon as the tingling faded he said, "Hamish, I need to get into the air above her. Let's go."

Briet blocked him. "What are you doing? Why aren't they attacking?"

"You said you'd trust me. Now get out of my way before we miss our chance. As soon as you see your opening, hit her with everything you've got."

"You're not making sense," Mattias said.

Connor grinned. "Sensible solutions won't win the day."

Then he ran to the Hawk with Hamish. Well, he tried to run, with Hamish half-carrying him. He felt immensely frustrated by his weakness, and hoped he had the strength to actually make his attack on Harley.

His control wavered over the illusions, so he sent Evander jumping behind a building, then erased him. He sent the Kilian illusion around another building and dropped that one too.

"Where'd they go?" Hamish asked as they settled into the front row seats.

"I'll tell you later. Now get us up there a hundred feet and swoop over her. Make sure when I jump out I'll land on her."

"You can't fight her, Connor. You can barely stand up."

"Please trust me."

Hamish looked torn, but ignited the thrusters. Connor silently thanked him. Hamish didn't understand the potential, and the deadly risks of his last option.

If either diorite or blind coal refused to answer his call, Harley would kill him. He only had a little of each stone. He would only get one shot at her.

The Hawk rose straight up a hundred feet. Hamish paused, one hand over the control to ignite the rear push thrusters. "If you get into trouble, you realize I'm going to come help."

"Don't. I've got this."

He'd better, because he could read Hamish's determination. He'd come, even if it meant a suicide dive.

Hamish touched the lever and the Hawk leaped forward. It'd cover the distance in seconds.

Harley had lunged around the building after Evander, but paused in confusion when he'd disappeared. Connor read her growing worry. She hadn't felt Evander touching the earth, had to be wondering why not.

He planned to try planting another thought, but at that moment his chert expired, the little stone crumbling to dust. It was the only one he had. Hopefully it had accomplished enough.

As they shot over the city, Connor twisted the light again, summoning Evander's illusion standing a block away from where Harley last saw him and causing her to turn away from the Hawk bearing down on her from the other direction.

Her voice boomed across the city. "I warned you that the next time we meet you will die."

"You first," Connor breathed as Hamish tilted the Hawk over and snapped off the wind shields.

Connor grabbed his one piece of blind coal in one hand and a tiny bag of diorite in the other. Then he jumped. As he fell, he absorbed the powder.

Hamish had positioned him perfectly. He plummeted down, aimed directly at the back of Harley's giant suit. He still couldn't tap his tertiary powers, couldn't call upon water or fire or air to slow his fall. He'd turned himself into a human catapult shot.

This had better work.

Connor tapped blind coal, felt its slipperiness coating his skin. He only barely bit back a shout of triumph when he felt the affinity come fast and strong, but that would give him away. That would be a stupid way to die.

Connor swallowed the snake and applied it to his bones. Just in time. He tapped diorite and unleashed all of its power in a single mighty curse-punch as he slammed into Harley's giant like a meteor.

The explosion tore through him, not quite able to rip his insides apart. It roared past, leaving him feeling empty and completely wrung dry, and exploded out from his fist with brutal intensity against Harley, as if taking out its frustration at not being able to kill Connor on her.

Her suit shattered and the impact blasted her out the front side, blood spraying from dozens of gashes in her skin. She lay still for a moment, eyes wide with shock from the unexpected, brutal blow.

Connor rolled the other way, somehow slipping through the shrapnel storm uninjured. He lay dazed for a moment in the rubble of the street, staring up at the late morning sky.

So he got a perfect view of three Tabnit projectiles arcing high into the air.

"They were supposed to wait for my signal," he muttered to himself.

He'd consumed all his diorite, and only a tiny bit of blind coal remained. Connor watched the projectiles reach the apex of their arc and begin the downward journey toward Harley and himself. He also spotted a huge ceramic sphere soaring in from the direction of the Althin researchers. At least they'd timed their strikes well.

Harley staggered to her feet, dripping blood. Connor marveled that she could stand at all. She looked terrible, but her wounds began healing, flesh knitting before his eyes. In seconds she'd be completely whole.

She turned a furious gaze on Connor. "You've annoyed me for the last time, pup."

The Tabnit projectiles and the Althin ceramic bomb struck.

She spotted them too late. The projectiles exploded with fire and jagged steel shrapnel that shredded her leather jacket and tore enormous chunks of flesh from her body.

Connor tapped blind coal at the moment of impact and its slippery protective blanket wrapped over him just as the fire and fury and deadly steel rolled over him to snuff out his life. Somehow it all missed, and he felt it sliding past his skin, leaving him whole.

Then the blind coal ran out.

Intense heat threatened to suffocate him, and he buried his face in the broken dirt, trying to reach for marble. For a second he connected, and he pushed the heat away. Fire appeared in his mind, still wearing the robe of conflicting power frequencies, scowling as if it was Connor's fault they could no longer walk together.

Then the connection snapped, and Connor blinked through the smoke and haze as debris fell all around. Harley had fallen to one knee, savagely torn by the explosions and covered by a thick layer of clinging, gray liquid. It began to smolder and her skin started to melt away, just as the buildings had fallen to her sandstorm.

Harley screamed, pawing at her skin, but the gray chemical clung to her like glue. She couldn't cover herself with protective earth because the acid was already sinking in.

As she tore at it in growing desperation, chunks of flesh started sloughing off like outer layers of half-rotten lettuce. Connor grimaced, horrified by the sight. They needed to defeat her, but that was a disgusting way for anyone to die.

Then the smell punched him right up both nostrils. The sick stench of rotting meat, mixed with a sharp, stinging scent that had to be the acid, layered over a smell like an open sewer pit. He grimaced and tried to connect with earth, hoping to simply squash her and end her suffering. Again the connection splintered and faded before he could use it.

What was going on? The thought of losing his affinities terrified him more than Harley ever had.

Harley abruptly stopped screaming, dropped her hands away from her ruined face and turned toward him. Even though her skin was still melting, her clothing smoking, bones visible through the horrible rents in her torso, she smiled.

It was ghastly. Her face was so badly melted he could see the white of her skull in several places where her hair and skin had slid off. One eye was gone, a bloody, melting socket, her nose was melting away like butter on a hot stove, and only part of her mouth seemed to be working.

"Perhaps you do have potential after all," she rasped in a barely understandable croak.

Connor gaped, his sense of victory evaporated, replaced by renewed fear. She should be dead, or screaming her lungs out at least. He still couldn't feel the elements, so he absorbed a bit of granite and stumbled to his feet. He swayed, barely able to stand, but determined to curse-punch her into oblivion.

Harley melted into the earth.

For a second, he hoped she had simply died, that the Althin acid had reached the critical point where it could finish her off, but that was a desperate hope. She had sunk into the earth using slate.

He couldn't connect with the earth.

She could destroy him easily, drag him under and crush or suffocate him. Or worse, she could cart him back to Donleavy so the queen could brain-wipe him.

Terrified, but unable to connect with marble or soapstone or quartzite to try to escape, Connor walked a slow circle, granite-enhanced fist ready to strike. She might be hurt badly enough that she'd make a mistake and let him hit her.

She did not reappear. Instead, a narrow tube of earth rose next to him and tipped toward him.

Connor stumbled back, but Harley's voice echoed out of the tube. "Congratulations on your ascension, pup. My lady queen suggested you were motivated by need. Today you took a necessary step toward preparing yourself to serve her. I've chosen to spare this worthless rock of a nation in case my lady approves of your development."

Then Hamish swooped out of the sky in his battle suit and ripped Connor off the ground. The abrupt motion strained his neck, and if he hadn't been tapping granite it might have broken bones.

Connor groaned as the world spun around him and the ground fell away.

Hamish asked, "Is she dead?"

"She's gone."

"You sure?"

"I think so." He frowned as Hamish banked back toward the command group outside of town. Was she telling the truth about leaving? He hoped so, but her reasons for breaking off the attack seemed ridiculous. If she was lying, why would she do that, and what were her real reasons?

If she wasn't lying, she was even more cracked than he'd imagined.

47

NO TIME TO PARTY

Two days after the battle, Harley still hadn't returned. Connor started to believe maybe she'd told him the truth and left. Who took that kind of punishment and simply walked away?

They left the remnants of the army still stationed in Raufarhofn and returned to Dagmanson to small but wildly enthusiastic crowds. So many had sailed downriver, it would probably take weeks to get everyone back.

In the meantime, the people who were in town were treated to a series of sumptuous banquets to celebrate their victory. Connor was treated like a national hero. In a pompous formal ceremony in the upper halls of the Logretta, the lawgiver awarded both Connor and Hamish honorary military titles of commanders, and promised to make one of his mansions overlooking Dagmanson available to them any time they visited the area.

All of the attention was overwhelming and a bit embarrassing. Although they'd hurt Harley badly, Connor couldn't help but feel like they hadn't actually defeated her. He kept his doubts to himself. They would only cheapen the ultimate sacrifice that so many had made standing against her.

Hamish's well-known love for food earned them a second, very tasty, award. The lawgiver granted them as much free food as they wanted from any eating house or bakery in the kingdom. Hamish looked close to tears as he accepted the award. As soon as they escaped the stuffy, formal meeting, they headed into town to sample everything.

The next day Connor asked Eystri, Mattias, and Wolfram to meet him in a cozy, book-lined study in the beautiful palace on the eastern hills above Dagmanson where they'd all been granted rooms. Hamish arrived last, walking a bit painfully. He hadn't donned his battle suit yet, and Connor wondered if he'd even be able to put it on. He'd eaten himself sick. Twice.

Word of how much Hamish loved the local cooking had spread like wildfire through Dagmanson and it seemed every chef, baker, or house-wife in the city was clamoring for him to try their specialty. He'd tried to oblige them all. Connor had helped as much as possible, but no one could match Hamish in full feeding frenzy.

Mattias beamed as they all settled into comfortable seats around a crackling fire in the study. "Negotiations are going better than we ever imagined. Nothing like facing total catastrophe to motivate people to accept favorable terms."

No doubt Mattias expected to present the final mutual defense accord between Granadure and the Arishat League to the crown prince and take all the credit for it. Connor didn't really care. He couldn't stomach all the political maneuvering that was clearly involved. He was glad Mattias liked it.

Eystri said in her timid voice, "Now that you having rested much, Jonida, the Alrun of the vault, has many wishings to scheduling you for interviewing."

The Althins were an information-driven people, and they'd want to know everything about him. They'd probably expect that he'd feel indebted to them for all the honors they'd lavished on him and tell them everything they wanted to know. Connor didn't believe they planned to hunt for information to use as leverage to influence him in the future.

He didn't disbelieve it either.

"I'm deeply honored by the invitation, but I'm afraid we'll have to postpone it until my next visit. I have to leave immediately."

Mattias exclaimed, "We can't go now. Not until the treaty is signed."

"And there's a chance Harley will return," Wolfram said.

"No one has ever denying the Alrun," Eystri said, her voice quivering with worry.

Connor glanced at Hamish, but he'd fallen asleep holding his stomach. Connor poked him with a foot. Hamish awoke with a start.

"Is it time for lunch?"

Connor laughed. "I didn't think you'd be able to eat again for a month."

"Haven't you ever noticed that after a huge feed you get hungrier than ever?"

Actually, now that Hamish pointed it out, he had noticed that. "We'll grab something from the kitchens before we go. I need you to fly me back to Drumwhindle."

That woke him up. "What? Why? We can't insult everyone by not eating all their food."

"We have to. I need to meet with Kilian right away."

Wolfram stroked his long mustaches and said, "There's something you haven't told us about your ascension, isn't there?"

Connor hesitated. He didn't want to reveal that he'd lost the ability to use his tertiary powers. Saying it aloud might make it permanent. He'd confide in Hamish during the flight, but no way would he let Mattias know.

"After that ascension, some of my affinities are acting differently," he admitted. "I don't want to hurt anyone. Kilian had mentioned there were dangers ascending. I need his advice and some more training."

"We can't go," Mattias declared, folding his arms and looking ready to argue all day.

Wolfram said, "Negotiations will take some days to conclude, no doubt. Then there will be the celebration feasts. I'm sure Hamish can send another Builder back for us."

Mattias frowned, but couldn't find a reason to argue. He finally said lamely, "It'll look bad."

"I'm sorry, but it has to be done." Connor couldn't bear to wait any longer. He had to talk with Kilian. "Eystri, will you convey my sincere apologies to the Alrun?"

Her face shivered, her expression hardening, her back straightening out of the timid slouch she'd huddled in. She spoke in Student Eighteen's voice. "Mattias can tell her. I'm coming with you."

"Are you sure? There's lots to study here."

Student Eighteen shook her head. "It's better if we leave with you. Now that the excitement's fading, people might remember what we did in Raufarhofn. It's a wonder Eystri's cover wasn't completely destroyed. Better if we don't return until memories fade."

"We'd love to have you," Connor said sincerely.

"Good because on the trip we need your help."

"With what?"

"It's time to try resurrecting Aifric."

48

TOTALLY MENTAL

B y noon they were speeding west over the Kalfafell mountains, the cabin of the Hawk awash with mouthwatering aromas. The entire cargo area in the back was packed with foodstuffs, from bags of cookies and sweetbreads to soups and roasts, packed in insulated, cast-iron pots.

Five huge cakes took up most of the extra seats in the second and third rows, although the nearest one was already half consumed. It was a delicious, dark confection that the Althins called chocolate. Connor hoped they never realized how much he and Hamish loved it, or they'd probably make access to chocolate a condition of a future treaty. Leveraging that clause could win them lots of concessions.

Hamish whistled softly as he flew, looking as happy as he could be when separated from Jean. Student Eighteen sat on the opposite side of Hamish from Connor. She said, "We're ready, Connor. Time to try rebuilding Aifric."

He dearly hoped they could really somehow bringing Aifric back, but felt nervous too. How could they 'rebuild' Aifric? She was a person, not a crafting like the little squirrel with big feet that he sometimes conjured.

"You're sure it's possible?" he asked.

"You're the only person who might be able to do it, and we need to. The sooner the better." She did not try to hide her concern.

"Her death somehow hurt the rest of you, didn't it?" Connor asked.

Hamish looked surprised by that, and he stopped whistling to listen.

Student Eighteen nodded. "Queen Dreokt crushed Aifric, and she caused some collateral damage, although I don't think she understood what she was doing. We've tried to stabilize our mind, but without Aifric, I'm afraid the damage may continue to spread."

"You mean more of you might die?" Hamish echoed Connor's fear. Connor couldn't bear the thought of seeing more of their friend fade away.

Student Eighteen gave them a brave smile. "There is danger. We need you, Connor, and I believe you need something to take your mind off your troubles."

"I'll be fine when I get to Kilian," he insisted.

"Are you having other problems?" Hamish asked, sounding surprised. "Did Harley leave you oozing somewhere unmentionable?"

"No, it's nothing like that."

He grinned. "Did she fill your ears with wind from that earth tube she raised at the end? Is it still rushing around in there? I bet the echoes are terrible with all that unused space."

Connor chuckled. Hamish's good humor helped take the edge off his worries. "I'm fine. It's just, something's different. It's like I've got access to another power source, but it cancels out my normal affinities, especially the elements."

Hamish grimaced. "I thought you were just suffering from lack of sugar when you mentioned that at Raufarhofn. Wow. You take that breaking things talent of yours to some pretty disturbing levels sometimes."

"I just need help figuring out what's going on. Student Eighteen, that's why this might not be the best time to try helping you."

"Your secondary affinities are still accessible?"

"They seem stronger than ever."

"That's all we need. What else do you have to do for the next day and a half?"

"Eat," Hamish said immediately.

"If this works, Aifric will challenge you to a sausage eating competition. She's our champion, and I saw a box full of smoked sausage in the back."

Hamish grinned. "Now you're talking. Connor, what are you waiting for?"

With the Hawk cruising high over the nearest peaks, Hamish wasn't really needed at the controls, so Connor switched seats with him. He still felt hesitant until Student Eighteen said, "Aifric's already dead, Connor. It's not like you can kill her again. As long as you focus on that one segment of our brain, the danger to the rest of us should be pretty minimal."

"And you're all willing to take this risk?"

"Like I said, it's necessary. Aifric's partition was centrally located." She tapped the side of her head. "If we don't get her restored, at least some of us will most likely die too."

Connor's problems didn't seem so desperate compared to hers. He didn't think he could handle dealing with a close friend's death if they died in his mind. "Why don't you do it yourself? You're the one who knows what you're doing."

She shook her head. "I haven't ascended. I don't have access to the abilities required to partition or re-partition a mind. Only you have that power."

He took a deep breath to settle his nerves. "All right. What do I do?"

She extracted a couple small pieces of chert and handed one to him. "We'll link our thoughts, like we did on the speedcaravan when I was helping you hide your porphyry memories. This time, I'll draw you into my head. The tricky part is to link to all of our minds, not just Student Eighteen. You should be able to sense all of our partitions. Aifric's spot is pretty obvious."

That could be intriguing or unnerving. He decided to pick intriguing. "What do I do then?"

"I'm going to cede that area to you."

"So Connor can mess with minds like the queen?" Hamish asked.

"Not quite, but better than anyone else."

"You're trusting me in your head, knowing that I could scramble things worse?" Connor felt the weight of responsibility resting heavily on his heart. The queen had killed Aifric. He could do the same, or worse, to the rest of her.

"We trust you, Connor."

The simple declaration buoyed his confidence. Good friends were far too rare to lose simply because he was poking around in her head with powers he'd never used before, in an attempt to resurrect an imaginary person and give them control over part of her fractured mind.

Actually, when he thought about it that way, it sounded totally mental.

"Wait, I thought you said creating a new personality takes weeks of preparation."

"We're not creating a new personality. We know Aifric. She was part of us. We have all the information about her. We just need you to help prepare that segment of our mind and rebuild the container for her. We'll fill in the rest."

Hamish asked, "You can really do that? You can make her exactly like before?"

"This is the first recreation attempt, but we think so."

"Could you make her better?"

"You didn't like her?" Connor asked.

"It's not that. I was just thinking if I ever got the chance to make myself from scratch again, I might like to slip in some improvements. You know, like deciding right from the start never to willingly eat boiled radishes ever again. Think of all the suffering that could be avoided."

That was a good point. Connor wouldn't have thought of it, but

Hamish had developed the curious inventor side of his mind in the months he spent working with Verena.

She hesitated. "We'd be happy just getting old Aifric back."

So would Connor. Aifric was a long-time, trusted friend. She'd risked everything helping him and had paid the ultimate price. He might be the first person to ever have the opportunity to restore a lost loved one.

"Don't limit yourself," Hamish urged. "There has to be something. She's already the best eater, so she's got good talents, but what could she do better? Can she speak a lot of languages?"

"She's fluent in Obrioner, and knows a bit of Grandurian."

"So what if she ends up assigned to heal a Varvakin? She wouldn't know how to ask them what they had for breakfast or anything."

"Do you have people in there who speak Varvakin?" Connor asked.

"Between us, we know all the continental languages."

"So you could give her a language upgrade," Hamish said excitedly.

"We'll think about it." She closed her eyes for several seconds then said, "Let's focus first on restoring the same Aifric. That would be a spectacular success."

"You're missing an opportunity."

"It's my head, Hamish," she said, a hint of warning creeping into her tone.

"Fine, but when we get back, maybe I'll do some exploring with Connor and see what else we can do."

"Please don't try quickening chert. We have no idea what that might do to your mind."

"I'll try it on Dierk first."

She glared and Hamish raised his hands in surrender. "Just kidding."

Connor wasn't so sure. One more reason for Verena to awaken soon. She could help nudge Hamish toward more productive ideas and keep him from some of his wilder suggestions, like the flap-jacker. That one was supposed to capture pigeons, pluck them, and make pies all in a self-contained package. Connor had seen the plans and shivered to think what would really happen to a pigeon caught in that contraption.

"Connor, are you ready?" she asked.

"Yes." He swore to make it work. Somehow.

She gripped his hands, with the chert between them. "Then let's do it."

Connor focused on the little stone. Almost immediately the sound of rushing wind began whooshing through his mind. He liked it, but still didn't understand it.

As soon as the chert activated, his gaze locked with Student Eighteen's. Her big, brown eyes seemed to grow wider and deeper, until they consumed his vision. The rest of the Hawk's cabin faded away as her aura intensified into a bright, golden glow like it had in the speedcaravan.

The link between them snapped into place and it dragged his mind forward, plunging his thoughts through her eyes and into her head. He landed on his feet on a soft surface, but couldn't see it. Deep, brown shadows, exactly the color of her eyes, obscured everything.

"Hello?" His voice echoed back, as if he stood in a vast cavern. Was that her mind? With nineteen people living in it, he'd expected it to feel crowded.

A very faint aroma of mixed spices tickled his nose. He couldn't quite identify it. He caught a whiff of clean cotton, stone baking under a hot sun, and a dash of spice root, but there was much more. The scents blended into a unique aroma that he decided he liked. It smelled like all of her, wrapped together.

He felt kind of dumb standing around waiting for something to happen, so he willed himself forward. It helped to imagine himself walking, as if he stood in her mind in a tiny body. The soft ground gave slightly underfoot, reinforcing the illusion. Was he stepping on her brain matter? How would that feel to her? He decided he was wearing soft shoes.

Through the brown gloom, a huge shape began to materialize. As he approached, he eventually realized it was a gigantic wall, extending out of sight above and to both sides.

"Welcome to the common area, Connor." Student Eighteen's voice echoed out of the gloom, as if emanating from the wall.

Rith's confident voice sounded from his right. "The link is strong. Come a bit closer, Connor."

Other voices whispered from the shadows to either side, not quite clear enough to make out, but Connor didn't see anyone. That common area seemed uncommonly creepy with those voices echoing all around like spirits.

As he drew closer, he realized the wall wasn't a single, unbroken expanse. It was all fashioned of perfectly cut stones. A seam of different stones met directly in front of him and ran vertically up the wall. To the right, the wall was built of immense basalt blocks, while the left was fashioned of a mixture of glittering obsidian, gray flint, and the distinctive, mottled pattern of serpentinite.

As he scanned the wall, he caught sight of a large door set into the basalt of the wall to his right, shadowy in the distance, about fifty yards away. An identical door broke the wall to his left. Both were made of a dark wood, covered with ornate carvings of flowing, geometric patterns. The ancient symbols of the affinity stones were carved into the center of each one.

Connor walked to the right to inspect the one set into the basalt wall. A shiny, gold plaque was inset above the swirling, circular symbol for basalt.

Rith.

Connor touched the door and immediately felt Rith's personality snap into sharper focus. Her thoughts rushed into his mind as fast as she rushed around the outside world. Her overwhelming confidence radiated through everything, but he clearly read her sorrow at Aifric's death, her nervous hope that they might succeed in restoring her, and her burning desire to find a way to exact revenge on the queen.

"This is my partition, my personal mind space," she told him.

"Wow." Connor was tempted to push the door open and peek inside, but would that plunge him into Rith's mind and knock him out of this weird limbo common area?

"So who's over there?" he asked, pointing back to the mixed obsidian wall.

"I am," Student Eighteen said.

Now it was starting to make sense. "The walls are built with your individual affinities?"

"Very good," Student Eighteen said. "We all start with a blank, wooden wall, but as we establish affinities, it changes."

That was so fascinating. He wondered what his mind might appear like to her if she visited. Maybe a high mountain peak, with spectacular vistas over Alasdair before it was destroyed. It would probably have a fresh kill roasting over a fire next to a huge pot boiling with all of Hamish's jokes.

"Where do I find Aifric's area?"

"Farther to the right, past Cacilia and Tresta."

Connor jogged in that direction. The basalt wall of Rith's partition ran for another fifty yards before transitioning to a mixture of granite and limestone. The door bore Cacilia's name, and when Connor placed his hand on it, her mind touched his gently, like the caress of a rose against the skin.

First he sensed only the demure, polite facade she portrayed to the world of lords and ladies of Granadure. Then she allowed him to sense the adventurous, rebellious side bubbling underneath. She loved those moments of delicious daring when she pushed the boundaries of expected behavior. She loved even more how furious her father became when he heard the rumors her escapades generated. Connor felt his face redden as he caught glimpses of some of her more scandalous adventures.

She spoke to him then, a wicked laugh in her voice. "The others will never admit it, but that Kilian's got mystery and style dripping off him in waves. I don't think he's had a girlfriend in ages, but I'd love to find out how to catch his attention."

Connor fled.

He tried banishing the astonishing suggestion while her soft laughter chased him right past Tresta's solid, granite wall. How would anyone even attempt to date the fractured woman whose head he was running around in? Would Kilian even consider it? What if . . . No, he forced the thoughts away.

When he reached the next partition, he stopped and stared. Tresta's wall ended in a jagged seam that seemed to be flaking and crumbling along the edges. In the far distance, he could just make out another similar, crumbling wall where the next partition started.

The space between was simply gone.

Stygian shadows swirled in that empty area, obscuring everything. The air around him chilled as he cautiously stepped along the perimeter. The ground felt hard and brittle. When he crouched to peer closer, it looked charred, and the finger he slid across the surface came away streaked with soot. It was like the queen had detonated one of Hamish's enormous diorite bombs in there.

"She's completely gone," he whispered into the stillness.

"But not forgotten," eighteen voices whispered back in their various tones and accents. The sounds swirled around him softly, but with unshaken hope.

"How can we rebuild this?" He felt totally out of his depth, as if he was again sinking into Loch Sholto above Alasdair, but with no lifeline tied around his waist. He definitely didn't want to blast his way out this time.

The other voices faded away and Student Eighteen spoke close behind him. "The walls are illusion, Connor."

He spun in surprise and found Student Eighteen standing next to him. She was dressed in a soft, black, silk gown with golden pedras stitched all down the length of the fabric.

She chuckled. "You look like you're seeing a spirit, Connor."

"I just, I mean, I didn't expect to see you standing inside your own head," he stammered. The idea was so weird, he wondered what trips down memory lane looked like for her.

"It's not so surprising. We all create images in our minds all the time. We have this common area to share and we project ourselves here in bodily form sometimes. It makes holding conferences feel a little less schizophrenic."

"I imagine." Actually, he wasn't sure he could. "Where are the others?"

"They don't want to distract you, but they'll appear when we finish." She gestured toward the broken expanse of her mind-scape that had housed Aifric's mind. "We decided to present our mind to you like this to help you relate. It's an illusion, an image we agree to project here, but inside our mind, images are thoughts and thoughts have power."

"Is this how you built the others?"

She shook her head. "Mister Five preferred a different image. I don't think it worked as well, but he was the master so we ceded to his will. This wall feels better."

She stepped to the edge of where the wall should stand and extended a hand. "You are the Builder here, Connor. If you focus, you should be able to sense the dimensions of this partition. It'll be easier for you than creating a new one since our other partitions help delineate the boundaries."

"You can't feel those boundaries, even though you created the illusion?" he asked with a frown.

She shook her head. "We sense the blank space, but we lack the power to build the framework we need to rebuild Aifric."

So Connor focused. He tried to extend his thoughts to the space around him like he did when tapping tertiary stones. He'd practiced extending his mind like that so many times that it came easily.

Chert reacted differently than the elemental stones. With those, he pushed his thoughts through gateways to the elements beyond. With chert, he was already standing in Student Eighteen's mind so there was no gateway. It took a few seconds, but Student Eighteen seemed willing to wait forever.

After a long moment, the common area seemed to grow lighter, and he felt like he was starting to rise, although he never left the brittle ground. The sensation was strange, like standing on a high plateau when suddenly the rest of the expanse in front of him split off and fell away.

He started, hands reflexively extending to balance himself.

"You're feeling it," Student Eighteen said eagerly.

"It's weird, like I can see more all of a sudden."

"Good. You need to understand how the partitions connect."

The view continued to expand, his perspective rising high above the wall. A pure white light lit the brown twilight from far in the distance and cast streamers through the gloom, illuminating the partitions.

Each partition was roofed in the same stone as the front walls. He gazed out over those long expanses of stone toward that white light. He sensed that although the wall looked flat and straight when he stood in front of it, it was actually curved like a many-faceted crystal with nineteen faces.

Her face was superimposed over the stone, each slightly different. Her expression changed in subtle ways, as did the intensity of her gaze, her posture, and the aura she emitted.

Well, eighteen of the faces did. The last one was a blank hole, a chunk gouged out of the greater crystal.

"I've got it, I think," Connor said, amazed by what he was sensing. Was it really how her mind was built, or was it merely a deeper illusion? Did it matter?

"Good. Now focus on Aifric's partition and rebuild the wall."

"Just like that?"

"Don't over-think it. That's a problem when using chert."

"Works for me. I try not to over-think anything." Then he frowned. "Wait, I just realized I don't know what Aifric's primary affinity is."

"Granite."

"Really?" He'd never considered her a Boulder.

"She almost never taps it. Her entire focus is her healing."

Connor absorbed those facts and tried to bring to mind the many cherished memories he had of Aifric as he focused on that gaping hole in the perfect crystal of Student Eighteen's mind. For building materials, he imagined the project was like raising a structure with slate. He just needed to seize what he needed from below and push it into the right spot.

As soon as he thought it, he felt stone blocks rising out of the gray matter under his feet. Grinning, he willed them to stack into walls. Dozens of blocks rose out of the ground and floated into the blank partition, but as they touched that central darkness, they fizzled and faded away."

"Don't build the center, build the container," Student Eighteen said. "We'll fill the center."

Should mind-fragmenting powers make that much sense? He changed focus anyway, calling forth more stone and laying blocks along the front wall. He tried to will the door into existence in the center, but nothing happened and again his connection with the rest of his building blocks wavered and melted away.

"Why can't I build the door?"

"The door is the entrance to her mind. Her mind doesn't exist yet. You're just creating the bucket we'll use to fashion her mind. Only then will the door come into existence."

That sounded more like it. He didn't understand what she meant, so it was probably exactly what they needed to do.

Focusing again, he rapidly formed the outer wall, packing stone atop stone, mixing granite and sandstone, but using twice as much sandstone since she preferred that affinity. If only manual labor in the quarry moved so fast. As the wall rose, Connor quickly grew bored with alternating the stones so regularly. Since he controlled the way the stones were placed, he began shifting the pattern.

He started with wavelike patterns, then incorporated some of the geometric shapes they seemed to like on the doors. As he completed the front wall and began extending the side walls behind, he continued working with those patterns. When he started in on the roof, he thought back to the many magnificent frescoes he'd seen in the Carraig and Altkalen.

So he added some of those. He couldn't make them so complex or colorful, but he did the best he could. The creative process captivated his attention so completely that he was surprised some unknown time later when Student Eighteen clapped three times loudly and laughed.

"I feel it! The partition is complete."

It was. Connor slipped his thoughts along the new container and felt a flash of pride. He'd done pretty good work, considering it was all illusion in someone else's mind.

"Why does it feel different? Aifric's partition feels far more . . . I don't know. It's subtle and complex. What did you do?"

"Just what you asked."

She raised one eyebrow.

"Well, maybe I spiced up the pattern of the stones a little, but that's no big deal, right?"

She frowned and the voices of all of the other personalities began whispering rapidly around them. Connor caught glimpses of their shapes drifting through the brown twilight.

After a moment Student Eighteen said, "We're not sure. Mister Five was always very methodical and strictly economical in building the partitions. We never tried it this way before."

"I'm sure she'll like it," Connor assured her.

He did. The partition seemed better somehow than the simple, plain ones the others lived in. He didn't want to tout his accomplishment too much, however. They might all want new houses and he wasn't sure he was up for attempting extensive remodeling.

Although the work was purely mental, when he extended a thought back to his own body, he could feel himself sweating, muscles aching as if he'd been running for hours. They needed to wrap up their work soon. Messing with people's heads was a lot harder than he'd ever imagined. Shona made it seem effortless.

Student Eighteen raised her hands, and said loudly, "All right, ladies. Let's bring our girl back."

"What do I do?" Connor asked.

"Maintain the partition. Each of us holds specific aspects of Aifric's personality, along with portions of memories of her life. Combined, they should create a new whole."

As she spoke, the other personalities all appeared, dressed in their favorite outfits. Rith wore her Strider leathers. Cacilia wore a stunning satin dress that revealed far more skin than any outfit Connor had ever seen Aifric wear.

The sight of it made him blush again and she sidled up next to him with a soft laugh and touched his cheek. "You're such a dear, Connor. Too bad Verena's got your heart all wrapped up."

Student Eighteen scowled at her. "Cacilia, we agreed not to strut your peculiar vices in front of Connor. You'll damage all of our reputations."

"You're such a stuffy old spinster," Cacilia muttered, but strode off, moving with a sensual grace that tempted Connor to keep watching.

He looked away.

Tresta marched past in her Boulder battle leathers, with Eystri creeping in her shadow, looking nervous even in the protected environs of her own mind. Mariora rushed past, dressed in her courier uniform, followed by Isabell, who wore a Healer's jacket covered in dancing, multi-colored flames. She winked at Connor as she passed. More of them followed, personalities Connor hadn't yet met. He wanted to ask their names, but Student Eighteen drew his attention back to the wall.

She stood in the center, right where the door should be. She held an ornate wooden box, completely smooth, lacquered with black and orange clouds.

She pressed it to the wall and said solemnly, "I grant to you birth and family, your deepest desires and your most crushing defeats. I bequeath your name. You are Aifric."

Intense white light erupted from the wooden box and it melted into the wall. Through his connection with the stone, Connor felt it fuse, becoming one with the stones. A ripple of power coursed all around the partition and a candle-worth of light began shining in the blackened heart at the center. He felt it like a whisper against the hair of his arm.

Rith took Student Eighteen's place. She held a similar box, but lacquered in crimson and green streaks that formed a bold, exciting pattern.

"I grant to you memory of your first affinity. You are a Boulder! You wield the strength of the mountain to nourish and shelter all who know you."

She pressed her box into the wall with another flashing brilliant light. Connor felt the granite in the wall begin to glow in his mind. Its affinity had activated.

The tiny glow inside the partition grew brighter.

Rith stepped back, and only then did Connor realize the wooden boxes they'd pressed into the wall had transformed into pieces of a beautiful doorway.

Surprisingly, Tresta took the next turn. Her normally stoic expression looked exultant as she pressed her box to the wall. She intoned, "I grant you the heart and soul of your work. Your second affinity. You are a Healer! You live to help others, to brighten the world with your smile, and to spread compassion to all who suffer pain and hurt."

The sandstone of the wall seemed to quiver as the affinity activated. The light in the center of Aifric's being intensified dramatically, and Connor sensed Aifric's legendary smile flicker around the boundary. He smiled in response, and he felt his throat growing tight with growing emotion. She really was coming back!

Each of the other personalities stepped up to the wall in turn. Each pressed a box into the wall, building the doorway to Aifric's mind and bequeathing memories, attributes, and pieces of Aifric's personality.

Connor watched and listened in amazement, moved by the solemnity of the moment. Student Eighteen was creating a new person, birthing

Aifric within her own mind. Many of her personalities wept with emotion as they performed their parts of the ceremony.

As the door slowly grew, the light inside the partition intensified, driving back the black emptiness and taking ownership of the wall.

Connor was still deeply connected with the partition when Isabell, the last of all, pressed her box into the wall, completing the doorway and granting to Aifric friendship, the memory of healing her first broken bone, and the day they'd won their appointment to the Carraig.

Isabell pressed her hand to the center of the door and whispered, "You are Aifric."

The others crowded in, all pressing hands over the same spot, repeating the words in unison. Their voices melded and grew, somehow magnifying each other until the common area reverberated from the thunder of it as the name echoed over and over.

Aifric. Aifric. AIFRIC!

Connor couldn't help himself. He joined in the final resounding chorus, his voice swept into the mix. With a blinding flash and a final thunderclap, a golden plaque materialized under their palms. Connor staggered from the mental jolt. The blazing light filling the partition pulsed with Aifric's first heartbeat and all of the pieces that had been offered by the other personalities fused together and became a solid whole. Aifric touched Connor's mind and he felt the question in her thoughts.

"I'm Connor. Welcome to day one."

Then Student Eighteen tackled him in an exuberant hug. She would have knocked him from his feet if he was really standing up.

"She's here! Aifric's Back. Thank you!"

"What are friends for?" he asked, hoping she'd regain her normal air of maybe-I'll-kill-you-today-anyway attitude he'd grown to expect.

All of her other personalities piled on, hugging and laughing together.

The door began to open.

Immediately the brown twilight of the common area disappeared, replaced by a long lawn of thick, luxuriant grass, ringed with towering oak trees. Connor couldn't see beyond the trees, but didn't care.

Bright sunlight spilled out over the grass, and several long tables rose up from the ground. They groaned under the weight of every single one of Connor's favorite foods.

All of the personalities flickered momentarily, changing in the blink of an eye into formal gowns. He'd always loved Aifric's ready smile and friendly face, but he'd never really considered just how lovely she could look when she tried.

With a thought, he changed out of his everyday clothes too. Aifric was Obrioner, so he switched to fine linen pants, a soft cotton shirt, and a long, russet jacket with deep pockets.

They all faced the far end of the clearing where Aifric strode eagerly toward them. She wore an emerald robe with a wispy pattern of grays that somehow gave the impression of hands extending to heal.

All of Student Eighteen's personalities swarmed around Aifric, welcoming her back and talking at the same time. They all seemed to understand it all, and they laughed and joked and reminisced at a speed that left Connor completely behind.

So he walked over to the nearest table and found a huge chocolate cake, with a fork already sticking out of it. The entire scene was an illusion, so he ate the entire cake.

It was delicious. No, it was better than that. Somehow the taste seemed to shoot right into the center of his brain, clearer and more incredible than any taste that had to pass through his mouth first. He grinned as he shoveled in enormous mouthfuls, wishing he never had to stop.

When he finished, he turned to find all nineteen women who lived in Aifric's head approaching, grinning at him.

Aifric stepped to the front and hugged him, laughing with joy. "Thank you, Connor. I remember you now. I cherish our friendship now more than ever. You've given me the gift of life."

The emotion pouring off of the women made him distinctly uncomfortable. He shook his head. "I'm just the builder. The ladies gave you life."

"Thank you."

Student Eighteen joined him, grinning way too happily. "We declare you an honorary Mhortair, Connor. We adopt you into the family."

"Isn't your family trying to kill you?"

"At the moment."

"And they'll try to kill me too."

"Definitely."

He shrugged. "That's how our friendship started. They'll come around."

Laughing, she kissed his cheek.

And suddenly the chert connection broke.

Connor fell out of his chair and groaned. He was drenched in sweat and every muscle ached.

Hamish sighed. "Finally. Are you all right?"

"I think so," Connor said, righting himself with another groan.

Hamish looked immensely relieved. His fingers were stained with chocolate, and he brushed crumbs from his shirt. He noticed Connor looking and said, "What? I eat when I'm nervous. If you hadn't returned when you did, I might have eaten myself sick. You've been gone for hours."

"Feels like I've been bash fighting for a week."

"Did it work?" Hamish asked, glancing at Aifric, who hadn't moved yet.

"Better than I ever imagined it might."

Aifric suddenly blinked and laughed, a bubbly, happy sound full of pure joy. She helped Connor rise and hugged him again.

Then she turned to Hamish and said, "We're starved. Where are those sausages?"

49

WE PLANNED TO LAND HERE. REALLY.

Connor slept for twelve hours.

He didn't even finish his sausage. Between bites, a wave of exhaustion struck him like an avalanche. The next thing he knew, the Hawk pitched violently and shook him awake. He blinked sleep from his eyes and climbed up from under the second row of seats. He groaned as stiff muscles complained while the little craft pitched and shook. He only barely managed to climb into the middle seat without tumbling around the cabin.

Luckily, the cake that had been sitting in that seat was gone. Hamish and Aifric had eaten it. They'd also finished the entire three-level, honey-glazed cake that had been sitting on the left-hand seat.

Connor glanced toward the rear, half expecting to see the piles of food completely gone, with Hamish and Aifric sprawled amid the last crumbs, pots and pans licked clean, and empty bags that had held hundreds of sweetbreads.

The image was so vivid in his mind that he felt a bit disoriented when things looked about the same. Two of the cast iron pots were empty, and one of the bags of sweetbreads was crumpled up nearby, but the rest looked fine.

Thank the Tallan. He was starving.

"I thought you were going to sleep all the way to the border," Hamish called as the Hawk shuddered violently.

He sat in the pilot seat. Aifric was sprawled to his left with several pillows and blankets propped against the shimmering window shields. She looked determined to try to sleep, but was failing. She flashed Connor her trademark smile, and he wanted to whoop. Aifric was back.

The Hawk pitched heavily to the left, knocking Connor right out of his seat.

"Hey, what was that for?" he asked, scrambling back into the seat and reaching for the safety harness.

The Hawk pitched the other way and dropped straight down in a stomach-lurching dive. Only then did Connor notice they were flying through a dense cloud, with snow whirling around every side. Wind howled outside, the sound muted by the shielding over the windows.

Hamish was hunched over the controls, hands flicking between control rods, a look of intense concentration on his face. "Major storm hit just a few minutes ago. I don't think it's quite as bad as that big one that brought winter with it, but it's close."

"Can't we fly above it?"

"I tried, but ran into fierce headwinds up there. Even with the push thrusters maxed, we barely made any headway. We'd run out of power before making it back to Badurach."

Every window showed billowing clouds of whipping snow. Hamish could just as easily be flying straight down for all he could tell.

That thought worried him, so he decided to test their direction. He picked up a big crumb of cake still stuck to the seat next to him and flicked it at Hamish. It struck the back of his neck, just above the collar of his suit.

Hamish glanced back. "What was that?"

"Just checking to see if we're flying straight."

"Good idea. I tried a spit test earlier. Since then, I've just watched Aifric's hair in case it starts falling up or sideways." He considered the control panel thoughtfully. "We need to install some kind of horizontal check to help with that. I wish we'd hung out in Althing a bit longer. I heard they have really good compasses in their ships. That would help make sure we stay on course."

Connor hadn't considered that. In the past, they'd always flown in weather that allowed them to see sun or moon or stars regularly. Now he had no idea where they were. It was like flying underwater.

That gave him an idea. Connor downed a vial of soapstone mixture and tried tapping elemental water. For a second he connected and Water appeared, standing in front of him. She still wore that coat of conflicting power frequencies, though. Connor reached for her extended hand, but the red and green power sparking and sizzling across her hand shorted each other out, snapping the connection.

The red-frequency power felt more familiar somehow, so he tried grabbing only a part of her thumb where the red power seemed to hold sway. For a second, he connected, and she smiled encouragingly. He managed to pulse his water senses out in every direction. The landscape unfolded to his mind, like a map in his thoughts. They were flying along a rugged mountain range. He hoped those were the Maclachlans.

Then a new wave of green energy swept across Water, momentarily swamping the red power he was connected with. The connection shorted out and the connection jolted him, knocking his hand away. He muttered a curse.

"What?" Aifric asked.

"Still having trouble with the elements. I connected for a few seconds, though. We're flying over a mountain range."

Hamish looked relieved. "I had worried we'd drifted off. The Maclachlans should take us right to Drumwhindle."

"If you can hold this course, we should get there. I'll try again when you think we're close."

"Give it three or four hours. This storm is slowing us down a lot."

That gave Connor time to rummage for food. Hamish and Aifric were both still stuffed from their epic eating competition. Connor settled back into the second row with a pot full of glazed ham and potatoes. Despite being packed carefully in the cast iron pot, they were pretty cold. He didn't dare attempt touching fire, but Hamish dropped an activated bit of marble into the pot to heat it up.

That helped, but heated things unevenly. The meat closest to the marble got charred, while the food on the opposite side stayed cold, despite his attempts to stir it. He would have tried heating the pot over the little marble burners, but the Hawk was pitching so badly, he'd never keep it in place.

In fact, trying to eat during that storm became a test of his agility and timing. He had to pull open the lid just long enough to take a bite before the bucking craft splattered the food all over him. He managed only a few bites before giving up. The wild motion was starting to make him feel sick, and this was not the time to try for the puke-distance title.

After securing the pot under his seat, he asked Aifric, "How are you feeling?"

"Great. My memories are still settling into the proper sequence. I'll be working with the other girls for weeks to fill in all the gaps. Other than those fuzzy memories, I feel amazing."

"I'm really happy to hear that," Connor said sincerely.

Her expression turned thoughtful. "One thing surprises me, though. I've been feeling a growing urge to tap granite, but from my memories, I don't think I used to ever actually use my primary affinity."

Hamish grinned. "You did include some improvements, then. Excellent."

"Not on purpose," Connor said.

"Maybe not, but another thing is weird too. When I tapped sandstone to reconnect with my Healer gift, my affinity seems exceptionally powerful. I suspect I'll be able to heal better than ever."

"Double enhancement," Hamish said. "Good job."

Connor thought back to the creative liberties he'd taken with designing the affinity stone walls of her mental partition. Might that have enhanced her affinities? The idea was intriguing.

"Let me know what you find out when you get to test it," he said.

"I will." She shrugged and smiled again. "I don't mean to sound ungrateful. I'm alive again and my affinities seem to be stronger than ever. It's just, I'm trying to settle back into being myself, and any changes make that process harder."

"I'm sorry if I did something wrong. I'm just thrilled your back," Connor said.

"Me too. Thank you." She lifted a chain of steel links over her head and handed it to him. Little silver clasps connected to every fourth links. Three were filled with pieces of chert, serpentinite, and limestone.

That was a clever way to carry power stones. When he tried to hand it back, she shook her head with a smile. "A small token of appreciation for helping bring me back from the dead."

Hamish chuckled. "So you're a resurrectionist for hire now? Can you resurrect that second chocolate cake? That one was worth eating twice."

"Not unless you want to return all the pieces," Connor laughed.

Aifric grimaced. "Don't you dare. Connor, I hope you find that necklace useful."

"Thank you." He hadn't expected any sort of gift. Friends helped each other out. That should be enough. The gesture meant a lot, and he'd cherish it.

Hamish said, "We've been talking about Donleavy and what happened when you tried sneaking in. Sounds like an amazing place if you ignore the whole reign-of-psycho-terror feel."

"Have you been talking with Mariora?"

She shook her head. "The girls suggested I hold the reins for a while. The closer connection with our body helps ground me to myself. Mariora shared her experience through me, and the others added their thoughts. We can all see what's going on, so we all have variations of the same memories. Melded all together, they're pretty accurate. That's how they'll restore me so completely."

"What does dying feel like?" Hamish asked, fascinated.

"That part I don't remember, thankfully. The others decided not to include that memory. Probably a good idea. We may revisit those final moments in detail once the rest of my memories are restored."

Connor said, "Good. My own memories of the last minute or so before she let us go are still fuzzy."

"Well, I was dead, and the other girls were in shock, so their accounts are pretty jumbled. That's another reason we've avoided those moments so far."

"I'd just like to understand why she let us go. It could be important."

Hamish asked, "Connor, couldn't you go back in and see it for yourself?"

He wasn't sure he wanted to. He'd witness Aifric's death, and that was traumatic enough from the outside.

She said, "I don't think we'd let him. I died, and that's not something you should focus on, Hamish. Better to concentrate on living."

After that, the storm intensified and they didn't talk much for the next three hours, but just held on while Hamish tried to keep them aloft. Connor tried connecting with water again, but failed to link to it at all. So Hamish resorted to slowing and descending carefully to check their position.

As the Hawk pitched and bucked in the turbulent air in the lower altitudes, Hamish looked nervously at Aifric. "Got anyone in there with soapstone who can help scout where we are? I don't want to fly into a mountain."

"We've been discussing that. Nuzha's got the best water affinity, but she doesn't really like Obrioners."

"Does she like to live?" Connor asked.

"Good point. We'll let her out and we'll do our best to keep her calm, but just be cautious not to insult her. Her honor is very touchy."

Connor glanced at Hamish, who shrugged, not looking concerned. Most of Aifric's personalities were dangerous so they were used to that feeling of danger around her.

Aifric's face shivered and her expression turned disapproving. Her eyes seemed to darken, her brows creasing into a scowl. Her voice came out harsh, with an accent that could have been beautiful if it wasn't so full of disgust.

"Figures, Obrioners aren't smart enough to avoid a storm like this. And of course you got lost. If my father knew you men asked help from a woman, he would slit all our throats."

Hamish grinned. "I think I like you, Nuzha."

She produced a knife from somewhere so fast Connor barely followed it. "If not for the life debt I owe Connor for restoring my sister, I would not have agreed to sully my lips speaking with Obrioners. Know that it is forbidden for an impure swine of Obrion to touch a daughter of the sands. Try it and I'll cut out your heart."

Connor liked her strength, but decided it was probably best that they interacted with Nuzha as little as possible.

Hamish gave her an incredulous look. "If you don't like our company, you're free to go."

The shielding over the window directly in front of Nuzha disappeared and the blizzard roared in. Blinding snow poured in, scattered her pillows, and bitter cold sucked the heat away in an instant.

Nuzha screamed and the snow rebounded away. She glared at Hamish. "Water that freezes and flies above the land is unnatural, but it still obeys my command. A city lies directly beneath us. Land there so we can get out of this abomination."

"What city?" Connor asked. He'd hoped they had reached Badurach pass, but it was guarded by only a tiny garrison.

Nuzha shrugged in abundant disgust. "The cities of you coldlanders matter little to me. We never raid this far north. It sits on a bluff beside a river, with high walls." She cocked her head, as if listening. "Tresta believes it's Merkland."

Hamish restored the window shielding and Connor said, "Thank you, Nuzha. You upheld your family honor perfectly. Would you send Aifric to speak with us?"

Her face shuddered again, her scowl replaced by Aifric's ready smile. "Nuzha's right. We need to set down."

Hamish said, "Of course we do. Trying to fly up to the pass through this storm would be suicidal, especially with Connor's affinities broken and Nuzha sharpening her dagger in that head of yours."

Connor added, "Ivor is here. We can find out how his planning with Rory is going."

Aifric's voice changed to Student Eighteen. "Hopefully it's going well. If they were discovered, we might get thrown into prison."

Connor chuckled. "If they were discovered, there wouldn't be anything left of Merkland after Ivor and Rory finished with it."

Hamish's expression turned to mock outrage. "They wouldn't start without us, would they?"

"Let's find out."

They almost crashed into the palace before they saw it. Even though many lights glowed in the windows, the raging storm obscured them until the last moment. Hamish fought to keep the Hawk descending slowly through the bucking winds. Even though Connor couldn't tap his tertiary powers, he swapped to limestone and called forth a burst of light.

The reflection off the snow blinded them, but they did catch sight of buildings looming all around like shadows. Hamish dropped through, shifting right to avoid some lower houses, and found a wide open space. The Hawk thumped down hard on a cobbled plaza, empty of people. Connor doubted anyone had heard the thrusters through the wind.

Hamish sighed and leaned back in his chair. "That was worse than digging ourselves out of that manure pile."

Connor laughed. "I'd totally forgotten about that."

Aifric grimaced. "I'm not sure I want to know."

Grinning, Hamish explained. "When we were six, we wanted to be adventurers, but our mothers wouldn't let us leave the fields around town. So we decided to tunnel into a huge mound of composted manure and dig out a cave in the middle. Figured no one would bother us there."

Aifric laughed. "I guarantee you would've been alone."

Connor said, "Unfortunately, the mound was not exactly stable so as soon as we dug four feet into it, our tunnel collapsed on top of us."

Hamish grimaced. "Everything I ate for a week afterward tasted like moldy compost."

She frowned. "What made you think about that in the middle of a snowstorm?"

Hamish laughed. "As if I could explain. I thought girls were supposed to be champions of intuitive leaps. Now you know how weird it feels trying to keep up."

They donned heavy jackets, then Hamish dropped the front window shield. As soon as they clambered out, he restored it. At Connor's questioning look he said, "I don't want anyone stealing our food. That stash was a gift from the people of Althing. I wouldn't want it wasted on just anyone."

"Good point."

They discovered they'd landed in a side courtyard of the northern wing of the main palace. The first three doors into the palace that they tried were all locked and no one answered their knocking.

Finally, they circled around to the main entrance hall and pushed open one of the huge doors there. Two sleepy guards roused themselves to help slam the doors shut. Only then did they challenge them.

"General Connor here to see General Rory," Connor said in a crisp, authoritative voice. "Quick, man. Take me to him."

"General Rory's not in the palace at this hour, sir. Best bet for finding him is in his office in the military command building." He pointed back out the doors. "Across the square, past the Hall of Lords. It's the big castle with four turreted towers to the south of the training fields."

The other soldier considered them suspiciously. "Why doesn't a general know that?"

Connor gave him a disgusted look. "Last time I visited Merkland, I spent most of my time with High Lord Dougal."

The first guard said quickly, "If you wish to speak with Lord Nevan, his palace is east of the command center, across the speedcaravan tracks."

"Thank you." Connor spun and led the way back out into the storm. The blowing snow and darkness made it hard to find their way, but they eventually found the command building with the help of a couple other soldiers they ran into on patrol.

It really did look like a castle, although it lacked an outer curtain wall or moat. It reared out of the snowy darkness in six imposing stories of thick stone, with crenelated towers and a parapet along the roofline.

Inside the main gate, they were again challenged by a pair of guards, who seemed a bit more competent. Before they could digest the fact that Connor wasn't wearing a uniform under his coat, he called upon limestone to make his eyes glow as he again ordered them to lead him to General Rory.

They seemed willing to believe him and summoned a third soldier to take them up to Rory's office on the top floor. The hallways of the castle were mostly bare stone, with the occasional military-themed tapestry. Lanterns lined the walls precisely every thirty feet. The air was noticeably chillier than in the main palace even though every fireplace was lit and additional brass braziers of coals were positioned every fifty feet.

Connor wouldn't be surprised if they still needed the Firetongues to help take the worst of the chill off. Heating the huge building in that kind of bitter cold must be a constant challenge. His family's home in Alasdair had always felt snug and warm, but their entire house would fit inside many of the vaulted rooms they passed.

It was early evening and the halls were mostly empty, but they did pass soldiers and servants, all hurrying about their business, most wearing jackets and gloves to keep warm.

At a junction of four corridors at the base of a long flight of stairs leading up to the higher levels, Aifric stopped. A flicker of worry momentarily crossed her face.

Her face shuddered as she shifted to the cold-eyed stare of Student Eighteen. "You two go ahead. I have something to deal with."

"What?" Connor asked, glancing around but not seeing anyone threatening. That wouldn't be a great place to get into a fight.

"It's a girl thing." She gave him an apologetic smile. "I'll find you later." Then she hurried away down the corridor to the right, not looking back.

Hamish asked, "What was that all about?"

"I don't know, but I don't like it. She looked worried."

"And since when does Student Eighteen talk about girl things?"

The soldier didn't look happy about the delay. He'd started up the staircase and now looked back from the top, clearly wanting to urge them to hurry, but not quite sure he dared.

Hamish said, "You go meet with Ivor. You don't really need me the whole time. I'll keep an eye on her and make sure she doesn't let Nuzha out."

Then he slipped down the hall after Aifric, moving slow along the wall. He managed to not quite look like he was sneaking. Connor wondered how long it would take for Aifric to spot him.

Hopefully they were overreacting, but he was glad Hamish was going after her. Connor climbed the stairs quickly and followed the guard deeper into the heart of the palace.

50

KEEPING A LOW PROFILE WILL BE EASY

Rory was not in his office, a long room on the top floor, with a huge window, covered by thick, insulating drapes. The view would probably be great on a clear day. Connor asked the guard to summon Tomas or Cameron.

Several minutes later, Tomas and Cameron burst into the office, grinning.

"Connor, me lad," Tomas exclaimed, pumping Connor's hand hard enough to dislocate the shoulder of someone unprepared.

Cameron clapped him on the back, knocking him forward a step. "How by the Tallan's warted backside did you slip into Merkland?"

"I bet he summoned the blizzard," Tomas suggested.

"Actually, we were aiming for Drumwhindle, but the blizzard blew us off course."

Cameron gave him a disgusted look. "Lad, next time let me take that bet afore you prove I would've won."

Tomas said, "The pass is already broken, Connor. What you want to be flying up there through a blizzard for?"

"Doesn't matter now. I need to speak with Rory. Do you know where he is?"

"Secret meeting with Ivor," Tomas said immediately.

Cameron leaned in closer and added in a conspiratorial whisper. "No one's supposed to know."

"But of course you two do."

"Of course," they said together. Tomas added, "On account of us being the new captain of the Fast Rollers, we need to know all the goings on around here."

"You're captain?" Connor exclaimed.

"We're captain," Cameron clarified. "Old Rory couldn't decide which of us to promote, so he made us joint leaders."

"Congratulations!" He wasn't surprised they'd been promoted together. Neither of them did anything without the other, so promoting just one would result in a never-ending barrage of arguments. He wasn't entirely sure the Fast Rollers were quite ready for Tomas and Cameron as captains, but he hoped Rory knew what he was doing.

They led him back to the main palace again, then up to a top-floor observatory in one of the lesser towers. The glass-lined room was chilly, despite a roaring fire, and the panoramic view showed nothing but darkness and swirling snow.

Rory and Ivor sat before the fire on either side of a table cluttered with papers, maps, and scrolls.

Ivor laughed and rose. "Connor? What are you doing here?"

"Checking in to see how things are going." He enthusiastically gripped hands with Ivor, then Rory. "Sort of missed our target in the snow."

Ivor asked, "How can you miss anything in the snow? You're even better with soapstone than me."

"It's kind of a long story."

"We have time," Rory said. He thanked Tomas and Cameron and sent them away, with a stern warning to make sure no one else interrupted his secret meeting.

"I still can't figure out how those two always seem to know what I'm up to," he said with a shake of his head.

"I'm glad they're on our side," Connor said.

"Are they?" Ivor asked. He didn't look so happy. "We can't afford word getting out about what we're planning before we're ready."

Rory said, "Don't worry about those two. They're loyal to me and they're far more capable than they pretend."

Connor glanced down at the paper-covered table. "How are things going?"

Ivor dragged a third chair from the other side of the room for him. "Rory is committed. We're trying to figure out the first stage."

Rory said, "Problem is, we've got twenty thousand troops housed in and around Merkland for the winter. Many of them are from other realms. I'm confident that once they know the truth, enough local troops will join us that any who oppose the idea will be compelled to silence. If not for all those other troops, we could take Merkland tomorrow."

Ivor shook his head. "We're not ready. Not only am I not sure yet how to manage Lord Nevan, we need to get word out to the other realms first so when we ignite the spark here we're ready to move everywhere."

Rory said, "Nevan's smart enough that he won't cause problems. Lord Tocall and Lord Logan can be convinced not to interfere if I promise no raids against their towns. The other lesser nobles and ladies will follow their lead, but Craigroy will need minding. We've got a bold plan in the works. The question is timing and coordination."

"Ailsa's network will play a critical role," Ivor said.

"You've been in touch with her?" Connor sat facing the fire so his front side was comfortably warm, while his back side already felt chilly. Those big windows allowed far too much cold to seep in.

Ivor nodded. "She's got contacts everywhere and she's positioned perfectly in Donleavy. She's feeding us daily reports and we've already started identifying key individuals to help spread the word about patronage. Without her network, it would take months or years to make this work."

"I'm assuming something significant happened in Althing," Rory said.

"You could say that." He told them about it. They listened in attentive silence as he related Harley's lone assault on the entire kingdom and their fight at Raufarhofn.

"So she just left?" Rory asked incredulously.

"Yes."

"Why? She held the advantage."

Ivor frowned. "She's a new element we haven't been planning for. If she can fight Evander to a draw and defy you and all the might of Althing, she and the queen together could squash our revolution before it gets off the ground."

"I'm hoping Kilian has ideas about dealing with her."

Rory frowned as he glanced out one of the nearby windows. "I don't like the fact that you left Hamish and Aifric loose in my city. I don't need new problems right now, lad."

"I'll find them after we're done here," he promised.

Rory raised a single eyebrow to show how little he believed that. Ivor chuckled. "Easier said than done." Then he leaned back, studying Connor with an unreadable expression. "And you ascended with marble? Are you insane?"

"It was my only choice."

"You're lucky you didn't die. Marble is a purifying fire. Most people don't survive."

"I almost didn't." He hesitated then added softly. "Have you heard anything about the second threshold? About changes or risks to your elemental powers?"

"What happened?"

"I can't seem to make my tertiary powers work."

"What?" Rory exclaimed, looking more startled than any time Connor had ever seen him.

"They're still there," Connor explained quickly. "It's just, now I sense two different power sources that fuel them."

Ivor looked fascinated. "What do you mean? I've never sensed a power source driving the elements. They're the source of it all, aren't they?"

"I used to think so, but now I'm not sure. I can feel something now. It's like waves of energy that seem to give the elements life, but there's a second power source with a different intensity. It seems to have enormous potential, but the two sources cancel each other out. It's like they can't coexist."

"Or you can't use them both together," Ivor suggested.

"Something like that. We were heading back to speak with Kilian to figure out how to handle it."

Rory said, "Make sure you do. We're standing on the brink of revolution, civil war, and open confrontation with the queen herself. We need you at full power."

"I know. Trust me, it's my entire focus."

Ivor said, "I'm sure Kilian knows what to do. He's ascended the second threshold, after all. So have Evander, Harley, and the queen herself. There has to be a way to manage it. But for tonight, help us review these plans."

They spent the next couple of hours reviewing their progress. They'd made a lot. Ivor's clever brilliance and Rory's attention to detail complemented each other well. They had listed every major city, important nobility, officers, and Petralists, and the likelihood they'd join the revolution.

The plan called for establishing contacts with as many of their strongest potential allies as possible and revealing the truth of patronage to them. They allocated time through the winter for recruiting those initial contacts and helping them carefully spread the word throughout the Guardian ranks.

By the first spring thaw, they planned to launch a coordinated strike, starting in Merkland. The next day, their allies would strike across all the realms of Obrion. The scope of the plan was breathtaking, and if they could pull it off, it would throw every high house into chaos. They hoped to win time to consolidate their forces into four strategic locations. With that many Guardians concentrated like that, they hoped to survive long enough for attacks from Granadure and the Arishat League to deflect the queen's wrath and put her on the defensive.

Connor was impressed. "We'll need to coordinate closely with Wolfram and Mattias. They should have a military alliance treaty in place this week."

Rory rubbed his face. He looked tired, but determined. "That's good news, lad. We'll need them if we hope to avoid unnecessary bloodshed. Problem is, we haven't faced revolution since the Tallan wars. It's hard to know how fast people will join up. Knowing patronage is a lie will not immediately lead everyone to the decision to risk everything for freedom."

Ivor said, "We need to inspire them, give them a reason to hope we might succeed. That's why we have to start it all by taking Merkland.

We'll control one of Obrion's key cities and command an entire army on day one."

"Or we'll face pitched battle, with the possibility of needing to kill at least ten thousand of our own countrymen just to survive day one," Rory said gravely. "I don't like those odds. We need a way to tip the balance in our favor before it'll work."

"We've been over that before," Ivor said, looking a bit frustrated.

"And we'll go over it as many times as we need to until we find the answer," Rory retorted.

They ended the meeting after that and Ivor invited Connor to bunk in his rooms in the southern wing of the palace. "Best we don't let too many people know you're here yet."

"They'll know something once they see the Hawk sitting out in the courtyard."

Rory grunted. "I'll have Tomas and Cameron move it to a storage barn and keep it out of sight for now."

"Good. I'll contact Hamish via speakstone. Hopefully he's still with Aifric."

"We'll keep you all concealed until after the storm, but then you need to leave. Quietly."

Connor gave him a confident smile. "No one will know we've been here until after we leave."

51

FAMILY PROBLEMS

Hamish decided that trying to hover in place above the towers of the Merkland palace was like trying to nap in the center of an avalanche. Wind gusted in every direction around the towers. It pushed and pulled, sucked him down, and tried to throw him right over backward. If not for the additional directional thrusters Jean had built into the new suit, he'd never have managed it.

On top of gusting insanely, the wind howled worse than Stuart that day Clifden's prize cow kicked him in the sweets. Snow whipped past in a blinding cloud, and the bitter cold seeped in, despite the heated water he kept circulating through his entire suit.

All those reasons forced him to creep ever closer to the top of the nearest tower. He needed to see what Aifric was doing up there and who the two men were who had just appeared in front of her, as if out of thin air.

One was tall and clearly a warrior. He faced Aifric, profile to Hamish. His face was all hard angles and weathered experience. Despite the storm, his head was bare. His hair was cut short, and he showed no indication that the bitter cold affected him. The other man was barely average height. His back was turned to Hamish, so he couldn't see much of the man's face, but something about him looked familiar.

They were speaking, the two men standing in aggressive postures. Aifric looked nervous but defiant. It looked like a fight could break out any second.

As Hamish drifted closer, the sound of his thrusters masked by the howling, whipping wind, the shorter man turned a bit and Hamish recognized his face.

Sir. The Assassin team had tracked Aifric down.

How had she known? Why hadn't she said anything? He and Connor would have gladly helped defend her until she could explain things.

The tall man pointed at her and began speaking rapidly. Hamish had drifted to within about twenty feet of the tower. He didn't think either of the men had spotted him yet. He could hit them with a barrage of mechanicals, but didn't want to start a fight with a pair of Mhortair until he absolutely had to.

The wind suddenly gusted directly away from the men, right into Hamish's face and carried with it their words. Whatever language they spoke, it was unlike anything he knew. It sounded like whispers on the wind, and the bits he caught were light and lyrical and fast. He wished he understood more.

Aifric, who must have shifted to Student Eighteen, shook her head violently and her hand reached for a dagger sheathed unusually visible on her belt.

Time to intervene.

Hamish landed in a whoosh of thrusters near the two Assassins and shouted, "Hey, does she owe you money too?"

Neither one of them so much as twitched.

Student Eighteen sighed. "Hamish, you're such a fool."

Even though Hamish stood near the outer edge of the roof over a hundred foot drop and that area had looked completely clear before he landed, someone seized his right arm and twisted it brutally up behind his back into a strange lock hold. If not for the protective bulk of his suit, the hold would have completely immobilized it.

Hamish turned in amazement to find a short, swarthy-skinned fellow, swathed in furs and an enormous hat that looked like it was trying to eat his head.

"Where'd you come from?" Hamish demanded, trying to shove the man away, but the fellow was very light on his feet and he shifted with Hamish, still pulling on his arm, but not quite able to twist it far enough to control him.

The man drew a short knife with a high, flat point from a wide, cloth belt at his hip. He looked confident, almost bored, and it was obvious he felt he could dispatch Hamish easily.

With a flicker of thought, Hamish fired little jets of quartzite, flipping his arm back around and locking the wrist and forearm straight.

The little fellow, short knife poised to strike, glanced to the tall man and asked in Obrioner, "Shall I dispatch him?"

"Do you think that ridiculous hat will help slow your fall off the roof?" Hamish retorted. The fellow clearly didn't consider him a threat.

Time for some education.

As the little man again tried twisting his wrist, Hamish was tempted to let him work at it for a few seconds. With the pieces locked together, he could wrestle it all night, but Hamish didn't want to give the others time to get bored so he activated two tiny bits of quartzite in the front of his helmet. They squeezed a little pouch of liquid between them and shot a jet of concentrated lemon juice into the man's smug eyes.

Grunting what had to be a curse in that beautiful language of theirs, the man side-stepped, slipping right behind Hamish.

Perfect.

Hamish triggered a small piece of quartzite concealed along the bottom hem of his armored jacket at the small of his back. It fired off a sharp piece of metal.

Jean had figured most attackers would be big, so that stabbing mini knife would catch them in the groin. That short fellow took it in the stomach.

He grunted in pain, but amazingly did not drop his knife. Instead he plunged it into the leather outer layer of Hamish's suit and scraped against a hardened granite leaf underneath.

The fellow was trying to kill him.

That simplified things. Hamish ignited a bit of marble between his shoulder blades, triggering a jet of fire that should roast the man's eyeballs. The man retreated with a muted cry, but the flames leaped away, soaring into the air to hover around the tall leader's head. His eyes filled with crimson flames, and Hamish tensed for a desperate fight.

Student Eighteen raised her hands and cried, "Stop! Mister Two, he is a friend only trying to protect me."

Mister Two? That sounded even worse than he'd feared. The title was still stupid, but it meant the tall fellow with fire mastery was one of the senior kill leaders of the Mhortair. Hamish had dropped right into the middle of the fire this time. Literally.

Maybe he should have thought that through a bit more.

Mister Two spoke in cultured Obrioner, sounding like a high lord. His dark hair was graying, and his black eyes held no hint of mercy. "Do not attempt any further interference. I agree to allow you to share my daughter's fate."

"Daughter?" That made twisted Mhortair sense. Nothing like a daddy-daughter murder date.

Mister Two gestured and the short Assassin pushed Hamish over to her. That was fine with him. That was right where he wanted to be. The man had sheathed his knife, but his hand lingered on his wide, cloth belt. No doubt he could draw the blade fast if talks broke down.

Sir said, "This is the Builder friend of the Tallan's heir."

"But no friend of betrayers." Hamish said. Facing three Assassins was usually a recipe for guaranteed suicide, even with Student Eighteen to help. He considered possible attacks. He'd only get seconds before they destroyed him, but he wouldn't make it easy for them.

Mister Two said, "We also honor loyalty and punish betrayers. That is in fact why we are here."

"I did not dishonor the clan," Student Eighteen insisted, standing proud before her father.

Sir stepped closer. "Mister Five changed your orders, but the Blood of the Tallan still lives, and you remain his companion. That suggests you lie."

"He did not understand the situation, but came to realize that the danger we face is not Connor, but Queen Dreokt herself."

"We know the dread queen has arisen. That does not excuse disobedience," her father said.

"I will defend myself with his own words." She extracted from a pocket a geometric crystal, and a deep voice, etched with worry, echoed out of it.

"Kilian doesn't matter. The Matron of Evil is our ultimate target and ever has been. Connor may be our best hope for stopping her."

"Wow. Play that again," Hamish said. That was a really neat trick. He wondered if he could create a voice-recording mechanical. He needed to convince her to share a bit of serpentinite with him.

"Not now," Student Eighteen said softly, not taking her eyes from her father.

The short Assassin frowned at the crystal. "I find it hard to believe he spoke those words."

"You call me a liar?" Student Eighteen asked in a deadly cold voice, one hand slipping to her own knife.

By his expression, the short guy would eagerly escalate the argument into a fight. Hamish knew Student Eighteen's deadly skill with her knives, but that little guy was more dangerous than he appeared. He had slipped his hand under his wide belt, as if grasping a weapon there, although Hamish had never heard of anyone fighting with a belt.

Sir spoke before he could. "Patience, Daulah. Guilt is not yet confirmed and I want neither of you dead before it is."

Daulah gave Student Eighteen a contemptuous look. "She is no threat to me."

Mister Two spoke softly, but his voice slid into Hamish's ears like an icy blade. "You insult my family?"

That made Daulah nervous. He made a strange gesture with his hand, ducking his head a bit in what Hamish assumed was a sign of apology. "I mean no disrespect, but I do not believe those are his words."

Sir said, "Share the first sentence again."

Again Mister Five's voice echoed out from the crystal. "Kilian doesn't matter. The Matron of Evil is our ultimate target."

Sir raised his hands, making little motions, as if he was parting a piece of invisible cake hovering in the air in front of him. After a moment he nodded. "I confirm these are Mister Five's words and they are unaltered."

Daulah looked disappointed.

Mister Two motioned Student Eighteen closer, his expression unreadable. She obeyed and he placed hands on her shoulders and said, "You recognized the truth even before the ultimate threat was clear. Mister Five confirmed your choice at the end. I declare the blood quest complete and find you innocent."

He pulled her to him in a fierce hug, which she enthusiastically returned. Tears stood in her eyes, but she blinked them away quickly. Sir looked pleased, Daulah glum.

"So this is a happy family reunion now and not a mass funeral for foolish Assassins?"

Mister Two barked a laugh. "I have heard of your confidence. Tonight it bordered on recklessness, but I salute you as a true friend."

Student Eighteen said, "Father, will you come inside and meet with Connor? He helped me restore Aifric when the queen killed her mind. I named him family."

"You didn't!" Daulah exclaimed, looking furious. "You've forever tainted the honor of the entire clan."

She rounded on him. "I used to respect you, Daulah, but now I see you speak before you think."

He glared, but Sir waved him to silence.

Mister Two said, "Such a use of that honor is unusual, but I will consider it."

"So you'll come meet him and ally with him?" she asked expectantly. Hamish held his breath. A formal alliance with the Mhortair would be a huge victory.

But her father shook his head. "Not yet, daughter. Like Mister Five said, the Matron of Evil is our target. We leave as soon as the storm blows itself out."

Hamish asked, "You're really planning to attack the queen? In her seat of power?"

Mister Two nodded. "That is usually the best place. She will be over-confident and not expect danger. The speed of her takeover has thrown every other potential enemy on the defensive. We will take her. Daughter, you will guide us."

Student Eighteen smiled coldly. "I am eager to avenge Aifric."

Hamish said, "You're eager to die then. Remember what happened last time? She spanked you and Connor and Ivor. She could have killed you all. Do you think she'll make the same mistake twice?"

Mister Two said, "For any others to undertake this mission, your fears would prove accurate. We possess secrets that should tip the scales in our favor. We cannot ignore this opportunity to strike now before she consolidates her hold or raises any other ancient servants."

Hamish shuddered to think of a dozen more Harleys running around Obrion. The four of them turned toward the door to get out of the brutal weather. Maybe Mister Two was right. Maybe they could kill the queen.

That made his choice easy.

He caught up with Student Eighteen and said, "If you have the tools to kill her, I'll take you there."

"We don't need your help," Daulah snapped.

Sir shushed him again. "You mean to fly us?"

Hamish nodded. "Best flyer alive. We can set down anywhere in or around Donleavy. I can get you there in a couple of days instead of weeks."

Mister Two smiled. "Done."

ONLY TRUST BREAD YOU BAKED
YOURSELF

T he next morning, Connor allowed himself to sleep in late. He still felt exhausted. Ascension, battling Harley, and restoring Aifric all took a toll. By the time he arose, Ivor had already left the rooms. When he wandered into Ivor's sitting room, he noticed a note on a small table.

It was from Hamish, and all it said was, *"I've taken the student on a little family trip. Should be fun. Be back in a few days."*

That did not sound good. No, it sounded terrible.

Connor studied the note. It suggested that Student Eighteen's family had tracked her down right there in Merkland. That would explain why she'd acted afraid, but he felt angry that she hadn't invited him to stand with her. It sounded like she'd convinced them she hadn't betrayed the family honor, and that perhaps they'd reconciled, but what did Hamish mean by a little family trip? What was Hamish thinking?

The outer door opened and Tomas and Cameron entered without knocking. They were bundled against the bitter cold, their faces red as if they'd just come in from morning exercise.

"Good morning," Connor said, motioning them toward the fire.

Cameron grunted as he removed his woolen hat and extended his hands toward the fire. "Woulda been better if we hadn't wasted sleep time traipsing through the tail end of that blizzard before dawn."

Tomas said, "Well, if you hadn't irritated the general, he wouldn't have sent us on that fool's errand."

"I didn't irritate him. You're the one who left his knife in that tankard."

"He wanted a drink. Just didn't know it yet. Fishing out that knife woulda forced him to do a bit of self-reflectioning." Tomas tapped the side of his head knowingly.

"What errand are you guys talking about?" Connor asked.

"That flying wagon. General told us to hide it before anyone spotted it this morning on account of your clandestine arrival and all," Tomas said.

Cameron grunted again, looking grumpy. It wasn't as if a little extra beauty sleep could help that brutish face, but Connor would have resented getting ordered out into that storm before dawn too.

"But Hamish lifted into the sky just as we arrived," Cameron said.

"Where'd he go?" Connor asked.

Tomas shrugged. "Took off south. Maybe he's going to hide it in the forest."

"I don't think so." Connor glanced at the note again, his worry spiking higher. "Was anyone with him?"

"Hard to tell with those shimmering windows, but might've been at least a couple," Tomas said.

Cameron asked, "Why? What's he up to?"

"I'm not sure. Probably something dumb."

The two big soldiers exchanged a knowing look. Tomas said, "Gotta be a good mission if it's so secret even his partner on this secret mission doesn't know."

"A double secret mission would be good, but Connor probably just sent him away so he can do all the breaking himself," Cameron replied.

"I'm not planning on breaking anything. I'm just going to meet with Rory and Ivor."

"And break the entire kingdom," Tomas finished for him.

Cameron shook his head. "With goals that big, Merkland doesn't stand a chance."

Connor gave up. Those two would make up their minds about what they expected him to do, and he'd never change them. The unnerving thing was how often they guessed right. This time they were just teasing, though. There was no reason to destroy Merkland.

"Where's General Rory?"

"Up in that tower with Ivor again," Tomas said.

"He should try a different secret meeting place," Cameron said. "That one's been used so much, people are starting to request time with him up there instead of waiting till he returns to his office."

"I'll suggest it," Connor promised.

The two Fast Rollers led him to the kitchens to grab some breakfast. He felt starved and piled an enormous platter with bacon, sausage, meat pies, a huge piece of some kind of delicious egg-baked pie, an entire honey cake, and a couple apples. The cooks protested, but Cameron insisted he was filling an order to feed the general and ten assistants.

"Althing food kind of thin?" Tomas asked as they escorted him up to the tower meeting room.

"I've been busy," Connor said between mouthfuls of honey cake.

Cameron chortled. "Can't wait to hear that story."

They left him at the door and headed back to oversee shift rotations along the city walls.

Connor watched them march back down the stairs, wondering at Rory's decision to appoint them captains. They were deadly fighters, with penetrating insights into political intrigue and masterful battlefield strategies, but could they really manage the day-to-day affairs of the Fast Rollers? If things got confused, they'd just order a general bash fight.

Rory and Ivor were again sitting around the small table in the tower room, near the fire, but Connor paused to stare out the huge windows. The spectacular view of the snow-covered city took his breath away.

The storm had finally blown itself out and bright morning sunlight set the pristine snow glittering like millions of diamonds. The palace and city gleamed like a fairy tale. Across the river, the township, snow-covered fields, and forested hills looked surreal under their blankets of fresh snow. Even the river that curved around Merkland before running south looked bluer than Connor had ever seen.

"I see why you like meeting here," Connor said as he joined them at the table near the fire and balanced his platter on his knees.

Rory, who sat facing the northern window and its view toward the Maclachlan mountains said, "The view helps us remember what we're fighting for."

Connor glanced toward those distant mountains. The Drumwhindle Pass was too far to see without quartzite, but he bet that was what Rory was looking toward. Was he fighting for freedom of his nation, or was his a far more personal motivation?

Ivor reached for a sausage, but Connor slapped his hand away. "Get your own breakfast."

"You can't possibly eat all that," Ivor laughed.

"I'm training for my next meal with Hamish."

Ivor snatched a sausage and took an enormous bite. "Too bad. Friends share."

Rory took a breakfast meat pie with a grin. Connor sighed. Sometimes friendship carried a heavy price.

"Tomas and Cameron reported that Hamish lifted off this morning just as the storm broke," Rory said.

"What's he up to?" Ivor asked.

Connor handed him the note. "Not sure, but it might not be good."

He explained briefly about Student Eighteen's situation, the expected threat from her family, and his hope the note suggested they'd reconciled.

"So he might be caught up in Mhortair business?" Rory asked gravely.

"Possibly."

Ivor grimaced. "Not good, although if we could secure an alliance with the assassins, we'd win a critical advantage."

Rory didn't look convinced. "I don't think we can count on them, but we'll keep an open mind for an opportunity. For now, we need to focus on timing for the first strike."

Connor asked, "How soon?"

Ivor gestured toward the maps and parchments on the table. "That's what we're working on. We'd like to move up the timeframe and launch our first strikes during the dead of winter, maybe even during another big storm. That would make it harder for the high lords under attack to get communication out."

"Or for reinforcements to marshal," Rory said.

Connor frowned. "But that would make it harder to time strikes from abroad. You'd have to stand alone against the queen and all her loyal forces for longer."

Ivor shook his head slowly as he considered their charts. "There has to be a way."

As they discussed different ideas, Connor again felt impressed by their detailed planning. With Ailsa's network of contacts, they already had communication established with every major city. Between them, Rory and Ivor knew a lot of people who would likely join the movement once they understood the truth.

Connor had definitely chosen his leaders wisely. He wouldn't have planned nearly so much, but would have leaped into action with his first idea. He'd proven that wasn't the best way to start a revolution.

With their help, Connor polished off the entire tray of food and even convinced Rory to order some more while they worked. Several trays of bread, meat, and cheese were brought in, along with bowls of fruit and tankards of mulled cider to help chase away the chill.

"That's more like it," Connor grinned.

Ivor leaned back with a tankard in one hand and a warm sweetbread in the other. Between bites he said, "Our biggest challenge is still figuring out how to convince everyone beyond any doubt that we're telling the truth."

"And convincing the local lords to throw in with us, or at least not openly oppose us. It's a hard sell," Rory agreed around a huge chunk of cheese. "The lie is so ingrained. Some days I still feel doubts creeping in, and I've seen Connor transform into that rampager and return."

Ivor said, "Not enough have. We should push the story of that transformation at the Carraig. Several hundred people saw that, so it won't be hard for folks to find independent confirmation."

"Except most of those witnesses are heirs of noble houses. They'll be motivated to downplay what they saw, or even lie about it when they realize the stakes," Connor said.

He considered the challenge as he downed a couple of sweetbreads. They were still warm from the oven, and they had a wonderful, spicy flavor. He'd never tasted any quite like that.

He held up a third one. "This is really good. I don't think—"

Pain erupted through his innards, and the bread fell from his hand. Groaning, he clutched his stomach.

"Connor?" Ivor asked, concerned.

He couldn't answer. The pain blossomed through every limb. It was almost as if something was eating at his flesh from the inside.

Then the pain reached his heart and flared to blinding intensity. As if from a great distance, he felt his limbs snap out, his head whip back, and a scream rip from his lips. Raw emotions boiled through him and the beast in his heart flexed and rose.

With horrifying clarity, he understood.

Porphyry.

RAVAROOROO

I mpossible, but it was happening.

Panic fueled Connor's intensifying emotions. His muscles convulsed and his second scream deepened and shifted into ranges of sound beyond the realm of the human voice.

Somehow he'd ingested porphyry, and he couldn't stop the transformation. He hadn't absorbed it through his skin, but that didn't seem to matter.

His vision clouded as a purple haze descended over everything. Rory and Ivor leaped to their feet, shouting words he couldn't understand.

"Get back," he managed before his jaw expanded, becoming a fanged maw. His hands and feet transformed into clawed paws and his muscles expanded beyond the limits of granite, stretching his skin until it split and transformed into thick animal hide.

Then the pain disappeared, replaced by pure euphoria. Strength and power flooded through him, so strong he gasped a ragged, panting breath. The transformation completed two seconds later, and he rose on all fours, flexing his mighty limbs and flicking his long tongue across massive jaws.

Fury enveloped him, a purple, unfocused rage that sought a target.

He found two of them.

Fear hung on the air as two puny humans stumbled back, their heartbeats accelerating. His rampager vision tracked the pulsing of their blood as it coursed through their thin hides. The sight ignited his hunger.

He took a single step toward them, intent on ripping out their still-beating hearts and consuming them.

No.

A tiny voice somehow penetrated the purple haze of fury and bloodlust. It was weak, but still compelling, and he growled with renewed fury.

He was the deadliest hunter in the world, perhaps the last of the mighty rampagers. No one told him no.

No, the voice came again and he recognized the voice of his weak, human self.

Shrugging off that pitiful resistance, he took another step toward the humans, who had retreated to the door. One swelled with granite, a meaningless gesture, while the other stood defiant with hands encased in water and fire. He must die first. He was the greater threat.

His puny Connor voice returned, stronger. *I promised Verena. I will not surrender to this again.*

Verena.

An image blossomed in his mind. Verena, lying lovely and peaceful in her bed in Altkalen.

The rage subsided enough that he recognized Ivor and Rory and understood the words they shouted at him, but he ignored them. The inner struggle for dominance consumed his full attention.

Could he allow the puny human to dictate his actions? The thought made him growl with anger and glance hungrily at Ivor again. If he ate that one, he could silence his Connor self forever.

I am pack leader. He threw the thought into the space he seemed to be sharing with his human self. *All challengers must be destroyed.*

His human self threw back, *You serve me, and I dictate who dies.*

With a howl of animal rage, he smashed the seat where Ivor had sat a moment ago, prowling circles around the table as he strove to drive the infuriating human from his mind.

The conflicting wills crashed and beat against each other in his head with satisfying fury, triggering a skull-splitting headache. He smelled anger and felt his own blood surging in battle lust, even though his limbs barely moved.

His human self was far stronger than before. It withstood his assault, even though he drove every ounce of rage and fury against it. They clashed, committed absolutely, and for a second their two selves melded together.

His vision blurred and his head felt like it was about to split asunder.

Then Connor's mind snapped awake and he looked out through rampager eyes. He now controlled his body, and it was glorious. Every muscle thrummed with strength. His paws could smash stone, and his jaws could rend granite flesh. Scents poured in, clearer than any Pathfinder could hope to experience. He turned, and his body moved like a coiled spring.

But somehow he was still Connor. The beast prowled in his heart, pushing him to release it and destroy everyone in the city. It was so strong, its hunger so intense, Connor had to fight with all his will to hold it at bay.

But he managed it. He scarce believed it, but couldn't risk doubting himself or the beast would take control again.

The door banged open and Tomas and Cameron entered, carrying a long length of chain. Ivor waved the others back and took a step closer, water and fire still rippling along his hands.

"Connor, can you hear me?"

His heartbeat had slowed after the initial rush of panic. Still elevated above normal, he faced Connor in rampager form with remarkable calm.

Connor tried to say, "I'm all right." It came out as, "Um-arr-rah."

Ivor seemed to take that as a good sign. "What happened?"

Connor wasn't sure. His thoughts still felt sluggish, clouded by the purple haze of porphyry. In rampager form, it was so much easier to feel than to think, to rend than to sit.

So he padded across the room away from the others and their tantalizing scent of fear and warm flesh. He'd transformed, but something was different this time.

His mind seemed more awake than ever before in rampager form, even though the beast also felt more alive, more real than ever.

As he considered that monster in his heart, he suddenly became aware of the power that fueled it. Always before, transformation into a rampager had been so raw and so wild that he barely managed any coherent thoughts. It was as if his mind was plunged into turbulent waters that flooded his mind and drowned him in rage.

This time he floated on the surface and got a glimpse at the river of power he rode. It glowed green in his mind's eye.

As soon as he focused on that, he became aware of the dual currents of magic, just as he had when trying to tap his tertiary powers. This time though, they did not collide inside of him and cancel each other out. The reddish current flowed past, close beside him, but not quite touching. It was the greenish current that fueled his rampager heart, through the porphyry.

He was stronger. He wasn't sure how he knew it, but he did. Recognizing that greenish current unlocked deep reserves of strength he hadn't known he'd lacked.

Was his clarity due to his sworn promise to Verena, his repeatedly declared resolve to die before surrendering to the monster in his heart? Or was it somehow tied to his ascension and ability to sense those different power frequencies?

He didn't know, and it didn't really matter. Connor's mind rode that green current as even more strength poured into him, until he felt he might simply explode. He breathed deep, savoring the movement of thick muscle across his torso and haunches. Even if any other rampagers still existed, he no longer feared them. They were like pups compared to his new strength.

Ivor called from across the room. "Connor? How did this happen?"

There was no way he could pronounce sweetbread with his monstrous maw, so he tried to say muffin.

It came out as, "muffa."

Ivor glanced at the table and nodded. "I thought those tasted different."

Rory grunted. "That means Craigroy. Shouldn't be surprised that he knows you're here, or that he'd make another play to control you."

"How are you still in control, though?" Ivor asked, edging closer and studying his enormous form with fascination. "Last time, just seeing the powder nearly overwhelmed you."

He couldn't explain it, but he wasn't about to miss the opportunity. They'd just been discussing the need for more witnesses to the lie of patronage.

No time like the present.

Connor tried to say, "Revolution," but the word came out like a growled, "Ravarooroo."

Ivor grimaced. "I'd ask you to write it, but what's the point?"

Connor gestured toward the main square far below.

Then he leaped through the window.

As he soared out over the hundred foot drop he clearly heard Rory's muttered, "You've got to be kidding."

At the same time Cameron sighed. "I liked Merkland. Pity."

54

FEAR IS A GREAT MOTIVATOR

As Connor fell toward the huge, peaked roof of the southern wing of the palace, he unleashed a full rampager roar.

He had really good lungs. The sound reverberated through the city, the echoes building upon themselves, seemingly magnified by the crisp, clear air. The sound seemed to seize people and freeze them in place. He landed and sprang to the outer edge of the roof and roared again, drawing every gaze.

That's when the screaming started.

Fear boiled into the air all around Connor like smoke from a thousand tiny fires. Connor threw his head back and howled louder still, exulting in the power to terrify an entire city. Rory and Ivor wanted witnesses of the lie of patronage. He planned to round up as many as possible.

So he raced down the length of the roof and vaulted from the southwest corner, easily crossing to one of the mansions clustered near the palace. He crossed several roofs in a flash, then jumped to the high, peaked roof of the imposing Hall of Lords.

Loving the unrivaled power of his mighty limbs, Connor shot up one of the high towers in enormous bounds, claws tearing into the stones and easily finding purchase. At the top, he howled again, then unleashed his tightly-coiled muscles in a mighty spring. He flew all the way across a stone-paved square to the roof of the military command building.

Soldiers were already pouring out of every doorway, many stamping feet into boots or struggling to don armor. He spotted Boulders tapping granite and a Spitter gathering snow and compressing it into water.

Useless. He ignored them and raced the alarm bells through the city, using the rooftops as his highway. He crossed one long barracks, scattering terrified soldiers, who were then chastised by officers trying to mobilize the city defense. He soared across wide avenues, howling all the while, making sure everyone saw and heard him. Fear grew so intense from the populace that it made his head spin and sparked a ravening hunger. He almost detoured into a small courtyard to eat a couple of slingers who began casting stones at him.

Civilians fled in every direction, like goats caught in the open during a pedra bloodlust. Soldiers were shouting the alarm and trying to get organized, but he moved so fast he left them in a constant state of frantic confusion.

As Connor neared the huge outer wall surrounding the city, one Firetongue on duty struck at him with several whiplike tendrils of fire. Connor simply vaulted the flames and landed atop the wall next to the surprised soldier. The man stumbled back, flames exploding from his hands.

Connor stepped through the fire, his thick hide smoldering but protecting him from harm. He hooked a long claw under the man's chest plate and tossed him off the wall.

The soldier used flames to slow his fall, but Connor was already tearing along the top of the wall, scattering soldiers. A Sentry tried to intercept him with a grasping column of earth, but he plowed through it and leaped back to the nearby rooftops.

Connor laughed with the thrill of simply running, the sound like the rumbling of a hundred battle hounds. His muscles bunched and flexed tirelessly as he crossed the city, spreading panic on all sides.

He worked back around to the enormous main square facing the inner wall of the central palace and stopped in the center, near a tall, four-tiered fountain, its waters frozen for the winter. Soldiers poured into the square from every side, forming into nervous companies. They hesitated to advance, wise enough to fear engaging the monster.

Connor's long ears weren't quite as good as a Pathfinder's, but he easily heard whispers of unclaimed. Soldiers watched him with fearful curiosity, while civilians peeked out windows or craned around corners. With so many soldiers between them and danger, for the moment their curiosity overcame their fear.

It seemed every eye in the entire city was focused on him. So far so good.

Now for the hard part.

Connor took a long, slow breath, closed his eyes, and tried to untap porphyry. He needed to transform back to human form, but he'd never done it on purpose before. Always he'd burned porphyry to exhaustion. He couldn't wait for that, but needed to prove he could step back to humanity now while everyone was watching, but before the soldiers worked up the courage to attack.

The beast chained in his heart immediately erupted into a frenzy of rage, resisting the decision. Only through porphyry could it be released, and although he was controlling it, it was awake and it exulted in the might of his transformed state. It attacked his control, striving to seize dominance again.

For a moment, Connor groaned as he struggled to impose his will upon the fierce monster in his heart. His muscles quivered from the inner battle and he growled low and threatening, triggering a ripple of nervous shuffling from the soldiers creeping slowly closer. They'd attack any second. He needed to transform now!

So Connor focused on Verena. He filled his mind with the last memory of her, lying peacefully asleep in Altkalen. He'd memorized every facet of that moment, and now he brought it to vibrant life in his mind. As the image took shape, that same peace that she radiated settled over him and helped him rein in his unbridled fury.

Releasing porphyry was immensely difficult, worse than waking up in a tub of bacon and not even licking a single piece. Transforming back hurt just as much as turning into the monster had. His window-shaking roar changed mid-howl into the far weaker scream of a human in terrible pain.

He staggered and fell to one knee, panting. Luckily the pain faded quickly and he returned to himself, feeling whole, but woefully weak. He laughed and raised a fist in triumph.

He'd not only controlled the beast, but caged it and returned on his terms. That victory was more amazing in its own right than beating that elfonnel at the Carraig.

Gasps of surprise reverberated around the square, but Connor barely noticed.

He was freezing.

As a rampager, he'd ignored the cold as easily as he'd ignored the Firetongue's flames. Standing on the snowy square with no boots, no shirt, his pants ripped up to the knees, he started shaking with cold in seconds.

That was so miserable, he nearly transformed back. Luckily, Tomas and Cameron charged into the square at the head of a forty-man company of Fast Rollers. They pushed through the soldiers, formed up their squad closer to Connor, then the captains approached together.

Tomas tossed him a spare battle jacket, which he gratefully donned. Cameron passed him his belt with his pouches of affinity stones, then beckoned a mature woman with the insignia of a Firetongue closer.

"Heat up the air a bit, will you, love?"

She glared. "I told you I'm not dating you, Captain."

"It's just an expression," he protested.

"I've learned not to let you get any ideas." She crossed her arms and waited.

Cameron sighed, then made a rather gallant bow. "I apologize, oh lady of the blistering fires. Will you please warm things up a bit?"

Tomas added, "You want to irritate the lad and give him an excuse to transform again?"

"Fine, but no more flowered prose. Ever." She raised a hand that glowed with inner fire. The air warmed and Connor sighed with relief.

"Thanks."

She retreated a step, as if afraid he'd bite her, then glared at him for frightening her.

Cameron said, "Just because he's been a raving lunatic monster this morning doesn't mean he can't be polite, does it?"

A knot of nobility and high-level officers approached, followed by pairs of each of the tertiary affinities. The soldiers included a mixture of Dougal's forces and those from other realms, and they all looked nervous and a little confused. Connor hoped most of them were Guardians.

Connor recognized Lord Nevan at the head of the nobles and waved. "Hello, Nevan. I hear you're in charge of the city these days."

Lord Nevan drew a bit closer, while most of the other nobles hung back. "Connor? What happened to you?"

An older lord with graying, brown hair and sharp, blue eyes that glowed with unmistakable Pathfinder light, trailed close behind Nevan. He carried himself with the self-assured swagger of a man convinced he was important. "What is the meaning of this? You, soldier, why haven't you detained that unclaimed yet?"

Tomas asked, "What unclaimed, Lord Torcall?"

That was the name of one of the central players in Dougal's court. Torcall pointed at Connor. "Him, of course."

"I'm not unclaimed," Connor told them calmly.

Another lord, younger, with thick, black hair, who wore an ankle-length fur coat joined Torcall, making sure to stand exactly even with him. "We all saw you."

Lord Nevan glanced at the other two, who stood barely half a step behind him. "Torcall, Logan, please allow me to handle this."

"What exactly did you see?" Connor asked, tempted to absorb a little granite. His tertiaries might be problematic, but he might need his primaries and secondaries. He didn't want to tempt porphyry again. With so many potential hostiles, he might not be able to control the urge to destroy them all. That would create exactly the opposite effect he wanted.

The senior officers spread out, flanking the three nobles. Connor didn't have to be a rampager to read their nervous tension.

A woman with the rank of chornail took a step closer. She also wore the tower symbol of a Sentry, so that would make her an earth-nail. Her uniform was trimmed in High Lord Feichin's crimson and steel. "We saw you transformed into a monster. What else could we assume?"

"Because you've seen so many unclaimed, right?" Connor prodded.

When she hesitated he asked, "Have any of you actually seen an unclaimed?"

They exchanged glances, but none of them spoke.

"Of course you haven't, because there is no such thing."

"He's barking mad," Lord Tocall said.

"Not today, not in this. My name is Connor and I am Blood of the Tallan."

That elicited a round of excited murmurs, which grew even louder when Lord Nevan said, "I know you, Connor, and I can confirm you speak the truth."

The earth-nail's glare deepened and she accused, "I thought you looked familiar. I saw you at Altkalen, allied with the Grandurians."

The murmurs turned ugly.

"I was there, fighting Dougal's lies."

Lord Torcall took an angry step forward, bringing himself even with Nevan. Lord Logan quickly followed suit as Torcall snapped, "That's more than enough."

"Let him speak," the woman said. He might be a lord, but she was a senior officer and her high lord was a vocal opponent of Dougal. She seemed eager to hear more.

"Might we speak in private?" Lord Nevan asked urgently

Connor felt bad for Nevan. His world was about to get shaken to the roots. He liked the man, but change had to hurt sometimes. So he shook his head. "I'm afraid not this time, my lord. We're beyond plotting in secret. Everyone needs to hear this. Like I said, there is no such thing as unclaimed. There is no such thing as patronage. It's a lie known only to the high lords. They use it to enslave the rest of us."

Lord Nevan blanched. Lord Torcall looked furious. Interestingly, Lord Logan looked intrigued. Most of the officers looked stunned, but Connor studied their reactions as they started understanding the ramifications of that declaration. The noble-born Petralists would focus on the threat to the establishment, while the common-born Guardians would begin to realize their entire lives were a lie and perhaps new options were available.

Quite a few looked like they weren't ready to believe, though. One of them, a beefy Sentry asked, "How do you explain that monster?"

He hadn't even bothered to make the question indecipherable. That was a good sign. "There's a secret affinity stone called porphyry. I am perhaps the only person alive with an active affinity to it. It causes that transformation. We call them rampagers and Dougal has used them for years to reinforce the illusion of unclaimed and to remove his enemies."

Lord Torcall grew visibly angry and pointed at Tomas and Cameron. "Seize him and throw him in irons."

Lord Nevan looked annoyed, but Tomas spoke before he could chastise Lord Tocall for overstepping his authority. "Can't do that, sir. He's telling the truth."

"I'll have you whipped."

Cameron took a slow step closer and nodded toward the force of Fast Rollers. "I wouldn't recommend anything so foolish, sir. Not if you plan to live 'till lunch."

"You dare threaten me?"

"Oh, shut up, Torcall," Lord Nevan barked. "You're making things worse. Connor is beyond your authority."

"But these lies are dangerous," Torcall insisted. He was a clever man.

"If they're lies," Logan said, generating another wave of murmurs through the officers. Some of them began arguing among themselves. Good. Connor needed them to think, to dare consider the truth.

Just then, Ivor appeared, sliding into the square on a pedestal of mixed water and fire. Soldiers scrambled out of his path as he slid toward Connor and the assembled lords and officers. General Rory stood beside him, one hand gripping the collar of a miserable-looking Craigroy, whose hands were bound in chains.

Connor wasn't surprised to see Craigroy. They'd probably caught him lurking around, waiting for Connor to murder them all and exhaust his porphyry. Then he could have approached with a bit of porphyry in hand and sealed his mastery over Connor's soul.

The plan would have probably worked just a couple days ago. He couldn't have known Connor had ascended and gained a bit more control over the rampager.

When they dropped to the ground, Rory gave Connor an annoyed look, then surveyed the assembly. "What's going on here?"

Lord Nevan raised one eyebrow and looked down his long nose at Rory. "I might ask the same question. It appears you've taken a senior member of my staff into custody."

Rory scowled at Craigroy. "For his own protection."

Connor chuckled. Right. Otherwise, Craigroy would already be dead, which wasn't a bad idea with that devious fellow.

Lord Torcall pointed at Connor. "This miscreant claims to be Blood of the Tallan, claims there are no unclaimed, that patronage is a lie fostered by the high houses to keep commoners in slavery, and that High Lord Dougal uses rampagers to murder his enemies."

Rory grunted. "He covered a lot of ground already. Have you kept up?"

"You believe him?" Lord Nevan asked, looking stunned.

"Of course I do. Didn't you see him transform back?"

Ivor held up a little leather pouch. "And we confiscated a bit of the secret affinity powder Craigroy used to force Connor to transform. He'd planned for Connor to lose control, kill us, and probably quite a few of you, all in an effort to contain the secret."

The lords exchanged incredulous glances, while several of the officers started arguing heatedly. Rory spoke over them. "Connor is Blood of the Tallan. I've seen his full range of affinities in action. I've witnessed the truth about patronage, and I for one am disgusted by the lie we've lived under all these years."

Craigroy tried to object, but Ivor jabbed him in the ribs.

Connor beckoned Lord Torcall closer. He seemed eager to step in front of Nevan, while Logan looked annoyed he wasn't also summoned. "Will you enhance my voice?"

"Why can't you do it yourself?" Torcall asked suspiciously.

"I was focusing on not transforming back into a rampager and eating your still-beating heart, but if you prefer I take the risk, it works for me."

Lord Nevan chuckled and Lord Logan called, "Don't let him cow you, Torcall. Call his bluff."

Lord Torcall glowered back at Logan, but wisely chose not to rise to the taunt. As soon as Connor felt the telltale tickle of quartzite against his vocal cords, he spoke, his voice magnified until it boomed across the square.

"My name is Connor, and I am Blood of the Tallan." He waited a few seconds for that to sink in. After the initial wave of shock, most of the soldiers and civilians drew closer, unable to resist the lure of seeing a legend come to life. Too bad he looked so bedraggled.

"I gathered you here to reveal a lie that has kept our nation shackled, our people enslaved to the high houses. Patronage is a lie!"

Connor explained, his booming voice drowning out the growing tumult as some people gaped, others shouted their refusal to believe, and many began arguing among themselves.

"You saw the truth with your own eyes. I turned rampager but returned. The transformation is difficult, but it's possible due to a secret power stone. Many of you are Guardians. You've dedicated your lives to honorable service to protect everyone you love from your curses raging out of control and transforming you into the monster you just witnessed." He pointed to the bag of porphyry that Ivor held aloft. "Patronage is a lie. Now that you know the truth, you are free!"

That generated ripples of conversation all around the square as soldiers discussed, debated, and argued with each other. Connor easily picked out the Petralists among the crowds. Those were the ones shouting that he had to be lying. The foundation of their entire world was threatened and they reacted exactly like the men and women from the Carraig when he shared the truth with them outside of Altkalen.

Many of the Guardians looked doubtful. He didn't blame them. Patronage was such an enormous lie, the truth changed everything.

Ivor stepped close and muttered, "You realize you've wrecked our timeline, right?"

"The opportunity is here. Take it," Connor urged.

Ivor sighed and gave him an annoyed look. "Next time we agree that I'm responsible for overthrowing the current world order, don't feel like you have to help, all right?"

"Are you going to whip them all into a revolution frenzy, or do I have to get even more creative?"

"Oh, no. Do not even consider leveling this city."

Connor made a sweeping bow and gestured Ivor to take his spot, with every eye fixed on him. "Be my guest."

55

THE HAMMER FALLS

Connor allowed a smile as Ivor said, "Torcall, please magnify my voice."

The man glanced at Nevan and demanded, "Aren't you going to do something?"

"What would you have me do?" Lord Nevan asked, looking shaken, but still remarkably calm. He'd proven himself a level-headed, competent administrator at the Carraig. Connor felt grateful that he wasn't calling for armed resistance to silence them.

Rory said sternly, "Torcall, you either do what you're told, or I'll throw you in jail right now."

Torcall paled under Rory's threatening stare and surrendered. Ivor's voice boomed across the square. "This is Commander Ivor. You all know me. I've investigated these claims, and I confirm what Connor said. Patronage is a lie."

Rory spoke next. "And as your commanding general, I also confirm that patronage is a lie."

Those announcements fueled a flurry of growing arguments. Connor watched the crowd closely. The huge square was filled to bursting, while more people were pushing in from every street. Ranks of soldiers formed the inner cordon, and they had drawn to within fifty feet on every side, thousands of men and women who looked stunned by what they were hearing.

Connor doubted anyone had contemplated over breakfast how best to react to world-shaking news if it got dumped in their laps. He'd have to encourage Rory to train his forces to be a bit more mentally flexible. More and more of the Guardians looked like they were believing. With so many witnesses from men they trusted, how could they not?

"You're all lying," Craigroy stated, his voice disgusted. "And as High Lord Dougal's chief adviser, I have no choice but to order your arrests."

Connor advanced on him. "I'm going to give you one chance to speak the truth for the first time in your life. You confess, or I'll transform again and rip out your throat."

"That would prove nothing," Craigroy scoffed.

"Wouldn't it? If unclaimed is real, then I'm not responsible for that action. It's High Lord Dougal's fault for denying me patronage. I'd remain a monster and I'd have to be destroyed."

He stepped closer. "But if I kill you then return to human form again, I prove you're a liar. Either way, you're still dead."

Craigroy seemed to deflate. "I hate working with amateurs. You don't understand the rules at all."

Connor smiled. "Today all the rules change. Now confess."

The spy master still hesitated, so Connor took the bag of porphyry from Ivor. At that, Craigroy glared but said, "Fine. I'll say what you want." He looked to Nevan and the other nobles. "Connor is right. Patronage is a lie. Now you all know the truth."

While they digested the forced confession, he added casually, "And now your lives are forfeit."

Lord Nevan did not look surprised, but Lord Torcall demanded, "What do you mean?"

Craigroy laughed derisively. "Patronage is the foundation of our society. What do you think the high lords will do when they hear about this little uprising? They'll raze Merkland to the ground and kill everyone who's heard so much as a rumor of this truth. They can't afford not to."

"Unless we stomp it out first," one of the officers suggested. The man wore an under-general's insignia with the soapstone symbol. He was tall, with a face lined from outdoor life, although his midsection was a bit soft. He probably enjoyed an office job now, but he looked ready to fight.

"Are you saying you plan to mutiny against me?" Rory asked in a deadly, soft voice.

The man hesitated and glanced to his companions for support. The group consisted of about a dozen high-ranking officials. The earth-nail woman looked like she agreed with him, but eight of the others were Guardians and they shifted around to stand behind Rory. The balance of power supported him, and the four remaining Petralists recognized it. For the first time, they looked afraid. Others across the square were coming to the same conclusion.

That small quartet of supporters loyal to the status quo slipped into defensive stances. They looked ready to fight for their lives, and the Guardians now standing behind Rory looked eager to oblige them. Many of those men and women were looking angry as they realized how they'd been duped all their lives.

Given even a hint of encouragement, Connor suspected they'd

unleash all that rage on every noble-born person in the city. That kind of bloody purge would quickly take on a life of its own, and it could turn the day into a horribly bloody revolution.

Maybe Connor should have thought his plan through a bit more before jumping out that window.

"Stand down," Rory ordered.

The officers standing with him seemed reluctant to obey, but they did so. The four noble-born Petralists looked relieved, but still nervous.

Rory gestured to the opposite side of the fountain. "You four, wait for me there."

When they cautiously moved away, he summoned the Fast Rollers to surround Lord Nevan and the half dozen other lords and ladies.

"Do you plan to execute us?" Lord Nevan asked calmly.

Rory shook his head. "I need you, Nevan. Give me a minute."

He gestured for Tomas and Cameron to take their noble prisoners a few paces away, then returned to Ivor and Connor and let them see his frustration. "This situation is about to spiral out of control."

The thousands of other soldiers in the square were beginning to separate, just as the officers had. Small clumps of nervous, noble-born Petralist were forming, surrounded by hundreds of increasingly belligerent soldiers. If Rory didn't do something to regain control, he'd face the first battle of the revolution right there.

The commoners outnumbered the nobles many times, but enough of the noble-born were Petralists that if battle erupted in the square, hundreds could die in the first minute.

Ivor said, "We can't afford open fighting in the streets yet. We need to consolidate our hold with volunteers."

"But we can't let the Petralist officers run free, or they'll plan an insurrection within the hour," Connor pointed out.

"Let me handle this," Ivor said. He gestured a Guardian Pathfinder to magnify his voice. She did so eagerly.

"Attention!"

Soldiers snapped into ranks, and silence descended over the square. They might be struggling with the ramifications of the momentous news, but they were still soldiers. The command in Ivor's voice brooked no hesitation.

Ivor rose on a pillar of mixed water and fire. "You are all privileged to learn the truth first, but truth can be dangerous. The high houses have kept us all enslaved to their will through the lie of patronage. They will fight to silence all who know the truth and dare speak it."

He gave them a moment for that to sink in. "They face a bigger problem, though. Their corruption has resulted in the return of Queen Dreokt from a centuries-long slumber as an elfonnel. She may be in human form, but she's still a monster. She's in Donleavy right now, murdering her own lords and ladies or brain-wiping them, ripping out everything that makes them who they are and turning them into dumb slaves with no minds of their own."

Most of the gathered had already heard rumors, and now Ivor was confirming their worst fears. The truth about patronage threatened their livelihoods at some point in the future, but the queen threatened their families and their lives now.

Craigroy tried to protest, but Rory cuffed him. Connor edged closer. He planned to volunteer if Craigroy needed more pummeling to keep him quiet.

Ivor continued. "How long do you think it'll take for her to enslave all the high lords to her will? Who next will become her target?"

Again he paused, letting the worry grow.

"We have a choice," he declared. "Today is the day each one of us can choose how we will face the difficult times to come. Struggle is upon us. There is no way to avoid it. The queen is intent on total domination of every soul in Obrion. Then she'll launch a war of conquest across the rest of the continent, using our blood to fuel her war."

His voice rose in strength, echoing across the square. "But today we have a choice. You all know the truth. You all know how deep and absolute the corruption runs. The leadership of Obrion is festering like a rotting wound, but our country is better than that. I for one am choosing to stand up and make a change."

He raised a fist high. "Today I throw off my shackles and fulfill my oath as Guardian. I swore to defend Obrion from all enemies, and today it's clear that our greatest enemies are our own queen and high lords. Today begins the revolution. We will fight! We will free our nation and build a free Obrion!"

Cheers erupted from the crowd, with many of the soldiers raising fists like Ivor, shouting their oaths.

Ivor lifted Rory to stand beside him. Rory too lifted his fist and the Pathfinder magnified his voice without needing to be told.

"I am your general. I too swore to protect Obrion and I've dedicated my life to protecting and defending this nation. Today I stand with Commander Ivor and join him in raising the flag of revolution. We will topple the reign of the dread queen and save Obrion from our own high lords. We will make Obrion free!"

Connor exulted that the revolution was really starting, but as he surveyed the crowd, he realized with a heavy weight of dread that many of those cheering so enthusiastically would pay a heavy price to win freedom.

He was willing to risk his life, so he would not deny them the right to do the same. It was worth fighting for. That helped him feel better and he cheered along with the others. The soldiers knew and respected Rory, and many soldiers from other realms joined the locals in cheering him.

Connor whispered to the Pathfinder, who looked moved nearly to tears by the bold speeches. She nodded and started a chant, her voice rising loudly over the assembly.

"Freedom! Freedom! Freedom!"

Soldiers took up the cry, the sound building to a crescendo that shook the air. Although many soldiers seemed wildly eager to join the revolution, those little knots of noble-born officers were looking fearful. The four standing across the fountain were trying to slip back toward the crowd, as if hoping to escape into the city before Rory noticed.

Ivor raised his hands for quiet. "There are some among us who do not support the cause of freedom. They would continue to uphold the corrupt status quo, continue to support enslaving Guardians and support the insane monster who has taken the throne."

Angry muttering rippled through the crowd, and soldiers again focused on those knots of nervous officers. An ugly feeling settled over the square, and Connor began to fear Ivor planned to execute them all right there.

He had to find a way to stop that. They couldn't start the revolution this way. He might not be able to use his tertiary affinities, but he'd fight to prevent such unnecessary bloodshed.

Ivor pointed back at Craigroy, who was looking decidedly worried. "This man will attempt to twist the truth and regain control over your lives if allowed to remain."

A pair of Boulders flanked Craigroy and they swelled with granite power, looking ready to smash him to pieces on Ivor's command.

Rory said something to Ivor, who nodded. Connor moved toward them. Were they really going to unleash violence upon the city?

Ivor spoke again. "Our cause is just. We will fight for freedom, but we will not force anyone who prefers to live in slavery to join us. Study your hearts and ask yourselves what you believe. What is worth fighting and maybe dying for?

"To me it's an easy choice. I've been to Donleavy. I've seen the insanity of the queen, felt her influence smothering my thoughts. She could have destroyed me if she chose, but she allowed me to live. Many are not so lucky. Despite the risks, I will fight for freedom."

A fresh wave of cheering.

General Rory now spoke. "Any of you who doubt our cause have one hour to vacate Merkland. Some of you soldiers who have served so faithfully are from other realms. You are welcome to join us, but if you prefer to leave, do it now. Any who refuse to support the cause of freedom will be treated as enemies after that one hour window closes. Again, please help us liberate our nation. If you leave, I hope you will return to your homes. Stay out of the fight because we cannot afford to show you mercy if you choose to interfere."

The gathered soldiers looked pleased by the offer. Over a third of them, including most of the noble-born Petralists, turned and fled.

Soldiers could pack a few things and leave in less than an hour. They looked eager to escape the insanity that had just swept Merkland.

Craigroy looked stunned by the offer and when Ivor and Rory returned to the ground he said, "You idealistic fools. You should have executed all of us immediately."

Connor scowled at the man. "It's not out of the question in your case."

Rory added, "You think rule comes from maintaining a stranglehold over people, but trusting people accomplishes so much more."

Craigroy's expression turned crafty. "So trust me, Rory. Let me go with them."

Rory barked a laugh. "I trust people, but I'm not an idiot. No, you're far too dangerous to release. You've won new quarters in the prison."

"Wait," Connor interrupted before Craigroy could protest. "First you take me to the cache of porphyry."

Ivor hesitated. "Are you sure that's a good idea?"

"I don't plan to use it, but I don't plan for anyone else to get the chance either."

Craigroy gave Connor a knowing smile. "Of course you won't. Fine, boy. You've proven yourself exceptionally resistant to porphyry, but you'll fall eventually. Then you'll kill these fools, break me out of my cell, and swear fealty to get the powder you'll need to survive."

"You never give up, do you?" Ivor asked with grudging respect.

"Never. That's why I always win in the end."

Rory said, "I hope that thought helps keep you warm at night. I hear the dungeons are chilly."

"Such a pity. You were a great man, Rory. I hate to see you fall," Craigroy said.

"Not the way I see it."

"Come along then," Craigroy said brusquely, turning toward the palace and striding away. Connor and a pair of soldiers assigned to watch Craigroy had to hurry to keep up. "I believe the dungeon may get many new residents today. I know those cells, and I plan to get one of my favorites before they're all filled up."

"You're taking this awfully well," Connor commented as they strode into the main hall.

"You don't survive high-stakes political intrigue as long as I have without learning that you control far less than you imagine. Flexibility is the key to survival."

"I'll remember that." He never would have imagined Craigroy might offer good advice. That whole be-my-slave-or-die mentality tended to get in the way. Maybe he liked motivated slaves.

They climbed to Craigroy's office, a plush set of rooms high atop the central tower, only two levels below Dougal's own private office. The man snatched up several articles of clothing and a pillow.

Connor watched him closely, and the Boulders who would escort him to his jail cell made a point of checking those clothes to ensure no power stones were concealed in the pockets. They seemed innocent enough.

In a cramped little closet full of old files and dusty paperwork, Craigroy slid aside a panel in the back wall and extracted an iron-banded box. He hesitated for a moment before passing it to Connor.

"This box might as well hold chains around your heart, boy. I don't care how strong you are. No one survives the transformation without losing pieces of their humanity. Soon nothing is left but the fury and insanity."

"You're waxing pessimistic. Not the best mental state to begin a jail sentence," Connor said, taking the box and carrying it to a table.

Craigroy grimaced. "Do you have to remind me?"

"Absolutely. You plotted to kill me, so I get to enjoy your failure every minute."

"I knew I didn't like you, boy, and that was before I knew you."

"The personal connections are the most meaningful."

Connor unfastened the latches and threw open the lid. Inside he found ten leather pouches, all carefully tied, each containing about a pound of porphyry powder.

"That's it?" He'd expected a lot more.

"The supply is small to begin with, and High Lord Dougal strictly manages production. He alone knows where it's quarried."

Connor didn't believe him, so he slipped his hand into his belt pouch and touched a piece of chert. Immediately he felt a chill across the skin of his arm closest to Craigroy. The man was hiding his shock at the abrupt reversal of his fortunes pretty well, and his thoughts remained fuzzy and elusive. Craigroy had learned how to shield himself somehow. Connor really needed to learn that technique.

The shielding wasn't perfect, though, and Connor picked up whispers. Craigroy was definitely committed to destroying him and the revolution. He was frustrated that the truth had been revealed to so many and annoyed by how much work it would take to put things right.

Unfortunately, Connor got no sense about whether or not Craigroy knew where to find more porphyry. It didn't matter in the immediate future. Only Connor could tap it, and he didn't plan to use it unless he found himself facing Harley or the queen herself.

He closed the lid and said, "Good-bye, Craigroy. The next time we meet, I'll most likely have to kill you."

Craigroy chuckled without humor. "The next time we meet, I'll own you."

"Get out," Connor growled, pushing Craigroy toward the door and carrying the chest of porphyry after.

He watched as the two burly Boulders led the old spymaster toward the exit, wondering if they'd made the right decision in letting him live. They might need more information from him. Once Connor found more time to practice with chert, he might be able to defeat Craigroy's mental shielding. No doubt the man possessed critically important information.

So he returned to the square. The city was in tumult as soldiers fled before the deadline, while other companies monitored their progress suspiciously. The air was filled with a strange combination of exultant celebration and nervous worry, but no open fighting had started yet.

He eventually found Rory and Ivor in Rory's office. He showed them the porphyry.

"What are you going to do with it?" Rory asked. He looked like he wanted to toss it into the fire.

"You should destroy it," Ivor said.

Connor shook his head. He was pleasantly surprised that he hadn't suffered any major craving since transforming back. He'd purged the last bit of porphyry from his system after leaving Craigroy's office and he didn't plan to ever use it again. At the same time, he felt a dangerous reluctance to destroy this last known stash.

He'd mastered the beast. Could he do it again? He wouldn't admit to either of them that he was tempted to try. He hesitated even admitting that truth to himself, but luckily it was a bridge he didn't have to cross yet.

"I'll bring it to Faulenrost. I'd like the Builders to study it and see what else they can learn about it."

Rory said, "Keep it tightly controlled. That powder is dangerous."

Connor knew that better than anyone.

Rory leaned back in his chair and frowned at Connor. "Have I told you yet that we weren't ready for this revolution?"

"You've thrown the whole plan on its head," Ivor added grumpily.

"No, I gave you what you needed."

"Panicked, sleepless nights?" Rory asked.

"Witnesses. You said one of your biggest hurdles was convincing people that unclaimed are false. Today I gave you over twenty thousand witnesses. They saw me transform and they saw me return, and thousands of them are leaving. Whether or not they support the revolution, they'll tell people what they saw and that will help."

"You realize you actually sound like maybe you thought this insanity through before you jumped out the window?" Ivor asked with a slow shake of his head.

"I think before I act," Connor said.

"Sometimes," Ivor acknowledged.

Rory sighed. "We'll work with it. We need to move fast, regardless of how you look at things. So far Nevan is cooperating. Torcall may cause issues, but when he realized I didn't plan to execute them all, he settled down. Lord Logan might actually join our cause enthusiastically."

"He seemed pretty excited in the square," Connor said.

Rory nodded. "He's very wealthy, but has no affinity. His town has a very productive gold mine, but no quarry. I think he sees our revolution as the chance to finally get the respect he's always wanted."

Ivor said, "We'll work that angle. I'd love to have active support from Nevan too. He's very skilled. On the broader front, I'm already sending Striders to all our contacts in every city. I've got some agents embedded in the forces leaving the city. They shouldn't have any trouble getting accepted into our enemies' camps since they walked away from the revolution when they had the chance."

That was clever even for Ivor.

He continued. "We'll work with Ailsa's intelligence network to push the information faster through Guardian ranks. We need to secure allies before the high lords can seal off access."

Rory said, "They'll send an army. We'll need reinforcements."

"I've got to get back to Granadure to speak with Kilian," Connor reminded him. "I'll see if he can send help."

Rory sighed. "That's good, but come back soon, lad. We'll need you."

"As soon as I can." Once he stabilized his affinities.

"Do me a favor," Rory said, suddenly looking nervous.

"Of course."

"Will you invite Anika to come for a visit?" His face reddened as he spoke. That look did not sit well on the stony-faced general.

Connor grinned. "I'd be honored."

Ivor rose. "Very well. I'll leave you to secure the city, Rory."

"Tomas and Cameron are overseeing the evictions to make sure we don't end up with a revolt. I promised to send a small allotment of tertiary stones along with those who are leaving, if they all leave peacefully."

"Are you sure that's a good idea?" Connor asked.

"It won't be much, just enough to help them make the journey south. Not enough to go to battle, but enough to encourage them to play fair."

Ivor rose. "Clever. I'm heading to my new office to get to work."

Rory raised a questioning eyebrow. "New office? Whose did you confiscate?"

"Craigroy's, of course," Ivor said with a grin.

"I should have known. It's one of the best."

"Why do you think I chose it?"

5 6

SOMETIMES YOU GET TO LIVE UP TO YOUR REPUTATION

Jean stared into a fascinating, invisible world of tiny proportions, so enthralled she barely dared to breathe for fear of shaking the delicate focus and ruining the image. She leaned over a work table in a corner of her office, elbows pressed against the surface to brace her view as she held the newest near-vision goggles to her eyes and stared in wonder.

"This is amazing," she breathed for the tenth time. "I never imagined mold could look beautiful."

Karlmann, the Healer, sat in a chair beside her, craning over the table with a second pair of the goggles. He muttered with abundant frustration in Grandurian, "I can't get it to focus. My hands are too shaky."

Jean's fluency was progressing rapidly and she could understand most of what he said.

"We'll have to secure the goggles onto a base to stabilize the view," she promised, not taking her eyes off the incredible sight.

A tiny sample of mold sat on a flat piece of quickened limestone on the table, magnified hundreds of times through the marvelous goggles. She felt like her vision was plunging down and down until the tiny piece of mold filled her gaze. With her normal vision, the mold looked a bit fuzzy and completely unremarkable. Through the near-vision goggles, it looked like a fantastic forest, complete with flowering stems, slender stalks, and oval-shaped seeds.

She was the first person to ever peer into that tiny world, and that feeling of pure discovery sent a chill sliding down her spine. With her many other administrative duties, she missed far too much of the wonderful work of discovery happening all across Faulenrost in the barns and improvised workrooms. Now she no longer envied the other researchers.

"Please, tell me what you see," Karlmann urged.

Jean wrenched her gaze away from the mold and tried to explain, but realized it would be simpler to ask Dierk and his team to add a base to the goggles for the old Healer.

They'd be happy to help. Once they'd figured out the trick to making the near-vision goggles work, they'd finally understood the brilliance of her plan.

Hamish had offered the suggestion that paved the way for the break-through. Even though he'd spent so little time with them, his brilliant inventor's mind had seen what she hadn't.

Karlmann examined the goggles closely. "I still can't pretend I under-stand how this works."

"It's so new, I doubt any of us understand all the ramifications," Jean admitted.

Hamish's idea had been so simple, but still so hard. Quickened quartzite worked best magnifying a view across a flat area, which worked great for wide vistas, magnified ten or twenty times. But they needed to magnify tiny things hundreds of times, and they hadn't figure out how to focus the quartzite properly.

Hamish had asked, "Can't we bend the view somehow to focus it tighter?"

That idea provided critical, especially when Jean had noticed a magnifying lens used by one of the Althing researchers. That had given her the insight she needed to figure out the new goggles.

Now she pointed to the curved lenses on each end of the goggles. "We use these to help bend the light shining up through the sample. We run that image through four sets of quickened quartzite, each increasing the magnification five-fold. Using that combination is far more stable than anything we've tried so far."

She felt impatient to get the next iteration of the goggles complete so she and Karlmann could really study the mold, and hopefully begin to understand what made diseases work. One Althin research team was already scheduled to help. In their studies of chemicals, they already suspected that many aspects of life were simply too tiny to see, and they were excited to get a chance to start proving some of their hypotheses. She was happy to have them available. Their work would save her years of research and hopefully kickstart the understanding of infectious diseases.

Karlmann rose and rubbed his back. He gave Jean a warm smile. "It appears you are once again on the verge of making the impossible a real-ity. Well done, my dear. I only wish I was a few years younger so I could keep up with you. I suspect the pace of our research is about to accelerate exponentially."

She took his hand and escorted him to the door. He was such a good-hearted man. She loved the chance to work with him and benefit from his many years of experience. "I doubt we'd make half as much progress without your wisdom guiding our path. I'll inform you the moment the new prototypes are ready."

After he left, she allowed herself to drop into an overstuffed chair near her crackling fire and savor the moment. Right then, her little office felt more like a Builder shop than an administrator's workplace.

She smiled when she realized she'd thought of her office as little. It was almost as nice as Lord Gavin's personal study in Alasdair. She'd never lived in such finery and she felt a little ashamed at how quickly she had grown accustomed to it.

As she held her hands out to the fire, she thought of Gran and wished she could share the marvelous days with her. She'd long dreamed of opportunities to learn and to challenge her mind. Now that she was nearly drowning in those challenges, she wondered how long she could keep up the pace. So many people were relying on her to lead and to make decisions, but she felt so inexperienced. All she could do was follow her heart and stay true to the principles Gran had taught her.

Bruno's heavy knock on the door interrupted her reverie. His huge hands simply couldn't knock softly, so even a polite tap shook the door like he was trying to knock it off its hinges.

"Come in," she called.

Bruno entered. In his big winter coat, he looked like a bear. He bowed a little as more and more people were doing of late, despite how often Jean reminded them she was still just a commoner.

She gestured him to join her by the fire, and the large chair he chose creaked under his bulk. She spoke in Grandurian before he could initiate a conversation in Obrioner. They vied for opportunities to practice each other's language.

"I'm glad you stopped by. I haven't had time to review your latest report, but I prefer to hear about your progress in person anyway."

Bruno loved working with the Builders and he'd assumed the unofficial position of supervisor of the many teams working on the various components of the enormous armored mechanical they were building for Hamish. He'd taken to calling it the Juggernaut.

"The armor is stronger than we hoped. The components are progressing rapidly. The Althin draftsman is struggling to keep the specifications current."

"Good. Tell me about it," she encouraged, and decided she'd make time to tour the various workrooms personally tomorrow.

Bruno explained how they were using both quickened granite and steel to create the curved outer shell of the spherical Juggernaut.

Jean frowned and interrupted. "The quickened granite is very hard, so that's a good choice, but could a powerful Sapper or Sentry manipulate it?"

Bruno shook his head. "Dierk tested that theory. Most Petralists lack ability to walk with solid stone. Even if Hamish faced one who could, it appears that by quickening the stone, its power is engaged and inaccessible to Petralist manipulation."

"Really? Is that principle true across all power stones?" What an intriguing idea.

"I don't know, but I'll make a point to assign a team to research that."

"Thank you. Keep me posted on developments, please." Jean grabbed her ever-present notebook from the nearby table and jotted a note. Then she said, "Sorry for the interruption. Please continue about the armor."

Bruno explained that individual sections were being developed to house various weapons that would drive through movable joints. Another team was working on a flexible harness to suspend Hamish in the center, where he would control all the various thrusters and components. The harness would turn to keep Hamish upright, even while the sphere rolled.

The engineering challenges were immense, but the various teams all saw it as the symbol of their entire rebuilding effort. They threw themselves into the project with remarkable zeal.

"The Juggernaut armor is the one way we can feel empowered against the supernatural forces threatening our nation. Perhaps we can help save our home from getting destroyed again," he explained.

That made sense. No one liked to feel helpless, and the Juggernaut could produce a fundamental shift in the balance of power.

"I'm impressed by how much you've all done. My biggest worry is how much power stone it will consume."

Bruno shrugged and switched to Obrioner. "It is very large. We will need mighty fire to make move."

His Obrioner was progressing a little slower than Jean's Grandurian, but he was definitely making solid progress.

She waved toward her desk where she'd just read a report from a different research team. "There has to be a way to harness the raw power more efficiently. These reports about pulleys and gears prove it's possible to take a little force and make it bigger."

Bruno nodded, his expression thoughtful. "Pulleys and gears are good for some things, but would need different fuel to make the fires burn hotter."

Jean rose and paced away, hands itching for her pencil and notebook. The many concepts they were studying were fascinating, and she firmly believed that all of that focused knowledge had to produce important new breakthroughs, but hated the rushed pace. They needed months to study and experiment, but she felt driven to hurry. Hamish might need the Juggernaut any day.

"What are you thinking?" Bruno asked.

She blew out an exasperated breath. "I don't like the idea of introducing new fuels, if we can avoid it. There has to be a way to improve performance, though. I know it. Pulleys and ropes would burn if we tried to use them to harness activated marble, but there has to be something. I mean, even a little fire produces a lot of force. We should be able to take that, control it, and magnify . . ."

She trailed off as an idea struck. She gasped and gripped his enormous hands in hers. "I think I know how to make this work!"

"How?"

She tugged him to his feet and headed for the door, sweeping her coat off a peg without slowing. "Come on. We have to get to the workshop."

She wasn't sure when she'd return to her office, and the thought of all of those reports piling up on her desk unread didn't bother her at all.

She had work to do.

57

SOME PROBLEMS ARE AS SIMPLE AS THEY APPEAR

Connor jumped out of the windrider as soon as it touched down outside of Emmerich. Even though he'd caught a ride from the border with a different Builder, he couldn't help but think again about Hamish's cryptic note. He wondered where Aifric had led him off to, and hoped they were all right.

Villagers of Emmerich were still not accustomed to windriders, so locals flooded in from every side, gawking at the huge flying wagon. Children whooped and waved and swarmed up onto the wagon, despite the Builder's calls to stay down. Their mothers tried to corral them, but also pleaded with the young pilot for just one ride for their little ones. He looked completely overwhelmed.

Connor's mother rushed up and wrapped him in one of her famous hugs. He really needed to get to Altkalen, but he hadn't been able to resist the urge to detour east to see his family. Some crazy things were going on. He'd just kicked a revolution into high gear, Verena was still asleep, and his powers were not functioning properly. He needed a reminder about what was important. As he hugged his mother, his problems seemed less dire.

"What's wrong, son?" she asked as Connor's siblings and Hamish's family swarmed around him, clamoring for news and asking about Hamish and Jean.

"I don't have much time. I've got to get back to Altkalen."

He spent several minutes catching up with everyone, his heart full as he enjoyed the company of so many people he knew and loved. It seemed like his siblings as well as Hamish's had all grown since he'd last seen them. He didn't like that feeling of disconnect. It seemed wrong that he was missing so much of their lives, but he couldn't see how to do things differently.

Lord Wenzel was at the quarry with most of the men, but Hamish's mother pointed north, toward the highest hill overlooking the town. "Stuart hurt his arm yesterday, but that's not enough to interfere with his daily walk with Stefanie."

The two were heading back toward town and altered course to join Connor and the crowd around the windrider. Stefanie seemed like a good, dependable girl, so he had no idea what she saw in Stuart.

When they drew near, he was surprised to see Stuart looking grumpy and Stefanie frustrated. Not a good idea for Stuart to anger his girlfriend. As a Rumbler, she could throw him over a building.

Stefanie seemed preoccupied, then surprised him by asking, "Have you ever heard of rocks that make a non-Petralist feel bad?"

The image of all the rocks Hamish had accidentally swallowed as a child immediately came to mind. He glanced at Stuart, who was scowling. "Have you been eating rocks?"

"No," he said tersely.

Stefanie said, "Nothing like that. Is only, Stuart insists our lookout rock makes him sad."

Her judgment in boyfriends might be suspect, but her Obrioner was getting pretty good.

It was clear Stuart was smitten by the girl, so why would he ever tell her he was sad? He said, "There's something weird about that spot. You're supposed to have a special talent for rocks, Connor. Come take a look and see if you can prove I'm not making it up."

The last thing Connor wanted to do was spend lots of quality time with Stuart. They weren't rivals any more, but they weren't exactly friends, and he had a lot on his mind. He started to shake his head, but both of them looked so crestfallen, he stopped. Seeing them arguing over something so foolish reminded him of his own arguments with Verena. The topics had been more weighty, but they'd let their disagreements become dangerous wedges.

He couldn't imagine how a long-term relationship between Stuart and Stefanie might actually work out, but he still wanted to help ease the current, foolish tension. It seemed a waste for them to argue about a rock when there were so many more glaring faults of Stuart's for Stefanie to focus on.

"All right, but only if we make it quick. I don't have much time."

"Thank you." Stefanie hugged him enthusiastically, and he was grateful she didn't tap granite. He'd been hugged almost to jelly by Princess Catriona more than once.

They had a little time before lunch, so the three of them ascended the hill and Connor saw immediately why Stefanie liked it so much. He had always loved the lookout rock high above Lord Gavin's plateau, with its fantastic view of Alasdair Valley.

This hill did not command such a magnificent view, but it was the best around Emmerich. The town spread beneath them, a well-ordered, tidy community, with a number of new buildings under construction and several domed, temporary earthen shelters on the outskirts.

Stefanie gestured to the large, rounded rock that they stood on. "Best place for view."

As soon as Stuart joined them on the rock, he glowered down at it. He did look sort of depressed. "Connor, can't you feel it? It's like this rock is trying to suck all the joy out of the world."

Connor didn't feel anything. It was just a big rock. Then again, he had spent enough time around Hamish and Verena to know that sometimes rocks were more than they seemed. He had no idea why Stuart would feel something that he didn't. Stuart was no Builder.

"I don't feel it," he admitted.

Stuart looked disgusted and Stefanie angry so he added quickly, "But maybe there's more to it than we think. I'll take a piece with me to Jean. She can have one of the Builders check it out and see if there's something wrong with it."

Stefanie did not want to damage her rock, but Stuart insisted it was a good idea. So she tapped granite and peeled back the frozen ground to snap off a jagged corner. When they replaced the earth, it concealed the damage.

"I'll make sure to let you know what we find."

That seemed to help, and the two of them walked hand in hand back down the hill. Stuart's good humor improved as they walked.

Connor convinced the Builder pilot to stay for lunch. Well, the sight of the feast being prepared by the village women, under the direction of Connor's mother, convinced him. Blair had rushed to the quarry while Connor was up on the hill. He returned with their father and the other cutters. Connor hugged his dad, grateful that he could see him before flying north again.

"How is your girl, Verena?"

"She was still sleeping the last time I saw her, but she might be awake by now." Speaking about her made him more anxious than ever to get back to her.

His mother squeezed his shoulder encouragingly. "She'll wake up son, and everything will be okay."

As Connor flew north in the windrider later, he hoped she was right.

58

A MOMENT WORTH SAVORING

Their detour to Emmerich brought them far to the east of Faulenrost, and the Builder pilot did not want to add yet another detour to his already delayed trip. Connor wanted to visit with Jean, but he wanted to see Verena more, and he needed to speak with Kilian most.

The pilot promised to deliver the wooden box of porphyry and the little piece of stone from Emmerich to Jean and her Builder teams in Faulenrost on his way back south the next morning. Connor decided that was probably the best compromise. Then he hunkered down against the wind as the young man coaxed every ounce of speed from the long wagon.

Altkalen looked unchanged. The city and the plain to the south were devoid of snow, warmed by the thousands of hot springs bubbling just under the surface of the rocky soil. The snow-covered hills ringing the wide plain stood out in sharp contrast to the brilliant blue sky.

As they swept over the enormous city, Connor focused only on the citadel where Verena slumbered. As soon as the windrider touched down, Connor leaped out, waved thanks to the pilot, and rushed inside.

Kilian intercepted him in one of the long halls on the second level where several hallways intersected. Kilian wore a black leather vest over a white shirt with the sleeves rolled up, despite the chill. He didn't look happy.

"Connor, I'm surprised to see you back so soon."

"I really need to speak with you."

"I figured you probably would. Come on." He gestured for Connor to follow. As they detoured into a smaller hallway that led to the northern wing of the citadel, Kilian asked, "Did you have a good reason to leave the others in Althing?"

"Several, actually."

Kilian raised an eyebrow in question, so Connor told him about the trip, Harley's surprise attack, and his decision to ascend in order to stop her.

Kilian pulled him to a stop, but before he could browbeat Connor for not listening to his advice, Connor insisted, "It was the only way. She would have destroyed Althing."

Kilian took a deep breath, one fist slowly clenching, then relaxing. He spoke in a resigned voice, "I know you felt justified. Perhaps you were. Time will tell. What happened to Harley?"

Connor explained about the strange ending to the battle, then tried to describe the weird feeling of those two clashing sources of power that collided in his tertiary affinities and shorted them out.

Kilian nodded slowly. "I had hoped to prepare you for that before you ascended. Harley's reaction makes me wonder if she had ulterior motives for that invasion, but how could my mother have known you would be in Althing?"

"She couldn't have. We travel too fast."

Kilian considered that as he resumed their journey, and Connor followed close behind. "Perhaps she just recognized an opportunity your action presented."

"What opportunity?"

"My mother wants your service. That's clear, or she wouldn't have left you free. She believes she can fetch you later, and now you've ascended successfully again. That suggests you might prove even more useful to her if she can win your loyalty."

"How could she imagine I'd ever willingly follow her?" Connor asked with a shudder. What would the world look like if she succeeded?

"She can be very persuasive," Kilian warned.

"She's also completely insane."

Kilian cracked a smile, and Connor felt relieved. A smiling Kilian was a lot less intimidating than the Kilian with fire blazing in his eyes. "So I'm not going crazy about my affinities being weird?"

Kilian chuckled. "I didn't say you're not crazy. Most people would say you're definitely crazy for choosing to ascend rather than turn and run like any sane person should have done in that situation."

"You know what I mean. I didn't break my affinities?"

"No, you didn't. We need to talk in private." When Connor hesitated, glancing in the direction of Verena's room, Kilian added in a kind but firm tone. "The last report I received, she was still slumbering peacefully. You'll have time to visit her later."

As they continued through the citadel toward Kilian's apartment, Connor asked, "Is this whole ascension thing the reason I could control myself better when I transformed into a rampager again in Merkland?"

Kilian stopped and spun toward him, looking shocked. "You can't just casually drop a comment like that, Connor. What happened in Merkland?"

Connor hesitated for a second, simply enjoying the moment. Kilian now understood how he felt. Maybe he would think twice before dropping earth-shattering secrets so casually.

Then he told Kilian about the trip to Merkland and Craigroy's trick with slipping porphyry into his food. He described his surprising new level of control, and his decision to start the revolution.

"Rory and Ivor approved of that?"

"Well, approve is kind of a strong word."

Kilian rubbed a hand through his hair, looking for a second like he wanted to rip at it instead. "That kind of rash action is not the way to begin a successful revolution."

"Maybe not, but I gave them twenty thousand new witnesses to the truth of porphyry to work with. That's something they didn't have before."

Kilian took a long slow breath. "Tell me the rest."

Connor explained how they had taken Merkland, ejected everyone who did not support the revolution, and imprisoned Craigroy. He finished with Rory's request that Anika come south along with some reinforcements.

They reached Kilian's apartment and dropped into chairs in his sitting room next to a cold fire. Kilian flicked a hand in that direction and the cold wood burst into flames.

"Usually I would hesitate to send Anika. Joining Rory at the head of a revolution would usually make me worry that they might do something rash. Since you've already taken care of that part, I see no danger in it. In fact, her presence might encourage Rory not to hesitate."

Connor was not so sure that was a good thing. He imagined Anika and Rory leveling an entire wing of the palace in their enthusiastic reunion.

Kilian continued, "They will definitely need reinforcements. I'll send Ilse and Lucas and the Crushers. They can help Rory organize his forces and prepare to defend Merkland. With the weather so bad, and with a little luck, they might get until spring to prepare."

"If your mother doesn't decide to intervene personally, or send Harley against them."

"I'm working on ways to draw Harley out. I'm hoping to secure assistance from my nephew first, though."

"You're recruiting Evander? Didn't work out so well for Harley."

"He's always tried to stay aloof from the conflict, but after defying Harley, he might finally see there's no other alternative but to destroy my mother."

"When do you think he'll make up his mind?"

Kilian grimaced. "Probably some point after I finally track him down.

He's gone to ground, and no one is better than Evander at staying concealed when he wants to."

Connor thought about that for a moment. "Where would you even start? The Carraig?"

Kilian shook his head. "No, that area is too unstable. I received reports that a slate quarry in southern Obrion experienced an elfonnel event, and I sent messengers to try to establish contact with Evander there, but so far no success."

Connor was glad he wasn't the one trying to establish contact with an elfonnel. He wondered who Kilian had sent.

Kilian asked, "Where are Hamish and Student Eighteen?"

That reminded Connor of his one piece of good news. "We resurrected Aifric!"

Kilian blinked. "Really? How?"

Connor explained briefly about the experience, but did not share a lot of details. Much of that experience was far too personal.

Kilian said, "It's good that you've already discovered your deeper ability with chert."

"Yeah. I can hear thoughts sometimes now."

"And you'll have limited ability to influence those thoughts, although you won't be able to wipe minds like my mother. That terrifying ability cannot be accessed until after the third threshold."

"That must be how I made such a good mirage in Raufarhofn," Connor realized with a grin. He loved new affinities, and he loved discovering new aspects to existing affinities.

"No doubt, you're right. Thankfully my mother never bothered practicing with limestone. Why play with mirage when you can simply grab another's mind and make them think whatever you want?"

"It helped me turn the fight against Harley."

"Keep practicing. My mother won't fear anything but the strongest elemental attacks, but that's always been her greatest weakness. No one can defeat her with the elements alone, but through careful cooperation and using some of these more subtle aspects to your other affinities, we might stand a chance. But we're getting side-tracked. I'm happy that Aifric is back, but where is she?"

Connor shrugged. "I think her family caught up with her in Merkland. Hamish left a pretty cryptic note suggesting he and Student Eighteen were leaving with her family."

Kilian grimaced. "I can't think of a single scenario that might turn out well. With Hamish providing transportation, they could strike almost anywhere. I wonder what target they chose."

Connor hadn't thought much about that. Who was an enticing enough target that Hamish would have agreed to go without waiting to discuss the idea with Connor?

The only idea that came to mind ratcheted up his fear for them a thousand times, even though he tried to convince himself Hamish couldn't possibly be that reckless.

He shared a glance with Kilian, who said softly, "If he takes them to Donleavy, I'll kill him myself. But we can't do anything about that right now. We need to get you stabilized."

"How?"

Kilian stared into the fire for a moment before answering. "Few Petralists have ever ascended through the second threshold and survived. Only my parents and Tallan could even attempt the third. My parents were not good at sharing their past or the deepest secrets of affinity stones, but they had to share some once I ascended. I gathered additional bits and pieces from Harley and some of their earliest supporters."

Connor shifted his chair a little closer, eager to hear more.

"As you have already discovered, the power that fuels our affinities is not generated by the stones we use. That power flows through the stones and they act like filters, making that power available to us."

That confirmed what Connor had sensed, but he still found it disturbing. It undermined the fundamental definition of affinities. "How does it work? How do stones—"

"I don't know." Kilian sounded frustrated, as if he had asked himself the same questions thousands of times. "But you've already sensed the truth. Whatever that ultimate source of power is, it's not a single entity. It's fractured into different frequencies, sort of like light split by a prism."

It had felt like that. "The two frequencies don't get along, though. They felt like different colors in my mind. One red, the other more greenish."

"I don't sense them as colors, but your description is valid. I suspect there may be more than two frequencies, but the others lie outside of our ability to sense them."

"So how come your affinities don't short out like mine?"

"Despite how difficult this has been for you in recent days, perhaps this is the best way to learn. Until you experience it, it's hard to grasp what we're talking about. The thing you need to understand now is that different affinity stones are tuned to different frequencies. Most are tuned to the lower intensity power source, the red one. Trying to hold onto both frequencies at the same time is what's creating that canceling effect."

Connor frowned, hating the new complication. His affinities had always felt so natural. He felt a headache growing.

He'd found in the past that the more he tried to understand his affinities, the less effectively they worked. Going by feel and pure instinct had always served him best. That green-tinted frequency had thrown off his inner balance. It was like throwing berries into one of his mother's nut-filled glory cakes. They might be great on their own, but together they wrecked the perfect balance of sweet and crunchy deliciousness.

"Why haven't I had this trouble before? And why don't the different frequencies seem to affect my primary and secondary affinities? If anything, they seem stronger than ever."

"Because until now, you were tuned only to that red frequency. It's like when Mattias taught you to see only one color as a Pathfinder, but imagine that's all you were ever able to do. Now suddenly you can see another color. The second ascension tuned your senses to the higher green frequency."

"So are any affinities tied to the green frequency?"

"I suspect porphyry may be, but my parents squashed all knowledge of porphyry so I can't be sure."

Connor nodded. "That's how it felt, actually."

"That would explain why it's so wild and addictive and hard to control in the lower thresholds, but responds better now that you've ascended and tuned to that same frequency."

"So how do I fix this?" Connor asked. All this talk of frequencies and colors and deeper truths of magic was all fine and good, but he needed access to his affinities again.

"Practice."

LEARNING CAN BE SCARY

K ilian extended a vial of soapstone mixture. "I found it easiest to work with my strongest tertiary."

That made sense. Connor's connection with water was deep and personal. When he tapped soapstone, he felt one with the water in a way he couldn't quite match with the other elements yet. He wasn't sure he ever would.

So he downed the vial. As soon as he focused, Water stepped into view in his mind. He snatched for her hand, and for a moment his senses expanded into the room. A pitcher of water on a nearby table glowed in his soapstone sight. He also sensed a wooden tub of soapy water in the next room and several bottles of wine in a cupboard behind Kilian.

Water still wore her coat, covered in swirling, clashing red and green power. Where they crashed over her hand, the connection vibrated violently, and he managed to hold on for only a second before losing connection.

Frustrated, he looked at Kilian who was calmly tossing a globe of water from one hand to the other.

"I can't get a solid connection," he complained.

"Think back to the day you trained with quartzite with Mattias. How did you narrow your vision to only see a single color?"

Connor thought about that. "I sort of unfocused my eyes."

"You stopped trying to see everything. This is the same principle. By touching both frequencies, you magnify the disruption."

That sort of made sense, but it would probably work better if he saw Water as a simple gateway instead of a woman. He tried explaining to Kilian what he saw when he tried tapping soapstone.

Kilian leaned forward, looking intrigued. "I've never seen the elements in human form like you describe. They started as gateways, like we've practiced. Over time, my affinity has become such an integral part of me that I no longer see the elements as external forces. They're more like invisible muscles that respond as easily as flexing my fingers."

That was fascinating, but not entirely helpful. "I haven't internalized my affinities so well yet, and I don't want to wait a hundred years to figure it out."

"No, we definitely don't have that much time," Kilian agreed. "But see if you can improve your vision. Can you separate the colors to different sides, then grip Water's red hand?"

"I'll try." That was a good idea. Connor hadn't realized he controlled how the elements appeared to him. They'd seemed to choose their own form, but maybe he could control at least some of it. Could stabilizing his affinities be that simple?

Connor closed his eyes and drew upon soapstone. Again Water appeared before him, her expression encouraging, her hands outstretched toward him. She seemed as eager to connect as he did. The problem was, as hard as he focused, he couldn't get the two conflicting power frequencies to separate cleanly to either side of her.

So he focused on her left thumb and bent his entire will into seeing that one little digit clear of green power. He wasn't sure how long he concentrated, but suddenly the swirling green power moved away, leaving her thumb clear. Connor lunged for it.

Even as he connected, the green frequency power swirled back across her thumb in a golden, crackling line that shorted out his connection. Water gave him an annoyed look, then faded from sight.

When he grumbled in frustration, Kilian asked, "Do you have to think about eating sweetbreads?"

"Around Hamish I do. If I'm not really alert, he eats them all before I get any."

Kilian chuckled. "Well, for the purpose of this exercise, imagine you're eating a platter of sweetbreads alone. How hard would you have to focus to ensure you eat them properly?"

Finally, something made sense. "I just let myself do it. I don't need to think about it."

"Exactly. Try again."

So he did. Unfortunately, walking with water wasn't quite as second-nature as eating. He spent the next hour and a half trying to make it work. He had felt frustrated by the several minutes it took to learn to split light those weeks ago. That was ridiculously easy compared with trying to tune out the powerful green power frequency. It was just so enticing, so insistent. Part of him felt that if he could just understand it, he could connect with it and unlock far more power.

Unfortunately, Kilian was right. The more he focused on it, the less he accomplished. He proved that point dozens of times. Even when he succeeded in distracting himself by thinking of Verena while reaching out to touch Water, he only managed the briefest moments of contact.

Soapstone was tuned to the lower, reddish frequency. He couldn't explain it, but he sensed it. And yet, the green frequency seemed to also want to claim her.

Eventually Connor sagged back in his chair, feeling exhausted. "I can't manage more than a second."

"It will take time. You'll need to practice every day. That connection should improve until you can walk with the elements better than ever before. In fact, we need to meet every day to continue your training. Now that you've ascended, there are new nuances and abilities tied to many of your affinity stones that you must understand."

"Soapstone doesn't feel very different when I can connect."

"That's probably the only one that will feel that way. You ascended in soapstone first, so you achieved a far more intimate connection with it. You saw lesser improvements in your other affinities. Now that you've ascended with marble, you'll find your connection with it has become almost as strong as soapstone. You'll also discover that it no longer hurts to tap marble."

"Finally some good news. I love marble spiciness." Unfortunately tapping had always been a bit insane. The deeper he drew upon it, the more it hurt. He always feared that he'd accidentally burn himself to a crisp.

Kilian grinned. "I've never found anything else that quite matches up to it."

Connor loved spicy food, and he would gladly taste marble all the time if it didn't burn so bad.

Before he could dig a piece of marble out of his belt pouch Kilian said, "As important as practice is with the tertiaries, don't forget your primary and secondary affinities. They are powerful tools that are unfortunately ignored too much by the very Petralists who could do the most with them."

"What do you mean?" That sounded foolish.

"My mother and Harley in particular have always focused on the elements to the exclusion of most other affinities. So they trained me and Evander with a similar mindset. I like to think we fall into that trap to a lesser degree. One of the most important benefits of your ascension is that you can now tap two igneous stones at the same time without suffering double-tap sickness."

"Wow!" That was great news. That limitation had always rankled. He'd discovered it the hard way shortly after establishing affinity with basalt.

He couldn't wait to try them both together. What would it feel like to run with Strider speed, but protected by granite-hardened skin?

Kilian said, "There are other subtle new aspects to the primaries and secondaries, and they might prove critical when we face Harley or my mother again."

"Harley seemed to like sandstone a lot. She somehow used it to melt buildings in seconds."

"That was her invention and is one of her favorite abilities. I don't know any other Petralist to accomplish much with it, other than perhaps Evander. He spent so much time with her while they were dating that he learned the trick."

Connor gaped. "Evander dated Harley?"

He had thought Rory and Anika were a pair that inspired fear. Thinking of Evander and Harley together was like imagining an earthquake dating a tornado.

Kilian chuckled. "The match always seemed strange to me, but they made it work for a few years. When the war turned fierce and Evander hesitated to support my mother as completely as Harley demanded, they split. It wasn't pretty."

"What city did they destroy?" Connor asked, thinking about their recent squabble that leveled the Carraig.

"It was a small, seaside town. Used to be a gem of the Sea of Olcan. It's nothing but piles of jagged rock now."

And Connor thought he had family problems.

Kilian said, "I know you're eager to go visit your girl, but before you go I want to teach you how to use one deeper aspect of basalt."

"Can we run even faster now?" Connor asked, excited by the idea. He'd definitely need to get a helmet and goggles to protect from the wind and the bugs. Then again, he could now harden his skin. Just thinking about it made him itch to go running.

Kilian shook his head. "Just the opposite."

The cryptic answer surprised Connor. Basalt was all about speed. "You mean, you use it to slow down?"

"Most Striders would feel offended to even consider the idea, which is why almost no one has mastered what I am about to teach you, but it could prove very useful. And the very fact that no one uses it means they won't be prepared to defend against it. I'm showing you this to help open your mind to new, subtle, and potentially critical nuances to your affinities."

Kilian drew from a drawer in a little table next to his chair a small pouch of basalt. He absorbed a little then passed it over to Connor. The exhilarating feel of basalt rushing through his system made Connor grin, and he had to fight to remain seated. One leg started to twitch, despite his best efforts to keep it calm.

"Basalt has an external ability which you can now access. Like other affinity stones, the external ability produces the opposite effect as the internal. It is available now because it's tuned to the higher-frequency, green power source."

Kilian gestured toward the fire, and it suddenly froze. The flames stopped moving mid-flicker and the entire fire seemed frozen in absolute stillness in a way Connor could not quite describe.

A second later the fire began flickering again, faster, as if trying to make up for lost time.

"What did you do?"

"It's called Stilling. Concentrate the power of basalt in your hand, almost as if you're about to purge, but then open yourself to the green power source. Focus on something external like the fire and push that power to it. External basalt acts like a smothering blanket, an invisible shackle that completely immobilizes your target."

Wow. That sounded impressive, but also felt like a terrible waste of basalt speed. When Connor focused the energy of the basalt into his hand, it started to shake, his fingers quivering so fast they seemed to blur in front of him. His hand began to ache with the need to move and he suppressed a groan.

While tapping a primary affinity, he could feel both power sources rolling through him like endless waves of two very different oceans, but they did not interfere like they did when tapping tertiary affinities. Strange. He couldn't explain it and didn't dare question it, lest by focusing on it he'd invite it to not work. The red frequency touched his mind where he tapped basalt, fueling the unrivaled need to move and run.

He had to get rid of it. Holding that power condensed like that would tear his hand apart. So in his mind, he imagined turning away from the red power source and extending his hand holding basalt out the opposite window, the one connected to the green frequency. As soon as he connected basalt to it, the green frequency of power supplanted the red, snapping into connection and thundering into him with astonishing strength.

Amazingly, that didn't dissolve his connection with basalt. It flickered for a second, and as the green power source locked onto it, the feel of it changed. The energy paused, like the coiling of a snake, ready to strike.

"Release it now, before it catches you in the effect." Kilian urged.

Connor focused on the fire and cast that power out of his hand. The coiled basalt energy sprang away in an invisible stream, almost like his ethereal senses when he tapped elemental powers, and encircled the hapless flames.

Instantly they froze into absolute stillness. Since he was controlling it, Connor felt what was happening. The energy and heat of the fire dissipated into the enshrouding basalt, sucked away completely.

Stilling the flames was so much more than simply dousing the fire. That would leave the wood available to burn again in the future. Basalt stilling instead stole that energy, draining it away and leaving the fire empty, almost more an illusion than a real flame.

"Hold it," Kilian ordered.

Connor did not want to. He could feel the energy draining away from the fire. But he held on as ordered and the energy drained away just as he expected. Five seconds later, the wood expired, and both the wood and the flames simply disappeared.

Shocked by the fire's abrupt demise, Connor released basalt. All that remained in the fireplace was a small pile of white ash.

He had completely destroyed the fire.

"That's horrible."

Kilian nodded. "It really is, but it may prove useful."

"Are you suggesting I try that on Harley?"

In some ways it was more terrifying than her sandstorm. That tore at things, reducing them to rubble, but basalt stillness simply robbed things of the ability to exist.

"I doubt you could maintain it long enough to kill her, but you might be able to use it in other circumstances. For example, I've used it here in the valley south the Altkalen to block a couple of eruptions that were threatening. When you learn to master this ability, you can actually draw into yourself the energy that the stillness robs."

Connor doubted he'd ever enjoy sucking the life out of things, like the ultimate leech.

"I think you've absorbed all the deeper truths you can handle for today. Go check on your girl and we'll speak again tomorrow."

As Connor hurried away from Kilian's apartment, he was starting to wish he had never ascended. Petralist powers had always seemed exciting, but now he was learning there was a darker aspect to affinities.

Now that he knew, he feared what else Dreokt or Harley might have planned for their subjects. He also feared what he might have to do in order to stop them.

6 0

LEAVE SOME THINGS TO THE PROFESSIONALS

Hamish looked up when Aifric slipped into the small culinary storage room where he was hiding with the other three Assassins. She'd discarded her normal healer whites and replaced them with a fine burgundy gown. He made a point not asking where she got it.

The room felt crowded with Assassins, rolling cabinets of silver trays, and carts with leftovers from some recent feast. Hamish alone had bothered exploring the food remnants on the carts.

That seemed like a professional oversight on their part. What if they were unexpectedly invited to attend a banquet? Not knowing what foods were popular could be a critical mistake.

"What's with that ridiculous hat?" Hamish asked as Aifric swept the wide-brimmed thing from her head. It was colored a garish, bright green, with an enormous red eoin feather hanging off the right side.

"It's apparently the height of fashion, and it helps conceal my features."

She dropped a bundle of clothes on top of the nearest food cart. Mister Two looked pleased and ordered them all to don the clothes. Hamish was already wearing a billowing, black cape to conceal his battle suit.

"What did you learn?" Mister Two asked softly.

"No sign of alarm. No one noticed our entry into the city."

That helped Hamish feel just a bit better. Donleavy was a beautiful city, but it felt wrong. Almost half of the desserts were left on those silver plates. Many of them looked like they'd only been nibbled at, even though they tasted perfectly fine. Even nobility could be counted on to finish quality sweets.

They had flown in during the hour prior to dawn. Hamish had ghosted up along the steep eastern escarpment, the sound of the Hawk's thrusters easily drowned out by the thunder of all those waterfalls. He'd found a low garden, heavy with trees, and dropped the others off, then left the Hawk hovering under an overhanging ledge near the top of the cliff, tethered to the rock. They'd easily slipped into the city and the palace after that.

"How about the throne room?" Sir asked.

"I foresee no issues gaining access."

"Are you completely insane?" Hamish demanded. "The throne room? Really?"

Aifric rolled her eyes. "I only checked the entrance. There are guards at the door, but they barely look at the people entering. People are desperate to avoid the throne room, so no one expects anyone to go who doesn't absolutely have to be there."

"Sloppy," Mister Two said with a tight smile. "Exactly what we hoped for."

They were all cracked. Hamish had realized that early in the flight and now wondered for the thousandth time if he'd made a colossal mistake. He also wondered if Connor had damaged some important self-preservation aspects of Aifric's personality when they resurrected her. Aifric was supposed to be a Healer, not a spy.

She also wasn't supposed to be Agor.

Hamish doubted Connor had any idea what he'd done in that head of hers, but on the journey south, she'd revealed that although the memory of her previous affinities existed, she still needed to reestablish them. While she'd worked on that, she'd exclaimed that she'd managed to establish primary affinity with two different stones. Apparently, despite her many personalities and their various affinity arrangements, she'd never managed an Agor gift before. She hadn't revealed which primaries she now enjoyed, but had confirmed she'd reestablished her very strong affinity with sandstone.

She'd also revealed that she'd managed to establish affinity with quartzite for the first time. Hamish had encouraged Connor to help her come back better than before, but it still unnerved him to see her changing so drastically. What had Connor done? Was his tampering the reason she'd kept up so well in the sausage eating competition in the Hawk? That could almost be considered cheating.

It did make sense that she become a Pathfinder, since her mission was to eavesdrop on the queen. He still thought her daft, cracked, and stir-fried for approaching the throne room. From everything he'd heard, that was the heart of darkness that few people escaped unharmed.

They all gathered around Aifric as explained how the corridor where they hid emptied into one of the main hallways that led to the central palace main atrium. The description of the waterfall plunging through the center of the building intrigued Hamish, as did the many hollow stairway columns leading up to the throne room perched high above.

"Harley wasn't there, and she's not expected to return to the throne room until tomorrow."

At least they had that going for them. Attacking the queen was crazy, but attacking her and Harley together was an entirely different level of insanity.

"I heard there are fewer nobles in attendance than usual, but High Lord Dougal and Shona are with them."

Mister Two smiled grimly. "Good. They would prove exceptional secondary targets if we get the chance."

Hamish hoped they'd kill Dougal, but he'd feel better if the man was not in attendance. Dougal was too smart by three servings. They didn't need the complications. Shona was an arrogant, heart-twisting cobra of a girl, but Hamish wasn't sure he wanted her dead. Shaved bald, maybe, but not dead.

Daulah took a step toward the door, his expression grim, but eager. "What are we waiting for? Now's the time to strike."

"Wait a minute. You're not going to attack her right now? Right there in her own throne room?" Hamish asked. Somehow, despite the whole reconnaissance mission, he'd assumed they needed more time to prepare.

Daulah's favorite expression was looking disgusted, and he used it again on Hamish. Mister Two looked surprised by the question.

Sir said, "Of course."

Aifric explained. "Her throne room is her seat of power. It's the place she feels most in control, therefore the place she will least fear an attack."

"You'll have to fight through everyone to get to her," Hamish protested.

Sir asked, "Do we question how you do your work, Builder?"

"You probably could if my work was about to get you killed."

Aifric said, "The queen has so dominated everyone that she has beaten all independent thought out of them." She hesitated for a moment before adding, "Except perhaps for Dougal and Shona. Those two are exceptionally clever."

Sir said, "What's important to understand is that not only will the speed of our strike shock them, they will hesitate out of fear of the queen. In those seconds, we will either destroy her and cow them all, or she'll destroy us."

They were even more insane than Hamish had figured. "Oh, when you put it that way, it sounds like a great idea."

"It does not concern you anyway. Your mission is to stay back and provide the escape route for any of us who survive." Mister Two said.

He turned to Aifric and added, "You will wait with him."

She looked shocked, as if he told her she had to serve them all sweetbreads without getting one herself. Her expression shivered and hardened as Student Eighteen took control.

"You need me. I have the right—"

Mister Two held up a hand to cut her off. She silenced immediately, although it looked like it took all of her willpower to do so.

"Your mission is to observe. Should our assault go poorly, you must bring word back to the people."

"Father, please let me stand with you," she begged, her expression agonized.

"I have spoken," he said, his tone unbending, but his gaze softened.

She still looked upset, but did not protest again.

Sir looked like he approved, and Daulah just gave her a superior look, as if somehow he was scoring major points by getting to risk his life while she waited behind. Hamish bit back a mirthless laugh. He'd almost considered the rear guard position he and Aifric would take as 'safely behind'.

Without further ado, they left the supply room and walked purposefully up the hallway. Student Eighteen lagged, twirling her fancy hat in her hands, with Hamish trailing behind.

"From what you've told me, there's little chance they'll even get into the throne room before she realizes something is wrong," Hamish said softly.

She slowed, letting the other three Assassins draw farther ahead before whispering, "They'll get in just fine. We have access to a power that has been lost to time."

"Another secret affinity stone?" He wondered how many they had. "Tell me about it." When she hesitated, he added, "If this goes really badly, and if I'm the only one who escapes, I need to understand what I'm seeing so I can explain it to others."

"That's not the reason you want to know, and you know it."

Hamish shrugged. "I know that, and you know that, but if we have to explain ourselves to your father later, it'll be a good excuse."

She grinned, and he knew he had won.

"Pumice."

He stared, expecting her to laugh, but she looked like she had just shared her mother's favorite secret cookie recipe, passed down for fifteen generations and shared only with the eldest daughter of the family.

"Pumice? You've got to be kidding."

"Like I said, lost to time."

Hamish tried to believe her, but pumice was only used in helping to quarry granite as far as he knew. Otherwise, it was completely useless. It was dry, tasteless, and made him cough when he tried it.

"What does it do?" He asked.

"It conceals. When tapping pumice, a Petralist is invisible to the senses of other affinity stones, particularly the elemental powers. It's like you don't even exist."

"Are you sure Connor didn't accidentally break something when he was in your head last time?"

"I'm fine. Think about it. Pumice is an unusual stone. It's a rock, but it floats. It acts differently than any stone should. Affinities with pumice create a similar effect magically. The Petralist skims across the senses of others instead of sinking into them where they can be felt."

"That's why you weren't afraid to get close to the throne room," Hamish guessed. "On the flight over, you were establishing that new affinity."

She nodded. "Whatever Connor did, I'm Agor for the first time."

"So pumice is a primary affinity?"

"Yes. It's paired with granite." She looked extremely pleased about that.

"Can I have a piece of pumice?"

She gave him a warning look instead of a rock. "I can't allow you to start experimenting with a new affinity stone, Hamish."

He gave her the 'I'm innocent' look that he always used on his mother. It did not work on her either.

"I'll give you one on the return flight," she promised.

Hamish wanted to ask more, but they reached the main atrium and he nearly stumbled into her as he gawked at the huge, vaulted room, with the magnificent waterfall plunging past the wall of protective glass.

They started up one of the many staircases to the throne room. The three Assassins moved purposefully, but outwardly appeared calm. Hamish and Aifric followed at a slower pace to allow some space between them and the lead strike team.

At the top of the stairs, they reached a glass-walled antechamber paved in blue and silver tiles, with a final wide set of white, marble stairs leading up to the gilded double doors of the throne room. A pair of guards stood at attention, but did not challenge them as they entered, exactly as Aifric had predicted.

Hamish tried to look calm, but his heart raced and he wished he could wipe his sweaty palms within his gloves. They were really doing it. They were insane. He was cracked for going in with them.

Then he stepped across the threshold and stopped to stare again. The stories he'd heard of the wondrous room completely failed to convey the majesty of it. The rare, transparent crystal floor took his breath away as he stared down toward the main palace far below. The domed ceiling of blue crystal made him feel like they'd somehow stepped into the rushing current of the falls.

It took a couple of seconds to notice the people. About thirty people stood in the huge, vaulted chamber. Many of them glanced in his direction, but they quickly dismissed him as a nobody. Probably because he lacked a feathered hat.

Queen Dreokt sat on her throne, listening to a florid-faced, beefy lord, who was petitioning for the reduction of taxes levied on Raineach to help accelerate production of power stone.

High Lord Dougal stood to the queen's right, along with Ailsa. The previous royal family stood to the queen's left, several paces behind the throne, looking as empty-headed as Connor had described.

The way Shona was standing, listening to the high lord's petition, she was looking almost directly at the door. So it was only natural for her to glance up at the newcomers.

Her gaze locked on Hamish's and she could not entirely suppress a look of shocked surprise, then fear before she again schooled her features to neutral. Hamish realized with a cold sense of impending doom that he and Aifric should have waited longer before following the other Assassins in. The three men had crossed almost half the hall, without drawing any attention.

High Lord Dougal noted his daughter's surprise and followed her gaze. Hamish tried to duck his head and slip behind a fat lady with an extremely wide skirt, but he wasn't quite fast enough.

"Builder!" Dougal shouted, pointing.

Aifric was gone. Hamish had not even seen her move, but she had luckily slipped away.

The queen leaped to her feet and pushed past Dougal, her expression enraged. "A foul Builder here? Where?"

Everyone scattered from her angry glare, including the fat woman shielding Hamish. He moved with her, keeping her between himself and the queen.

The ruse would not work for long, so he glanced at the outer doors and prepared to activate his thrusters. He could escape in just a couple of seconds.

The solid quartzite floor beneath him and the fat lady simply disappeared. She screamed as she plummeted through. Hamish instinctively ignited his thrusters, caught her by the many layers of fabric billowing around her, and hauled mightily, throwing her back up into the room.

He wanted to turn and throw wide the release rate on every thruster and escape, but Aifric was in there. Maybe he could keep the queen distracted long enough for the Assassins to complete their mission.

As he rose back through the floor, cloak billowing dramatically around him, every eye focused on him. The queen was glaring so hard, he immediately second-guessed his choice. By her expression, he wouldn't live much longer.

So he waved and said in a cheery voice, "I'm sorry, I thought this was the banquet hall."

That surprised her just long enough for him to trigger one of the diorite missiles embedded in the left arm of his suit. It tore through the sleeve of his cloak and leaped away in a rush of air, shooting across the throne room toward the queen's cold heart.

Air gusted around her, deflecting the missile away. It struck the enormous windows behind her and exploded in a very satisfying explosion of fire and glass.

In that same second, the Mhortair struck.

Daulah stepped out from between a pair of huddling lords, not twenty feet away from the queen. His cloth belt fell to the floor behind him. Under it, he'd actually worn a second belt. It looked to be made jagged lengths of steel. As he stepped from cover, he grasped the buckle and gave it a flick, and the entire thing slipped free and fell in coils around his feet.

It wasn't a belt, but some kind of bladed whip sword.

Daulah lunged and swung his arm around and forward. The whip-sword lashed out, slashing across the queen's stomach with a soft *snicking* sound.

It cut her completely in half.

Hamish was already turning to flee, but he paused to gape, horrified at the blood and entrails erupting from the queen's severed torso as she fell, as if in slow motion. Her scream of pain was lost among dozens of other screams from shocked lords and ladies.

Daulah swung the belt around again, even before the queen struck the floor. She raised her hands to protect her head, and his awful weapon snicked past twice more, severing her arms at the elbows in sprays of blood.

On the dais, Ailsa remained remarkably calm, expression intent as she watched the assault. Shona was stumbling back, her form already shifting into the perfect lines of max-tapped granite. Dougal was crouching in a fighting stance, hand snatching for a dagger on the nearby weapons rack next to the throne.

Mister Two and Sir charged from the opposite side. White-hot flames erupted around Mister Two and he hurled the deadly fire at the mortally wounded queen. Sir raced past with obsidian grace, twin swords already raised to take off her head.

It was actually going to work! In less than three seconds, the Assassins would kill the most powerful Petralist in the world.

Hamish couldn't breathe, couldn't blink, seemed frozen in position as he watched. Could she really die that easily?

No.

As Daulah's whip-sword flicked back toward her again, the stones beneath her brutalized body erupted into protective walls. The whip-sword slashed cleanly through one of the blocks of stone, but could not reach her. Mister two's fire rebounded from an invisible wall, changed direction, and speared toward Sir.

He leaped through the flames without harm, but the royal family charged in, screaming, "Save the queen!"

Sir cut down both of King Turriff's sons in an eyeblink and kicked the enslaved king and queen to the floor. Then with two quick steps, he leaped high. It looked like he would clear the protective stone barrier.

It exploded.

Stone shards tore him to pieces, and more ripped the air in a deadly, outward ring. The overwhelming barrage caught Daulah, and his body seemed to simply disintegrate into a cloud of bloody mist.

Why hadn't their pumice saved them?

Many other people, most of whom were scrambling toward the exit, cried out in pain and fell to the ground with bloody wounds from the indiscriminate spray of stone. Hamish blasted himself above the storm with a brief but powerful gust from his thrusters.

Encircled within white-hot flames, Mister Two managed to deflect the deadly spray of stones. He dove forward, propelled by fire so hot that Hamish felt the heat fifty feet away. He flashed across the distance to the queen, who still lay prone on the floor, and slammed into her, driving a long dagger into the center of her chest.

He stabbed her again and rose to his knees above her. As he ripped the knife out of her chest in another spray of blood, he shouted, "Tainted blood to purge!"

Those words seemed important to him, but Hamish willed him to strike one more time and remove her head. Maybe that would kill her.

Mister Two leaned forward to strike a third time, but the blow abruptly stopped with the knife still poised high over his head.

Then he slowly toppled to the floor. High Lord Dougal's blade rasped against bone as it slid free of his side. Hamish had not even seen Dougal move, but he'd slipped the narrow blade between Mister Two's ribs, straight to his heart.

High Lord Dougal dropped to the floor beside his queen and cried, "I'm so sorry, my liege. Know that I avenged your death."

The throne room fell silent, so Hamish clearly heard the queen's response as he settled back toward the floor.

She spoke in an annoyed tone. "Stop being so melodramatic, Dougal. Be so kind as to position my arm back into place so I can heal myself."

Hamish gaped, more shocked by that matter-of-fact statement than anything else he had witnessed. Could she really heal from such horrific injuries? Blood and gore drenched the floor all around, although it no longer gushed from her ghastly wounds.

He readied another missile. Maybe she was distracted enough for this one to work. He imagined the diorite exploding her head. No way she'd outlive that.

But suddenly Student Eighteen appeared, leaping the gap in the floor, and landing on his back. Her weight drove them down through the opening in the floor before he could compensate.

As he increased thruster, she slapped him on the side of the helmet. "Are you daft? Dive! We need to get out of here."

She was right. She was also shaking so hard as she clung to him that he felt it right though his suit. Hamish pivoted in midair and dove down the waterfall. Within seconds, the waters sprouted dozens of tentacle-like arms that whipped out and grasped at them.

Hamish banked and turned, dodging with every bit of agility his suit offered. Student Eighteen shrieked with fear as she clung to him. Impossibly, they avoided those deadly watery arms.

She shouted into his ear, "I'm tapping pumice. She can't sense me. My proximity to you must be helping to shield you too, but get us out of here!"

So Hamish used another diorite missile to blast through the bank of windows shielding the main atrium from the waterfall. He erupted through the cloud of glass, then cut to the left to avoid the horizontal waterfall that the queen threw after them. She might not be able to sense them, but that explosion wasn't the most subtle use of diorite he'd ever tried.

The water swept everyone in the atrium off their feet in a screaming, tumbling tide, but Hamish and Student Eighteen were already gone. They swept out through the speedcaravan tunnel, raced across the city under full power, and dropped over the edge of the cliff where the Hawk was tethered. Hamish activated the thrusters of the Hawk almost before Aifric slashed the tether line, and they rocketed away as fast as the nimble little craft could go.

The air buffeted them from every side in a sudden storm. The sky darkened and rain lashed out in blinding sheets. If not for their safety harnesses, they would have smashed themselves to pieces against the Hawk's shielding.

"She can sense the Hawk with air," Hamish shouted as he fought the controls.

"Must fly faster," she said in a remarkably calm voice, gripping the sides of her seat with a white-knuckled intensity. She'd switched back to Aifric, but tears still dripped down her cheeks. She did not seem aware of them.

"I am." He angled downward, sacrificing altitude for speed, and the little craft shot down along the mountain, far too close for his liking. With the right gusts of wind, the queen could dash them to pieces against the rocks.

"Give me a piece of pumice!" Hamish shouted.

She pressed a small piece of the remarkably light stone into his hands. He'd played with pumice all his life, but he'd only ever licked it once. Pumice dust made him sneeze terribly, so he'd never trusted it.

Hamish felt into the stone with his Builder senses and sure enough, he felt the crack that held its power in check.

Hamish wasn't sure what it would do, but the storm was quickly rising in intensity and they needed something. He had enough blind coal to escape one or two crashes, but that would not be enough to elude the queen's wrath.

Hamish threw wide the release rate on the pumice.

Every mechanical stopped, and the Hawk plummeted straight down.

Aifric screamed as the Hawk fell like a rock along the cliff face. Even though the storm still raged all around, they fell in complete, eerie silence.

After the first stomach-flipping lurch, Hamish ignored the view outside, his entire focus on the many stones accessible through his Builder senses. Pumice slid along those senses, like little bubbles trickling out his nostril. For several terrifying seconds, he felt nothing else. It was like all the thrusters and other power stones had simply fallen away.

"What are you doing?" Aifric shrieked. She clutched her seat and looked like she was deciding whether to throw up on him or switch to Student Eighteen and murder him in his seat.

"Working on it!" he cried. He was tempted to shutter the pumice, but if he did that, the queen would shred them in seconds.

If he didn't, they'd splatter at the base of the cliff almost as fast.

He could still feel the power stones in his suit. So he could grab Aifric and try flying out into the storm and leave the Hawk to crash, but they'd die just as fast.

"I hate grumpy old ladies," he muttered as he tried for the tenth time to reconnect to the thrusters.

And suddenly there they were, like little vortexes in his mind. He had no idea what changed, or why the connection was back, but he didn't have time to question it. With a shout of triumph, he activated the puking dooms on the underside of the Hawk at the same time he activated the lift and directional thrusters.

The stones all activated together, the sound like the roaring of a hundred nuall hunting cats, and their descent slowed, the pressure driving them down into their seats. He adjusted thrusters to angle them away, then activated the push thrusters, changing their downward speed to horizontal and shooting away from the cliff.

They knifed through the storm, with lightning and rain and misty clouds splitting around them, and somehow not quite touching them. Thunder pealed all around, but they flew through absolute calm.

Hamish exchanged an amazed look with Aifric, who pushed her wildly bedraggled hair away from her face.

"Will the pumice last long enough to escape this storm?" Aifric asked in a soft voice as the Hawk accelerated through the eerily calm, stormy skies.

"I think so." Hamish grinned at her. "This is amazing. I bet I could sneak right up on Kilian and surprise him so bad, he'd jump right out of his socks."

She smiled at the mental image, then asked, "How long do you think you'd outlive that prank?"

6 1

THE ONLY THING BETTER THAN ONE BIG DISCOVERY IS TWO

With Dierk hovering expectantly nearby, Jean secured a sample of mold on a clear dish over a piece of glowing limestone. She then slid both into position. The newest near-vision goggles, now secured onto a stable platform, actually looked like a serious research device. No doubt Verena would come up with a proper name for it when she awakened.

Healer Karlmann shifted his chair closer to the table, his expression eager. "Today perhaps we begin the journey of finally understanding the diseases we've fought for so many generations."

Jean exchanged an excited glance with Dierk and said, "I sincerely hope so."

Karlmann peered through the soft, leather viewports, and Jean said, "You can adjust the focus with this little knob. It moves the platform tiny degrees." She showed him how to manipulate it.

"Ah, that's better," he said after a moment.

Dierk looked pleased. "I figured it would allow for more consistent analysis and easier duplication of tests if the settings could be adjusted mechanically."

"Brilliant thinking," Karlmann said softly, his eyes pressed to the viewports, his wispy hair settling for once to complete stillness as he focused. "This is remarkable. I never imagined we could ever see its structure so clearly."

Jean agreed. She'd studied several samples of the mold. Each was a little different, and each time she peered into the viewports, she'd felt like an explorer entering a brand new world. "I tried looking at a piece of infected skin too. Although I saw amazing detail of the skin itself, I didn't get a good view of the disease."

Karlmann finally pulled his gaze from the viewports, his expression thoughtful. "Why do you suppose that is?"

"I'm not sure yet. I've seen some things that I haven't identified yet, but it's possible some things are still too small for us to make out."

"It's hard to imagine things that small," Dierk said. "We're already magnifying the view over five hundred times."

"We might need to go deeper," Jean insisted.

"How much more can this setup allow?" Karlmann asked, gesturing at the device.

"I'm not sure yet. I've got an entire Althing research team testing different samples. They're so excited to catalog tiny materials and chemical samples, they're working on it day and night. They'll help us document our findings and confirm the maximum effective magnification we can achieve with this approach. Now that we understand the basic principles, adaptations usually come more quickly."

Karlmann rose to unsteady feet and pulled her into a warm embrace. He smelled faintly of the cleaning solutions the Water Moccasins used while cleaning the hospital. He kissed her forehead and smiled. "I am proud of you, my dear. I doubt we yet understand the importance of the work we do here today, and I thank you for leading us into areas of research I was convinced were impossible."

Jean felt deeply moved by his words and thrilled that he appreciated their work. She expected many important breakthroughs were now on the horizon. It was like standing in a vast cavern with a single candle lighting her way. She sensed there was so much more to discover, and she vowed to figure out how to illuminate the entire area for all to see.

"Thank you, Karlmann. I wanted you to be among the first to see it."

"I would like to participate in the research with your team," he said eagerly.

"We'd be honored to have you."

Dierk added, "We're already working on additional devices. I plan to have one installed in your office so you can collaborate without having to cross the town ten times a day."

"Thank you." Karlmann chuckled. "I'm not as young as I like to think I am."

Jean escorted him to the exit of the manor house and arranged for a soldier to escort him back to the hospital. It was cold outside, but no longer snowing. Wrapped in his enormous fur coat, with a thick hat pulled low over his face, and a scarf wrapped tight around his neck, the old man still looked frail, and she silently wished him a safe journey home.

Bruno waited in her office when she returned. "How did mold test go?" he asked in his rapidly improving Obrioner.

She beamed. "Amazing! We're making almost as much progress as the Juggernaut teams."

"Do you have time to inspect the work?"

She nodded, grabbed her coat, and joined him in the hall. The enormous blacksmith towered over her as they walked toward the exit, and he insisted on walking half a step behind. She knew it was a sign of respect, something more people were insisting on around her. It was immensely annoying.

She wasn't nobility, no matter what titles Lord Eberhard bestowed upon her. Of course, Bruno insisted he was just giving her enough room so he didn't knock her into a wall by accident. He did have a point, so she didn't complain.

"Do you have the reports about the sound levels of the new thruster configurations on the Storm?" she asked. They'd rebuilt the original fast-flying craft, reshaping the body, adding newer, longer wings than they'd used on the Hawk. They'd reconfigured the thrusters to test whether it was possible to improve flight performance without losing any of the Storm's impressive speed.

Bruno nodded and shifted to Grandurian. Some of the technical details were still beyond his Obrioner skills. "Using clusters of smaller thrusters instead of the larger ones for liftoff, hovering, and landing is showing excellent performance and nearly a thirty percent reduction in wind noise. The larger thrusters still perform best for high-altitude, fast travel."

She frowned as she considered the report. "Not as good as I'd hoped. If they have to approach an enemy position at night, they'll still make too much noise."

"The team is still testing, but this was Verena's specialty."

Jean sighed. "I know. We need her. We need Hamish." She needed Hamish, felt his absence more every day. He and Verena possessed unrivaled intuitive brilliance which could accelerate so many of their research projects. Even more than that, she longed to fly with Hamish, feel his strong arms around her, and savor the incredible happiness she always felt in his presence.

"We'll keep working on it," Bruno promised.

She placed a hand on his arm. "I know. We'll get there, but I keep feeling like we don't have much time. I'll keep chewing on the problem. How do you reduce noise levels in your smithy? Or are there techniques used for insulating homes from storms that we might adapt for quieting flight noises?"

"That's a good question. Smithies are loud, but I'll ask Artur about insulation techniques and get back to you."

"Thanks."

They exited the manor house and headed across town. Jean breathed deep the cold, clear air, and enjoyed the picturesque town. She loved Grandurian architecture. The steeply pitched roofs included ornate gables, and the exposed timber design of some of the structures appealed to her. The brighter colors used for the doors, window shutters, and even some of the walls helped keep the town feeling festive, even in the depths of winter.

On the western outskirts of town, they entered one of the large Builder workshop barns. Most of the enormous main floor was filled with different teams, working in cramped open areas. They were surrounded by piles of materials, tables covered in designs, and racks of equipment and partially-completed mechanicals.

Jean loved the smell. As she ascended a ladder up to an observation catwalk twenty feet up the wall, she breathed deep the scent of fresh-cut lumber, hot steel, broken stone, and dozens of other scents that mixed together into the unique smell of Builder creativity. The area thrummed with energy, and she smiled as she surveyed the workroom, notebook in hand. From that vantage, it looked like a beehive of activity. Builders and craftsmen and workers swarmed in little vortexes of energy around each of their projects.

The framework of the Juggernaut was nearly complete, a complex skeleton of steel that would support the outer shell as well as house all of the weapons, thrusters, and other components being developed. When completed, the Juggernaut would span over twelve feet in diameter. With Hamish strapped into the middle, it would transform into a giant wrecking ball of destruction. She couldn't wait to see his face when he saw their progress.

Dierk arrived and rushed up to join her, looking excited. He held a small piece of obsidian in his hand, roughly carved into the shape of a Sentry tower. She recognized it as a piece that Gisela had been working on before she left for Althing.

Dierk held up the little sculpted stone, as if it were an incredible treasure, even though it was far from finished. Gisela had mentioned that she had done enough work on it to amplify the vortex found in that little piece of stone three or four times. That was impressive, but less than half of the magnification she would achieve with the finished product.

Dierk exclaimed, "I've discovered something amazing. I've been experimenting with quickening this obsidian."

"I'm surprised you're spending time with that."

Most of the other power stones created measurable, useful effects when quickened, but obsidian was a strange stone. It did not act like the others. When quickened, it did nothing.

Dierk said, "Most obsidian is still pretty useless, but this one, this one is a whole different matter. When I quicken this sculpted stone, I can sense other pieces of quickened obsidian in the vicinity. I almost missed it because we don't really use obsidian yet, but I noticed the effect when I was checking on the production of Karlmann's near-vision goggle. Somehow this allows me to link to the other quickened obsidian remotely."

That was fascinating and unexpected, but did not seem to represent anything useful, and unfortunately Jean did not have time for anything that wasn't useful.

Dierk continued. "What makes this find important is that when I place those other pieces of quickened obsidian next to other power stones, I can link to those power stones too, as if I was touching them."

"What?" Jean gasped, immediately grasping the profound ramifications of that discovery. Ideas began crowding in faster than she could jot them down in her notebook.

Builders could trigger incredible mechanicals, but only when they could touch the stones. Until now. "Dierk, this is amazing! We could remotely activate mechanicals!"

Dierk grinned. "It opens up so many possibilities."

Artur the carpenter scrambled up to the catwalk to join them. Jean wished he'd waited a few more minutes. He was interrupting their moment of discovery. But he too looked excited, so she asked, "What is it, Artur?"

He held up an iron-banded, wooden box and a small piece of stone. "I apologize for interrupting, Lady Jean, but these packages just arrived on the latest windrider. Sent from master Connor."

Jean eagerly took the box and opened it, wondering what Connor would have sent. She hadn't heard from him since they left for Althing. She'd expected them to be gone for a lot longer. Hopefully that meant Hamish would be returning soon.

She peered in one of the nine carefully tied pouches inside and gasped at the sight of the purplish powder. "Porphyry!"

Dierk looked as excited as he had about the obsidian discovery. "We need to test it." He stared at the little box eagerly, in a way that made Jean just a little nervous.

Artur held up a note. "The pilot said that's exactly what Connor directed."

"In Hamish's and Verena's initial testing with porphyry, it proved extremely dangerous. It triggered uncontrollable rage. We need to exercise extra precautions around that stone. I want it secured in our strongest vault."

Dierk closed the box and tucked it under his arm. "I'll take care of it."

Jean scanned the note. "Is that the rock that Connor picked up in Emmerich?"

"I assume so. It's the only other thing that came with the shipment."

Jean took the little rock and examined it "I don't recognize it, but Connor said in his note that Stuart thought it might have some kind of active properties."

She handed it to Dierk who took it distractedly. He looked eager to begin experimenting with the porphyry.

Dierk suddenly peered closer at the little stone. "This is a power stone, but not one like anything I've ever felt before."

"What is it?" Jean asked.

Dierk did not respond for a moment, eyes half closed, as he examined the little rock with his Builder senses. Sometimes Jean envied him that extra sense, but she chided herself for the thought. She didn't need all of everyone else's talents. He'd share what he learned soon enough.

After a moment his eyes widened and he said in a tone of wonder. "I may be mistaken, but I suspect this stone is the anti-obsidian stone we've been hunting."

6 2

KIDS DO THE DARNDEST THINGS

Verena felt it, felt her consciousness, as if from a great distance. An old friend, now strangely foreign after so much time away. Verena stirred.

A flick of her fingers, a twitch of one foot, a soft murmur escaping her lips. Those tiny movements felt like momentous victories after her long struggle up from the black depths of her mind.

For a long time, she hadn't expected to ever make it. She'd been lost in the labyrinth of her own mind, her thoughts muddy and unfocused, unable to reach consciousness. It was like she was sunk in a deep pool with her arms and legs tied, unable to claw toward the surface.

She'd heard distant voices, tried to call out to them, but lacked the ability to do so. Many people she loved had spoken to her. Although she couldn't retain most of the words, their sorrow, and their fading hope trickled down to her. She had begun to despair.

Mattias's voice eventually penetrated the drifting haze of her thoughts. His beautiful voice, which she had loved for so long, was like a lifeline to her heart and she clung to it. He spoke of love, of his confidence in her recovery, of the wonderful life they'd enjoy together, of his ambitions, and how their union would help them achieve political greatness.

Then Connor came, his voice like a distant light beyond the next range of hills. He couldn't match Mattias's angelic tones, but the sound of his voice made her heart sing. He spoke to her with love and hope so strong, it buoyed her spirits. She shouted at him, strove with all her might to reach him, but the pathway from where her consciousness paced, trapped like a caged animal, to the outside world was broken.

Connor had poured in rivers of healing and they had streamed across her mind like glittering rainbows in a darkling sky. It was beautiful, but untouchable.

When he left, she fell into even deeper despair. She wanted only to see him again, touch his face, feel his arms around her.

Her anger had fizzled out and she felt only sorrow and regret. He'd acted the fool, but perhaps she had too. She needed to return to him, to set things right.

When he returned again, his voice had sounded closer, at times almost like he spoke directly to her mind instead of her distant, numb ears. More healing power had slipped into her mind, and this time when she reached for it with all her strength, all her will to live, she had somehow touched that intangible warmth.

It was real! She'd never felt healing power as an energy that she could manipulate. She didn't understand how she could now, but she grasped it with all her might. He'd poured so much into her that although most of it eventually drained away, she managed to hold onto a little.

She began to build bridges.

That wondrous healing light spanned the gaps in her mind, mending broken pathways and lifting her slowly toward the surface. Each time he came, she grew stronger, and better utilized the vast quantities of healing that flowed through her mind.

She was nearly there. With a final focused effort, she blinked her eyes open for the first time.

Light dazzled her and she tried to turn her head away. It moved only a little, the muscles stiff from disuse. She managed a soft groan and tried to speak, but not even she could hear the shadow of a whisper that emerged.

She lay prone on a soft bed, covered to her chin in a thick, warm blanket that smelled of rose water. Her clothing was soft, caressing her skin under the comforter. She felt clean, despite her long sleep, and she took a long, slow breath, inhaling the scent of clover and indoor, winter flowers.

A shape bent over her, blocking the light and she blinked a couple of times to bring it into focus. It belonged to a mature woman she did not recognize. She wore a white Healer's robe, but scowled in a very non-Healer way. Her dark blue eyes were hard, her expression cold.

Hers was the face of a killer.

Verena tried to move, but the woman pressed down, pinning her under the thick blanket.

She spoke quietly, her voice surprisingly gentle. "You should have slipped away into oblivion. My orders were to allow you to die naturally, if possible. Death will hurt more this way, but I appreciate the chance to earn my reward after wasting so much time watching you sleep."

"Wait," Verena gasped, trying to get her muddy thoughts working, trying to grab for her satchel, but finding nothing but smooth sheets under her fingers.

The woman leaned harder over her, squeezing the breath from her lungs. Then she calmly placed a hand over Verena's mouth and nose, blocking her air.

"Good-bye, Builder. Dougal always wins."

Verena thrashed under the blankets. Her body was healthy, but her muscles responded only fitfully and she was too thoroughly pinned.

She tried to scream, but only a muffled moan escaped. The woman pressed harder, preventing her from twisting her head, even though she tried until the muscles of her neck threatened to tear.

This couldn't be happening! She'd fought so hard to awaken. She couldn't die now.

Connor! She shrieked the thought out of pure desperation as black spots began to dance in her eyes and she felt herself fading back to oblivion. Only this time, she would never awaken.

Something blurred past, so fast she couldn't register it. The false Healer staggered back from the bed with a grunt of pain and an angry curse.

Someone was pushing her.

Connor?

No. It was a boy. She blinked in confusion.

Nicklaus?

He pressed something to the assassin's chest and wind erupted from it. The woman, who was just reaching to grab Nicklaus, rocketed backward, her expression stunned. She flew through the door, arms and legs flailing behind and sailed across the sitting room beyond. She shattered a glass balcony door and whooshed over the railing.

Her legs caught the rail, tumbling her sideways, and she lost the quartzite, which flew away as she tumbled out of sight. A loud cry of pain echoed back up a moment later.

"Where are we?" Verena asked.

Nicklaus was staring after the woman, wide-eyed. "That's a long fall. I floated it once, and Connor and I made a snow slide, but that bad lady just fell." He gave her a grim smile. "Bad people get hurt sometimes."

Tears welled into her eyes and she struggled to push back the constricting blanket. "You saved my life, Nicklaus."

The outer door of the apartment burst open and Connor rushed in, wild-eyed, fist already raised to strike. "What's going on?"

Verena just stared, filled with joy. Their eyes met and she easily read his surprise and elation when he realized she was awake.

"Verena!" he shouted, rushing toward her.

Nicklaus stepped in the way and gave Connor a disgusted look. "No smooching until you catch that bad lady who was trying to kill her."

"What?" Connor exclaimed and a look of feral rage swept across his features.

Nicklaus pointed toward the shattered balcony. "She was only pretending to help."

With a shout of fury, Connor leaped across the room and plunged over the railing.

Things were moving so fast. Verena closed her eyes to try to ground herself. The air seemed too cold, the lights too bright. Voices still rang too loudly in her ears.

Nicklaus spoke close beside her. "Oh, no, Lady Verena. No sleeping. You've been napping for weeks. It's time to get up."

She blinked open her eyes in surprise. "That long?"

He nodded gravely. "You crashed your flyer and hit your head."

"I did, didn't I?" she said softly, frowning as the jumbled memories slowly oriented themselves properly.

"You probably shouldn't crash again," Nicklaus said with absolute sincerity.

She laughed softly, amazed that she felt whole, if a bit fuddled still. "I think that's an excellent plan."

Angry shouting echoed up from the courtyard outside, followed by a shriek of pain. It sounded like it came from the the assassin.

Nicklaus said, "I just had a lesson on interrogating prisoners instead of killing them. Sometimes that's more important, you know."

"This might be a good time to use that one."

Nicklaus leaned closer and said in a conspiratorial whisper. "I'm thinking Connor might have failed that lesson. Don't sleep any more. I want to fly with you."

Then he zipped away with wingrunner speed and leaped off the balcony shouting, "Connor, catch me!"

More people rushed into the room a moment later. A soft-spoken Healer with gentle, brown eyes that Verena instantly trusted, several soldiers, then Saskia.

"Oh, Verena! You're awake!" Saskia cried, flinging herself onto the bed beside her, weeping with joy. They shared a long hug, laughing and crying together.

"Wait till Mattias hears. He just returned from a successful mission to Althing," Saskia exclaimed, moving to get up.

Verena grabbed her hand. "Wait. Deal with that assassin. Once things calm down, I want to speak with Mattias and Connor together."

"Are you sure that's a good idea?" Saskia's expression made it clear she thought Verena was insane.

Verena nodded and sat up. The Healer immediately propped her with several pillows. "I couldn't wake up, but I heard them both. We all know what they want, and we need to settle the question once and for all."

"Verena, dear, you just woke up. Don't you think you need some time—"

"No. I had more than enough time trapped in here." She tapped the side of her head. "Please, Saskia. Do this for me."

"All right." She squeezed Verena's hand one more time, eyes brimming with emotion.

After she left, the Healer shooed everyone out of the bedroom. After checking Verena thoroughly and forcing her to eat a bowl of chicken broth with soft bread, she allowed Verena to rise and dress. The only outfit on hand was a soft, green woolen dress.

"Where's my satchel?" Verena demanded as she turned to a nearby mirror. Then she exclaimed, "Who dyed my hair?"

It was midnight black, and trimmed shorter than she liked. It barely reached her shoulders and hung in bouncy black waves around her head. The effect was honestly quite striking, but she didn't like someone making decisions about her hair.

The Healer said, "The color changed on its own while you slept. We haven't yet determined why."

Verena frowned, fingering a lock. It felt silkier than before. "I've never heard of such a thing."

"I've heard of hair graying or falling out after severe trauma, but never changing color to black. It is very possible it will revert back over time."

"Well, if that's the worse scar I have to bear, it's an easy one to handle," Verena said.

Other than her hair, she looked well rested and her body felt strong. She remembered most of what happened at Alasdair, but her memory ended abruptly in a collision with the ground. She asked again, "My satchel?"

"That old thing?" the Healer asked with a look of disapproval. "I sent it to be laundered last week."

"Send someone for it, please." The woman turned to leave but Verena asked, "And can you tell me . . . where are we?"

63

LIFE ADVICE FROM A GRUMPY OLD LADY

"A re you ready, my dear? We can't afford to be late," High Lord Dougal called.

Shona emerged from her bedroom, dressed in a fine blue-and-gold gown. It didn't exactly match her wide-brimmed hat and ridiculous purple eoin feather, but then no one's hat really matched. Her father was resplendent in a rich green jacket over a blue doublet. He beckoned her urgently toward the door.

Shona said, "I'm still amazed she's holding court again so soon."

Her father scowled. "I still can't believe she survived."

"Why did you save her then?" Shona demanded. That was still easily the stupidest thing her father had ever done. Usually he was the most clever man in the realm, but service to the queen had changed him.

She still barely believed she'd seen Hamish and Aifric in the throne room. Aifric was supposed to be dead, and Hamish was supposed to be in Granadure with Connor. Mysteries multiplied around everyone who associated with Connor faster than linn at a Sogail feast. She didn't know the other assassins, but they'd struck with such overwhelming, brutal ferocity that she still shuddered at the memory.

Her father sighed. "I thought she was done for. Killing that foul assassin was logical. I'd avenge her death, prove my courage, and could take the throne with little opposition. Even Harley would have to respect my actions. She's more a follower than a leader. We were so close!"

Shona regarded him with concern. "Father, you can't allow yourself to think any of that around her. If she reads your ambition, she'll kill you."

Dougal shook his head. "No, Shona. She's read deep enough. She knows my ambition and she counts on it. I'm motivated to serve her because of what she can do for me. She might have survived against all odds, but my actions were still worthy. She'll reward me for them.

Perhaps we can arrange to rule one of the conquered lands under her direction once the continent is again brought back under her control."

"If there's anything left."

He gave her an encouraging smile. "Don't give in to despair like so many weak-willed fools have done. The queen's tactics may seem brutal now, but she gets things done. Once opposition is rooted out and peace enforced upon everyone, she'll need rulers to support her reign. We are perfectly positioned to step into those roles."

Shona didn't respond as they walked the wide hallway that led toward the central palace and the throne room stairs. She'd long dreamed of ruling. She'd even shared that dream with Connor. She would be good at it. Now she was starting to wonder if the price required to obtain that power might be so high she wouldn't recognize herself after paying it.

What choice did she have?

At the moment, none. She schooled her features and her mind the way she had trained herself to do in recent days. The guard at the throne room doors was doubled and they scanned everyone who entered with far more attention than before.

It was laughable, really. The assassins had failed. Who else would attempt something so rash and daring? Word had spread of the queen's ghastly injuries, as well as her miraculous healing. She'd reattached severed limbs, reconnected her legs to her torso, and stood upon her own feet within minutes of her injuries.

Covered in blood and gore, she'd raged as she inspected the fallen assassins and confirmed they were Mhortair. She'd ordered Turriff to collect their power stones, then she'd incinerated their corpses and dismissed everyone from the throne room.

Now as Shona followed her father back inside, she felt a little nervous about what they'd find.

The throne room looked immaculate, as if nothing had happened. The broken floor was perfectly repaired, the bloodstains gone, and the windows blocking the waterfall restored.

Queen Dreokt sat on her throne in a silver-and-gold gown, her hair intricately braided. She looked regal, and furious. She scowled at the gathering lords and ladies, most of whom looked terrified. Few volunteered to attend the queen, but none dared fail to appear when ordered.

Shona and her father took their regular places to the queen's right. Ailsa was already there, quietly waiting to serve, to advise, and to provide the power stones the queen insisted on receiving from her hand alone. Dougal bowed low, while Shona curtsied.

"I am delighted and amazed to see you in such good health," Dougal said in his rich, sonorous voice.

Queen Dreokt waved away the compliment. "Save the platitudes, Dougal. I'm not in the mood."

He bowed again, his expression locked into a well-practiced look of subservient eagerness.

The queen huffed impatiently. "Where is Harley?"

"Here, my queen." Harley marched into the room, looking rough and dangerous in a fur-lined jacket, her black hair windblown as if she'd just come in from the cold.

"Well?" Queen Dreokt demanded.

"No sign of wreckage at the base of the cliff. I fear the last two escaped."

The queen's scowl deepened. "Builders here in my throne room. I shall not tolerate such betrayal."

She seemed more upset about the presence of a Builder than in getting quartered and nearly killed by a trio of deadly Mhortair.

"Shona, you know that Builder?"

"Yes—" Her words cut off as the queen thrust her thoughts into Shona's mind with the force of a sledgehammer.

Shona rocked back with a groan, clutching her temples as the queen fished through her mind for the memories that rose in response to the question. It took only a moment, but Shona felt nauseous by the time the queen finished. The woman had never brutalized her mind like that before and it was a terrifying experience that left her feeling deeply violated.

Queen Dreokt surprised Shona by laughing, as if suddenly delighted. "He's such a dear friend of the boy, Connor. Ha! Justice will feel so exquisite on the day his disgusting life is snuffed out."

High Lord Dougal spared a concerned look for Shona then offered, "My liege, might I suggest the Mhortair represent a far more pressing danger."

"You know less than half of what you think you do. The Builders must be crushed. I've set in motion the pathway to their destruction, but perhaps I must accelerate my plans." She paused for a moment, then shouted, "Turriff, fetch me Captain Aonghus."

As the empty-minded former king scurried off to do her bidding, she glared at Harley and added, "And the beggared offspring of Mhortair? How dare they? I gave them purpose, but they've fallen so far." She rose, hands clenched into fists. "And they dare strike at me and use the very secrets I taught them? No. It shall not stand. I shall wipe them from the world."

Harley grimaced and muttered, "What a waste."

Dougal said, "Our intelligence suggests their lair resides somewhere in Ravinder, but we're not sure exactly where."

"I'll find it," Queen Dreokt promised. "Marshal all available forces to Raineach. I'll march against Maninder and raze it to the ground. That will draw them out. Or I'll rip the secret from someone's mind. Dougal, I want an army."

Dougal started listing off available forces, but Harley cut in. "My queen, there's another matter that we must also consider."

"Why do you interrupt my fun?" the queen asked in a suddenly petulant little girl voice. Her abrupt shifts still startled Shona, despite how many she'd seen.

Harley took it in stride. "Just this morning I received reports of an uprising in Merkland."

"What?" Dougal exclaimed. With his extensive spy network, he usually prided himself on learning all important news first.

Shona noted with interest that Ailsa didn't look terribly surprised.

"Apparently your commanding general, Rory, has allied with Granadure. He declared patronage a lie, unclaimed a ruse, and Queen Dreokt the greatest threat to Obrion. Half the army stationed there has thrown in with him. They forced out the remaining loyal troops, who are marching south toward Crann."

"Revolt? Among your people?" Queen Dreokt rounded on Dougal in a fury, fires burning in her eyes.

For the first time in his life, Shona's father stammered, struggling to find the words. He held up a placating hand. "I had no idea. I've always trusted Rory."

The queen's fury evaporated as quickly as it arose. She gave Dougal a compassionate smile. "I know exactly how you feel. My own son betrayed me." Then her fury returned in a flood and she shrieked, "And all who dare defy me must die!"

"Of course. Please grant me leave to deal with the insurrection. I promise to root out and destroy all who defy your rule," Dougal said quickly.

Shona was glad she didn't have to speak. She was still reeling with the news. Rory a revolutionary? The idea stunned her. He was the epitome of Obrioner loyalty. He was one of the rocks upon which Dougal's army rested. If Rory was breaking away, who could they trust?

Queen Dreokt settled back into her throne, actually looking concerned. "You realize my son will likely choose to meddle."

"That is likely," Dougal admitted.

The queen leaned forward a little, her voice softening. "You know you cannot beat him, that he will kill you when you two meet again."

Dougal's expression hardened and he said simply, "He killed my wife."

The queen nodded. "I saw the memory. Kilian is a troublesome youth, but your wife was an idiot. He was right to put her down. You two were meddling in your own destruction."

Dougal's face flushed with anger, but he managed to say in an almost respectful tone, "As you say, my queen."

She sighed. "Dougal, I see greatness in you, but you've allowed that cankered memory to define your life. If I let you face him, my son will kill you."

Shona felt surprisingly moved by the queen's compassion. She knew the depth of her father's anguish for the loss of his first wife. It had haunted him all her life, had made it impossible for him to truly love Shona's mother.

He hesitated for a second before spreading his hands in a helpless gesture. "I cannot abandon my realm to rebels and traitors, my queen. I have to try."

She clapped her hands together, suddenly enthusiastic. "Good for you, Dougal! Yes, you must fight to protect what is yours. And I am going to give you the tools to face my son on equal terms."

"What tools?" he dared ask, desperate longing in his voice.

"I will share the secret with you once we are alone, and you must swear to keep it secret from all others on pain of death. It would be a most gruesome death too."

"I swear," he said eagerly.

Shona wondered what secret could give him an advantage against Kilian. The ancient Dawnus was so powerful, she doubted anyone but the queen herself could face him with any real confidence in victory.

The queen's expression turned serious. "See that you do not waste the boon I will grant you. You've proven yourself once, but you must pass this test to find stability of heart to serve me at your best. Return to me victorious and you will be rewarded beyond even your impressive ambitions. Take the army from Crann and those troops loyal to me now fleeing Merkland. Take the city and execute all who breathe out threats against my rule."

Dougal bowed low again. The queen glanced at Shona. "Go with your father. See how law and order are established. If you prove yourself, I'll grant you the boon of a tertiary affinity."

Shona stammered, "Thank you!" She'd long dreamed of a tertiary power. Now it was almost within her grasp.

All she had to do was help her father destroy their home and kill a man she'd looked up to all her life.

"Harley, you go with them."

"I'd rather kill Mhortair."

The queen leaped to her feet, spitting with fury. "Don't second guess my orders!"

Harley didn't look concerned. She made an attempt at a curtsy. "Sorry, my liege, but do you really need me to go spank that rabble?"

The queen sat and spoke in a fierce whisper. "You will support Dougal in his attempt to retake the city and destroy my irksome son."

"Kilian does need dealing with," she said softly, eyes lighting with anticipation.

The queen waved them away. "Go. Do my bidding." Her voice turned deadly serious. "Do not fail me like you did with Evander. It irks me to no end that we have yet to discover his hiding place."

For the first time, Harley betrayed a hint of nervousness. Not even she was immune to the queen's wrath. "I swear my life to the task."

The queen's grim look evaporated and she grinned and rushed off the dais to give Harley a warm hug. "Take care, my dear. Be safe, and mind the cold. It's winter out, after all."

"Thank you, Your Majesty. I will."

The queen waved everyone else away, ending the audience early.

"I know he's infatuated with the Grandurian wench, but I never imagined Rory could be such a legendary fool," Dougal hissed as the rest of the assembly headed for the door.

"Are you really going to kill him?" Shona asked. Somehow she hoped they could save Rory. He'd led the team to rescue her in Alasdair. He was almost like an uncle to her and the thought of having to kill him nauseated her more than she'd ever admit.

Her father snapped, "Of course. He's done this to himself, Shona. I'll make it quick, though. After all, he's given us the perfect opportunity to prove ourselves. With this victory and with Kilian destroyed, nothing can stop us!"

Assuming the queen dug Evander up from wherever he was hiding and destroyed him too. Or mind-wiped him. Somehow, Shona could not imagine Evander as a mindless slave. A martyr, yes, but not a slave.

How many people they cared about would they need to sacrifice to climb the ladder of their ambition?

"I'll find you soon," he said, pushing her toward the door and turning expectantly back toward the queen. Shona was tempted to linger, but wondered if that would trigger the queen's volatile temper.

The throne room had emptied remarkably fast and she found herself alone in one of the stairways leading down to the central palace. She descended slowly, mind whirling.

Ailsa caught up with her a moment later, looking grave. "I imagine you must be worrying for all those you care about in Merkland."

Shona felt a little embarrassed. She hadn't really thought much about the people whose lives and homes were now in danger. She'd been wondering if Connor was somehow involved in Rory's change of heart and if he would dare stand against Harley and the army about to march north to crush the rebellion.

"Do you know where Connor is?"

"You and I both know he'll end up in the middle of whatever ends up happening."

"That's what I'm afraid of. He's such a fool! They all are. Can't they see that they can't fight her?"

"Not alone, they can't."

"What do you mean?"

"You're a bright girl, Shona. One of the brightest I know. Today you stand on the cusp of the future, with perhaps your best opportunity to decide your fate and that of many others."

"How?" Shona's voice fell to a whisper and she glanced around fearfully. "Even thinking the questions I want to ask could get me killed."

Ailsa winked. "Every path is overgrown with risk these days, but you already see that surrender to evil and tyranny is not the only answer."

"It is if I want to survive."

"Is it, though?" Ailsa held her gaze. "As you pointed out, no one can stop the queen alone, but that is not the choice you face. Perhaps the right group working together could defeat her."

Shona found herself wanting to believe that. She cast another worried glance down the stairway. They would not remain alone for long.

Ailsa added, "Perhaps they will fail, but perhaps with the right help, they might just succeed. The question you have to ask yourself is do you prefer surrendering to slavery until the day the queen grows tired of you and executes you out of hand? Or reshapes you, body and mind, into what she considers more worthy on that particular day? Or do you prefer to stand for Obrion and liberty while it's still possible?"

Shona opened her mouth to speak, but wasn't sure what she intended to say. She needed time to think. The faint hope of freedom from the insane queen's rule that Ailsa suggested tempted her mightily, but could she risk everything chasing such a flimsy dream?

On the other hand, if she steeled herself to help her father destroy those who dared fight for freedom, if she killed people she cared for, she would win the coveted tertiary affinity. They might die anyway, so perhaps their deaths wouldn't really be her responsibility . . .

She had long since accepted the potential need to sacrifice many to bring peace and prosperity to the nation and even the continent. There were always those who fought to thwart progress, but always in the past those sacrifices were made by political enemies and nameless individuals she didn't know and didn't care about. Now, as she faced the true cost of her ambitions, doubts began creeping in like the canker of rust spreading over bright steel.

Ailsa patted her hand and gave her an encouraging smile. "I don't need to know your choice. You do. Consider my words and do not hesitate when the moment comes. You'll know it, and I doubt you'll get a second chance."

She turned to leave, but Shona grabbed her arm.

"What else are you involved in, Ailsa?"

"I am proud of my sculpting work," Ailsa said with a smile, her green eyes glowing with good humor, and Shona suspected with many secrets.

"But that is not the full picture of who you are." Shona leaned closer, realizing that Ailsa was perhaps an even more powerful ally than she had suspected. "How much have you told Connor?"

Ailsa concealed her surprise well, but Shona caught a hint of it. "You are indeed a clever girl," Ailsa said approvingly.

"When I see you again, we have much to talk about."

"We might indeed."

"Tell Connor to stay away. I don't want him hurt."

Ailsa chuckled. "Since when does Connor do anything any of us tell him to?"

Shona frowned. She had a good point.

Ailsa added, "But I will warn him and the others of the danger. Be careful, Lady Shona, and be sure to look deep and see clear in the days to come."

64

WHEN YOU CAN'T GO BACK, GO FORWARD BOLDLY

Hamish lounged on a couch in Lord Dougal's personal study, high atop one of the tallest towers above Merkland's enormous palace. For the first time in the last couple of days, he felt almost himself again. He patted his stomach contentedly. "I like eating like a high Lord. The cooks in the palace are exceptional."

"Well you've eaten enough to keep them all busy," Rory said. He sat in an overstuffed chair closer to the fire and glanced at the silver tray cluttered with empty dishes on the little table beside Hamish's couch.

Ivor, who had taken high Lord Dougal's tall, padded leather chair behind his desk said, "I'm still amazed you survived."

Aifric, who sat in another comfortable chair near Rory, a glass of mulled wine clutched in her hands said, "I barely believe it myself."

The miraculous effects of activated pumice still amazed Hamish. Aifric had seemed reluctant to share the secret with anyone else, but Hamish had insisted. If they were going to have any chance against the queen, they needed to stop keeping so many secrets from each other.

Hamish extracted a little piece of the porous stone and tossed it to Ivor. "Quickening it changed everything. We flew right through that crazy storm, but it couldn't quite touch us. It was almost like we had shifted into a different piece of sky."

"Is that how it is when you tap pumice as a Petralist?" Ivor asked.

"Not really. Elemental powers seem to evaporate when they make contact, almost like they get drained away."

Hamish said, "I definitely need to do some serious testing with this thing. I can't wait to get back to Faulenrost. Jean will be thrilled." He couldn't wait to see the look on her face.

Rory looked grim. "Despite her injuries, it sounds like the queen will recover. She'll be furious."

Hamish grimaced. "I'm worried she'll come after us, or send Harley."

Ivor leaned back in Dougal's big chair, his expression thoughtful. "It's definitely a risk, but I suspect she'll be more focused on exacting revenge against the Mhortair. Hopefully she'll ignore us for a while."

Aifric said, "That's what I'm afraid of. I need to return to my people and warn them."

Hamish wanted to help her, was tempted to offer to fly her into Ravinder. He would love to get a glimpse at the Mhortair's secret base, but he could not take the risk that they would react badly to his presence. He had learned too much and needed to talk with Jean, Connor, and Kilian.

"We'll help you in every way we can. In fact, we'd like to establish communications with your people to make it easier to help each other out," Ivor said.

They were already hard at work making plans with contacts all across the kingdom. From what Hamish had seen so far, their network was amazingly extensive.

The door to the office opened and Tomas stepped inside, grinning. "General, she's here."

Rory leaped to his feet, looking nervous and excited at the same time. Ivor rose and headed for the door.

It flew wide before he reached it and Anika leaped through, leading with her fist. Ivor stumbled aside, barely avoiding getting trampled. Already tapping granite, her body transformed into perfectly-sculpted lines, Anika sped across the room to Rory and punched him right off his feet.

Rory rebounded from the ground, laughing like a fool. He slipped inside her next punch, wrapped his arms around her torso, and pulled her tight. They embraced in a passionate kiss, holding it long enough that even Hamish started feeling uncomfortable.

When they finally broke for air, grinning like idiots, Rory laughed. "It's about time. I thought you were waiting until spring time."

Anika took an angry step back, but her retort was cut short by Rory's fist. He seemed to have expected her to move that way because he caught her under the chin with a fierce uppercut that lifted her off her feet and smashed her head through the ceiling.

She dropped to the ground and the two pummeled each other with fierce passion, scattering the rest of them and smashing most of the furniture in the room.

Ivor finally interceded by wrapping both of their heads in ice. They smashed their heads together to break the ice, but did not resume their playful, destructive bashing.

"May I suggest that you pick a less important room to trash?" Ivor asked with a grin.

The two of them looked ridiculously pleased with themselves, but settled for holding hands instead of punching. Anika glanced around the room and noticed the rest of them for the first time.

Hamish waved. "No need to crush my skull. I'm only a casual friend."

Anika laughed and said in Grandurian, "It's good to see you, Builder. Might need your help finding Erich. He was supposed to be stationed at Badurach, but we couldn't find him when we flew in."

"We?"

Captain Ilse and her husband Lukas stepped into the room over the shattered remains of the door. "I'm assuming it's safe to enter now." They both saluted to Ivor and then to Rory. Ilse gave Rory an approving smile. "Congratulations on your bold move, general. We've been ordered with a full company of Crushers to assist you with the revolution."

Rory turned back to Anika and took both of her hands in his. "We'll get to that business soon enough. But there are more important things to deal with first."

Looking nervous again, he took a deep breath, then continued in a rush. "Anika, if I'm throwing caution to the wind, declaring revolution against the dread queen, rising up against everything I was taught all my life, I can't do it alone. I need you by my side."

He sank to one knee and finished in a rush, nearly choking on the words. "Will you marry me?"

Anika gasped, color rising in her cheeks. Then her smile ignited like a max-tapped Solas, growing so wide they were going to need a bigger door to get her out of the tower.

She started to nod, but then her expression fell and she looked crestfallen. "Mine capitan, in Granadure we no make question like this. Brother must approve."

"I've already dueled with Erich, remember?"

She nodded but still looked sad. "Must ask parents. They are many far."

That was right. Hamish had forgotten all about that tradition. Rory's audacity, bravery, and suicidal infatuation had eclipsed any kind of normal thinking. In Granadure it was considered extremely bad for a bride to accept a marriage proposal before her parents gave permission.

Instead of looking upset by the challenge, Rory rose and smiled. "In that case, don't you think we should invite them in to hear what they say?"

Ivor moved around to an inner door that led to another room and opened it. An elderly couple, both short and wizened, stepped into the room hand in hand, grinning widely. Erich followed them, towering over the aged couple.

Anika gasped, her hands coming to her face. "Mother? Father? How?"

Rory looked immensely pleased with himself. "Ivor was familiar with your customs, and he was kind enough to enlist Erich's aid in fetching your parents. They just arrived last night."

Anika laughed and rushed to hug her parents. Hamish was immensely impressed. If Rory kept thinking that cleverly, he might just survive the first month of marriage to the deadly Grandurian woman.

Anika's parents hugged her excitedly and spoke in rapid Grandurian. They were both elderly, but still spry. Her father's hair was mostly white, his face weathered, but his blue eyes sparkled with joy. Her mother was a petite woman, with long, silvery hair that she styled in loose curls. They both dressed well, like wealthy merchants or minor nobility.

Her mother passed her a delicate little glass bottle with a painted label that looked like some kind of flower. "We brought some of your best perfume, just in case you've run out."

She accepted the bottle with obvious pride.

Hamish approached, studying the perfume. "You like to buy perfume?"

Anika's mother shook her head. "No. My daughter designed this perfume. It is a best seller across all Granadure."

"Really?" He struggled to picture Anika doing anything with flowers other than crushing them. Then again, wasn't perfume made from crushing flowers?

Anika flushed and handed the bottle back to her mother. "Keep an eye on this for me. I don't want to break it."

She then turned to Hamish and added, "I wasn't always part of Ilse's team."

He tried to ask another question, but she made a shushing gesture. "Now's not the time. Please translate so my Rory can understand our conversation."

"I'd be honored."

Anika's mother said, "Erich explained the situation with this handsome general, but are you sure you want to marry a southern barbarian?"

Anika laughed and assured them she did. Her parents did not look surprised. No doubt they had grilled Erich already about the strange relationship. Together they turned to Rory and bowed over his hands.

Erich translated this time. "We give blessing to union. Is very strange, but eldest son swears you are man of strength and honor, and daughter loves many deep affection. Is only way to win this precious girl. Cherish and keep each other safe."

Hamish nearly laughed at that last. Didn't they know Anika? Hadn't they heard the exuberant greeting and seen the smashed furniture?

Anika hugged her parents again, still blushing and breaking into wide grins that she seemed to be trying unsuccessfully to control. At the same time, she looked close to panic.

She faced Rory, who looked eager for a response. "I have much sorry, but must needs special dress." She gestured at the plates and straps of her leather battle armor. "No can accept in this."

"Nay, lass," Rory said, gently taking her hands again. "You look most beautiful dressed as a warrior maiden, with battle lust in your eyes. I prefer you answer me exactly how you are."

Her blush deepened and her hands gripped Rory's tight. Her smile grew radiant and she exclaimed, "Then I accept!"

Rory looked like he could not believe it, and Hamish was right there with him. Starting a revolution was not enough for the general. He needed to risk his life in a far more intimate way. Hamish wished them luck.

The happy couple embraced passionately again. Hamish tensed and prepared to duck when they launched back into another lover's bash fight.

They didn't.

When they finally broke the kiss a long, long time later, Rory swelled with granite power and threw a punch. Anika grabbed his hand in both of hers and just held on, laughing.

"No, mine Rory. We no must fight. I accept. I surrender."

He looked thunderstruck. "Really?"

She laughed again, looking like a happy girl. Well, an extremely deadly happy girl. "In Granadure, battle maidens must fight many strong to show her man she is strong and no will surrender ever to another. But accept mean we no have to fight anymore."

"Oh. That's great." He tried to look enthusiastic about the abrupt change in their relationship, but wasn't entirely convincing.

Anika winked then. "But now we can train together every day!"

She punched him in the chin.

Ilse looked close to tears, and she clutched Lukas's hand in far too ladylike a fashion. Anika's parents looked so proud they might burst, and Erich look resigned.

Laughing, Rory rose and reached for Dougal's desk.

Ivor shouted, "Oh, no you don't. You two go practice outside."

"But—" They both cried together, then looked at each other and laughed.

Ivor groaned. "You're making me positively nauseous. In a good way. If that is possible. Enjoy yourselves."

Then a wave of water blasted in through the smashed doorway and swept them both out the window. They laughed all the way down the outside of the tower, already pummeling each other with unrestrained enthusiasm.

Hamish lost sight of them after Rory threw Anika through the wall of a smithy. He charged in after her, and by the sounds of it, they started fighting with all the metal implements in there. Within seconds, hammers, tongs, and an entire oxen yoke harness burst out through the walls. That building was doomed.

Erich moped by the window nearby, with his parents comforting him.

"She is a battle maiden, son. You can't imagine she'll quit the company and settle down to the life of a housewife," His mother was saying. "Look at how they beat on each other. I've never seen her happier."

"I need to hit something," Erich said.

When Hamish translated that, Tomas and Cameron perked up immediately. They'd drifted over to Dougal's private stash of expensive liquor to celebrate the engagement, but Cameron chortled, "I've got just the thing. To celebrate the insanity, eh, engagement let's host a general bash fight between the Fast Rollers and the Crushers."

Tomas added, "Since we've got to start working together, there's no better time to really take the measure of each other."

Erich loved the idea, and neither Ilse nor Lukas seemed inclined to get in the way. The trio trooped off together, already singing a loud battle song together.

Hamish watched them go, wondering if any of Merkland would survive the night. Luckily Ilse ordered them all to fight in the open squares and they more or less obeyed.

Granite powder flowed like wine that night and citizens cowed in their homes while elite warriors beat on each other, singing the most boisterous battle songs they knew while Rory and Anika proved to the world that they were meant to be together.

The festivities eventually spread through the entire city. Everyone seemed eager for something to celebrate. Hamish wasn't sure if the magnitude of signing up for a revolution against Queen Dreokt and High Lord Dougal had started settling over them, or if they just admired Rory's courage. Either way, few people got much sleep.

Late the next morning he was finishing a large breakfast in the main hall, which was still remarkably intact and very empty. Too many people had stayed up too late and were sleeping in.

A tired-looking Strider jogged into the hall and glanced around. He spotted Hamish and stumbled over, looking on the verge of collapse. Hamish gestured him to a seat and pushed the last two sausages in his direction. The man grabbed one gratefully and saluted with it, then gobbled it down in one bite.

After downing half a pitcher of juice he asked, "What's the celebration for?"

"General Rory got engaged."

"To that scary Grandurian woman?"

"The same."

The Strider saluted again, with the pitcher this time, and took another long drag. "Everyone says he's the bravest man in Obrion."

Hamish chuckled and decided not to tell the man he'd heard that joke seven hundred times during the last night. Instead he asked, "How is it that you don't know anything about it?"

The man pulled from inside his jerkin a scroll wrapped in waterproof oilskin. "Important message for the general."

"I doubt he'll be in any condition to read it any time soon."

"I figured as much, that's why I'm handing it to you."

"I don't actually have any official rank here."

"I know, but I recognize you, Builder. This news needs to reach Granadure too, and I hear you're the man who can do that."

So Hamish unwrapped the scroll. It was from Ailsa, and as he scanned the contents, his good humor evaporated.

He found Ivor sleeping under High Lord Dougal's desk up in his tower, and kicked him awake.

"What makes you so mean in the morning?" Ivor grumbled as he sat up and rubbed his eyes.

Hamish pushed the scroll in front of him. "You need to read this. Celebration is over. Harley is bringing an army to crash the wedding."

THERE CAN BE ONLY ONE

Connor eagerly pushed open the door and slipped into Saskia's personal library. The note Saskia had sent to him had suggested Verena was finally ready to see him. He'd been so anxious, he'd barely resisted the urge to storm her rooms by force. But she'd sent word that she needed some time before accepting visitors.

If only he'd lingered a few extra seconds when he first arrived. The memory of her sitting upright, conscious, and happy to see him still filled him with exultant joy. He couldn't imagine not going after the assassin who had dared assault her, though.

When he had leaped over the balcony after the assassin, he had landed on the woman as she tried to rise in the snowy courtyard. Connor had not bothered tapping one of his inconsistent tertiary powers, but had simply attacked with fury so deep and raw, it made the rampager rage seem flighty.

To think Abigail had been so diligent in watching over Verena only to ensure she never woke up. He shuddered to think of the many hours Abigail had spent alone near Verena. She could have ended her life and no one would have doubted that Verena simply succumbed to her injuries. That betrayal of trust fueled his rage even hotter. He'd been tapping basalt at the time, and in his rage he had remembered the time that Lorcc punched a Blade in one of the student battles, hitting him so fast the man could not fall to the ground fast enough.

Connor had actually managed to frack his upper arms. He had not even known that was possible, but all of a sudden his hands were striking the pretend Healer so fast they blurred. Connor didn't usually like hitting women, but he'd felt no hesitation whatsoever as he beat down Abigail.

He'd broken every one of his fingers before he could stop himself. That just made him angrier and he kicked her several times in the ribs, breaking most of them. He would have surely killed her if not for Nicklaus's suicidal leap off the balcony.

He'd reluctantly left the bloody and unconscious Abigail with officials of the citadel guard, but hadn't been allowed to see Verena again until now. So he pushed through the doorway, already grinning, imagining her there, moving to greet him.

It was not Verena who waited on the far end of the room, standing in front of the fireplace.

It was Mattias.

Connor frowned and crossed the room. "Where's Verena?"

If Mattias thought he could play silly games and keep Connor from seeing her, Connor would find out if Mattias knew how to fly.

Mattias frowned, looking just as impatient as Connor felt. "I was informed that she is completing a series of tests to verify she is of sound mind after her long sleep. She has asked that we both go in to see her together."

"Why would she do that?"

"As if I've ever understood why Verena does anything," Mattias said with a sigh. He paced away before turning. "Don't forget our deal, Connor. Verena appears to be fully recovered and healthy, but she's been through great trauma. She doesn't need—"

Connor interrupted him impatiently. Mattias seemed to like that angelic voice of his far too much. "I know. I'll honor our agreement as long as you do. Let Verena choose who she wants to be with. You couldn't force her to accept someone she doesn't want anyway."

He almost wished Mattias would try it, and imagined some of the different mechanicals that Verena might employ to remind Mattias that she had a mind of her own. Most of the ones he considered resulted in several of those beautiful, glowing teeth getting knocked out.

Then he remembered Mattias leaning over Verena while clinging to the back of the Swift, kissing her on the lips. Verena had not beaten him senseless that time.

He tried to drive that memory from his mind, but it clung to his thoughts like a leech. Thankfully the outer door opened and Nicklaus trotted inside. He waved enthusiastically when he saw the two of them standing near the fire and rushed over.

"Connor, is now a good time for you to teach me how to punch someone so fast?" Nicklaus asked excitedly.

"Only if Mattias volunteers to be the punching dummy," Connor said with a straight face.

Mattias glared at Connor. "Don't be stupid."

Nicklaus looked dejected. "Come on, Mattias. It won't hurt for too long. I bet Connor would even heal you afterward."

Connor grinned as Mattias tried to stammer an excuse that would make sense to the disappointed six-year-old. "Come on, Mattias. Don't disappoint Nicklaus. You're a better friend than that."

For a second, Connor dared to hope that Mattias might actually give in to Nicklaus's pleading, but Mattias said, "I have a better idea. After I speak with Verena, I could go find that knife I promised you."

Nicklaus immediately forgot about learning to frack punch. "That's right! You promised. If I had a knife, I could have stabbed that mean lady."

Promising that little boy a knife was a singularly bad idea. Connor said, "You did a wonderful job, Nicklaus. I need to find out what that assassin said when they interrogate her, so I'm glad you didn't stab her."

Nicklaus nodded, but suddenly looked worried. "Mother said I shouldn't hate people, but I hate that bad lady."

Connor dropped to one knee and gave him a quick hug. "It's all right, Nicklaus. I bet even your mother will hate her."

The door opened again and one of Saskia's handmaidens entered. "Lady Saskia asked me to summon you to her study. Lady Verena's ready for visits now."

Connor hurried for the door with Mattias close beside. They nearly trampled the handmaiden at the door, neither of them willing to cede the opening to the other. She sensed the danger just in time and backpedaled into the hallway, hurrying back toward lady Saskia's study, just barely keeping ahead of them. Connor was tempted to break into a run, but no doubt Mattias would do the same thing. Verena had asked for both of them to come in together, so unfortunately that's what they were going to do.

Saskia's study was the same vaulted room where Connor had first met her. Mattias managed to slip through the doorway first, only because Connor refrained from punching him in the back of the neck.

Connor stopped in the doorway and stared.

Verena sat in an overstuffed chair, drawn up close to the crackling fire on the opposite side of the room, near the tall window trimmed in colorful stained-glass. She was dressed in a burgundy dress that made her look elegant, noble, but somehow vulnerable all at the same time.

Connor had grown used to seeing her in her fantastic, custom battle armor. Her hair hung in gentle black waves that seemed to caress her face, and her lips were curled back in that familiar little smile that he loved so much.

Seeing her sitting upright, smiling, alert, and apparently herself again filled Connor with unrivaled joy. For a moment he could not move, could not hope to speak, but tried to fix every particle of that moment into his mind to remember forever.

Then Nicklaus poked him in the back. "Get out of the way Connor. You're blocking the door. Saskia said she would order some cake for us. Do you see it?"

Connor shifted to the side to let Nicklaus race into the room. The little boy gave a casual wave to Saskia, who stood near the mantel.

Connor followed him farther into the room, but by that time Mattias had already reached Verena. She rose to greet him, but looked a little unsteady on her feet. She extended a hand toward him, but he ignored it and wrapped her in a tender hug.

He leaned down to kiss her, clearly aiming for her lips, his teeth already glowing. She turned her head so that he kissed her cheek instead, and she gave him a warm hug.

The sight of the two of them embracing terrified and enraged Connor all at the same time.

"Verena, you look wonderful," Mattias said, pulling back enough to hold her at arm's length.

"I feel remarkably well. I'm a little shaky still, but everything seems to work."

He embraced her again, and she let him, but then pushed him away and gestured toward a seat to her left side. He instead took the one to her right, pulling it close beside hers.

She then turned toward Connor and gave him that special smile that he still firmly believed belonged only to him, and perhaps to her favorite mechanicals. He crossed the distance to her in a flash and wrapped her in his arms.

She hugged him back, burying her face against his neck, and he breathed in the scent of her, wanting to shout with joy. She smelled clean, but was missing that scent of untamed mountain peaks and high altitudes. He held her for a long moment. He imagined she was hugging him tighter than she had Mattias.

When she pulled back just a little, he leaned down to kiss her. His heart fell when she turned her head again to let him kiss her cheek.

She was acting perfectly fair to the two of them. He hated it. He had secretly hoped she would slap Mattias on the face the first time he tried to touch her, call him a cad, a waste of breath, and a dishonor to his house.

A tiny part of him that was far too reasonable realized that dream might have been a little optimistic, but he still felt disappointed.

"I'm so glad you're awake. We missed you."

That sounded lame, but he could not get any more words out. Powerful emotions choked the rest and he didn't want to say too much with Saskia and Mattias watching. Nicklaus ignored them all, busily consuming a tall cake on a little table nearby.

Verena wobbled and Connor quickly eased her back into her seat. She looked healthy, but clearly had not regained her full strength yet.

He dropped into the open chair next to her, across from Mattias, and held onto her left hand. "If you're too tired, we can come back later."

Mattias mirrored Connor's move, grasping her right hand. "What did the Healer say?"

Before she could answer, Saskia laughed.

"Look at you two silly men.
Worrying like a pair of old hens.
Verena is fine. Just give her some time, and soon she'll be flying again."

Verena smiled at her friend. "Thanks to all your care."

Saskia drew closer and placed a hand on her shoulder, her expression tender. "We would have done ten times as much if needed."

Mattias said, "She's right. We love you, Verena. You're family."

Connor wanted to kick him between the knees. That was a smooth, crafty way to declare his feelings again and remind her in not so many words that all she had to do was say yes and she would be part of their family.

She glanced at Mattias and smiled warmly, and Connor racked his mind for something to say to pull her attention back to him, but none of his thoughts seemed to work. All he could do was listen in horrified anticipation as she spoke to Mattias.

"I heard you when you came and sat with me every day. I don't remember all the words, but I remember you did it. You gave me hope in moments of absolute darkness, when I could not find my way. I don't think it's possible for you to understand how much that means to me, or how much I appreciate it."

Mattias grinned, his teeth glowing softly again, and he looked ecstatic. "Of course. I thought I made it clear that I would do anything for you, Verena. I'll speak with you and encourage you every single day of your life if you let me."

Connor coughed, hoping to pull her eyes away from his, but she did not even seem to hear. He wanted to punch Mattias in those perfect, glowing teeth, but that would require him to let go of Verena's hand, and he refused to do that. He may never get another chance. The thought paralyzed him with icy terror.

Verena said, "Mattias, you and Saskia are like my brother and sister. There's no family I have that I love more."

Connor's heart began to beat again. Girls did not marry their brothers, at least not anywhere he'd ever heard about.

Mattias seemed to agree. His teeth stopped glowing and a flicker of doubt clouded his expression. "I don't think any brother ever loved his sister the way I love you, Verena."

She patted his hand. "I can't imagine my life without you as my dear friend."

He opened his mouth, but no words came out. His eyes flickered to Connor's, and Connor could not suppress a smile. That made Mattias glare, but then Verena turned to Connor, and he forgot all about Mattias.

He gazed into her eyes, and he forgot about everything else. Verena was his entire world, and her voice seemed to reach the center of his heart without even having to go through his ears.

"Connor, I was lost. That accident broke something in my mind, and I was trapped in there. Like I told Mattias, I could hear a little, but nothing else. I was stuck in a deep, dark well, without any way to escape. You saved me."

Connor felt horrified. He had thought she was just sleeping, but as he listened to her description of the long struggles in darkness, alone, he had to blink back tears.

"You gave me the tools to free myself. All that healing power made the difference. Somehow, occasionally, I managed to grasp that healing power and use it to repair the broken connections." She squeezed his hand with her warm one and he read a depth of emotion there that he had feared lost forever.

"It must have been the chert. I felt connections too, but how is it possible you felt the healing power? You're not a Petralist, are you?"

She shook her head. "I asked for a piece of sandstone when I woke up. I tried to connect with it, but I couldn't. There's a whisper of something, maybe, but it's not an active affinity. I don't know what it is."

That was amazing. He'd desperately hoped that his efforts with chert and sandstone were helping, but part of him had feared he was wasting time and wasting that precious resource. What if he had listened to those doubts? Verena might never have awakened. The thought chilled him.

"As I was working to heal myself, I heard everything you said. I heard about your struggles, the terrible trials you had with porphyry, and your vow to fight it to the bitter end. I'm so proud of you Connor. I love you."

Then she leaned forward and kissed him tenderly on the lips.

Connor felt like he had swallowed the sun and it exploded through his chest. That was the only way to describe the all encompassing feeling of joy and love and relief that swept through him. He kissed her back, and all of his fears melted away.

Verena was awake, she was healed, and she still loved him. He couldn't imagine anything ever going wrong again.

"So this is your decision?" Mattias asked coldly, rising abruptly and glaring down at Connor.

Connor blinked up at Mattias. He had forgotten that anyone else was in the room. Mattias looked angry, bitter, exactly the way Connor would probably feel if Verena had chosen Mattias instead.

Connor's hatred of Mattias vanished. He felt like maybe he understood the man, at least a little. As much as he disliked what Mattias had done in trying to steal Verena back, he found he pitied Mattias now.

Verena rose and reached toward Mattias, her expression apologetic. "I never wanted to hurt you again, Mattias."

He retreated, pulling his hand away. "Is that why you called us in here together, to give Connor the opportunity to gloat?"

Verena frowned and gave him that look that she had so often given to Connor. "You know me better than that, Mattias."

"Maybe I don't know you as well as I thought," he snapped.

Saskia came around the back of Verena's chair, also looking upset. "Mattias, Verena's had a long and difficult day. She woke up with an assassin trying to kill her."

Mattias took a deep breath, clearly fighting to control his emotions. "You're right. Now is not the time." He bowed to Verena and said, "I'm glad you're in good health, but I can see you need some time alone."

Then he turned and left. He walked a bit stiffly, but did not run to the door, and did not look like he was crying. Connor was not sure he could have maintained his composure so well if Verena had rejected him. She had asked Mattias to be a friend and a brother, which was something, but Connor was not sure he could spend time with Verena and only act like a brother. He loved her too deeply for that.

Saskia sighed and glanced at Connor, but he could not read her. Was she angry? Sad? Surprised?

She said, "I'll take my leave too. You two have much to discuss." She gripped Verena's hands and added, "I know you feel you made a decision here, but it does not have to be final. If you have any second thoughts or doubts, don't feel like you have to rush."

Connor started to protest but she held up a hand to silence him. "Like I told my brother, Verena has been through a terrible ordeal. You two both should be willing to give her the time she needs to make sure she knows her heart."

"Thank you, Saskia. You are a true friend, but I know my heart." Verena hugged her.

"Perhaps."

Saskia turned and followed Mattias out of the room, dragging Nicklaus with her.

He took the cake platter with him, waving to Connor on his way out. "Let's practice that punching move with Mattias later."

Connor laughed. He would love to, but maybe they could find a different dummy. Mattias had already been beaten enough for one day.

As soon as they were alone, Verena wrapped her arms around Connor again and squeezed him tight enough that he worried one of his ribs might crack. They held each other for a long time, not speaking, just reuniting.

Finally, she spoke softly. "I told you the truth, Connor. I was lost and you saved me."

He cupped her lovely face in his hands and stared deep into her eyes. "I feel like you saved me too. I don't think I would've survived porphyry without you."

They sat down together on a couch, holding hands, and Verena sighed. "I'm so glad we get this chance to make things right, Connor. I acted foolishly, and I nearly drove you away."

Those words were like a balm to his heart, but he shook his head. "I was an even bigger fool. You're everything to me, Verena, and I let Shona drive another wedge between us. I should have known better."

She grinned. "Yes, you should have."

"It'll never happen again. I saw her in Donleavy. I broke all ties with her. I'm yours and yours alone."

Verena gave him that special smile, and it lit up her whole face. He could have stared at her for hours. Her expression turned more serious. "Every relationship requires work to stay strong. I promise to work at us every day."

"Me too," he promised. He'd never felt so committed to anything or anyone in his life. "So tell me more about what you felt in your mind."

"It's hard to explain." She tried to relate her ordeal, and Connor tried to relate what she went through with his experience in Aifric's mind.

"After you're feeling stronger, maybe we can explore your memories with chert and see if that gives us any new insights," he suggested.

"That's a good idea. I need to get a piece to study anyway."

He grinned. Of course Verena would want to leap back into her research. "Everyone will be happy to see you get back to work."

"I miss my workroom so much," she admitted. "But first, I want you to tell me everything you've been involved in. I want to make sure I didn't miss any of it."

So he did. They talked for hours. He barely noticed as the afternoon faded into evening. He would probably have stayed there and talked all night, but her stomach rumbled loudly.

"I'll go find someone to bring you some dinner," he offered immediately.

"Have them bring dinner for six."

"Are you really that hungry?" He'd never known Verena to eat that much, but she had been sleeping for several weeks.

She laughed softly. "No. My family is supposed to be arriving tonight. Saskia said they would get here at around dusk. That should be any minute. I can't wait to introduce you to them."

Connor felt the familiar sense of uneasiness at the mention of her family, but he squashed it. He and Verena were reunited. Nothing could get in the way of that. He decided he would choose to accept and love her family. Until they did something to make him choose differently.

He rose and kissed her one more time, then hurried from the room to find a servant to summon dinner. As he closed the door behind him, a soft footfall sounded nearby, drawing his attention.

Mattias stepped out of the shadows nearby, his expression determined.

6 6

SOME DREAMS REALLY CAN COME TRUE

"Have you been waiting out here all this time?" Connor asked, although from Mattias's haggard look, the answer was obvious.

"Is she asking for me?" Mattias asked, not able to hide the desperation in his eyes.

"I'm sorry, but she's just asked me to set up a dinner for six."

"Six?"

"Her family's arriving."

Connor didn't think that was information he should keep secret, but Mattias's eyes suddenly glowed. Literally. He stood taller, his shoulders squared out of their previous slump, and a new hope infused his voice.

Definitely shouldn't have told him.

"We need to talk," Mattias said, gesturing down the hallway.

Connor hesitated, but Mattias impatiently gestured him to follow again. Wary, but curious, Connor decided to see what he wanted.

As they walked away from Verena, Mattias said, "Don't worry about the dinner. We'll find a servant for that."

"You mean I will. Verena's hungry and I want to make sure it gets done right."

"You don't think I could handle such a simple thing?" Mattias asked, and his veneer of calm slipped for a second, revealing his seething anger. If he attacked, he'd hold the advantage. Connor didn't have an active primary affinity stone, and his tertiaries were still acting erratic.

So he shrugged and said, "We've traveled together, remember? I've seen you try to cook."

"And you left us behind to fly home in a drafty old windrider," Mattias griped.

"Cold air is good for the complexion."

As they descended to the next lower level, Connor slipped a hand into

461

his belt pouch and absorbed a little granite, just to be safe. He still felt pity for Mattias, didn't want to fight him, but sensed Mattias wasn't yet ready to surrender to Verena's will. He was trying to act calm, but Connor sensed his fury.

Connor spied a serving girl in the next hallway and gave her Verena's request. She seemed to be expecting it and hurried off.

They reached a large window, shuttered against the cold. Through a crack in the slats, Connor saw the window looked out over a courtyard two stories below, with a low, slanted roof directly below them. It felt like the perfect place to get to the bottom of what Mattias wanted.

So he stopped and asked, "What do you want to talk about?"

Mattias turned to face him and asked hopefully, "Did Verena say she wanted me to join her?"

Connor felt sorry for Mattias, but coddling him wouldn't help, so he shook his head and said simply, "No."

"Did she—"

He looked so beaten down, Connor had to say, "Look, Mattias, I think I understand a little how you feel—"

"Can you?" Mattias snapped.

"Sure. I've worried right along with you that she might die, that we'd lose her. Even thinking it was devastating."

"Well, I've lost her. To you. That's worse." Anger was creeping into his voice.

"Worse than her dying?" Connor demanded, incredulous.

"In some ways," Mattias admitted dejectedly. "If she had died, I could fool myself into thinking she still loved me."

He actually had a point. That was annoying. "She still cares for you. She said so."

"As a brother." He filled the word with abundant disgust.

"I don't recommend pulling her hair. Have you seen how fast she is with those throwing knives?"

"Not funny," Mattias snapped.

"At least I'm trying. I didn't have to follow you down here. We agreed to let her decide. She decided. I'm not about to try to convince her to change her mind."

"I know what I agreed to. I don't need you to remind me."

"So, why are we here?"

Mattias had probably waited with the hopes of seeing Verena. Connor was impressed he seemed to be trying to handle Verena's decision like a man. After the underhanded way he had tried to lure Verena back, that was a refreshing change.

So Connor made a supreme effort and said, "I never wanted to be rivals. You're a true friend to Verena and you helped me when some guys might not have. Thank you for not making things hard on her."

Mattias nodded acceptance of the praise and said loftily, "I would never do anything to harm her. I gave my word of honor not to interfere . . ." His words trailed off and his expression changed to anger again.

Uh oh. That look spelled trouble.

Mattias growled, "But you. You cheated."

"What are you talking about?"

"We both promised not to interfere, but you kept trying to heal her. You heard what she said. She felt it and that swayed her decision."

"If I hadn't, she might never have woken up."

"You broke your word of honor. You're no gentleman. You sneaky, underhanded liar!" Mattias exclaimed, growing visibly angry and suddenly shifting into the graceful stance of an Allcarver tapping obsidian.

Connor prepared to tap granite, his own anger flaring at the stupid accusation. "Says the guy who tried to illegally move the entire Builder compound to his estate to force Verena to live next to you."

Good thing he absorbed granite a moment ago because he bet the Tallan's dirty socks that Mattias would never grant him time to absorb some for a fair fight. A fight was clearly Mattias's intention.

So Connor tapped limestone. The little stone was still hanging under his shirt on the steel-link neck chain that Aifric had gifted to him. He smiled, applying limestone to his teeth.

"You thief!" Mattias exclaimed. "That's my move."

"I perfected it, though." Connor tapped more limestone and twisted the light in front of Mattias into a mirage. He felt the image forming and pushed his thoughts onto it to give it clear direction.

Captain Ilse suddenly appeared in the hallway near them. Mattias started at her sudden appearance and did not look happy at the intrusion.

Connor reached for serpentinite and managed to connect with it long enough to craft some words in Ilse's voice. "Lord Mattias, all the Crushers have voted. We've decided to appoint Connor as our new liason with—"

Then the crashing waves of red and green power interfered with each other again, despite his efforts to focus only on the red frequency. The rest of the sentence faded away, but Mattias didn't seem to notice.

His face flushed with affronted rage and he cried, "You can't do that!"

Connor shrugged. "Of course she can't. I was just practicing."

Maybe he'd pushed a little too hard. Connor hadn't wanted to fight Mattias, hadn't wanted to gloat or remind Mattias of his shame at losing Verena to an Obrioner commoner. He'd won Verena, so he didn't need anything else, and he honestly hoped Mattias would learn to live with her choice.

Mattias threw a punch.

After practicing with Tomas and Cameron, Connor easily slipped the blow, but suddenly all of his suppressed anger at Mattias's attempts to force Verena to submit to his will, bubbled over.

Mattias's hand went to his sword. "I've had enough of your foolishness. I formally challenge you to—"

Connor stepped closer, tapping granite just as Mattias drew his sword in a flash. It rasped loudly as it cleared the scabbard, and it seemed to blur through the air, slashing through Connor's shirt and scraping across his stomach a split second after it hardened.

Mattias was a champion Allcarver, and he could kill Connor, despite the protection of granite, if Connor gave him any chance at all.

So Connor crowded close, pinning Mattias's arm to his side, and grabbing him by the collar. Mattias struggled to bring his sword up to stab at Connor's vulnerable eyes, but Connor seized his arm.

"We're supposed to start at ten paces," Mattias protested.

If he gave Mattias that much space, he'd get sliced to ribbons. So Connor said, "I never accepted your challenge. I have to admit, I prefer ending things this way."

Connor threw Mattias out the nearby window.

Mattias cursed as he smashed through the window and the shutter behind in a satisfying explosion of glittering shards of glass and splinters of dark wood. He still somehow managed to slash his sword across Connor's stone-hardened cheek. The scraping sound of steel on stone rang loudly in his ears as he twisted his head away to protect his eyes. Mattias really was a gifted fighter.

He wasn't good at flying, though.

Connor immensely enjoyed watching Mattias tumbling through the cloud of debris, limbs flailing, priceless expression of shocked disbelief on his face.

Their eyes met. Connor waved.

He'd dreamed of throwing Mattias out a window for so long, and the wait was worth it. Mattias plummeted to the little, sloped roof directly below them. He bounced and rolled wildly down the snowy pitch and tumbled off the lower end. Connor tried to burn the moment into his memory to enjoy all his life.

"You Obrioner lowlife rock pounder!" Mattias shouted as he disappeared from view.

That was a good one. Connor tried to tap serpentinite again to snag the words, but the dual frequency power sources immediately interfered and snuffed out his connection. He sighed. What a loss. Hamish would have loved to hear that one.

"What's going on here?" a cultured voice demanded in Grandurian from behind him as a muffled thud and long groan echoed up from the courtyard below.

That was one of the few phrases Connor had learned. He turned to find a finely dressed, elderly gentleman approaching. Clearly a nobleman, he did not look pleased. He was probably one of Mattias's friends.

"Settling an agreement," Connor responded in Obrioner, a little harsher than he intended. "Who are you?"

The man drew himself up proudly. "I am Lord Heilwig."

"Am I supposed to know you?" Connor demanded, not feeling very subservient at the moment. The stuffy lord had interrupted his long-dreamed-of moment of glory. His anger at Mattias's idiocy and ridiculous accusations was still building. Some of it slipped into his voice as he confronted the proud old lord.

Lord Heilwig sniffed in abundant disapproval. "Apparently you are more unrefined than my daughter led me to believe."

"Who's your daughter?" Connor demanded.

"Verena, of course."

Oops.

Connor's anger evaporated in a flash. He was such a grouted fool.

SAVED BY INTERNATIONAL WARFARE

Verena's father eyed Connor critically, then glanced out the broken window. "Was that Mattias?"

"You know him?" Connor asked, cursing the Tallan's bad luck that Verena's father had to show up just then.

"Indeed. I have found him a most remarkable young man."

"I guess you didn't know him that well, then."

"What are you talking about?" Lord Heilwig demanded angrily.

All he could do was rely on truth to help smooth over the awkward introduction. "I don't know what you've heard about him recently, but just now he made false accusations about me, suggested Verena might be better off still in her coma, and tried to kill me. Throwing him out the window was the gentlest way to deal with him."

Plus, it was so incredibly fun.

Verena's father frowned, not looking convinced, but said, "I will reserve judgment until I speak with Mattias again."

Hopefully he avoided staring into those hypnotic, glowing teeth, or he might believe whatever lies Mattias tried to invent to justify his actions.

"Fair enough." Connor tried to compose himself and said rather lamely, "It's a pleasure to meet you, sir. Verena is expecting you."

Still frowning, he said, "She requested that I invite you to join us for dinner so the proper introductions could be made, but if you prefer to carouse in the streets with the drunkards, I would be happy to make apologies for you."

That didn't sound like he'd made a good first impression. Well, thinking of returning to Verena filled Connor with so much happiness, he didn't really care. So he gave Lord Heilwig a happy smile and extended a hand to shake.

"Not at all. I love eating after exercise."

Lord Heilwig did not look inclined to shake, but Connor grabbed his hand anyway. He had a pretty good grip for an old guy.

"Verena has informed me of her choice of suitors. It is my opinion that she chose foolishly."

"How can you say that? You don't even know me."

"But I know Mattias." He glanced at the window and scowled.

"If you always settle for what you know, you'll never experience anything better."

Connor released his hand and led the way back to Saskia's study. He kept his expression neutral, but slowly clenched his fists on alternating sides. He recognized the superior look and disdain in Verena's father's eyes. He had seen that same look from nobility in Obrion all his life.

Verena was exceptional, so perhaps once they smoothed out that bad first meeting, maybe her family would come around. He'd won the hearts of the spoiled noble students at the Carraig. He'd give Lord Heilwig time before throwing him out the window after Mattias.

He was amazed to discover that in his brief absence a table had been set up for dinner, complete with six chairs, entire place settings, and at least eight different courses. The long table groaned under the weight of silver platters and crystal goblets, roasted pork, some kind of vegetable soup, a type of sweetbread twisted into braids, with jelly and cream filling, and several other platters with covered lids.

Verena was standing near the table with three other people who Connor assumed must be the rest of her family.

The woman standing beside her could have easily been mistaken for her older sister. They looked so much alike that Connor had to look again before he saw the lines of age mostly concealed under cosmetics, and the wisps of gray at her temples that faded away under whatever hair dye she used to keep herself looking young.

Verena's smile chased away Connor's lingering irritation at her father. She rushed over and greeted her father with an enthusiastic hug, then took Connor's hand. "Father, I'm glad you two already met."

"I doubt you intended us to meet as we did," her father said, although he couldn't maintain his frown around her.

"What happened?" she asked.

"Mattias wanted to talk," Connor said.

Verena's father raised one eyebrow. "I thought you said he tried to kill you?"

"Oh, no," Verena exclaimed. "Are you all right?"

Connor loved the look of worry on her face. He assured her, "I'm fine. Mattias is a bit bruised, but I figured out how to force him to take a time out."

The rest of the family had approached while they talked. Verena refrained from asking the questions she clearly wanted to. Instead she said, "Mother, this is Connor. Connor, this is my mother, Lady Christel."

Connor bowed over her hand and said, "I thought you two were sisters."

Verena gave him an approving look, and her father almost smiled.

Lady Christel took Connor's hands in hers. They were just as warm as Verena's. Her voice was rich and warm, and her expression welcoming. She glanced to her husband, then said, "I am so pleased to meet you, Connor."

The girl who crowded in close on Verena's other side, who Connor assumed must be her sister, said in a disapproving tone, "Is poor Mattias okay?"

Maybe thirteen, she was tall and gangly, with long, thick, blond hair, styled perfectly around her face and dropping halfway down her back in obedient layers. She looked at Connor with her nose turned up just a bit, regarding him with the superiority of someone born to power, who knows to the deepest corner of their heart, and all the way down to their tiniest, perfectly manicured toenail that they are better than everyone else.

Connor gave her a reassuring smile. "It looked like he knows how to bounce pretty well, so he should be okay."

"I'm sure he's fine, Ludmilla," Verena assured her, then gave Connor a warning look. He wasn't sure what she was warning him about. He'd already thrown Mattias.

The last person in the family, a tall, handsome man, with broad shoulders, brown hair and eyes, and a smile that most girls probably fell for immediately, chuckled. "Looking forward to our honor duel. I'm starting to think I might even want you to win."

Verena flushed just a little, and that soft, creeping color in her cheeks was extremely distracting. "Connor, this is my brother, Vincenz."

Vincenz shook hands with the grip of a Rumbler, but he made a point to not crush Connor's fingers. Connor sensed that he was going to like Vincenz. As for the rest of them, he wasn't sure yet. Her mother seemed nice, if a bit subservient to her husband, and her sister seemed far too much like the spoiled nobles he'd known at he Carraig. No wonder Verena was so eager to escape to Schwinkendorf valley with the Builders.

Lord Heilwig directed them around the table and three serving girls scurried to dish out the various courses. Connor eagerly sampled them, which was apparently necessary before really digging in. He felt almost as hungry as Verena, and as soon as she began attacking her dinner, he did too. The two of them ate far more than the rest of the family combined.

That seemed to annoy her parents and please her brother in equal measure. Ludmilla seemed torn between digging in like Verena, who she clearly looked up to, and wanting to emulate her parents' restraint.

Connor said, "You must be hungry after your journey. Don't feel like you have to hold back on my account. I'm used to eating with Hamish. He could out eat all of us together."

Ludmilla's air of stiff superiority evaporated. She gasped. *The Hamish?* You're friends with him?"

Connor laughed. "You must be talking about a different Hamish."

"The Builder who works with Verena, the one who flies like an eagle and is so brave he fought rampager monsters with his bare hands."

Connor looked to Verena who shrugged innocently. "You've been telling stories, haven't you?"

"I love Verena's letters," Ludmilla gushed. "We love reading her adventures, don't we mother?"

Lady Christel looked a bit embarrassed, but also seemed to realize she couldn't avoid the subject. "Your letters are a wonder, dear. We love the insights into the exciting life of invention and adventure you've lived."

"A little too much adventure," her father grumbled.

Verena chided, "You're acting grumpy, Father. What's the matter?"

He glanced from her to Connor and said, "I can't help fearing you've made a rash, hasty decision."

Vincenz chuckled, "Father's in mourning. He was looking forward to spending the summers in Mattias's palace outside of Edderitz."

"Don't be insolent, boy," Lord Heilwig said with affronted dignity, but Ludmilla concealed her grin behind a napkin, and Verena's mother couldn't suppress a smile.

She placed a hand over her husband's. "I know you were already prepared to grant Mattias your blessing, but we cannot ignore Verena's will in the matter."

He grunted and frowned. Verena said, "Please, Father. Just be happy today. We're all together. Please withhold judgment until you get to know Connor better."

"This situation is highly unusual," he muttered.

So it fit Verena perfectly.

But even though he looked like he wanted to refuse to accept that his daughter had chosen an Obrioner commoner over his favorite Grandurian nobleman, Lord Heilwig sighed. "Very well, dear. You've been ill. I will humor you."

Connor was impressed. Maybe there was more to Verena's father than he'd feared.

Verena gave her father a dazzling smile. "Tell me about your journey. This is a terrible time to travel."

That was a safe topic, one they all seemed happy to linger on. They spent several minutes discussing the deplorable conditions of the roads and the fact that they never would have made it without their escorts of Water Moccasins and Flame Weavers to help make the journey bearable.

Verena polished off her second heaping plate of dinner while they talked. She said, "If we have time, I'll give you a ride in the Storm. It's our fastest flying machine. You'll love it."

Most of the family looked thrilled by the idea, but her father's good humor cracked and he shook his head. "Members of high society do not go around flying in Builder mechanicals, Verena."

That was such a stupid statement Connor spoke before he could stop himself. "Are you kidding? Kilian flies all the time. Mattias himself flew with me to Althing to secure a treaty along with General Wolfram. While we were there, that ability to fly played a critical role in helping to repel an invasion from Obrion that could have destroyed their entire capital city."

Vincenz asked, "What invasion? We never heard about that."

"Just happened. We only barely returned from that and from helping to start a revolution in Obrion."

Lady Christel gaped. "Revolution? Oh, my. You've been busy."

Verena chuckled. "I fall asleep for a while, and Connor starts meddling in politics."

Politics? He liked that. Glancing at Lord Heilwig Connor said, "I've always had a gift for breaking things. I've never broken an entire country before, though."

"Tell us?" Ludmilla asked eagerly. A good story was clearly the way to get to that girl's heart.

So Connor told them a little bit about the desperate fight against Harley in Althing. He probably played up some of his involvement just a little, but even being completely humble he had to admit that he had saved the day.

As he spoke he watched their reactions carefully. Vincenz was nodding, as if imagining himself there, fighting at Connor's side. Ludmilla listened, rapt, her big blue eyes starting to glow a little. She must be a Solas, and no doubt if she practiced that look on the lordlings in Edderitz, she was already starting to win a huge following of devoted suitors.

Lady Christel also seemed to appreciate the story, but she kept glancing at Verena's father, who looked impressed, and equally annoyed to feel that way.

"I suppose you provided a valuable service to our allies," Lord Heilwig finally conceded, eliciting loud laughter from Vincenz.

"Oh father, stop being so dour. I'm starting to see what Verena sees in this guy."

Before her father could answer, the door banged open and Mattias swept inside, hair wet from melted snow, clothing disheveled from his fall, and with a noticeable limp on his left side. His right hand dropped to his sword and he glared at Connor.

"You owe me a duel."

Verena's father looked pleased by the idea, although her mother looked shocked by the interruption.

Vincenz jumped to his feet, his expression amused. He intercepted Mattias with an outstretched hand. "Mattias, is this any way to greet us after so long?"

Mattias seemed to realize where he was and who he was with for the first time. He dropped his hand from his sword and tried to compose himself, but got distracted when Connor waved.

"We don't have another chair, but if you want to wait until we're done, you can use my spot," Connor offered.

Verena slapped him lightly on the shoulder. "Stop teasing, Connor. Most people don't fall out windows as often as you. It's hard on them."

She rose and went to Mattias, taking his hands in hers. "Please stop fighting. I don't want to see either of you hurt."

His anger deflated as he stared at her, but Connor saw more bitterness than anything. He had to wonder if Mattias was thinking only about the loss of political connection and the imagined slight on his honor for having lost her to an Obrioner commoner.

Lord Heilwig rose and greeted Mattias like a long-lost son. "I'm glad you're not hurt from that fall, my boy. Come, join us. We'll send for another chair."

He was laying on the favoritism pretty thick. Connor wondered if he really did love Mattias so much, or if he was testing Connor. More likely, he was testing Verena's resolve.

The door opened again and Connor was startled to see Hamish and Aifric burst into the room, followed closely by Kilian. They all wore winter travel apparel, and looked windblown, as if they had only just landed.

Verena's family focused on Kilian, bowing or curtsying to him. Then Ludmilla noticed Hamish. She gasped with wide-eyed wonder, as if she'd seen the Tallan himself return from legend.

"Verena!" Hamish swept her off her feet in an enthusiastic hug and they laughed together. When Hamish set her back down he said, "About time you woke up. I was starting to think you were waiting until all the rebuilding was finished, lazy bones."

She grinned even wider. "How is it going?"

"Faster than anyone imagined possible. With Jean at the helm, New Schwinkendorf is going to be amazing."

Mattias frowned at the mention of Jean's name, and his frown only deepened at what Hamish said about all the progress made in rebuilding the town.

Lord Heilwig frowned too. "Mattias, what happened to your plans to move the Builder township to your estate near Edderitz?"

Mattias grimaced and glanced guiltily at Verena, who rounded on him and demanded, "What are you talking about?"

"I thought you might prefer living closer to your family," he said a bit lamely.

Connor wasn't about to let him get away with lying to Verena, but he hesitated. Would calling out Mattias further damage his already-rocky start with her father?

Hamish didn't have any of those concerns. He barked a humorless laugh. "He meant to say he tried to illegally order the entire town moved to his estate so he could control it all and force you to live under his thumb."

Mattias's hand moved back to his sword, but he turned his guilty gaze toward Lord Heilwig, who stared at him like he was seeing him for the first time.

"You would do such a dishonorable thing?" the old man asked, sounding crushed.

Mattias stammered, glancing from Lord Heilwig, to Verena, then to Connor. His anger returned, but before he could make another stupid accusation, Kilian placed a restraining hand on his shoulder and shook his head slowly.

"No fighting. Not today. Today we celebrate Verena's return." Kilian then pushed Hamish aside and hugged Verena, grinning like a proud uncle. "I'm so happy to see you awake."

Hamish waved to Connor as he grabbed half a ham and began chewing on it. Glancing around the table, he started to grin. With a mouth full of food, the affect was a little disturbing.

He swallowed a huge mouthful and pointed the ham at Christel. "Verena told me she looked like her mother. She didn't tell me her mother looked like her twin sister."

Christel blushed, then rounded the table and gave him a hug. "Hamish. I feel like I know you already. Verena told us so much about you."

"All of the good stuff was me. I blame Dierk for everything else."

He actually made a little bow to Lord Heilwig. "It's a pleasure to meet you. It's a rare thing for a father to trust his daughter so much and encourage her to push the limits and embrace her passion. Connor, have you met Verena's father?"

"We were in the process," he said, smiling at his friend who had so utterly interrupted the meal.

"He's a good man. Always supports Verena, no matter what."

Lord Heilwig was looking decidedly uncomfortable by the praise. Connor loved it.

Vincenz greeted Hamish like an old friend and introduced himself. Hamish laughed and pumped his hand. "Have you beaten Connor up yet?"

"Haven't had time to schedule it."

"Can't wait. Connor, Vincenz is the bash fighting champion of Edderitz. Trained under Erich himself."

No wonder Connor liked Vincenz so much.

Hamish turned to Ludmilla, who was staring at him with a look of adoration. He took her hand and said, "And you're the lovely Ludmilla.

Verena talks about you all the time. Have you conquered every heart in Edderitz yet?"

She stammered, switching to Grandurian probably without realizing it. Connor couldn't make out what she said, her face flushing bright red. Her air of haughty, superior nobility was gone, leaving her simply as an early teen struggling to figure out what to say to someone she clearly regarded as a hero. Maybe she'd turn out all right after all.

Hamish seemed oblivious to Ludmilla's discomfort, pumped her hand again and replied in Grandurian. Her blush deepened and she looked awed that he spoke her language.

Hamish patted her shoulder with his greasy fingers and said, "I hope you visit us at New Schwinkendorf when it's finished. Get out of stuffy old Edderitz for a while."

"I will," she promised, glancing at her mother, who looked eager to join her for the visit.

Verena broke away from Aifric, who she was hugging enthusiastically. She looked vibrant with joy. "You all just landed? Did you fly in just to come say hello?"

Hamish shook his head. "Glad you're awake, but unfortunately that wasn't the only reason we came. There's an army headed for Merkland, moving against Rory. We need Connor."

Connor winked at Verena's father. "Sorry for the interruption. Guess I've got to jump into another round of international warfare."

OLD SECRETS. NEW SECRETS. STONE SECRETS. BLUE SECRETS.

Verena surprised Connor by saying, "I'll need a little time to pack."

"You can't be going," Lady Christel exclaimed.

"I have to."

Connor felt immensely proud of her, but what was she thinking? She'd just broken out of a coma. She needed a little time.

Lord Heilwig declared, "You are not going to risk your life defending Obrioner barbarians. I forbid it."

Connor grimaced. Didn't he know forbidding Verena from doing something was the best way to guarantee she did it anyway? He'd hoped to convince her to stay behind, but her family was making his job ten times harder.

Lady Christel implored, "Verena, think about what you're saying. You can't rush off to battle so soon. You're not ready."

"Mother, you always encouraged me. Father, you've never interfered with my work before. You commissioned my armor, by the Tallan's mercy!"

"I never imagined you'd ever actually use it. Your work is supposed to be inventing, not fighting. You're no warrior, Verena. Leave the fighting to the professionals."

Connor didn't want Verena anywhere near Harley, but he could not bear to hear them criticize her. "Verena's more a warrior than anyone I know. Have you ever seen how she fights? How amazing she looks in that armor?"

Maybe he should have left out that last bit.

Lord Heilwig glared at him. "You stay out of it, young man. You are not part of this family, and at this rate I cannot see how you could ever persuade me to bless such a ridiculous union."

Verena's initial surprise at their reactions was quickly turning to anger. "Connor risked his life many times for me. He's the only reason I was able to wake up. Don't you dare insult him."

Her father sighed. "Perhaps I was a little ungrateful, my dear. I'm sure the boy has offered valuable service to you and to our nation, but you must see that this silly infatuation would prove a disadvantageous match."

Mattias nodded enthusiastically, standing a bit straighter. Connor would applaud his tenacity in any other situation.

"No, I don't. I'm not looking for a political union, father." She stepped to Connor and took his hand, eliciting a simultaneous scowl from her father and Mattias. Connor figured he might as well get used to that look. "Connor and I have built something special, and I won't abandon it."

Connor said, "I love you, Verena, but maybe your father is right about not coming to Merkland."

"What? You doubt me now too?" She looked so hurt, he promised to beat himself with a stick later.

"Of course not, but you've just woken from a long coma. You're still a bit shaky. You said so yourself." He added softly, "I couldn't bear to see you hurt again because you pushed your limits too soon. Please wait until you've recovered your strength."

She hesitated and her mother spoke. "Listen to Connor, dear. Once this emergency is resolved, we'll have time to discuss your future more calmly."

Verena looked from her to Connor, and the anguish on her face tore at his heart. "I just escaped the prison of my own mind. I'm not about to accept a new one so soon."

Kilian spoke for the first time. "Perhaps there's a way to avoid that. Verena, come with us to Faulenrost."

Her parents both started to protest, but Kilian continued over them. "There will be no fighting there. She can visit with Dierk and with Jean and see the amazing progress they've made in rebuilding. There is much work that needs to be done there that has nothing to do with the fighting at Merkland. Frankly, they need Verena. She's my lead researcher and she's been sorely missed. She'll be safe, but productive. I think she'll recover faster there than anywhere."

That was a good idea. Connor should have thought of it. Verena's father looked like he disapproved so that pretty much guaranteed it was the right choice.

He started to protest again, but Lady Christel actually interrupted him. "It's all right, dear. I think Kilian is right."

The entire family looked thunderstruck, as if she'd never expressed a contrary opinion in front of them. Verena's father looked so shocked that he couldn't seem to find the words.

Connor took that as agreement. "Great. We'll head for Faulenrost tomorrow."

"I appreciate your flexibility and your support of Verena's Builder work," Kilian told her parents. That seemed to ease Lord Heilwig's grumpiness, and he stood a bit taller. It looked like getting a compliment from Kilian carried a lot of weight even in high social circles. "We'll need to discuss our plans tonight in my tower."

That sparked another round of protests from the entire family. They'd just barely seen Verena. So the group ended up lingering for another half hour of tense smalltalk. Connor felt relieved when he and Verena finally joined Hamish, Aifric, and Kilian in Kilian's tower and sat around the fire in his cozy sitting room.

"What happened to you two in Merkland?" Connor asked.

"Merkland was the fun part. It was Donleavy that nearly killed us," Hamish said with a grimace.

"Donleavy? What were you thinking going there?" Connor demanded.

Aifric said calmly, "Trying to kill the queen, of course."

He listened in growing dismay as they described the incredible, but ultimately failed attempt on the queen's life. Verena rushed to hug Aifric and comfort her when she heard about the death of Student Eighteen's father.

As Hamish described their harrowing escape from the city, Connor exclaimed, "Pumice? That's an affinity stone?"

Aifric hissed, "Keep your voice down. It's a jealously guarded secret. Student Eighteen is trying to reconcile with her people, so we can't blab their secrets to the world."

"We're alone in Kilian's suite," Verena said.

Hamish said, "Just humor her. She's had a difficult week."

Connor had been impressed by how well Aifric seemed to be handling the tragedy, but Mister Two wasn't her father. Connor wondered if Student Eighteen was a hidden wreck, with a dozen or more other personalities all gathered around as she wept. Given their profession, the Mhortair probably had to deal with a lot of untimely death, but she'd lost her *father*.

He leaned back in his chair, considering the startling secret. "But we use pumice in quarrying."

Kilian looked equally shocked, and that reinforced Connor's sense of amazement. "Pumice was never used for anything until after the Tallan wars. I knew my mother kept many secrets, but hadn't expected this one."

That's where he got his habit of holding back information. At least he hadn't adopted her psycho world domination problem.

Connor thought back to Alasdair and how often he'd handled pumice. He even hid in that barrel of pumice before starting his journey downriver and crashing into his first adventure.

"That's why you didn't find us in the river," he exclaimed to Kilian. "I had worried I'd somehow broken my curse. It felt wrong, somehow, but that's because I was using pumice, not granite!"

Verena said, "You were Agor first with pumice and never knew it?"

Kilian nodded thoughtfully. "That would explain it. I wondered how you slipped past."

"We were right in the river, not twenty feet away from you at one point."

"I thought I heard a cough, but I sensed nothing in the water."

"We submerged and that's when my curse was acting so weird."

"That would explain why I didn't sense you, but I should have sensed Shona."

"She ran out of air and I seemed to have a lot more than I should have. I shared some with her."

That was the first time he'd kissed Shona. Even though it hadn't really been much of a kiss, he'd touched lips to the high lord's beautiful daughter. He'd cherished that memory for a long time until he'd realized the truth about Shona.

Verena jabbed savagely at the fire with the iron poker, looking disgusted. He didn't really think she'd use the poker on him, but he watched her carefully anyway.

Hamish said, "So breathing in that pumice-enhanced breath somehow shielded her too?"

"It must have," Connor said. That breath had linked them for a moment. "We'll have to test it."

Verena raised one eyebrow. "You think I'm going to jump in the river and kiss you underwater, Connor?" Her voice made it clear what she thought about that at the moment.

"I'd never kiss anyone else, so it would have to be you."

That softened her frown into an almost smile.

"Kiss in the river next summer," Kilian said. Then he slapped his knee. "That's how he did it."

"Who?" Connor and Hamish asked together.

"Old Mhortair, of course."

Aifric's face shuddered slightly and her voice changed pitch, assuming the intensity of Student Eighteen. "You knew Mhortair, the First and Great One?"

Kilian chuckled. "He added those titles after he abandoned Stornoway in the waning days of the war, after my mother disappeared."

"What was he doing in the capital?" Student Eighteen asked with a frown. "Our great mission is the destruction of the house of Dreokt and removal of any direct relations and those with the Tallan's own curse."

"That wasn't his mission originally. He was my mother's personal bodyguard and devoted servant"

Student Eighteen gaped, her shock changing quickly to outrage. One hand dropped to the hilt of her dagger and her voice grew deadly soft.

"Watch your words, Kilian. Any other Mhortair would have slit your throat already for such an insult."

Kilian held her with a steady gaze. "Calm yourself. I spoke no insult, only the truth. Mhortair was as deadly as your legends claim, but he was one of my mother's first supporters and came with her from whatever lands they haled from. Despite his powers, he never achieved the same status as Harley and some of the other first generation Petralists. I think he resented that."

"How is it possible?" Student Eighteen asked, her voice shaky as Kilian calmly undermined the entire foundation of her life.

"I don't know why he chose to dedicate his life to the exact opposite of his previous purpose. I suspect he feared the return of the Blood of the Tallan might reunite Obrion, which could threaten his new-found freedom."

Student Eighteen whispered, "'Tainted blood to purge, evil hearts to pierce' is the heart of the Mhortair creed. I don't think anyone else will believe what you say."

"I don't need them to believe me. I need them to help us fight my mother."

"I guarantee the full might of the Mhortair will embrace that mission. Our ultimate purpose is to prevent the return of the Matron of Evil."

That was such a good title. Connor wondered if they had one for him yet. Maybe it was better if they didn't, but he still had to wonder what it might be.

Hamish chuckled. "If she's the Matron of Evil, does that make you Mister Evil, Kilian?"

Verena threw a pillow at him. "Not funny, Hamish."

Actually, it wasn't bad.

Still grinning, Hamish asked, "So what were you saying about Mhortair?"

"He was one of my battle instructors."

Student Eighteen looked awed by that.

"Sometimes he challenged me to find him somewhere in the castle grounds before he could close and touch my throat with a wooden sword. I never once beat him. I never knew he was cheating with pumice the entire time."

His expression turned more serious. "I'm glad you shared the secret with us. I wonder if Harley knows it."

Student Eighteen said, "She might be the only one besides the queen. I doubt Dreokt would share such a dangerous secret with anyone else."

"No, she wouldn't," Kilian agreed.

"We can use it, though," Connor said excitedly. "It could give us a huge advantage."

Student Eighteen said, "With extreme caution. We can't share this secret beyond those sitting in this room."

"But . . ." Connor started.

She cut him off. "No, Connor. It's too dangerous a secret, and could too easily be turned against us. Besides, if we share the secret widely, my people would swear a blood oath against all of us, despite the threat the queen poses."

"We'll keep the secret for now," Kilian assured her. "But after we repel the attack on Merkland, we'll need to consider how best to treat it in the future."

She didn't look pleased by the limited promise, but she accepted it.

Hamish rubbed his hands together near the fire, then said, "Back to the story. When we escaped, we returned to Merkland."

As he described events in Merkland, Verena exclaimed, "Rory proposed? Oh, I wish I'd been there! I've wished those two could be together for so long, but never imagined it was possible."

Connor laughed as Hamish described the singular engagement party. It sounded like they'd need weeks to repair the damage. He wished Rory and Anika all the luck in the world. They were perfect for each other. He doubted anyone else could survive a courtship with Anika anyway.

Kilian eventually interrupted their happy talk. "We'll have time to catch up with them in Merkland. It's getting late and we need to start early tomorrow. Get some sleep and pack for battle. We'll only have a few days in Faulenrost to gather what supplies we can."

Verena said, "I can't wait to get back. It'll be so good to get home."

Connor felt happy to think of Faulenrost and New Schwinkendorf his eventual homes. He was committed to Verena, but felt relieved she didn't consider Altkalen her real home. Living in the same city as Mattias might not be wise.

Kilian ushered them to the door. "I'll speak with Saskia and Wolfram. We lack time to marshal an army to send to Merkland, but they must prepare Altkalen's defenses in case the fight goes poorly."

Those sobering words dampened some of Connor's good humor. Then Verena took his hand as he escorted her back to her room, and he just couldn't worry. She kissed him tenderly at her doorway and he savored the memory of her soft, minty lips all the way back to his room.

Tonight, all was right with the world.

Tomorrow he'd worry about how to face Harley.

TOO MANY VOICES

A ifric waited just inside Kilian's outer door until the others disappeared from view. She doubted any of them noticed she'd lingered behind. They were far too focused on each other.

Student Eighteen's mind-voice was disapproving. *Sloppy. We'll have to remind them of the importance to remain aware of their surroundings, even when walking with their beloved.*

Later. We have more important things to deal with, Aifric reminded her.

A chorus of agreement sounded from the other ladies.

Kilian glanced at her with a question in his eyes as he held the door open. "Do you need something else, Aifric?"

Cacilia immediately suggested, *Ask him what he does for fun, and if he needs company.*

Hush, Aifric chided her, thankful Kilian couldn't hear her words.

She told Kilian, "Yes, actually. I need to speak with you on a matter of grave importance."

He closed the door and gestured her back to the fire. They took seats across a small table from each other, and he said, "Very well. Since you waited until the others left, may I assume Student Eighteen wishes to discuss old Mhortair further?"

Yes! Student Eighteen cried immediately. She moved to take control, but the other ladies pulled her back. They could discuss Mhortair later. First, they had far more important things to deal with.

"Actually, that will have to wait. After Connor helped bring me back, we've been rebuilding my memories." She tapped the side of her head.

Kilian leaned a little closer, looking intrigued. "So each of you maintains separate memories of events?"

Aifric nodded, ignoring Cacilia's suggestion that they explain how the best memories were ones where each of them got to experience it in turn while controlling their body. Of course Cacilia urged her to suggest they experiment with a fresh kissing memory. Aifric felt her face begin to flush from the mental images Cacilia was passing around with the other ladies. If Kilian noticed, he made no indication.

She only said, "We do, although each of us often focuses on different aspects of events. The one in control, of course, perceives events most clearly, but each of us ends up with partial memories of most events. That allowed us to rebuild most of my memories."

"So have you remembered something important?"

"Very. I've built a solid memory of the encounter with your mother in Donleavy, including the moments after the queen snuffed out my life."

"Go on," Kilian urged when she hesitated. He looked enthralled by the conversation, and his intense gaze really was alluring. He was a handsome man, a mystery unlike any other.

Cacilia, stop whispering, she chided.

I haven't said anything, Cacilia replied with laughter in her voice. *That last was all you. I feel proud of you, Aifric. Finally recognizing a real man when you see one.*

As the other ladies giggled and threatened to make her really start blushing, Aifric focused on her tale, but tried not to get too distracted by Kilian's eyes. A spark of fire had ignited inside his left eye, like a will-o-the-wisp trying to draw her in again.

"It was challenging because all of the other ladies were in shock from my death, and our system was very chaotic in those moments, but we pieced together enough that I feel confident the account is accurate. You need to understand what she did to Connor and to Ivor."

"What did she do?" Kilian asked, his tone grave. Crimson flames boiled in his left eye, while tiny waves crashed in his right. Aifric could watch those eyes for hours.

Instead, she told him about those terrifying moments when it appeared Queen Dreokt would kill both Ivor or Connor, or at minimum wipe their minds and make them empty puppets to her will.

The truth was even worse.

Kilian hissed a sharp breath when she related the queen's command to spy on him through the winter, then murder all the Builders at the first Spring thaw.

"You're sure?" was all he asked when she finished.

"Certain."

Kilian mouthed a near-silent curse. Student Eighteen took control long enough to tap serpentinite and snatch the faint words across to their ears. It seemed a heartfelt curse, but was one she'd never heard before.

Aifric took control again. They could swap places in the blink of an eye. She doubted any of their friends understood just how fast they could exchange. It was one of the secrets they still kept to themselves.

"I believe you," Kilian said. "It's just like my mother to do something so vile. Worse, she removed the memory of what she instructed them from their minds, so they don't know they are soon to commit mass murder and betray their closest friends."

Aifric nodded. "That's why I came to you. What are we going to do? How do we break it?"

"Do you have the ability to enter his mind like he did to yours? Can you find that memory, that directive, and remove it?" Kilian asked.

Student Eighteen slid into the control position to answer. "I cannot. I haven't ascended, and I doubt anyone below the third threshold could countermand an order delivered like that."

"That's what I feared," Kilian said, leaning back in his chair and drumming his fingers on the arm of his chair. Little figures made out of flames began appearing above his knuckles, like men and horses galloping in a circle. He did not even seem to notice.

Student Eighteen said, "There may be hope, however. Connor himself might be able to resist the order with my assistance. He has ascended the second threshold. He'll naturally want to resist, but would need to recognize the danger. That means we can't intervene until the order is triggered."

"So if it triggers before we're ready to intervene, it is likely he would be unable to resist the order."

She nodded, hating the horrid queen for inflicting such a torture upon him. "He would murder Hamish and Verena and the other Builders."

Kilian considered that for a moment. "If we timed our intervention properly, we might have a chance. Every fiber of his being will fight the impulse to kill them."

She nodded again. "That's my hope. If I can help him recognize the foreign nature of that impulse, link to his inner horror at such a thought, and tap into his love for those two in particular, we may be able to break the queen's hold."

"Ivor would prove more difficult. He lacks the same level of motivation with Verena and Hamish."

She considered that for a moment, holding a quick conference among all of the ladies living in her head. They reached consensus and she reported, "We'd have to leverage his anger at Dreokt over the mind-wipe of Alyth. With that powerful motivation, once Connor is free, together he and I may be able to break Ivor from the queen's control."

"How confident are you in that assessment?" he asked, holding her with his incredible gaze again. "If you fail to free him, Ivor's life would be forfeit."

"If we fail to intervene, many lives would be forfeit," she pointed out. "I believe we can do it. I really do."

"Good. Keep this information secret between the two of us. After we complete our business in Merkland we'll have time to formulate a plan of intervention."

"I've considered trying to warn them," she admitted.

"Don't. It is possible my mother included other commands you did not hear. She has done so before. If they learn of her secret directives, she may have implanted other back-up measures that would then trigger. We would not be prepared to respond to those."

"I could try to ferret them out," she suggested.

He considered the idea before shaking his head again. "No. There are too many unknowns. My mother is the master of mind manipulation. If we allow these directives to trigger without tampering, any peripheral directives would vanish."

"What if we both fall in the battle? No one would know the danger."

Kilian shrugged. "If we both die, chances are good the revolution is broken and nothing could stop my mother from winning. The Builders would be executed before spring thaw in that case."

She shuddered to think what might become of everyone she loved if that worst possible future transpired. "Let's not die, then."

They both rose and Kilian took her hand. His skin was warm. "Thank you for telling me. You're a remarkable young woman."

She wasn't able to do more than mutter her thanks as he led her to the door. Cacilia was clamoring for control, begging her to reply with an invitation to get to know her better. Student Eighteen was arguing just as strenuously against closer involvement with the son of the Matron of Evil. The rest of the ladies got sucked into the argument, taking different sides and filling Aifric's head with a cacophony of noise that made it impossible to know how to act.

She fled his rooms, grateful for the cool air of the corridor. She glanced back once, and he stood in his doorway, watching her with an unreadable expression on his face.

"Oh, my," she muttered.

70

HARD CHOICES

Verena loved the Hawk.

Although the loss of her precious Swift left a constant ache in her heart, the Hawk fulfilled her deep-seated need to take to the skies. She exulted in the unrivaled freedom of the high places, and once she ascended above the highest peak around Altkalen, she felt truly whole.

Maybe once her family experienced the joy of flight they would finally start to understand her. Unfortunately, that would have to wait. Securing aid for Merkland superseded every other need.

If anyone had suggested she might be willing to risk her life, Connor's life, and the lives of so many other people she loved defending High Lord Dougal's home, she probably would've punched them in the throat. Twice.

"You do realize that I'm the main pilot for the Hawk?" Hamish asked from his seat beside her, his feet up on the front rail.

"I love it, but I'm still planning to build a new Swift." She couldn't imagine not rebuilding it. Her memories of flight were so intimately connected with it that the Hawk, despite its amazing enhancements, simply couldn't compare.

"You'll have to include some of these new enhancements," Connor echoed her thoughts from where he sat on her other side. Kilian and Aifric sat in the second row, with the rear of the craft stuffed to over-flowing with supplies and a remarkable amount of food.

"I'm amazed by how much they've done. Jean isn't even a Builder, but she's taken so many of our ideas and improved them and pushed them to the next level." Verena couldn't wait to return and see all their accom-plishments first-hand. She felt deeply grateful to hear all that Jean had accomplished.

The Hawk was a marvel. It powered through the clear winter sky nearly as fast as the Storm, but consumed only a fraction of the power stone. It handled far more nimbly too. Not nearly as responsive as the Swift, but for such a large vehicle, it amazed her how connected she felt with the air.

The shielded windows built upon the work that she and Hamish had done and made the trip far more pleasant, as did the little marble heaters. She wondered what the next generation of flying craft might accomplish, and looked forward to diving back into her research to figure it out.

When they eventually soared over the last row of hills blocking their view of Schwinkendorf valley, the land opened up into the beautiful expanse that she knew so well. Even though it was covered in snow, she grinned with delight to see her home again.

Hamish was right. Construction had progressed incredibly fast. As they swept over the valley, she descended and slowed, studying the orderly layout of the streets.

Hamish pointed at the huge building that was already complete. "That will be the central hall, and it'll include four different kitchens and dining halls. It's going to be amazing."

"I'm sure the inaugural feast will surpass even your dreams," she assured him with a smile.

He grinned. "I hope so."

She banked the Hawk and headed for Faulenrost, nestled in the hills on the east side of the valley. The town looked bigger, with several large new barns on the outskirts and two entirely new streets on the south side of town with homes packed around them. Several huge, earthen buildings butted up against those new streets.

A crowd was already gathered, waiting for them to land in the windrider parking field on the outskirts of town. Hamish had called ahead via the speakstone. Jean, Gisela, and Dierk stood at the forefront of the enthusiastic crowd.

Verena jumped from the Hawk as soon as it touched down, her heart nearly overflowing as she waved to all the enthusiastic, smiling faces of so many people she knew so well. They surrounded her in a happy throng, calling out greetings and pushing for a chance to hug her and welcomed her back.

It took several minutes for everyone to greet her, and she loved every second of it. She wanted to speak with all of them, hear about their ordeals, their struggles, and their triumphs. Many of them mentioned with great pride their current projects.

Most were things she knew nothing about. It was a strange feeling. As the lead researcher, Verena had always known all about every project, had helped her people make critical breakthroughs, and was usually there to celebrate every success. Now she felt a twinge of sadness as she realized she had missed so much, She promised to make it up to them.

Finally Kilian and Hamish broke up the crowd, assuring them that Verena would get to speak with them more as she toured their workrooms. Connor stayed close, hovering as if worried she might suddenly disappear.

She squeezed his hand, relieved to have him by her side, united again in purpose and love. Their arguments had threatened the foundation of their relationship and wounded them both far too deeply.

Now that she thought back, she could see how they had both acted foolishly, with too much pride, too much judgment, and not nearly enough forgiveness or understanding. She felt hopeful they'd keep their mutual promise to listen more and judge less.

Of course, the fact that he had told Shona to her face that he wanted nothing else to do with her and had broken his promise to kiss that vile woman again helped a ton. It seemed that Connor had finally recognized his priorities. She dared hope they'd escaped the last of Shona's manipulations.

Jean pushed through the thinning crowd and gave Verena another hug. "I'm so happy you're awake and feeling so well. We missed you, and we really need your leadership."

"I doubt that. From everything I see, you're a gifted administrator. You've done miraculous work here, Jean. Thank you for taking such good care of everyone."

Connor asked, "Jean, did you get my deliveries?"

She nodded excitedly. "That rock that Stuart discovered is the anti-obsidian stone!"

Verena gasped and shared a surprised look with Connor. He said, "That's wonderful. I'm still trying to figure out how he sensed there was something special about it."

That caught Verena's attention. "What do you mean?"

Dierk interrupted and gave Verena another hug. Connor motioned that he would explain more later. The question tugged at Verena's mind, but it had to jostle with the dozens of other questions she also needed to follow up on.

Dierk said, "Jean's done a brilliant job, no doubt about that. We need you too, though. Our work seemed empty without you. It's good to have you back."

"So tell me what you've all been working on. I didn't understand half of what everyone was so excited about," she said as Kilian led them into town toward Lord Eberhard's manor house.

Jean said, "There's so much to tell. We'll need half the day to catch you up on everything."

Dierk nodded. "We've got production for most of the important mechanicals up and running again." He clapped Hamish on the shoulder. "But the majority of our efforts have been focused on developing your new Juggernaut armor."

"Juggernaut? I like the sound of that," Hamish said. Then he wrapped Jean in an enthusiastic embrace.

She glowed with joy. They'd greeted each other with unabashed joy, and their happiness warmed Verena's heart. Jean said, "Wait till you see what we've done! We should have a prototype ready for testing in the next month."

"Whatever you've got, I'll need it within a week."

"A week?" Jean gasped.

"We also have a lot to talk about." Hamish gestured at Aifric. "Her family tried assassinating the queen. They nearly succeeded, but 'nearly' doesn't work with that woman."

Aifric looked grave. "Student Eighteen's father and two other senior assassins lost their lives in the attempt."

"I'm so sorry," Jean exclaimed. She touched Aifric's arm and said with heartfelt sincerity, "Is there anything we can do to help her?"

"Just knowing you're all here to support her is enough for now."

Sometimes Verena found it a bit mind-bending to think about all the different women living inside Aifric's head, but Jean seemed to have no trouble treating each version of Aifric as a separate, beloved friend.

As they entered Lord Eberhard's manor house and proceeded to Jean's spacious office, Hamish and Aifric together told the harrowing tale of their failed assault on the queen in Donleavy. Dierk looked horrified, and Jean gripped Hamish's hand with white-knuckled intensity.

"You could have been killed," she whispered.

"It was a close thing. I have no idea how we're going to stop her, but at the moment we need to focus on stopping Harley. She's leading an army against Merkland. Rory will be outnumbered and underpowered."

Verena frowned. "It sounds like Harley could probably destroy his entire army by herself. I still don't understand whys he's bothering with an army."

They glanced to Kilian who said, "Without us to aid them, she definitely could. I'm hoping Ailsa can shed light on the details in her next communication, but I suspect my mother is sending a message to the rest of the nation that any army with Harley at the head is invincible. It helps motivate them to support her."

Connor grimaced. "And keeps them afraid of giving her a reason to lead the army against them instead."

"If she wins, she'll lock down the entire country under her thumb. No one will dare challenge her," Verena added. That only heightened the desperate need to send her loved ones into harm's way. The stakes were higher than ever.

Hamish nodded. "That's why I need whatever you can get done within the week."

Jean looked terrified. "You can't mean to challenge her. The armor won't be done, won't be tested. You won't be ready."

Kilian said, "He won't be alone. We have a few days to plan how best to take her down. She's a very experienced general. She survived all the pivotal battles of the Tallan wars, so she might underestimate the danger she'll face in this little clash for Merkland."

He surveyed them all seriously. "I'm not going to lie to you all. We face a dire threat. We lack the time to mobilize enough forces. Rory's already got Ilse, Lukas, and the Crushers. We're the only other ones coming."

Verena knew he was right, but she couldn't shake a feeling of shame that she'd agreed to let them face their deadliest fight without her.

Kilian added, "This battle could very well determine the fate of the entire continent. If we lose, the revolution will die in its infancy. Harley and my mother would no doubt build on that momentum to invade Granadure, and we are far from ready to stop them."

He did not point out that if they lost in Merkland, there was a very good chance all of them would be dead. If that happened, Verena wasn't sure she would survive the heartbreak. No doubt the rest of the continent would fall. They needed Kilian's leadership and Connor's curse if they wanted even a glimmer of a chance at defeating Queen Dreokt.

Verena squeezed Connor's hand, drawing comfort from his presence. He glanced at her and gave her an encouraging smile. She tried to return it, but she felt sick with fear. She hadn't struggled to hard to return to him only to let him die alone without her.

Jean took a long, shuddering breath and managed a weak smile. "Then we have a lot of work to do."

Dierk spoke for the first time. He sat at the end of the table, looking deeply concerned, but resolute. "All of our lives and the lives of everyone we love hang in the balance here. We cannot hold back. We must destroy them, fight them with every weapon at our disposal, no matter how horrible."

"What are you suggesting?" Verena asked. She had never seen Dierk look so miserable but determined. He had taken Ingrid's death very badly, but she read an iron-hard resolve in his eyes.

"Porphyry."

She did not like where the conversation was going.

Kilian asked, "What about porphyry?"

"I've been experimenting with the powder Connor sent to us."

"You haven't," Verena gasped. Connor had mentioned he'd recovered some, but in the blur of everything else that had happened, she had not considered what that meant. "We did some initial testing at the border when we captured those rampagers, but porphyry is so incredibly danger-ous. When we quickened it, it triggered uncontrollable rage."

"Exactly," Dierk said grimly. "I plan to unleash that rage upon Harley and her army."

Verena shuddered, imagining the horror that would sweep across that army as thousands upon thousands of soldiers were swept up in rampager fury.

Hamish looked ashen. "They would tear themselves apart."

Dierk nodded, looking sick, but resolute. "Better they tear themselves apart than tear Merkland apart."

Kilian sat back in his chair and said softly, "I don't like it." When Dierk started to protest he added, "But I'm willing to consider it."

Jean exclaimed, "You can't be serious. It's insane. You told me you were exploring how to safely handle porphyry. You didn't say anything about building a rage-murder weapon."

Dierk regarded her gravely. "I did what I had to do. Would you feel better killing them all yourself?"

Kilian spoke into the silence that fell over the group as they considered that ugly question. "Many battles are won with only a fraction of either army actually dying, but in this case I suspect Harley will not allow her forces to retreat. That means a fight with no quarter given from either side. Rory and Ivor and their supporters cannot retreat either. One side or the other must conquer in Merkland."

Dierk nodded. "We face a terrible choice. Do we meet them on the field of battle and commit to killing each one of them individually, or do we consider unleashing this horrible weapon with the hopes that they'll damage themselves sufficiently that the survivors will retreat and leave us alone, at least for a while?"

Verena squeezed Connor's hand, feeling close to tears as she considered the terrible decision. They had faced battle and war together, had seen people they knew and loved die in the fighting, but they were considering death on a whole new scale.

No one spoke for a moment, but finally Jean said softly, "There has to be a better way. Couldn't we target Harley specifically, try to isolate and remove her? If we did that, might the rest of the army retreat?"

"Are you willing to risk the lives of everyone here who depends upon us for their safety?" Dierk asked softly. "If Merkland falls, Altkalen will be next. Where do you think they would strike after that?"

Jean rose and paced slowly around the table, clearly struggling with the same concerns that swarmed through Verena's mind. The rest of them sat quietly as they considered the terrible choice.

Connor finally spoke. "I vote that we attack Harley. I don't know if we can kill her. I was not able to the last time I faced her, but if we work together we might be able to."

The others started to nod, except for Dierk, who did not look convinced. Verena wanted to go to him, hug him, try to reassure him that they would not let the other helpless people they knew die like Ingrid had.

Kilian spoke. "I support the plan, and I'm proud of all of you for working so hard to defend our land, but not getting caught up in the bloodlust that destroys so many during wartime. However, it's unwise not to have a backup plan. Dierk, prepare your weapon, but hold it in reserve. If we're blessed with a bit of Tallan's luck, maybe we won't need it."

That was not a great solution, but perhaps it was the best one. Dierk nodded and rose.

Verena hated that they were faced with such choices, but she stiffened her resolve to do everything in her power to help safeguard her friends against the dangers they were willingly confronting. She rose and said, "Like Jean said, we have a lot of work to do."

Jean grinned at her suddenly. "And we also have a little surprise for you."

71

AFFECTIONS ARE FLIGHTY

Connor walked hand-in-hand with Verena down the cobbled streets of Faulenrost as the group followed Jean, who seemed ready to burst with excitement. Snow clung to the edges of the streets, but the foot traffic had cleared the main lanes. It was cold, but calm. Columns of smoke rose straight from chimneys into the crisp, blue sky.

The picturesque little town looked even more appealing under a coating of snow, and the townsfolk went about their daily routines with smiles and jokes, most of which Connor couldn't understand. He really needed to start learning Grandurian.

"Do you have any idea what this surprise is?" Verena asked as they rounded a corner and headed toward a large barn near the outskirts of town.

"I haven't got a clue."

He'd ask Hamish, but his friend didn't look like he wanted to ever let Jean's hand go. They were talking and laughing together, despite how often Jean urged the others to hurry. Kilian, Aifric, and Gisela rounded out their little party.

As they neared the barn, one of the massive doors slid open and Dierk stepped out. He waved enthusiastically and beckoned them on.

Verena grinned and said, "It has to be one of their new projects. I hate how little I know about what's been going on."

"I'm sure you'll pick it all up before nightfall," Connor assured her.

He was glad she'd come with them. Walking among the Builders and refugees of Schwinkendorf seemed to fill her with vibrant energy. Her eyes glowed with joy, and she kept breaking away to rush over to greet people as they passed.

When they followed Jean and Dierk into the barn, Connor paused to let his eyes adjust to the dim light. After the bright winter sunlight outside, the barn seemed shadowed.

Jean grabbed Verena's other hand and tugged her forward, between stacks of wooden crates. The huge barn was warm, and it rang with voices and the banging of tools. Connor caught sight of several groups working around heavy wooden tables, but didn't pause to see what they were doing. Walls of supplies separated each group and formed a warren of little hallways that Jean whisked them down.

After a moment, they neared the rear of the barn. Another set of doors stood closed there. When they rounded a final corner, Connor stopped to stare.

In a large open space near those outer doors stood a sleek little flying craft.

Verena gasped, one hand going to her mouth, and both Jean and Dierk laughed with joy.

Jean proclaimed with obvious pride, "Behold the Swift reborn!"

"Oh, Jean, it's beautiful," Verena exclaimed. She gave Jean an enthusiastic hug.

"Dierk led the team that did the work. I just helped with planning," Jean explained.

Verena hugged him next, and the bespeckled Builder flushed with embarrassed pride. "You didn't think we'd let you awaken without a personal flyer, did you?"

Verena looked close to tears as she rushed to the craft and slid a hand along its gently curving flank. "I thought I'd have to rebuild it myself."

Dierk huffed. "Fine friends we'd be if we let you do all the work."

Jean said, "I hope you don't mind, but we took the liberty of adding some of the enhancements we developed for the Hawk."

Dierk nodded toward the enclosed canopy. "Your original Swift left you too exposed."

Connor agreed with that. If Verena had been riding in this new Swift, she might have better survived that crash. He followed her to the new Swift and together they inspected it as Jean and Dierk talked over each other in their excitement to explain all of its components.

It was a marvel. The little craft was a little larger than the original Swift, with that enclosed canopy instead of the simple front and back supports. In addition to a comfortable, padded pilot seat for Verena, it included one other cramped little seat close behind. That would be a lot more comfortable than the little stirrups they'd used on her original Swift for passengers.

Jean and Dierk were quick to assure Verena that the bigger Swift lacked none of her original craft's mobility. They had packed thrusters into every plane, allowing the nimble craft to twist, turn, roll, and spin just as fast as the original ever had. The new one was significantly faster, safer, and more stable. The stubby wings, packed with weapons, would certainly help.

"And Dierk himself tested it," Jean said eagerly.

That was a surprise. Connor had always heard that Dierk was a terrible flyer. Hamish started to laugh, but cut it short when Jean shot him an angry look.

Verena looked startled. "Dierk, you used to hate flying boring old windriders."

"After Ingrid died, I dedicated myself to mastering flight. If I had been a better flyer, I might have been able to help her, or at least train her better so she wouldn't have died."

Sorrow etched his features, but he looked unusually resolute. Connor felt proud of him for working so hard to overcome his grief. Verena hugged him and said softly, "Ingrid would be so proud to know how well you've honored her memory."

"Thank you."

Jean added, "Dierk now acts as our lead test pilot. He might give you and Hamish a real challenge in the air."

"Good for you, Dierk!" Hamish laughed, clapping the smaller Builder on the shoulder. "We'll have to race."

"When we can find the time for it," Jean interjected.

Verena completed her initial circuit, looking as happy as Connor had ever seen. She didn't speak, but simply walked around the new Swift, touching it, smiling so wide her cheeks looked permanently locked back.

"What do you think?" Jean finally asked.

Verena flung her arms around Jean and hugged her again. "I love it."

She hugged Dierk again and tears shone in her eyes. She spoke with a voice heavy with emotion. "You are the truest friends. I feel like you don't even need me any more."

"Nonsense," Dierk said. "We've only continued the work you started."

Jean nodded, her expression warm and serious. "We need you now more than ever, Verena. We've pushed the limits of what we can do with the research you'd done, but we need you to help us make the next break-through."

"We'll work on it together."

Kilian said, "Jean. Dierk. Thank you both. I couldn't imagine a better way to show Verena how much we care for her and how happy we are to have her back."

Connor took Verena's hand. "What are you waiting for? I know you can't wait to get that thing into the air."

She laughed, glancing longingly at the Swift. "I do." She hesitated and asked, "Would you like to come?"

He wanted nothing more than to join her, but sensed it wasn't yet the time. So he shook his head. "Next time. I think you need some time to just fly alone. You and the sky and the new Swift."

She smiled. "Thanks."

"Have fun out there."

She scrambled into the Swift and caressed the control rods, familiarizing herself with the many components. Connor and Hamish pulled the heavy doors wide as the thrusters ignited with a whooshing of air. The craft lifted off and the shield windows flowed across the wide window openings in the canopy. Verena waved once more as she hovered out through the doors.

Then the thrusters roared like exultant pedras and the Swift leaped into the sky with startling speed. Connor watched her ascend at a steep angle, growing smaller and smaller until she disappeared from view.

He wedged a piece of quartzite into his cheek and sucked on it. As soon as he felt the liquid warmth begin pooling in his head, he tapped it to his eyes. His vision sharpened and the distant speck of Verena's Swift grew until he could watch her diving, spinning, and rolling, putting the craft through its paces. He was glad he hadn't joined her. He would have reached the stomach-lurch point by then.

After a few seconds though, his vision started to flicker and dance. He'd felt the green frequency of magic rolling past, but had expected internal-focused quartzite to act like his primaries and secondaries, without interference from the higher-frequency power source.

It wasn't as bad as when he tried to tap elemental air, but the interference did creep in, like oil slithering across the calm surface of a loch. He lost connection with quartzite and his vision snapped back to normal. Then the connection returned and his gaze swooped back into the sky. Frowning, he tried to stabilize the connection, but it continued to flicker. As his gaze shifted repeatedly back and forth between normal and Pathfinder enhanced, the effect made him feel a bit dizzy.

Releasing quartzite, he frowned. Turning, he saw Kilian watching him and said, "I can't even keep quartzite stable with internal focus."

Kilian gave him that roguish smile and said, "Then I guess we'd better practice."

72

WHEN INSPIRATIONAL SPEECHES
ARE NOT

It was actually a great time to practice, with everyone scattering to their various duties. So Connor asked, "Where to?"

"Come on. We need a bit more privacy," Kilian said.

Together they absorbed a bit of basalt and raced out of town, down through the foothills, and across the wide, snowy valley toward New Schwinkendorf. Connor grinned as they flashed across the top of the snow, kicking up sprays of fine powder, moving too fast to sink in. Connor laughed into the cold wind that whistled in his ears as he ran. He loved that sound.

That was it! That's why he heard wind every time he tapped serpentinite. It was the sound of running with basalt, the sound of freedom.

Feeling exultant that he'd figured that out, he barely noticed the cold until they slowed in the cleared streets of New Schwinkendorf. Only then did he remember he could have tapped granite at the same time. He'd been so looking forward to trying two primary-affinity stones, he felt annoyed that he'd missed his chance.

The streets were all laid out in an orderly grid pattern, so unlike the original town that Connor had to wonder if the eventual residents would like it or hate it. Kilian led him at a trot past the nearly completed assembly building, dodged workmen and wagons laden with supplies, then entered the shell of another building just up the street. The outer framework was complete and much of the sheathing was finished. The interior was little more than a skeleton of beams that suggested a complex arrangement of multiple floors and rooms.

"What is this building supposed to be?" Connor asked.

"One of the administration buildings, I believe," Kilian said.

"Why isn't anyone working on it today?"

"I'm not sure, but it makes a perfect place for a little practice."

"Far from Faulenrost and a lot of innocent bystanders, you mean?"

Kilian shook his head. "I don't think you're a danger to people, Connor. I do think you need the least amount of distractions possible while you try to stabilize your tertiary affinities."

That was definitely true. The other truth was that he was freezing. He hadn't exactly dressed for a Strider sprint across the winter landscape. He said through chattering teeth, "Maybe I'll start with marble."

Kilian placed a hand on his shoulder and warmth flowed into him like an invisible river. He sighed as the chill faded and said, "Thanks."

"I forgot you couldn't keep yourself warm. It's second nature to me," Kilian said with a rueful smile.

"Any suggestions?" Connor asked as he downed a vial of soapstone and water.

"You've been practicing daily in Altkalen?"

Connor nodded. "Didn't seem to help much. I still can't keep an elemental connection more than a couple seconds."

"Have you gained any other insights about how the higher frequency power source interferes with you?"

"I was hoping you could tell me."

"It takes time, and unfortunately the threshold affects different Petralists in different ways."

"Really?" That seemed weird until Connor considered that they would have established different affinities, in different orders.

"Few Petralists have succeeded in ascending twice. Of those who did, we all faced varying degrees of interference from the two conflicting power frequencies. One that I knew of never managed to figure out how to overcome that challenge and died in battle shortly after ascending."

"You really need to work on your inspirational speeches," Connor grumbled, feeling even more desperate than ever. He couldn't imagine not figuring out how to stabilize his precious tertiary affinities. They played such a critical role in battle planning. He'd never survive another encounter with Harley without them.

"So what can I do? How long does it usually take?"

"It varies. For some it's taken weeks or months," Kilian admitted.

"I can't wait that long!" Connor exclaimed.

"Why do you think I told you not to ascend?" Kilian asked, sounding a bit exasperated too.

As if he'd had an alternative. As much as the current situation frustrated him, dying at Raufarhofn would have been worse. He tried to calm his racing thoughts. He'd faced many difficult challenges. He could figure this out. As he considered Kilian's words he suddenly got an idea.

"If the second threshold messed everything up by tuning my affinities to the higher-frequency, green power source, what would the third threshold do? Would it grant access to another frequency?"

"Good question, but no. Tallan once explained that the third threshold seemed to bring stability. It helped balance the two different frequencies and smoothed out the troubles he'd encountered after the second threshold."

That was even better than Connor had hoped. "That makes it easy, then. I just need to ascend the third threshold right now."

Kilian surprised him by shaking his head. "Not if you want to live."

"Why not?"

"You can't tempt the third threshold until you're stabilized. Otherwise the attempt would almost definitely kill you. At the least, you'd burn out all of your affinities and never again manage to touch the power of any stone."

His words chilled Connor far worse than the run down from Faulenrost had. "So if the third threshold is out, what else can you suggest?"

Kilian grimaced. "I'd hoped to locate Evander by now, but he's concealed his location from my messengers. From what Ailsa's reported, my mother has not had better luck. I had hoped he might have discovered better techniques in his deep studies at the Carraig."

"Well, I need to do something. Maybe I should go look for him," Connor suggested.

Kilian chuckled. "Leaving you to run alone into Obrion would be a singularly bad idea, I think."

"I'm not helpless," Connor grumbled.

Kilian raised one eyebrow and asked, "How well did your last excursion go?"

That was a good point. Connor sighed. "So do you have ideas? I'll keep practicing, but trying the same things doesn't usually produce different results."

"Agreed. I do have one idea we can try."

"Name it. I'd kiss a pedra or play tag with a torc if that would help."

Kilian chuckled. "I'm tempted to watch you try."

Connor grimaced. A pedra had once tried to rip his head off. He knew all too well how disgusting they were up close.

Kilian said, "It's possible that if you actively tap a green-attuned power stone, you may be able to keep the green frequency from interfering. Then maybe you could establish red-attuned connections at the same time."

The idea actually had merit, but he only knew of one green-attuned power stone. "Tempting porphyry again is a really bad idea."

Just thinking about the dangerous stone was like throwing open the door to the wild hunger that had assaulted his will so much in recent weeks. Connor's vision blurred as the need for porphyry erupted through him, so strong his hands began to shake and he growled with the need to embrace it. He had some porphyry. He'd kept one pouch of the dangerous powder when he sent the rest of Craigroy's stash to Jean.

The abrupt need startled and terrified him. Ever since he'd managed to control porphyry in Merkland the craving for it had subsided to a dull ache. He'd dared believe that after his ascension it would no longer pose such a threat.

Kilian placed a strong hand on his shoulder and he glanced up. He hadn't realized he'd doubled over, clutching his stomach. Kilian's gaze was penetrating, but compassionate. "Are you all right?"

"I'm not sure. All of a sudden I feel the craving for porphyry stronger than I have in days."

Kilian frowned as he helped Connor stand straight. That unnerved Connor as much as anything he felt from porphyry. Kilian was supposed to have all the answers. Connor couldn't tempt porphyry again without knowing for sure Kilian was confident it would work.

Kilian said, "You've established a deep affinity with porphyry. If you can control it, I suspect it would indeed help stabilize your tertiary affinities, but it is not the only green-attuned power stone."

"Really?"

"Indeed. Both obsidian and pumice have partial links to green-frequency power."

"How can people establish affinities with them, then?"

"Because those connections are not exclusive. Obsidian was the first-ever power stone, the only igneous stone that has its own threshold. I don't think my parents understood how to tune power stones to the different frequencies yet, and obsidian ended up somewhere in the middle of the two lowest frequencies, allowing both the red and green to flow through."

"What about pumice?" Connor asked.

"Another unique stone. From Aifric's description, it actually absorbs red frequency power. To do that, it must funnel that power elsewhere. I suspect it does so by linking somehow to a higher frequency power source, most likely the green."

Connor frowned as he considered the new information. "I definitely vote trying one of those first."

They made a quick basalt-fueled dash back to Faulenrost for the stones they would need, and that time Connor remembered to tap granite at the same time, hardening his skin against the cold. Running while tapping both basalt and granite was an amazing experience, and he wished for more time to explore the different possible combinations. He was only tapping a little granite, just enough to harden his skin, but what if he tapped more? Would swelling his muscles allow him to run faster, or would the expanded bulk actually slow him down?

He'd test it later. He collected some stones, including that secret stash of porphyry. He didn't want to use it, but he'd keep it close, just in case.

They returned to the empty shell of the building in New Schwinkendorf and Connor purged his active igneous stones, then absorbed a little pumice. Immediately he recognized its strange feel, like hundreds of tiny bubbles under his skin. His mind returned to that night he'd saved Shona from Ilse's band and hid from Kilian in the Wick.

In the past, when he thought of that memory, he'd always just thought about that first kiss with Shona. Now he felt relieved to have other aspects of the memory to consider.

Tapping pumice seemed to accelerate the intensity of the bubbles bouncing around under his skin, and like that time in the Wick, he seemed to have a lot more air, even though he slowed his breathing. Now that he'd ascended, could he actually breathe underwater? That would be fun to try out.

With pumice active, he also tried tapping soapstone. As soon as Water formed in his mind, he felt the two conflicting frequencies crashing through her, mixing and colliding across her robe. But with pumice active, the red-frequency power source seemed a lot stronger and as covered most of her hands.

She gave him an approving smile, her long, blue tresses waving like a gentle tide. Connor eagerly took her hand.

He connected!

His senses radiated out beyond the building and mapped the snow-covered streets of New Schwinkendorf. The green frequency power still collided with his grip, but only briefly. That contact shook his connection with Water, but did not quite sever it.

"It's working!" Connor exclaimed. He tugged on the snow just outside the building, melted it, and fashioned a globe of water over his palm. With the green interference, it shook and nearly dissolved every couple of seconds, but each time he managed to catch it and reform it.

Kilian watched closely. "It's not great, but it's better."

"A million percent better," Connor laughed, trying to pull on more water, but he timed the pull badly, just as another wave of green-frequency power swept across Water's hands, and he lost the connection. The globe of water splashed down over his hand before he could save it.

Kilian clapped him on the shoulder. "We'll need to keep practicing, but maybe we've found the way to accelerate your stabilization."

Connor took a deep breath and reached for a piece of marble. Time to push the limits a little.

73

EXTREME ALONE TIME

Hamish, did you decide to take a nap in there?"

Dierk's voice startled Hamish awake as it boomed into his helmet through a speakstone. He actually had nodded off, held up by the complex harness securing him in place in the tight cockpit of the amazing Juggernaut.

"Just double-checking access to the components," he replied quickly. "Give me another minute."

The past five days had sped by in a blur of activity and strudel-induced creative frenzy. Hamish had worked with Dierk, Jean, Verena, and dozens of Builders, researchers, and workers on the monumental task of completing the Juggernaut. It seemed the entire town turned out to support efforts to finish other mechanicals and provide whatever supplies the tiny strike force could bring south to Merkland.

Verena's presence invigorated everyone. Working with her again was like a breath of cool air on a hot afternoon in the middle of summer. Every time she entered the workroom, she infused it with new life. But even so, their work was daunting. Hamish caught far too little sleep and had to eat far too many smashpacked meals.

They'd done it, though.

Hamish glanced around the cockpit at the center of the twelve-foot tall, spherical wonder. By now he knew every component as well as he knew his personal battle suit, but it still amazed him.

He'd helped design the initial concept, but they'd taken those rough ideas and given them wings. How they powered the suit was simply brilliant. Jean and her team had developed an entirely new way to harness affinity stones.

The engineering master still left him gaping. To his right sat the marvelous new furnace. All it burned was a small piece of marble. That constant fire was then mixed with single grains of diorite, released one at a time through a clever set of rotating canisters. The explosive result produced tiny but fierce bursts of power that drove a series of gears and pistons that in turn powered most of the ingenious mechanicals. Hamish controlled the flow of that power with a series of brass knobs and levers arrayed all around him.

He spun a complete circle, touching each one, connecting with the many components and weapons built into the armor. His harness was suspended from brass casters set into a complex pattern of channels that allowed them to spin in any direction. In testing, they'd proven that he could remain upright as the armor rolled, except for in the most abrupt changes of direction.

Dierk, Jean, and their teams had packed a remarkable amount of mechanicals into the armor, including drills, thrusters, missiles, and battering ram arms. The armor could roll at impressive speeds and even fly short distances. Even the Althing researchers had presented him with a small vial of highly corrosive acid that he could spray up to thirty feet.

He'd expected to need wagonloads of power stone to fuel the massive juggernaut. Some of the individual components did consume marble, quartzite, or diorite, but that little central furnace powered most of the mechanical's ravenous needs.

Jean's voice interrupted his inspection of the mechanical wonder. "Hamish, are you eating in there?"

He laughed. He'd consumed dozens of smashpacked meals in the cockpit over the past few days, but he'd always offered to share. "Come on in and find out."

He activated one of the last components they'd gotten working. They called it a sightstone. It was another clever use of quartzite that Jean had decided must be possible. Hamish and Verena had figured out how to make it work just the day before. Little pieces of quartzite were embedded in the outer shell, and they could act as remote eyeballs for Hamish.

He activated the one closest to Jean. One side of his visor shimmered as the quartzite linked to that outside sightstone revealed the image of what its paired stone could see. It was sort of like using long-vision goggles, but seeing objects visible only to that outer stone.

Through it, he could see the cluttered jumble of benches, tools, and empty crates that had held power stones. The team was gathered near Jean, who stood facing the Juggernaut, her expression a bit impatient.

"No. You come out. It's dinner time. I promised Verena and Connor we'd join them at the inn."

"Coming!"

He released the sightstone, unbuckled, and scrambled out the access tunnel to the round exit door. Jean had been incredibly optimistic in her declaration that they needed another month. Hamish figured they needed six to do things right, but all they'd had was five days.

The frantic pace their teams had sustained around the clock through all of those days inspired him. Hamish had only ever achieved that state of complete focus and inexhaustible enthusiasm during the construction of his initial battle suit, fueled by hundreds of smashpacked meals and secret trips into the kitchen for buckets full of sweetbreads.

Jean helped him crawl out and stand. She looked tired, but her smile still lit up his soul. Spending so much time with her during the final assembly and exhaustive testing had made it all worthwhile.

Dierk and the rest of the team looked worse. Dierk's glasses were a bit askew, and he had dark circles under his eyes. Twenty men and women, most grease-stained and disheveled, gathered around in a tired but enthusiastic circle.

Hamish glanced at the glittering out shell, made of steel and hardened granite plates. The Juggernaut was rough and raw, but ready for battle. He wasn't sure he could destroy Harley, but he could sure keep her busy until the rest of the team figured out how to take her down.

"Well done, everyone. I think it's ready!" Hamish proclaimed loudly to enthusiastic cheers.

Dierk sighed with relief and added, "Go get some dinner and a good night's sleep everyone. We'll celebrate properly tomorrow."

Hamish clapped hands with each person as they left, thanking them for their hard work. Jean stood close beside him, and he kept getting distracted just wanting to look at her. Her thick, blond hair had come unbraided, and wisps of it seemed to caress her cheeks and throat.

"Stop dawdling. I'm hungry," Jean said after the last of the team left the large workspace and he finally got to simply stare at her.

Hamish wrapped an arm around her shoulder as they headed out through the cold twilight toward the inn across town. Connor and Verena were waiting for them outside, holding hands. They too looked tired, but happy. Hamish had seen little of Connor in recent days, and not enough of Verena once final testing commenced.

Verena had spent most of her time supporting and assisting, well, everyone. She seemed to be involved in everything, lifting spirits and helping drive projects forward. And of course she spent every bit of extra time flying in her new Swift. Hamish was starting to fear that if Verena was ever asked to choose between her new Swift or Connor, she'd leave him in a heartbeat.

Connor spent the bulk of his time practicing with Kilian. It sounded like that second threshold made life complicated. Some of what Connor tried to explain challenged some of Hamish's basic beliefs about how affinity stones worked. When they found more time, they needed to dig into some of that weirdness and see if there were deeper truths to Builder powers too. They might be able to unlock even more potential from affinity stones, and that was worth embracing a little weirdness.

Verena greeted them with enthusiastic hugs, and Connor gestured them toward the entrance. "We already ordered a meal. Should be ready."

Hamish and Jean led the way into the inn, with Connor and Verena on their heels. A wave of golden light and heavy warmth embraced them inside the huge common room. Hamish breathed deep the smell of meat pies and fresh-baked bread.

Although it was late, the inn was packed with people, and they all turned, as if they'd been waiting. Liesa and Evert, their innkeeper aprons somehow still spotless white, raised wooden tankards high and shouted the new cheer they'd invented that week.

"For Faulenrost and Builder glory!"

Everyone raised glasses and tankards and shouted the cheer, shaking the inn with the thunderous noise. Jean flushed. She still seemed surprised by the attention. She'd confessed she'd love more quiet time to simply focus on research.

Hamish doubted she'd get much peace. Too many people knew how brilliant she was.

He raised a hand, and calm slowly settled over the crowd. "Thank you all for your help. We could not have succeeded without you all."

Another round of loud cheering.

Connor added, "We have to leave tomorrow."

That surprised Hamish. He glanced over as a somber hush settled over the crowd. Connor said softly, "I'll explain while we eat."

Plump Liesa cried, "You'll trounce those Obrioner Petralists, you will!"

That elicited another loud cheer, and Hamish grinned at their enthusiasm. "Many of you helped build the tools we'll use. Faulenrost is going to battle with us, and it's your hard work that will turn the tide in our favor."

The crowd cheered louder than ever as the four of them headed for the back dining room. Many of the locals rose to shake their hands and wish him and Connor luck, although they seemed more eager to speak with Jean and Verena, both of whom were town favorites.

The table was already heaped with the inn's best food, and a roaring fire in the hearth warmed the room to sleepy levels.

"How did the testing go today?" Verena asked as they took their seats.

"We're not ready," Jean said, her voice nervous.

Hamish said, "Maybe not entirely, but enough of it works that I won't be facing Harley unarmed."

He loved his personal battle suit, but he'd need the Juggernaut to hope to survive even a little while against Harley.

Verena said, "It's incredible. I can still hardly believe how much you've accomplished."

"It was a group effort. New Schwinkendorf might become the official Builder compound, but Faulenrost is the heart of the Juggernaut."

Connor said, "I'm glad it's ready. We received word from Ivor today. Harley is close. That's why we need to leave tomorrow morning."

"I still can't imagine how she moved nearly thirty thousand troops all the way from Crann to Merkland through the dead of winter so fast," Verena said.

Connor said, "Probably used wagon loads of tertiary stones. I'm glad I don't know how many soldiers died on that march."

They all served themselves large portions of roasted pork, beef medallions in a delicious dark sauce, bratwurst, dijon-dill chicken, and sauerkraut. Hamish sighed with bliss as he polished off his first plate and returned for more.

After sating his initial hunger he said, "Jean, you and Verena will need to keep everyone focused. If things go badly, Altkalen will need all the help you can send. If things go well, it means we'll be facing the queen next, and we'll need all the help we can get."

Facing Harley was truly terrifying, even with his Juggernaut armor, but he trusted Connor and Kilian, as well as the rest of the team already in Merkland. They had survived other long odds.

He hoped their luck held out.

Verena leaned back in her chair, her food only half gone and said, "I'm coming to Merkland."

Connor tried to object, but choked on a piece of ham he'd been about to swallow. Hamish beat him on the back while he coughed and asked, "What's wrong with you, Verena? Usually your timing is better. You can't make an announcement like that when people are eating. It's dangerous."

Jean said, "Well, I'm glad you said it because I'm coming too."

The thought of Jean in danger killed Hamish's appetite and he sighed. "I'm so disappointed. Couldn't you wait until after dessert?"

Connor recovered from his coughing fit. "Verena, we talked about this. You're not ready."

"I wasn't ready five days ago, but I am now. I've got the new Swift and I plan to tow a full windrider full of extra mechanicals." She met his gaze firmly. "We're a team, Connor, and I'm coming with you."

Verena was deadly enough that Hamish wasn't really all that worried for her. Jean was another story. "Why do you have to come too?"

"I know the Juggernaut better than anyone. It's still so new, we barely got all the pieces fitted together. If something goes wrong, I can help you troubleshoot it."

"If something goes wrong, I doubt Harley will give me time to troubleshoot anything."

Her expression turned stubborn and although he tried several more times to discourage her, in his heart he knew she'd never change her mind.

Finally, Verena grew exasperated with the argument. "Stop it, Hamish. We're going, and that's that."

The door opened and Mattias stepped through. "And I'm coming too."

Connor started to rise, but Hamish pulled him back down. If he and Mattias started fighting, they'd wreck any chance of getting the feast going again. Besides, there weren't any good windows in the room.

Verena looked as surprised as the rest of them. "Mattias, what are you doing here?"

He approached and faced her, pointedly ignoring Connor. "I figured you'd do something foolish, although honestly I suspected Connor would encourage your lunacy."

"We don't need you," Connor said coldly.

Mattias dropped into a chair across the table from him. "We both know that's a lie. You're undermanned, facing the queen's strongest Petralist. You need all the help you can get."

Mattias looked far too calm. Had he hatched a plot with Verena's grumpy father to try persuading Verena to dump Connor?

"Did you bring any of your troops?" Verena asked, again composed.

He shook his head. "Taking anyone else would have triggered a blizzard of questions and delays. I just slipped aboard the daily windrider. Good thing too."

When both Verena and Connor started to protest again, he held up a hand to forestall them. "I'm not here to make trouble for you, Verena. You made your choice, and I'll honor it. I still think you'll change your mind, and I'm willing to wait until you do, but I'm here only to make sure you return home safely. The only way to stop me is to return to Altkalen with me."

"I can think of other ways," Connor said softly, angry gaze locked on Mattias.

Hamish said, "Mattias, you're ridiculous, but you're right. We do need the help." They could deal with any underhanded ploys after they survived Merkland.

Connor looked at him like he'd betrayed his trust, but Hamish shrugged. "You can't stop the girls, and you know it. Mattias is experienced working with the Crushers and we can use another good Allcarver."

Jean squeezed his hand in thanks. He might not be able to stop her, but that didn't mean he wouldn't spend the entire trip down to Merkland trying to think of the best way to keep her safe during the fighting.

Verena said, "I don't need your protection, Mattias, but I'm glad you're coming to help."

Connor looked like he'd taken a long swig of sour milk, but still managed to say, "Thanks for your help."

Jean ordered in another plate and insisted that Mattias join them for the rest of the feast. She was always thinking clever thoughts like that. It was a lot harder to remain angry with someone while enjoying a huge meal together, and they couldn't afford any hesitation when facing Harley.

As they resumed eating, Hamish noticed Connor seemed a bit preoccupied. He'd only eaten half of one of Liesa's famous walnut strudels and stared down at his plate with a frown. Definitely not natural, but he wasn't glaring at Mattias either.

"What's wrong?" he asked quietly.

"Oh, nothing," Connor said, shaking himself out of his reverie.

Hamish chuckled. "Something's eating you, Connor because you're not eating your dessert."

"It's just, today in our training, Kilian taught me another of those really strange new affinity powers. It's one of the ones that seems tuned to the green power source."

"That's the new one, the more powerful, but unstable one, right?" Verena asked.

"What are you talking about?" Mattias asked.

Connor hesitated then said, "I'll explain later. You taught me quartzite so I'll share what I've learned about the second threshold when we have a little more time. There are a couple of new abilities I can access through limestone."

That kind of mature response was no doubt inspired by the strudel. Desserts of that caliber lifted everyone to a higher state of being.

Mattias looked eager to hear more as Connor continued. "This effect is really strange."

"Stranger than mirage?" Jean asked.

Connor chuckled. "Most Solas have a complex. They think their power is kind of lame, but limestone is really amazing and really scary, honestly. It's possible, although extremely difficult and time consuming, to focus light into a super-compressed beam that can slice through just about anything except for mirrors. I haven't mastered that one yet, and I'm not sure how useful it would be in a fight with how long it takes to prepare."

Mattias hung on every word. "I've studied every scrap of information we have in the king's own library in Edderitz about ascended powers, but I've never heard about that."

"Few know about it. Kilian said a lot of these secrets were jealously guarded by his parents."

Verena said, "I wonder if we could tap something like that with a quickened stone?"

That would be amazing. Hamish eagerly said, "We'll have to practice. But you said there was another effect that's even stranger?"

Connor nodded. "Limestone focused internally."

"Doesn't that just make your teeth glow?" Verena asked.

Mattias shook his head. "The glow effect is just internalizing the external generation of light, like swallowing an invisible lamp. I never knew limestone had an internal effect."

Connor said, "It's completely opposite."

Hamish frowned. "Limestone produces light. So that effect creates darkness?"

"Darkness to every sense. It's complete sensory deprivation. Kilian demonstrated it on me for a couple seconds." Connor shivered.

Jean and Verena exchanged uneasy glances, but Hamish said, "Wow. Try it on me."

Jean asked, "Are you serious? Why would you want to experience that?"

"It didn't hurt Connor. I want to feel what he means, see if I get the same effect."

"It's not pleasant," Connor warned.

"Neither was smelling the mega-stench, but that was a life-altering experience. Maybe this will be too."

Verena grimaced. "I still can't believe you took off your mask."

"You're just jealous you weren't brave enough to do it too."

"Not hardly."

When Connor still hesitated, Hamish held up another of the walnut strudels. "I just don't believe you could really block me from tasting this amazing dessert." He popped it into his mouth and savored the explosion of deliciousness.

Mattias said, "I want to experience it too." He looked resolute, as if willing to fight over the point.

Connor couldn't resist an opportunity like that. He made no outward move, but all of a sudden the taste in Hamish's mouth faded away to nothing. The rest of the strudel in his hand faded from his sense of touch. Then he couldn't feel the chair he sat in, then lost all feeling entirely. It was like his skin fell asleep.

Complete blackness dropped over his vision. His sense of smell snuffed out as if he had never smelled sweetbreads fresh from the oven in his entire life. All sounds ceased to exist, and Hamish felt like he'd dropped into the deepest, blackest abyss, except he could not see or hear or feel or taste any aspect of that abyss. It was beyond black, beyond quiet, beyond empty. He was locked completely and utterly alone, with no sensory input whatsoever.

It was so fascinating.

He figured most people would begin to panic almost immediately. It was pretty disturbing if he let himself think about it. He tried screaming, but made no sound. He could still hear himself think, though.

So he tried imagining the smell of fresh sweetbreads, the feel of Jean's hand in his, and the incomparable experience of kissing her beautiful mouth. The memories felt weaker somehow, like pale shadows of what they should be, but they still existed. Whatever Connor was doing could steal away his external senses, but it could not rob him of his mind.

Only the queen could do that.

Then all of his senses came rushing back, and all Hamish could do was exult in the explosion of taste in his mouth, as if that pastry had been concentrating its flavor until he could enjoy it again. The colors of the room seemed brighter than ever before, and Jean's voice sounded like the pure singing of angels as she leaned closer and asked, "Are you all right?"

He grinned. "Ask me again."

She smiled and the curve of her full lips mesmerized him, as did the sculpted perfection of her features. She looked more beautiful than ever. The sight of her took his breath away.

Across the table, Mattias suddenly pitched backward, arms flailing out wide, his teeth erupting with blinding brilliance. He shouted a long, wordless cry, overbalanced his chair, and toppled with a crash.

Verena rushed around the table. "Are you all right?"

She helped the shaking Mattias to his feet and righted his chair. He glanced at Connor, shuttered his glowing teeth, and shivered. "I didn't think you could really do that to me, not while I was tapping limestone."

"I tried to warn you," Connor said apologetically.

Hamish said, "Next time I need to test it with a power stone in hand to see if I can still reach it."

"Next time?" Jean asked.

"Of course. I'm fine. In fact, we should do that at least once a week."

Mattias shook his head. "Once was enough for me."

Verena asked, "Why would you want to go through that again? I was trapped in my mind too, and I never want to experience that again."

Hamish shrugged. "It just seems that everything is more vibrant and beautiful now that I've experienced what it would be like without it. Especially you, Jean."

For that, she gave him a spectacular kiss that took his breath away again.

74

SOME MOMENTS NEED MORE HAPPY-THOUGHT THINKING FOOD

Merkland glittered in the bright morning sunlight, snow and ice reflecting the light like millions of diamonds scattered across the snow. Connor admired the beautiful river valley as they flew in over the township, toward the majestic city on the bluff on the other side of the river.

No doubt word was quickly spreading of their approach. They made a strange procession, even for Builders. Verena, Hamish, and Dierk each flew a long windrider, piled so high with mechanicals and supplies that there was barely room for the pilots on their high benches. It was a wonder they managed to lift off at all, and if not for a steady tailwind, they might never have made it to Merkland before exhausting the thruster blocks.

A second string of windriders floated behind each of them, tethered to the first and just as heavily loaded with equipment. In Hamish's case, his trailing windrider was an oversized model and all it carried was his enormous Juggernaut armor.

Trailing behind that enormous wagon came the Hawk, with Jean at the controls and Connor perched on the front row beside her. Jean wasn't doing much flying, although she had used her keystone to adjust the thrusters so they floated out wide and slightly above the obstructing view of the Juggernaut. Verena's new Swift floated tethered behind her trailing windrider.

Kilian rode in the second row, feet up on the seat to Jean's right, munching on a sugar-coated strudel he'd pilfered from one of the high-piled boxes of provisions that packed the rest of the craft. Aifric and Mattias shared the second row with him. They passed the time discussing strategies for the upcoming fight and exploring ways Aifric could use her

Mhortair affinities to support them. And of course, they did their best to consume as much of the food stores as possible.

Connor did his part to help while trying not to feel guilty that he rode in comfort, shielded from the wind in the comfortable, warm cockpit while Verena rode in the open windrider.

The people of Faulenrost had worked through the night to pack those windriders. Connor appreciated their diligence, although he didn't fool himself into thinking any of it was for him. They loved Jean and Verena like local heroines and treated Hamish like a favorite celebrity son. Gisela, who remained in Faulenrost with Jean's leadership team, promised to keep production going during their absence.

She'd gifted to Hamish and Verena a pair of small, sculpted obsidian stones. Those tiny stones excited the two Builders more than the packed spare windriders they towed. Hamish had explained that sculpted obsidian allowed them to control other mechanicals remotely and would prove extremely useful.

Kilian passed Connor another strudel, and he saluted in Verena's direction before taking a big bite for her.

They slowed to a hover above the huge square in front of the central palace. In his suit, Hamish flitted to all the tethered windriders and reduced their lift force so everyone could settle for a landing together. Huge crowds gathered along the fringes of the square, craning their necks to watch the marvelous flying wagons. Flying was becoming a commonplace part of Connor's life, but to most people it was still a miraculous new wonder.

Anika waited for them in the square, dressed in her normal battle leathers, with an additional, fur-lined cloak. She actually bounced on her toes in excitement. With her long, braided hair, cheeks rosy from the cold, and ridiculously happy smile, she looked a lot younger.

Tomas, Cameron, and Erich waited nearby, looking completely at ease with each other. They'd battled each other as enemies enough times to learn to respect one another. Connor wished he'd been around to join in their recent training bouts.

As soon as they landed, Verena rushed to Anika, who lifted her off the ground in a bear hug, laughing loudly. They talked and laughed in fast Grandurian. Connor caught the words "engaged", "happy", and of course Rory's name a dozen times.

He'd long marveled at the budding romance between the two, but had never imagined they'd actually find a way to legally get together. Well, Rory had been forced to start a revolution and declare war on the queen and all the high houses to do it. Connor hoped that Verena wouldn't expect him to overthrow any other sovereign nations to prove his love for her.

As Connor and the others all shared happy greetings with Anika and the three warriors, Mattias held back, looking surprised by their evident friendship.

Erich saluted him and said in his broken Obrioner, "No have fear, Lord Mattias. Many good bash fight prove strength. Is good revolution."

Mattias scanned the square and grinned ruefully. "The wonders will never cease."

Tomas said to Connor, "We'll assign guards to watch your wagons until you're ready to unload. General Rory wants to speak with you right away."

His tone seemed unusually grave, so Connor asked, "What's the situation?"

Cameron said, "Raiding party just returned."

Erich added, "Commander Lukas and his men are missing."

Connor exchanged a worried look with Verena. "Take us to them."

They hurried into the central palace and up one of the two central high towers. Rory and Ivor were meeting in Ivor's plush office with Ilse. They all looked relieved to see Connor and the others, especially Kilian. Ilse nearly burst into tears of gratitude when he entered the room.

Verena rushed to Ilse and hugged her. "What happened?"

Ivor gestured them all to take seats near the fire. When Mattias hesitated he said, "That's about all the protocol you'll probably get here, Lord Mattias. We save it for the parades. We know who you are, and you know us. Since you're here, we'll assume you're here to help."

Once they sat, Ivor said, "We've been sallying out of the city to monitor the advancing army and to harry and delay them when possible."

"Harley's with them?" Connor asked.

Ivor nodded. "Caught a couple glimpses of her in the distance. Wish I'd had a pair of those long-vision goggles."

Kilian said, "Captain Ilse, your team is specially trained for these types of high-risk missions. What happened?"

She said, "Our initial excursions went exactly as planned.

Ivor added, "I wouldn't want to tangle with Harley over dry ground, but this time of year, with so much snow everywhere, I could shield us entirely from her senses. We used the underwater Slide to move through the river to get close enough to observe and to strike."

"She must have Spitters," Mattias said.

Ivor nodded. "Several, but at first they weren't focused on defending against our incursions. I managed to slip through their perimeter without too much trouble."

Rory said, "They gained critical intelligence. High Lord Dougal himself leads the army. Shona is with them too."

"So is Harley in charge, or Dougal?" Connor asked.

Rory said, "It's not entirely clear, but that's an important question. Harley might be happy to level Merkland to drive us out, but Dougal will want to preserve it, if possible."

Ilse said, "Once we realized we could slip close to them without detection, we risked sallying from the river with Ivor shielding us through the snow. We took down two Spitters and a Firetongue who got lazy."

Ivor grimaced. "I'm afraid we got a bit overconfident. Lukas took a four-man squad back for another strike at a Sentry who had drifted from the main camp. It was a bold move, but could have won an important victory."

The Crushers, led by Ilse and Lukas, were trained specifically for those high-risk attacks against tertiary Petralists, but Connor still felt impressed. Lukas had dared to try attacking a Sentry just outside of a huge army led by none other than Harley herself.

"What happened?" Verena asked.

Ivor shrugged. "Not entirely sure. The Spitters in camp struck out in their first well-coordinated effort to sweep the area for our team. They caught a hint of us and we were forced to dive back underwater in the Slide. Once we started moving, I made sure to give them a hint of our presence to keep them focused on us instead of Lukas. It got rough."

He grimaced and Ilse blanched. Connor had seen her face terrifying odds against powerful armies unafraid, but he'd noticed on their trip away from the Carraig that she hated riding on the Slide. Floating so completely disconnected from the earth seemed to rattle her.

Ivor continued, "They came at us with a vengeance. Spitters hit the river hard and Sentries struck too, blindly driving earthen obstructions up from the bottom. Nearly skewered us. We only just barely escaped."

"So Lukas might have slipped away during all that commotion?" Connor asked. He would have assumed the worst for anyone else, but the Crushers' tenacity and cleverness was legendary. If only they knew the secret of pumice. Their chances of survival would climb dramatically.

"It's possible," Ilse said, but looked like she didn't quite dare believe it.

"What can we do to find him?" Verena asked.

Ilse said, "We've got Pathfinders scouring the countryside, but if he escaped, he would have struck west to get as much distance from the army as possible. The hills and forest are too thick that way to see him yet."

Hamish immediately offered, "We'll scout from the air. If he's out there, we'll spot him."

"Thank you," Ilse said with obvious relief.

Kilian said, "If there's any chance at recovering his team, we'll take it. This is only the first challenge we'll have to overcome in the days ahead. Thank you Ilse for risking so much to help."

She nodded her thanks and Kilian said, "What is the status here in the city, and how long before Dougal and his army arrive?"

Ivor said, "They've been pushing hard. They could potentially launch their first assault as early as tomorrow some time."

Rory said, "Looks like they've stripped Crann and picked up everyone we released. They're pushing close to thirty thousand troops, with maybe two thousand Petralists in the vanguard."

That was fast. Connor hadn't expected them to draw so close for at least another week. They were about to face an army as big as the one that had attacked Altkalen, but without a carefully planned defense. Plus, there was no guaranteeing all of their troops supported their cause with enough commitment to face those type of odds without cracking.

As if reading his thoughts, Mattias asked, "And what of Merkland? How are all of Dougal's lesser lords and ladies positioned?"

Rory said, "We're actually in better shape than I had expected. Lord Nevan is Dougal's administrator, a clever fellow who I've always respected. He doesn't approve of the way we're challenging the status quo and is still resisting the idea that patronage is an entire fabrication. However, he supports the idea of resisting the queen's usurpation of the crown and her assault on the noble houses. She represents a clear enough danger to the future of Obrion that he has thrown in support with us, especially after he learned Granadure would support our effort."

Connor was surprised. "Really? He's willing to risk his neck to help Guardians revolt?"

Ivor shook his head. "He doesn't like the idea of Guardians gaining freedom, but the queen's worse. She could easily kill him, mind-wipe him, or cast him out of his comfortable life."

Rory said, "Lord Logan eagerly joined us, and with those two on board, Lord Torcall couldn't bear not to throw in his support. He bears watching, but as long as the other two remain firm, I don't think he'd dare cross us unless the situation turns so dire he'll see advantage in taking the risk."

Ivor said, "We've got over ten thousand troops, with over a thousand Petralists and Guardians."

"That's a huge disadvantage," Mattias muttered.

Ivor nodded. "Dougal's army will hold a clear advantage if we have to meet them in a head-on bash fight, and with Harley they'll own earth. We control soapstone, though, and with all the snow and with the river right beside the battlefield, that may give us a critical advantage."

Connor nodded slowly as he calculated different ways they could plan for the battle. Between Kilian, Ivor, and himself, plus the Spitters in Rory's army and the pair of Water Moccasins in the Crushers, they could spank Dougal's Spitters. Even if Connor and Kilian had to focus entirely on countering Harley, Ivor and the others could own water.

Assuming, of course, that he could get his tertiary affinities to work. In the last five days of frantic practice, he'd managed a little better. Pumice was the critical element, and he had plenty of that, but he still didn't consider himself ready to face Harley. Any hesitation, any flicker of his tertiary powers, and she'd crush him.

Ilse gestured toward the large desk near the window. "We were beginning to run possible battle scenarios just before you arrived. The key will be to isolate Harley and deal with her. If we can accomplish that, we stand a better than even chance of winning the day."

Kilian said, "That will be our greatest challenge. Harley was a top general and veteran of the Tallan wars before her long sleep. She's as crafty as she is powerful. Taking her will prove challenging."

"More than challenging, and that's if things go well," Connor said, thinking back to his fight against her in Althing. She'd absorbed terrific amounts of damage and healed remarkably fast. She'd toyed with him for most of that fight. He doubted she'd give him that kind of leeway again.

Her abrupt departure from Raufarhofn still bothered him. Was she really just respecting the queen's wish to develop him into a worthy servant, or had he really hurt her? Was there a key to defeating her in that previous battle somewhere?

If it was, he couldn't see it yet.

"Has Craigroy said anything useful?" Connor asked.

Rory grunted. "Not hardly. That man is a crafty Tallan spawn. Even though he's locked up, I sometimes think we'd be better off having thrown him over the wall."

Ivor added, "We've tried talking with him, but get nothing useful. Lord Nevan even offered to try, but he reported no better luck."

Kilian's expression turned thoughtful. "Keep him in isolation until this battle is over. We don't want him confusing anyone or trying to pass information out to Dougal."

"I'll make it happen," Rory said. He rose and fetched the papers, spreading them on a smaller table that they positioned between all of their chairs.

They spent the next hour reviewing the intelligence that Ilse and Ivor and the Crushers had gathered with so much risk. They reviewed lists of resources in the city, discussed the city's primary defensive strategies, and reviewed the many mechanicals Connor's team had brought with them from Faulenrost.

Eventually Kilian leaned back in his chair and said, "We've got the makings of a solid plan here, but don't underestimate Harley. She's a battle-hardened Petralist, with a hundred years' experience more than I do. She was one of my battle instructors, actually."

Connor grimaced, struggling to wrap his thoughts around that fact. Kilian had always seemed a man apart, someone who the regular rules did not apply to, someone who could accomplish whatever he decided to do.

Was he suggesting Harley might be tougher?

Most of the others exchanged uneasy glances. Hamish broke the silence. "You can defeat her, though. Right?"

"Perhaps." Kilian let the single word hang in the air, and Connor's sense of dread deepened. Kilian finally added, "She'll have to limit how much she draws upon earth, and that might offer us our best advantage.

Still, she wasn't my mother's most trusted general for no reason. Of all the mightiest Petralists, she was always considered the most dangerous."

Hamish grimaced and said, "I think we need better thinking food. Happy-thought thinking food."

Connor heartily agreed, and the others chimed in support. Ivor ordered some refreshments and he was happy to see a lot of desserts on the trays sent up from the kitchens.

As they ate, Verena gestured at the papers and notes scattered all across the table. "We understand the challenge, so how do we isolate her and remove her?"

That was the big question. As they all considered how best to answer it, a knock sounded on the door and Tomas pushed it open without waiting for a response.

He saluted, then held up a scroll in a waterproof case. "General, we just received a messenger from High Lord Dougal."

Rory took it and Connor was tempted to read it over his shoulder, but forced himself to wait as Rory scanned its contents. His craggy face fell into a frown.

"What?" Connor and Verena asked together. He almost didn't want to know. Dougal was devilishly clever and had a way of twisting situations to his benefit, even when it seemed impossible.

"It's not from Dougal. It's from Harley."

He handed the scroll to Ilse and said, "She has Lukas, and she's coming to parley."

75

PARLEY WITH HARLEY

As the mid-afternoon sun plunged toward the distant horizon, Connor stood five miles south of Merkland on the wide road to Crann, dressed in his battle leathers, affinity stones ready, nerves knotting his stomach. The air had grown colder, and heavy clouds darkened the sky to the north. He smelled snow on the stiff wind blowing south from the Maclachlan mountains. Another storm would strike during the night.

Kilian and Aifric flanked him, while Rory and Ilse stood just in front, with a dozen Crushers and an equal number of Fast Rollers in twin formations close behind. The grim soldiers fingered weapons, all eyes locked on the road to the south where Harley's company was approaching for the parley, riding atop a wide, squat tower of earth.

Connor glanced up to check that Verena, Hamish, and Dierk were ready. Verena held position over their left flank, above the river in her new Swift, quadruple speedslings already tracking toward the distant Harley. Hamish and Dierk rode in the Hawk a hundred feet above, and fifty yards to their right.

Harley had stated she wished to talk and to offer an exchange for Lukas's life, but if the meeting turned violent, they were prepared to hit her with overwhelming force before she could do the same to them.

Verena had distributed to everyone the mini-hubs they'd developed during their fighting against Dougal in Granadure. The clever mechanicals each had several small speakstones attached in a circular pattern, with a rotating keystone in the center. Turning the keystone could activate the various speakstones they wanted to use. Connor wore his mini-hub strapped to his arm, and he turned the dial to Ivor's paired stone. "Ivor, are you in position?"

"Ready and monitoring," came the immediate reply. Ivor was

concealed under the river in the Slide, ready to strike from the flanks with water if it came to a fight. Kilian would take fire.

That left Connor to help Ilse face Harley with earth. He tried not to show how much that though terrified him. He was already tapping slate. Earth stood before him, feet sunk into the frozen ground, looking as indomitable as ever.

Those waves of red and green energy swirling across his back made Connor nervous, though. He had already activated pumice, its power bubbling through him like the energetic Upper Wick. His earth senses extended in a half circle from the river on his left, arcing across to the hills a mile to his right. The connection wobbled with every fresh wave of green power, though.

Ilse had glanced at him twice already, worry creasing her brow in a silent question. He'd smiled and insisted he was fine. She knew the truth, but would not allow her worries to interfere with getting her husband back, no matter the danger.

Harley had probed his outer perimeter a couple of times, but had not pressed farther. If she planned to hit them by surprise, he'd hopefully sense it early enough to shout a warning.

Luckily Ilse walked the earth with him, and her presence boosted his confidence. Harley might fool him, but not Ilse. The Grandurian captain watched the approaching force with stony-faced calm. Connor dearly hoped they could find a way to secure Lukas's release. If they didn't, Ilse would no doubt challenge Harley directly, even though she couldn't hope to beat her.

That would trigger the fight that might actually offer their best chance at beating Harley. They'd discussed that possibility, but Kilian had pointed out that she understood the situation and would be ready to counter any surprise aggression.

Connor's tension grew as Harley's tower drew to within a hundred yards, then stopped and sank into the ground with a soft rumbling and spray of disturbed snow. Through his earth senses, he felt her presence like a shining beacon.

Connor tapped quartzite to his eyes while the others raised long-vision goggles that the Builders had already set to five-times magnification. Tapping multiple tertiary stones simultaneously was especially challenging. It was almost as if the green energy resented his tightening bond with red and increased its efforts to interfere.

So he watched Harley and her party with stomach-flipping lurches, his vision zooming in, then dropping back to normal, again and again. If he got sick, he should absorb some diorite so he could explosive-vomit at Harley.

Lukas stood in front of Harley, battered and dirty, lips swollen, left cheek bruised, blood matted on his scalp. His hands were chained in front of him and he looked exhausted. He had clearly not surrendered without a fight.

Connor saw no sign of his men.

Ilse sucked in a long breath as she studied her husband. She spoke with icy calm. "He lives and appears mobile."

Connor hoped he could be as tough as Ilse when he grew up.

Shona stood to one side of Harley, dressed in Boulder battle leathers under a long, white fur coat, looking as elegant and beautiful as ever. High Lord Dougal, wearing armor under a long, leather jacket, stood beside her.

Shona had once forced Connor to look on Verena, chained and bloody, at the Carraig. He'd been filled with such rage, if he'd had access to power stones, he would have laid waste to everyone who tried to stop him from going to her. Shona had used Verena to force him to consent to marrying her.

She'd eventually released him, sent him north with Verena to escape the disgusting second-breed rights proclamation from the king. He appreciated that, but it didn't change the memory of what she'd done.

"They're keeping a respectable distance," Rory muttered.

Harley's voice boomed into the cold, dry air. "You came at my bidding. That's a good sign. Now, surrender and let us be done with this farce of an uprising."

"So Harley's in charge today, at least," Kilian commented.

Rory grunted, "Marching makes a lot of people grumpy, but she seems to have handled it well. Do you mind, lad?"

He gestured toward his throat. Connor managed what he hoped was a confident grin and applied quartzite to Rory's throat. The connection felt shaky, so he dropped his connection to earth and max-tapped pumice. He focused with all his will, determined to keep Rory's voice from shaking. That would convey the wrong message.

Praise the Tallan, it seemed to work. Rory's deep voice boomed back. "Freedom is no farce. Justice for crimes committed against this people is no farce. If you supported either, you would join us now."

Connor bit back a laugh. If Harley suddenly found a conscience and actually offered to join them, what would they do?

Dougal spoke next. "Rory, you've dishonored yourself, man. Are you really willing to sign the death warrants for so many good men and women whose only crime is their loyalty to you?"

Rory shook his head, even though Dougal probably couldn't see the gesture. "You are incorrect, my lord. It is you who has dishonored yourself and your entire house. My troops dedicated our lives to serving you and our nation only to discover you lied to us the entire time. You enslaved us through false patronage, destroyed men and women who counted on you for their livelihoods, and forced some to become abominable rampagers, knowing they would have to die in your service. You built your life upon a web of lies and blood. You know me. Can you honestly believe I would not stand against such corruption?"

High Lord Dougal looked annoyed, but Shona looked troubled. Connor had told her the truth about patronage, but had she doubted his word? What did she believe now? Would it make a difference? Ailsa had suggested she might become an ally, but he couldn't imagine Shona sacrificing her privilege and position for any cause, no matter how noble.

Harley only laughed. "Pretty speech, General. I see why those poor wretches cowering behind Merkland's walls follow you. Speak about honor and choices all you want, but today you face but a single choice. Surrender and enjoy the potential for life once you've been re-educated . . ."

"She means mind-wiped," Connor said.

". . . or stand against us and die in misery and agony. It's your choice, and honestly, I hope you choose to fight. I haven't destroyed an entire city full of fools in a long time."

Connor frowned. "What about that town in Althing? Doesn't she even remember that?"

"Probably not," Kilian said. He motioned Connor to enhance his voice too.

Connor silently prayed he could keep the solid connection, and tentatively pushed quartzite power out to Kilian and wrapped it around his throat. For the moment, it seemed to be holding.

Kilian said, "Harley, this fight is folly. Return to my mother and tell her I will no longer allow her atrocities in my homeland."

"Kilian, your foolish pranks have gone too far. Your mother sends her final regards. Boy, it will be my pleasure to share your final lessons tomorrow."

Ilse growled and took a step forward, but Rory held her back. He said, "You offered to release our men if we met to parley with you. We've met, so release them."

Harley chuckled, the sinister sound rolling like thunder across the valley and echoing from the hills. It sent shivers down Connor's spine. It was amazing. He needed to develop an evil chuckle of his own.

"I did offer to release your men from all pain. All but one have been released. This last scrapper might just manage to survive the long walk between us."

Kilian muttered, "She likes that term 'release from pain.' Death is the ultimate release, and that's what she offers to us."

"My other men are dead," Ilse said with perfect calm, then shouted, not bothering to wait for Connor to enhance her voice. "Let him walk!"

Harley said, "Even better. Your own strong woman is here for you. What is your name, oh beloved one?"

She prodded Lukas, who looked willing to endure her worst tortures without saying anything. She frowned at his silence and struck a casual backhand blow that flattened him to the ground.

"Lukas!" Ilse shouted. This time Connor enhanced her voice so it cracked like thunder across the valley. "His name is Lukas. Release him, woman."

"Lukas. A strong name for a strong man with a strong woman," Harley said approvingly. "Do you trust your woman, Lukas?"

"With my life," he said through bruised lips as he stumbled back to his feet. Someone enhanced his voice so they could hear. Connor had to wonder if it was Harley. She'd enjoy ensuring they heard everything.

"Well said, indeed. What is your woman's name?"

"Ilse."

"Here's the deal, Ilse. I will allow Lukas to walk back to you on the condition that he must walk at standard parade march and not deviate."

Connor exchanged glances with Rory. He couldn't believe that was it.

Lukas started forward, but the ground rose up and grabbed his legs. "Not so fast. To make things fair, I will take a little sport in exchange."

"What sport?" Rory asked, although Connor wished he hadn't.

"Lukas will walk. Every tenth step, I will try to stop him. Ilse and only Ilse is allowed to defend him from where she stands."

Kilian shook his head and muttered, "She'll never allow him to return. She'll use this as a test to probe your strength, Ilse, and she'll cheat. No doubt she plans to murder him within arm's reach of you."

"What choice do I have?"

"None."

She spoke, her voice firm and calm, as always. "I accept."

Lukas looked immensely proud. "I trust you, love. I know that if you cannot save me, no one ever could."

He spoke softly, calmly, in a voice that did not waver.

Ilse's expression turned fierce and she nodded and whispered to herself, "I'll see you soon, love."

Harley said, "Remember control, Ilse. This area is dangerously unstable. If you escalate this into an underground bash fight, I'll destroy you both and we'll most likely trigger an earthquake that will leave Merkland a shattered wasteland like Alasdair."

"How intense we fight is entirely up to you," Ilse shouted.

"Oh, no. It's your call, Ilse. I will start small, but every time you save his life I will intensify the next round. I leave it to you to decide when the worth of your man no longer outweighs the risk to tens of thousands of others."

"That's barbaric," Aifric whispered in a tone of disgusted awe.

Connor saw it differently. Harley was actually playing into Ilse's hand with that taunting twist to the game. No one could match Ilse for clever uses of small amounts of applied power. If only he could believe Harley would keep her word.

"She's just teasing. She can't allow Lukas to live," he said softly.

Ilse glanced at him and said, "You know me better than that, Connor. Of course she plans to kill him. Are you ready?"

"Ready for what?"

She gave him an annoyed look. "Whatever you plan to do to yank him out of that queen-loving toadie's grasp when I tell you."

Oh, he was so grouted. "Of course I'll be ready," he assured her with what he hoped was convincing sincerity.

She held his gaze for another second and said gravely. "My husband's life is on the line, Connor. I trust your cleverness will not abandon you in this moment of need."

He nodded. That Ilse trusted him so much gave him confidence, but could he really trick Harley?

"I will help too," Kilian offered quietly.

Ilse shook her head. "She'll expect you to interfere. She knows you and she will be on her guard. Probably has Petralists monitoring you from afar. She might underestimate Connor."

"Perhaps," Kilian acknowledged. He too glanced at Connor, raised one eyebrow, and asked, "Are you ready?"

"Working on it," he said although he wanted to shout at Kilian that of course he wasn't ready. Kilian knew better than anyone how much he was struggling.

So what could he do? He could barely tap any tertiary stones. He definitely couldn't use slate. With both Harley and Ilse grappling along the road, they'd already be taking a terrible risk of destabilizing the area.

Lukas stood calmly in front of Harley, his expression grim, his eyes locked on Ilse.

"Start walking," Harley ordered simply.

Connor felt a flash of panic. He wasn't ready, and had no idea how to help.

Lukas began to walk.

76

LUKAS'S WALK

As Lukas began walking in a steady, measured stride, Connor tried to think, tried to plan, but his mind felt frozen, his enhanced gaze locked on Lukas's feet. Lukas was starting his walk about a hundred yards away. Standard parade march was short steps, maybe two feet maximum. That meant over a hundred and fifty steps. That could be as many as fifteen attempts on his life.

No way he would survive so many.

Kilian spoke softly into his mini-hub, relating the situation to Verena and asking her to pass word to Hamish and Ivor. The situation could easily escalate into full-blown battle.

Aifric started counting the steps aloud when Lukas reached his seventh step.

Eight.

Ilse crouched slightly, hands half raised, palms down.

Nine.

Pillars of earth rose to either side of her and she plunged her hands into them to strengthen her connection to the earth. Connor touched slate and felt a flicker of her presence, like lightning across his earth senses.

Ten.

The ground softened under Lukas's boot. Harley simply liquefied ten feet of earth below Lukas. He'd plunge into it and drown.

His foot came down upon a single flat rod of earth that extended across the mire, just in time to catch him. Barely three inches in diameter, it was just enough to support his weight and allow him to continue over the trap.

Lukas never slowed, his expression never changed. He kept his eyes locked on Ilse and continued to walk with the same measured strides.

Aifric started her count over again.

One.

Two.

Three.

"Don't tempt earth," Kilian said to Connor.

"I'm not planning to."

"What are you planning?"

"Working on it," he repeated tersely.

Nine.

Ten.

Again Ilse's presence leaped across the distance just as the ground beneath Lukas dropped away into a spike-lined hole. With his next step, he'd fall and impale himself. This time, the outer edges of the hole began to spin. If Ilse attempted the same simple trick of spanning the hole with a supporting rod of earth, it would get chopped off.

For a second Connor felt a surge of panic. If Ilse needed him now, what would he do? He could access soapstone, marble, or quartzite, at least for a couple of seconds, but which? Nothing felt right.

Lukas's foot plunged down into the hole, but a tentacle-like rope of earth erupted up between two of the spikes and caught his boot. It quivered, but held, and a second slender tentacle rose to catch his next step. He continued, trusting the unsteady footing as the tentacles of earth slid beneath him, catching his feet for two more perilous strides until returning to the solid roadway.

"Good move!" Hamish's voice spoke from Aifric's speakstone.

The count began again.

"Focus, Connor," Kilian urged. "We're ready to help, but you must get Lukas out of there."

"I'm focused." Connor considered and rejected a dozen ideas, from simply wrapping Lukas in water or fire, to complex plots that not even he could keep straight, and which would never work.

The problem with using soapstone, other than his fear that it simply wouldn't work, was that Harley would see the snow or river water moving. He had to assume even a fraction of a second's warning would be too much. If only Lukas had a bit of quickened pumice.

Aifric probably intended her steady count to help, but the numbers rang in Connor's ears like drumbeats of doom. When she hit seven, he couldn't concentrate. All he could do was watch.

Ten.

A single spike of earth erupted out of the ground behind Lukas, spearing up at his back with enough force to shatter his armor and his torso.

Another spike, topped with an open hand, erupted right up between Lukas's feet and intercepted the first bare inches from his back. The first spike plunged into it, but the hand wrapped around the spike and dragged it sideways so that it scraped past Lukas's shoulder, showering him with dirt.

He kept walking without slowing, without flinching. In fact, he flashed his wife a tight smile. Connor didn't think he could have maintained that steady pace, knowing that every tenth step might kill him. Lukas had crossed almost a quarter of the distance, and the tension was making Connor want to pant. The remaining distance seemed like miles.

Sweat beaded Ilse's forehead, despite the chill, and she leaned forward, her expression fierce, her lips curling back just a bit in a defiant snarl.

Harley's voice boomed across the road. "Very good, Ilse. For a weak young thing, you're clever. I'll give you that. It's a pity you prefer to die along with your beloved instead of simply surrendering to our queen and swearing loyalty to her."

"She grows annoyed," Kilian warned.

Ilse nodded. "Once more. After that, Connor?"

"I'll be ready," he promised, and as Aifric counted off the steady marching steps again, he forced himself to focus.

He was tempted to tap obsidian, but maybe the entire elaborate, twisted game had been devised by Dougal as a way to force him to do just that. They were close enough that Dougal might be able to seize his mind if he dared obsidian, so he couldn't take the risk.

He could try stilling, but he'd never still Harley enough to matter. The light-burst attack might hurt her, but he didn't have the time required to gather and condense the necessary light.

"Ten."

He had so focused on his problem that he'd blocked out Aifric's slow count. So he glanced from Harley to Lukas, completely unprepared for what might happen next.

Wide slabs of earth pivoted up out of the ground to either side of Lukas. Six feet wide and seven feet tall, they slammed inward with bone-crushing force.

Dozens of wrist-thick bars of earth leaped out of the ground at Lukas's feet, rising into the air all around him, ends pointed at the slabs and barely wider than his shoulders. They reached the apex of their short flights just as the two slabs of earth crashed together.

Earth billowed around Lukas in a blinding cloud, obscuring him for a moment. Connor tried to feel what was going on through the earth, but Ilse and Harley were squabbling over the ground directly beneath Lukas.

Harley wasn't limiting this attack to a single strike. She battled Ilse, their clashing wills like water and ink mixed violently in a glass, and he couldn't tell what was going on.

Then Lukas erupted out of the cloud, tumbling wildly through the air. He was covered in dirt, and one arm was twisted awkwardly, while blood was spreading across a ragged hole ripped through the left side of his armor.

"Connor!" Ilse shouted through another angry snarl.

Good thing he hadn't settled on a plan yet, because he never could have planned for the ten spikes of earth erupting out of the ground. They shot into the air from all sides, all aimed at Lukas.

Connor reacted on pure instinct. He switched to marble. The flame-haired youth appeared in his mind, and Connor tackled him. He couldn't afford a timid connection now. He seized the flames and yanked hard.

Fire burst out of thin air, surrounding Lukas with a twirling, round cage of sword-like flames. As the earthen spikes drove up toward him, Connor spun the cage violently, scything across each one.

Both Ivor and Kilian were already drawing upon water, so he let them have it. Despite his lingering fear of failure, he dared tap quartzite.

She appeared, hovering nearby, and he grabbed her hand before she could flit out of reach. Instantly he tasted the gusting north wind. He gave it a sharp tug, and one strong current whipped around and caught his fiery cage, fanning the flames and lifting Lukas higher, giving him a few more precious seconds.

That was all he was going to get. The next wave of green-frequency power inundated both Fire and Air and severed both connections. His flame cage winked out, leaving Lukas tumbling helplessly.

The ground rumbled, cracking the road and shivering snow into the air. Ilse snarled, "You cannot have him," and plunged her hands down through the supporting pillars, driving them into the earth.

"Cheater!" Harley's voice boomed. "I will squash the life out of your man!"

No matter Ilse's determination, she could never stop whatever devilry Harley was intending.

Connor couldn't feel any of the elements, so he tapped limestone. The light all across the valley appeared streaming past in distinct layers. He gave them a savage twist.

"Aifric, I need death cries," he hissed. "Kilian, pull him into the river!"

At that moment, a ten-foot-thick trunk of earth erupted out of the ground and reared high toward the falling Lukas. The hideous head of an earth-bound elfonnel formed at the tip, and the enormous jaws gaped open, revealing stalactite teeth and several snakelike tongues that snapped out and seized Lukas by the arms and legs. Those horrible tongues yanked him, struggling and screaming, into the maw.

It crunched closed in a spray of blood and gore.

The enormous, snakelike creation trumpeted in victory, then sank back into the ground with an ominous rumbling of earth.

Ilse fell to her knees, hands still buried in the earth, screaming with rage and grief. Fat flakes of crimson snow fell over the road, stained by Lukas's life blood.

Harley's voice boomed across the valley again. "That concludes today's lesson. Think tonight on how badly you really want to share that fate. Tomorrow you join me or join your beloved."

Connor shouted angrily back at her, "You're a cheat and a coward, Harley! Shona, leave now or tomorrow you die with Harley and your father!"

Harley's evil thunder-laughter boomed across the valley as her tower slid south, back toward her army.

Ilse turned to Connor, her eyes mad with grief and fury.

He winked.

She blinked at him, confused and angry. He dropped to his knees and hugged her. "Aifric, use that new tertiary of yours and create a shielding wind for us, please."

"Of course." Immediately wind began whistling around them. Hopefully it was enough to block Harley's ability to eavesdrop.

"That was my best mirage ever," Connor said with well-deserved pride.

Ilse frowned through tears, and the flicker of impossible hope lit in her eyes. "Connor, now is not the time to be vague."

He leaned close and whispered, "Lukas is in the river with Ivor."

"How?" she stammered, looking toward the placid waters that showed no signs of any recent disturbance.

"Mirage." The others knelt beside them and Connor grinned at Kilian and Aifric. "I'm so glad you two didn't hesitate, or it never would have worked."

"You're lucky you have friends who can think fast on their feet," Kilian said with a smile.

Aifric said, "If I didn't know you were manufacturing those images, I would have believed them."

"That death scream was perfect," Connor congratulated her.

"I can always be counted on for a good scream."

"How?" Ilse asked again, laughing through her tears.

Kilian said, "I yanked Lukas to the river and Ivor sucked him down. Connor slapped a mirage on the scene, changing it so that everyone saw Lukas get eaten instead. Harley struck with such overwhelming force, I doubt she noticed the lack of resistance."

Ilse hugged Connor and he was astonished to feel her arms shaking. She clung to him and sobbed. Just once, but it wracked her entire body.

He held her, not sure how to react. Ilse was not supposed to feel emotion, was not supposed to feel cowed by any challenge, no matter how difficult. She was the unflappable, undefeatable, clever Sapper. She wasn't supposed to be a woman too.

So he held her as she took a long, shuddering breath, then pushed away, her expression calm and in control once more.

He said, "You're getting sloppy, Ilse. I expected you to hold her off for at least fifty more steps."

She laughed, the last of her tension draining. "Keep talking like that and I'll have Erich and Anika beat you with another tree."

"You say the nicest things." He helped her to her feet.

Then the Swift swooped low and settled into a hover. Verena shouted, "What are you waiting for? We have to go after her!"

Connor ran to her and explained the ruse while Kilian informed Hamish, who was apparently racing toward the windrider hovering high above with his Juggernaut armor inside.

"So Lukas is still alive?" Verena asked.

Connor nodded, happy she hadn't swooped in to attack Harley on her own. That would have wrecked their little victory.

Verena sighed with relief and wiped her eyes. Then she glanced at Connor with new danger in her gaze. "So why did you feel the need to warn Shona away? I'm looking forward to killing her tomorrow."

77

SPEEDSLINGS AND SPECULATION

Thankfully Verena didn't mention Shona again when they returned to Merkland, and Connor made a point of trying to not even think about her. He still couldn't help worrying that if things went poorly, she and Verena would finally get the duel they'd both been so eager for.

Verena had only just returned to him. He hated the thought of her involved in any direct fighting. He didn't think he could handle losing her.

If only Shona would leave them alone, he wouldn't wish her harm. His relationship with her was so complex, the only thing he knew for sure about Shona was that he never understood her and never would. Now that he'd broken off contact, there was no further reason to quarrel, was there?

The rest of the day passed in a blur of frantic activity as the city prepared for siege. Many of the lesser nobility and merchants fled, taking the chance that if Merkland fell, High Lord Dougal would sate his anger on the fools who remained, and spare the rest of them.

Sentries peeled back the ground over one of the practice fields, revealing enormous doors to two huge underground bunkers. They held the city's arsenal of siege weapons. Giant catapults and deadly ballistae rumbled up long, wooden ramps into positions flanking the huge gates.

Connor grimaced when he inspected the iron shot that would be fired from the catapults. Formed like spike-tipped, little pyramids, they'd no doubt inflict severe damage on anyone not protected by granite-hardened skin. Even Boulders might fall if struck in the face.

Worse, when the projectiles fell to the ground, their construction guaranteed one of the spikes would always point up. They'd create deadly tripping hazards and threaten to impale the feet of charging soldiers.

Since they were metal instead of stone, Sentries would not feel their approach.

The ballistae hoisted onto platforms atop the wall were like giant crossbows. They fired spears thicker than Connor's forearms, capped with deadly steel tips. The soldier in charge of one of the siege weapons assured Connor those spears could punch right through half a dozen armored knights or a single max-tapped Boulder.

"If they get this close, they'll wish they hadn't," he said simply.

Connor appreciated his optimism, but if the attacking army got to the walls, that meant their plans had failed miserably and he doubted a few siege weapons would hold back the tide for long.

Connor was impressed that Lord Logan insisted on remaining in Merkland. The young lord shrugged when Rory questioned why he would risk so much to help Guardians and said, "My Lord Dougal will know I supported your effort. Even if I leave now, I'd never escape punishment. He always treated me like a lesser lord anyway. Now is the time to take a stand."

Lord Nevan's insistence on remaining also surprised Connor. Nevan said stubbornly, "Merkland is my city. Lady Shona herself appointed me administrator and I'll spit in the Tallan's eye before abandoning my post."

"Even though she's returning with an army to kick us all out?" Rory asked.

"Even so. Some things are right, and some things are wrong, and sometimes we have to take sides."

So of course Lord Torcall felt pressured to stay too, even though he didn't make any bold speeches, and looked increasingly sick as the afternoon wore on.

Although badly hurt, Lukas survived. Ilse stayed by his side in the hospital while Healers worked on him. She looked so happy gripping his hand that Connor didn't have the heart to even tease her about acting so un-deadly-captainish.

Rory and Ivor met in council with all of their senior officers. Anika refused to leave Rory's side. Jean spent time in the hospital wing, and Connor gave up trying to figure out where Aifric got to.

So he helped Verena, Hamish, and Dierk unpack the windriders. Erich assisted too, overseeing the mixed company of Grandurian and Obrioner soldiers assigned to the effort.

They distributed nearly one hundred speedslings, splitting them between the various forces tasked with sallying forth against the enemy and those assigned to defend the walls. They supplemented the stores of projectiles for the catapults with diorite bombs.

Dierk pointed to bits of obsidian worked into the plugs sealing the bombs closed. "Remote activation. Any of us Builders can quicken the bombs just before they're needed."

That would also help prevent theft by troops secretly loyal to Dougal who might want to sabotage their efforts. That was a very real risk, although Rory didn't like to admit it. They had no way of proving their troops' loyalty before the moment of battle.

When Connor mentioned his worries to Verena she said, "This battle is the test of their loyalty, Connor. This is a revolution so no one's tested until they are."

"That's a really big help," he grumbled.

So she kissed him. That did help.

As he poured hundreds of deadly hornets into one of the speedsling drums, he wondered how the fledgling revolutionary forces would do. Many were veterans of the invasion, but this fight would be very different. Hopefully they'd feel even more motivated by freedom than by conquest.

JUSTICE IS FOUND IN STRANGE PLACES

A messenger arrived, calling Connor to meet with Kilian. He left Verena and Hamish with half the mechanicals still to unload. Kilian and Ilse waited for him inside an enormous warehouse at the edge of the market district. Piles of clay were heaped on the stone floor. They smelled like they had only recently been dredged from the icy river. Five pallets of canvas sacks rested nearby. Connor's father's clean handwriting noted the weight on every one.

"Alasdair White? What are we going to do with so much?"

Those pallets represented months of work from the entire village. Standing beside them, Connor felt connected with his home in a way he hadn't since Alasdair valley was buried under half a mile of rubble.

Kilian said, "One of Harley's favorite tricks is unleashing a horde of summoned creatures during key moments of battle. From the reports we read, it sounds like Evander used that trick against her at the Carraig."

Connor frowned. "How can they do that? It's hard enough controlling one. Trying to control an army would leave her totally vulnerable."

Kilian shook his head. "Not these creatures. One of the new abilities available after the second threshold is to create a summoned creature that can act autonomously, within strictly defined parameters."

"Whoa! Really?"

Ilse also looked amazed. "You've been holding out on me, Kilian. I can think of a few times we really could have used that ability."

"I'm sorry. The major drawback with this technique is the preparation time. We rarely seem to have that luxury."

He added to Connor. "I have no doubt that Harley will hit us with an army of earthen creatures. She'll point them at us and they'll attack on their own, although she can seize control over individual creatures if it suits her. Usually it's not necessary, though. They are incredibly effective and very deadly."

Connor shuddered. He bet they were. He'd summoned creatures a few times and still marveled at the experiences. The thought of giving life to creatures that could destroy on command without needing specific direction scared him more than a little.

"What happens if they accidentally attack friendly troops?"

"It's possible. They're not thinking, intelligent creations, so they need to be aimed carefully. The trick is to unleash them only when the enemy is obvious."

"Like at the start of a battle?"

"Or against a stubborn knot of resistance. She likes to divide her enemies and strike with her autonomous creatures through that confusion."

"That makes it harder for us, since our whole plan depends on dividing her and Dougal."

Kilian nodded. "If we can manage to separate her, we could expect an attack from any autonomous creatures she might still have in reserve."

"Wonderful," Connor said dryly.

"Better if we have our own army of creatures ready to counter hers," Kilian said with a grin. Flames began billowing inside one of his eyes, and the other filled with miniature cresting waves.

Connor really needed to learn that trick. The effect was always striking. Those little nuances of style set Kilian apart from everyone.

Harley was even older, but she lacked his refinement. She was like an angry bear crashing through the woods, while Kilian was more like a wolf, slipping silently through the trees, closing on his prey with deadly stealth.

The problem was, wolves couldn't usually take down a bear alone. Hopefully Connor could trip her up and expose her throat for Kilian to lunge in for the kill.

Ilse looked thoughtful. "So will this be similar to how we summoned that great stone pedra in Alasdair?"

Kilian nodded. "I cannot summon alone. I lack a granite affinity. You'll provide that part, and I'll craft the elemental portion. Connor, I'm hoping you can manage enough control to create your own summonings."

"I'll do my best," he promised, eager to learn a technique that only a handful of the mightiest Petralists had ever mastered. Summoning a little squirrel, using the strength of granite to encase an elemental heart, was easy, but Kilian had grander plans.

"We'll be summoning big, powerful creatures that can overwhelm Petralists and withstand Harley's creatures."

Connor asked, "How can we do that? Just summoning that stone pedra exhausted you, but now you're talking about scores of monsters."

"These types of summonings aren't as tiring. We don't need to worry about maintaining the link to our creations or actively controlling them. Autonomous creatures are far simpler. We design them with the ability to destroy. Period. Then they wait until we call upon them."

"Could you create some for other purposes besides war?" Connor asked.

"I've never heard of anyone doing so. They're expensive in affinity stone and in Petralist energy. In most other circumstances they're not considered worth the price. Why? What do you have in mind?"

Connor shrugged, thinking that if his little brother, Wallace, ever found out about this ability, he'd insist on a permanent summoned squirrel pet. He could never give him one created with the sole purpose of killing whatever Wallace pointed it at.

"I don't know. It's just sort of a shame we can't use them for good. Like when those Boulders fell into that pit under the road near Altkalen and drowned. An autonomous creature fashioned with quartzite could have jumped in and given them air until they could be fished out, or a soapstone one might have been able to fish them out."

Something like that could have saved fifty lives.

Kilian clapped him on the shoulder. "I like the way you think. If we survive tomorrow, let's explore that idea."

With that gentle reminder of the very deadly stakes they faced, they got to work. The early stages of the process were similar to what he knew. Connor absorbed huge quantities of precious Alasdair White, grateful that Merkland enjoyed a ready supply.

For the first attempt, he chose soapstone as the element that would give the creature life. With granite and pumice both active, he tapped soapstone. Water appeared, smiling and extending a hand mostly covered in red-only magic. Connor took it, hoping he was finally getting the hang of managing the weird dual power sources.

With focused care, he drew from a deep well behind the warehouse a barrel-sized globe of water and plunged it into the nearest pile of clay. As a muddy shape began to rise out of the pile and flow into the shape he held in his mind, Connor concentrated the granite into his chest and drove it out to the construct. Granite infused it with power, clay with bulk, and water with life.

That's when things got interesting. In the past, a part of his attention would be consumed managing and directing the creature. If he concentrated, he could step fully into it, becoming the creature. He'd done that with the squirrel in Alasdair and still loved the memory of the little animal's sharp senses and agile movements. Unfortunately, such a close connection left his own body defenseless.

With this first autonomous creature, he instead pushed into its head a simple set of instructions.

Destroy anything I point you at or that gets in your way or that tries to injure you.

With a muted thunderclap, a large nuall snapped into final shape in front of him and fell to its haunches. About the size of a large dog, it sniffed the air, turned to face him, and crouched, ready to spring at his command. He did maintain a whisper-thin connection to it, a conduit he could focus on to activate the creature or take control over it, as if it were a regular summoning.

"How do they know how to move and to fight?" he asked. Kilian stood beside Ilse, who was petting a huge, bearlike creature with a fanged maw like a rampager.

"Your subconscious mind knows and conveys those expectations to your creature. I don't know exactly how, but I've seen it enough times to know it works."

"What is that thing?"

"A whim. I think of it as Justice."

"I'm glad it's on our side."

Kilian inspected Connor's nuall. "Well done. Make the next one twice as big. Harley likes powerful creatures so our army needs to be nimble and deadly."

Ilse looked grimly pleased. "Thank you for inviting me to participate. Harley needs a taste of Justice for sure."

The next hour passed quickly as Connor, Kilian, and Ilse immersed themselves in the effort of creating the first unit in their army of elemental-powered, granite-hardened battle monsters.

He made it to ten before collapsing, exhausted.

Impressive, really. He'd never imagined he could create so many. He was quickly mastering the technique, and each of his monsters was bigger and deadlier than the last. Partly because of his growing confidence, and partly because he didn't want Kilian to feel he couldn't keep up.

Ilse seemed inspired by the danger Harley represented. After four identical siblings for Justice, she insisted they try even bigger creations. She and Kilian created more fantastical creatures, all fueled by water or fire, all deadly variations of creatures Connor knew or had heard about.

Two of them looked like miniature variations of wolf-like, fire-bound elfonnel, and they crouched in the center of the warehouse, fiery eyes pulsing, radiating gentle heat. Another looked like a sea serpent with six legs and three heads, all with long, needle-sharp teeth. Their final constructs were a pair of four-armed, seven-foot humanoids with bulging muscles. Connor recognized them as tiny versions of the giant elfonnel that Evander had raised at the Carraig.

"What do you call them?"

"Little Nephews." Kilian blew out a breath and dropped onto the clay beside Connor. He and Ilse had created thirteen.

"They're perfect," Ilse said. She too looked tired, but the determined set to her features suggested she planned to keep working until she passed out.

Connor said, "There's no way we can create an army in one night. We'll kill ourselves trying, and won't have the energy to fight Harley tomorrow."

"Not by using only our own strength."

Connor groaned. "Is there another secret new ability that will give us strength?"

"Don't tempt earth," Ilse warned. "The land is even more unstable after my confrontation with Harley."

"The energy we'll use to build our army will come from the earth, but not through slate," Kilian said.

"How, then?"

"Basalt."

Connor blinked at him a few times, too tired to make the connection.

"Stilling. We're going to apply stilling to the ground under the city. We need to calm it down and dampen the area to reduce the chance that tomorrow's battle might trigger a catastrophic response directly beneath us."

Connor grimaced. He didn't like stilling. It made him feel like a leech. He'd killed that fire in their first practice session so fundamentally that the memory still disturbed him.

"You said you used it in Altkalen to settle the ground there too. What would happen if you held it too long?"

"Even if I could seize the land under Merkland securely enough to still all the life out of it, I'd need years to try. Luckily, we only need to apply it for short durations to draw off the extra energy threatening to destabilize the area. Instead of releasing that energy the way you did with the fire, we'll draw it into ourselves to replenish our own strength."

Connor the Leech. Sounded more sinister than epic. He really needed Harley's evil laugh to go with it.

"What about me?" Ilse asked. "I can't use this stilling effect."

"No, you can't. But if you keep a hand on my shoulder as I use it, I can share energy with you too."

Connor wouldn't have thought of that, although it made sense. He'd shared healing power with many people, and both he and Kilian had shared heat with friends.

The best part about Kilian's plan was that they didn't have to move. Ilse fashioned more comfortable chairs out of the piles of clay, then Connor and Kilian both absorbed enough basalt to sprint to Altkalen and back. The coursing energy helped revive Connor and focus his mind.

Anchoring that wonderful, rushing basalt energy to the green-tinted power source came far easier than the last time he'd tried. That green-attuned basalt power coiled inside of Connor, filling him with a sense of foreboding. He followed Kilian's lead, driving it out through his hands and down into the earth below the lowest basements, past the foundations of the city.

The earth trembled.

It felt different through basalt than with his earth senses. Through slate, he would have felt the trembling like quivering of his own fingers. With basalt, that trembling radiated through his senses like the shaking of a fish on the end of a long line.

Kilian spoke, his voice soft and distant. "Spread your influence to the north. I'll take the south."

He guided Connor in the effort of extending his basalt sense out through the earth and stone beneath the city. They allowed it to drift deeper, to seep into the roots of the bluff.

Then they activated stilling over that entire area. Kilian was right. The area was far too immense to seize like Connor had that little fire, but they could latch onto the extra energy bubbling in the land. The earth under Merkland was like a soup pot threatening to boil over. By siphoning off the extra energy, he was saving dinner from getting wrecked. He no longer felt like a thief cautiously siphoning power out a window.

"Let your basalt sense cling to that energy, like a barge floating on the Wick, using its strength for movement," Kilian explained.

Or like that time Connor lowered Hamish headfirst off the roof of Neasa's bakery on a rope when they were ten so he could lick the icing off the top of a special five-layer cake she'd made for the Saorsa.

As the energy rose like a mist from the deep places beneath Merkland, Kilian said, "Now draw it to you."

"How?"

"Will it in. Invite it to join you. Energy needs a home, and flowing into your willing body is easier than other alternatives."

Connor managed it when he imagined that energy mist like the aroma of a fresh-baked apple pie. He'd always wished he could just keep breathing in when sniffing a pie, without having to pause to let all the air back out again and interrupting the experience.

With stilling, he didn't have to breathe out ever. He just inhaled through invisible basalt lungs, drawing the energy into him in a long, continuous breath. It didn't smell as good as apple pie, but it felt incredible. Energy poured into him, first erasing his exhaustion, then replenishing his strength.

It kept coming.

He felt alive and healthy, as if he'd used half his sandstone pendant. His muscles quivered with energy that had nothing to do with granite. This was pure energy from the natural world, and it filled him to overflowing.

"Enough," Kilian said after an unknown time.

Connor blinked open his eyes and only then realized he'd risen to his feet on that tide of power and stood stretched tall on his toes, arms thrown wide, head back, exulting in the glorious, unrivaled feeling.

Ilse was starting to look concerned.

It took a few seconds to convince himself to release the stilling and let go of basalt. If he held on much longer, he wouldn't destroy the ground under Merkland, but he'd probably explode like a pig bladder, sewn into a Sogail ball and inflated too much.

"That was . . ." Luckily he didn't have to explain it to Kilian. It was an amazing thrill that he didn't like admitting he liked so much.

Kilian studied him for a moment, as if reading his thoughts. Wait, did he have chert? Could he?

Connor created an image of Harley kissing Evander in his mind. He tried not to shudder at the image, and watched Kilian closely. Kilian made no indication that he read that thought.

Kissing Verena was a highlight of his life, but that image was just gross.

"How are you feeling?" Kilian asked Ilse.

"Like I could challenge Harley directly," she grinned.

He smiled in turn. "Well done, Connor. You seem to have a knack for stilling, and together I think we siphoned off enough so that we shouldn't fear a catastrophic event unless someone draws very deep from the ground tomorrow."

Connor grimaced to think of Merkland suffering the same fate as Alasdair. "Let's hope Dougal convinces her to spare Merkland."

"And keep her distracted with other things," Ilse added.

Kilian gestured toward the waiting piles of clay and rubbed his hands together. "Shall we get back to work?"

79

SCULPTED SCONES - THE ULTIMATE
SECRET WEAPON

Connor slipped through the main doors of the central palace, pushed by the howling wind that seemed eager to finally sneak inside. A guard slammed the door, squashing that dream flat. Connor paused to stamp his feet and beat at his clothing with his hat to knock away the snow that clung to him.

He could have tapped soapstone, but had run out after completing his sixty-fifth summoned creature. He felt so tired he couldn't stomach the thought of attempting another one. At least his connection with soapstone had held. He hadn't dared try switching to anything else for fear of losing that stable link. He hoped tomorrow he'd enjoy the same success.

All the energy he'd siphoned from the earth beneath Merkland was gone, spent to give life to all of his fighting monsters. They crouched in the warehouse, awaiting his call, their presence like a comforting memory flickering at the back of his mind. He smiled as he slipped his thoughts across them, particularly the last one.

He'd named it Mouth, and he'd poured every last bit of his energy into finishing it. As big as a torc, it lacked a head. Instead, the entire front half of its torso could gape open into an enormous maw, ringed with icy fangs. He couldn't wait to see it gobble up Harley's creatures.

The guard recognized him and saluted. "Is the storm natural, sir?"

"I think so."

Those dark clouds he'd spotted earlier on the horizon had decided to make a mad dash south, bringing another wave of brutal winter along for the ride. The blizzard had roared in over Merkland as he and Kilian completed their work. Winds tore at the city, rattling the walls of the warehouse, while the temperature plummeted to well below freezing.

It was an impressive display of nature's fury, but neither he nor Kilian had sensed any Petralist wills whipping it into a higher frenzy. Harley and her army would have been fools to do so anyway. They'd suffer even more out on the open road.

All that blowing snow might actually prove an advantage if the storm continued into the next day, but Connor felt too tired to worry about it.

"Do you know where Builder Verena is?" he asked the guard.

"Yes, sir. She's taken up residence in Lady Shona's apartment."

"Um, are you sure?" That sounded wrong on multiple levels.

"Yes, sir." He pointed Connor in the right direction.

Basically all he had to do was keep climbing. Shona's apartment occupied the entire top floor of the southern high tower that reared above the central palace.

As he climbed the many steps, he wondered why Verena would choose Shona's room. She and Shona hated each other. They weren't the same size, so Verena couldn't steal her clothes or anything. Maybe she just wanted to destroy everything.

He knocked when he reached the elegantly carved wooden doorway at the top of the long stairs. He doubted Verena would bother climbing all those stairs. She'd just fly up in her Swift and land it inside Shona's parlor.

"Come in," Verena called.

Connor entered a wide sitting room with southern-facing windows and an enthusiastic fire casting a warm glow over a couch and several comfortable chairs. Verena sat on the couch in men's breeches and an open leather vest over a long, white blouse that fell untucked to her thighs. She looked adorable like that, with one foot drawn up under her.

Hamish and Jean sat in chairs pulled close together. Hamish had removed his flying suit and both he and Jean looked like normal Alasdair youths in their casual clothing. The sight of them dressed like that made Connor smile.

Verena beckoned him. "We were wondering where you got to."

He dropped onto the couch beside her and she took one of his chilled hands in her warm ones and massaged it gently. He could have enjoyed that gentle touch for hours.

"I've been busy with Kilian building an army of summoned creatures. All we have to do is point them in the right direction and they'll rush out and destroy anything that gets in their way."

They all looked astonished. Jean said, "I thought summoning was difficult."

"It is." He told them about his day.

Verena said, "We should warn Rory. If Harley hits his forces with her creatures before you can stop her, they could do terrible damage."

"One more complexity to worry about," Jean said with a frown. "I sat in on some of Rory's planning meetings. This battle is going to have a lot of moving parts."

Hamish said, "It has to. We can't just wait behind the walls for them to come up and start beating on the doors. We'd lose that fight for sure."

"I know. I support the plan, but the more complex a mix, the more likely something will go wrong."

"Something always goes wrong," Connor said with a rueful chuckle. "We've learned that the hard way. All the planning we do is just so we're better prepared to be flexible when nothing goes according to plan. Can one of you tell me what the plan is? I sort of missed all that."

Verena sat up straighter and explained. "We need to split Harley's forces and hopefully isolate her. Rory will lead a large company into the western hills to launch an ambush after the vanguard passes."

"I'll be with him," Jean said.

Hamish frowned. "I still think you should stay in the palace."

"I'll be fine. It's not like I plan to lead an assault, or anything. Aifric offered to act as my protector. My job is to help subdue captives."

Hamish still didn't look happy, but Verena continued. "The bulk of the army will defend Merkland, but Kilian will lead a strike force directly against Harley."

"That's where the rest of us will be, right?" Connor asked.

She nodded. "Hamish and I will provide support from the air, and Ivor will hold the river. He'll be positioned to support whoever needs help. Most of the Fast Rollers and Crushers will sally out with Rory and Anika. Ilse, Lukas, and Mattias will lead the remainder in our strike force."

"Who will command the city garrisons?" Connor asked.

"Lord Nevan has command. We'll all be linked via speakstone, so he can send out reinforcements if needed, or provide safe routes of retreat."

It actually sounded like a good plan. "And if Harley throws her own summoned creatures at us like Kilian suspects, we'll be ready to surprise her with our own army of creatures."

Verena gripped his hand, her expression fierce. "It'll work. All we need to do is take down Harley and we can defeat the rest of them." She didn't say it, but Connor could tell by the predatory look in her eye that she was thinking about Shona.

Hamish's expression turned thoughtful. "Connor, you said you used clay for mass. Could you use something else?"

"Sure. It's possible to just use granite and the elements, but that requires a lot more granite. We could use stones, I guess. They'd be stronger, but unwieldy."

"Could you use bread?"

Verena and Jean both laughed at the idea.

Connor said, "I once considered trying it with bacon."

"Except that would have encouraged the rampagers to eat you," Verena reminded him. She looked so beautiful when she smiled, for a second all he could do was stare.

"Why bread?" Jean asked.

"It makes so much sense!" Hamish grew excited. "Think about it. If we could create little bread creatures, we could send them to infiltrate the enemy kitchens."

"And do what? Wait until soldiers ate them, then attack their guts from the inside?" Jean asked, then grimaced. "Forget I ever suggested that. It's disgusting."

Verena smiled again. "You'd have to call them sculpted scones."

"Yes! Our little army of sculpted scones could win the Battle of the Belly. Think how many lives we could save," Hamish said excitedly.

"Think how many latrines they would need," Connor commented, and the girls grimaced again.

Verena punched him lightly on the shoulder. "You would have to go there with the image, wouldn't you?"

He shrugged. "Only logical."

Hamish nodded agreement.

Jean said, "For a boy, maybe."

"Well, at least I'm thinking creatively," Hamish said defensively.

Verena chuckled. "Try thinking outside of the stew pot for once."

The conversation fell into one of those occasional lulls, and they sat for a few minutes, just soaking in the warmth of the fire and enjoying a quiet moment. They knew what the next day would bring, although they'd never battled in a blizzard before.

Connor glanced around the opulent room, but the door that led deeper into Shona's apartment was closed. "Why'd you pick Shona's apartment, Verena? Are you going to destroy it?"

She shook her head. "Oh, no. I love these rooms." She pointed to a spot near the drape-covered window. "Right over there is where Ilse hit Shona with the weakening powder that night we kidnapped her." She sighed contentedly and smiled at the memory. "I love how many times we got to use that on her."

"She did like to fall on her face a lot," Hamish said with a grin.

Smiling, Jean rose and drew Hamish to his feet too. "It's getting late. I think we all need some sleep. Tomorrow will be difficult and some of us have to head out before first light."

Hamish started to grumble, but she held a finger to his lips. "Hush. I know how you feel, but I'm going. I can help, and I won't be in too much danger. Plus I've got a bunch of mechanicals in case we get in trouble."

"You know how to activate them all?" Hamish asked.

She gave him an annoyed look and he raised his hands in apology. "Just making sure."

Verena rose smoothly to her feet and reached for her ever-present satchel. "Do you have sandstone?"

Jean looked startled. "We've never tested if I can quicken sandstone with my keystone."

"You've been busy," Hamish said.

She took the sandstone gratefully, then she and Hamish left. Jean had been assigned rooms below Verena's. Connor and Hamish would share a plush apartment near Ivor's rooms.

Verena settled back to the couch beside Connor after the other two left, tucking both feet up so she could sit sideways on the couch and face him. She took both of his hands in hers and gave him a serious look.

"I worry for you tomorrow, Connor."

"And I worry for you. I don't want you doing anything too crazy. You just barely woke up and—"

"I'm fine," she interrupted, pressing one finger to his lips. He kissed that finger, then the palm of her hand, then drew her to him to kiss those soft, minty lips.

Verena wrapped her arms around his neck and leaned into him, kissing him slowly, thoroughly, with building passion that took his breath away. He held her tight, savoring the feel of her in his arms, inhaling the clean scent of high places that again clung to her hair.

After a long, delicious moment, she sat back, blue eyes sparkling in the firelight. He lost himself in those eyes and drew her toward him again. He wanted another one of those kisses.

But she shook her head and settled back cross-legged facing him again. "You're the one who will have to face Harley with Kilian. She could kill you."

Her voice shook a little, and she dropped her gaze, suddenly looking smaller, vulnerable.

"We'll be fine. I'll be fine." He squeezed her hands.

"But you're still struggling with your elemental affinities."

"I seem to be getting better at it. Tonight I only lost connection with soapstone half a dozen times while summoning."

She frowned. "I don't like it. Any weakness could be fatal."

He gripped her hands and said, "Together, we can do this. Let's both promise to be fine."

She met his gaze again and her smile lit up his heart. "Deal."

Later, as Connor walked the chill halls back toward his room, he hoped their plans proved more clever than Harley's. He believed he could make his elemental affinities work with the aid of pumice, but he would keep his secret stash of porphyry close, just in case.

If she got the best of them, how many of his friends would die tomorrow?

80

TRUST IS UP IN THE AIR

Connor slept deeply, but started awake several times. Each time, he listened and scanned his unfamiliar room. It was dimly lit by the dying embers of the fire, but he spotted no danger. Hamish's form was a dim bulk against the far wall. Once the wind that rattled the window sounded almost like distant voices, and he lay for a long minute, worried that Harley had attacked in the night.

Eventually he forced himself to relax, annoyed at his nerves. Hadn't he and Verena both promised to be fine? Repeating her name to himself helped him finally drift off to sleep again.

Just a few hours later, he stood with the Ivor and the central command group atop the great outer wall above West Gate, feeling tired and chilled. Fighting for freedom was supposed to be an adventure, and adventures were supposed to be fun. He decided that whoever had spread that lie must have been working for High Lord Dougal.

In the fuzzy gray light of dawn, Rory marched out through the open gate beneath them at the head of a mighty force, with Anika at his side. Jean and Aifric flanked them with Erich, Tomas, and Cameron, followed by five hundred granite bash fighters, including most of the Fast Rollers and Crushers. The strike force included a handful of tertiary Petralists and a hundred Striders, who disappeared into the impenetrable gloom of the blowing blizzard.

The air was bitterly cold, and Connor wished he'd added to his regular battle armor more than an extra pair of socks, warm leather gloves, and a woolen lining to his helmet. He usually maintained his warmth with a constant, low marble burn. With his tertiaries still unpredictable, he didn't like tapping them too much. He hoped the fierce heat that always seemed to accompany battle would keep him warm. He pitied the poor soldiers without even inconsistent marble who stood in ranks along the parapet, or down in the courtyards below.

Verena leaned against him, gorgeous in her custom battle armor, but looking tired and worried. Hamish watched long after Jean disappeared into the night. Dierk stood nearby, gripping in his gloved hands a steel cylinder warmed from within by quickened marble. He still looked cold, but faced it with resolute determination.

As soon as the last of Rory's battle force faded into the billowing white and blackness of the storm, and the huge gates started to close, Ivor gestured to Dierk. He gratefully activated a piece of quartzite, and a shielding dome shimmered into existence around the group, sealing out the blustering storm.

Hamish said, "I wish we could just shield the whole city."

"We'd need a piece of quartzite so big it wouldn't fit on a windrider," Verena said.

"What if we linked a bunch of small ones together, like the way that false ground concealed the hidden city under the Carraig?"

Ivor said, "Figure it out, but not today. Rory is away. Soon it will be time for the rest of us to take our positions."

"Any sign of the army?" Lord Nevan asked. He wore a thick fur coat, but Connor caught glimpses of glittering steel beneath it. He was taking his military duties seriously.

Connor had tempted soapstone for a moment earlier and managed a quick scan of the land. "They're about five miles south, already preparing to march. Pretty much exactly as expected."

With the blizzard filling the air with snow, scanning for enemy forces was far easier than normal. Dougal's Spitters were blocking the worst of the weather, but weren't holding a solid shield across their forces, so it was pretty easy to scan their lines.

"What are the chances they're deceiving you and really planning to attack the township or circle the city and hit us from the north?" Lord Torcall asked.

Kilian appeared out of the sky, descending in a swirling storm of orange flames and crystallized snow. Dierk dropped the shielding before he landed atop it, and he settled to the parapet with a flourish of twining elements. As usual, he seemed to ignore the weather, dressed in his leather jacket, with no hat and no gloves. A longsword and dueling dagger swung at his waist.

A frigid gust of snowy wind blew across the wall before Dierk could replace the shield. Some of the Pathfinders in the city were trying to encourage the storm to split around Merkland, but hadn't found much success yet. Connor didn't even bother trying to dance with fickle Air. He wouldn't unless absolutely necessary.

As snow leaped off of him, Kilian said, "I completed a circuit of the city. There's no indication of treachery yet."

"It'll come though, won't it?" Verena asked.

"Undoubtedly. Rory's away without issue?"

Ivor said, "In this storm, and with his Sentries and Spitters helping a bit, they should remain concealed in the hills to the west. I'm already actively monitoring the river."

"Good. I don't expect Harley will try splitting forces until they reach the southern bridge," Kilian said. The bridge spanned the Macantact two miles south of the city.

"Should we drop the bridge?" Lord Logan asked.

Lord Torcall gave him a disgusted look. "Are you insane, man? Ten thousand gold staters a week in trade cross that bridge, minimum."

Ivor said, "It's a valid question. What do you think, Kilian?"

He shook his head. "Splitting their forces and sending a strike team to occupy the township only weakens them."

The workers, merchants, and sailors who made up the bulk of the population in the township had evacuated. Most fled into the city, swelling the ranks of frightened citizens huddling behind Merkland's famous walls and Rory's determined troops. Some had fled toward nearby towns, hoping to escape the fighting entirely. So the township was empty, a waste of effort for the invaders.

Lord Nevan asked, "When do we launch the next phase of our defense?"

"When they hit the southern bridge," Kilian said. He turned to Dierk. "Are you ready? Is your bomb ready?"

He nodded, looking nervous but determined. Verena scowled at Kilian. "I thought we were going to wait until we had no choice before using the porphyry bomb."

Kilian sighed, looking older than usual. "I consider the southern bridge a point of no return. They will attack and try to kill everyone behind these walls. That bomb could save all of our lives."

"By killing thousands of theirs," she said softly, frowning.

Kilian nodded, holding her gaze. "Yes. It might. I hope that the effects wear off fast enough that the army will be crippled by injuries more than death, but some will die. If we do not drop that bomb, we'll be trading some of their lives for some of ours."

Verena looked like she wanted to argue, but held her tongue. Connor felt the same conflict, undiminished since the last time they argued the terrible choice. That porphyry bomb was so horrible because it robbed those soldiers of the ability to decide their own fates. Then again, any kind of warfare did the same thing in varying degrees.

It was easy to blame High Lord Dougal or even Harley for all the death and suffering about to descend upon Merkland and both armies, but life wasn't that simple. By rising up in rebellion, they'd declared their willingness to pay in blood and lives the cost for freedom.

He still felt fervently that cost was worth paying, but now they had to choose which lives paid the bill. It wasn't fair, but it was a choice they couldn't ignore.

So Connor said, "Kilian is right. We need to use the bomb."

Ivor solemnly nodded agreement. Hamish muttered, "Should have tried the sculpted scones first."

Verena sighed, still looking anguished by the choice. "I know you're right. I also know this moment will haunt me all my life."

"Me too," Kilian said softly.

Ivor said, "That's the next step, then. Dierk, prepare your windrider to deliver the bomb."

Kilian frowned and asked, "Are you sure you don't want someone else to fly that windrider, Dierk?"

"I can do it," the bespeckled Builder assured him. "I've trained hard to develop the skills to fly into this storm, and I wouldn't feel right asking someone else to assume the danger in my stead."

Before Dierk had become an accomplished flyer, it would have been folly to allow him to fly that bomb against Harley, no matter how much he wanted it. Even for Verena or Hamish, that mission would prove extremely dangerous.

"Hamish, are you ready?" Dierk asked.

"Absolutely."

"Ready for what?" Connor asked.

Hamish pointed up into the sky. "You don't think we'd let Dierk fly a windrider into that storm, over that woman, without some support do you? Ivor and I will make a distraction pass over the army to keep their attention."

Hamish knew better than anyone how dangerous it was to try flying anywhere near Harley, but he was still willing to do it anyway. Brave, sure, but crazy as a one-legged Strider running circles around his wooden leg.

Verena said, "I'll go too. That'll keep the pressure from getting too bad."

Connor's good humor evaporated. He started to protest, but Verena shook her head. "We talked about this, Connor."

"We didn't talk about this!"

"I'll be fine. You'll be fine." She placed her hand over his heart. "Trust us."

He wanted to argue, wanted to shield her from danger. For once he wished Mattias was with them to help him convince her, but that was foolish thinking. He hated to admit it, but she was right. They all needed to take risks to win. So he placed his hand over hers. They'd faced so many dangers together, it was foolish to hope she wouldn't have to take any risks.

"Be careful."

Hamish snorted. "Tell Dierk to be careful." He gripped Dierk's shoulder and added, "No offense, but I still worry you'll revert to old habits and forget how to fly."

Dierk didn't return the smile. His expression was all grim business. "I can do this. I've never wanted to fly into battle, but I have to do this. For me. For Ingrid."

Connor gripped his hand, moved by Dierk's determination. He might not seem the ideal person for this mission, but he'd do it anyway.

But he couldn't sit by and idly watch his friends fly into danger. He'd find a way to connect with his tertiaries. Today of all days, he had to make it work. He said, "I'll see if I can shield you from the worst of the storm."

NO SHELTER FROM THE STORM

For the first time, Verena wished the Swift was heavier. The nimble little craft pitched and bobbed in the turbulent wind, thrown off course by every gust. With snow whipping from every side against her shielded front window, she lost all sense of direction.

If not for the compass mounted on the front rail, and the leveling bubble beside it, she'd never maintain her flight path. For the first time in her life, she felt a bit air sick by the unexpected bouncing, jouncing, and stomach-lurching spins.

Then she managed to hit an exhaustion pocket in the middle of that whirling storm, and the craft simply dropped under her. The snug restraining straps seemed to drag her down. She quickly adjusted power to the various thrusters, grateful for the extra stability her little wings offered.

If she was having that much trouble, she feared for Dierk. They had lifted off in close formation from the central square. Hamish and Ivor took the lead. The plan was for her to follow them, with Dierk tailing her.

That lasted about five seconds.

Even with speakstones allowing constant communication, Verena suspected their little formation was scattered too far apart. She couldn't see anyone or anything in the blowing snow and gray nothingness. Dawn had supposedly arrived, but all it did was turn the billowing blackness into billowing gray, filled with angry wind and whirling snow.

She shouted into the dedicated speakstone linked to one in Hamish's helmet. "Hamish, are you there?"

"Pastry."

"I thought we agreed to change that stupid code word."

"Oh, right. Sculpted scone."

She sighed. It was probably good she couldn't see him, or she'd be tempted to fire a diorite missile up his backside.

"I thought Ivor was going to keep the snow in check."

A brief pause. "He can't do too much or it'll draw attention the of the Spitters."

"We need something. I can't see anything, can't tell where I am or how close we are," she insisted.

Another pause. "How's this?"

A shape formed in the air in front of her, snow condensing into a long, white arrow that pointed slightly left and down of her current course. Verena blinked a couple of times in surprise. The surprise tactic made perfect sense. Ivor was brilliant. Feeling a little more confident, she adjusted thrusters. As she pulled the Swift into line, the arrow straightened out.

"Follow the arrow and you should be fine. We're about a mile from contact."

"Sculpted scone," she acknowledged, then bit her lip trying to call back the words. He'd never stop using the stupid acknowledgment phrase now.

The air seemed to settle down a bit all of a sudden and she took the opportunity to twist her mini-hub to Connor's paired stone. "Connor, are you able to tell how Dierk is doing?"

"He's not far behind you. I've managed to smooth out the current you're both riding. As long as you don't deviate course, you should be able to slip through the storm okay."

"You managed all that with a shaky connection?" she asked, amazed.

"You needed my help," came the simple answer.

Connor was a good man. He was far from perfect, but knowing he was watching over them from a distance helped calm her nerves. "Thank you."

Hopefully he'd eased Dierk's flight quicker than he had hers. Dierk might have become the best flyer in Faulenrost, but that still didn't mean a whole lot. She still worried about him, especially in those stormy conditions. Still, with Connor and Ivor to help support his efforts, she decided he'd make it.

She had to believe that. Verena grieved Ingrid's loss too, but it had devastated Dierk. He wasn't a fighter, hadn't prepared himself mentally for the likelihood of losing loved ones in the struggle like she had. In his festering anger, he'd developed an angry bomb. She dearly hoped that when it detonated, it might extinguish his anger too and free him to heal. If he didn't learn to manage Ingrid's loss, the grief and rage would tear him apart.

A moment of smooth flying later, Verena unexpectedly burst out of the obscuring clouds into clear morning sunlight. The abrupt change shocked her so much, she didn't react for a critical second.

Blinking against the unexpected light, her hands instinctively tensed on her control levers as she looked down. High Lord Dougal's army marched up the road directly below her. The blizzard simply ended, snow and wind splitting around the army.

Verena barely caught a glimpse of the thousands of marching troops before spears of fire lanced up toward her. She threw the Swift into a banking roll and increased power.

She caught sight of the Hawk banking away in the opposite direction, water and fire spraying all around it, but not quite touching it. Without Ivor on board, Hamish would probably already be dead.

"Connor, they've split the storm! They see us. We're under attack!" She cried as she unleashed the puking dooms along the underside of the Swift to throw herself higher.

Firetongues in the army below stole those flames. She screamed as the fire condensed into white-hot spears that leaped up after her.

The fire deflected away as if striking an invisible barrier.

Connor's voice came over the mini-hub, tense and worried. "Try not to give them more ammunition, please. It's tough enough for Kilian and I to cover you and Dierk from here. Those Petralists are working unusually well together."

"Thanks! They almost crisped me."

"Can you get out of there?"

She reached at least a thousand feet and banked the Swift over. At this height, she doubted anyone could reach her with elemental attacks. The army was enormous. Even though she'd seen the huge force marshaled against Altkalen, this army somehow seemed more threatening, appearing suddenly out of the storm like that.

The Hawk still banked and turned in a dizzying display of aerial acrobatics as Hamish tried to keep the enemy's attention and Ivor fought to protect them.

Then a bomb fell from the back of the Hawk.

Verena activated her long-vision goggles and focused on it. No, it wasn't the porphyry bomb. They hadn't lied to her after all. It was a normal diorite bomb.

She shouted into Hamish's speakstone, "Hamish, pull up!"

"Working on it," he replied, strain evident in his voice. "Harley's messing with the air. I don't know if we can get out of here. Where's Dierk?"

She didn't see him yet. Without hesitating, Verena rolled the Swift into a steep dive and activated the four large speedslings mounted on her wings.

As she dove, Connor's voice boomed into her cockpit. "Verena, what are you doing?"

"I've got to help Hamish. Harley's hitting them with air. Can you block her?"

"Not while protecting you."

"Do it, Connor! I'm fine for now."

Hamish's bomb hit and detonated huge, creating a deep crater in the center of the road and blasting hundreds of soldiers off their feet. Verena didn't have time to see if they were Boulders or regulars. Fire boiled over the army, but Dougal's Firetongues swept the flames into the air to spare their soldiers.

Those Petralists really were working well together. She shuddered to think about Harley as a battle instructor. She'd be horrible, terrifying, and yet probably inspirational. She hadn't considered what Harley might do during the long march up from Crann.

That she'd apparently used her time wisely did not bode well. Dougal's army easily included many more Petralists, but they had counted on the critical delays that usually occurred when multiple Petralists tried walking with the same element at the same time.

Verena scanned the army as she plunged toward them, hoping the distraction of the bomb might give her a better chance for her own strike. With her entire front shield transformed into a long-vision viewport, she easily focused on Harley. The deadly woman stood atop a low earthen tower, one hand partially raised toward the Hawk, a little smile playing across her lips.

Verena was diving from the opposite side, almost directly behind Harley, and it appeared Harley hadn't noticed her yet. So Verena unleashed the hornets. In a five-second burst, nearly a thousand deadly projectiles erupted from her speedslings. They tore through the air in a blurring cloud, reaching out to rip Harley to pieces.

She must have sensed them because she suddenly twisted to look up.

Verena launched two diorite missiles. They leaped away from the Swift, quickly accelerating to five times her speed, driven by powerful quartzite thrusters. These were the newest model, complete with little stabilizing fins.

The hornets deflected away from Harley, and Verena muttered a curse. The woman's mastery over air was far greater than any Pathfinder she'd ever known. Still, Harley couldn't stop the deadly projectiles entirely. They tore apart the edges of her tower and ripped into the troops massed around her.

The ones that contained grains of diorite erupted with satisfying explosions that ripped holes in the tight-packed ranks. Firetongues quickly snatched away the fire, but they couldn't stop the sheer force of the detonations.

The two missiles veered away while still more than a hundred feet above the army. They shot away to the left, and Verena lost sight of them as she banked the Swift to the right. Not a bad first attack. She decided to risk coming around for another speedsling strafing run.

Hamish said, "Thanks. We broke through her restricted air space during that distraction. I think . . . Look out!"

She glanced back and gasped. Her diorite missiles had somehow banked around after her and were closing with terrifying speed.

On pure instinct, Verena called upon every thruster and flipped the Swift into a backflip so that she was flying upside down, facing the onrushing missiles.

Hamish shouted, "Get out of there!" But she had already read the truth in the winds. She'd never escape impact.

So she activated the speedslings again.

A thousand hardened projectiles shot from the wings in less than two seconds, forming a wall of deadly granite. The missiles plunged into the hornet cloud and detonated with enough force to shake the Swift.

Verena flipped the craft over again and accelerated higher, barely believing that worked.

"I see Dierk!" Hamish cried.

She spun the Swift and looked back. Dierk had indeed burst free of the storm, about five hundred feet above the massed troops, his huge windrider barreling through the clear morning sky right over the army. He stood in the bed of the wagon beside the bomb.

"He's a sitting eoin," Hamish cried, banking the Hawk hard over and unleashing a distracting stream of hornets. His aim wasn't great, but the soldiers on the left flank of the army didn't know that. They still dropped behind shields or Boulder friends, while a Sentry on that flank started raising shielding walls.

Too slow. Hornets tore down the ranks of the soldiers, dropping at least twenty of them.

Verena banked the Swift over hard and tried to add more power, even though the main thrusters were already maxed. She needed to get to Dierk, offer him cover, maybe unleash her own hornets again.

Harley began rising majestically up into the air. Straight toward Dierk's wagon.

It was flying slow and straight, and he was still standing beside the bomb in the back.

Verena activated the speakstone paired with his. "Dierk, drop the bomb and get out of there! She's coming."

Dierk glanced over the side, but he was looking away from Verena so she couldn't read his expression. She couldn't imagine what he was waiting for. He was supposed to have overcome his fear of flying, but why would he hesitate?

"Dierk?" she called, hating the fear creeping into her voice.

"I can't do it." He spoke in an anguished tone and he dropped to his knees beside the bomb. "Tallan forgive me, but I can't kill so many."

"Oh, Dierk, no," Verena breathed, suddenly terrified. She loved that he'd rediscovered his gentle heart, but he should have picked a better time.

"What's he doing?" Hamish cried, spinning in a long barrel roll, the

Hawk blasting through half a dozen grasping ropes of water and fire.

"He can't do it!"

Her heart racing with terror, Verena changed her angle of attack, heading straight toward Harley. The Swift tore through the cold air, as if the little craft sensed the danger Dierk faced and wanted to help her save him. Verena wanted to shout to Dierk to flee, but he'd never escape Harley in that windrider.

Harley had to die.

"Connor, Dierk's in trouble! I need everything you and Kilian have got."

"No, Verena, get out of there! She's activated heavy shielding along the edge of the storm. We need a few seconds to break through."

"We don't have that long. Harley's coming. I have to stop her."

Harley was barely a hundred feet below the windrider, rising fast. Verena was closing from her left side, but still nearly a quarter of a mile away. Despite the distance, Verena fired the speedslings, praying with all her heart that they'd arrive in time.

Harley looked right at her. Through the magnification of her long-vision goggles, Verena felt like she was sitting right in front of the woman.

Harley smiled.

And the wind suddenly hardened under the hornets, deflecting them slightly higher.

Time seemed to slow as Verena realized with icy horror what she'd done. She watched in helpless anguish as the hornets, her hornets, tore into the front of the windrider in a storm of destruction that ripped the flying wagon apart. Explosions blasted flame and smoke and splinters of wood in every direction.

"No!" Verena screamed, pounding on the dash of the Swift with impotent fury.

Abruptly the storm closed in around her again, buffeting her with crazy winds and blinding snow. Verena drove through it, adjusting course on pure instinct, her eyes locked on the spot where Dierk had disappeared.

A moment later the winds parted the storm and she flashed within ten feet of Harley. She passed so fast that she caught only a glimpse of Harley standing calmly on the air, waving to her.

Hovering just above her head was the porphyry bomb.

Dierk hung upside down below her feet, writhing in apparent agony, although Verena didn't glimpse his injuries.

Then the Storm closed in on her and Verena wept freely as she fought for her life against the elements unleashed. The storm howled and screamed along with her, but the glacial cold of that storm could not match the freezing horror that chilled her heart.

Dierk was Harley's prisoner. So was his terrible porphyry bomb.

Verena wept to think what Harley might do next.

THINGS AREN'T AS BAD AS THEY SEEM.
THEY'RE PROBABLY WORSE.

It took five eternal minutes for Verena to land in the main courtyard of the central palace. Connor paced nervously every second. The news that Harley had both the bomb and Dierk had rattled him so badly that he'd completely lost connection with quartzite.

Terror that Harley might somehow catch Verena and yank her out of the air helped him connect with soapstone. Water had appeared, but seemed insubstantial. The connection was weak, but he'd touched her hand long enough to cast his thoughts into the air to find Verena. She was alive, but buffeted by the storm. He'd thrown every ounce of will into calming the storm around her, but wasn't sure how much good he'd managed with his connection wavering so badly.

He exulted when she finally landed. Verena stumbled out of the Swift, her expression anguished. She threw herself into his arms, sobbing, and he tried to comfort her through the torrent of his own emotions.

"I'm so sorry," he finally managed to say. "Harley sealed the air around the army in a way I've never seen before. With her Spitters and Firetongues supporting her, they locked us out for a few seconds."

The explanation sounded weak. He should have found a way. With the mighty Kilian at his side, they should have done more. Unfortunately, with Harley at its head, the army was far better prepared to defend against them than anything Dougal had thrown at them during his invasion of Altkalen.

Verena clung to him for another moment before wiping her eyes. "I know you tried. We all tried, but we were fools to let Dierk go. He couldn't do it. He wasn't a warrior or a killer. He was just a good man, driven too far by grief."

She was right, but she was also wrong. Dierk's failure to act put every one of them at greater risk. Dierk was a good man, a man brave enough to understand his own boundaries at the last. Now his foolish insistence that he fly that critical bomb against the enemy might have condemned thousands.

"She'll kill him," Verena said, wiping at her tears, but only leaving glittering tracks that froze to her cheeks.

"Or worse, she'll force him to tell her what the bomb does. Come on, we need to get to Kilian and the others."

As they raced for the military command building, Mattias appeared out of the snowy, early morning gloom and fell into step beside them. He clearly wanted to speak with Verena, but she said nothing while they ran.

Breathless from the fast run, they met with the central command a moment later atop the southernmost tower. On most days, its flat, crenelated roof offered a spectacular view over the outer wall and across the lands south of Merkland. The blizzard had lost some of its strength, as if exhausted by the Petralists fighting to control its heart, but snow still fell steadily, sheathing the distance in softly falling curtains.

Ilse and Lukas had joined the group, both dressed for battle. Lukas still looked pale and a bit battered, but he looked determined to not leave Ilse's side.

"Glad to see you on your feet," Connor told him.

"We'll take her next time," Lukas promised fiercely.

So far, she'd taken more from them than they had from her.

Ivor and Hamish arrived seconds later with Kilian, all looking grim. Ivor wasted no time with pleasantries. "So Harley has the bomb?"

When Verena nodded he asked, "Can you sense anything about it?"

"No. I've already tried, but I feel nothing."

"Is that good?" Connor asked.

"I doubt it," Hamish said. "It had an obsidian plug for remote detonation. I've tried to sense it too, but I get nothing. If we could link to it, we could still trigger it."

"Since you can't, we must assume Harley removed it," Kilian said.

"How would she know? We just discovered that secret about obsidian recently," Hamish asked.

"You said she captured Dierk alive," Kilian said gravely. "She is expert at extracting information."

Verena looked close to tears again. "Dierk's no warrior. He wouldn't be able to resist that kind of interrogation."

"Then we have to also assume Harley knows what the bomb does," Ivor said with a grimace. He looked around the somber company and added, "That could have gone better."

That was an understatement big enough to swallow Merkland. Connor said, "I can't imagine how it could have gone worse."

"If only he hadn't insisted," Hamish said. He looked deeply shaken and paced the perimeter of the tower, hands clenching and unclenching, scowling.

Kilian said, "We took a daring gamble. Had it worked, we might have avoided the desperate struggle we now face. It didn't work. The fight is upon us and we lack time to second-guess ourselves."

Connor didn't want to ask the next question, but couldn't help himself. "Dierk's probably already dead, isn't he?"

"Almost for sure," Kilian confirmed.

Verena savagely wiped away her tears, her sorrow transforming to resolute fury. "Then it's up to us to avenge him."

Connor squeezed her hand reassuringly. Victory was far from sure, but they had to remain confident, or Harley had already won.

Ivor said, "I'm scanning the lands to the south. They're advancing more quickly. They'll be here in less than an hour."

"Not much time to prepare," Lord Nevan said, exchanging glances with Lords Torcall and Logan. Connor wished he knew what they were thinking, but before he could reach for a piece of chert, Ivor spoke again.

"Kilian, they worked together far better than I've ever seen. Does that change our strategy?"

He shook his head. "Our job might be harder, but it is unchanged. Don't despair. Remember, you fought clear, despite their numbers. Connor and I helped, even across that great distance. They capitalized on the advantage offered by their proximity, numbers, and surprise. The closer they get, the stronger our advantage, particularly in soapstone."

Connor hoped he was right. They'd thought they were the ones about to surprise Harley and Dougal, but the crafty old hag had flipped the geall right back on them.

"Then we prepare secondary measures," Ivor said. Turning to his officers he began issuing orders. Then he gripped Lord Nevan's hand. "When we take our positions, you will play a critical role. We'll funnel communication back to the city through you. Hold the city, but be prepared to send out reinforcements as we've discussed."

Lord Nevan said confidently, "I know what to do. You're the ones taking the great risks today." He gestured at Lord Torcall and Lord Logan. "We are committed. There is no turning back now. We will not fail you."

"Good, then get to your posts. I'm heading for the river."

Connor gripped Ivor's hand. "Good luck." He'd be responsible for holding the entire left flank alone.

Ivor flashed a predatory grin and said, "Don't hold back today, Connor. We need that creative brilliance you showed at the Carraig."

"We'll beat her," Connor promised with a lot more confidence than he felt.

As officers and lords scattered to their appointed positions, Hamish said, "Verena, let's go."

"I'll be right there," she promised. Then she hugged Connor fiercely.

He held her close and assured her, "You did everything you could for him."

She leaned back to look him in the eye, fresh tears making her beautiful blue eyes even more mesmerizing than ever. She shook her head slowly and her voice cracked with sorrow. "No, Connor. I did too much. I knew Harley could deflect my hornets, but I fired again anyway. She used them to destroy Dierk's windrider. I helped her take him."

He read anguish and self hatred in her gaze. He gripped her shoulders and said strongly, "It's not your fault that Dierk hesitated. It's not your fault that Harley took advantage of the moment. Blame Harley and Harley alone."

Verena nodded and sniffled loudly. "You're right, Connor. Promise me we'll kill her."

Usually Connor tried to avoid killing, but he did not hesitate now. "We will kill Harley today, Verena. No matter what."

She kissed him fiercely, but as she turned to go, Kilian hissed, "Connor, she's unleashed the hounds."

Ilse frowned. "Her summoned monsters?"

Kilian nodded. "A little earlier than I expected."

"Has she discovered Rory?" Verena asked, her voice thick with worry.

"I don't think so. They're coming fast, straight up the road."

Ilse said sharply, "Lukas, call up the Crushers. I need to get down to the ground. Lord Mattias, will you join us?"

"Of course." Mattias looked grateful for a chance to look useful. He and Lukas hurried off, but Kilian held Ilse back for a moment.

"Harley obviously wants us distracted. Just as obviously, we have to deal with the threat."

"So what's she distracting us from?" Verena asked.

"I'll tell you as soon as we stop her hounds and figure it out. Get into the air, Verena. Watch yourself and do not allow your anger to cloud your judgment. Harley is a master at rattling her opponents into making stupid blunders. She rarely offers a chance to make a second mistake."

Connor watched her go, full of conflicting emotions. He loved her strength and determination, but sometimes in the grip of battle fury she made reckless decisions, like her strafing dive against Harley's army. He worried what she might do when she spotted Harley again.

Kilian clapped him on the shoulder, his expression eager. "Let's bring out Justice and his friends."

JUSTICE'S LEAGUE WOULD HAVE BEEN A BETTER NAME

Connor embraced his growing battle excitement, using it as a shield against his worry for Verena and his fear that his tertiary affinities would fail him again at a critical moment. Determined not to falter, he focused on the slender thread of thought still connecting him to his summoned creatures. The links blossomed in strength, filling his mind with an image of the scores of monsters awaiting his command, crouched in the dark warehouse.

Connor tugged on them.

"You forgot to send one to open the door," Kilian commented as a tide of ferocious elemental creatures shattered the wide sliding door and bounded up the street, led by Mouth and Justice. Terrified townsfolk and startled soldiers scattered out of their path.

Connor didn't want anyone hurt, and he didn't want to damage the city walls yet, so as the tide of summoned creatures swarmed toward the gates, he tapped pumice and then managed a decent connection to inner-focused quartzite. He applied it to his voice and shouted, "Open the Army Gate and get out of the way!"

Soldiers scrambled to obey, and they moved a lot faster when they caught sight of the tide of terrifying creatures bearing down on them. Connor pushed the thought to his monsters to slow to give the gate a little more time.

He switched to soapstone, and thankfully Water appeared in his mind, looking regal and stable. Her hair billowed around her beautiful face like deep blue tides, while her red and green cape fluttered behind her sea-foam white gown. She gave Connor an approving smile and stepped close to embrace him.

The connection felt stronger than any time since his ascdension. He took that as a good sign. He waited a couple of heartbeats until after the next wave of green energy swept across her cape. It barely shook the connection. So he swept his soapstone senses south, across the landscape. With snow piled on the land and still falling in heavy sheets, he could see everything mapped clearly to his water senses.

Harley's horde of monsters was pounding up the road in a dark tide of enlivened earth. Connor suddenly worried that maybe he should have made Mouth twice as big. Most of Harley's creatures were the size of horses, and they all moved with deadly speed. He sensed mostly predator shapes, like pedras and nualls, and decided to think of them collectively as her hounds.

But he hated the icy fear that slid down his spine as he considered her larger army of creatures. Then Ivor's parting words came to mind and he allowed a fierce grin.

Ivor was right. Connor needed to embrace the same unpredictable state he'd sought at the Carraig. He'd faced far stronger armies and won because he thought creatively and found ways to enjoy the journey, despite the risk.

He couldn't refer to those monsters as Harley's hounds. He needed something simpler, something that poked a mocking finger at her tyrannical power. So instead of Harley's Hounds, he'd call them Hahos. Except that sounded a bit juvenile. Hayhos. That was it.

Connor's creatures poured through the still-opening gate, with Kilian's mixed in among them. The Hayhos were charging up the road on a wide front. The deep snow did nothing to hinder them.

He twisted his mini-hub. "Ivor, are you sensing this? Harley sent her summoned creatures. When we engage, feel free to take any that wander too close to the river."

"Sculpted scone."

Ilse frowned at Connor. "Who came up with that ridiculous codeword?"

"Verena, I think."

"That girl's been spending far too much time with you lot," Kilian said.

Connor smiled to himself as he spread his creatures out and sent out the order, *Destroy everything on the road south.*

He decided he also needed a name for his little army. Too many of the ideas he considered based on Mouth made him want to snicker, so he decided to use Justice, which raced beside Mouth at the vanguard of the host.

He was tempted to call it Justice's League, but that didn't feel right. So he settled on the Freakishly-Awesome-Monsters-Connor-And-Kilian-Each-Summoned. Famcakes sounded right. Giving them a name definitely helped cut through the fear that threatened to rob him of his ability to think clearly.

The Famcakes sprang forward with remarkable speed, racing to meet the Hayhos. There might be almost twice as many Hayhos than

Famcakes, but Connor felt optimistic they could tear her summoned army apart. He couldn't fathom how she alone had produced so many.

"Kilian, are you reading the counts?"

Both of Kilian's eyes were filled with blue flames that transformed his face into an intimidating mask. His fierce grin added to the aura of danger suddenly surrounding him. "She'll try cheating. Ilse, are you ready to play catch-the-devil with her again?"

"It will be my pleasure." Ilse rushed for the stairs, leaving Connor and Kilian alone atop the tower.

"Connor, you'll have to support Ilse's efforts this time. Harley won't be holding back."

"How deep do you think she'll risk drawing?"

"Not too deep at first, but she'll hit harder than yesterday."

"I'll deal with it. She won't squash our Famcakes."

"Our what?"

"Never mind. I'll deal with the earth," he promised.

Ilse was far craftier, but if he could secure a solid connection, he could sling earth around with more strength. He wished they hadn't used up his slate sculpted stone. It might have offered him a tremendous advantage against Harley.

"Ivor and I will push with soapstone and marble," Kilian continued. "She's a lot closer now and her army is almost as far from the hounds as we are. She has to know the situation isn't ideal."

Connor was tempted to ask Kilian to refer to her hounds as Hayhos, but it was better to fight from two very different mental states.

Kilian added, "Whatever she hopes to gain from attacking so far out, let's crush her hounds and stop her. This might be the break we need."

The Famcakes crashed into the Hayhos, and the fierce, brutal struggle that erupted a mile from Merkland totally captured Connor's attention.

The two lines of monsters tore into each other with terrifying intensity. They held nothing back, were not limited by pain or fear of getting hurt or killed. They launched themselves at each other with single-minded intensity.

Connor caught flashes of images from his Famcakes. One tore out the throat of a bearlike creature with two heads, and air erupted out the breach, shrieking a high-pitched death wail. The dying monster's second head ripped its attacker's foreleg off in turn with a spray of fiery blood.

Another nuall-shaped Famcake landed on the back of an enormous doglike beast and ripped out its spine in a spray of dirt, then leaped away toward the next attacker.

Connor couldn't sense the earth well enough from up there. He hesitated just long enough to ensure a strong connection with marble, then threw himself off the tower with a burst of fire. He shot high over a row of long barracks and a wide, paved yard full of soldiers. He planned to drag the flames along with him to form a fiery net to break his fall, but his connection wavered, Fire gave him a jaunty wave, and the flames winked out.

Luckily, he had already absorbed granite. He max-tapped it just before plowing into the ground near Ilse. He blasted through a foot of snow and bounced off the frozen ground. The brutal impact rattled him, but he forced himself to roll over and press his hand against the ground, seeking a connection with earth.

"Don't get sloppy, Connor," Ilse warned from where she stood nearby atop a squat Sapper tower, hands embedded into earthen rails.

He decided it was better she think him nervous rather than realize how unstable his tertiary affinities still were. Mattias, Lukas, and a dozen Crushers were spread out to either side in four-man squads. They included a Water Moccasin and a Flameweaver, and the falling snow parted around them, leaving them in pockets of calm.

Luckily, Earth rose out of the ground in front of him and gripped Connor's shoulder, his solemn expression encouraging. Harley and Ilse were already clashing under the raging battlefield a mile to the south. Earth bubbled and rippled beneath the battling creatures, who all ignored the threat. Where Harley gained advantage, Famcakes died, sucked into the earth or impaled and ripped apart by vicious, grasping fingers of earth.

But Ilse refused to surrender easily. For every two Famcakes that Harley destroyed, Ilse shattered the life out of one of her Hayhos.

Not good odds.

Connor hesitated to throw himself into that fight, though. The two women were interlinked under the area, their wills twisting and weaving around each other in an intricate pattern as they tried to block each other's moves while gaining advantage for themselves. The delicate balance moved remarkably little earth. Neither of them had yet abandoned caution and risked drawing deep enough that they might trigger catastrophic disaster.

No, if Connor threw himself into that mess, he might hinder Ilse as much as help her. So he jumped on top, just like when his younger brothers were squabbling in their loft bedroom.

Connor thrust his earth senses down the road, limiting himself to the top two inches of dirt. He didn't push into the area in a single wide sheet of influence, like sliding a mattress across a floor. Instead he focused his will like the prongs of a really long pitchfork and punched through the weave of the women's battle.

The next wave of green power swept across Earth's cloak, shaking his connection, but not quite severing it. Connor cursed softly, hating the limitation. He felt like the second threshold had lied to him.

He forced himself to think. Kilian always said how one applied force was more important than how much force they brought to bear. So as his connection solidified between waves of green magic, he plunged his narrow bands of influence into the battlefield. Everywhere his earth senses touched one the Hayhos, he grabbed at whatever part was touching the ground and sheared it off.

That helped a little by distracting the creatures or knocking them down for a Famcake to destroy, but it wasn't enough. Connor sprayed earth into the air to better sense the battlefield and began focusing on individual contests. One Hayho had knocked down a Famcake and was snapping in for the kill. Connor grabbed its jaws with slender fingers of earth and wrenched it off. That gave the Famcake the chance to lunge back in and rip out its throat.

With each wave of the green-frequency magic, his connection wavered, but he threw himself back into the fray as soon as it stabilized again. His limited approach didn't give Harley enough time to counter him well, and Connor grinned.

Kilian joined the fray with his usual flair. Fire swept across the battle-field like a bowl of spaghetti thrown into a hurricane. The long, thin tendrils of fire whipped around the hounds, driving into eyes and ears and throats, disabling, distracting, and piercing from the inside.

Ivor struck with a cresting wave of water that snatched everything fighting within ten yards of the Macantact, Hayhos and Famcakes alike. A second later, the dark, cold waters spit the Famcakes back out, but none of the Hayhos ever surfaced.

The next two minutes passed in a blur as Connor immersed himself in the effort of maintaining those brief, intense strikes against the Hayhos, and tried to block Harley's attacks on the Famcakes. He even tried to think in confusing sentences to encourage a tighter bond with Earth, who seemed to approve. His affinity strengthened, the interference fading from the green-frequency magic. The ground under that section of road became one with him. Summoned creatures tore each other apart and he felt every claw, every stumble, every broken body.

Earth buckled, oozed, and churned under the creatures as Connor and Ilse fought Harley. Carefully. Fire and water ripped across the battle lines, tearing at Harley's monsters.

Some of Harley's other tertiary Petralists joined the fight against Kilian and Ivor, and their opposing wills shredded the air above the monsters, showering the land for a quarter mile in every direction with sprays of fire and glittering, icy shards of broken water.

Ivor and Kilian gained an early advantage, smashing down nearly three dozen Hayhos before Harley's support solidified. After that, the elemental battle grew in intensity but faded in effectiveness as both sides spent the majority of their strength countering each other.

That gave the monsters time to rip each other apart.

Although the Famcakes fought with inspiring ferocity, the Hayhos outnumbered them and often exceeded them in sheer mass and power. Connor recognized the looming outcome thirty seconds before Justice and Mouth, the last of the Famcakes, both exploded under the combined onslaught of five Hayhos.

All of their creatures were dead, shattered into wet piles of broken clay, their elemental lifeblood sucked away by Petralists in the intense battle over their corpses. Nearly thirty Hayhos still remained, although several of them were badly damaged.

Harley's thunder-chuckle echoed across the valley as her hounds began to retreat.

If only Connor could mix multiple elements, he could probably smash most of those remaining creatures before they could retreat, but he didn't dare.

He did have friends handy, though.

"Kilian. Ivor. Help me. Mix your elements with mine and we can make a final strike."

Without waiting for a reply, Connor flung a long rope of earth into the air above the battlefield. Many of the other Petralists seemed to be beginning to withdraw, so the move must have caught them by surprise. Ropes of crimson fire and black water shot across the battlefield and twined around his earth.

"All together!" Connor cried, and heaved on his piece of the combined elemental weapon. Kilian and Ivor sensed the movement and reinforced it with their own.

Their twisted elements slammed down over the retreating lines of Hayhos, swatting them like a line of ants under a long boot. They caught a dozen of them in that strike, splattering their corpses across the road. The rest of the hounds galloped away while Harley and her Petralists surrounded them with heavy shielding.

Connor let them go. They'd accomplished what they needed. Harley now knew that she wasn't the only one with tricks up her sleeve. He, Kilian, and Ivor released the elements, and Connor switched to quartzite.

Fickle Air appeared, flitting around his mind, hands outstretched, but spinning to make a connection difficult. Connor lunged and caught one hand. He laughed and unleashed his own thunder-chuckle.

Air wrenched her hand away and blew him a kiss as the valley boomed with what sounded like an enormous choking cough.

"Did you do that?" Ilse asked with a frown.

"Trying to keep them unbalanced."

Mattias said, "It probably worked. I have no idea what that was supposed to be."

Next time, he'd use serpentinite.

IDEAS WANTED. NOW.

onnor turned his mini-hub to Verena's stone. "Are you in
position?"

"What happened down there? I couldn't make out specifics
through that elemental storm."

"We destroyed almost all of her Hayhos. Our Famcakes are gone."

"What?"

"She's got about twenty hounds left. Keep an eye out for them."

"Why didn't you say so?"

"Sculpted Scones."

Kilian landed nearby on a pillar of intertwined water and fire. "That
went about as well as we could have hoped."

"Any idea why she initiated that?" Ilse asked, then she frowned and
said, "Connor!"

He tried tapping slate again, but this time, despite max-tapping
pumice, the gateway simply refused to open. The interfering green magic
seemed to bounce around in his head between waves, completely
canceling out his ability to connect with earth.

"Do you feel her?" Ilse asked.

"Not really. What are you sensing?"

Ilse frowned. "What's wrong with you today, Connor? I thought you
were stable."

"Mostly. For now, just tell us what you sensed, okay?" He hated that
Lukas and Mattias had to hear that he was struggling. He didn't want the
team to fear he might become a liability.

Thankfully, Ilse didn't press him on it. "She's coming. She knows we'll
sense her so she's not even trying to hide. She's about a mile and a half
down the road, and she's infused the ground with so much of her will that
I can't penetrate the area close to her. She's so strong."

"How about the rest of the road around her?" Mattias asked.

Ilse shook her head, her frown deepening. "It's weird. I don't sense anything else around her, but why would she approach alone? She's got an entire army with her."

Kilian looked troubled. "I sense something for a second, but not enough to get a clear idea what she's up to. Her Spitters are shielding heavily now."

Mattias asked, "Does she really think she can fight us all alone like she did in Althing?"

"Was this why she was distracting us, so she could advance closer without us realizing it?" Ilse asked.

"Perhaps," Kilian said slowly, still frowning. "She may be trying to prove she's the strongest Petralist after my mother. It would help secure their control over the nation."

That didn't sound right. Harley might challenge all the rest of them combined, but surely she didn't think she could take them all. Not with Kilian on their side. Connor said, "Maybe she figures if she defeats us the rest of the city might surrender."

"She has to be planning more than this," Kilian said.

The words barely left his lips when a distant crack sounded through the snowy air, like a far-away thunderclap.

"Inbound," Ilse warned. "Earth projectiles, maybe a dozen of them, just cast into the sky."

"I feel them. Enemy Spitters are trying to guide them in," Kilian said.

Connor tried to connect with earth again, but again he failed. His frustration was growing to open worry.

Ilse said, "They just cast a second wave. I sense other Sentries sliding their influence along the flanks of the road. We may be facing a full earth barrage."

Verena's voice spoke over the speakstone on Connor's mini-hub. "I'm spotting dozens of earthen projectiles, maybe two or three yards in diameter."

"We're tracking them too," Connor replied.

Kilian raised his own mini-hub. "Ivor, help me deflect these away." Then he glanced at Connor. "Get connected to soapstone. We'll need your help."

"I'll try," he promised.

Kilian held his gaze, pinpoints of white-hot light glowing in his eyes. "No, Connor. Don't try. Do."

Connor nodded, his resolve growing. Soapstone was his most stable element. He could do it. He closed his eyes and focused on it, building a clear image of Water in all her majesty in his mind.

Nothing. The green magic blocked him again.

As he silently cursed his weakness and tried again, Kilian was saying, "Our Sentries behind the wall can shield Merkland from underground incursion. Ilse, watch our feet. As long as we knock the missiles out of the air, the attack accomplishes little."

Connor took a deep breath, trying not to get distracted as Kilian conferred with Ivor, discussing how many missiles they were deflecting. They were holding them off, but only barely. They needed him.

Driven by that need, Connor focused on soapstone again. He took a long, slow breath, even though with pumice max-tapped he almost didn't need to breathe. He waited between green waves of power and then plunged his senses through the soapstone gateway.

Finally, Water appeared, although her form seemed indistinct, as if he was viewing her through a screening waterfall. Still, it was something, so Connor plunged a hand into that waterfall and grabbed for her. He managed a weak connection. It was enough to cast his water senses up into the storm. The earthen missiles tore through the falling snow, drawing his attention like ants crawling across his scalp.

He felt the influence of the Spitters, surrounding many of the missiles with protective bubbles. There weren't enough Spitters to protect them all, though, so he grabbed at the ones flying without aid, forming nets of water, and yanking them off course. He aimed them east to crash into farmers' fields.

"Don't waste ammunition," Kilian said and Connor felt him form the snow in front of one earthen missile into a curving tube. The projectile shot into the tube, which redirected it right around, shooting it back down toward Harley.

Connor grinned. That looked like a lot of fun.

Thinking of fun seemed to help solidify his connection a little. More projectiles were launching constantly, so Connor threw his will into the fray against enemy Spitters. He managed to break through a couple of the protective barriers and knock the missiles off course, although the enemy Spitters broke apart his curving tube before he could send missiles shooting back at Harley.

So he changed tactics, forming blades of ice and shearing several projectiles into little pieces. He noticed that the enemy Spitters immediately lost interest in the broken ones. So he yanked the pieces back around and slammed them into the next missile, shattering it too.

"They're trying to overwhelm us with volume," Kilian said. Ilse, get your tertiaries into the fight and ask Verena to pass word to Nevan for their Spitters to stand ready. If any get past us, they'll have to deal with them."

As everyone scrambled to obey, Mattias said, "If they keep us busy long enough, Harley will have time to close on us."

That was an unpleasant thought, but Connor lacked the time to think about it. Over a hundred and fifty heavy earthen projectiles were in the air, shooting toward Merkland.

"Verena, where are you and Hamish?" he asked after successfully knocking another one from the sky.

"We're monitoring from over the township. Do you need us to intervene?"

"No. Stay back. The elements are getting twisted into knots up there. You'd get crushed."

"Copy that. We'll monitor for any other surprises."

That was comforting, but as Connor fought an enemy Spitter for control over yet another projectile, he realized the approach was not working well enough. His connection with soapstone was not nearly strong enough to dare a second element, so he turned his mini-hub to Ivor's speakstone.

"Ivor, try mixing water and fire. See if that gives you an advantage."

"Good idea."

Kilian overheard, and he nodded approval.

Immediately, Connor felt the difference as both Ivor and Kilian switched to mixed elements. With fire intertwined with their water, they stumped the enemy Spitters long enough to gain critical advantage and knock even more missiles from the sky.

Ilse said, "Harley is still approaching. Less than a mile now."

They really needed to figure out a plan to take her, but just then another wave of projectiles burst out of the ground, fired all along the road, from back near Harley, all the way nearly up to their own position.

"I've got two projectiles fired from the east and west," Ilse said.

"Only two?" Connor scanned that area, which was far beyond where the others had come from. He found those projectiles, but whoever had thrown them into the air wasn't very good at aiming. They would both fly right over the city. In fact, they might just smash into each other. If they missed, they'd crash down harmlessly in fields on either side. If those Sentries could fire projectiles from those sides, why hadn't they sent more?

"Ware!" Ilse cried, suddenly looking tense. "Harley just threw a hundred more projectiles herself, and the other Sentries doubled their volume."

Connor left the two mis-aimed projectiles and turned his attention to the new swarm of earthen missiles arcing up into the air. The sheer volume daunted him. Harley's Sentries must have pushed themselves to the limits.

Could so few stop so many?

Hundreds in Merkland might die if they failed. Connor could no longer afford to hesitate. He tapped marble, trying to achieve that same dual-element advantage as Kilian and Ivor.

Immediately his connection with Water shattered.

"Tallan's boiled socks! Why is this so hard?" he cried as he released soapstone altogether and switched to marble.

Fire popped into his mind, laughing with wild insanity. Perfect. Connor grabbed hold of his arm, savoring the explosion of deep, spicy flavor from the stone in his mouth. Most of the Petralists shepherding the missiles toward the city were Spitters, so he struck with fire.

Fire seemed to like him embracing that wild and unstable element, and the connection felt strong. Riding that wave of intense flames, Connor threw himself into the effort of spearing missiles, shattering them, or knocking them off course. There was no time for tricks of finesse. He attacked like a battering ram of white-hot fire.

The rest of the team fought beside him in a frantic effort to quell the tide. Connor allowed a fierce grin. They were going to do it!

The two mis-aimed projectiles did smash into each other high above Merkland.

One of them exploded.

"Did you feel that?" Connor asked. Since when did earth explode?

"Kind of busy," Ilse muttered.

"One of those projectiles just blew up over the city."

The others exchanged confused looks. As Connor scanned the air over the city, he found dust and debris filtering down. Harley had concealed a bomb inside one of those projectiles. She must have intended for it to explode above the city, but why?

Connor understood a second later, and his heart chilled with dread. "Harley released powder with that bomb."

He wrenched his mini-hub to Verena's stone just as she shouted, "That was Dierk's bomb! She's raining quickened porphyry over Merkland. They're going to tear themselves apart!"

Connor turned to look up at the high, white walls behind them, indistinct through the sheets of heavy snow, horrified by what was about to happen.

Lukas frowned. "Would Dougal allow her to use it?"

Ilse said, "If she chose to send it, do you think he could stop her?"

Verena asked, "Can we do something to stop it? Can you push the dust aside?"

Connor was already trying, but his connection to quartzite was so unstable he barely felt Air laughing at him as she dodged his grasping hands. Every time he made brief contact, his air senses radiated out over Merkland, and he hated what he felt.

Harley was there, riding those currents, twisting them so they sucked the powder down toward the helpless populace. She definitely knew what the bomb did.

"Harley's driving it down. I can't stop her," Connor exclaimed, hating his weakness. Hating Harley more.

He tried switching back to soapstone to help Kilian try to whip the blowing snow across the city and drag the dust away with it. Harley responded by calling forth powerful downdrafts that sucked everything down into the city.

Connor muttered a curse as he tried to reverse the currents, but she was prepared, while he was scrambling to react with weak affinities.

"The Sentries have retreated," Ilse reported.

Connor didn't care. His connection was just solid enough that he could feel those deadly grains of powder settling down over the city.

"It was all a distraction so we didn't intercept that bomb," Mattias stated.

Three seconds later, the first scream of rage echoed across the city. Even before it died out, more howls of mindless fury rose over Merkland, mixed with screams of mortal agony and fear.

Verena cried through the speakstone, "No! I knew using porphyry was a mistake. The city's going to tear itself apart." Her voice fell to a horrified whisper. "The children."

Connor struggled to comprehend the vastness of the disaster Harley had just dropped on Merkland. Now it made sense why she was coming alone up the road. She'd just struck a crippling blow.

The city was going to rip itself apart.

They had to turn back, had to try to save as many as possible. If they did, they'd never stop Harley and her army. If they didn't, there'd be no city left to save.

Either way, Merkland was going to die.

No. There had to be a way.

Connor purged granite, thrust a finger into a pouch of obsidian at his belt, and risked absorbing just a little. He hoped Dougal couldn't sense him across the distance, but he had to take the risk. He couldn't think of a way out of the trap they'd just allowed Harley to catch them in without it.

He tapped it, and his thoughts accelerated tenfold.

And all of a sudden he realized what he had to do.

Ilse started to speak, but Connor cut her off. "I can save the city."

More screams echoed into the sky, followed by a series of fiery explosions.

"How?" Kilian asked.

"Stilling."

The others looked confused, but Kilian nodded in understanding. "Covering the entire city is ambitious."

"Failing to cover the entire city is not an option."

"Can you do it?" Ilse demanded, looking back over her shoulder. Harley was still invisible through the blowing snow, but she had to be drawing close.

"Yes." He had to. "You'll all have to hold Harley until I get back."

Ilse nodded, her expression fierce. "We'll stop her."

Kilian said, "Focus on your task, Connor. Save them. Leave Harley to us."

CLOSING THE TRAP

Hamish circled high above the city in his Builder suit, aghast at the chaos sweeping the city. Soldiers were fighting each other with unrivaled savagery. Even common citizens were leaping upon each other, ripping at each other with hands and makeshift weapons.

He'd once felt the unbridled, unstoppable rage that quickened porphyry unleashed, and he felt sick with horror.

"Hurry, Connor," he whispered. He couldn't imagine how Connor could stop that mess, but he believed in his friend. If Connor failed, the battle was lost. Merkland would tear itself apart, killing the revolution and everyone who believed in it.

Even if Hamish and their little core team escaped, how could they approach another city and ask the people there to join them? Who would ever believe again that they stood a chance against the queen? It didn't matter that they'd given Harley the weapon used to destroy them.

Even though he hadn't been affected by the porphyry bomb, simmering rage swept through Hamish. Harley needed to pay. He powered higher into the early morning, snow-laden air, seeking the enemy. He soared east, out over the river, breathing deep the clean, cold air as he approached the township built along the far bank. He doubted any Petralists would attempt to attack him so far out, but kept his counter measures ready, just in case.

Kilian and his small team were south of the city, moving down the road to face Harley. It seemed strange that she'd left the bulk of her army behind, but that was a perfect set-up for Rory and his forces to launch their flanking attack. If they kept the element of surprise, they could keep the far larger army busy until the real battle with Harley ended.

Hamish turned south toward that impending fight. He felt eager for a chance to strap into his Juggernaut suit and join the fight, but Kilian had ordered him to stay aloft until they knew for sure Harley wasn't planning any other surprises.

Hopefully she'd used them all up. Hamish really wanted to beat some comeuppance into her face for the death and destruction she'd unleashed on the city. Mostly, he wanted to pound her to a bloody stump for killing Dierk.

He banked out over the abandoned township, planning to circle back to the windrider hovering high above Kilian's position, where his Juggernaut armor waited. That's when he spotted hundreds of soldiers marching up the road toward the township. He blinked, at first wondering if he'd imagined them, but the indistinct shapes far below him grew clearer as he approached, seeming to materialize out of the fog.

One more surprise from that Tallan-cursed woman. They must have crossed the river far south of the city. They'd pass Kilian and his team while they were distracted by Harley's approach.

They must have seen him too, because the gently falling snow suddenly formed into grasping hands that snatched him and sought to yank him out of the sky.

Hamish cried out in surprise, firing thrusters in a vain attempt to break free. He triggered three puking dooms to cut through the snow, but the flames leaped away and turned back against him.

"Cursed Petralists," he muttered and activated his safety plan.

Pumice.

Water and fire tore the air to shreds around him, but he slipped through, invisible to the elemental senses. Calling for maximum power from his thrusters, Hamish shot higher and banked back toward the city.

"We've got a large force moving up toward the township across the river! Just tried to ambush me," he cried into the speakstone that linked him to Kilian's mini-hub.

"Ilse doesn't feel anything."

"They're across the river."

A second's pause, then Kilian said, "I found them. They're very well shielded. I hadn't noticed them during all the distractions."

"That's what they were concealing. Everything else was a ruse. This part of the army's going to hit the township."

"We'll deal with them later. Harley is our first priority."

Almost immediately Kilian spoke again. "Harley just disappeared from Ilse's earth senses. It's like she was never there."

Hamish spun in the air and focused on the distant force marching toward the township. Maxing his long-vision goggles, he scanned them.

Kilian said, "Ilse just caught a glimmer from Harley. She's shielding, but looks like she's with that strike force you spotted. I knew this was too easy. She's played us for fools. Get to your armor, Hamish. We'll need it shortly."

"How did she do that?" he asked as he accelerated toward the hovering windrider. He hadn't seen her down there, but the ruse actually made sense.

"Clever shielding tricks. I'm coming. Verena and Mattias will support me while I intercept Harley."

"Alone?" Hamish exclaimed. He'd seen Kilian in action, but standing in front of an entire army led by Harley was a bit ambitious, even for him.

"That's all we've got until Connor gets the city calmed down. Rory and his company have their own jobs. Ivor will support them and me, as needed. I'm leaving Ilse and the Crushers to guard the main road. I can't imagine Harley doesn't have plans to send in the rest of the army once we're committed. Your job is to support Ilse when Harley springs that next phase on us."

Hamish muttered a curse as he landed on the windrider, hovering over a thousand feet above the southern edge of the city. His huge, spherical armor, covered in a dusting of fresh snow, loomed in the oversized wagon bed. They'd hoped to divide and distract Harley, but she'd done it to them instead.

"I'll maintain watch from here. If you run into trouble, I'll help you. If something hits Ilse first, I'll help her."

"Very well. I'm heading across the river now."

A new note of predatory anticipation had crept into his voice. When Hamish looked down toward the bridge over the Macantact, connecting the southern end of the township to the road encircling the city, he easily spotted Kilian.

All pretense gone, Kilian skated over the river, twenty feet in the air, ringed in orange and red flames, sliding across glittering, icy pavement that materialized in front of him and faded back to falling snow behind.

Hamish suddenly felt more optimistic.

Kilian was going to war.

He was glad his name wasn't Harley.

* * *

Jean crouched in the snow beside a towering maple tree, so like the ones she loved outside of Alasdair. There, among the trees at the border of the hills four miles south of Merkland, the storm seemed far less intense.

Trees creaked under the occasional gusts, and fat flakes of snow drifted down all around, making that peculiar, barely audible hissing sound unique to snowstorms. The cold air bit at her nose and cheeks, but she felt warm. Anticipation accelerated her heart rate and flushed her with energy.

Rory's strike force crouched along the tree line to either side. Aifric waited near Jean. Rory and Anika stood arm in arm next to her, while

Erich, Tomas, and Cameron stood a little farther back in the shadow of an oak tree.

They all looked as anxious as she felt. Ivor had been providing updates, and Rory had nearly ordered the entire command to run for Merkland to try to help, but Ivor had explained that Connor had a plan to save the city.

She was already lifting her mini-hub to her mouth to ask Ivor for an update when his voice echoed up into the silence.

"Start your advance. Kilian is moving to intercept Harley and a large host we just discovered on the eastern shore. Connor's trying to help the city. Ilse is covering the main road."

Rory turned to one of the Spitters, a senior officer with plenty of gray in his beard. "Talk to me."

"The army's not scanning in this direction any more. We've held careful shields with slate and soapstone. I don't think they know we're here, and they're definitely not acting like they expect to get hit on the flanks."

"Move out then," Rory ordered.

Taking Anika's hand, Rory led the way out of the trees. Jean felt a rush of anticipation as she followed them into the open. Several soldiers carrying large packs full of mechanicals followed her. They really were going to attack an army more than fifty times bigger.

Soldiers all down the lines moved when Rory did, without the need for verbal commands. They emerged silently from the tree line, along the first row of hills, over a quarter mile west of the main road to Merkland. The soldiers looked like dark wraiths through the snow and the morning gloom. Jean walked close beside Aifric, who flashed an eager grin.

"Aifric, keep us quiet," Rory ordered.

"Already on it, General," she said in Student Eighteen's voice. Jean hoped to find time to meet all of her fascinating personalities and delve deeper into how she crammed so many women into that single head.

As the army advanced, they broke into four-man squads. Tertiary Petralists were sprinkled down the ranks, each supporting several squads. With so much snow in the air and on the ground, the Spitter officer assured Rory they were maintaining an excellent shield against both Sentries and enemy Spitters.

"Just get us close," Rory said softly, his voice like the scraping of pebbles in a receding tide.

The Spitter saluted but did not speak. Silence was of paramount importance, even with Student Eighteen snatching the little sounds they made.

Anika gave Rory a quick kiss, then trotted ahead to join Erich and a couple Crushers. Tomas and Cameron moved up as well, with a couple of Fast Rollers flanking them.

Jean found it hard to breathe as they slipped through the gray morning like ghosts in the snow. She clutched a satchel filled with her healing supplies, her precious keystone, and special tonics she'd worked up for the stealth assault.

If the plan worked, they could distract the entire enormous army long enough for Kilian and Connor and the others to defeat Harley.

If it failed, they could get surrounded. Everyone else was committed, so no one could come to the rescue.

BAD GUYS AREN'T SUPPOSED TO BE CLEVER, TOO

Hamish scrambled into the entrance tunnel of the Juggernaut and activated a bit of limestone. Its soft, green-tinted light made the marvelous mechanical seem wonderfully sinister.

He patted the heavy steel plates and quickened granite slabs that formed the outer skin. Each plate was octagonal-shaped, fitted closely together in an alternating pattern of steel and granite, forming an extremely durable barrier. He briefly inspected the weapons, thrusters, and other components on their racks behind the plates. Everything looked just as ready as the last time he checked it before dawn, and he allowed a grim smile of anticipation.

Let Harley come.

The Juggernaut smelled of steel and stone, oil and dust, leather mingled with the fresh scent of quartzite. He breathed deep and allowed himself a moment to simply feel it.

He loved the Juggernaut. It was an engineering marvel. As he crawled through his access tunnel past a long, sharp drill to his left and battering-ram arm on his right, he paused to touch the top of the furnace and activate the marble inset into that lid. The furnace rumbled as the fire inside began to build pressure to power the many massive components.

Then he climbed into the pilot chamber at the heart of the armor. After those long days of practice in Faulenrost, it took only seconds to secure all of the straps that held him suspended in the center. He firmly believed the Juggernaut was ready to withstand brutal damage. He double-checked the brass casters that secured his harness to the hull, making sure they'd roll unhindered through their complex array of iron tubing.

Hamish gripped a pair of control handles, set with pieces of sculpted obsidian that Gisela had crafted for that purpose. They'd never equal one of Ailsa's finished pieces, but they didn't need to. They acted as the lynch pins that allowed the Juggernaut to work.

He opened the release rate on those sculpted obsidian stones just a fraction, and the Juggernaut came alive in his mind. No longer simply an external framework, the armor became part of him. The outer hull was like an extension of his own skin, the many weapons and components like fingers, flexed and ready to punch. Hamish flicked his Builder senses across everything, linking to them through tiny pieces of obsidian connected to each one.

With a thought, he activated a couple of sightstones. His visor shimmered, then two separate views of the outside appeared. The forward-facing one took up the top half of his visor, while the backward-looking one took the bottom. He could activate others if needed, but viewing too many at once still gave him a headache.

Those sightstones looked out over the gently falling snow to either side of the windrider. That wasn't terribly helpful, so he activated a lever that drew upon the power building in the furnace to roll the Juggernaut to the edge of the long, flat bed of the windrider. The movement tipped the view downward and he immediately spotted Kilian.

The Dawnus had reached the road near the southern edge of the township. He and Mattias faced over a hundred soldiers about a hundred yards away, with a billowing wall of flames between them, across the road. Those soldiers broke into a charge.

Kilian was going to need Hamish's help.

He rotated the Juggernaut and found Ilse and Lukas moving cautiously south along the wide Crann highway. They'd just about reached the southern end of the long, elevated speedcaravan bridge that rose up from the ground near their position and extended up to the bluff. The Crushers flanked them on either side, their small squads keeping fifty yards apart.

They looked fine. Hamish activated the speakstone paired with one on Ilse's mini-hub to warn her of his plans.

The ground directly beneath Ilse and Lukas erupted in a huge explosion of dirt, sending the two flying. Hamish blinked in surprise and instant fear. He'd never seen Ilse thrown around by earth. Then the same thick-bodied, earthen serpent with the elfonnel head that tried to eat Lukas before erupted from the ground, massive jaws gaping wide.

Crushers swarmed in toward the unexpected attack, but their dispersed grouping worked against them that time. They needed several seconds to react and close on the monster.

They didn't have that much time.

Lukas rolled to his feet, several yards away from Ilse, whose hands were already buried back into the earth. He drew a heavy mace and lunged at the earthen beast, clearly trying to keep it distracted until Ilse could dispatch it.

Whatever she tired, it wasn't enough.

The hideous monster lunged at Lukas, its massive jaws gaping wide. He struck a mighty blow with his mace, snapping off one enormous fang, and knocking its entire head away.

"Kill it, Lukas!" Hamish shouted, even though he didn't have a speak-stone connection.

Then his glee evaporated as the serpentlike monster whipped its massive tail around at Ilse. She raised a hand, and Hamish shouted again with victory as the beast's heavy body split, two massive pieces tumbling past either side of Ilse. But then he noticed two details that cut his victory cry into a joked shout of warning.

Ilse looked surprised by the monster's sudden splitting.

And Hamish saw no blood, no spray of elements released.

Those two broken pieces of serpent abruptly stopped moving, trans-formed into huge blocks of earth, and slammed together, with Ilse caught in the middle. She tried throwing herself clear with a burst of earth.

She almost made it.

The blocks smashed together with terrific force, catching Ilse's hips and legs between them. She screamed again, this time in pure agony.

Lukas shouted a furious battle cry and struck the monster's back. Its flexible body coiled, then struck like a cobra, catching him in the ribs and tumbling him away.

Things were happening too fast. Hamish couldn't believe what he was seeing, but one thing was abundantly clear. They needed him far more than Kilian did.

The Juggernaut pitched off the windrider before he realized he'd willed it to move, and huge quartzite thrusters ignited, blasting it down-ward like an enormous stone from the world's biggest catapult.

Harley rose out of the ground as her mini-elfonnel serpent dove down into the earth, then re-emerged onto the road beside her, looking whole and undamaged. Twelve legs sprouted from its belly and it lunged toward the charging Crushers with astonishing speed.

Those soldiers didn't flinch, didn't show any fear, but reacted with instincts honed from years of training and dangerous missions. Fire and water struck at the monster's face while Striders raced around it, striking at the joints of its legs.

The Boulders couldn't move fast enough. It reached the first squad and consumed two Boulders, even though the valiant pair smashed at its jagged teeth and darting tongues with fortified hammers. Their blood sprayed wide across the snow, and Hamish was glad he couldn't hear their cries.

He accelerated. The Juggernaut tore down toward Harley, who stood on the roadway, watching the carnage. He raged at how high he'd been hovering. It was taking him precious seconds too long.

The mini-elfonnel snapped its long, whiplike tail to the side, catching a Strider and shattering the man's ribs. He fell tumbling, and the creature leaped upon him, gobbling him up in an eyeblink. Then it turned toward the Spitter and Firetongue, who were attacking it viciously, but with no apparent success.

Lukas charged in, alone, mace held high in both hands, shouting defiance. The monster turned toward him and he delivered another mighty blow, slamming it across the head hard enough to shatter stone, beating its head into the ground.

That blow should have broken something, but somehow it didn't. The monster knocked Lukas stumbling back a step, opened its enormous maw wide, and struck.

Lukas raised his weapon to strike, but moved a fraction of a second too slow. The monster snapped that huge maw around Lukas with terrific force. Hamish cried out in horror as the monster crushed out Lukas's life in a single powerful bite. Blood sprayed across the snow and Lukas's death cry echoed through his helmet, along with Ilse's scream of horrified denial.

Hamish blinked, trying to believe what he'd seen. How could Lukas be gone so fast, so brutally? If Ilse hadn't been so badly injured, she would have saved him. It was a miracle she was still conscious.

Harley turned toward Ilse and bore down upon her where she lay on the ground, still screaming, her legs and hips clearly broken, crying Lukas's name.

"You demon spawn," Ilse cried between sobs. "I'll rip out your heart."

Harley laughed and grabbed Ilse by the throat. Ilse's speakstone picked up her voice, passing it to Hamish. "I promised no quarter, fool. You're going to die slowly, with a perfect understanding of what it means to anger me."

Ilse gasped. "You're healing me?"

"Just enough to keep you alive and less distracted by your own problems so you can enjoy watching what happens to the fools who follow you."

She dropped Ilse to the ground and walked a few paces toward the minielfonnel, which was devouring another Strider. One Water Moccasin was spearing at the monster's eyes with spears of ice. Harley raised her hand, and spikes of earth erupted from the ground all around that Water Moccasin, driving in at the surprised woman. She convulsed under the onslaught, falling limp over the blood-soaked spears that propped her off the ground.

The Flameweaver, a stocky veteran with graying, brown hair, erupted into the air before he could be similarly speared.

Ilse screamed again with rage and tried dragging herself toward Harley.

Hamish reached her first.

He fired an enormous puking doom just before impact to slow his descent enough to not destroy the Juggernaut. Harley glanced up just in time to take the full ferocity of those flames full in the face.

Then the Juggernaut slammed down onto her head, crushing her down into the ground so hard that the armor drove two feet into the frozen earth after her.

The impact brutally jarred Hamish, despite the protection of his suspended harness, which stretched under the incredible force but couldn't absorb all the shock. He bounced and rattled so hard he strained his neck, and all the breath exploded from his lungs.

The armor didn't crumple, though. The spherical design helped dissipate the impact remarkably well, although the support girders thrummed and flexed under the strain.

Still blinking dizziness from the sudden stop, Hamish rolled the Juggernaut out of the hole and activated another sightstone, expecting to see only a splattered smear of blood where Harley had stood.

She wasn't there.

The mini-elfonnel had collapsed into a pile of dirt nearby, but Harley was gone.

"Tallan's ugly grandmother," he muttered and rolled the Juggernaut abruptly to the side.

Just in time. A pillar shot up out of the ground, right where he'd just been. Harley stepped out of the pillar, face bloody, her entire right side looking broken. That arm hung limp, while a bone of that leg jutted out through the flesh of her thigh.

"Oh, I'm grouted," Hamish muttered. She should not be alive, should not be standing.

Hamish activated a long drill, planning to drive it into her chest and rip her to pieces. Before the drill could even spin up, or the outer hull plate slide aside, the ground under the Juggernaut buckled, sending it rolling aside. He activated thrusters, accelerating, and shifting to other sightstones to keep Harley in view as he rolled in a circle around her.

She ignored him, but grabbed her leg with fingers of earth and pulled, extending the leg and sliding the bone back into position. She never screamed, didn't even flinch.

In fact, she just looked annoyed.

As Hamish circled around for another attack, he activated a speak-stone so she could hear him. "Hey, psycho hag lady, at your age you should take up knitting or something less strenuous than world conquest."

He activated pumice, ready to take a huge hit.

Instead, the ground fell away beneath the Juggernaut into a huge pit, lined with spikes.

With thrusters already active, he quickly increased the release rate. Although the huge weight settled a foot into the pit before the blasting air caught it and threw it into the air again. He added rear thrusters, aiming for Harley's head again.

This time earth rose up in grasping fingers to catch him. With pumice activated, he slid right through.

Harley looked surprised.

Hamish activated a battering ram. The steel plate at the front of the Juggernaut snapped aside and the quartzite-driven steel ram erupted out the gap. It caught Harley in the chest and Hamish clearly heard breaking bones.

Then the Juggernaut slammed into her and rolled over. Hamish activated directional thrusters, rolling it around for another pass.

Harley was struggling to rise, fresh blood on her angry face, but she still hadn't screamed. How did she do that? How could she still be living? Connor could manage impressive healings, but nothing like that.

Hamish started to fear the Juggernaut was not nearly powerful enough to kill her.

Snow suddenly condensed into long ropes that snaked across the ground to wrap her legs and yank her feet out from under her. She scowled, and more grasping fingers of earth ripped the watery bonds free. With the Water Moccasin dead, who was controlling the snow?

Ivor.

Hamish ignited thrusters, accelerating toward Harley to hit her while she was distracted. Before he could reach her, the Crusher Flameweaver who had shot into the air a moment ago slammed down onto her like a meteor storm, piercing her in a dozen places with white-hot flames and driving his sword into her heart.

This time she did scream as her skin blackened and blood fountained out of so many wounds. The Flameweaver shouted in victory and raised his sword high. It looked like he planned to take off her head.

Harley sank into the ground.

The Flameweaver cursed and erupted into the air, but a grasping hand of earth caught him and yanked him back down. Cursing and shouting defiance, flames blackened the ground all around him as he clawed at the the bonds dragging him down into suddenly-liquid earth and out of sight.

Hamish arrived a second later, but no trace of the man remained. That was simply not fair. How could Harley have survived those wounds? What was her limit?

"Take away her sandstone, I guess," he muttered.

Hamish prowled the area, but saw no sign of her. Maybe they'd injured her badly enough that she'd retreated.

He was just about to go check on Ilse when Harley rose out of the ground closer to the river, right at the point where the speedcaravan track began its steep ascent up the elevated ramp toward Lord's Gate.

Her clothing was charred and ripped, but she looked whole. And really angry. She glared at Hamish and spat, "I've always hated Builders."

Then she ripped forty feet of ramp out of the ground.

"No fair," Hamish cried, activating thrusters, but the Juggernaut didn't accelerate quickly enough.

Harley slid across the ground, legs not even moving, and struck him with the bridge like a batter in the Sogail cammag ball game. The impact rang through the Juggernaut, sending it bouncing and tumbling away. The little brass casters made a surprisingly cheery sound as they spun along their tracks, keeping him upright while the armor tumbled.

Hamish couldn't bring it under control for a couple hundred yards. He swung around in a long arc back toward Harley, who gestured him closer, hefting the bridge like it weighed nothing at all.

"Okay, hag lady, how by the Tallan's twisted memory do I kill you?" he muttered.

As he accelerated toward her again, snow condensed in front of him, forming a ramp. Hamish grinned. Had to be Ivor.

The Juggernaut shot up the ramp and arced into the air. Hamish activated thrusters and accelerated the outer shell spin while flipping a lever to snap into place seven blades.

Harley wound up for another hit as Hamish hurtled down toward her in the spinning, bladed armor.

Game on.

PEACE, BE STILL

Connor rushed back toward the enormous Army Gate set into the thick outer wall. Screams and shouts echoed from behind the closed gate in a steadily rising tempo. The soldiers on the wall no longer stood at attention, but fought with insane ferocity.

Two of them fell screaming from the walls. They hit the ground hard, but didn't seem to register their injuries. They leaped upon each other, snarling like animals. Connor rushed up to them with basalt speed. He tapped it to his arms and cracked their skulls together. Their eyes rolled up in their heads and they collapsed to the snowy ground.

He didn't have time to knock out everyone individually. As much as he disliked stilling, it offered the one chance for Merkland.

Stepping right up to the heavy gates, Connor max-tapped basalt, letting the rushing freedom of the stone fill him with its boundless energy. His entire body quivered with the need to run.

He took a deep breath to focus on the daunting task. He'd struggled to maintain the stilling effect over half of the ground under the city the previous night, but he couldn't afford to fail.

Connor needed every advantage. So he tapped pumice too. The stone again helped him connect with the green-frequency power, and that seemed to magnify his connection when he transitioned the basalt energy to that same green frequency.

Green-tinted power thundered through him, bolstering his hopes that he could make this work. Driven by the intensifying sounds of battle within the walls, Connor drew upon all that energy coiled inside of him like a mighty spring.

And unleashed it upon Merkland.

The city spread under his senses like a map in his mind. Every living thing seemed to glow in his sight as his basalt energy flowed past.

Hating what he had to do, Connor pressed basalt to every single living soul.

It latched onto them so much easier than it had the more subtle energy of the ground beneath Merkland. Living things burned their life forces so fiercely, they seemed to draw the basalt power like lodestones.

Their rage was like a living thing. Most of them were locked in mortal combat, and even as he connected with them, he felt dozens die. The candle-fires of their lives snuffed out. He needed to move faster.

Sweat trickled into his eyes as he pushed that stilling energy farther across the city. The first few blocks went easily, but the farther he extended his influence, the slower it crept. He could feel the men, women, and even children savaging each other, but didn't dare activate the stilling power to steal their energy until he connected with all of them. He wasn't sure he could connect to more of them once he activated it.

Every second seemed to take forever as he extended his influence farther and farther. His will soon blanketed the entire military section, with thousands of soldiers locked in mortal combat, but as he pressed farther into the residential districts, he reached his outermost limits.

He could feel more people beyond the fringes of his control. He couldn't reach farther, but needed to. He could sense them fighting, killing each other. The destruction sweeping Merkland tore at his heart and tears froze on his cheeks.

He couldn't reach them all. Could he still the ones he could reach, hope that he could move on to the others before they all died?

No, there wasn't time for a piecemeal approach.

Connor focused on his affinities. He was max-tapping basalt and pumice both, but he needed more power. He sensed that more was available, but he couldn't seem to access it. Pumice seemed to help boost his connection to the green energy source, but it wasn't enough.

Through his external basalt senses, one of the lives he was brushing against drew his attention. A child, barely more than a toddler, was biting her mother like an angry nuall. Her mother snatched the child into the air and spun toward a nearby window.

She was going to throw the child out, was going to murder her own baby.

For a moment Connor forgot all about the thousands of other death battles occurring across the city. He seized the woman and activated stilling. She managed three quick steps toward the window, with the furious child raised overhead, ready to cast her away and dash her onto the cobblestones below before.

One pace shy of the window, stilling robbed her of the energy to move. She slumped to the floor, and Connor caught her daughter with stilling too. For three long seconds, he held them, drawing their life force away, but could not spare more time for them alone.

How many more children would die while he was distracted? The thought tortured him. He had to find a way to get more energy. Pumice was insufficient. He needed a stronger green-frequency stone.

The solution was clear, and he was out of time. Only one stone might offer a chance to save those helpless people.

Porphyry.

Even Kilian had agreed it would probably grant him an even tighter connection to the green-frequency power. He could no longer hesitate.

Connor extracted the bag of porphyry from his belt, grateful that he'd kept it close. Every scream that echoed from the city drove him to move faster. He purged pumice, then slipped a hand into the bag and willed porphyry into him.

The hard, little grains bit into his hand, and he groaned as the pain intensified. The feeling of teeth gnawing up his arm distracted him so badly, he almost lost connection with basalt.

He could not afford that. He'd spent far too much time already spreading his will across the city. Starting over would cost too many lives. So as the porphyry reached his heart and his limbs shot out in convulsive shudders, he screamed with the effort of holding in the rampager. He could not afford to transform, did not want to become a raging monster. All he needed was the connection to the green-frequency power.

For several seconds, his vision blurred, turning purple. His limbs trembled as porphyry poured through his bloodstream, driving every muscle to transform. The beast in his heart awakened and raged against his constraint.

I cannot release you now, he snarled. *Do my bidding, and maybe we can run together one night, but not now.*

For a moment, he teetered on the brink, his skin rippling, his bones feeling like they were liquefying in preparation for the transformation. His connection to basalt faltered, then snapped.

"No!" Connor shouted, desperation giving him the strength to fight down the porphyry. The beast paced in his heart, but he held it prisoner, refused to listen to its calls for release.

His skin stopped bubbling, and the pain subsided. Connor took a deep breath, closed his eyes, and cautiously tapped porphyry while still in human form.

The affinity was bound to his heart, and it felt like a cage rimmed with white-hot fire. Connor pressed his mind to it, but refused to open the door to release the rampager coiled within.

As soon as he touched it, his connection to the green-frequency power source snapped into place. Like the waterfall of Donleavy, power thundered through the center of his being with unimaginable force. Funneled through his porphyry affinity, he could tap that stream, draw upon it.

Connor laughed, exulting in the moment, but unable to take the time to really enjoy it. With that green-frequency connection so strong,

Connor again tapped external basalt and cast his influence across Merkland.

This time, fueled by that flood of higher frequency power, he spread his will over the entire city in seconds. The fighting was still raging. Even though to him it felt like half an hour had passed, the bomb had probably exploded less than a minute ago. He could sense many dead, but fewer than he had feared.

As soon as Connor linked to every living soul, he activated stilling.

All across the city, the invisible influence latched onto every life and began to suck away their energy. More precious seconds crept by as it took effect, and half a hundred more people died needlessly violent deaths. There were just too many of them, and his attention was spread too thin, but Connor refused to falter.

Finally, stillness crept inside and denied them the ability to move. They stopped punching, kicking, stabbing, screaming, and trying to kill each other. The strongest of them lasted a few extra seconds, but they all settled into perfect stillness, not even breathing. Forty thousand souls languished, prisoner to his control.

They no longer killed each other.

Now he was killing them all.

Vast amounts of energy drifted into the air from them, like smoke from tens of thousands of individual campfires. It coalesced over Merkland, then began drifting toward Connor, drawn to him by the invisible cords of his influence.

He didn't want to accept it, but his body quivered under the strain of holding such a vast stilling in place, even when fueled by so much green-frequency power. Hating himself for needing to do it, he drew that stolen energy closer and breathed it in.

The smoke touched him, and energy pounded into Connor, filling him with life and with strength, everything that he was stealing from them. Connor gasped at the incredible influx of energy, feeling more alive and more horrified than he ever had in his life. It felt so much more alive, more vibrant than the energy he'd taken from the earth beneath Merkland. The feeling was intoxicating, and for a second he loved it.

Then the first person died.

The young soldier had already been bleeding out when Connor caught him in the stilling web, but his magic snuffed the man's life out several seconds before it would have escaped on its own. Connor had killed him.

Dozens of others were fading fast, reaching the limits of no return. Healthy bodies could survive several minutes without air, but he was forcing perfect stillness upon them, denying their blood the ability to pump, their hearts movement. The strongest would last a few minutes.

The weakest might not recover, even if he released them now.

He found the life force of the little girl he'd saved from her own mother. She was fading quickly, too young and weak to withstand his assault for much longer.

The porphyry madness would not last much longer either, but he could feel it thrumming through them still. If he released them, more of them would die than if he maintained the effect.

He forgot about Harley, about his friends, about the battle. His entire focus became the city of Merkland with those slowly dimming lives flickering in his mind.

Tears stung his eyes as he held on while the second person expired. Then the third. Each time, a final burst of energy rushed into him from them.

That little girl would be next. He could feel her life force drop to that critical point, on the cusp of snuffing out entirely.

Connor released her.

He hadn't even realized it was possible to release an individual from the stilling web, but he couldn't take it any more. He did not care if it was possible. It had to be done.

Before the little girl faded from his mind completely, he felt her take a breath, felt her begin to cry.

She would live.

He sagged with relief. Bolstered by that success, he swept his thoughts across the city, trying to touch each person, to gauge their strength. The city was mapped in his mind, each life force like a candle, but the weakest were flickering, nearly exhausted. He released them before their candles snuffed out.

Hearts racing, blood pounding, many of their first breaths came out as porphyry-induced rage-howls. But they were the weakest, the wounded who lacked the strength to kill. Others were the children caught in the porphyry disaster. It would take critical seconds for them to regain strength to try hurting others. Hopefully by then the rampager madness would pass.

Connor lost track of time as he slowly extracted life after life from his own influence. With each one, the energy and glorious life force pouring into him reduced by a fraction.

A part of him that he did not like to recognize even existed hated to see that power go, but Connor refused to acknowledge the whispered thoughts that maybe he should hold on a little longer. He could not live with himself if he did that.

All of a sudden, the porphyry madness evaporated, its course exhausted. Connor felt the change in the energy he was draining from the city. Relieved, he prepared to release the stilling.

But he hesitated. In that moment of letting go, he found it incredibly difficult to release that glorious lifeline that held him in the sunlight of all that energy. Releasing it was like consciously choosing to plunge into the cold depths of a black well.

With a wrenching effort, Connor broke the connection and released basalt. He collapsed to the ground, trembling, feeling cold and miserable now that the flood of new life was gone.

"Stop it," he chided himself, leaping to his feet. What would Verena say if she knew he was moping about the fact that he'd just saved the entire city from destroying itself?

He might have severed that connection, but every inch of him thrummed with strength. Even more remarkably, he felt stable. Frowning, Connor scanned himself. Beneath the pure, raw power he'd stolen from all those lives, he still tapped porphyry, and the green-frequency power source still thundered through him with undiminished force.

It no longer felt disruptive like it had even while tapping pumice.

Connor touched the rampager heart of his porphyry affinity. He sensed that coiled beast there still, but for once it seemed content to wait. The rage of the rampager still burned within that porphyry affinity, but it no longer clouded his emotions. He realized with a thrill that somehow he could now use that rage as a weapon without losing himself to it.

A thought floated to his consciousness. He wasn't sure where it came from, but he felt it as clearly as if he'd spoken it aloud.

Now we hunt as well in your weak form as we do in ours. Let us continue the hunt!

Connor grinned and turned south toward the crashing sounds of desperate struggle. He drew upon the inexhaustible strength pounding through him and focused it into a stone-hardened resolve.

Harley had brought the fight to them, chosen to unleash porphyry upon the city. She'd unwittingly forced him to learn the secret to stabilizing his affinities. Now she'd pay the price. He swore upon all the lives just lost that he would not stop until she died.

Connor leaped into a run.

WHEN IN DOUBT, CHARGE!

Only minutes had passed since they started the slow, silent advance against the enemy army, guided by the Spitters, to close on the left rear flank of the much bigger army.

Rory's force spread to either side of Jean in a rough line of small squads, fading to indistinct figures in the early morning heavy snowfall. She stayed close to Rory and his central command group, with Student Eighteen ghosting along by her side, one hand gripping the handle of one of five daggers on her belt.

Ivor's voice suddenly boomed from Jean's speakstone, sounding extremely loud in the quiet. Jean jumped in surprise and tried to cover it, but that didn't muffle it at all.

"Harley just exploded out of the ground! The army moving on the east bank was a diversion. It's bad! If you can strike, do it now!"

"What's happening?" she asked.

No response.

Jean looked at Rory, who was frowning at the noise, but Student Eighteen gave her a thumb's up. "No one outside of this group heard that."

"This sounds bad," Jean said, worry making it hard to breathe. Wasn't Hamish supposed to be helping guard the main road? He couldn't face Harley without Connor and Kilian.

"We can't do anything to help them from here. Best we can do is keep to the plan and break her momentum." Rory turned to the Spitter officer. "How far?"

"Two hundred yards."

"Perfect." Rory raised two fingers high. The four-man strike teams accelerated into the gloom. The storm provided the perfect cover for their assault.

Jean strained her ears, listening for the sounds of fighting, for the cry of alarm to echo through the thick snow.

Nothing.

She glanced at Student Eighteen, whose brows were furrowed in concentration, and felt like a fool. Of course she wouldn't hear anything.

Several seconds later, the first of the strike teams appeared through the gray sheets of snow, dragging the first catches of the day. Some struggled and shouted, while others hung limp in their hands. Rory had explained that often the rear flanks of the army spread out, producing stragglers, so the first few contacts should prove easy snatch-and-grab encounters. With Aifric blocking sounds of the struggle, no one would know to look back or raise the alarm.

Jean moved to meet the soldiers and their prisoners, extracting the tonic from her satchel. The unconscious prisoners, most with bruises on their scalps or bleeding head wounds, were dropped to the snowy ground, hands and feet bound. The others were held still, their mouths forced open while Jean used a small leather pressure pump to force a squirt of tonic down their throats.

"What's that poison?" one panicked soldier exclaimed.

"It's not poison. It will help you relax."

"Relax, my kidney stone, wench! You filthy Grandurian Tallan-loving—"

The Boulder holding his left arm slugged the man in the side of the head hard enough that he probably cracked the poor fool's skull. "Sorry about that, miss. Guess he don't need the tonic after all."

The other prisoners accepted their tonics with a lot less fuss, although they still looked terrified. She tried to soothe their worries, but she felt a bit nervous too.

The tonic should do exactly what she said, calm their nerves, settle them into a lethargic stupor for a couple hours, making them sleepy and compliant. She hated how fast she'd needed to develop it, and worried about administering it to so many different people with such different sizes, weights, and metabolisms.

There was a chance it might permanently injure or even kill some of them, but the alternative was worse. Every one of those soldiers beaten unconscious faced far greater chances of permanent damage. So she concealed her fears, spoke soothing words, and gave them the tonic she hoped might save their lives.

She quickly lost track of time as the trickle of prisoners increased to a flood. Anika arrived with one struggling, bound soldier thrown over her shoulder and dumped him into the snow in front of Jean.

"You'll have to speed up. We just rushed an entire squad that had fallen behind the main company. An excellent little fight," Anika said happily in Grandurian.

"Did any of our soldiers get hurt?" Jean asked.

Anika shook her head. "We haven't hit the real resistance yet. I hope you have a lot of tonic."

So did Jean. At the rate they were going, she'd consume her five large bottles fast. She only hoped they captured many more before the army realized what was happening and the general alarm was raised.

After she doused that prisoner, she paused and raised her mini-hub. "Ivor, what's happening?"

"Busy," came the short reply. "Taking prisoners on the east flank, but we've got trouble. Kilian's facing a much larger force than we anticipated. Harley hit Ilse's team. It's bad. Hamish is fighting her in that huge armor. I'm trying to help."

"Oh, no," Jean gasped, her worst fears realized. The Juggernaut was a remarkable mechanical, but he couldn't stop Harley.

Ignoring the line of prisoners waiting for their tonic doses, she reached for her mini-hub. She had to know Hamish was all right.

Rory's large hand gripped hers, making her jump in surprise. She hadn't noticed him approaching.

"Don't, lass. If he's fighting Harley, he needs to focus."

"We have to do something," she begged. Suddenly she hated that she'd accepted this assignment. Hamish might need her, but she was too far away.

"Aye. We do." His expression turned grim. "We create a diversion and keep the rest of the army from storming Merkland."

He raised his voice and bellowed, "Phase two! Hit 'em hard. Aifric, distraction initiative."

Soldiers who had been shepherding prisoners toward Jean simply threw them into a pile, with a few guards overseeing them.

Everyone else charged into the gray, blowing snow.

WHAT GOES UP

Verena slid the Swift sideways through the air to the south, paralleling the course of the river. Kilian stood with Mattias near the southern end of the township, facing a couple hundred advancing soldiers. He'd called forth a barrier of fire, but they were still charging.

No doubt they included Spitters and Firetongues, but Verena wasn't really worried about Kilian's ability to stop them. Sentries worried her more. The ground was unstable enough that Sentries had been holding back, but would they still?

Her job was to identify them and hit them with overwhelming force from above. She'd try to kill them, but even just distracting them until Kilian dealt with the others would be enough.

She wanted to call Connor, ask how his efforts to save the city was going. If he failed . . . No, she refused to consider it.

Movement farther south behind the advancing soldiers, dim and indistinct through the snow, drew her attention. She focused her long-vision front window, then gasped. Hundreds more soldiers were charging out of the confusing grayness. They were about to snap closed a trap that even Kilian might not escape.

Merkland couldn't send aid in time.

"Kilian, you've got hundreds more soldiers coming."

Without waiting for a reply, she activated Hamish's speakstone. "Hamish, we're in trouble. Kilian's facing a much larger force. It's a trap."

His response was a grunt, accompanied by the sound of squealing metal. He panted, "No time to chat. I'm playing tag with Harley. Should have picked a different game."

Oh no. Anger and fear boiled through Verena. They had planned so carefully to trap Harley, but she was the one who had tricked them.

Worrying and wondering were not going to help. Kilian would never retreat. Neither would Mattias. So neither would she.

Verena dove, the speedslings already spinning up on the stubby wings. She was the reinforcements, and she'd make those new soldiers wish all they had to deal with was an army out of Merkland.

She wished she could return to the second windrider she'd set in a hover above the township. It was full of additional mechanicals, but she didn't have time for any of that.

Verena dove toward the second strike force, still a couple hundred yards behind the front company. They wouldn't expect an attack yet. Verena forced herself to forget all her concerns. The best way to help Hamish was to defeat this other army quickly and get back over the river.

The enemy troops came clearly into view as Verena swooped below five hundred feet.

She opened the speedslings.

Hornets tore out of the four speedslings, but at that moment, the storm whipped into blizzard intensity all around her. Verena shuttered the speedslings as the Swift bucked and spun halfway around before she caught it. The visibility out her windscreen fell to zero, replaced by a churning, solid mass of white.

It felt like every Spitter in Dougal's army was attacking her at once. Cold fear set her heart racing as she flicked her hands across the control levers, trying to gain altitude, but not quite sure which way might offer safety.

Annoyed, she activated pumice. Instantly her flight smoothed out as the Swift plunged through the raging storm that couldn't quite grasp it.

"Now show me your faces," she whispered as she used the leveling bubble on the front dash to straighten out her flight. The blizzard still howled around her. She managed to level, but even as she increased horizontal speed, she couldn't see anything.

She decided to rise up out of the storm, then come around for another pass. She'd have to strike from farther away next time. She applied more push thrusters and began to angle upward to ascend.

That's when she smashed right into a giant snowball. It had to be twice as big as the Swift, and even though it exploded to powder, the impact caught Verena by surprise and brutally jarred the Swift. Verena grunted as she slammed forward against her safety harness.

Luckily the shielding over the windows held, but even before the snow from that giant snowball blew clear, she struck another one. Then a third.

"How is this possible?" Verena shouted as she tried to bank the Swift away from the unexpected barrage. Pumice was supposed to allow her to slip right through any elements being actively controlled.

"Oh, no." She cursed herself for not realizing the catch.

Harley must have learned about pumice and trained her troops on how to circumvent it. They'd created those snowballs using their power, then simply thrown them into the path of the Swift. With no active magical control, there was nothing for pumice to shield her from.

More impacts shook the Swift, spinning it around and bouncing it violently. It seemed the Petralists had fine-tuned their attack, and they assaulted Verena without mercy. In seconds she lost all sense of which way might be up. The leveling bubble rocked so wildly and the little craft spun so hard, her instruments couldn't help.

Verena screamed as she tried to fight the controls. She tried maxing the push thrusters to escape, but the central thruster took a direct hit and broke free. The enemy were throwing chunks of ice now. The other thrusters soon followed, robbing Verena of the power she needed to escape.

Verena fought down a growing panic as she fought to bring the Swift back to a level flight path using the smaller directional thrusters. There had to be a way to salvage the situation. She glanced at he own hair and cursed again.

It was falling up.

By the Tallan's blessed memory, she was flying upside down.

She tried spinning the Swift back over, but more projectiles made of ice crashed into the crippled little craft. Verena caught sight of one projectile that looked like a giant sword, just before it speared into the front of the Swift with a brutal impact that dented the entire nose and seemed to knock the Swift backward in the air.

More ice smashed at her shielding windows and her armored sides. If she had been flying her original craft, she would have lost her head in a second. Verena increased the release rate on the shielding over the windows, extending the protective bubbles farther around the craft in overlapping spheres. They wouldn't hold for long, but all she needed was a target and she could fire her weapons.

She tried not to panic, tried not to think about another brutal impact with the ground. The terror of those broken memories of her last crash set her hands shaking, and she started to pant, unable to get enough breath.

All that kept her from descending into pure panic was her faith in Kilian. He would see what was happening, would sense it, and would help.

A flash of crimson across her front window shield brought a spark of hope. Kilian had come to help.

Actually, he hadn't.

A giant snowball exploded against the shielded sides of the Swift, releasing a burst of white-hot fire that had somehow been contained inside. They must be releasing active control only a fraction of a second before hitting her.

"Cheaters!" she cried as fire and ice smashed her little Swift relentlessly on every side, tearing at the wings and spearing into the craft. If they found a way inside, they'd incinerate her.

"Kilian! Can you hear me?" she shouted.

Abruptly the snow and fire snuffed out. Verena peered through the sudden stillness and screamed again. She was plunging at a steep angle toward the snowy ground, barely fifty feet below her.

Verena tried desperately to activate any thrusters she had left, but none of them responded. They'd all been ripped out. She hadn't even noticed when the smaller ones were destroyed.

A second before the Swift plowed into the ground, Verena threw wide the release rate on all of the shielding stones. Then she held tight as the Swift smashed nose first into the ground.

She slammed against her safety harnesses, crying out in pain and fear as the Swift tumbled and bounced madly a dozen times before coming to a rest on its side.

The Swift was dead. The main body was broken, the wings gone, every outside surface smoking. She flicked her Builder senses across it. Most of the amazing mechanicals she'd felt such confidence in were shattered or simply gone.

Fighting back tears and groaning as every muscle protested the abuse, Verena snatched up two of the shielding stones, deactivated the others, grabbed her satchel and her sword, and crawled out of the wreckage.

She looked around, and her heart sank.

At least three dozen soldiers were racing in her direction, weapons drawn, shouting with victory. She saw no indication that they intended anything but to hack her to pieces.

They'd driven the Swift across the front line of their ranks and crashed it at the eastern outskirts of the township. Two houses stood less than a hundred feet to her left, and a long warehouse squatted like a distant shadow through the storm to her right, but they were too far to offer any real shelter.

Kilian and Mattias were somewhere on the far side of town, and by the flames exploding high into the sky from that direction, they had joined in battle. The truth struck her with absolute clarity.

She was completely alone. Her Swift was destroyed, and those dozens of troops no doubt included many Petralists.

So she felt no pity for them.

Verena pulled out of her satchel a small piece of sculpted obsidian. She wrenched open the invisible crack of its power with her Builder senses and focused on it, losing herself in the stone.

The enthusiastic shouts of the fast-approaching soldiers faded away, as did the aching of her muscles from the brutal landing, and her own fears. Everything vanished as she threw her Builder senses into the sculpted stone and linked to the pieces of activated obsidian floating high over Merkland.

More than a thousand feet above her, beyond the attention of any of the Petralists, she connected with the windrider packed with weapons. Through obsidian, Verena touched a series of quartzite veins set in leather. She activated a sightstone in the link and viewed the chaotic scene below through its prism lens.

She also activated a series of thrusters, pushing the windrider toward the township and turning it, then tilting it slightly upward at the front. Seconds were ticking away dangerously fast, but she made sure everything was aligned properly.

Then she activated every single weapon.

Verena started a mental countdown as she returned to herself. She looked around and bit back a cry of fear. A pair of Striders were closing with superhuman speed, short swords already raised to deliver killing blows.

Verena activated the two shieldstones in her hand and crouched low so the two domes of protective air sealed her off completely.

The first Strider never saw the double-thick dome. Shouting with victory, no doubt thrilled that he would be the one to take the Builder's head to High Lord Dougal, he struck the domed shield at full speed. Bones shattered and he tumbled with a scream right over Verena. She lost sight of him as he rolled out into the snowstorm.

The second Strider, half a heartbeat behind the first, managed to leap and spring off the top of the dome. He soared a hundred feet before landing and sprinting around in a tight turn, kicking up sprays of snow. He shouted a warning cry to the other soldiers, and they slowed to a cautious advance.

Several soldiers moved to the front. Fire erupted around the hands of two of them, while a pair of women who looked so much alike they must have been sisters, started gathering snow between themselves and condensing it into water.

A grizzled veteran, with the huge muscles and overlapping leather plates of a Boulder drew a little closer. "You can't hope to escape. If you surrender, I can promise a quick execution. If not . . ." He glanced at the soldiers to either side of him. "If not, I can guarantee my men will make you wish you had."

His words sounded a bit distorted through the shielding, so Verena spoke loudly to make sure he understood her. "You realize Builders can fly, right?"

He shrugged. "You crash too."

"Do you think I don't have reinforcements?"

The countdown in her head reached zero, so Verena pressed herself flat, covered her head with her arms, and maxed the double-thick shielding protecting her.

Two heartbeats later, ten thousand hornets tore down out of the sky without warning, shredding the entire area around Verena. One soldier started to scream, but the cry cut off almost immediately. Deadly hornets ricocheted off the shields protecting Verena, punching so hard into them that if they hadn't been layered over each other, they would have failed.

One in a hundred hornets were tipped with diorite. A quick succession of powerful little explosions tore across the entire area with fire and destruction.

Two seconds later, twelve much larger diorite-tipped missiles struck all around Verena, vaporizing the snow and blasting huge craters in the ground. She'd aimed them to miss her shield, but there was still a chance one might stray off course and strike her directly. That would have obliterated her along with everyone else.

The thunderous detonations deafened her right through her shielding. In a blinding eyeblink that entire corner of the township transformed into a superheated oven and charbroiled everything beyond the melting point of cold steel.

The brutal onslaught drove the double-layered half domes of her shielding nearly a foot into the frozen ground. Verena shouted and clung to the earth, eyes squeezed shut, trying not to think about what she had just done.

She stayed like that for ten long seconds after the last explosion. She did not want to move, did not want to look, but if she hesitated, more soldiers might come and she lacked the weapons to defeat them all again.

As soon as she released the shielding, brutally hot air rushed in, sucking the breath from her lungs. Despite the bitter cold of the snowy day, the land for a hundred yards in every direction was now a blackened wasteland, pocked with craters. Even the topsoil had melted to a glassy crust.

No trace of any of the soldiers remained.

Verena refused to acknowledge the sorrow she felt for those deaths. She wasn't safe yet and if she stopped to think about the lives she'd just snuffed out, she'd break down into helpless tears. She refused to die that way. It was Harley's fault for sending those men and women into battle.

She'd find a way to make Harley pay for those deaths. Somehow.

First, she had to get out of there. She again tapped her sculpted obsidian and connected with the distant windrider. It wasn't a battle craft, but it was a flying platform, and that was better than what she had now. Trying to land the ponderous windrider through remote control would be tricky, but it seemed her best chance.

Before she could even try, the wagon suddenly shattered, as if a giant, invisible hand had squeezed it to pieces.

Verena cursed and released obsidian. She peered up through the curtains of snow, as if she could see up where the broken pieces of the windrider were already falling toward the river. Had Harley shattered it, or had one of her Petralists recognized what Verena had done and targeted the helpless wagon?

It didn't matter. The wagon was gone. That meant she was stranded on the ground, with too few power stones. Verena buckled on her sword belt, adjusted her satchel, then started jogging north toward the township, hoping to circle the fighting.

Kilian and Mattias needed her. She would not let them down.

THE CHALLENGE WITH JUGGLING

Using intertwined ropes of fire and water, Ivor slashed across Harley's face and neck from three sides at the same time. He snapped those ropes of elements against her like bullwhips, every strike powerful enough to decapitate any normal person, and most Petralists.

They just annoyed Harley.

The seared flesh and shattered bones healed as fast as he damaged them. She didn't scream, didn't even stumble, but she did swat at them with one hand. More importantly, the earth she used to defend herself from him was earth she couldn't use to crush Hamish's Juggernaut.

As the battered Juggernaut burst free of the earthen bands that had been tightening around it, Ivor added a fourth mark in the outer shell of the Slide. Hamish was doing a remarkable job fighting Harley, but that made four times he most likely would have died without Ivor's assistance.

Together they couldn't defeat her, but hopefully they could keep her annoyed and distracted until Connor or Kilian returned to help.

Ivor suspected Connor would get there first. Merkland had suddenly calmed a moment ago, and he took that as a hopeful sign that Connor had succeeded. They needed Connor badly. Harley had split them and played them for fools. If they didn't turn the tide on her soon, they'd lose any chance.

Ivor was already pushing his limits more than he ever had. If not for how deadly serious the situation was, he would exult in the moment. He'd never spread his influence so widely. While he sat in a comfortable chair on the deck of the Slide under the surface of the Macantact, he enjoyed unrivaled access to the landscape all around. Not only was he linked tightly to the river, but through the high-piled snow and ongoing snowstorm, his will permeated everything.

He wasn't alone, but he was as yet unchallenged in his mastery of the area. Kilian was already fighting Petralists on the east bank, and Ivor was eager to check in on him. Verena had crashed her new Swift, and he'd lost contact with her after that firestorm she'd unleashed. He wasn't too worried about her for the moment.

Rory's forces were attacking the western flanks of Dougal's army, and Ivor was striking at their eastern flank every chance he got. He kept the Spitters distracted by sending waves of water bursting the banks of the Macantact to drag soldiers into a holding cell deep in the river, or by striking at their ranks with the billowing snow.

They fought back, but didn't know exactly where to hit him. He kept himself carefully shielded, but had also created half a dozen fake Slides that he scattered down the length of river. He allowed those shields to slip a little, giving the Spitters targets, which they attacked with admirable tenacity and coordination. They even pulled in Sentries to help, spearing earth blindly up into the river to try to strike him down.

Ivor felt confident that between his and Rory's efforts, they could keep the main army distracted for a while, but that was but a lesser skirmish in the greater battle.

Hamish made a reckless dash back at Harley, firing a dozen diorite missiles to cover his approach. Harley deflected them away with powerful air currents, so Ivor struck at her back with a hundred ice balls, helping distract her long enough for Hamish to crash into her and roll clear again. The daring strike left her body gashed, but again she healed almost immediately.

As Harley slid across the ground after Hamish, Ivor left them to the chase for a moment and turned his attention to Kilian. The ancient Dawnus's presence was like a towering inferno. The man was so powerful, he inspired and intimidated Ivor in equal measure.

The enemy troops had slowed their advance in the face of Kilian's opposition, ceding the front lines to half a dozen Spitters and an equal number of Firetongues. The two groups were attacking him in ferocious, well-coordinated strikes that would have overwhelmed most Petralists in seconds. Ivor might have held his own for a while, but he would have been fighting a desperate, defensive battle.

Kilian was whistling.

He marched toward the enemy Petralists, ringed with fire and water that flowed all around him in intricate, ever-shifting patterns. The barrage of elemental attacks deflected away or parted around him without quite reaching him.

Ivor tried turning his mini-hub to Kilian's speakstone, but he heard far too much interference from the elemental storm to make out any words. So he switched to Mattias, who was flanking Kilian, about fifty yards behind, out of the worst of the elemental barrage. So far it looked like he'd been ignored as everyone focused on Kilian.

"Mattias, what's your status?" Ivor asked.

"Are you seeing this?" Mattias asked, his voice awed.

"I can sense it through soapstone, so I get a pretty good idea."

"He's teaching them," Mattias exclaimed in disbelief. "Can you believe that? They're hitting him with everything they've got, and he's congratulating them on working well together and encouraging them to try harder."

Ivor chuckled. "Maybe he's trying to intimidate them."

"With reverse psychology? Why doesn't he just kill them?"

"Maybe his fight isn't with them?" Ivor suggested. He didn't doubt Kilian could kill those Petralists if he really wanted to, but one of the things he really respected about Kilian was his restraint. He'd kill if he had to, but maybe he was looking for a way to spare those men and women whose only error was in following orders?

As Ivor scanned the area, he noticed a group of Striders sprint around the front of a warehouse at the trailing, southern end of the township to Kilian's right, blades and nets poised.

Attacking Kilian like that seemed awfully optimistic.

"Finally, something for me to do," Mattias said as he ran past Kilian, twin swords drawn.

Kilian threw out his hands, and Ivor felt the mighty surge of his will. It slammed against the ongoing assaults from the attacking Petralists, scattering their control and their elements together. Fire and water exploded away from Kilian in a blinding sheet, and he turned to watch Mattias.

The onrushing soldiers seemed happy to target Mattias first. Four cast nets to tangle him, while the rest threw knives or rushed in with short swords.

Mattias wasn't the champion of the Edderitz games for nothing. He twirled past the first two nets, tipped a third high enough to duck under, and simply slashed the fourth one to shreds before it could wrap him up. His swords blurred as he deflected knives with sharp clangs.

Some of the Striders seemed to recognize the danger and peeled away, but most of them did not. They rushed in, swords striking at Mattias's head and shoulders.

They never came close.

Mattias lunged through their midst, feet dancing, blades slashing like a sphere of deadly steel around him. Swords somehow missed by a hair's breadth, or clanged as he deflected them aside, more often than not to smash into one of their companions. His own swords whipped out, touching enemies gracefully for a split second.

Blood blossomed at every stroke and Striders cried out and fell, clutching at their bleeding wounds. In three seconds, only the Striders wise enough to flee remained standing.

Eight Blades took their places.

The twin-sword wielding warriors approached in a wedge formation, moving with the same deadly grace as Mattias.

He saluted them, and they saluted in return.

Ivor tensed to intervene. He appreciated Mattias's optimism, but not even he could stand against that many Blades and hope to survive.

"Mattias, get back," Kilian called.

In that moment, the Spitters and Firetongues attacked again, actually weaving water and fire together and driving the mixed elements at Kilian like a giant, elemental spear.

Ivor was impressed and suddenly fearful. That kind of combined attack could threaten even Kilian, couldn't it?

Kilian grinned fiercely and clapped his hands together, fingers pointed at the enemy. The elements swirling around him flowed into the shape of an enormous shield, and the attacking spear deflected high.

Kilian erupted off the ground, bursting right through his own shield. He made a grasping motion, and the enemy spear stopped in mid-air, then leaped into his hands.

He paused twenty feet in the air, reversed the spear, and threw it back at his attackers. It split into a dozen smaller spears, each aimed at one of the attackers. They either dove aside or raised hasty barriers.

Most of them managed to deflect or avoid the deadly attack. Two of them didn't. A pair of Firetongues tripped over each other and fell in a heap. The spears drove in for the kill, but abruptly paused, inches from their hearts.

Then every spear exploded in a blinding display of colored lights and sparkling ice crystals.

Kilian said, "Not bad, kids, but take a break for a minute."

They didn't take advantage of the reprieve, but re-formed their line, looking ready to resume the attack.

Kilian snapped his fingers. Twice.

One of the Spitters screamed, clutching at his head as steam boiled out of his mouth and eyes. He collapsed, and when Ivor scanned him, he recoiled with disgust. The man had boiled from the inside.

One of the Firetongues pitched over at the same time, body rigid. Ivor scanned that one too and found the body completely frozen.

Kilian had drained the heat out of that man in a heartbeat. At the same time, he'd set the other man's blood boiling.

A fearful silence settled over the entire company, and Kilian's voice sounded clearly through Mattias's speakstone for Ivor to hear. He spoke softly, but with deadly intensity.

"I told you to take a break."

One of the Firetongues held up his hands in a placating gesture. "Be our guest. We'll just wait till you're ready, I guess."

"Good lad." Kilian extracted a ceramic jar from his vest and added, "Danger lies not only in the elements you wield."

He threw the jar and pushed it high, past Mattias's head with blowing snow, then shattered it with a burst of fire. The contents sprayed all across the Blades, who had again resumed their advance.

One breath later they began to stagger. Two seconds later, most of them dropped their swords, looking confused and afraid.

"What was that?" Mattias demanded.

"Anti-obsidian powder. We only recently discovered it. This was the trial run. Looks like it works."

Ivor applauded from where he sat in the Slide. That was a brilliant move.

Mattias sheathed his swords and said with obvious disappointment, "I can't fight them now."

"You're welcome," Kilian said with a smile in his voice.

Seeing their Blades fall to the strange powder seemed too much for the Spitters and Firetongues, none of whom looked eager to attack Kilian again.

They retreated into the larger force massed behind them. Four soldiers rounded the same warehouse the Striders had appeared around a moment ago. Their leader spoke, and even though the voice only reached Ivor faintly through Mattias's speakstone, he recognized Dougal.

"Your time has—"

Kilian did not wait for Dougal to start monologuing. Instead he whipped out a spear of mixed water and fire and hurled it at Dougal and the three blades flanking him. Ivor gasped at the amount of power Kilian poured into that spear. He didn't want to just kill Dougal, he wanted to incinerate him to ash.

The deadly spear of mixed elements somehow slipped past the four of them, without so much as curling a single hair on their heads. It struck the warehouse behind them and vaporized it.

High Lord Dougal laughed, sounding overjoyed. "Your mother sends her best, along with this little secret that protects us from your elemental powers."

"It's so annoying when the enemy gets clever too," Ivor muttered.

Mattias drew his swords again. "I'll take care of the other three."

Kilian started to shout a warning, but Mattias suddenly staggered, his hands gripping his temples.

Dougal chuckled as he drew to within fifty feet. Mattias trembled violently and Dougal spoke, his tone gloating. "I have a better idea. Why don't you go take off the head of that annoying little Builder?"

"Oh, no," Ivor whispered. Dougal had seized Mattias's mind. He'd probably been waiting for a chance to take the mind of anyone tapping obsidian. Connor knew to be wary, but Mattias had apparently forgotten about the danger. Leave it to Dougal to complicate things. The man really needed to die.

Mattias dropped his hands from his face and Ivor could imagine murder in his gaze. Without a word, he turned toward the area where Verena had crashed.

Kilian wrapped Mattias with a constricting layer of ice. "Cool off a bit, Mattias. We'll talk in a minute. I should have saved some of that anti-obsidian powder. It would have simplified things."

All of the enemy Spitters and Firetongues who had made such a show of retreating a moment ago now attacked again. The Spitters struck with a blizzard of ice shards, attempting to overwhelm Kilian with the sheer volume of the assault, but they diffused their own strength so much that he easily deflected the ice away.

The Firetongues whipped out ropes of crimson fire, trying to seize his limbs and bind him. He swatted each of them aside, but they snapped right back at him with annoying persistence. None of the attacks threatened him much, but all together they seemed to finally consume a lot of his attention.

That's when the Blades flanking Dougal began to advance. And just to make it fun, an unseen Sentry joined the fray. The ground rumbled and thick earthen walls rose up twenty feet on either side of Kilian and ten feet behind him. The side walls that boxed him in extended all the way past Dougal before a back wall rose, completing the rectangle and locking him inside with the enemy Blades and High Lord Dougal.

Mattias ended up on the outside, along with the other tertiary Petralists. The unseen Sentry began dragging him away along the ground by the very block of ice that Kilian had used to bind him. The Spitters and Firetongues did not strike into the box, but they prowled the perimeter with their wills, ready to attack on Dougal's command.

Ivor prepared to intercept Mattias. He'd have to strike fast to overwhelm the Sentry and avoid interference from those Spitters and Firetongues. He'd have surprise on his side, but he also didn't want to kill Mattias.

But his attention was drawn back to Hamish. Harley caught up with him, bashing the Juggernaut brutally with a thrown boulder. The impact knocked it off course and dented a couple of the outer panels. He was in dire trouble and needed Ivor more than Kilian.

So Ivor left Mattias. He figured that the best way to save Mattias and Verena was to kill Dougal quickly. Kilian seemed eager to do just that. Instead, Ivor whipped up a mini blizzard and wrapped it around Harley, grabbing at her, spitting shards of ice into her eyes, and doing everything possible to distract and annoy.

It seemed to work. Hamish accelerated away and although Harley gave chase on her earthen chair, Ivor's distraction initiative kept her busy enough to allow Hamish to keep ahead.

Ivor grinned. He might not be in the middle of any of the multiple fights scattered along the river, but in a way he was in the middle of all of them. He swept another squad of soldiers into the river from the main army, then turned his attention back to Kilian, just as the ancient Dawnus drew his sword and his long-knife, his movements fluid and resolute.

Ivor turned his mini-hub to Kilian's stone and this time he managed to catch the words as Kilian said, "I'm afraid you've over-estimated your own cleverness today."

Dougal snarled, "Finally, we meet on equal terms."

Of course Dougal would consider it equal, with an army around them, Petralists poised to support him, and Kilian isolated and alone. Even so, Ivor couldn't quite believe he could destroy Kilian.

Kilian lifted his weapons and stalked forward.

Dougal pointed his sword. "Take him."

The Spitters and Firetongues attacked from the outside in blistering waves of ice and fire that poured in continuous waves over the earthen walls. The Blades charged.

"Time for your final exam," Kilian said. He stepped through the attacking elements, knocking them aside with an angry flick of his will. Ivor felt sure that he would not give those Petralists another chance to withdraw.

Ivor turned his mini-hub to Verena's stone. "I hope you're listening. Mattias is coming to kill you. Dougal will die soon."

Then he focused on Kilian again, who was leaping to attack.

CONNOR GETS GREAT DISTANCE

Connor flew over the ground, faster than he'd ever run. He tapped just enough granite to reinforce his fracked stride, and applied more to the rest of his body. His feet barely touched the ground as he sped south, his hardened skin impervious to the cold, his upper body straining the limits of his expandable armor.

The wind rushing through his ears seemed wilder than ever, fueled by so much energy, he felt he could run across the Sea of Olcan, all the way to Tabnit without stopping.

A laugh bubbled on his lips, but it died as he sped around the gentle curve of the road south of the city, heading toward the bridge and the bottom end of the speedcaravan ramp.

The road was broken and torn, with several limp bodies strewn across it. Ilse was dragging herself toward a bloody mess on the ground. Connor was shocked to recognize Lukas's face. Most of the rest of him was gone, savaged beyond recognition. Ilse was badly wounded, the lower half of her body crushed, and she trailed a wide swath of bright blood.

The sight sickened and enraged him. He embraced the rage of porphyry and scanned for Harley, intent on murder.

Hamish's Juggernaut was rolling fast toward Connor. The sphere looked dented and worn, but not broken. It looked like he'd taken the Juggernaut head to head against Harley and barely survived. Harley pursued, riding on her narrow sliding chair. She carried a long section of speedcaravan railing like a spear. Other shattered pieces of the speedcaravan ramp were strewn everywhere.

Seeing her in close pursuit of his best friend stoked Connor's anger to white-hot fury.

She'd usually move faster on that sliding seat that she rode straddled like a horse, but a mini blizzard of snow was whipping around her head in a blinding storm. She kept swatting it away, but it kept returning. Connor recognized Ivor's style.

Connor accelerated so fast he took his own breath away. He shot past Hamish's armored sphere, opening himself to all of his elements. Water, Fire, Earth, and Air stepped into his mind and gathered close, looking eager to walk with him again. When he touched their hands, the connections snapped into place, stronger than ever. The red-frequency power locked him to the elements, while the green-frequency power augmented his porphyry strength.

That new influx of power, added to the life forces of the forty thousand people in Merkland, made him feel like a living lightning bolt. He'd achieved stability, and Harley was about to regret it.

She swatted away the blinding snow one more time and looked up just in time for him to clobber her off her earthen chair with an enormous fist of mixed elements that he hurled in front of him. Even as she tumbled back into the air, Connor launched after her, leading with his legs.

He max-tapped granite as he struck at five times the speed of an arrow. The impact jarred him brutally, but he was so awash with energy that he ignored the blow that might have shattered even granite-hardened bones any other day.

Harley took the hit in her chest, and bones all through her torso were crushed. She screamed, blood spraying from her open mouth, her arms flying wide, her entire body seeming to crumple under the onslaught.

They tumbled apart, and Connor hit the ground running. He outran the fall and circled back around, looking for his target. Harley had tumbled when she fell, leaving a long, bloody smear on the snowy, frozen ground. She lay unmoving for a single heartbeat, but Connor tapped quartzite to his eyes and could clearly see her chest healing.

He accelerated toward her, but the ground heaved under him, sending him soaring. He tapped quartzite, seized a nearby air current, and used it to slingshot him back toward Harley.

She'd already sunk into the ground.

That reminded him that despite his rage, despite the energy boiling through him, she was still a deadly foe. If he underestimated her, she could still crush the life out of him.

So he tapped limestone. The snowy, gray air all around immediately glowed with streamers of light. They were softer, spread farther apart than on a sunny day, but there were enough. Connor gave them a twist and called upon mirage.

As he touched down on the ground as light as the falling snow, he tapped slate and applied a careful shield. At the same time, he used mirage to create the image of himself flying another twenty yards before dropping to the ground. With slate, he created ripples through the ground, emanating from that area, reinforcing the illusion.

Connor tapped serpentinite next and crafted words, which he released where the mirage of himself stood. "Harley! Come out and fight, you coward!"

He felt nothing, no sign of her anywhere, even though he scanned the area carefully. So he was completely taken by surprise when her serpent-like mini-elfonnel erupted out of the ground directly below his mirage. Harley had shielded it perfectly, and her control awed him.

The mini-elfonnel chomped down on mirage Connor, its jaws crashing together hard enough to crack its stone-hardened teeth. It bellowed with frustration as he allowed the mirage to disappear.

Tapping limestone again, Connor twisted the light around himself, bending it to turn himself invisible. He was tempted to surround himself with other elements, but that might give away his position.

The Juggernaut came tearing back toward the mini-elfonnel, firing diorite missiles and hornets in an angry stream. The swarm of projectiles tore into the mini-elfonnel, but it ignored them and plunged back into the ground. Connor realized that Hamish must think the monster killed him.

So he tapped limestone again, twisted the air, and formed five mirages of himself. Two he sent sprinting around the area with basalt speed. Two he sent leaping into the air, driven by elemental power, and the last one he sent stalking toward where the mini-elfonnel had disappeared.

The Juggernaut slowed, and Connor turned his mini-hub to Hamish's speakstone. He spoke into it, but using serpentinite, he caught the words and squashed them so only Hamish could hear.

"Hamish, it's me."

"Connor! By the Tallan's rotten cooking, it's great to hear your voice!" Hamish shouted.

Connor grinned to hear the relief and joy in Hamish's voice. "I'm using mirage. Back off until I find Harley."

"Sculpted scones."

The Juggernaut made an abrupt turn and powered back north.

Harley suddenly rose out of the ground, barely fifty feet away from where Connor stood in his protective, shielded, invisible hiding place. She looked completely healed, and furious.

She made a shooing gesture toward the mirage of Connor walking toward her. The ground erupted to either side, forming thick walls of stone that slammed together with a resounding crack.

Harley shouted, "Your Builder friend has annoyed me to no end, boy. Tell me how he blocks me from controlling the granite plates on that armor and I might let him live."

That was astonishing. Connor had no idea that was possible, although now that she mentioned it, they should have considered the risk that she might try turning those outer plates against Hamish. But she didn't need to know he was clueless.

"I'd be happy to explain it as soon as you surrender and swear fealty to me."

Harley's evil thunder-chuckle boomed all around. "My queen wishes to use you, but she didn't say I couldn't beat you to within a hair's breadth of death before bringing you in."

Connor really wanted to ask Hamish about his fight with her, but first he had to kill her. As she raised her hands and created whirlwinds to rip his two flying mirages out of the air, he considered the best way to attack her. Even hitting her with mixed elements didn't seem to damage her for long.

Then he remembered something he'd heard Kilian threaten to do with High Lord Dougal. Tapping marble, Connor focused on Harley's bloodstream. Seizing it through her body would usually be very difficult, but riding the wave of so much power, he easily connected with it.

Connor poured heat into it. In two heartbeats it began to boil.

It was disgusting, but nothing worse than she deserved. Harley convulsed under the sudden, unexpected attack. Lacking fire affinity, there was nothing she could do about it.

Earth rose all around her, forming a large, protective cube. More earth packed in until the cube swelled to over a dozen feet on each side. With so much earth insulating her, his connection to her faded. He should have known she was too clever to die that easily. He could feel her somehow cooling her blood too. Was she using a healing technique? She was just so fast with healing, it was really annoying.

Hamish said, "No way we can give her time to plot her next move. I'm going to draw her out." The Juggernaut accelerated over the frozen ground toward Harley's protective cube.

Her voice boomed out of it. "Have I told you I hate Builders?"

Connor couldn't let Hamish risk charging her like that. She had far too much time to anticipate the Juggernaut. So he directed one of his sprinting mirages to charge her protective cube.

The cube exploded, and Harley charged out to meet his mirage.

Well, the twelve-foot earthen giant she'd clothed herself with charged him. She'd used the same technique at Raufarhofn, and it still felt daunting standing anywhere near that giant.

"Look out!" Hamish shouted, and the Juggernaut launched into the air with a thunderous roar of thrusters. A long drill extended out the front, already spinning.

Harley turned with remarkable agility for such a huge giant. As she focused on Hamish, Connor dared start jogging toward her. He dragged his bubble of invisibility with him as well as his careful shielding. If he could close on her while she focused on Hamish, maybe he could hit her hard enough to do some serious damage.

As the Juggernaut powered through the air and slammed into the giant drill-first, Harley caught it. Even though the drill tore massive chunks out of her giant hands, she didn't seem to care. With a heave, she sent it soaring toward the river, but again the thrusters fired, arresting its flight and dropping it back to the ground.

She beat her hands together, the damage his drill had done already gone. "Come on, Builder! You'll run out of pumice soon enough. Then I'll crush that steel ball around your ears."

Connor's mirage raced past, but Harley ignored it. She had probably recognized that it lacked actual weight. Connor fumed and tapped marble, forming a spear of fire in the hands of the mirage, and making it look like it threw the spear at her.

She batted the spear away, and the earth swallowed up the mirage. The momentary distraction gave Hamish time to advance, and gave Connor time to creep closer. He was barely ten feet away from her. So it was a bit unnerving to have the enormous Juggernaut come barreling in, just to his right, aiming for the equally enormous earthen giant just a few feet to his left.

Hamish closed on Harley with no weapons of any kind visible. It looked like he planned to simply run her over. She crouched to meet him, hands outstretched. The front section of the juggernaut shot out into a battering ram that speared into Harley's giant chest as the Juggernaut slammed into the giant.

And stopped.

It was like she'd set down roots. Even impaled by five feet of steel and struck hard enough to capsize a sailing ship, her giant barely shifted backward. She lifted the Juggernaut high, and the ground opened into a huge pit beneath it.

It was an amazingly impressive stunt.

It took four seconds too long.

Connor purged basalt and absorbed a handful of diorite. He tapped blind coal, applied it to his bones, and prepared to unleash a diorite punch against the distracted Harley's face.

With diorite building through him, he leaped into the air, propelling himself with a bit of soapstone. He soared up, fist cocked back, ready to punch her to oblivion.

The ground erupted under the Juggernaut, sending it tumbling away instead of into the pit. A new hand emerged out of the earth giant's shoulder and caught Connor in mid-air. Earth flowed around him, pinning his hands to his sides and imprisoning him.

He was barely a foot away.

It might as well have been a mile.

The earth melted away from the giant's head, revealing Harley's grinning face beneath. "Did you really think I learned nothing from that squalid little town in Althing?"

"Did you think I didn't either?" He could tap his elements again, but he didn't need to. Diorite was building into a crescendo inside of him. If he didn't release it now, it would rip him apart.

So he explosive-vomited right in her face.

Diorite erupted from his mouth like a volcanic tide, driven by a full measure of diorite and by the incredible energy of all those lives he'd drained in Merkland. The heat reddened his own face, and the pressure knocked him right out of her restraining earthen grip.

The vomit-explosion blasted Harley out of her earthen giant suit. Her face melted under the onslaught. It looked like she tried to scream, but the overwhelming tide of explosive force crushed the sound.

That was so much more amazing than he'd imagined it could be.

Even better, Hamish shouted, "Explosion vomit! Best weapon ever!"

Knowing that his best friend was there to witness the moment, that he understood how incredible and life altering that ability might prove to be, filled Connor with as much satisfaction as watching Harley blasted back with a melting face.

Connor landed just as the diorite extinguished. He tapped marble, seized those superheated flames, and wrapped them around Harley. He could not allow her to touch the ground again, or he might undo all the progress he'd just managed.

Surrounding her with those flames, he poured in even more heat and lifted her higher, separating her from the earth. Then he tapped slate and scanned the area, just in case she could somehow still connect.

He felt the mini-elfonnel barreling through the ground toward him, seconds away from crushing out his life, just as it had his mirage form.

So Connor wrapped himself in more elements, creating his own giant suit of mixed water, fire, and earth. In that pulsing blue and crimson giant suit, he drove a spear of mixed elements down into the earth just as the mini-elfonnel lunged up toward the surface.

His spear punched through its head, splitting it right in half. The earthen beast convulsed, and Connor ripped it out of the ground. With so much energy from Merkland still coursing through him and fueling his affinities, he tossed the monster aside, then turned back to Harley.

Even encased in a superheated tomb, she somehow still found a way to fight. The air in front of Connor darkened and he recognized the cloud that formed and began rolling toward him.

Sandstorm.

It swarmed around him, tearing at his elemental suit, shearing off the outer layer, but it caused less damage than it had against the buildings of Raufarhofn. He drew deeper from the elements, replenishing what she stole.

She wanted to play with sandstone? He had more power than she could dream of at his disposal. Connor hadn't practiced sandstorm, but Kilian had explained the concept. It was a terrifyingly destructive power, so he couldn't think of anything better to rub her face in.

Connor tapped the sandstone pendant and mixed its power into the flood of energy from the lives he'd tapped in Merkland. He linked all that power to the green-frequency power source thundering through his porphyry heart, plunged it through the fires still holding her prisoner, and wrapped it around her burning body.

He didn't quite manage the deadly, elegant sandstorm effect like Harley did. Instead a blizzard of sand spikes materialized and ripped into Harley, puncturing deep and scouring away her already-blackened skin.

Air howled in, called by Harley to fling her free, but Connor tapped quartzite too and deflected the currents away. Riding the wave of power she'd forced him to take from the people of Merkland, he overwhelmed her resistance. She was far stronger than Connor alone, but not even she could beat the combined might of every living soul in Merkland, condensed into Connor's body and fueling his affinities.

Harley beat against the elements imprisoning her, but she couldn't touch the earth or the wind any longer. Connor intensified the already super-heated flames even hotter, until the air crackled from the heat.

Harley writhed in the flames as the heat grew hot enough to melt steel. She screamed again as her clothes melted, and her hair vaporized.

But as fast as her skin melted away, she somehow healed it.

"I'm impressed and disgusted at the same time," Hamish said, rolling close in his battered Juggernaut.

Connor only felt disgusted. He didn't like killing, and a long, drawn-out execution was even worse.

So he fashioned a dozen spears of ice and drove them through the intense flames, right through Harley's body. She convulsed under the onslaught, but although she opened her mouth, he heard no sounds.

Just then, Verena's voice echoed through Hamish's speakstone. She sounded panicked.

"Hamish, I can't reach Connor. Can you help me? Dougal took Mattias's mind and he's trying to—"

Her words broke off into a shriek, followed by a quick ringing of steel on steel, then a whooshing sound.

"Hurry! I'm almost out of quartzite. He catches up so fast. Kilian's fighting Dougal, but I don't know if he'll free Mattias in time. I don't want to hurt him."

Connor glanced across the river. It sounded like Verena was on the ground. Why wasn't she in the Swift? Had Mattias broken the thrusters somehow?

Dougal was there fighting Kilian? Why wasn't he dead yet?

It didn't matter. Mattias was trying to kill Verena. Under Dougal's command, he'd do it. He'd kill himself later if he regained his faculties and realized what he'd done, but that wouldn't change anything.

Towering rage boiled into Connor, hotter than the fires he was using to kill Harley. He fanned it, using it as a shield against his fear, and wrapped Harley in yet another layer of superheated fire.

"Where are you?" Hamish asked.

"North end of the township."

"I'm coming."

Connor said, "No. I'm going."

"Harley's not dead yet," Hamish protested.

She couldn't be far from it. She'd stopped struggling, stopped screaming, and her skin was blackened and peeling. Connor stabbed her again and she didn't twitch.

"I'm going. You finish her."

It took only a couple seconds to surround the boiling fire that was charbroiling Harley with an outer layer of ice. Just to be safe, Connor tapped limestone and hit Harley with sensory deprivation. Even if some spark inside of her still remained, she was locked away until her body crumbled to ash.

"If she stirs, smash her flat, but I think she's done for."

"I don't think we should underestimate her," Hamish warned.

"You can do it," Connor assured his friend. Then he threw himself into the sky, letting his giant suit peel away.

He needed to stop Mattias. He didn't plan to kill him, but if he had to choose between Mattias and Verena, Mattias would die.

THE GREAT MERKLAND BASH FIGHT

Jean ran after Rory and his army as they courageously made the quietest charge in history.

They weren't trying to be quiet. Soldiers shouted battle cries, while Crushers chanted their favorite Grandurian battle songs. Jean cringed, wishing she didn't understand the words.

Student Eighteen blocked all the sound.

In a silent wave, they charged into the swirling snowstorm. Then all of a sudden, Jean spotted the Obrioner army and she quailed with fear. There were so many of them!

Even though the charge was completely silent, the army noticed them and soldiers turned, swords and spears rising.

General Rory's voice boomed over the battlefield. "You are surrounded! Surrender!"

Some of them actually did.

Soldiers wearing High Lord Dougal's colors simply couldn't disobey an order from General Rory. They threw down their weapons and dropped to their knees, looking disgusted with themselves, but still defeated.

Their companions charged.

Tiny but intense bursts of light erupted among them. Rory's Solas's had been inspired by Connor's words that limestone could do more than anyone usually accepted. They scattered the blinding, distracting little lights all through the enemy ranks.

Then the air erupted with sound. Thunderous booms shook the air, as if every diorite bomb ever invented detonated just over their heads. Soldiers ducked instinctively, then crouched lower as thousands of invisible arrows swished past.

Then their officers shouted orders, just not the orders they intended.

"Fall back!"

"Every man for himself!"

"We're surrounded!"

"Surrender!"

Jean gaped and slowed as the confused soldiers milled around, glancing at officers for confirmation. The officers looked stunned and shook their heads, pointing and shouting, but couldn't seem to make the right words come out.

Rory and his five hundred slammed into their confused ranks. They plowed the first rows right under, driving deep into the enemy army. Non-Boulders simply collapsed under the onslaught, but granite Petralists rushed to block them far too soon. The stone-hardened warriors grinned as they closed, matching the jubilant expressions of Rory's forces.

The two groups crashed together, shouting, "Bash fight!"

Boulders and Rumblers beat on each other with unrestrained glee, using fists as much as clubs or swords. The cracking of stone fists against rock-hard faces echoed across the battlefield like continuous, rolling thunder. Soldiers beat on each other, laughing insanely as they all enthusiastically leaped into the fiercest bash fight Jean had ever imagined. They punched and elbowed, kicked and bashed with such intensity, Jean wondered if they feared the bash fight might end too soon, so they wanted to get in as many punches as possible before the dreaded order to stand down came from the officers.

Conflicting orders continued to be shouted from both their officers and Student Eighteen, but the granite warriors didn't seem to notice. They ignored the sounds of explosions and a few pedra screams that Student Eighteen threw into the mix. Bash fighting was the purest joy that Boulders and Rumblers knew, and they embraced it as the truest form of fighting, their greatest pleasure in life.

The rest of the enormous army retreated from the wild fighting. Tertiary Petralists threw elements at each other, and Striders sprinted around the perimeter, looking for other fast movers to duel.

The nearby river rose into a tidal wave and burst over the road, sweeping at least a couple hundred Obrioner soldiers off their feet. Fire erupted right out from the waters and speared at Sentries, keeping them distracted while the Crushers closed.

Ivor had joined the fray.

Jean was no soldier, but from where she stood, a little behind the furious bash fighting, she had an excellent view of the battlefield and she noticed a subtle shift. Rory's forces enjoyed the element of surprise and they'd struck the tail end of the Obrioner army, stretched thin along the road. However, their initial success was quickly being eclipsed by the sheer numbers of the Obrioners.

Most dangerous were the companies of tertiaries. They were fewer in number than she'd expected, perhaps because many of them were up front in the vanguard, but they still outnumbered Rory's few tertiaries many times over. After their initial surprise, they were counter-attacking with remarkably good coordination.

A group of Spitters began targeting Rory's Striders, turning the ground beneath them to slick ice, sending them tumbling, then wrapping them with icy bands before they could rise. Four Firetongues were whipping white-hot flames over the heads of the bash fighters, targeting Rory. He only had one Firetongue defending him, and it looked like that woman wouldn't last much longer. Jean was close enough to that fight that she felt the intense heat of their duel. It must be blistering poor Rory.

"Hurry!" Jean cried, gesturing the soldiers carrying her supplies closer. She directed them to drop their bundles, then thrust her hands into the first pack, keeping her keystone out of sight. With careful twisting motions of the keystone, she began activating mechanicals and handing them out.

"Those are speedcrack walls. Get some Striders to throw them. They'll make fast-sliding walls to interrupt enemy formations."

A sack full of round balls of slate, encircling marble, came next. She activated them and said, "Careful. Get some Boulders to throw these. When they hit, the slate will burst open and release blasts of fire."

Larger diorite bombs were easy to identify. She activated them and said, "These explode easily so be very careful and get someone to throw them far."

She hated the idea of helping hurt or kill, but Harley could kill Hamish any second, and if she had to fight through that entire army to get to his side, she'd do it.

Sounds of screams and clashing of steel weapons sounded from every side. With the falling snow whipping around and playing tricks on the eyes, it was impossible to tell what was going on beyond the closest sections of the battlefield. It sounded like the fighting had spread to every corner of the army, as if they really did have thousands of extra troops joining the fray.

Jean extracted her last group of mechanicals and cringed to think of the damage they were about to do. She directed seven soldiers to each hold one of the leather-wrapped balls, with the tiny pieces of quartzite aimed diagonally down at the ground. She moved down the line, activating each one in turn.

The quartzite whooshed loudly, flinging the balls high into the air. As they arced out over the army, the quartzite shrank just enough to slip inside through spring-closed flaps that prevented them from escaping.

The balls disappeared into the vast army surging toward Rory's embattled forces. Other bombs were detonating as Boulders flung them over the fighting, but the explosions seemed so tiny against so many. Jean waited eight seconds until the building pressure inside those balls ruptured the seams. Hundreds of hornets tore out, spraying in every direction. Waves of fresh screaming echoed across the battlefield.

Jean cringed. She'd done what she could, but she needed thousands more mechanicals to make a difference.

Student Eighteen patted her shoulder. "Well done, Jean. Now it's my turn. Don't waste the prisoners I send to you."

"What?"

She winked and her expression turned eager as she sprinted toward the still-raging bash fight. Instead of plowing into the fighting soldiers, flames erupted under her feet, throwing her into the air, aimed directly at those four Firetongues attacking Rory and advancing on his position.

They were so focused on their impending victory over the general that they never spotted Aifric. She crashed into one, knocking him right off his feet. As she rolled into the group, the earth buckled under them, knocking them flying, then grasping them with slender fingers and cracking them together hard enough that Jean imagined she heard their heads banging all the way across the battlefield.

Aifric barely paused. She sprinted with Strider speed toward those Spitters wreaking so much havoc among Rory's Striders, but then changed to granite just as she reached them and pounded them off their feet.

Jean frowned as she watched Aifric's solo assault on the enemy force. Jean knew many of Aifric's personalities, but none of them could tap all those powers. Aifric was changing personalities, using different aspects of herself to tap different affinities.

The display of absorption and tap rate management was awe inspiring. Jean had never imagined Aifric could switch between personalities so fast and change affinities so quickly. She looked more like Blood of the Tallan than a single person.

As Aifric disappeared into the distant gloom, beating a swath of destruction right through the heart of the enemy army, Rory's voice boomed over the battlefield from that direction. Aifric had borrowed it and enhanced until it cracked like thunder.

"Any who do not wish to die, report to Lady Jean at the southwest edge of the field and surrender to her. No others will receive any quarter."

Other officer voices began calling for their troops to surrender. The officers who owned those voices looked furious, trying to restrain their soldiers from obeying, resorting to hand signals, but unable to reach most of their men.

The waters flowing freely around the battlefield rose up around many of those officers, yanking them under the surface and out of sight. Jean had no idea how Ivor was coordinating his efforts with Aifric, but their combined assault on the command structure of the Obrioner forces was devastating. It left soldiers frightened and confused, and therefore not effectively fighting.

Jean stood in a pocket of calm at the outer fringes of the fighting. Rory and his command group were advancing toward the bash fight, leaving her standing alone with her few assistants. With her mechanicals mostly spent, she was a mute spectator to the chaotic insanity of that battle.

Now a horde of soldiers moved toward her. Some looked confused and frightened and eager to surrender. Others looked angry, weapons clenched, as if they were only coming to her because their officers ordered them to.

Jean swallowed her fear and assumed her Healer expression of confident authority that she used with difficult patients. She wasn't sure what the proper protocol was for accepting the surrender of enemy combatants.

So she pointed to the ground to her right. "You are all now under my command. Form ranks behind me and stand at attention until I deliver my orders."

Many hesitated. She needed to assert her authority, or she'd lose them all. So she extracted from her satchel the keystone and a piece of marble. Applying the keystone, she gave it a twist and generated a blast of fire that she aimed over their heads.

"I am accustomed to my troops obeying my orders at once. Snap to it, soldiers!"

That broke the spirits of enough of them that they scrambled to obey, dragging their companions along behind them. As they formed into companies behind her, Jean fought to suppress a smile.

She had just assumed command of what would soon become several hundred soldiers. Many were regulars, but some were Petralists.

What could she do with so many?

Student Eighteen raced up on Strider legs and skidded to a halt in front of her, saluting and reinforcing the illusion that Jean was some sort of officer. "Well done, Lady Jean. The hero of Schwinkendorf assumes yet another title, eh?"

"It is rather exciting," Jean admitted.

One of the soldiers in her new company said loudly, "What kind of officer are you? I don't recognize your uniform."

Jean was wearing her battle outfit, consisting of a form-fitting leather vest, with leather bracers on her forearms, a wide leather belt encircling her narrow waist, loaded with vials and pouches of medicine. Brown leather boots peeked out from under her dark green skirt, and a larger medical kit hung from a strap on her back. She'd braided her long, blond hair, and wore a leather headband. A long, blue woolen coat covered it all, but hung open in the front.

Student Eighteen stepped forward, her voice carrying easily to every ear, even though she spoke softly. "She's the Lady Jean, of course. Didn't you hear General Rory? Soldiers, you are privileged to now serve under the Hero of Schwinkendorf, the Healer of Alasdair. Lady Jean commands Builder mechanicals, but she is no Builder. She flies, but is no Pathfinder. She is the builder of cities, nobility seek her counsel, and she is the dread and glorious elfonnel's bane! She is the Lady Jean! Obey her commands, and you will see victory in every venture she directs."

They looked impressed and suitably cowed. Jean caught herself just in time before gaping in astonishment at the litany of her accomplishments. That would have ruined everything Student Eighteen had just accomplished.

The Mhortair turned back to her and winked. Jean said softly, "You make me sound as amazing as Connor and Hamish and Verena."

"You are. Keep them distracted. Run an inspection or something. This battle is far from over, but we've got them confused, and Ivor is a one-man army. He's dragged thousands into the river."

"He's not killing them, is he?" The thought sickened her.

"I doubt it. He's probably got them stuck in a hole in the middle of the river. Can't do any harm there. But several thousand soldiers broke away from the front of the army. That's their second wave, and they're charging upriver, but angling to the west. Looks like they're planning to circle around Harley."

"How do you know all this?"

Student Eighteen raised a single eyebrow. "Really? Keep your forces busy," she reiterated. "I'll be back."

She rushed off with Strider speed, disappearing into the snowstorm in seconds.

Jean turned to face her steadily growing army. Luckily she saw few officers of high enough rank to challenge her. She didn't exactly have a bellowing-level voice. The handful of soldiers acting as her assistants looked even more astonished than she did by the turn of events. So she beckoned a hulking mountain of a man closer. He wore the insignia of sergeant and the battle leathers of a Boulder. He actually saluted.

"You are now my caller. New battle plan. We will circle the fighting and render aid to the city."

"But my lady, we were supposed to—"

She gave him the look she'd used on Connor and Hamish all their lives, and it cowed him just like it had them. "Do you want me to send you back in there against Rory?" She pointed at the insane bash fight.

"No, ma'am."

"When this is all over, we'll sort things out, but right now we have work to do. Sound the charge and follow me!"

She began to run out around the main army, her assistants close on her heels.

Her new caller's voice boomed so loud, he sounded like he'd eaten a

Pathfinder for breakfast. The bellowing order to follow the Lady Jean snapped the troops out of their milling indecision.

Three hundred soldiers charged after Jean.

With heart beating wildly from excitement, Jean left the Great Merkland Bash Fight behind and led her army in a desperate charge to help Hamish.

9 3

SOME FRIENDS ARE TERRIFYING. IN A GOOD WAY.

Hamish peered through his sightstone viewscreen at the sphere of translucent ice that held the white-hot flames burning Harley alive. He could barely see her, and he was grateful for that. The hints he did see of her blackened corpse threatened to make him sick. He loved watching a good ham roast slowly over a fire, but this was totally different.

As much as he wanted to not look, he increased the magnification factor and peered closer. Her body seemed to be swelling inside the fire. That was weird. Was she filling with fire, about to explode?

Gross.

He tore his gaze away and spun the Juggernaut toward Ilse. She had somehow dragged herself all the way to Lukas. She clung to his remains, weeping, a piece of sandstone clutched in her fist.

All of a sudden her head snapped up and she shouted, "Hamish, look out!"

Twenty snarling demon hounds, the size of horses, galloped out of the blowing snow. They swarmed the Juggernaut like a living tornado, knocking it rolling west, away from the river and Harley's burning prison.

Two more hounds plunged through the sphere of fire and ice holding Harley prisoner. They disintegrated in the resulting elemental explosion, but Harley's blackened corpse dropped free onto the earth. It had definitely swelled to nearly twice its previous size. Connor had gotten something wrong in his Petralist fricassee recipe.

"You've got to be kidding me," Hamish cursed as he tried activating thrusters to regain control, but the hounds beat and battered the Juggernaut so hard he couldn't turn it about.

So he started activating weapons. He'd exhausted his supply of diorite missiles and hornets, but many of the mechanicals were multi-use weapons. The battering ram caught one hound in the face, crushing its skull. Its head was packed with earth. The spinning drill caught another monster through the torso and ripped it to shreds. Its death howl shrieked through the Juggernaut, echoing painfully back and forth through the hull.

The hounds were pressed close, so Hamish dropped his last two small bombs out a hatch. As the armor rolled under the ferocious onslaught, he triggered them. The explosions knocked three hounds aside, but did not appear to do any serious damage.

The summoned beasts tore at the outer hull with superhuman ferocity. Their claws actually ripped into the steel or screeched as they scraped hardened granite plates. The sound made him shiver.

He opened one hatch to extend an articulating arm, but a hound seized the arm and ripped it right off. Then the beast shoved its head through and tried crawling inside with Hamish. It smelled like charred earth, and its dead, black eyes sent a shiver of fear through Hamish. They remained fixed on him while it snarled and snapped deadly jaws, trying to enter his armor. If it got inside, it would rip him to shreds.

Its huge shoulders got stuck in the opening, but it blocked the hole and the little quartzite thrusters that moved the plate lacked the power to shear through its hide. It snarled and lunged, stuck barely six feet away.

"Bad dog," Hamish said, throwing a diorite dart.

It snapped its huge jaws over the dart. An eyeblink later, those jaws exploded and it tumbled back out the hole.

Another, smaller hound took its place and scrambled wildly to get in. For a second, Hamish feared it would make it into the armor.

Then with a yelp of pain, it was sucked back out the opening. Hamish caught a glimpse of earthen fingers ripping into its head.

"Ilse, was that you?" he shouted as he sealed the hatch and focused on his sightstones again. The earth really had risen up against the hounds. Fingers of earth were ripping them off the Juggernaut, while soft, bubbling ground was swallowing a couple more.

Despite her ghastly injuries, Ilse had rejoined the fight. Propped up on one elbow, her other hand was driven into the earth. Her expression was a mixture of agony and fury. Her determination awed him. She should be unconscious, if not dead.

He wasn't about to complain. With the hounds momentarily distracted, Hamish activated thrusters and set the armor rolling in a wide circle, picking up speed as he went. As he roared back in toward the pack, he snapped spinning blades into place.

He struck the pack like a crazed butcher, shredding summoned bodies and plowing others under. With Ilse's help, he'd rip those hounds to pieces in seconds.

That's when Harley's corpse split down the middle and she rose up from her own ashes.

"Tallan take it and burn it to cinders," Hamish shouted. He didn't want to believe what he was seeing, couldn't imagine how she wasn't dead. Any sane person would have just accepted they'd died.

Harley looked much smaller, a skeletal, almost childlike version of herself. Bald, with earthy skin, she was dressed in a layer of concealing earth.

She took a faltering step, looking like she barely had the strength to stand. Her second step looked stronger though, and she squared her shoulders and glared at him.

Pure hatred burned in her eyes. She didn't look human any more, but more elemental than anything. She hadn't gone elfonnel, but she had abandoned much of what made her a woman when she'd slipped out of her former body.

"I'm going to rip off your head and eat your eyes, Builder," she growled.

"You first," Ilse said from behind.

Hamish activated a side-view stone. Ilse had risen to her feet and stood facing Harley defiantly.

Impossible.

Hamish zoomed in and realized the truth. Ilse had summoned new legs for herself. Her crushed, crippled lower half was wrapped in earth.

He'd never heard of anything like it. Sure, Harley had surrounded herself with the elements, but Ilse had been crippled, on the brink of death. Now she faced Harley with vengeful determination.

Ilse had always scared Hamish. Now she terrified him. In a good way.

Even Harley looked impressed. She saluted Ilse with one skeletal, childlike hand.

Then the ground erupted under Hamish, tossing the Juggernaut into the air and flipping him over, despite the efforts of his leveling casters. His view blurred for a moment and something struck the Juggernaut with terrific force, shattering one granite plate and collapsing a couple steel ones in shrieking protests of grinding metal.

The Juggernaut slammed into the ground so hard, Hamish was nearly ripped out of his retraining harness. Another brutal strike dented the sides farther. One of the thick support girders began to bend with a shriek of protest.

What was going on?

One of the sightstones was gone, knocked out by the brutal attack. Hamish frantically activated all the others and they formed a grid of six images across the inside of his visor.

"I'm grouted," he whispered.

The mini-elfonnel was back. Its head had grown large enough to grip the entire Juggernaut in its massive jaws. The dents were caused by those stalactite teeth grinding down with the power of an avalanche. The long, serpentlike body was wrapped around the Juggernaut, and the snakelike tongues were batting at the outside, ripping at the bent metal, seeking a way to slip inside and tear him asunder.

A couple of the views offered glimpses of the area beyond the mini-elfonnel. Inhuman-Harley and Ilse had both risen on Sentry towers, and the ground rippled and bubbled between them.

For the moment, Ilse was holding her own. Was she angry enough to win? Was Inhuman-Harley weakened enough to give her the chance?

He activated every speakstone in the Juggernaut, linking to every member of the team and shouted, "Anyone who can hear me, Harley's back! Now would be a great time to get back here and help."

Then as he focused on trying to figure out a way to escape his predicament he muttered, "Should have used the sculpted scones."

94

PLAYING CATCH-THE-DEVIL WITH
SWORDS IS NOT AS FUN AS IT SOUNDS

Verena sprinted around the corner of a long warehouse. Mattias couldn't be far behind and she panted with fear that he'd catch her again. She was quickly running out of power stones, but none of the tricks she'd used had helped her escape for more than a moment. He pursued with single-minded, murderous intensity.

She hated Dougal more than ever for turning a cherished friend against her. She had so far refused to hurt Mattias, but if she didn't figure out a way to elude him, she might not have any choice. The thought that she might have to put him down like a rabid dog made her shudder with horror between ragged breaths.

A sound caught her attention. It sounded like something banging lightly behind her. She spun and looked around, but couldn't see through the snowy grayness. Maybe that was Mattias vaulting the fence she'd just scrambled over. That meant he was too close. Again.

She glanced up at the warehouse looming over her and decided to risk using a precious piece of quartzite. She jumped and activated it, using it like a mini thruster. The tiny stone had barely any power left, and it didn't produce a lot of force. She carefully managed the release rate, applying just enough force to augment her leap and pull her high enough to grab the outer edge of the gently-sloped warehouse roof. She pulled herself up with desperate strength, barely yanking her torso up over the edge before the little piece of quartzite exhausted its strength and crumbled to dust.

She scrabbled for purchase on the slippery roof with her gloved hands and teetered precariously on the edge for a breathless moment, legs hanging over the space.

Then one of her hands slipped, and she started to slide.

With a muttered curse, she snatched a throwing dagger from her belt and drove the razor sharp blade into the roof. That anchor gave her the leverage she needed to climb up.

Moving carefully, she crept up the shallow roof, grateful it wasn't pitched steeply like many of the other buildings. The long warehouse was three stories tall and she hadn't spotted any exterior stairs or ladders.

It might offer a respite from Mattias's relentless attacks.

Verena lifted her mini-hub, already pointing to Connor's speakstone. "Connor, where are you?"

"I'm at the north end of the township. Where are you?"

"I'm not sure. I'm on top of a tall warehouse. Give me a second to get oriented."

She wished there were better landmarks. The township was a working community, so it left the ornamentation to the city across the river. Most of the buildings looked the same. Crowded tenement apartments for the workers, warehouses for goods, and the occasional freestanding house for the merchants.

Verena reached the peak of the roof and looked around, trying to gauge her position. The past few minutes were a blur of terror, punctuated by brief flashes of desperate struggle and escape. She'd used up most of her tiny store of power stones. Maybe she should have disabled him. She wasn't sure she had enough stones left to stop him.

He was just so fast. He'd leaped a speedcrack wall and dodged jets of fire. He'd nearly taken off her head three times as she fled. He'd scaled buildings when she tried to use the roofs for cover, and ran right up a wall that got in his way when she used a hand thruster to fly over.

This warehouse was a little taller than the others she'd tried, so maybe he wouldn't find a way up. If she'd finally managed a bit of the Tallan's luck, he might not have realized where she'd gone.

She tried to calm her rapid breathing as she oriented herself. "Looks like I circled farther south and east again. Hurry."

"I'll be right there."

Verena turned at a slight noise and terror spiked anew. Somehow Mattias had climbed to the roof and was stalking toward her, twin swords at the ready.

"Mattias, I'm getting tired of this," she said as she backed to the end of the roof and pawed through her satchel, trying to formulate a plan to keep herself alive, but not kill him.

He paused and spoke. "Time to die, Builder witch."

"I'm going to kill you, Dougal," she snarled.

Mattias laughed evilly and charged, feet effortlessly finding purchase on the slippery surface.

Verena jumped.

She only had one tiny piece of quartzite left, a piece too small to fly with, but she quickened it to help slow her fall.

Mattias threw himself off the roof after her in a face-first dive, swords driving for her heart.

Verena shuttered the quartzite, dropping faster, and just barely keeping ahead of him. She hit the ground hard and rolled, spraying snow in every direction. She drew her sword as she staggered to her feet.

Mattias landed a second later, making a graceful roll and returning to his feet even before she did. Nearly within arm's reach, he slashed his deadly swords without any hesitation.

Verena threw herself backward and managed to deflect one sword with hers. The other skipped across her armored shoulder with a shriek of metal.

Mattias pursued, blades whipping like living things. She retreated, focusing on deflecting the strikes aimed at her face and neck. He connected several times against her armored torso, his blades shrieking as if with anticipation of the kill as they scraped her armor.

Verena threw a knife, then dropped a piece of quickened soapstone.

Mattias deflected the knife that would have otherwise plunged through an eye. She threw a second knife a split second later, and he deflected that one just as easily.

The soapstone hit the ground, and all the snow piled along the street whooshed in from every direction. She dove backward through the inrushing blizzard that seemed to swarm Mattias.

He plunged through the snowstorm after her, swords already slashing before she even realized he'd arrived. The first one slapped her hand, numbing it and knocking her short sword away. The second one slashed across her chest as she spun, scoring her armor deeply with another shrieking clang.

Mattias followed through, driving one sword straight at her throat.

Verena screamed and punched out a hand, quickening the blind coal in her gauntlet.

Mattias's sword skipped across her throat, not quite able to cut the skin, although she felt the deadly cold of the steel. The blind coal would only last a couple of seconds, and Mattias knew it. He raised his swords to cut her down when she tried to flee.

Verena did the only thing she could.

She charged.

And quickened her last, tiny piece of quartzite. She dropped it at his feet as the two of them collided. She shivered at the creepy feeling of sliding right through Mattias and running three long strides beyond before the blind coal ran out.

Verena spun to face him. Mattias turned at the same time, swords ready to slash out her life. He didn't speak, didn't gloat or hesitate, showed no recognition in his murderous eyes.

He took a single step closer. And collided with the shimmering shield that appeared around him.

Mattias snarled with rage and beat on the translucent shield with his swords. The quartzite was so tiny that the shield was barely large enough to hold him, and his swords struck the curving boundary both in front and behind.

"This little shield won't hold me for long, Builder."

Verena didn't waste time responding. She grabbed her sword from the ground and ran, swearing vengeance on Dougal for what he'd done to a good man.

She called back over her shoulder, "You are my dear friend, Mattias. I know this isn't you. If you survive me, know that I forgive you."

Then she focused on running. Forgetting tricks and stealth, she rounded the building into an empty street and ran for her life. If Connor didn't arrive soon, Mattias would kill her.

Five seconds later, the shield sputtered out and Mattias shouted in victory. She didn't bother to look behind, but tried to accelerate. Her legs ached, her breaths came in ragged pants, but she refused to slow.

She stayed ahead of him for a full block before his rapid footsteps drew close enough that she had to slide to a stop and spin to face him. He was closing fast, both swords raised to strike. She readied herself for one final attempt at defense.

As Mattias rushed in for the kill, blinding light erupted in the air between them. Verena threw herself to the side, covering her face with one arm.

Crimson flames blasted the air above her, and Mattias cried out in pain. He'd leaped through the light, swords slashing after her, but the flames seized his arms and wrenched them back. His swords tumbled to the snowy pavement with a muffled clatter.

Then the snow whipped around Mattias, sealing him in a column of ice from toe to neck.

Connor landed next to Verena, riding a column of mixed elements, and cried, "Verena! Are you hurt?"

Relief made her weak and she sagged against the cold paving stones, savoring the fact that she wasn't dead. Tension melted away and she laughed before she could decide to cry.

"You arrived half a heartbeat before too late. Help me up."

Connor lifted her easily to her feet and pulled her close. She clung to him and tried to banish the terror of the last several minutes. She'd survived. He'd survived. They were both okay. Connor's arms quivered, rattling their armor a little.

"Are you all right?" she asked, touching his face.

"I nearly lost you." His voice shook, and she loved him for the depth of emotion he didn't try to hide. She kissed him, drawing strength from his presence. He grinned and added, "But you're fine, Merkland is safe from the porphyry bomb, and I finally figured out how to stabilize my affinities."

"Wow. You've been busy."

Before she could ask for more details, Mattias shrieked, "You filthy Builder witch! You will die, along with all other abominations!" He struggled vainly within the ice, face twisted with rage.

Verena sighed. "I hate what Dougal has done to him."

Connor said, "I'm just surprised Kilian hasn't killed Dougal already. He must have used some kind of trick."

"He does that," Verena agreed. She stepped closer to Mattias and placed a hand on the ice. He tried snapping at her fingers, but couldn't hope to reach. "What can we do for him?"

Mattias suddenly calmed, his expression fading to complete neutrality. Verena exchanged a worried look with Connor.

Mattias spoke, his voice calm and haughty, just like Dougal. "Bring this waste of an Allcarver to the southern edge of town or I will crush his mind right now."

"What do you want?" Connor demanded.

"An exchange, of course."

"What sort of exchange?" Verena asked, but Mattias did not respond. His eyes closed and he seemed to have fallen asleep.

"Just like Aifric," Connor muttered.

"Should we go?" Verena didn't want to do anything Dougal said, but simply defying him could cost Mattias his life.

"Kilian's there. I can't imagine Dougal has defeated him, but something's afoot. We have to go that way anyway to get back to Hamish. Let's find out what's going on."

She took his hand and together they headed south, with Mattias sliding along the street behind them, sleeping in his icy prison.

But Verena kept her sword out, just in case.

95

WITH GREAT POWER COMES GREAT AWESOMENESS

Ivor rose to the surface of the river and slid toward the bank closest to where Kilian faced Dougal. They could no longer delay. With Harley impossibly risen again, full scale battle joined between Rory and the main Obrioner army, they needed to defeat Dougal and join forces to stop Harley.

Even though he kept up a distraction attack against the eastern flank of the Obrioner army, he turned his main focus toward Kilian and brought that entire area, just south of the township, into clear focus through his soapstone senses.

Kilian was advancing toward Dougal and the three Blades who supported him. The two men and one woman moved in perfect unison. Clearly they'd worked closely together before. They advanced in an inverted curve formation, with Dougal and the woman in the center. The other two led on either side. This way they could encircle Kilian and strike from every side.

The long, rectangular "room" the unknown Sentry had raised to box them in was plenty big enough for a duel. The cobbled pavement was swept clean of snow and ice by the fierce elemental fighting, and the air was comfortably warm.

Ivor decided he needed to focus on turning the tide on that fight first. The annoying young tertiaries still hammered at Kilian's defenses with high volume strikes meant to distract. Once he closed with the Blades, he couldn't spare the attention to deal with them, and they could actually prove deadly.

First, the Sentry. The man was easy to spot, standing alone near the western wall of the dueling room, atop a squat Sentry tower. He seemed to be focused on the fight inside his kill box.

So Ivor seized some of the falling snow near the Sentry, condensed it into ice, and slammed it into his head from three sides. The unexpected strike knocked the Sentry right off his tower. Ivor caught him with snow, preventing him from touching the ground. The man appeared knocked out, or at least stunned, but Ivor wasn't about to take any chances. With fingers of water, he stripped the man's boots off to remove his slate, then dragged him around the earthen duel "room" and into the river. There he dropped the slumbering Sentry into one of several prison rooms he'd hollowed out of the river.

Inside the kill box, Kilian had wrapped fire and water around himself to ward against the ongoing elemental attacks as he faced Dougal and the three other Blades closing on him.

Ivor accelerated onto shore, sliding on a sheet of snow, aiming to land behind the long line of distracted Spitters and Firetongues. He kept himself carefully shielded and felt fairly confident none of them yet realized he was there.

Time to say "Hello."

Ivor pulled hard on the river. The surface near the shore erupted in an enormous geyser. He coalesced the waters into an eight-foot tall shapeless blob and sent it rolling onto the bank, accelerating toward the line of tertiaries attacking Kilian.

They couldn't miss noticing its approach. The watery blob sounded like it had swallowed a hundred crashing ocean waves. Ivor grinned as he drove it forward. He was enjoying this construct immensely and needed to remember to use again some time. Maybe he'd introduce Connor to it the next time they practiced together.

As the blob bore down upon the tertiaries, the Spitters rushed to the front, forming a defiant line, throwing their combined wills into stopping the surprise assault. Ivor did not cede control, but pushed it on even faster.

As the blob closed on them, Kilian noticed what he was doing and joined in, striking at the distracted Firetongues, snapping a whip of mixed elements across all their backsides.

Ivor grinned as the young Petralists yelped and jumped, grabbing their backsides. That was too much dishonor for one of them. He blasted off the ground on a column of crimson flames and arced high over the blob, back toward the opposite side of the river and the main army.

Kilian snapped the whip back at the others, aimed at their heads this time. Most of them ducked, but one tried to catch it with his own flames, but ended up taking the whip in the face. The blow toppled him unmoving to the ground. The other four Firetongues erupted off the ground, following their cowardly but inspired comrade back to the safety of the main army.

Good decision for them, although it meant Ivor would need to hunt them down again later. Unless Aifric in her super-schizophrenic battle frenzy took them out first.

The blob of water thundered toward the row of defiant Spitters, but Ivor allowed them to beat through his control and stop it several feet short of where they stood. They raised victorious fists.

So none of them noticed Ivor as he sprinted out of the shadows on fracked legs, meteor hammer already spinning. Ivor flashed down the line of the Spitters before any of them realized a new threat had appeared.

He'd practiced a lot with that meteor hammer. He loved the deadly weapon and he'd mastered enough technique for what he planned. He spun it as he sped down the ranks of the Spitters, clunking it into the back of every one of their helmets.

Direct hits. Each of them pitched forward, sprawling on the ground. Most did not move. A couple groaned and sat up. So Ivor returned and hit them again.

Kilian spoke through the mini-hub. "Took you long enough."

Ivor chuckled. "I've been busy. Finish playing. Hamish needs help with Harley."

He didn't quite dare imprisoning a bunch of Spitters in the river with his other prisoners, so he wrapped them all in cages of crimson fire to block them from easily reaching their affinities when they awakened. Then with a blast of mixed fire and water, he swept away the earthen walls surrounding Kilian so he could see with his own eyes what was going on.

Dougal and his Blades had nearly reached Kilian, who waited for them, sword and dagger at the ready. It seemed wrong somehow to watch Kilian fight with steel instead of elements, but he did not look concerned. In fact, his expression looked eager as he faced opponents who should be able to easily cut him down. He wasn't a Blade, after all. Enhanced by obsidian, they moved too fast, too gracefully, too balanced. Whatever Kilian had in mind, Ivor approached, ready to support him.

Kilian saluted, and the trio returned the salute. Dougal only scowled. The leading Blades were barely six strides away and four paces to either side of Kilian, just wide enough to make it hard to know where to strike first. An optimistic fighter might try to leap between them and try to strike at Dougal or take down the woman before they could close from either side.

That meant she was probably the deadliest of the trio.

If Kilian turned to the left or the right in an attempt to remove one of the flankers, again the others would sweep in behind and cut him down.

Ivor had studied enough battle lore to recognize the time-tested tactic. It would work against almost all foes caught alone. He hoped Kilian had a plan because otherwise he was about to die.

If only they could strike them down with elements. The queen must have made them Agor so they could tap protective pumice. If he rushed in with his meteor hammer, they'd carve him to pieces. He wasn't sure how to help.

The two flanking Blades drew even with Kilian, swords ready, and Dougal and the woman approached Kilian directly. Still looking calmly confident, Kilian stepped into the kill circle between all four, facing Dougal and the woman in the center, who both looked eager to cross swords with him.

Suddenly the woman froze in place, one foot raised slightly as she prepared to take another step. She looked completely immobile, and Ivor realized Kilian had hit her with stilling.

Why hadn't he done the same to the others?

Dougal and the other two Blades leaped at him in unison, swords slashing. Ivor opened his mouth to shout a warning, but his voice died on his lips, his mouth hanging open in astonishment instead.

Kilian erupted into a blur of motion. Ivor was an accomplished Strider and he recognized that Kilian must have applied basalt to every limb, but Ivor never would have imagined anyone could move so fast.

Kilian's sword and long-knife whipped around with superhuman speed, clanging against his attackers' weapons, deflecting them wide as he spun out of the way.

They responded without hesitation, flowing around him and each other, swords dancing out, fast as viper strikes. Even Dougal leaped into the fray, moving with the same deadly grace, face locked into a mask of hatred as he struck with terrifying speed.

Kilian deflected them all.

Ivor watched in awe as Kilian flowed around his opponents, moving with even greater speed. Blades were supposed to be the fastest and therefore the deadliest, but Kilian was taking away that advantage. He was demonstrating a mastery over basalt that eclipsed anything Ivor had ever heard.

As the four of them whirled and spun, twisted and slashed, blades moving faster than sight, Ivor read the Blades' surprise. They were all fighting so fast, even enhanced by obsidian, they were moving on instinct alone, reading the next strike through long training and perfect under-standing of fighting forms.

Kilian wasn't a Blade. He shouldn't be able to keep up.

Somehow he did, and he grinned as he fought. Ivor found his own pulse quickening as he watched the epic duel. The group of blurring fighters seemed to meld together into a confusing view of slashing steel and clanging swords.

Then the woman shook off her stillness and leaped into the fray with a shout. Maybe Kilian couldn't keep it in place while fighting so fast. Now Kilian fought four Blades together, the group swirling around with even greater intensity, swords clanging a staccato rhythm. Dougal and his three Blades worked well together, trying to box Kilian in to hit him from all sides at once, while he moved among them, trying to keep at least one of them between him and that one's companions.

He managed it for five glorious seconds, using basalt speed and his long years of training to counter their enhanced abilities.

Then they finally moved together in the perfect chorus of deadly steel and dancing feet, and for a split second Kilian ended up in the center, with his four opponents spread evenly around him. He was facing Dougal, and Ivor saw victory shine in Dougal's eyes.

Not even Kilian could avoid all of them striking in unison now.

But Kilian winked.

And he fracked.

As his opponents closed with perfectly coordinated attacks that no living being should be able to survive, Kilian exploded through them, arms and legs all fracked, every limb moving at whirlwind speed.

Ivor shouted with exultant disbelief, eyes glued to the fight, not sure he could feel any deeper awe. The clatter of swords became a long, continuous peal of steel thunder. Kilian's entire body blurred as he entered a super-fracked state that Ivor had not imagined possible, and doubted any other Petralist had ever achieved.

Kilian was the ultimate Strider and he introduced the Blades to what speed in battle really meant. His weapons hummed through the air as he broke out of their circle, slashing the woman's hands and arms twenty-six times in a single heartbeat. She screamed and fell back, swords flying from her nerveless grips. Blood covered her from shoulder to fingertip and she stared at the wounds that to Ivor looked like they'd struck like a single blow.

Kilian continued to accelerate as he swept back around Dougal and the other two Blades, settling into a whirlwind spin of arms and steel. He caught Dougal across the chest, cracking his armor and sending him tumbling away. The next Blade tried to accelerate to match, but Kilian blasted through his defenses, slashing his arms and hands exactly the same way he had the woman. He also sliced the man's hamstrings and toppled him screaming to the ground.

The final Blade, with those two extra seconds to realize what was going on, recognized he couldn't win and tried to retreat.

Kilian reached him in a blink and whirled an entire circle around him, steel whipping in a frenzy of cuts that slashed every tendon. The man screamed and fell limp to the ground, unable to move.

Only then did Kilian return to normal speed with a final sliding stride that placed him in front of the fallen woman. She faced him defiantly.

Kilian saluted. "You kids are pretty good. I left you alive because your high lord has brought death to too many of his best followers. Think about which side you really want to be on."

The man gasped, "How did you do that?"

"It's all in knowing how to apply your strength to best effect. Now, if you'll excuse me."

He left them open-mouthed, and marched toward Dougal, who was staggering back to his feet, gaping at his abruptly defeated champions.

Kilian said, "I think perhaps now you're finally beginning to understand your folly."

Ivor drew closer as Dougal faced Kilian with hatred burning in his gaze and spat, "Your problem is that you never think ahead."

"And your problem is you're about to die."

Dougal chuckled and pointed his sword north. "Did you forget about precious Mattias? Are you ready to sentence him to death too?"

Connor and Verena were approaching from that direction, with Mattias encased in ice sliding right behind. Ivor should have known Dougal would try a final bid for freedom.

When the trio arrived, Connor glared at Dougal. "Aren't you dead yet?"

Kilian said, "I figured you'd want to be here for the big moment."

Dougal frowned at them. "You're all fools. You stand here celebrating the chaos you've unleashed upon our homes."

"Not the way we see it," Kilian said.

Verena said, "Release Mattias and we might let you return to your army to die with them."

Dougal gave her a disgusted look. "Oh, no. I make the terms. You will cede to my demand, or your beloved Mattias dies in front of your eyes."

"What do you want, Dougal?" Kilian asked with a tired sigh.

Ivor couldn't imagine they'd reach an accord, but maybe they could use the time they wasted arguing about it to figure out how to free Mattias.

Dougal gave Kilian a victorious smile. "I want nothing."

EVEN EVIL PSYCHOPATHS LOVE SOMEONE

Connor glared at Dougal. He was one of the few people Connor truly hated. Dougal's thirst for vengeance and ambition had twisted him into a monster. How many thousands of lives had been destroyed, how many families shattered all to feed his selfish goals?

"What do you mean, nothing?" Connor demanded.

"I want you to do nothing more in Obrion. Leave. All of you. Take all Grandurian forces with you."

"We won't surrender to you," Verena hissed.

"I'm not asking for surrender, Builder." He infused his voice with such disgust, Connor longed to punch him back to Donleavy. "You've invaded my home and corrupted many of my best people. You've done enough damage. Leave now and I'll let you go in peace. Try me. Release your precious friend from the ice. He is yours to take home, as long as you leave now."

Connor slid Mattias around until he stood a little behind and to the side of Dougal, then drained the water away. Mattias did not lunge, but dropped to his knees, completely docile.

"Rory won't go, nor will the troops loyal to him," Connor said.

"Ah, those traitors are a different matter. They must stay and pay the price for their insurrection, but that's none of your business."

"The future of this nation is our business," Kilian said evenly.

"So stay and fight, but Mattias dies." Dougal pointed at Mattias, who was staring at Verena with pitiful, imploring eyes.

"Please, Verena. Please save me. Don't let me die like this," he begged.

Verena looked horrified by the choice they faced. The three of them could kill Dougal for sure, but could they do it fast enough to prevent him from killing Mattias too?

Connor tapped chert and focused on Mattias. He sensed two different pulses of emotion from him, one calm and calculating, the other enraged. He heard two different streams of thought.

One, clearly Dougal's, was whispering, *Beg for your life. Make that vile Builder suffer for you. The sentimental fools will play right into my hands.*

Mattias could not deny him. Under the obsidian force of Dougal's will, he maintained his imploring look and begged again, "Verena, if I mean anything to you, please let us just leave."

But in his mind, Mattias was raging. *I'm going to rip out your heart, Dougal! Give me just a second, and I'll kill you!*

Connor wanted to warn Verena that Dougal was making Mattias beg, but he hesitated. She might already see the truth. She knew Mattias, and as much as Connor disliked him, he'd never seen Mattias act the coward in the face of danger. Could he somehow help Mattias escape, use the deception against Dougal?

Options flitted through Connor's mind, but he rejected one after another. Elemental attacks would need a second or two to destroy Dougal. How much time did he need to kill Mattias? The queen had snuffed out Aifric's mind in an eyeblink, but did obsidian mind control work just as fast? He simply didn't know.

Kilian said, "You're clever, Dougal, but you're assuming we believe the life of one man is worth the lives of the thousands we'd be sentencing to death if we left now."

"That depends on how dearly you love the one," Dougal said smugly.

That gave Connor an idea.

He focused limestone, gave the light a wrenching turn, and tapped serpentinite at the same time. Then he pointed toward the river. "Some are more dear than others."

The waters of the river bubbled, and a motionless body floated to the top, then slid to the shore. It approached over a thin coating of water, limbs lifeless, skin cold and blue, eyes staring. The waters bubbled softly over the paving stones.

Shona was clearly dead.

The mirage was so lifelike, so exquisitely perfect that for a second, Connor nearly believed it. The sight of Shona lying cold and dead on the ground shocked him to the core.

It shocked Dougal more. He gasped and screamed, "Shona!"

Mattias blinked and swayed where he knelt. Then his eyes focused on Dougal and a knife appeared in his hand. He lunged with startling speed even as Dougal swung toward Connor, sword sweeping up, murder in his eyes.

Mattias struck first, his knife plunging into Dougal's back. Dougal gasped, and Mattias collapsed, grabbing at his head.

Verena struck half a heartbeat later. She threw the knife she'd held close to her side. It plunged into Dougal's eye.

Kilian reached him at about the same time and punched him in the center of the chest. Dougal exploded. His body ruptured, spraying blood and gore and flesh back across the snowy ground. He simply ceased to exist.

Diorite was a really fast, but really gruesome death.

Mattias convulsed on the ground, oblivious that the man who had held him prisoner was gone. His hands and feet twitched, head rattling against the earth. His eyes stared blindly up at the sky, mouth wide in a silent scream.

Verena dropped to her knees beside him, clutching his head. "Mattias! Mattias, are you all right?"

He kept convulsing.

Connor crouched on his other side and tapped the sandstone pendant, then directed the healing power into Mattias's head. At the same time, he tapped chert and focused on Mattias's mind.

It was broken. Not a vacant, blasted crater like Aifric after the queen struck her down, but shattered like a glass vase dropped onto a stone floor.

Connor recoiled and met Verena's eyes. He couldn't keep the horror of what he found in there from his expression.

"Oh, no. Not like this," she moaned, tears flowing down her cheeks.

Mattias mumbled as he twitched, and Connor focused on his fractured mind, clinging to the hope that he might find some unbroken core still intact that he could attempt to rebuild.

He found only one coherent thought. As soon as he touched it, Mattias shouted the words. "I killed Dougal. Verena, I killed Dougal for you."

Verena smiled sadly down at him, her right hand pressed to his cheek and said softly, "You should have let us deal with it, you big idiot. We could have saved you." She looked at Connor again. "Please, don't let him die like this. Help him."

He couldn't speak the words to describe the utter destruction he felt in there. He also couldn't deny Verena. He again bent his will to Mattias. Maybe it wasn't as bad as he first feared.

It was worse.

Dougal hadn't killed Mattias outright, but the damage was so severe, the broken pieces of his mind were collapsing, his bodily functions shutting down. Connor tried seizing those pieces with sandstone, tried fusing them together with chert like he had with Aifric, but he didn't understand what he was doing and he couldn't stem the tide.

Eight seconds later, Mattias convulsed violently, then lay still.

"Connor?" Verena asked in a soft, fearful voice. She looked like she understood what had happened, but didn't want to believe it.

Connor didn't want to say it either. He had felt Mattias slip away, had been linked to those broken shards of his mind when they faded. For a second, he'd felt something stir, and he decided that must have been

Mattias's spirit departing. Feeling death so intimately shook him, and he felt crushed by grief.

He forced himself to meet Verena's gaze and said softly, "I'm so sorry. He's gone."

Her anguish turned to anger and she shouted, "Why didn't he run? Why didn't you do something else? We could have saved him!"

The words cut him deeply, but not as much as the anger in her teary eyes. He couldn't bear it. "I was trying to distract Dougal. I'm sorry. I—"

"You never think, Connor! Do you suppose you can make things up at the last second and everything will just work out? You can't play with lives like that!"

Connor recoiled from her anger, all of his fears of maybe losing Verena thundering back into him. Part of him wanted to defend himself, to point out that he'd freed Mattias, but Mattias had attacked and drew Dougal's attention again. He could hurt her as much as she was hurting him.

No, that was the last thing he wanted. That's what they'd done at Altkalen and they'd nearly wrecked their future.

"Verena—"

"You wanted him to die, didn't you?" she shrieked.

"Of course not. You know me better than that." Connor felt only grief for Mattias. He'd been mostly a good person, and in time he would have probably accepted Verena's choice. He'd died helping them strike down High Lord Dougal. Maybe he could have chosen a different course, but at least he would be remembered as a hero.

Tears coursed down her cheeks, but he held her gaze and tapped chert. The link snapped into place far stronger than he expected. He felt her anger and her overwhelming grief, understood in a heartbeat that she was only lashing out because she didn't want to accept the facts.

His thoughts also touched her. He could see it in the look of surprise on her face that broke her anger.

"Oh, Connor. I'm so sorry," she sobbed, flinging herself into his arms.

He dropped chert, not wanting her to think he was trying to influence her, or spy on her. He held her as she sobbed and simply focused on comforting her. She'd lost a dear friend.

But they'd finally killed High Lord Dougal.

That thought helped turn his own grief. Losing Mattias was a high price to pay for that victory, but it was still a great victory.

Kilian placed a comforting hand on Verena's shoulder. "Do not lay blame on anyone but Dougal. We lack time to properly grieve Mattias now. Connor, you and I must return to finish Harley."

"But she's dead. I defeated her," Connor protested.

Ivor said, "She broke free somehow. Hamish sent word. I thought he broadcast that to everyone."

Connor exchanged a surprised look with Verena, suddenly terrified anew. He couldn't imagine how she could have escaped. He'd been convinced she was finally dead. Hamish was in terrible danger, and it was Connor's fault.

Verena said, "We were kind of busy, but how did we miss that?"

"It doesn't matter," Kilian said. "Hamish and Ilse need our help. Ivor, take Verena with you. Support Rory's efforts. Connor and I will deal with Harley."

Ivor nodded. "Come on, Verena. We have an entire army to deal with still."

She straightened and nodded, sniffling back tears. She kissed Connor briefly, fiercely. "I'm sorry, Connor. Be safe and kill that woman."

"I swear it. We'll both be fine, remember?"

She smiled through her tears and jogged off with Ivor.

Kilian turned toward the bridge and the far bank. "Focus, Connor. Hamish and Ilse are in mortal danger. Pray we're not too late."

Connor had spent much of the energy he'd stolen from the people of Merkland, but he swore that he still had enough to finally destroy that cursed woman.

He would not allow Harley to kill another friend.

"Let's kill her this time," he said.

Together they blasted off the ground, driven into the air by white-hot fire.

JUST WHEN YOU THOUGHT YOU KNEW WHAT SHONA WAS GOING TO DO NEXT . .

S peak to me," Shona demanded.

She stood just forward of the mid-point of her army, surrounded by her personal guard and by seven high officers, responsible for coordinating the entire mighty host.

Her Pathfinder commander, a severe woman with piercing gray eyes named Bethia said, "Three thousand troops, including a large percentage of our remaining tertiaries broke off from the main army and are moving against Merkland under the command of Captain Aonghus, as planned."

As if anything was going according to plan. That force would supposedly circle around whatever fighting Harley was doing and take the city. Reports were confused as to what exactly Harley was doing, or what had happened to Shona's father and the force he'd led across the river.

That left her to deal with the surprise attack that seemed to be devastating their rear and flanks.

"Does no one have a clear idea what is going on?" she demanded. Every report they received seemed to contradict the last.

Some claimed only a small army of Boulders and support troops had driven deep into the left flank. Others reported the river bursting its banks and swallowing thousands of troops, despite everything the Spitters tried to do to stop it. Still others reported hundreds of troops surrendering and Builder mechanicals exploding through the ranks of the army.

Those were the ones that almost made sense. Others suggested the Blood of the Tallan was leading the charge, and that Connor was somehow a woman. According to Bethia, many officers had defected to Rory or were ordering surrender. It didn't make any sense. The army had seemed so strong, so united. She'd never seen such a cohesion of purpose.

As her commanders began arguing about the conflicting reports, she waved them to silence. "That's all useless. We'll have to go find out for ourselves."

Shona headed south, with all of her senior commanders and a protective detail of Blades and Boulders in tow.

"All captains report to me directly. No orders are to be given except face to face. Relay those commands individually to every officer you can contact," she ordered.

Her Strider commander grimaced. "That'll take precious time, my lady."

"Do it. Our communication lines are suspect. I need order, commander."

He rushed off with his Strider corps and Shona pressed through the ranks of soldiers, peering south through the storm, trying to understand her enemy.

Commander Bethia suddenly pulled her to a halt. "Lady Shona, I just received a report from a captain across the river. The incursion force there is falling back. They suffered major casualties." She hesitated, her face turning as pale as the still-blowing snow. She added in a voice that trembled with shock. "They report your father fell in battle against Kilian and the Blood of the Tallan."

Shona had thought herself well-prepared for that eventuality, but the news seemed to punch her right in the heart. Tears welled in her eyes, but she fought them back. She'd known he might die. Despite the queen's secret gift, the in-person confrontation was fraught with danger.

"Do you believe the report?" she demanded, barely daring to breathe as she held onto the hope that they were receiving yet another bogus report.

Bethia nodded. "Nothing seems sure tonight, but I know the Pathfinder who called in that report. I believe it."

So her father was dead. Probably.

The news was like a crushing weight on her mind. She suddenly felt like her entire world had shifted subtly, the solid foundation of her life now gone, leaving her feeling exposed and vulnerable. She drew in a long, shuddering breath and closed her eyes for a moment, shutting out the chaos of sound echoing from the battlefield to the south. Her father was dead.

She no longer had parents to guide her, to tell her what to do. But she was the high lady of her father's realm and rightful ruler of Merkland. Everyone in the army depended upon her for direction and survival. She now needed to decide the fate of so many lives, and the course of her own future. The weight of responsibility settled on her shoulders like a heavy, mail coat.

She'd wielded power and authority all her life, had trained for years for this moment. She would not fail, would not show weakness.

Shona opened her eyes and said, "Keep me informed of progress on all fronts."

"Yes, ma'am." Bethia saluted with new respect.

"Can no one push this storm back so I can see?" she demanded, glancing back at her Spitter captain, a long-time veteran who had spent too much time in his office in recent years. His large belly and long white beard gave him a jolly look most of the time, but at the moment he looked rattled.

"We can't, my lady. There's too many conflicting fingers in the air, so to speak. Besides, we're too focused on trying to block whoever's controlling the river."

"I bet it's Ivor," she muttered. That made the Spitter captain look even more nervous. Well, knowing the truth, however difficult, was better than guessing.

She hated that she had to guess about everything else, but tried to apply what she knew. If both Connor and Kilian were spotted fighting her father, who then was attacking their rear?

After pushing through another column of heavily-armed regulars, Shona finally drew close to the heart of the fighting. Hundreds of Boulders were locked in furious battle across the road. The snow had been trampled to mud, and all the combatants were covered with it. She couldn't tell who was who, and wondered if they could.

Probably not. Not that Boulders would let that trouble them much. They were enjoying one of the best bash fights she'd ever seen, and the granite part of her yearned to leap into the middle of the fray and pit her strength against all others.

As she drew closer, followed by her high commanders, a pair of Boulders bashed through a line of fighters and trotted in her direction.

Even beneath the layer of mud and grime, she immediately recognized them.

Tomas and Cameron.

The sight of them gave her pause. This really was a pitched battle between Rory's revolutionary forces and her army. That was an annoying thought. They should all be her army.

Her Sentry and Firetongue commanders stepped in front of her, but she waved them back. "I'll deal with this."

Tomas and Cameron trotted up to Shona and saluted together. "Beggin' your pardon, my lady, but seeing as you haven't surrendered yet, we'll have to shackle you now."

"You insolent dogs," the Firetongue exclaimed, crimson flames erupting around his hands.

"I told you to stand down," Shona snapped. She faced the two Fast Rollers who she knew so well, and couldn't suppress a smile at their boldness. They also offered possibly the best opportunity to put an end to the chaos and resolve this mess.

She spoke with all her regal authority. "Shackles will not be needed. Take me to General Rory."

Tomas sighed. "That opportunity was just too good to come true, I guess."

Cameron agreed. "You'd think revolution would make things simpler, not more confusing."

Bethia said, "My lady, what are you thinking?"

"I'm thinking it's time to stop this foolishness before it goes too far."

"Shall we send in reinforcements?" the Firetongue asked, gesturing at the nearby fighting.

"Don't bother. No one's had this good a bash fight in years. Let them have it. Wait here and try to keep anyone from doing anything too stupid. I'll return shortly."

Then Shona urged Tomas and Cameron toward the line of fighting. "Stop dawdling. I need to speak with Rory immediately. Haven't you noticed there's a battle on?"

"Of course we have. We started it," Tomas said proudly.

"Well I'm going to finish it."

Cameron grunted. "Leave it to Lady Shona to take all the credit for all our hard work."

FREAKY BABY DEMON CHILD OF DOOM

As Connor shot across the river toward where he'd left Harley imprisoned in that burning ice tomb, he rose high enough to see Merkland atop the bluff. He noticed several things at once. First, a large force of several thousand soldiers from Dougal's army was charging the Army Gate.

Second, the gate was open. Third, the entire western half of the city was overrun by intense fighting. Fourth, the groups fighting in the city were all revolutionary forces.

Someone had betrayed the revolution. Merkland was heavily embattled, and could be overrun. The thought infuriated Connor. He hadn't worked so hard to save the city for someone to waste all those lives through some secret plot. He'd find out who was responsible, and maybe he'd let the rampager out to deal with them.

But as Connor descended toward where he'd left Hamish, suddenly none of that mattered. He spotted Ilse first. She was lying prone, one hundred feet in the air, beating futilely against the unyielding air that held her prisoner.

Hamish's Juggernaut was pinned in place by the enormous, snakelike mini-elfonnel. The summoned monster held the giant armored sphere in its jaws, and some of the outer plates had crumpled under the pressure.

Harley had just reached the Juggernaut, but Connor frowned as he studied her with Pathfinder eyes. She looked much smaller, a skeletal figure no bigger than a bald youth. She wore only a concealing layer of dark earth. She crouched over a steel plate and heaved, straining mightily for three seconds before ripping it free. She tossed it aside, then crouched and stepped inside.

Connor's pulse raced with fear and he tried to accelerate. He wouldn't arrive for three or four more seconds, though. She could rip out Hamish's heart as easily as she had ripped off that steel plate long before Connor could help.

He twisted the mini-hub to Hamish's speakstone and shouted, "Hamish, are you alive?"

The top plate of the Juggernaut burst free with a gush of air and Hamish erupted up through the gap, every one of his thrusters firing at max power.

Harley's bellowed curse chased him into the sky, and the mini-elfonnel released the Juggernaut, turning to follow.

"Stay back!" Hamish shouted over the speakstone.

The Juggernaut suddenly glowed with white-gold lightning, then every plate burst free, releasing an enormous firebomb. The mini-elfonnel shredded under the onslaught of steel, quickened granite, and incandescent fire. The thunderclap shook the air, knocking snow sideways for a couple seconds, and sent Connor tumbling backward before he could tap quartzite and split the blast around himself.

Kilian passed him in that second, plunging into the firestorm. Connor seized some of the flames and pulled against them to slingshot himself after Kilian. Together they landed in the blasted crater where the Juggernaut had stood.

Harley was gone.

Connor muttered a curse, then coughed at the acrid smoke hanging thick over the crater. Kilian swept it aside under a spray of billowing mist while Connor tapped granite, questing into the ground for Harley.

He heard her before he felt her. The high-pitched scream, sounding like a child's shriek, began wailing from about thirty yards away.

"That doesn't sound like Harley," Kilian muttered, rising again on a pillar of fire to see better.

Connor followed, and grimaced at the sight. Harley's youth-sized body lay on the ground, broken and blackened, its chest a gaping hole, its sightless eyes filled with black earth. The limbs and visible skin was all smoking, and looked to be melting into a puddle of sludge.

Hamish swooped down to hover nearby, carrying Ilse in his arms. She looked exhausted, but still glared with undying hatred at Harley. Hamish pushed up his visor, looking disgusted but satisfied by the gruesome sight. "Those Althins make the best acid ever."

A hideous creature, about the size of Nicklaus, was wailing as it crawled off the other corpse and grasped at the clean earth. Its torso was roughly rectangular, pocked with oozing blisters, with eight short tentacles sprouting from the perimeter. The head looked like a squashed rock, with only one narrow eye that Connor could see, and a round mouth, full of sharp teeth.

It glanced back at them and hissed. Amazingly, Harley's voice, sounding weak and faint, emanated from the disgusting thing.

"No more restraint. You all die now."

"Is that really Harley?" Connor asked, feeling like he might puke.

"What's left of her," Kilian said with a grimace.

Hamish said, "I hate that woman, but what is she?"

Connor felt overwhelming relief to see Hamish apparently unhurt. It seemed impossible that he'd survived a head-on clash with Harley, even after all Connor had done to injure her before.

Kilian regarded the freakish Harley-child with disgust. "She was the first Healer and rivaled my mother for pure healing talent. She lacks access to all the healing power my mother can tap, but she made up for it with raw determination to stay alive. As you can see, she's discovered a way to abandon her body, distilling her essence into a smaller core that's easier to regenerate, but every time she does it, she loses more of her humanity."

"You mean she can heal that thing?" Hamish asked.

"If we gave her enough time."

Just then, Connor felt Harley's will slam down into the earth beneath that thing. She was trying to reach the deeper earth, probably trying to trigger a catastrophe similar to what she and Evander had done at the Carraig.

"Oh no you don't," Connor said.

He yanked on all four elements, mixed them together, and flung out a whiplike rope of intertwined elements. It struck the child monster, yanking her off the ground and severing her connection. He dared to hope he'd blocked her in time.

Harley's eyes began glowing with inner fires, one red and the other green. Connor wasn't sure what that meant, but he wasn't about to let her reach the ground again. She opened her mouth wide and screamed inhuman fury at them.

Air whistled around her, a whirlwind that held her aloft and rotated her to face them from fifty feet away. She spoke, and her voice was surprisingly human, her tone calm and conciliatory. "You've again impressed me with your bravery and relentless determination, Connor. I cede the fight and will return to my queen with news of your worthiness."

Kilian laughed, but the sound held no humor.

Connor didn't doubt for a second that she was lying. He would never trust her to reach the ground again, and he definitely didn't want her anywhere near the queen, who could probably heal her a lot faster.

So he said, "Good-bye, Harley."

She shrieked again and dove toward the ground, propelled by her whirlwind.

Kilian intercepted her with a column of fire that roared up out of the ground directly below her, driving her screaming back into the air, her little tentacles whipping around in fury.

Connor coiled the rope of mixed elements, and as her tumbling spin brought her around to face him, their eyes locked and he read undying hatred in her gaze. He drove his mixed elements right down her throat, shoving it in with all the energy he'd siphoned from the people of Merkland. Her body convulsed as he filled it with elemental fury. It swelled, as if about to explode.

Connor hardened all the water inside of her, including her own blood, to ice.

Her little body swelled even more, and Kilian wrapped her in a cocoon of mixed water and fire. Then he shot across the distance, propelled by a blue-white mixture of superheated flames and ice.

Somehow she must have sensed him coming because the wind whistling around her carried a whisper-thin plea. "Kilian, show mercy. After all these years—"

He reached her and struck with an explosion of elemental might and diorite fury.

For a second, Connor lost sight of Harley in the smoke and fire and haze. He dropped to the ground and quested for her, but sensed nothing.

The smoke cleared and Kilian stood alone on the blackened ground. He didn't look exultant, though, but was pacing around, hand raised with fire crackling around his fingers, his eyes studying the ground.

"She couldn't have survived that!" Hamish shouted.

"I won't believe she's dead until I see her burned to powder," Connor said.

"Finally, you say something smart," Hamish said in an attempt at humor, but he was right. Connor should have dealt with her and sent Hamish to save Verena.

Then he felt her. She was small, barely the size of a child, slipping fast through the earth toward the south.

"She's trying to flee," he shouted, turning in that direction and grabbing for her with earth. He snarled with frustration when she slipped through his elemental fingers. She'd been wounded enough to kill dozens of Petralists, but somehow she was still stronger than Connor in the earth.

"Can you get her?" Hamish asked eagerly. Kilian was already rocketing south, driven by white-hot flames. Maybe he could catch her if Connor could ever force her back to the surface.

He tried again, but couldn't quite hold onto her. "No!" he cried, banging his fist into the earth. She was already over a hundred yards away, accelerating fast.

Connor refused to give up. He quested after her a third time, pouring all his determination, all the energy he could summon into the effort to break through her shielding and grab her for just a second. He felt her, ringed her with his power, but still felt her sliding through.

Then she jarred to a stop. For a second, Connor felt an invisible wall in front of her. He had no idea where that came from, hadn't thought Ilse was well enough to lend a hand, but he wasn't about to waste that precious chance.

In that second, he could grasp her.

He ripped her out of the earth.

What remained of Harley burst into the air and soared up to twenty feet. She was a baby-sized . . . something. The creature looked even less human than the freaky tentacled shape that Kilian blew up. Now she was little more than an oblong mass that oozed blood and puss through its black skin. She lacked arms and legs, but did have a flat, fishlike head. A rank stench drifted to Connor, making him gag. It stunk like an open sewer full of dead skunks.

Was that really Harley? Could she really be considered alive? Could she actually try healing herself after falling so far from humanity?

He wasn't about to give her the chance to try.

"You should have kept sleeping," Connor said, propelling himself toward her along the ground with slate. Kilian closed on her, flames already building for yet another strike. Connor had to wonder how many times they'd have to kill her. How much smaller could she go before turning into a puddle of goo and ceasing to exist?

The creature's fishy eyes still burned red and green, and its little mouth opened, revealing pointy teeth. It spun in the air at the apex of its arc to face Connor.

It laughed, and the sound that bellowed forth had lost none of Harley's potency. The evil chuckle-thunder boomed across the valley.

"You're all going to die, fools! I'll regenerate and return stronger than ever, but you'll spend the time grieving the idiots who believed you could save them."

Then Harley-demon-baby abruptly stopped laughing and looked down, shock on her hideous face. The ground beneath her erupted and a giant figure burst into view, aimed straight at her.

Evander.

His massive hands were clenched tight together, enormous arms quivering with strain. He held light between his hands, so condensed and so bright that it shone right through his skin, illuminating the bones with blinding intensity.

He released it, and the slender blade of light shot up so fast and so bright, it left an after-image hovering in Connor's eyes for several seconds. The golden blade of light sheared right through Harley, cutting her completely in half. Without slowing, the light shot into the gray sky and looked like it would continue up until it struck a star.

The two pieces of Harley-demon-child rolled in the air, held aloft by an invisible hand of wind. Evander pointed at them and said, "Connor, Uncle, incinerate them, please."

Kilian seized one of the pieces and surrounded it with white-hot fire, lifting it higher and burning it.

Connor grabbed the other. He saw no blood, but wasn't sure if that intense beam of light had cauterized the wounds it made, or if Harley was somehow trying to heal again. He wasn't about to give her the chance to try.

So he wrapped that broken monster body with superheated flames. He poured in even more heat and drove dozens of spears of white-hot fire through the globe of death-flames, piercing her half-corpse again and again. Kilian did the same on the other side.

Twenty seconds later, all that remained was a pile of ash.

Evander accepted the ash from both of them, holding it in his huge hands. He regarded it solemnly for a moment before the earth under his feet shook and formed into a roughly-humanoid figure with huge hands.

For a second, Connor worried Harley might have somehow returned, but Evander did not look worried. He carefully passed the ash to his construct and it turned and trotted to the nearby river. It leaped impossibly high and plunged into the waters, carrying the ashes with it.

Kilian blew out a breath and clapped Evander on one leather-clad shoulder. "Late, as always, but that was one impressive entrance."

Connor exchanged a happy look with Hamish, who laughed with relief. He looked exhausted. "I'm so glad that old hag is gone forever."

Ilse hugged Hamish, then glanced back toward Lukas's body. With tears glinting in her eyes she said, "Thank you, Hamish. Thank you, Connor. Thank you, Kilian. We've avenged my love. He can rest in peace."

Connor joined them. "Are you in pain?"

"I am stable. I fear you won't be able to do any more for me. Focus on the things you can do."

Her bravery inspired him. "I'll check on your injuries soon anyway."

Then he turned to Evander. "I'm glad you came."

Evander shrugged. "The fury of a woman scorned eclipses the sun, but companions of fools suffer the greater harm."

Connor laughed, feeling his tension drain away. "Evander, I never thought I'd be happy to say this, but I don't understand."

Hamish suddenly pointed to the west and shouted. "Hey, that's Jean! Where is she leading all those soldiers?"

99

ANYTHING CAN BE STOLEN

Verena barely paid attention to the shouting soldiers, the clashing of weapons, and the tumult and noise accompanying the bash fight. She walked with Ivor, who guided her with a hand on her shoulder.

Mattias was dead. That fact shook her so deep, she found it hard to breathe. Tears threatened to burst free again, but she fought them back. She couldn't afford to lash out blindly at anyone again. The memory of Connor's shocked, hurt expression haunted her.

She felt horrible that she'd reacted that way. Sure, she was shocked and grieving, but that was no excuse. She felt so grateful they'd cleared that up immediately. She couldn't risk losing Connor too.

Mattias was dead, Dougal's final casualty. Mattias had been a major part of her life. Even now when she no longer thought of him as her potential husband, she loved him dearly and his death left a gaping hole in her heart.

What would Saskia say? She cringed, terrified of the moment she'd have to face Saskia and try to explain. If not for Verena, Mattias wouldn't have come, wouldn't have died.

If only she'd moved faster, sooner. She had to believe her blade had killed Dougal even before Kilian struck. She'd avenged Mattias even before his heart stopped beating, but why couldn't she have struck a heartbeat sooner?

Ivor's voice shook her out of her misery. "Rory, how's the fighting?"

"Never better," Rory boomed with such enthusiasm that Verena looked around and tried to figure out where they were.

Rory was battered, his battle leathers shredded and torn, his granite-hardened muscles gleaming through the rents. He was covered in mud, but grinning like a far younger man.

Anika stood at his shoulder, her long braid muddy and half undone, her armor also battered, but smiling just as wide.

The nearby line of muddy bash fighters, barely fifty yards to the north, looked like they were having the time of their lives. They pummeled and pounded against a roughly equal number of opponents, although Verena struggled to distinguish friend from foe. The bulk of Dougal's army had drawn back from the furious bash fight and seemed content to let it run its course.

They might have to set up tents if they planned to wait that long.

The snow had slackened to gentle sheets that no longer obscured the landscape. The sky was still a solid gray blanket, but it seemed lighter than before. Verena could see thousands of enemy troops, poised to descend upon them when the order was given. Most of them were assembled in long ranks on the western side of the battlefield, farther from the river. The entire eastern flank was gone, flooded under, a testament to Ivor's effectiveness.

"Verena, what are you doing here?" Rory asked, clearly surprised to see her. "What happened?"

She tried to say, "Mattias is dead," but choked on his name, and fresh tears flowed. Anika rushed to her side and held her as she sobbed again, hating her weakness, but unable to stop herself from crying.

Ivor briefly filled them in.

Rory's expression turned grim. "Battle is an ugly business, Lady Verena. I'm sorry. Mattias was an honorable man, but this day isn't over."

Ivor started to speak, but then exclaimed, "Shona?"

Verena blinked away her tears as Shona marched up to them, flanked by Tomas and Cameron, both filthy and grinning from the fighting. She did not look like a prisoner.

The sight of her ignited Verena's rage. Dougal had killed Mattias. Shona was his wicked daughter. She'd plotted for so long to destroy Verena and enslave Connor.

As if moving with a will of its own, her hand flashed to the last of her throwing daggers and flung it. The little knife leaped from her hand and buried itself in Shona's leather armor.

Unfortunately, Shona must have been tapping at least a little granite because it stopped without sinking deep. Shona yanked it free and glared at Verena.

"You've grown ruder than ever, wench."

Verena reached for her sword, but Ivor grabbed her arm. "Don't. Let's find out why she's here first."

"I'm here to stop the fighting," Shona declared.

Rory chuckled. "Are you saying you wish to surrender your army, Lady Shona?"

"It's High Lady Shona now. My father is dead."

"You bet he is. I killed him," Verena declared.

Shona regarded her with open scorn. "I heard Kilian and Connor defeated him." She looked sad, but not heartbroken. As if the cold-hearted viper had a heart.

"They were there, but my dagger took him first."

"One more reason I'll enjoy crushing your skull, but all in good time."

"Oh, you're actually going to fight me, not send an assassin to smother me in my sleep?" Verena demanded. She'd received reports of the interrogation of Abigail the false Healer. The woman had confessed to taking a substantial payment from Dougal to ensure Verena never woke up.

Shona made a dismissive gesture. "I knew an attempt would be made. It seemed a valid strategy at the time, but today is a day of change. Don't live in the past."

Verena made a beckoning gesture, filled with an overwhelming urge to wipe that self-assured smirk off of Shona's hated face. She didn't have many stones, but she'd figure something out. "How about we focus on the here and now? Given the circumstances, I can't think of a better place for you to die."

"I don't have time to waste on petty squabbles," Shona said. Then she turned away from Verena to face Rory. "The army is mine, general, as are these lands."

Verena clenched her fists, filled with rage. How dare that murdering vixen dare dismiss her? She reached for another knife, but Ivor grabbed her hand.

When she turned her angry gaze on him, he shook his head slightly and said in a whisper, "Calm, Verena. We need peace now. There will be time to settle scores later."

The fact that he was right only irritated her more, but she drew upon her years of training in the Grandurian court to school her features and settle her breathing. She would deal with Shona soon enough.

Rory was saying, "I cannot abandon our cause, Lady Shona."

"You've done well for yourself today, Rory. I have to believe that between them, Connor and Kilian will defeat Harley, which would leave me alone in charge. We can stop the fighting on my command."

"Why would you choose to do that?" Verena asked suspiciously.

"Because today is a day of choices. Today I choose to end this battle and join your cause. Obrion must be free, and if I don't see to it, I doubt it'll be done right."

Verena gaped, momentarily speechless. The others looked equally surprised.

Shona added, "I will join you. I will stop the fighting. I will bring victory to our cause. I have one condition, however, and you must all agree to it now, in advance."

"What condition?" Verena demanded. That was the Shona she knew and hated. Shona would never make such a bold and dangerous move without seeing benefit for herself, although Verena couldn't imagine what

Shona might think they'd give her that would be worth risking the queen's wrath.

Then she did.

"Oh, no," she said between clenched teeth. "You don't get blanket terms like that."

Shona had tried everything to win Connor back, but Verena had never imagined she'd attempt something this daring. Was she really so arrogant she thought it would work?

Shona sniffed. "You do not speak for the revolution, witch. What do you say, generals? Rory, Ivor, you have accomplished great things today, but two-thirds of my army yet remains and as we speak, my vanguard is taking Merkland. My condition is simple. I require only that you accept me as a full partner, a commanding general of the revolution."

Verena blinked in surprise. She scarce believed Shona wasn't demanding Connor swear fealty to her again.

Rory looked equally surprised, but Ivor started to laugh. He clapped a couple of times and took Shona's hands in his. "This revolution just got very interesting. Welcome aboard, Shona."

Rory chuckled. "How can I refuse partnership with our own high lady?"

"And of course, you'll recognize my claim to my realm and this city."

"Let's discuss that once we salvage the city," Rory said, once more serious.

Shona extended a hand and Rory took it with a rueful grin. "I can't say I ever imagined you'd join us, but I'm grateful you have, Lady Shona. I'm proud of you."

She gave him a dazzling smile, as if his words actually mattered to her. And then, incredibly, she began to glow.

Rory looked stunned and Ivor exclaimed, "When did you achieve a secondary affinity?"

"Recently. Do you like it?"

"It fits you perfectly," Rory said with a straight face.

Shona's glow brightened, no doubt fueled by their fawning approval. It made Verena seethe with renewed fury. She thought they all hated Shona, but she was worming her way back into their affections with that unmatched deftness that had twisted Connor's heart into knots so many times.

If Shona ever tried to leverage her newfound position of authority within the revolution to make another play for Connor, Verena would kill her, no matter what anyone said.

Shona declared, "Win or lose, this land no longer belongs to my father. Come, I'll need an escort to speak with the rest of my army."

Tomas whistled softly and shook his head with admiration. "Doesn't that beat all? She just stole our whole revolution."

"And Rory locked the gates behind us and everything," Cameron agreed.

100

LADY JEAN

Jean ran toward Merkland with over three hundred soldiers at her heels. Her heart raced with nervous excitement. She barely believed she could really be in this situation. Everything happened so fast.

They'd passed the broken ground near the bridge, covered in shattered pieces of speedcaravan ramp and seething with raging elements. That had to be where they were fighting Harley.

Jean longed to lead her troops there to give battle to the dread Petralist, but she couldn't throw away so many lives. She forced herself to trust Hamish and trust that Connor and Kilian and Ilse and Verena could keep each other safe. She couldn't really do anything to help them.

But she could help save Merkland.

One of her Pathfinders had reported that somehow the Army Gate was open and intense fighting was raging all around it and into the city. She didn't understand how the enemy could have breached the city, unless the people in there hadn't recovered from the porphyry bomb. They needed help, and she was the only one positioned to offer it.

As they raced up the curved road around the city, with the towering white walls of Merkland soaring high above, she finally caught sight of the gate. It was indeed open, and thousands of soldiers were pushing their way inside. Screaming and clashing of arms rang through the still air.

"What are your orders, Commander?" her caller asked.

"We liberate the city, of course."

"I thought that was our original orders."

"Same orders then, just liberating from a different group." She gave him an encouraging smile. "Let's just fight that group at the gate and sort everything else out after we've won, all right?"

"As you say, Lady Jean," he said, looking a bit confused, but willing to accept her orders. He bellowed, "Charge!"

The army accelerated, weapons at the ready, Striders racing around the flanks, and Boulders swelling with granite power. Her few tertiaries prepared their elemental attacks.

Only then did Jean realize she might not want to be running right in front of them. As the army accelerated, a wall of steel and affinity stone, she had to run faster to keep from getting trampled.

That meant she'd be the first to crash into the enemy soldiers. They had seen her little army, and the rear guard was turning to face them.

Jean was about to run right into the middle of a pitched battle, and she'd used up most of her weapons. She couldn't show cowardice or the entire charge might falter. So she reached into one of her pockets and drew forth her last mechanical and her keystone.

Her caller shouted a battle cry, and her troops took up the cry. It rose into the air and thundered through her, filling her with wild elation and a notable lack of common sense.

"For Lady Jean!"

Jean sprinted up the road, hand raised high, shouting with her troops, and led the charge.

Fire and water began whipping back and forth between her troops and the rear guard blocking their path. The ground rumbled dangerously underfoot, but did not suck them down to their deaths. Twenty feet from the wall of armor and sharp steel waiting to rip her to pieces, Jean placed the keystone against the little piece of slate and diorite, twisted it to quicken the mechanical, and tossed it in front of her.

A two-foot speedcrack wall erupted out of the ground. Twelve feet wide, it shot across the distance and smashed into the gathered ranks of soldiers, sweeping aside the first three rows, tumbling screaming soldiers off their feet and into the tight ranks behind them.

Then it exploded.

Jean cringed as the concussion threw soldiers in every direction, knocking weapons flying and shredding armor. She was a Healer, not a warrior. She wasn't supposed to hurt people.

If she didn't, how many thousands more would die?

"Lady Jean!" her troops shouted and surged past her on either side. Her caller swooped her off her feet and she cried out in surprise as he carried her back through the army, which split for her, shouting her name.

She felt immense relief. They weren't forcing her to leap into battle after all. But her brave troops charged ahead and plowed into the ranks of the enemy. The air split with fresh screams, the hard crashing of steel on steel, and the sickening thud of steel rending flesh.

Fighting back tears, Jean forced herself to watch, to encourage her soldiers. She spotted two Healers at the tail end of her company and excitedly waved them over. She hadn't noticed them before, but felt immensely relieved by their presence.

"Make sure all the wounded are brought back here so we can tend them," she ordered her caller, who saluted and rushed into the fray, bellowing orders as he closed on the enemy with his huge sword.

Then strong hands grasped her by the shoulders and lifted her into the air again. This time she soared ten feet up and her cry of alarm faded to a shout of joy as she realized who had taken her.

"Calm down," Hamish shouted. "I'm trying to save you."

She twisted in his grasp and clung to him. She felt an overwhelming sense of relief. "I'm so glad you're all right, but please put me down. I need to lead my army."

"Have you cracked?" He slowed to a hover, looking confused.

"I don't have time to explain. Can't you see the city's been breached? We have to help."

"Fine, but you stay at the rear."

"That's where I was when you arrived," she reminded him, exulting in the joy of knowing he was safe.

He lowered her to the rear of her little force, where the wounded were being dragged. She began extracting her herbs and medicines while her Healers placed hands on the most grievously wounded.

"Do you know what's happening in there?" Jean asked.

He shook his head. "We were busy. Just finished defeating Harley. It was a close thing, but we got her."

"Thank the Tallan. Let's hope we can sort the rest of this battle out soon too."

Connor and Kilian flew overhead, wreathed in fire and ice, and landed atop the wall.

Hamish had also spotted them, and she read the conflict in his eyes. "Go. I'm fine here. You can do more at their side. Just stop the fighting soon."

"Let's hope we don't have to kill a lot of people."

Jean hoped with all her heart that he was right. Far too many had already died.

Hamish shot into the air, aiming for the wall.

Three seconds later, A Firetongue burst out of the melee and rose several feet into the air amid an explosion of orange flames. Soldiers recoiled from him, and Jean recognized him as the wild, flame-haired Captain Aonghus from General Carbrey's army.

He looked furious, and he bellowed, "You fools! We're on the same side. You're interfering with our invasion."

Jean's huge caller stepped to the forefront of the crowd and shouted, "We serve Lady Jean now!"

That started a renewed chant of "Lady Jean!"

Aonghus snarled and made a clutching gesture. Flames appeared around the caller and yanked him into the air. He screamed as blades of fire materialized and slashed at him from every side. Jean felt horrified by the display. Her troops stopped chanting and retreated.

Did Jean have no Firetongue who could stop Aonghus's murdering?

She turned her mini-hub to Hamish's stone, but before she could speak, Captain Aonghus shouted, "There you are, you wicked little imposter!"

"Hamish!" she shouted, suddenly terrified.

Aonghus launched himself over her troops, driven by crackling flames. He swooped toward her, fire billowing from his mouth, his expression completely insane. He laughed maniacally and shouted, "Now you pay the price for everyone's follies, *Lady Jean*!"

Hamish's voice rose from her speakstone. "Run! Jean, I'm coming!"

She glanced up and saw him shooting over the wall, thrusters roaring, aiming for Aonghus's back. The sight of him filled her with joy, but he'd never make it in time.

Jean stepped away from her Healers and the fallen wounded, moving to a clear bit of ground, and turned to face Aonghus. She couldn't outrun him, and she refused to endanger her patients.

She hoped to try speaking with him, but Aonghus formed an enormous spear of white-hot fire and threw it from fifty feet away.

Terrified, Jean screamed and tried to dodge. The spear split into many fiery shards. Those smaller spears plunged into her body, and flames boiled over her.

Intense pain exploded through her as superheated air singed her lungs and turned her world into an inferno. She clenched her eyes against the burning fires. As she fell to the ground, writhing in pain, with horrible crackling and sizzling sounds filling her ears, the clinical part of her tried cataloging all of her injuries.

She couldn't focus on the effort and screamed through the pain. More screaming echoed all around, but she couldn't tell if it was her voice, or others.

Her last thought was that Aonghus had better spare her patients.

Then she fell into blessed oblivion.

101

THE COST OF FREEDOM

Verena insisted on joining Ivor and Rory and their small company as they marched through the center of the fighting to return to Shona's command. She didn't trust Shona farther than the depth of an open grave.

Ivor plowed a path through the fighting with a literal plow made of water. Most of the Boulders he knocked aside didn't stop fighting, but just rolled over each other, still bashing with unbreakable enthusiasm.

Rory shouted, his booming voice piercing the din. "Wrap it up, boys. Bash fight's over in one minute."

The fighters redoubled their efforts.

"Can't we just stop it now?" Verena asked.

"Don't be so mean," Tomas protested.

Cameron nodded vigorously. "You can't go snatching a man's fun right out of his fingers. Change is hard for a lot of people. Gotta give 'em time to get used to the idea of doing something different."

Shona's officers looked eager to fight Rory and Ivor, but Shona said loudly, "Stand down. Order all troops to stop fighting. We've reached an accord."

They looked shocked, but obeyed her. Officers began shouting with Pathfinder-enhanced voices for soldiers to stop fighting, to stand down.

No one believed them.

Shona scowled at Rory. "However you've been managing to confuse everyone, it's backfiring now."

Ivor shrugged. "We weren't sure we'd ever get this far, so it sounded like a good idea at the time."

"Well it's no longer a good idea. Come on. Get me up there so they can see me and know it's me." She gestured into the air.

"But Lady Shona, I thought you didn't like flying," he said with a smile.

"Oh, shut up, Ivor. Help me."

Chuckling, he pulled her close. She wrapped an arm around his broad shoulders. They both looked comfortable in that position, as if they'd flown together before. Ivor threw them both into the air with a burst of flames, then fashioned crimson wings of fire on his back. Holding Shona tight, they glided over the fighting, and Shona began to glow like a golden-haired sun.

Flying on wings of fire with Ivor, the sight was truly breathtaking. Verena hated her all the more for how she could transform herself into the apparent embodiment of all that high ladies were supposed to be. Shona's voice cracked like thunder.

Her Pathfinder commander must have enhanced it. Verena certainly hoped Shona wasn't demonstrating a new tertiary power. She was already far too proud of her limestone secondary affinity. A tertiary would make her absolutely unbearable.

"Stand down. This is High Lady Shona and I order you to stand down. The fighting is over."

Echoes of her words bounced back from the hills but did not die away. Instead they magnified and multiplied until Shona's voice reverberated in every ear and shook the valley.

"Stand down! Stand down!"

The words began to change. Soon Shona's larger-than-life voice was shouting, "How dare you ignore the command of your high lady? Put that man down! You there, don't tempt my wrath. Stand down, oaf!"

Verena giggled and looked around. She didn't spot Student Eighteen, but she recognized her handiwork.

Ivor and Shona swooped back around and landed nearby a moment later as the fighting fell silent. Ivor was laughing, but Shona looked annoyed.

"I do not sound like that," she insisted.

Bethia asked, "That wasn't you, Lady Shona?"

"Of course not."

"I thought you went aloft specifically with that purpose in mind."

"I did, but oh, never mind." She scowled at Ivor. "Stop laughing like a fool. Come on, we have to get to Merkland. The fighting there needs to stop before they destroy my city."

They again shot into the air and swept north.

Verena rushed to Bethia. "I have to go help. I need quartzite."

Bethia glared at her until Rory said, "Go on. Give her what you've got."

She looked annoyed to be taking orders from the commander of what was supposed to be the enemy army, but she produced a pair of quartzite pieces far too small to actually fly with. Verena doubted any other

Pathfinders had larger blocks handy. They only needed small pieces to fit into their cheeks.

"I need a Strider. Get me some basalt in stone form, please," Verena asked Rory. Tomas and Cameron had rushed back into the Great Merkland Bash Fight to enjoy the last minute.

It took a moment, but Rory managed to get someone to find her a couple pieces of non-powdered basalt.

"What are you planning?" Anika asked.

"I'm not about to let that woman get anywhere near Connor without me around to defend him."

She rushed west, beyond the outer fringes of the army, and slid the basalt into loops built into the front of her armored shins. She quickened it, then quickened the quartzite. As air gushed out of the little stones, she leaped.

Verena landed on her knees and accelerated fast, sliding along the quickened basalt, propelled by the quartzite. It wasn't as graceful as flying, but it was nearly as fast as a Strider. The snow helped soften the bumps that would have otherwise made the journey painful.

In seconds, she slid past the huge army, marveling anew at the unexpected twist in the fighting. Shona had sided with them, had saved thousands of lives, and come out in open rebellion against the queen.

Why?

It had to be Connor.

Verena tried to tap more quartzite, and angled back to the road after passing the northern elements of the army. Once she reached firmer surfaces, she accelerated more. She flashed past the next bridge and the shattered battleground where Ilse was sitting awkwardly next a body.

Lukas was dead, and Ilse's hips and legs looked terribly crushed.

Fresh tears stung Verena's eyes. She understood a fraction of Ilse's pain, wanted to rush to her and comfort her, but she had to save Connor. She did turn her mini-hub to Rory's speakstone and passed word for Healers to be dispatched to help Ilse.

As she swept around the curve of the road, she caught sight of the open Army Gate. Soldiers were standing in a loose half-circle, not fighting, all focusing on a small group of people crouched over a blackened patch of ground.

It took a few more seconds for Verena to recognize them, and her heart raced with new fear. Hamish and Connor were crouched over a horribly burned person. Hamish looked devastated, weeping openly, and Connor was clutching his sandstone pendant, looking terrified as he worked on healing.

Verena wondered if he should bother. The victim looked badly burned, their hair gone, their scalp blistered. Their right arm was little more than a blackened, twisted stump that would definitely need to be amputated. If they survived. They had to be someone important to command so much attention, especially with Shona and Ivor already swooping over the walls, commanding everyone to stop fighting.

Then Verena recognized the green skirt and satchel of healing supplies and the truth struck her like a punch from a max-tapped Boulder.

"Jean!" she screamed as she closed the last few yards to the tiny group. "Oh, no! Not Jean. Please tell me she'll survive."

Hamish glanced up, his face grief-stricken. He spoke through his tears, his voice cracking with grief and fear and stubborn hope. "Connor will save her."

Connor didn't respond, but remained hunched over Jean's body, eyes closed, breathing slow as he tried to save Jean's life. Just as Verena arrived, another Healer pushed past Hamish and placed her own hands on Jean's head. She looked dirty and weary from the long morning, but just as determined as Connor.

A second Healer dropped to her knees beside Connor, but paused to stare in shock. Tears rimmed her eyes and she whispered, "Oh, Lady Jean."

"What happened?" Verena asked.

"Aonghus," Hamish growled, his expression turning furious.

"Where is he?" she demanded, hand moving to her sword.

"Gone," Hamish spat, looking south. "The coward fled after he struck down Jean. He was laughing like a madman, shouting that today we suffer, and soon we die."

"We have to catch him," Verena cried, reaching for her long-vision goggles.

"I'll kill him," Hamish promised with deadly sincerity. "But Jean's more important."

Verena pulled him close and said, "She'll survive. I know it."

She desperately hoped she was right. They couldn't bear to lose another dear friend so soon.

Hamish hugged Verena and sobbed into her shoulder. She held him, fighting back her own tears as she looked down on Jean's unmoving form.

In addition to the horrific injuries on her right side, her face was a mass of burns. If not for her clothing and healers bag, Verena would never have recognized her.

They sat there for several long minutes, quietly waiting for word from Connor and the Healers. Hamish stopped sobbing, but still clung to Verena as they watched, desperate to ask for an update, but fearing disturbing the healing process.

The noise of battle subsided slowly from the city behind them. Verena wished she knew what devilry Shona was up to, but that could all wait. Jean was more important.

Slowly, Jean's injuries faded. The blisters stopped oozing blood, closed, then faded to scars, and many of them were slowly replaced by clean flesh. Watching the healing progress was awe inspiring.

But it wasn't complete. It became obvious that not even Connor, with all his incredible healing powers, could restore Jean to full health. Although her scalp healed, her thick, beautiful hair was gone. Most of the burns faded from her face, but some scarring remained, and her right eye remained purple and slightly swollen. The worst was her right arm. It was so badly burned, it was clearly dead.

A moment later, one of the Healers reached up to Jean's right shoulder and placed her hands around that blackened stump. It came free, revealing pink, new flesh along the stump.

Hamish whispered, "Oh, Jean," as he watched the Healer slide the broken stump away.

Two minutes later, Jean suddenly gasped and her body convulsed. Her good left hand shot upward, and Hamish caught it. She blinked open her left eye, and Verena read fear and pain in her gaze.

"Jean!" Hamish exclaimed, leaning over her.

"Hamish, you came," she breathed, her voice raspy and weak. "I was so afraid."

The Healers sat back, looking exultant, and Connor sagged as he blinked open his eyes. Verena shifted quickly to him and he gladly leaned against her. Hamish held Jean where she lay, and they were both murmuring softly to each other. Seeing her alive and at least partially healed filled Verena with so much relief, she wanted to laugh.

"You saved her." She kissed Connor, then hugged him again.

"Barely." He looked troubled. "My pendant is nearly spent, but I wish I could have done more."

Jean extended her good left hand to grip his. "Thank you, Connor. I know how badly I was hurt. I felt you healing me. I should have died. It still hurts, but I'm grateful for getting even one more day."

One of the Healers said, "Lady Jean, you're stabilized, but you need rest and further healing."

Hamish lifted her easily into his arms. "I'll see to her."

Jean glanced to her right side, to where her other arm was missing. She didn't look surprised or grief stricken, but seemed to be simply examining herself. Verena didn't doubt the sorrow would come. Such a devastating would would take a mental and emotional toll. Jean would understand that better than anyone.

Jean said, "There are many who need critical care still. Hamish, where's my bag?"

Verena grabbed the satchel. The leather was charred, but the contents seemed intact. She passed it to Hamish, who draped it over his shoulder. Jean looked relieved.

"You can't think to help, not after what you suffered," Verena said.

Jean managed a weak smile. The right side of her mouth didn't seem to work well, and her right eye had still not opened. "I'm sure I can find something useful to do. I can't sit idly while my patients need me."

Hamish hugged her closer. "I'll help. You tell me what to do, and I'll be your hands."

Their love inspired Verena. She clutched Connor's hand in hers, and he said, "Jean, you're amazing."

As Hamish led the way into the city, the troops parted for him. Several hundred of them raised fists in salute and shouted, "Lady Jean!"

She waved weakly to them, and they cheered all the louder. Verena asked, "What did I miss?"

Connor shook his head in wonder as he surveyed the cheering soldiers. "Somewhere during all this, Jean won herself an army."

DARLING OF THE REVOLUTION

Connor walked with Verena through the Army Gate, following Hamish, who carried Jean like she might break.

She nearly had. Connor had never attempted to heal someone so badly burned before. Jean had suffered immense trauma, much of it internal. He'd poured vast quantities of healing power into her, reinforcing it with the last vestiges of the power he'd siphoned from the people of Merkland, and extra strength that he drew from the earth through slate.

He had refused to even consider the possibility that Jean might die, and had thrown himself into the healing with as much determination as anything he'd done in his entire life. If he'd needed more power to heal her, he would have stilled the entire city again without hesitating for a single heartbeat.

His biggest regret was that Aonghus had escaped. The flame-haired captain had laughed as he rocketed away after striking down their precious Jean. His final, taunting words made Connor wonder if he'd been given the specific mission to find and strike down Jean. He didn't doubt the queen would give such an order.

They hadn't dare waste time chasing Aonghus. His time would come. Soon.

Connor hated that he couldn't restore Jean to full health. Her entire right side was broken. He'd healed more bones than he could count, and managed to save her right leg, although she might not be able to walk for a while. With extra healings and time to rest, hopefully she'd recover. But she'd lost her right arm and her right eye.

Thinking of her injuries filled him with such fury that he hoped someone broke the truce and tried to start fighting again. Now that they weren't fighting, many of the soldiers seemed at a loss for what to do.

Hamish took Jean toward the hospital building, but Verena pulled Connor the other way. "We need to get to the square. We need to find Rory and Shona."

"Why would Rory be with Shona?" Connor asked, confused.

When Verena told him about Shona's surprise change of sides, he couldn't believe it. "You're right. We need to get to the square right now."

Pushing through crowds of soldiers would take too long. So Connor pulled Verena close and threw them into the air with a pulsing of the ground. Then he drew a current of air around them and glided over thousands of milling troops to the square. It too was full of soldiers, but they easily spotted Kilian, Ivor, Shona, Rory, and the local lords. Everyone looked battered and blood splattered. They had indeed participated in the fighting.

Shona stood at the ultimate center of attention, glowing with limestone light. Connor blinked and looked again, but she continued to glow.

Verena noted his look and muttered, "Yes, she has a secondary affinity. Don't mention it to her. Her head grows bigger every time anyone does."

Shona noted their arrival with a satisfied smile, and began to speak loudly. "My father is dead. Harley is dead. I am the High Lady of Merkland, and I've reached an accord with Generals Rory and Ivor. This conflict is over. I hope I've made myself clear. All fighting is to cease at once. See to the wounded, regroup in your companies, and send me your senior officers for further instructions."

"I still can hardly believe it," Connor said softly.

Verena was watching Shona with open disgust. "She waltzed right up to Rory in the middle of the fighting and told him she's switching sides. I wish my dagger had penetrated deeper."

"You stabbed her?" That didn't surprise Connor, but what did surprise him was that both Verena and Shona looked healthy. They'd wanted to fight so badly.

"Threw a knife. Her blasted stone skin stopped it." Verena frowned, and actually seemed to be pouting.

"Come on. I want to know what else she's planning," Connor said

The two of them pushed closer as Shona turned to Lord Nevan and gave him a hug. "Nevan, I'm so glad to see you."

"All in a day's work, Lady Shona. I have to admit, when we received your father's orders, I hadn't expected the battle to turn out this way."

"What orders?" Ivor demanded.

Nevan actually looked a bit sheepish. "Coordinated through Craigroy and his network of spies, High Lord Dougal sent orders prior to the start of battle. Lord Torcall and I were ordered to comply with your wishes, but to open the city gates when Captain Aonghus's force approached."

"You betrayed us?" Rory asked angrily.

"Of course, buffoon," Torcall sneered. "Did you really think we'd throw in with you lot?"

"I did," Logan said angrily.

"That's why you weren't invited to join us," Torcall sneered. "You're not worthy to stand on the side of victory."

Shona gave him a scornful look and said softly, "I joined the revolution too."

Torcall and Nevan both looked thunderstruck, and Logan chortled with glee.

Torcall exclaimed, "What? You fool!"

Shona frowned and Ivor cracked Torcall on the back of the head with a stone-hardened fist, dropping the man to the ground in a stupor.

Shona gave Ivor a warm smile. "It's so nice to have competent help on hand."

Verena leaned close and muttered, "I can't believe it. Shona's really doing something heroic, and not entirely for selfish reasons?"

Connor chuckled. "Well, not entirely selfless, either. Leave it to Shona. She's the only one I can imagine who could figure out how to switch sides in the middle of a pitched battle. She retained rule over her realm, snatching it right back from the revolution by joining the revolution."

"Is she really now one of the three senior leaders of the whole thing?"

"It appears so. Life is crazy."

Shona spotted them and gestured them closer, her expression serious. "Connor, I received word that you had a hand in the death of my father, as you had sworn to do."

"I was there, but it wasn't me who killed him," Connor admitted.

Her expression softened, revealing a hint of the grief she must be feeling. "We have much to discuss, but know that I do not blame you."

"Blame your father," Verena said shortly.

Shona met Verena's angry stare and the two enjoyed a hate-filled glare for a moment, then Shona turned back to Connor, her expression returning to neutral. "Will you be so kind as to enhance my voice for me?"

There were probably other Pathfinders nearby, and Verena definitely looked like she wanted him to spit in Shona's eye instead of doing her any favors. If the request was an opening bid to try reconditioning him to do her bidding, he promised himself it wouldn't work. Then again, as one of the commanders of the revolution, he'd have to figure out how to coexist with Shona.

So he said, "Of course."

As soon as he applied the quartzite power to her throat, she spoke, her voice booming over the expectant crowds. "Let it be known to one and all that I, High Lady Shona, ruler of this realm and ultimate authority of Merkland, support wholeheartedly the cause of Obrioner freedom!

Generals Rory and Ivor are visionary men, among the bravest I know. I applaud their leadership and command all forces loyal to them or to me to swear fealty to our cause. We will liberate our nation from the evil queen who has brutally stolen the crown from our rightful rulers."

As her voice echoed through the city, Connor easily read the disbelief on many faces. Those who had supported the cause of freedom were grinning with optimism, and those who had fought to crush the revolution looked like the world had just collapsed under their feet.

Shona continued. "I confirm the truth that these great men discovered. Patronage is a lie. I formally release all Guardians residing at this moment in my realm from their oaths of fealty, and I look forward to your new, freely-given oaths to serve as free men and fight to liberate the rest of our nation.

Verena said, "Connor, you realize she's leaving you out of all that praise."

"So?"

"So, you're a big part of the reason the revolution is happening."

"It doesn't matter. She didn't mention Kilian either, or you, or Hamish."

Shona spread her hands and said, "Come, my friends and freedom fighters. Let us celebrate our victory today and toast the lives sacrificed in our great cause. Their deaths were not in vain. We shall see victory and freedom for Obrion!"

The entire city burst into cheering. Verena shook her head slowly, clearly sharing Connor's disbelief. With that pretty speech, Shona had smoothly transitioned from the daughter of evil High Lord Dougal to the darling of the revolution. Soldiers would gladly follow her to their deaths.

He wondered how many would need to.

1 0 3

REASONS DON'T HAVE TO MAKE SENSE

Connor sat beside Verena in the great hall of the palace of Merkland, soaking in the warmth, enjoying the mountains of food, and simply savoring a happy moment with dear friends.

The storm had blown itself out the evening after the battle, and the next day dawned clear and cold. That day had passed in a blur for Connor, filled with helping to heal the worst of the injured as well as sitting in meetings with Shona, Rory, and Ivor.

It was a grand thing for Shona to proclaim she'd switched sides and to declare all Guardians free, but not everyone was as eager as she to join the revolution. A couple of different factions emerged, and some of the soldiers from Crann had revolted in ugly, but short fights that ended quickly when Connor, Kilian, and Ivor arrived. As a result, over a thousand captured soldiers were being held in the underground bunkers that had been used for the siege weapons.

Connor wasn't sure what they were going to do in order to sort out the loyal troops from those simply biding their time. If they had enough chert, and if he was willing to share its closely-guarded secret with Shona, he and Aifric could attempt to search for those harboring thoughts of insurrection.

Luckily, they didn't. That was too similar to the queen's evil tactics for him to feel comfortable with it.

A servant arrived with a note summoning Connor to yet another meeting. He gave Verena a kiss on the cheek and followed the young man back to the military command building.

As he walked, he wondered at Shona's change of heart. Was it real? Could she be faking?

The servant brought him to a small room on the third floor. Many of the meetings he'd attended in the past twenty-four hours had been packed with dozens of officials and officers trying to hammer out logistics, lodging, and the sharing of medical staff. This time, only Shona, Ivor, Rory, and Kilian were present. They sat in hard-backed chairs around a small table near a crackling fire.

Connor had decided not to spend time alone with Shona without Verena present, just to avoid any possible misunderstandings. Shona was far too skilled at manipulation to let his guard down. Still, he felt relatively safe in the present company, so when Ivor gestured him to the last empty chair, he joined them.

Shona looked regal in a blue and green dress, and Kilian looked comfortable in his scarred leather jacket over a freshly laundered white shirt. Rory wore a new set of battle leathers, while Ivor had changed into trousers, shirt, and vest cut in a popular fashion. He looked every inch a high lord. Connor had left his battle leathers in his rooms and wore clothing he'd borrowed from Lord Logan, so he didn't feet totally out of place.

"Thank you all for coming," Shona said graciously. "Reports suggest the city is secure and fairly quiet."

Rory nodded. "Indeed. I doubt we've rooted out the last insurrectionists, but hopefully they'll take a breather for a few days."

Ivor chuckled. "Said by one of the chief insurrectionists in Obrion."

Rory cracked a smile. "I'm all for revolution, as long as it's my revolution. Didn't you know that?"

Connor appreciated their levity. They'd seen precious little of that in recent days. They had beaten Harley and High Lord Dougal, but paid a heavy price for it. He'd tried healing Ilse, but her lower spine was crushed, and that injury was beyond the skills of any of the Healers he'd talked with.

She might never walk again on her own power, but she didn't let that slow her. With those marvelous summoned legs of hers, she lost no mobility. Word of her bravery and stubborn refusal to succumb to her injuries had spread throughout the city, and her already-respected reputation had grown to near legendary status.

Connor hoped that might help a little as she struggled with losing Lukas. He firmly believed the indomitable captain would recover eventually. For now, she needed time to grieve.

Jean's fame was growing even faster. The troops she'd commandeered were mostly from other high lords' realms. They'd unanimously abandoned their high lords and pledged service to Lady Jean.

She'd seemed embarrassed while accepting their oaths, but had not refused them. In fact, she'd insisted on Hamish carrying her to where their injured were being treated. She stayed with them, offering encouragement to those being tended, and consoling those who lost fallen comrades. Her compassionate interest in their well being won their hearts more completely than any other high lord ever could.

When Verena heard about it, she'd said, "Sounds like we'll have to find a way to make the title of Lady Jean permanent. It fits her, and she deserves it."

Connor agreed, and he loved the fact that Verena found something to smile about. Mattias's death had traumatized her. That grief would take time to mend.

Kilian brought him back to the present. He asked, "Shona, tell me why you chose to join us. The battle could still have gone either way, or you could have retreated with the bulk of your army intact."

She nodded slowly, her expression grave. "I could have, but I saw no long-term advantage in that."

As always, Shona sought advantage. That did not surprise Connor.

She must have noted his look because she added, "Not just advantage for me, but advantage for my realm and for the kingdom as a whole. I spent much time in the presence of the dread queen. I know her insanity, her instability, and her cruelty better than most."

"Doesn't she think those very qualities will force people to remain loyal?" Connor asked.

Shona nodded. "Many fall into line through fear, but I was taught to look deeper and study the long-term trends. Her policies are too destructive. She might beat us all. In fact, from what I've seen so far, I doubt we can really hurt her. I'm hoping you know things about her that I don't."

She looked to Kilian with tentative hope. He only said, "That remains to be seen. If you saw no hope, why make the choice you did?"

"Like I said, she may win, but she'll eventually destroy our people. I've worked my whole life to win power and station because I firmly believe I can make things better for everyone, not just for myself. If I chose to remain with her, there was no guarantee she wouldn't kill me on a whim tomorrow. But I faced near-certain odds that I would need to abandon every value I hold dear in order to survive. I was not willing to do that. Your little revolution offered me the best alternative. I hope you don't disappoint me."

Wow. Connor hadn't thought he could feel inspired by Shona ever again. She spoke with calm dignity, and rare sincerity. He wished he'd brought a piece of chert along because he dearly wished he could read her thoughts.

He actually believed her. Her startling choice to throw in with them made no sense any other way. He sat back in his chair, considering this new side to Shona he had never known existed.

He had to wonder if she had known about that part of herself either. Granted, she had many sides, and every time he thought he'd figured her out, she proved him wrong.

If she betrayed them, Verena would kill her.

Connor would help.

PLAIN-SPEAK IS SCARIER THAN SENTRY-SPEAK

That night, Shona proclaimed a feast to celebrate victory and to honor their fallen comrades. Of course, she sat at the center of the high table, flanked by Rory and Ivor. Ostensibly, they all shared the spotlight, but one could easily interpret their positions as the two soldiers supporting her central rule.

They could have the spotlight. Connor was perfectly content to sit with Verena at the second table, holding hands between courses. He only wished Jean and Hamish were there. Although Jean did not seem to feel ashamed to be seen with scars and handicaps, she'd chosen to spend the evening with Hamish in her apartments, enjoying a quiet dinner together. Connor didn't blame her. The feast was loud and boisterous, and Jean needed rest.

Aifric and Kilian sat a little farther down the table from Connor. Several of the Crusher officers sat nearby, along with Evander. Many seemed intimidated by his giant presence, but Connor loved the fact that he'd finally committed to a side and chosen to help them.

He caught Evander's eye and said, "I'd love to hear the story of your duel at the Carraig and what you've been doing since then."

Verena chuckled and whispered, "As if we'd ever understand his explanation."

A smile cracked the ebony facade of Evander's face and he said, "The heart that enjoys the warm fire during the cold nights of winter alone retains the strength to march into darkness."

Connor had felt strangely comforted by the indecipherable answer.

Kilian laughed and slapped his knee. "I never thought I'd admit it, nephew, but I've actually missed your twisted way of speaking."

"When light shines in the darkness, truth that once was clouded may glimmer with renewed hope."

"I hope that means you have some good news," Connor said.

He looked from Connor to Kilian and nodded. "I found the other slumbering elfonnel that the queen attempted to raise. A man named Tristan. His humanity was lost. He could never return."

Evander had never spoken so much so plainly. It had to be incredibly important.

Kilian frowned. "I heard of Tristan. He was one of my mother's original followers from across the seas. I never knew he had fallen to the long sleep."

"I put him down." Evander spoke the impressive feat simply. Then he added, "He was protecting a secret that may change our deepest understanding of the source of our powers and perhaps suggest a weakness of my grandmother that we can exploit."

"Wow! What?" Connor exclaimed. Why had Evander waited so long to tell them?

But Evander shook his head and made a quieting gesture. "We will speak soon."

"You can't drop hints like that, then not say anything!" Connor objected. What was it with really old Petralists? They didn't understand the finer points of sharing secrets.

Kilian chuckled and took a long drink.

Connor tried to get Evander to say more, but all he got was more indecipherable Sentry-speak. Verena finally said, "He's not going to talk here at the feast, Connor."

"Sometimes you're too wise," he grumbled.

She kissed him on the cheek and he couldn't help smiling. "But always adorable."

Every kitchen in Merkland seemed to have been tapped to assist with the cooking, and food flowed like the waters of the Wick. Connor ate his fill, then ate a little more, just to be polite. He hoped Hamish was getting enough. He'd hate missing such a feast.

As they talked and laughed together, trying to focus on their recent victories instead of the tragedies, Tomas, Cameron, and Erich joined their table. They related in boisterous detail the glorious Great Bash Fight of Merkland.

"That's what they're calling it already?" Verena asked.

Tomas thumped his fist on the table and proclaimed, "No better name for it. It was right nearly perfect."

Erich nodded enthusiastically and said something in Grandurian. Verena smiled and translated for him. "He plans to compose a new battle song to honor it."

"I'm sorry I missed it," Connor said sincerely. "Sounds like a lot more fun than some of what we had to deal with."

"It was, laddie," Tomas confirmed.

"Until General Rory went and canceled it early," Cameron grumbled.

Connor comforted them. "We're probably going to have to fight every high lord in Obrion. I bet at least one of them will be willing to try to put on an even better bash fight."

The the bash fighters loved the idea and left, discussing ways to convince Rory to use his network of spies to disseminate the challenge to every city.

Verena laughed. "You realize you might have just set in motion the greatest bash fight tournament in all of history."

"I wish we could settle this with simple, pure bash fighting," he said wistfully. "That would be amazing, and everyone would have so much fun, I doubt they'd really care too much about who eventually won."

Many of those present raised many silent toasts to missing comrades, and the solemnity of the gesture seemed very appropriate. Too many had fallen among their own close associates. He thought of Lukas and Mattias, and wished he could have done more. Maybe if he'd tempted porphyry sooner, stabilized his affinities back in Altkalen, the battle would have gone better.

Maybe not. There was no way of knowing. So he hugged Verena and decided to enjoy every day, while striving to win an even better future. That was the best they could do.

The remaining Crushers celebrated loudly, led by Ilse. The elite Grandurian company had paid a heavy price to help those they'd considered enemies for so long fight for liberty. Periodically, they observed somber moments of silence in tribute to their fallen brothers and sisters.

Then they rose as a company and raised their glasses high to shout, "Captain Ilse the brave! The hero of Merkland!"

She waved down their applause, but the cry spread to other tables and rose in a long chorus. Apparently Erich had already finished composing at least one other new song because the Crushers shifted smoothly from saluting their captain to singing a boisterous, lively tune in honor of Ilse's heroics and in remembrance of Lukas.

They sang so loudly that the words reverberated through the hall. Many Obrioners paused their conversations to listen and silently raised their glasses in salute. They might not understand the words, but they applauded the sentiment.

Connor watched Ilse joking with her men, happy to see her trying to celebrate those who still lived. He wondered if they could create some kind of autonomous summoning, perhaps linked with some kind of mechanical to give other crippled soldiers renewed mobility.

He mentioned the idea to Verena.

Her eyes lit up with Builder enthusiasm. "Yes! What a great idea. I just wish we could do more to help Ilse and Jean. Harley healed herself miraculously, and you've ascended as far as she had. Are you sure you can't . . ."

He hated to disappoint her, but he'd already pushed far beyond what he'd thought were his limits. He'd consumed the last of his precious sandstone pendant trying to further heal Jean and Ilse. He wasn't sure he'd ever find a way to reach Ailsa again, but maybe Gisela could help sculpt at least a partially enhanced pendant for him. They would need that advantage, and he felt exposed without the treasured pendant.

Kilian looked up from his conversation with Aifric. She'd kept him chatting for the last half hour, and the two seemed to have a lot to talk about. Connor had noticed her face shivering repeatedly as she shifted between her various personalities. Whatever they were talking about, a lot of the women in her head wanted a say in it.

Kilian said, "Harley was exceptionally gifted in healing. The help that Ilse and Jean need requires a tremendous understanding of human anatomy and structure. I support the idea of trying everything we can think of, but only my mother can craft new flesh."

"The third threshold," Connor said with sudden hope.

"You're not ready for that," Kilian reminded him immediately with a warning look.

"Some day I will be."

"For now, let's visit Ilse and Jean again. Together we can explore whether or not there are still things we can do."

"I'll come and help," Aifric offered immediately. "My healing powers are stronger than ever. That tampering you did while restoring me really helped, Connor."

"Glad to hear it."

Kilian said, "Perhaps between all of us we can find a way."

Connor dearly hoped they could.

"So what now?" Verena asked Kilian.

"We eat ourselves sick, I think. Isn't that what you and Hamish always do at a feast?" Kilian asked with a grin.

"I mean, Merkland is safe. Our army is bigger than ever. Ivor will make sure to spread the word far and wide. We're a threat now. Your mother will have to respond."

He nodded. "Indeed she will, but I hope not until springtime. She'll need time to marshal another army and position them for attack. She lost Harley and she cannot afford to lose any other critical resources."

"Will she raise any other ancient Petralists?" Jean asked.

Kilian considered that for a moment and glanced at Evander, who shrugged. "The lion hunts alone, but often steals the prey taken by the pack of jackals."

Connor chuckled. "Glad we waited for that one."

Verena elbowed him. "We need Jean here to help interpret."

Evander said with unusual clarity, "I believe we will have a little time."

"Wow, that's two clear sentences in one night," Connor told him. "Are you sure you didn't get injured fighting Harley?"

Evander chuckled. He made it seem somehow inscrutable.

Connor hoped he was right about the time. They needed rest and time to plan, but he secretly feared they wouldn't get nearly enough. How by the Tallan's twisted memory were they ever going to stop the queen? Even if they got a year of peace, he wondered if they'd figure out a solution to that one, overwhelming problem.

The outer door of the hall burst open and Frazier, the maze lord, burst in, covered in snow and looking grumpy. He scanned the hall, then marched toward their table.

"Evander!" he shouted.

Evander's deep, booming voice echoed through the hall as he pointed. "It's Connor's fault."

Thumbs Up?
Or Thumbs down?

How did you like the book?

Are you willing to take 5 seconds and share it with the world? Now, while it's still fresh?

Reviews help more than you imagine. How many times have you looked at reviews of books or products before buying?

If you've never posted a review before, it's super simple. Just two steps:

- •Rate the book 1-5 stars. Be honest. Be generous.
- •Write a short review. One or two sentences is plenty.

What goes in those sentences? Here are a few suggestions:
- •Your feelings about the book.
- •Something you loved about it. (no spoilers please!)
- •The fact that you couldn't put the book down all night.
- •Your favorite line of Sentry speak.
- •Who is your favorite character?
- •If you were a Petralist, what affinity would you most love to have?

Just pick one suggestion, or come up with your own. It's that simple.

And just like that, you really help me out, and help other readers considering buying this story.

To post a review on Amazon: http://smarturl.it/yv37jy

Thanks!

Frank

Do you want exclusive content?
First notification of new covers, new maps, and upcoming events?
Exclusive opportunities to submit your ideas and suggestions for future stories?

Join the Reader's Group!

To join: http://smarturl.it/4u6hmm

I send emails to the group on a regular (but not annoying) basis.

I hope you'll join the team. I look forward to your input.

Frank

PETRALIST STONES

Three for the masses
Two for the many
Four for the privileged few

IGNEOUS

Basalt
Speed, agility
Tapped: Powder
through the skin
Obrion: Strider
Granadure: Wingrunner

Granite
Strength, summoning
Tapped: Powder
through the skin
Obrion: Boulder or
Fast Roller
Granadure: Rumbler

Obsidian
Magnifies innate abilities
Tapped: Powder through the skin
Obrion: Blade
Granadure: Allcarver
Sedimentary

SEDIMENTARY

Limestone
Light
Tapped: Held or worn
Obrion: Solas
Granadure: Solas

Sandstone
Healing
Tapped: Held or worn
Obrion: Healer
Granadure: Healer

METAMORPHIC

Marble
Fire
Tapped: Under the Tongue
Obrion: Firetongue
Granadure: Flameweaver

Slate
Earth
Tapped: Soles of feet
Obrion: Sentry
Granadure: Sapper

Quartzite
Air, Senses
Tapped: Placed in Mouth
Obrion: Pathfinder
Granadure: Longseer

Soapstone
Water
Tapped: Powder swallowed
with water
Obrion: Spitter
Granadure: Water Moccasin

Secret Stones

Diorite
Igneous Stone
Explosive Power
Tapped: Powder
through the skin
Obrion: Unknown
Granadure: Unknown

Porphyry
Igneous Stone
Rage Monster
Tapped: Powder
through the skin
Obrion: Unclaimed
Granadure: Rampager

Anthracite (Blind Coal)
Sedimentary Stone
Aggressive Slipperiness
Tapped: Held or worn
Obrion: Unknown
Granadure: Unknown

Serpentinite
Metamorphic Stone
Sound
Tapped: Unknown
Obrion: Unknown
Granadure: Unknown

New Stones!

Chert
Sedimentary Stone
Empathy
Tapped: Unknown
Obrion: Unknown
Granadure: Unknown

Amphibolite Gneiss
Metamorphic Stone
Counters Basalt
Tapped: Powder
through the skin
Obrion: Unknown
Granadure: Unknown

Granite Gneiss
Metamorphic Stone
Counters Granite
Tapped: Powder
through the skin
Obrion: Unknown
Granadure: Unknown

ALSO BY FRANK MORIN

THE PETRALIST SERIES

Set in Stone — Book One
A Stone's Throw — Book Two
No Stone Unturned — Book Three
Affinity for War — Book Four
The Queen's Quarry — Book Five
The King's Craft — Book Six
Blood of the Tallan — Book Seven

OTHER PETRALIST STORIES

When Torcs Fly — Tomas and Cameron prequel
Game of Garlands — Anika prequel
Builder of Intrigue — Aunt Ailsa prequel

THE FACETAKERS SERIES

Face Lift — Prequel short story
Saving Face — Book One
Memory Hunter — Book Two
Rune Warrior — Book Three
Aeon Champion — Book Four

SHORT STORIES

"Odin's Eye" — Part of *A Game of Horns: A Red Unicorn Anthology*
"Only Logical" — Part of *Unseen: United! Box Set Anthology* to raise funds to fight plagiarism
"The Essence" — Part of *Dragon Writers: An Anthology*
"The Seventh Strike" — Part of *Cursed Collectibles: An Anthology*

Find all books here!

www.frankmorin.org

Amazon

About the Author

Frank Morin is an avid storyteller and story consumer. When not writing or trying to keep up with his active family, he's often found hiking, camping, Scuba diving, or enjoying other outdoor activities.

Frank writes all types of fantasy, from his exciting Facetakers time-travel fantasy thrillers, to these popular Petralist novels, and more. Check his website for updates and to sign up for his newsletter to receive the latest on all his releases, scheduled events, and insider information: www.frankmorin.org.

Or you can follow him on Twitter: @MorinWrites

Or like his Author Facebook page: www.facebook.com/authorfrankmorin

Frank lives in Oregon with his family, who are his most enthusiastic fans and his most brutal critics. In their home, storytelling is a cherished family tradition that keeps magic alive

www.ingramcontent.com/pod-product-compliance
Lightning Source LLC
Chambersburg PA
CBHW021239200726

48288CB00014B/15